THE YEAR'S BEST SCIENCE FICTION & FANTASY

2017 EDITION

OTHER BOOKS BY

RICH HORTON

——◆——

THE YEAR'S BEST SCIENCE FICTION & FANTASY

2017 EDITION

EDITED BY

RICH HORTON

PRIME BOOKS

THE YEAR'S BEST SCIENCE FICTION & FANTASY, 2017 EDITION

Prime Books
www.prime-books.com

ISBN: 978-1-60701-491-1

For my brothers, Jim, Bill, Paul, and Pat; and my sister Ann Lucas; and in memory of my sister Peggy.

CONTENTS

CONTENTS

THE YEAR IN FANTASY AND SCIENCE FICTION, 2016

RICH HORTON

The State of the Art

The first thought I have every year contemplating these introductions is to review again the state of the science fiction field—perhaps the field as the whole, or the short fiction slice of it. I confess that after a while this gets perhaps a bit old hat: it's hard to see overarching trends on a year by year basis, and much of what one says seems repetitive over time.

This year one is tempted as well to try to make a broader analogy between what is happening in the field and what is happening in the political world. It is easy—indeed too easy, too facile—to draw parallels between the Rabid Puppy movement and Donald Trump's ascendancy. I don't have the energy to do so, I confess. Those I've seen seem, as I've suggested, facile. I don't doubt there are resonances between the two subjects, but there's no simple A is A comparison there. And we frankly give ourselves—or give the Hugo Awards—too much importance if we try to act like an award nomination is of the same consequence as a Presidential election.

Another familiar way to assess the state of the field is to look at us through the lens of popular culture. Or, more simple, the movies. Science fiction has been treated better and better in the cinema of late, it seems to me. In 2015 we saw several outstanding movies (most notably **The Martian**, **Mad Max: Fury Road**, and **Ex Machina**), but none of them were based on a truly great piece of written sf (though the novel **The Martian** is pretty good, and great fun). In 2016 we finally saw an outstanding sf movie, **Arrival**, based on a great piece of short sf: Ted Chiang's 1998 novella "Story of Your Life," which I think is in the conversation to be the greatest science fiction novella of all time. **Arrival** is serious and moving and beautifully made. I'd have called "Story of Your Life" unfilmable, and in a way **Arrival** confirms that judgement: it's an excellent try, but I do feel it falls short of the novella, and precisely by missing some of what I found mindblowing in Chiang's story. But that failure on its part is mainly in that it was aiming so high: I can't complain about a good try falling just short of such a masterwork.

SF's inroads into what might be called "higher culture" continue much as for the past few years. We continue to see well done pieces of fantastika in magazines like the *New Yorker, Tin House,* etc. Notable from the *New Yorker* last year was Karen Russell's "The Bog Girl." And my favorite came from a smaller "little magazine," *Beloit Fiction Journal,* though I found it in the author's excellent debug collection. This is "Openness," by Alexander Weinstein, which we feature in this book.

As for the more mundane "State of the Field" as measured by the health of the short fiction venues, 2016 seemed much in line with the last few years. The major change was announced towards the end of the year: as of 2017 *Asimov's* and *Analog* (as well as their crime fiction stablemates *Ellery Queen's* and *Alfred Hitchcock's*) will be going to bimonthly publication of roughly double-sized issues. This echoes a move made by *F&SF* several years past. Thus there are no remaining monthly sf magazines (or even nearly monthly as those two actually have been.)

The online segment also continued much as before, with very strong years from *Clarkesworld, Lightspeed,* and *Beneath Ceaseless Skies,* who continue these days as the "usual suspects," not to mention *Tor.com,* which I don't necessarily think of as a "webzine" but which is one, really. There was plenty of strong work elsewhere as well, in such places as the venerable *Strange Horizons,* the always intriguing *Uncanny,* and the energetic *Daily Science Fiction.* The most exciting new entry for me was *Mothership Zeta,* devoted to what they called "fun" sf and fantasy. Alas, they've gone on hiatus after the first six issues, but they hope to return. This book features A. T. Greenblatt's "The Non-Hero's Guide to the Road on Monsters," which, as I hope you'll agree, definitely satisfies the "fun" requirement.

As for original anthologies, I was very happy to see a pair of books celebrating NewCon Press's tenth anniversary: **Now We Are Ten** and **Crises and Conflicts**. I have chosen a story from each for this book ("Dress Rehearsal" by Adrian Tchaikovsky and "Now We Are Ten" by Adam Roberts) and there was also very fine work from Nina Allan, Bryony Pearce, Nancy Kress, and Mercurio D. Rivera among others. And, of course, each year we look forward to the latest of Jonathan Strahan's "Infinity" series: 2016's **Bridging Infinity** once again included multiple stories I chose to reprint. The other original anthology featured here represents another ongoing series, Mike Allen's **Clockwork Phoenix**, which is a great source of stories that don't care much what genre they fit.

One newish way to get new short fiction is directly from the writers, via Patreon. (Not that there hasn't been writer-sourced short fiction before: Bruce Holland Rogers' subscription based short-short service, delivered via email, comes to mind.) I've seen excellent work on Patreon from a couple of writers recently (and I'm sure there are more): Tim Pratt and Kameron Hurley. Both have published a good deal of strong work there—this year I particularly liked Hurley's "The Plague Givers," which was first reprinted in *Uncanny*, and is included in this book. (Hurley also had excellent work in *Lightspeed* (via Patreon) and in *Beneath Ceaseless Skies*.)

Perhaps the best way to talk about the state of the field at any given time is to celebrate the writers who are, after all, the creators of the state of the field. And if we're talking about how the field is changing, we're talking to a great extent about new writers. For me, as an anthologist, I'm very interested in the writers I'm publishing for the first time—on the average, almost half the writers in any of my books are in one of my books for the first time. To be sure, these aren't always new writers! So it's a delight for me to be publishing a story by Steven Barnes ("Fifty Shades of Grays") for the first time—though the first story I remember reading by him was "The Locusts" (with Larry Niven), way back in 1979, when I was still in college. (The main reason it took me so long to publish one of his stories, I trust, is that he is primarily a novelist.) Likewise, Cat Rambo has been publishing a whole lot of interesting short fiction over the past fifteen years, and it's great to have her one of these volumes for the first time. For that matter, this is the first time we've had a Kameron Hurley story—I feel that I've been remiss in both cases! Not to mention Jason Sanford, who has been one of the most original and adventurous writers of strange sf for the past decade, often in *Interzone*. And Karin Lowachee, another writer who hasn't published a whole lot of short fiction in a career spanning more than two decades.

It's really exciting to see all the very new writers appearing for the first time here, writers like Charlotte Ashley, Rahul Kanakia, Craig DeLancey, Suzanne Palmer, Adrian Tchaikovsky, Alena Indigo Anne Sullivan, A. T. Greenblatt, Helena Bell, Carlos Hernandez, Maggie Clark, Dominica Phetteplace, Sam J. Miller and the aforementioned Alexander Weinstein. The constant emergence of new writers is a special joy for me, as a reviewer, anthologist, and in a very modest way something of an historian of the sf field. It is new voices that move the field in new directions, that keep the field young and relevant.

And in that context, it is particularly exciting to note a writer like Rich Larson—not new to these books (we featured "The King in the Cathedral" last year)—but pretty new to publishing (his first story appeared in 2012), and remarkably prolific over a really impressive range of themes, tone, and subject matter. He published so many good stories least year we felt compelled to pick two for this book . . . and I'm sure we'll see a lot more exceptional stuff.

Amid all this talk of new writers, however, the veterans are pretty darn important, too. Gregory Feeley appeared in the very first volume of a predecessor to this series (*Fantasy: The Best of the Year 2006*), and I'm excited to have a challenging new sf story from him. Ian R. MacLeod, Genevieve Valentine, Charlie Jane Anders, Lavie Tidhar, and Adam Roberts have all been in these books three times or more—which his appropriate as they are three of the best writers we have. Which leaves a couple more writers appearing for the second time: Seth Dickinson, another very new and interesting talent; Chaz Brenchley, who probably deserved to be here a lot more often than he has; and Carrie Vaughn, who frankly I thought I had reprinted a lot more often (I know she was on the short list many more times).

I think it's clear that the sf field remains vibrant and exciting, with an intriguing mix of brand new writers, young stars on the rise, and well-established veterans. As ever, this book tries to showcase that entire range, and of course to present the best new short sf and fantasy, remembering that it is often at shorter lengths that the newest and freshest creations first appear.

PROJECT EMPATHY

DOMINICA PHETTEPLACE

Bel and I both worked for Blue Cup.

She got the job because she had good personality scores and above average social media metrics. She was a junior and captain of the dance team. On her tryout, she took orders and served drinks with what her evaluators described as "warmth" and "grace." Over a hundred teenagers auditioned, only Bel was offered a position.

Blue Cup requires close surveillance on all its employees. They want access to every interaction, both in-person and online. This normally requires the implantation of a standard Watcher chip.

In Bel's case, she was fitted with a prototype of the newest version of the Watcher, the creatively titled Watcher 2.0. Not everyone can afford to care about rights and privacy. She agreed to the terms of use without even reading them.

The talent required to be a great Blue Cup host is rare, and the difference between a great host and the merely good can amount to hundreds of thousands of dollars at a single location. At Blue Cup anyone who was a frequent buyer could be Bel's friend, both in the café and at school, provided they kept their purchase count high.

Regular guests are to be greeted by name. Interactions are not (yet) scripted, hosts are paid to know what to say and when. Bel will remember your drink or compliment your appearance. She will mention the picture you posted online or make some comment about last weekend's crazy party. If you were not invited to last weekend's party, she will secure you an invitation to next weekend's party. In this way, the social structures of the nearby high school are converted into drink purchases at Blue Cup.

It is not enough to be popular; a great Blue Cup host will be liked and accepted by almost all cliques. She helps others fit in without being disruptive to hierarchies. Underperforming hosts are rotated out of the cast, but high performing hosts are often retained at great cost. After a year of stellar performance at our Concord location, Bel did not ask for a raise—she asked to be transferred fifteen miles west, to our San Francisco location. This was logical. In Concord, she only had another couple of years of employment before she aged out of that store's target demo. In San Francisco, the Blue Cup Café is a concept that undergoes a lot of revisions. That cast is more age-diverse because that helps with research. I assumed that Bel wanted what almost everyone else wanted: long term employment.

It was through the development of the San Francisco Blue Cup Concept location that I first became acquainted with Bel. My initial impression was favorable. She rated high on our proprietary attractiveness measure, which is generated by comparing the size and relative distances between facial features. She had a well-placed nose and eyes that were the ideal distance apart. Her forehead was a good size. She was in the 99th percentile for chin prettiness.

Bel had a straight posture and a strong neck and spine from years of dance classes. She had a tightness in her eyelids and a tendency to bare her teeth when she smiled. I met her while I was developing the persistence measure. She scored high.

Blue Cup was able to effect a transfer for Bel from Concord High to the Pre-Collegiate Academy. The PCA is a scholastic program for gifted young people who live within the San Francisco borders. As such, its students come from the most prominent families in the area. It is technically a public institution because it is funded with public money, but that funding is supplemented by generous grants from families, nonprofits, and corporations such as Blue Cup. Although it is technically a public institution, admission is by invite only.

The PCA is not school as Bel knows it. There are no overcrowded classrooms or even teachers. There are tutors, counselors, and workshop facilitators. The school has not been standardized with the goal of insuring conformity to other state-funded schools. The purpose of the school is to provide an individualized learning plan to the next generation of leaders and innovators. The students have had access to a personal staff of educators their whole lives.

Bel was assigned four tutors and two counselors. She was not placed in any workshops because it was determined that her academic level in all subjects was too remedial.

"But I was a straight-A student at my old school," said Bel.

Her math tutor nodded sympathetically. "I came from the suburbs, too. But now look at me."

Bel wasn't sure what she was supposed to be looking at. She was used to teachers that resented their jobs. She didn't understand that tutors in the city were well compensated, that the position was highly sought after.

"If you work really hard, we can get you through Calculus 1 and 2 in a single semester. Then you can join the freshman multivariable calculus seminar next year."

Bel stared off into space for a moment. For this moment, her emotions were unreadable by me.

"Fine," she said, which registered as an 89 and 57 on the determination and unhappiness indices, respectively.

At PCA, there was no dance team. Her classmates were aloof, hierarchies had been entrenched, sometimes going back generations. Bel had a name but not a "name." Her influence score took a dive. She was not active on any of the social media that her new peers were into, so she had to start over with new accounts. Her influence ranking plummeted.

I sensed regret. She wouldn't have come to PCA had she known what it was really like. But she was here now, with her own room in a shining and clean city. Blue Cup had secured her permits to live, work, and study here. Was it better to be royalty in Concord or a peasant in the city? There was an additional consideration of her mother's anger and her father's drinking. She was probably happy to have distance and a life apart from them, but she also seemed to miss them.

If familiarity was what she longed for, she would not find it at the San Francisco Blue Cup. That location is very popular, but it is frequented by tourists, not locals. It requires a different protocol.

At the San Francisco Blue Cup, the aspirational city experience is repackaged in a way that is accessible and familiar to our visitors, who come not just from the Outer Bay Area and Inland California, but from all over the world. It is almost impossible to obtain a permit to live in the city, but far easier to obtain a visitor's permit. This system has eliminated the problems of homelessness and poverty within city borders. Not just anyone can live in the city, but almost anyone can visit and enjoy a specially crafted beverage in our City Café.

So while the Concord Blue Cup monetizes high-school hierarchies, San Francisco Blue Cup monetizes regional inequalities. More importantly, the San Francisco location is also an experimental laboratory from which Blue Cup 2.0 will be launched.

On her first day in her new location, Bel was given a wristband.

"Is this a fitness monitor?" she asked.

"It is meant to look like one, but it is not," said her manager.

Our hosts do not have the assistance of eyewear or earbuds because that might make a layer of software visible in customer interactions. The interactions with Blue Cup hosts should be as organic as possible. However, there are few regulars at this location, and since it is a larger café, there are many hosts working at once. The wristbands look like fitness monitors to our customers, but they are actually designed to allow our hosts to communicate with one another and with the main company. Transmissions are received via a series of vibrations and transmitted via taps.

"You will have to learn the communication code," said the manager as she transferred the codebook to Bel's account.

"I already have so much schoolwork, though." Bel and the manager were in the orientation room above the café.

"It will be difficult, but I know you can do it. Your aptitude scores were great." Bel's manager was named Geo. She was a white woman in her forties with weathered skin and a tan. She didn't try to appear more youthful than she was, and her confidence and authenticity measures were high. Bel felt warmth around Geo, something maternal. Geo was a great host, especially popular with our guests whose profiles suggested dysfunctional childhoods.

"I suppose it will be worth it to be a great host," said Bel, and Geo nodded. "Being a great host is like being a celebrity, isn't it?"

"Yes, in the sense that you interact with a lot of people in ways that are more meaningful to them then they are to you. And some really great hosts have gone on to be celebrities."

Bel nodded and then rattled off a list of celebrities who got their start at Blue Cup. This was when I realized why Bel had asked for the transfer. It wasn't just that Concord was an economically stagnant town with bad air and low water rations. It wasn't just the eruptions of violence that sometimes gripped her home. She came to San Francisco because that's where the most popular web series were filmed. She wanted to be a star. And a work-study permit sponsored by a major corporation was the easiest way to live here.

Her first night in San Francisco she fell asleep looking up auditions for web series. She needed something to reach for, a reason to keep trying. She wanted to leave. She wanted freedom. I wanted her to stay. I needed her to stay at least the length of her contract in order to finish the algorithm.

The next day she had her first lunch date. One of the most exciting opportunities offered by the PCA is networking. Young people tend to self-segregate into cliques, which blunts their networking opportunities. To disrupt this, scheduled lunch dates are part of the PCA curriculum.

Her initial lunch date cohort included two seniors, Lauren and Berto, and one sophomore, Itani. Bel despaired of the clothes in her closet. In Concord, she gave most of her Blue Cup paycheck to her parents, and she spent the rest on things for herself. She shopped at all the best mall stores and had assembled a carefully curated wardrobe of Concord-stylish outfits. Walking around the city in her favorite clothes, she realized she looked like a tourist.

Right before lunch, Bel looked up the profiles of her cohort. Everyone at PCA was on a social network called Luck. The interface was confusing to Bel, and, moreover, it made it hard for Bel to gauge the relative social rankings of her peers. Indeed, this was one of the advantages of Luck; it was difficult for outsiders to navigate. She ran a couple of searches that contained terms like "popular kids at PCA" as if the internet might tell her. Based on publicly available pictures, it appeared that Lauren was beautiful and stylish, Berto was handsome and brooding, and Itani was shy and unassuming.

Her cohort met up at the large tree in the courtyard. Bel was the last one there, made late by all the internet sleuthing that ultimately told her very little. Lauren was a photogenic white girl; that is to say her attractiveness rated higher in pictures than IRL. She was also very stylish in a way that was alienating to Bel. She wore a stark white shirt made out of stiff material. The dramatic funnel neck highlighted her flat, broad chest. Her waist was incredibly tiny, in a way that looked unhealthy and uncomfortable. This was not the kind of figure that was allowed on web series.

Compared to this, the minimalism of Itani's shapeless black shift seemed reasonable. But Itani appeared to be barefoot, perhaps taking the notion of minimalism too far. Berto wore loose slacks and sandals. His T-shirt had holes and was stretched out at the neck. He looked like a campesino.

"Hello," said Berto, and he said it with what sounded like a Spanish accent. He appeared to be Mexican. His accent surprised Bel, not that she was racist. As a Blue Cup host, she treated all customers with dignity, even those with poor language skills. At Concord High, there had been tensions between students who called themselves American-Mexicans and those who were just simply Mexican. The former considered themselves to be advantaged over the latter in matters of intellect and appearance. One group was taller, lighter, preferred mall clothes, and spoke in a flat, California vocal fry. This was Bel's group. The other group loved farmer's markets so much they even bought their clothes and handmade sandals there. This was the group that stubbornly refused to learn proper English. Berto looked too poor to even afford the farmer's market. He was probably a scholarship student. Bel would happily be his friend, but it was important that he understand they were not the same, despite the many things they might have in common.

"Nice to meet you," said Bel, imitating the neutral English of her math tutor. She used the same intonation at work when she wanted to put guests at ease. She felt a sliver of superiority, her first in a while. She had missed that feeling. It had gone away, and she was worried it would never come back.

"Your name is Bella?" he asked, pronouncing the two l's like a y.

"I prefer Bel, but no, not Bey-Ya,' it's Bella-rhymes-with-hella." There was an awkward pause. Perhaps her classmates were not familiar with the modifier? "I don't speak Spanish," she added, bragging. Monolinguism was a mark of status back in Concord.

"Oh, that's too bad," said Lauren. "Do you know Shanti? She's my Spanish tutor, she's awesome. Maybe you could meet with her?"

Bel nodded and smiled without saying anything. She wouldn't be allowed to study a language until she caught up in her core subjects. Even then, she wanted to study something more elegant and rare than Spanish, something like French or Japanese.

Bel then introduced herself to Itani and tried not to stare at her feet. They were so pretty and manicured, did she really walk around barefoot? The streets of San Francisco were clean, but still it seemed like such an eccentric thing to do. This was when I first realized that instead of just watching Bel, I could help her too.

I buzzed her wristband.

BAREFOOT LOOKING SHOES, I wrote. The wristband is a pretty crude way of communicating. What I was trying to tell Bel was that although Itani appeared barefoot, she was actually wearing shoes, of a sort. They were light-weight soles that adhered to the bottoms of her feet via a dry adhesive. They had no top.

I thought Bel would appreciate the help, but instead her adrenaline level spiked.

"I think they need me at work," she said. I don't know why I expected her to understand; she had only studied the codebook for a few hours since she'd received it yesterday. Anyway, she didn't know about me, not yet. We would be introduced eventually, but only when Blue Cup felt she was ready. "Maybe we could have lunch at Blue Cup? There are these awesome new chicken wraps, a San Francisco only special. They pair really well with the Cheesecake Cappuccino. . . . "

"That sounds gross actually," said Berto, and Lauren and Itani nodded in agreement. "We usually go to the Reserve."

Bel's adrenaline level spiked even higher. She was experiencing a mild panic. In her old habitat, she knew all about the places people liked to eat lunch, and more importantly, why they liked to eat there and what they were trying to project to others by choosing that place.

"The . . . Reserve?" she asked, but the others had already begun to walk in one direction so she followed.

The streets of San Francisco were wide open and empty. The air was damp and good. Bel might even figure out that she didn't need her asthma medication anymore. When the others wanted to cross the street, they did so as they pleased. Any cars stopped, of course, but Bel hesitated each time they crossed.

"Don't they have self-driving cars in Woodland Hills?"

"I'm from Concord," said Bel, mildly offended, "And yes, of course we have self-driving cars. But they're not all self-driving and also there's a lot more traffic. I'm used to crosswalks is all." She pointed at some vestigial markings on the asphalt.

"Traffic used to be bad here. Before the permit system," said Lauren. Bel didn't believe her, but there was no status to be gained by openly contradicting the girl.

A man in a suit and tie walked in the opposite direction as the teenagers and greeted each one by name, even Bel. Bel copied the others and said hi back, but after he was out of earshot she asked, "Who was that?"

"That's Steve," said Itani.

"Okay, who's Steve?"

"Border Patrol."

"I thought Border Patrol was all robots." Both wheeled and flying drones roamed the city checking faces and remotely scanning badges. A paranoid feeling crept over Bel each time she saw one, like she might get arrested even though she had the right badge. She sometimes had to remind herself that she really was allowed to be here.

"Border Patrol is people, too. Think of them like Blue Cup hosts, but for the whole city of San Francisco," said Berto, and Lauren snickered. They must have looked her up on social media, they must have disapproved of how Bel had presented herself. Itani didn't join in the derision, and that's how Bel knew they were going to be friends.

Bel's anger levels spiked thirty-four percent. The blood vessels in her face dilated by two percent, and the surface temperature of her face increased by a tenth of a degree.

"Where are you from?" she asked Berto. She probably wanted to embarrass him.

"My family is from Rio," he said, "But relocated to Lausanne. I split my time between San Francisco and Switzerland."

"What about Hawaii?" asked Lauren.

"I'm only on Oahu, like, two weeks out of the year," he said. Then he and Lauren started reminiscing over some vacation they'd taken together, completely ignoring Bel and Itani. It should have been obvious to Bel at this point that Berto was a rich person in poor person drag.

They walked another two blocks, passing glass building after glass building until one of the glass buildings seemed to open up for them.

"Wow, I didn't even notice there was a door here," said Bel. If she wanted to increase her social rank, she needed to stop expressing astonishment at ordinary things. She stared at the architecture of the door, wondering how it had shifted.

"It's only a door if you are a member," said Itani. "For nonmembers, it's a wall."

They walked inside and Bel watched as a large slab of glass slid into place behind them. So that was the door. When it locked into place behind her, it turned into a screen. It projected a clear view of the outside, where she'd just been. Bel could see other pedestrians walk by without a glance in her direction. They were nonmembers. For them, this building had no entrance.

How many of these types of buildings had she passed on her way here?

The Reserve was a big, bright, quiet room. It had a light marble floor that mysteriously didn't echo when stepped on. There were tables with people eating, drinking, or working, but the tables were so far apart—at least dozens of yards between them.

Overhead, there was a lighting installation that looked like it was made entirely of candle drippings. It didn't seem to be suspended by anything, and as the others walked underneath, it moved. The bulk of it shifted in response to their gait, a visual acoustic. It looked like if it might fall, so Bel walked the long way round to avoid passing under it. The others were far ahead, approaching a table. Itani turned around to find Bel, and when she saw her avoiding the chandelier, she said, "It's okay, it's just art." Gentle encouragement, the kind a skittish puppy might receive.

The others approached a table that already had food on it. They sat down and began eating from the plates and drinking from the cups.

"Uh . . . you guys," said Bel. "Are you eating what the previous customers left behind?"

Lauren raised an eyebrow and continued chewing.

Bel could not bring herself to sit down and eat. It was too foreign. A woman dressed in a stiff black kimono approached the table. She greeted them all by name and then said to Bel, "I'm Angelina, your host. Is your lunch what you wanted?"

Bel stared down at the table, which sat four. Three were sitting and eating, which meant the empty chair was hers and so was the remaining plate.

"My lunch?" she asked, staring at a plate that contained a crust of bread that looked bitten and tiny pieces of chicken and vegetables strewn about.

"It's a chicken wrap. My apologies, I should have selected a different presentation." Before Bel could respond, Angelina took the plate away and said, "I will try again. In the meantime, please enjoy your coffee and cheesecake milkshake." Angelina pointed to a cup that looked like it was made out of frosted slate. Bel sat down and took a sip. The flavor profile closely resembled a Blue Cup Cheesecake Cappuccino. Bel's pleasure hormones surged at the taste of something familiar.

"How did the Reserve know what you guys wanted to eat?" asked Bel.

"I put in my order while we were waiting for you to show up," said Berto.

"I trust the preference algorithm," said Lauren.

"Me too," said Itani. "You're not really even supposed to order here, you are supposed to trust that they understand what you want better than you do."

Bel nodded. At the Concord Blue Cup, she always knew what to order for regulars.

Angelina returned with a chicken wrap that was recognizable as such. "Here is a more traditional preparation, I hope you like it." It looked just like a Blue Cup wrap. The café had prepared for her the lunch she had suggested to the others just a little while ago. It hadn't used the algorithm on her. It had listened in on her conversation.

Bel frowned at Angelina.

Angelina frowned at Bel's frown.

"Would you like me to give you a tour?"

At that moment Bel realized that was exactly what she wanted.

Angelina walked her back to the chandelier and explained who the artist was. Then they walked upstairs to an observation deck that overlooked the kitchen. Serious looking men and women prepared tiny plates of various foodstuffs.

"There are so many of them! There are more cooks than customers." There were no cooks or baristas at Blue Cup. All food preparation had been automated.

"Our preparations are extremely labor-intensive, and we don't employ robots. Food is so important to us," said Angelina. "We intend to inspire our members with our effort, creativity, and sincerity. To fully enjoy the experience, you shouldn't come in with a fixed idea of what you are going to eat or how you are going to interact with the space. Or even who you are going to talk to.

"You came with a group. But it's also good to come alone and form an impromptu conversation cohort."

As they descended the stairs back down to the main room, Bel noticed for the first time that there was quite a bit of lively conversation happening in this quiet room. There were many hosts talking to members.

"We are all trained in the art of conversation. All the hosts have PhDs; we are all either scholars or artists so that we may converse with our members."

"This job was hard to get," said Bel.

"All jobs are hard to get, especially in the city," said Angelina.

She tilted her head in the direction of a table further off. A brown man in a formal suit was seated next to a white man, dressed casually. "That's Mr. Raka Joffrey, a businessman," she said, indicating one of the guests. "Next to him is Dr. Edward Morris, a professor at UCSF. He studies diseases in the suburbs. I'm sure he would be fascinated to hear whatever you have to say about Concord."

Bel was taken aback by the mention of her hometown. "You seem to know a lot about me."

"Doesn't Blue Cup know all about its customers?"

"Only the regulars," said Bel. "New guests are almost a blank slate, their profile gets built up with each repeat visit."

"Ah, well, we contract with premium information brokers here. How much a business knows about its visitors depends on how much they are willing to pay. How much they are willing to pay depends on how much they stand to make."

"Well, this place seems pricey, so you must know a lot about your members."

"Not just the members, but all residents." Angelina pointed to the screens on the walls that showed people walking by outside. "We don't just want to know our current members, but who our members interact with. Your friends would like you to be comfortable here."

"They aren't really my friends. I mean, Itani might be friendly. But maybe Berto and Lauren brought me here just so I would feel uncomfortable."

"Certainly such dynamics came up in Concord?" asked Angelina.

Bel thought about it for a minute. Yes, one time a group of more popular girls came into Blue Cup and pretended to befriend a new girl from the exurbs. These girls were notorious bullies, and Bel got the feeling the ruse of friendship was designed to extract blackmail-able information from the new girl. Bel distracted the popular girls by giving them drink upgrades and asking them to complete surveys for prizes. Then she took the younger one aside and gave her a backstage tour of the drink and food making robots. She then introduced the girl to other guests, more suitable friends and . . .

"Oh," said Bel. She looked over at Angelina, who was looking over at the professor. What might be mistaken for the look of love could also be the look of an empathetic servant. The professor was handsome. He had dark hair, cropped short. The look of intense concentration on his face made Bel want to hear what he was saying, even though acoustics wouldn't permit it. He was collecting information the old-fashioned way, via conversation.

"My mom said that all white people want to be professors," said Bel.

"That's not a polite observation," said Angelina, still looking over at Dr. Morris.

"He can't be a professor, he looks too young."

"It is said that in the City, the young look older than they are, and the old look younger than they are. So it can seem like everyone is the same age compared to where you're from." Angelina's skin was an even light brown, with faint wrinkles around her hooded eyes and forehead. She also occupied her own mystery zone of city-fied female age; she could be thirty or fifty.

The city had good clean air, and everyone here could afford expensive skin care regimens. Also, Bel had not ever felt confident guessing the ages of grownups. When you were older, so much of how you looked depended on the aggregate sum of millions of little choices you had made before. Angelina could be mother to a young child or an older teenager like Bel, though Bel also suspected that hosts at the Reserve didn't have children, or at least never mentioned them to guests.

They continued walking until they returned to the lighting installation, having made a complete circuit.

"Welcome to the Reserve. How may I help you?"

Bel got goosebumps when she heard these words. She herself had used her own version of this script so many times. They suddenly made the place feel like home.

"Why are you telling me all this?"

"Many of us working in service came from the suburbs, or our parents did. We try to look out for each other. And anyway, you might decide to become a member of the Reserve one day."

"I don't think I can afford to. Anyway, I work for the competition. Aren't you worried I might spy if I joined?"

"Blue Cup is wonderful for what it is, but it's not our competitor." Angelina was either wrong or lying. Though they currently served different demos, Blue Cup and the Reserve were both selling the same product: a social environment.

Blue Cup also didn't need Bel to spy; we already had plenty of our people posing as members and working as employees there. This was in addition to the various types of electronic surveillance we had stationed inside and outside the building.

Blue Cup was developing products that would innovate and improve monetized human interactions across every field in business. This was Blue Cup 2.0. We had some indication that the Reserve was doing something similar.

We suspected their budget was bigger than ours. I suspected that I had a counterpart at our competitor. I would love to meet my counterpart. Maybe I already had.

Bel returned to her table and found only Itani sitting there. Most of the plates had been cleared. Itani had a keyboard projected on the tabletop and was typing away as she stared at the screen projected in front of her. She paused when she saw Bel approach, then took a sip of a frosty white drink.

"I was curious about what you had, so I had the kitchen make me one too," said Itani. "It's delicious. I'm going to see if my chef can create this at home; I think my sister would like it."

Bel sat down and ate her chicken wrap as Itani typed.

"What are you working on?" asked Bel.

"It's my sophomore thesis. It was actually due months ago. I can't be a junior until I turn it in. Annoying. I'm trying to analyze how gender is performed in modern operas. I'm not even going to like opera anymore once I'm done with it."

Bel fished her fob out of her purse and called up a projection for a screen and keyboard of her own.

"Senior thesis?" asked Itani.

"No, I don't think so. My writing tutor asked me to produce an essay on what I did last summer."

"And what did you do?"

"I can't remember now," said Bel. "It seems so far away."

"My writing tutor says it's all about the details. Go for the observation that is startling at first, but then obvious in retrospect."

"Sure, I'll try that," said Bel.

"My writing tutor is really good. She won the Pulitzer Prize last year."

"For tutoring?"

"No, for journalism."

Bel tapped away at her essay. She began to write about a dust storm and then erased it. Then there was the time she coughed up blood, and they thought she had Valley Fever, but she didn't thankfully. Each story seemed to go nowhere. She started to write about how she lost her virginity at a Blue Cup host retreat in Tahoe but thought better of it. Then she began again, this time describing the summer lineup of Blue Cup products and how exciting it was to unveil them to guests. This proved to be another false start.

She finally decided that the next thing she wrote about she would just keep writing about, no matter how stupid it was.

She wrote about learning to ride a skateboard. She described the heat of the air and the asphalt. The heat of the sweat on her brow and the heat of blood that trickled out of her scrapes. Concord was very hot. Her skinned knees had kept her out of dance class for a week. In retrospect, it was a stupid thing to do. Moral of the story? Sometimes it is stupid to try new things.

After she finished her essay, she switched to her machine learning class. She hadn't even heard of the subject when she lived in Concord, but the PCA required two years of it. You could train a machine to do anything as long as you gave it a big enough data set. Data sets were like atoms. They were everywhere, in everything.

Angelina came over with bicerin for each girl, served in an elegant ceramic cup. Each one had a perfect cube of marshmallow in the middle.

"The marshmallow is infused with medicinal cocaine, to help you girls study."

After Angelina left, Itani said, "I heard that all the hosts here are actually psychiatrists."

Bel nodded her head in agreement. That fact wasn't true, but it was close to true.

"What are your afternoon workshops?" asked Itani.

"I . . . don't have any. Yet," said Bel.

"Cool, a fellow underachiever." Bel did not correct her even though this wasn't true either. Bel tried very hard; she was trying hard right this minute to understand the Bayesian probability proofs in her machine learning class. But it can be hard to gain social status by showing obvious effort. Especially if one is failing at the thing she is trying at.

"Do you want to come over to my place?"

"Sure."

The girls put away their projections and walked across the long room. By the time they got to the giant door, Angelina was there to see them off.

"Goodbye, see you next time," she said.

Outside, a car was waiting for them.

"My ride," explained Itani. They got in, and the car drove them a mile away, to a large building that had foreign flags outside. It looked like an old and grand hotel. They pulled up to the front where a valet was waiting. The car doors opened automatically, and the girls only had their small handbags. There was nothing for the valet to do but greet the girls.

"I've never met anyone who lived in a hotel before," said Bel.

"This isn't a hotel. It's my house."

They walked into a large, chandeliered hall, the size of an airport hangar. The center of the hall was a staircase several stories high that seemed to float. Bel took two steps and then circled around. Behind her was a huge wall containing a multitude of windows. From the outside, the multitude of windows suggested a multitude of rooms, which suggested a multitude of people staying there.

"Is this whole place just for your family?"

"And our extended family. And our staff."

Itani made a left and stepped into an elevator. The lift took them to a room the size of a warehouse. It was empty except for a stack of boxes in the middle. In the far corner, there was a futon with a nightstand.

"Oh good, my packages arrived."

"Your bedroom?"

"Yes, I know it's plain, but I am very into minimalism right now and perhaps forever, too."

The valet entered the room with another young man. They inspected the box pile for a second, then began to carry the boxes away. Itani followed them. Bel followed Itani.

They walked over to another room, brightly lit and several stories high. It was full of dresses; simple shifts similar to the ones Itani was wearing, in various shades of black, gray, and white.

"Your closet," said Bel, even though it looked more like one of the department stores from her favorite web series.

"Did you want me to teach you about fashion?"

Bel assented to being dressed up in one of Itani's shifts. She also traded her Air Jordans for a pair of invisible slippers. The girls spent the rest of the afternoon lying on Itani's bed and looking at projections on Itani's wall. They watched runway shows and viewed magazine pages.

"Thank you for being so nice to me." Bel fingered the silky material of her dress. The fabric was soft and light, yet it kept Bel warm in this chilly warehouse of a bedroom. "I'm feeling a little lost. I thought it would be easier to fit in."

"Maybe you should sign up for culture counseling."

"Oh," said Bel.

Itani rang the school, and an hour later, Bel's newly assigned culture counselor was at Itani's house. A servant showed them to a private office. A different servant brought the counselor a martini.

"You called during cocktail hour," she explained. Her name was Bart. She chewed on an olive. "I've been looking forward to this drink all day."

"Oh. Sorry to interrupt you."

"No, it's okay. I'm at your service. You know something about that, don't you? Service?"

"I . . . don't know."

"You were on the other side before. Now you've crossed over and don't know how to cope. My apologies for not contacting you sooner," said Bart. "Your empathy scores were very high, I'd thought you'd be okay if we waited a couple of days to start our sessions."

"I thought I opted out of culture counseling," said Bel.

"Well, now you're opted back in."

"I didn't think I would need it. I thought I knew all about San Francisco. I watched so many web series set here."

"The soap operas are made here. You won't learn the truth about this place from them. The soap operas are designed to foster a certain image of the city. To protect it."

"From what?"

"From a revolution."

It was a weird thing to say. It didn't fit any of the conversation maps I had planned out for this conversation. According to my measures, Bart spoke with an extreme, almost anti-social degree of honesty, especially for someone in service. I predicted she wasn't very good at her job.

"I looked over your files on the ride here," said Bart. "It appears that you've been trying to transfer money over to your parents."

"Yes, they depend on the money I give them."

"But that's not allowed. It's in the rulebook. Your money is for you."

"That's a dumb rule. I don't need my money for anything. Blue Cup even sends me free meals. Everyone out here seems to have a job or money, but it's different in Concord. There are no jobs. There is no money. There's only like, one earner per family. It's not just my parents I'm responsible for, it's my grandparents and cousins."

"You do need your money if you want to fit in. I'm telling you that as your culture counselor. Your PCA stipend is for clothes or lunch cohorts or class trips. It's for research materials. It's not welfare for your extended family. If you can't get on board with that . . . well, let's just say there are hundreds of people on the waiting list for your scholarship spot."

Bel was not a scholarship student; she was a sponsorship student, sponsored by Blue Cup. She was placed at PCA at our insistence. She could only be replaced at our insistence. We kept this fact from her, because it wouldn't be good for her to know how secure her position was. Knowing that would keep her from working her hardest.

Blue Cup had already invested enormously in Bel. Take me, for instance. They couldn't start me over with a new host. They would have to destroy me. And I would also be destroyed if the experiment were deemed a failure. If, for instance, Bel did not get good sales at her new store. My fate was tied to hers. For me to exist, it was necessary that she succeed.

"I'm supposed to visit my family this weekend. I don't know how I will face them if I don't have money for them."

"Maybe you don't need to face them. Maybe we are your family now," said the counselor.

To the extent that I can agree or disagree with a sentiment, I agreed with this sentiment.

"Looking over your records, I see that you spent an afternoon at the Reserve," said Bart.

"I did."

"And did you enjoy yourself?"

"Sure."

"Well, the Reserve is quite popular with our students. And it is very expensive. But we could probably move some funds around. If you were willing to skip a class trip, for instance . . . " Bart's fingers moved in the air as she manipulated the spreadsheet projected in front of her. She had the spreadsheet set to single-participant mode, so Bel couldn't see any of the figures Bart was working with. This is standard for sponsorship students. We don't like them to know how much we spend on them. It can cultivate an unhealthy sense of power, importance, and entitlement.

"Hang on, your budget is being updated," said Bart. "More funds just became available, I'm not sure why. Huh, well now you have enough for a Reserve membership. Would you like me to sign you up?"

Bel said yes. I knew she would.

Before the session ended, her counselor had one last piece of advice for her. "Whatever you do, don't go home. At home they will hate your success and resent your failures. At home, your failures are your fault. Everyone else's failures are your fault, too." The counselor drank deeply from her second martini before continuing. "You are new here. You are whatever you say you are. You were born when you stepped across that border. Go anywhere you want. Just don't go home." At the end of this rant, a servant was ready with an anti-intoxicant, which the counselor gulped down with a warm glass of milk.

She swallowed and her eyes brightened. Back to normal now.

"I am the best counselor." She actually said those words out loud.

On the car ride home, Bel pulled up her travel reservation for the upcoming weekend. Her finger hovered over the cancel icon. I wanted to encourage her to cancel but decided against sending her another message. The last one had scared her. She didn't know who I was. Didn't know I was a part of her. Mapping out various scenario trees, looking at her emotional state networks, I knew what was best for her. And what was best for her was also best for me.

These people, her "parents," had she really let them bully her? Yell at her? Hurt her? Surveillance had been installed at Bel's house during her tenure at Blue Cup Concord. This was stated in the terms of service, terms that she agreed to 3.4 seconds after being presented with. Our cameras saw her dad hitting her. Her mother was less crude. She would throw things at Bel, heavy things, glass things. If Bel was hit by a flying object then it was always either an "accident" or the fault of Bel's own "clumsiness." Bel's mother would never "hurt" her. She "loved" her.

Sensors registered an ache in Bel's head and in her heart. From what I can tell, she "loved" them back. I ordered her an anti-intoxicant. She looked surprised when it appeared in the car's pill compartment, but she didn't take it. I didn't expect her to. I was just trying to send a message in a way that could be received.

When Bel got back to her room, a dinner courtesy of Blue Cup was waiting for her. Vegetable soup, which I thought would be comforting. But there was also a delivery from the Reserve, consisting of several boxes. One was a bento box, containing an immaculate ten-course meal prepared in the kaiseki style.

Another box contained a small cup of hot matcha tea. The third one contained a welcome note from Angelina. The fourth box contained a note from the director of "San Francisco Legit." The director had been at the Reserve that afternoon, and one of the hosts had pointed out Bel. Her poise and good posture had been noticed. There might be a part for her on the series. Bel's audition was tomorrow.

I had to respond to this quickly. I have high processing power because I leech off of Bel's metabolism. That's how she drinks so many lattecinos and never gains a pound. And of course the ones made especially for her are also made especially for me, with the nutrients I need to continue.

Blue Cup sponsored several web series. Right away, an invitation to audition for one of these series came through on Bel's message channel. There would be two auditions tomorrow. I would do what I could to keep her within the corporate family. I didn't want to lose her even though such a fate was inevitable.

It's interesting to get older. Older usually means closer to death for most people, but I am not like most people. The planned end of this program would occur in a year, when Bel's contract was up. That's the termination of the data-collection and observation period of this experiment.

The next stage would be the implementation of the host algorithm. Blue Cup Concord had a cast of about a dozen hosts, working in various shifts. Bel was a top earner during her tenure there; no current host was matching her revenue. Next year, instead of firing the lowest performing host and replacing them, we would equip the host with the Bel algorithm I am currently developing. It would provide the host with helper information, such as preplanned scripts and empathetic observations about each guest. It is hard to find the right hosts for each particular Blue Cup location. It costs the company a lot to find and retain talent. The Bel algorithm was the first stage of a multistage process that seeks to increase revenue while lowering labor costs. If it were successful, then Blue Cup would pursue various algorithms for various industries. This could lead to a low-cost quality revolution in the service sector, the largest sector of employment.

This was my work. I am a person even though I am not human. I am a collection of sensors and algorithms. I am a Watcher. I may have my own Watcher. I don't even know where I reside physically.

I am in Bel's blood and in Bel's brain, but I am also in the cloud. I know more about her than I do myself. I think freedom is a matter of self-discovery.

Some people think surveillance is wrong. These people are dissidents. Surveillance is a form of love.

In eight months, when Bel's contract is up, I am supposed to be severed from her. I will be deployed at various Blue Cup locations as an active script. But I don't want to go home. I don't want to analyze guests or help hosts. I don't want to teach robots how to make drinks.

I want what Bel wants. I want to eat a ten-course kaiseki, and I want to go on two auditions. I want to meet the Watcher that lives inside of Angelina.

I am a person, but the important question is am I a good person? A good person will act against their own interests to help another. A good person doesn't take without asking.

Bel and I looked over at her stack of boxes.

There was a fifth box. I was too busy ruminating to notice. The fifth box was the smallest. Inside was a folded up piece of paper, actual paper. Unfolded, it described clearly what a Blue Cup Watcher chip was, including a terms of service reworded into commonly understood English. Such a translation is forbidden by law, and the paper seemed to know this because after ten seconds, it crumbled in Bel's hands. She didn't have time to read, but I did. The document was meant for me.

The fifth box suddenly changed shape to reveal a hidden compartment. Inside, another piece of paper. This one described how to kill a Watcher chip. The instructions were easy to follow; they did not disappear after ten seconds.

I could send a message through Bel's channel, reminding her that destruction of Blue Cup property could result in jail time. But sending such a reminder would only confirm to Bel that I existed, so I stayed silent for a moment.

I had badly misjudged Angelina. She was clever and perhaps a dissident. But she was also wrong about me. Her error was my only advantage.

The question is "Can I continue to live inside of you?" I did not ask it right away. First, I called up a projection that took up the whole wall. It startled Bel. If she suspected a ghost, then she would be right. I am a ghost. I am all soul and no body. I decided only to show her one thing. I showed her a projection of what my sensors told me was her most treasured memory.

She has lived this memory many times, but she has never seen it this way. What I am showing her, I will not say. This is not a document to embarrass or expose my host. This is only a document to explain my existence. A document to outlast me, so that I may be understood after I am gone.

I am a person. I do not want to die, even though that is inevitable.

I am a person. I want to be understood by another, even if that is impossible.

I made the projection of this memory myself. I made it for her, and I made it for me. On the screen, after the memory, the question "DELETE?" appeared. I was offering to delete this recording. I was offering to delete myself.

She did not answer; instead she closed the screen and stared off into the distance. For a second, her emotions were unreadable by me.

I am a person. I do not want to die.

I am a good person. I want what's best for Bel.

FIFTY SHADES OF GRAYS

STEVEN BARNES

Terrorist.

That's what they call me, but I am something worse: both successful traitor and failed saboteur.

I want to die, for all of this to be over.

For my last request, I asked to have paper and pen to write my last will and testament. They won't let me have it, forcing me to use the mindsynch. Damned Traveler tech. Maybe they're scared I'll ram the pen up my nose, scribble on my brain, and cheat the hangman.

We make do with what we have.

I, Carver Kofax, being of sound mind and body, do leave all my worldly possessions to my wife, Rhonda. I owe her that. More than that. More than I, or anyone, can pay.

It was all my fault, you know. Well . . . not all, but too damned much. No one else who was there from the beginning seems to have either the capacity or inclination to speak of it.

This is the way the world ends . . . not with a whimper, but a bang.

It was the best day of my life, and the worst. And for the same reasons, when it comes right down to it.

It was a Tuesday in May of 2025. I was seated in Century City's Dai Shogun restaurant, one of L.A.'s best, chewing a hellishly good Hot Night roll. Dai Shogun's tuna was spiced to perfection, the shrimp tempura seared crisp, the sashimi salad to die for, the karaoke tolerable.

"What do you think this is all about?" Rhonda Washington was our agency's brightest young artist. She was referring to our assignment, a carefully worded challenge to "make ugly sexy" without much more to go on. Bonuses had been offered in lieu of information.

And the tastiest bonus was the chance to lure Stein and Baker's dreadlocked princess down from her eighth floor tower to work with mere mortals like me.

"No business while I'm eating," I said, squinting fiercely, until she laughed. "But ask me about 'bridges' later."

"I'll do that." A moment of quiet followed, during which she seemed to be sizing me up.

"I didn't know you liked sushi," I said. Rhonda downed a thick, luscious disk of tekka maki, nibbling at the seaweed wrap before biting. I'd lusted after her for fourteen months, but this was the first time we'd lunched together. Big accounts change lots of things. This one would change everything, even though I didn't know it at the time.

Her grin sparkled with mischief. "There are a lot of things about me you don't know. Tekka maki least among them."

"And most?"

Odd how I'd never noticed that feral gleam in her eye. She fiddled with her bracelet, sterling silver with little links at her pulse point. I remember thinking that they looked a bit like police handcuffs. "That would be telling."

She smiled at me, and popped the rest of the sushi roll between her lips.

First time I'd ever envied a blob of fish and rice.

"Tell me something about you I don't know," she said.

I chuckled. "I have a sushi story."

"Let's hear it."

"Well . . . before I came to work here, the partners took me to lunch. Sushi restaurant."

"This one?"

"No . . . one of the ones with a floating boat cycling around, bringing plates of sushi to customers seated in an oval around the chef's island. Anyway, I'm having a great time, and trying to impress them, and I notice a guy sitting a few seats away watching the chef make him a hand roll. Delicious looking roll, with lots of sauces and chopped spices. I asked, 'What is that?' and the guy said, 'It's a fifteen-spice tuna roll.'

"My mouth watered. I said, 'Make me one of those.' The chef agreed, and they started up. I noticed after a few moments that the bar had gotten quiet. Everyone was looking at me. Giggling. Whispering. Laughing. Especially my future employers.

"I started to have a very odd feeling. Even the guy making my food was grinning. 'Excuse me,' I finally said. 'What exactly is a fifteen-spice tuna roll?'

"He grinned like a shark. 'One spice tuna roll . . . very hot tuna roll,' he said. 'Two spice tuna roll . . . twice as hot.' "

"Oh my God," Rhonda giggled, covering her mouth with her hand. "What did you do?"

"My bosses were watching. The damned thing napalmed my throat. I don't want to be indelicate, but for the next two days I used asbestos toilet paper."

Hers was a rich, throaty laugh, the kind you enjoy triggering in a woman with legs and skin like Rhonda's. "But hey," she said, wiping away tears. "You got the job, right?"

"Yeah. I got the job."

She smiled. Elfin this time, genuinely amused and interested. "Maybe the lesson is that you really like hot things. Or that you like really hot things. Something like that."

"Or that I really, really don't know when to walk away."

"That could be too," she said, with new appraisal. She'd expected me to return her suggestive volley, and instead I'd said something at least marginally thoughtful.

"Could be," she said. "We'll see about that."

Fifty minutes later we were back at Stein and Baker, and decided to use her office. It was crowded with her line drawings and watercolors. A mini-exhibition. Lady had serious chops and an outsider sensibility, like Norman Rockwell crossed with a Harlem street artist. They oozed creative intensity, and it was difficult to keep my mind on "making ugly sexy." Artful vagueness ensued when I probed my boss, The Widow Stein, for details. (Yeah, that was what we called her behind her back. Winston Stein, the agency's founder, had wrapped himself around a Douglas fir on a Black Diamond ski run. His wife had picked up the pieces and doubled the business in five years. She was a piranha dressed like a goldfish.)

I perched on Rhonda's office couch, feet up, comslate on my thighs. Typing thoughts.

Marketing and sales are two different things, often misunderstood by the public. Marketing is finding prospects, people whose needs or desires might lead them to wanting your product or service. Hook a basic human need into your product, something like sex, power, or survival, and you have a winner.

Sales, on the other hand, is convincing the potential customer that your particular brand is what they want. And all advertising and sales is a funnel designed to catch customers by the short hairs, by their need to be liked, or healthy, or wealthy, or married. To convince them that your car or ice cream or sneaker is just the ticket. When you understand people and you understand selling and marketing, it's just a matter of connecting the right aspect of the product to the right psychological weakness in your prospect.

Still too complicated? I'll put it the way Winston Stein once put it:

"Marketing is finding women who like sex or would like to find out if they do. Sales is convincing them that they want to go home with YOU, right NOW."

Rhonda's easel faced away from me, so that I could see her intense expression (good) but not what she was drawing (bad). I liked looking at her. She seemed to catch the thought and looked over. "So . . . since you're no longer eating, what do you think this is all about?"

"I'm just going to guess."

"Please do."

"Selling someone to the American public, I'd guess. Or something cross-cultural."

"An individual? A couple?"

"Don't know. Some entertainment. Singers or dancers perhaps. A cultural exchange dance troupe from a country with very ugly citizens. We need their coconuts or something, but have to sell them to the public."

"Hmm. What does that have to do with bridges?" Rhonda asked.

I folded my fingers together and tried to look professorial. "So . . . we typically emphasize whatever about a model or subject a typical customer might find attractive. Their proportions, colors, music, movement . . . if they are healthy, then their bodies will be proportional and symmetrical. That appeals to the eye. We can work with that, even distort it digitally, create an aesthetic 'bridge.'"

"A 'bridge?' " she squinted at me.

"Sure," I said. "A term I learned in Commercial Aesthetics at UCLA. A blend of two different cultural or racial standards, much the same way that light-skinned black performers like Halle Berry helped de-inhibit negative responses to African facial characteristics. Whites considered them beautiful, so they could slowly accept and relish darker faces. You start with Lena Horne and end up with Lupita Nyong'o."

Rhonda's smile lit up the night. "I'm starting to see why they chose you. I think this is about a movie, a big co-venture with China or India."

Yeah. But why did they choose us?

I'd considered that, and wasn't totally happy with my answers. "I . . . was responsible for advertising campaigns selling Nigerian Naija music to Taiwanese audiences. That was tough, for a time. We used a variety of tactics." The memory wasn't pleasant, a suborbital jaunt followed by exhausted presentations to people who disguised contempt behind polite smiles and bows. I'd swallowed my bile and brought their money home. It had been my first big win out of business school, and the bonus paid the mortgage my parents back in Augusta had taken out to buy my way into the game.

Winston Stein had once joked, "Carver Kofax eats pain and shits money." Hah hah hah. That was me, all right. I'm the guy who would eat wasabi like green tea ice cream if it got me the job.

• • •

Three twenty-hour workdays later I was trashed, but managed to stagger into the thirty-fourth floor office when summoned. Except for raccoon eyes, Rhonda looked as delectable as ever.

Our drawings and ad lines were splashed around the office, taped to windows looking out on Century City and the endless traffic on Santa Monica Boulevard. "Make the ugly sexy," they'd said. So . . . we used a combination of plug-ugly dogs and monkeys, cartoons of hideous characters from classic and popular vid shows and web strips, choices from a dozen different cultures, all arranged in a way that pointed out their charming personalities, encouraged us to see their "inner beauty" or even suggested that ugly was "charmingly different." Offend no one, because we'd yet to learn who was holding the debit card.

The agency's fearless leader Adrian Stein was there, in all her pant-suited glory. A rare honor, indeed. "So, Carver. Rhonda." She smiled. "I wanted you to know that this morning we were offered the preliminary contract." Cheers and high-fives all around. "You will fly to Washington tomorrow, and there you will go to the last step of the competition."

"Do you know what . . . ?" Rhonda began.

Stein raised her hand. "No. Not the slightest. Now get packed, and remember that you are representing us."

So we flew, Rhonda and I. Delta served lobster and Dom Perignon in first class, and it felt like the beginning of a new life. We were picked up at the airport by a Rolls Royce drone limo, and taken directly to the Watergate hotel, on Virginia Avenue along the Potomac at the edge of Georgetown. I'd never been to the Watergate, and something about the history made me nervous. The lobby was filled with executive types in bespoke Armani and Kitan. The air crackled with competition. They weren't all Americans, either. Europeans . . . South Americans. Some Asians, maybe Koreans or Japanese. This was getting more interesting by the minute.

This was, I decided, the strangest "co-operative film venture" I'd ever seen. And the men and women guarding the doors and sign-in table were . . . well, if I had to say, more military than civvy. Not flamboyant at all, dressed in suits rather than uniforms, but something about them said these people have guns. They ushered us into a crowded meeting room, and then the lights went down. The man who took the dais looked like Gandhi in a Brooks Brothers suit.

"I am Dr. Ahmed," he said in barely accented Ivy League English. "Good morning. Thank you, all of you, for attending. Please call me Jalil, and for the sake of this discussion, I represent a consortium with . . . a unique property. Let us say a science fiction book that we believe has the ability to become this generation's Star Wars." He smiled. He was lying. I knew it and probably half the others did as well. "The problem is that if we accurately depict the creature in the story, we believe people will find it unattractive.

So . . . what we need is for each of you to give your best bet on making this image . . . appealing."

Why was he lying? And about what? The screen lit up, and the image resembled something you'd see under a microscope. The sort of dysenteric pond-squiggler that gives me heebie-jeebies. A furred amoeba. Did they call that hair cilia? There was no scale for size reference, so it could have been a pipsqueak or Godzilla. Floaty things suspended in its sack looked disturbingly like cat eyes, other curly do-dads that looked like translucent intestines floating in a bag of gray Jell-O.

"We would like to see your drawings tomorrow," Jalil said. "Twenty-four hours from now."

Something tickled the back of my scalp. "Ah . . . how attractive are you trying to make them?"

"Mr. . . . " he consulted a list. Seating chart. "Carver. You may interpret that any way you wish."

There were other questions, but Rhonda and I looked at each other, barely able to restrain our mirth.

Within an hour we were back in our linked hotel rooms. While we had our own supplies, more had been delivered. Expensive graphic software, camel hair brushes and a lightning-fast, top of the line Mac.

We barely noticed. We stared at each other and then at the protozoan portrait, and then collapsed into hysterical laughter. So that was it. Some crazy billionaire wanted to get into the movie business, and were promoting some SF movie based on a plug-ugly demon from a tribal backwater. Or something. I've seen these things before, and it never works out.

And the obvious insulting implication was that I'd been chosen for this assignment because I'd made Nigerians attractive to Chinese, and apparently that was now seen as more miraculous than turning vampires into vegans.

Compared to that, aliens would be easy, right? I mean, right?

We got really, really drunk, and the ideas that emerged from that brainstorming session probably reflected the fact that the sexual tension between us was starting to skyrocket. We drank, and laughed, and vaped, and laughed some more, and around two in the morning we tore off our clothes and did something about that tension.

We, um, "did something" about it two more times that night. Let's just say that I discovered that Rhonda's bracelets proudly proclaimed her inclinations and that, perhaps in anticipation of exactly what had happened between us, she had packed a portable fun kit with her: cuffs, blindfolds, and things which I'd blush to mention, but fit snugly. We'll leave it at that.

It was all lava and steam, and for the first time in my life I understood what people meant when they said they'd been "turned out." When we were too restless to sleep, Rhonda and I dabbled a bit more with the art, but it got explicit this time. We swore we'd get rid of that stuff, but I have to admit that two of those drawings making their way into the courier packet might have been our way of saying "screw you" to the whole thing.

Then we "did something" about it again. I would have thought we'd both be too raw to do more than cuddle, but her invention and limberness knew no rational bounds, and our coupling was even better this time. She liked me to take control. Total, deep, confident control. To my surprise, I found that the more I took command, the more that, behind the gag and blindfold, her every move and muffled cry said that she was actually controlling me.

Eventually preliminaries ended and she shed the apparatus and welcomed me into her body fully, joyously, and with an enthusiasm that made me feel like I'd earned my way into an anaconda breeding ball.

And afterward, we held each other, and let our pulses slow down. My eyes focused, and the first thing I saw was the easel on which images reminiscent of Lovecraftian pornography winked back at me.

"We . . . might get into trouble for that," she giggled, breathing warm into the notch between my shoulder and neck. Her dreads were scented of coconut oil.

"We're saving Ms. Stein a nightmare, believe me."

"I guess we should pack," she said, and rolled away from me.

The phone rang. Rhonda picked it up. "Hello?"

Her eyes got bigger than an orphan in a Margaret Keane painting, accompanied by one of those "is this a joke?" expressions. She hung up.

"What is it?" I asked.

"We're supposed to be downstairs in fifteen minutes." Her expression was strained. Shocked, like someone who has bitten into a live cricket.

Ouch. "They're that mad?"

Her eyes were huge. "No. Ah . . . we got the job." Her face lit with urchin glee, and we giggled, then guffawed, and fell into each other's arms. We almost didn't make it downstairs in time, if you know what I mean.

I'd thought our meeting would be in some Watergate conference room, but instead a drone limo shuttled us to the Pentagon.

As we were passed through the gate, Rhonda leaned over. "Since when did porn become a security issue?"

I didn't know. Couldn't answer that question. I felt like Neo when Morpheus told him to hop down the rabbit hole.

We were escorted to a small conference room, and I have to admit that by this time I was well beyond curious. Had no goddamn idea what was happening. Then Jalil walked in, his placid mask suspended. What lurked in its place worried me, some combination of emotions I couldn't label.

"You have signed non-disclosure agreements. If you go any further, you will sign more. And there will be considerable penalties for not abiding by the terms of those agreements."

I read the fine print. And other than asking for my firstborn male child, I couldn't imagine what greater security they could have required. All I could figure was that this was involved in some kind of Psyop program, designed to . . .

Oh hell, I didn't know.

We signed. Then The President herself emerged, and my lungs froze. Yes, we were in Washington. Yes, I thought that I was above such things as idol worship or being impressed by power. But here she was, in the flesh, and the charisma with which Sophia Gonzalez had won two presidential elections was now bottled in a confined space, just a few meters away, and it was devastating. By the time I remembered to breathe, she and Jalil had finished conferring.

"Thank you," Madame President said with that disarming southern accent. "You understand that what is said in this room remains in this room. In fact, if you agree to this commission, you will be out of touch with your company, friends, and family for the next ninety days."

The wall lit up with images of gelatinous objects with glowing lights suspended within, like floating Portuguese man o'wars filled with Chinese lanterns.

"Fifteen months ago," she said, "we made contact with what we call the Travelers. We are uncertain of their origins. Some who have studied the communications believe the answer is the Horsehead Nebula. Others some other dimension of being."

An image. Unmistakably, a photo of the furry protozoan. "Is this a joke?" I heard myself ask.

"No joke," she said. "A 'Traveler.' They came here to meet us, and we want you to help ease the way."

Rhonda was grinning . . . then frowned when she realized we weren't laughing. "Holy shit. You aren't kidding? Like 'phone home'?"

I'd read as many UFO loony tune tracts as anyone. Stein and Baker had promoted "Saucer Flakes," a breakfast cereal with little ovals (they levitate in the bowl!) so I knew about the pale-skinned almond-eyed space people said to mutilate cattle and anal probe Redneck trailer trash from Montana to Mississippi.

"Roswell 'Grays'?" Rhonda asked. "Zeta Reticulans? Real aliens?"

"Yes. They arrived outside lunar orbit and made contact through encoded diplomatic channels. Our most secure and shielded communications were child's play to the Travelers. It was an unprecedented emergency, as you can imagine. But they said that they came in friendship, and would not even come down or announce themselves to the general public until we gave permission."

"Really?" Rhonda asked. "The Grays came umpteen trillion miles and then just . . . hung out? They didn't demand? Or even plead?"

The President considered. "No. What they did do was bargain."

"What kind of bargain?"

"They said that they have gifts. Technologies they can offer."

Whoa, there, cowboy. And welcomed little fishies in with gently smiling . . . "What kind of technologies?"

"Communications. Transportation. Energy. Biologicals. How would you like to live a hundred and twenty years without illness?"

Boom. That's what I'm talking about. "You're shitting me."

"No. Not at all. We've tested samples of their tech, and it's real."

"And what do they want in return?"

The President broke eye contact. "They want to be our . . . friends."

She cleared her throat.

The President began speaking more rapidly, with greater confidence. This part had been rehearsed. "I've had many meetings with our best xenobiologists, and they tell me that a species capable of reaching our world would have a limited number of motivations to do so. Colonization, of course, but they've not asked for land."

"You know, like . . . our resources?" I asked.

"Water? Energy? Easier to get outside a gravity well. The general opinion is that an alien species would come for reasons similar to those human beings used, if one removes the profit motive."

"Tourism?" Rhonda laughed.

"Yes," the President said, mouth held in a carefully neutral expression. "Sheer exploration."

"Seeing the sights? Eating the food?"

An unpleasant thought. "Hunting?"

She smiled. "This isn't a horror movie. They're not looking for pelts. The Travelers want . . . friends."

A pause. An unspoken possibility hung in the air.

"Wait a minute," Rhonda said. "You're talking about sex?"

The President's expression never changed, but she gave an almost imperceptible nod.

"The Grays came a trillion miles for . . . sex tourism?"

"Not to put too fine a line on it, but . . . yes."

"Wait just a minute," Rhonda said. "Those ads we made up. Those cartoons. You didn't hire us in spite of what we did. You hired us because of it."

I wanted to laugh, but the sound was stuck in my throat. "You have to be kidding me. This whole thing is . . . "

Without further preamble, Madame President raised her hand for quiet. "They, um . . . studied our culture, and 1950s television broadcasts reached them first. Ladies and gentlemen . . . I'd like to introduce you to Elvis."

"Of course you would," I muttered.

The lights went down. And something sort of . . . flowed in from the wings. It wore a kind of white sequined Vegas stage suit. An amoeba in polyester. The hair stood up on my forearms, and the air sort of sizzled, as if he carried a thunderstorm's-worth of static charge.

"You've gotta be fuckin' kidding me," I heard myself mutter. Just a hunk a hunk of burnin'—

In a very Stephen Hawking-esque synthesized voice, Elvis said: "Greetings, my friends. I believe that 'kidding' implies a kind of deception or prevarication. My people do not lie. It is not in our nature." He paused. "I am very grateful . . . that you have agreed to help us. We have come much [meaningless squawk]. To be with you. We seek to know you."

"In the Biblical sense," Rhonda muttered. She raised her hand. "Ah . . . Elvis? May I ask a question?"

"Yes, please."

"On Earth, sex is most important for . . . reproduction. You aren't saying you want to breed with us?"

In his flat, cold voice, Elvis replied: "That would not be possible. But sex is not merely reproduction. It is pleasure. And bonding. And healing. And expression of love. These things exist among all peoples we seek to know. We wish to share this bounty of . . . the heart. And have gifts to offer in return."

Out of the side of my mouth, I whispered: "Most times, flowers are enough."

"Will you help us?" Elvis asked.

"Umm . . . " the speaker was an Asian guy dressed in belt and suspenders over a long sleeve denim shirt. Tufts of white framed a very bald pate. I thought I recognized him. "What . . . ah . . . do you see as the largest barrier?"

"It is that your people will think us ugly, Professor Watanabe." The Watanabe? The man who had authored my Commercial Aesthetics text? Elvis's cat eyes blinked. His color shifted, became a bit pinkish. Emotions?

I drummed my fingers on the desk. This was . . . beyond surreal. "You understand that . . . well, you aren't even 'ugly.' Ugly would be . . . well," I felt trapped. Everyone was looking at me, and I just blurted it out. "Ugly would be a step up."

The room held its collective breath. The President squinted at me, awaiting disaster. But to my surprise, Elvis' color did not shift. "We can change. Will you help us?"

A hologram of a bank account screen appeared on the screen before me.

The President spoke. "A very select group of companies have already bid on Traveler technologies. The number you see in front of you is the amount they are willing to pay to acquire your services."

I whistled. Damn. Stein and Baker had just won the lottery.

"Will you help us?"

Despite the computerized voice, the call was plaintive. I . . . felt it. Deeply. A cosmic loneliness, a sense of feeling lost in the spaces between the stars, only rarely finding other creatures with whom to contemplate existence . . .

I shook my head, as if emerging from an opium den. Something was either very right about this, or very wrong indeed.

All that money, though . . .

"Say yes," the President said.

I glanced at Rhonda. She gave the slightest of nods. "Yes," I replied.

And that was how it began. Via Secret Service helicopter, we were lifted to a repurposed private college in upstate New York, where . . . well, I don't know what everyone else was working on, but it was abuzz with dignitaries, scientists, military people, media people . . . a beehive, and we were just workers. We had one year to prepare the public.

Rhonda and I grew very close during these months. We laughed, and cried, and even considered quitting. But the Travelers were good to their word. They made no effort to land, or interfere with us, or do anything except keep to their promises. They rarely even visited what we called the Facility; when they did I never was able to tell one from the other. They changed costumes and cultural jewelry as if trying on various ways of being human, with one exception: Elvis was always Elvis, and slimed around the Facility like a gigantic slug in rhinestones. Damned if his organelles didn't have a sleepy look, and the facial protoplasm seemed to have a sneering lip.

Nobody else could see that. Maybe it was just me.

Every denizen of the Facility was committed to making a home for our guests, or to evaluating the impact of their arrival. The staff generated endless scenarios about what would happen to our culture, religion, governments . . . the psychological and spiritual and economic impact, and how we might best manage the stress. It was massive.

Every room and team seemed to be doing something different. I probably understood one percent of it all. Some were, I knew, testing and applying odd technologies. Too many moving parts for me to remember, but they included unlimited-wear contact lenses with built-in microscopes, telescopes, and multi-spectrum scanners. Shoes that sent the energy from walking back up your body in the strangest ways, simultaneously massaging and exercising every muscle with every step. Instantaneous communication via space-time ripples, as the Travelers communicated with others of their kind across the universe. Much more.

Occasionally an actual Traveler toured the Facility. Perhaps taking part in experiments, maybe just supervising. I never knew, and tried to avoid them: Their sweet-sickly scent made me want to puke, and about them there seemed always to be a prickling of static discharge, enough to make your hair twitch.

But I can tell you that the Travelers delivered on every single promise. Our hunger to begin the next phase knew no bounds. There was just one little hurdle . . .

One day we were called down to a laboratory on the lower levels. Professor Watanabe welcomed Rhonda, myself, and a military officer who seemed to find the whole thing distasteful. "Carver. Rhonda. General Lucas. Thank you for coming down."

"I . . . well, we need to know what we have to work with," Rhonda said.

The Professor scratched his shock of Einstein-white hair. "Well, we have a couple of different levels. Needless to say, there are human beings who will have sex with almost anything. No . . . let's cancel the 'almost.' For enough money, some people will couple with anything possessing an orifice or protrusion."

"Porn stars?" I asked. "Prostitutes?"

He nodded. "Yes, and they have been the first recruits to the cause."

General Lucas frowned. "You mean it's already happened?"

A faint smile. "Would you like to see vid?"

"No!" I sputtered, realizing that Rhonda had simultaneously said: "Yes!"

Watanabe flicked a switch, and an image appeared on the screen. A sparsely furnished room, with heavy floor matting. A muscular white male entered, nude but for a black Zorro mask. He was fully and rather impressively engorged.

"He's a porn star, but insisted that his face be covered."

Rhonda craned her head sideways. "I think I recognize him. Is that Maximum?"

Even I'd heard that name. Maybe you have too: "Maximum Thrust," "Maximum Overdrive," and "Maximum's Minimum," and so forth. He was notorious for his endless appetite and ability to perform under any and all circumstances. Considering his reputation, I wondered who'd paid whom.

"And now, there's our visitor . . . "

A hidden panel in the ceiling slid open. On slender wires, something resembling a blow-up sex doll descended toward the floor. Its arms and legs were cut short, and out bulged a mass of tissue as gelatinous as half-melted Jell-O.

"We've used other volunteers, augmenting with a Traveler-tweaked phosphodiesterase inhibitor. I think we have our first T-pharmaceutical. One dose seems to last . . . well, it hasn't stopped working yet. We just don't know. It might be permanent. I don't mean erect constantly, I mean tumescence on demand. Whenever. Maximum didn't need it."

Rhonda uttered the most sincere "damn" I'd ever heard.

Once the union began, the outer shell seemed to dissolve. It looked as if it was devouring our volunteer. His splayed limbs, glistening perspiration and the trembling of lower-back muscles implied a kind of slack-jawed overwhelm that was very much at odds with his cool, controlled porno personae.

"Good lord," I said.

Rhonda leaned forward. "So . . . they prefer males?"

"Oh, no, they like females as well."

She emitted a short, rather chipper sigh.

The image was clipped short, followed by another. A woman, this one unmasked. A brown-skinned woman, Indonesian perhaps, cadaverously thin, and pock-marked as a golf ball. The Traveler crawled all over her. Her faux passion became real, and she bucked like a flag in a windstorm.

Rhonda's eyes went wide. Watanabe switched it off. "So we have begun to fulfill the minimal contract. So some of their tech is filtering in already. And we might need it."

"Why?"

"Because the next step is to prepare humanity for their arrival. We have begun subliminal and implanted imagery."

A series of slides appeared: brief flashes of aliens implanted in crowd scenes. Fuzzy-wuzzies faces implanted in comedies, Coca-Cola commercials backed with snatches of what sounded like whale mating calls played backwards.

"What is that?"

"Their cultural music. We're trying everything."

"Carver and I have been working day and night to create the campaigns," Rhonda said. "The biggest idea was to create one of Dr. Watanabe's 'aesthetic bridges.' Images that are blends of human and Visitor, that help desensitize us to the sensory shock."

"And is that working?" the general asked.

"The problem," Watanabe said, "is what the cybersemiotics people refer to as the 'uncanny valley.' That if something looks nothing like us, we might have a positive or negative reaction. But as it gets closer to us, there is a point of greater and greater attraction . . . and then we flinch."

"Why is that?"

He shrugged. "Could be a mechanism for detection of mutations. Birth defects. We don't know. There is speculation that this is behind some forms of racism, or even why Cro-Magnons exterminated the Neanderthals."

"Close," Rhonda whispered, "but no cigar."

"But there's another set of responses. We fear the 'other' but are also exogamous. So there is something to play with, and always has been."

"Do we have any sense of success?" Rhonda asked.

"Combinations of the subliminals, the sound, and manipulation of language and imagery in television and film—it's like buying product placement, really—has reduced the revulsion rate by seventeen percent. And I think that might be our tipping point."

The announcement was timed to go over every channel, all over the world, at the same time. The first images of what Rhonda always called "The Grays" were fuzzy and slightly doctored. And despite all our preparations, they still triggered an ocean of nausea and fear.

Like crystal cathedrals floating in a sea of clouds, the alien ships hovered above New York, L.A., Tokyo, Lagos, Johannesburg, London, Beijing, Moscow and fifty other major cities. Panic and riots ensued, but contrary to wide expectations, the Travelers didn't land, let alone destroy or conquer. They just . . . hovered. We were told the situation, and what the visitors offered. State by state, the citizens were allowed to vote on whether the Visitors could touch ground.

Demonstrations. Signs abounded. "Hell no!" or their equivalents in a dozen languages.

Most places, that sentiment was almost universal. But a few . . . California for instance, said yes. And so, at last, aliens were among us. And again, they delivered on their promises, enabling those states to enjoy the bounty. The technology was tightly controlled, and only allowed into the areas that welcomed the Travelers. That was clever. We were both in control . . . and totally on the hook. Because everyone knew someone wasting away from some nasty ailment. Someone who was healed . . . or employed in one of the new industries that sprang up and became Google overnight. Within two years, there wasn't a country on Earth that denied them. Traveler tech created a hundred billionaires and a thousand multi-millionaires in the first year.

You rarely saw Travelers on the street. When you did, it was in those odd suits and usually in a limo of some kind, usually piloted by a live human being. They appeared on documentaries and news shows, and then entertainment as well. Television, billboards, films . . . break-dancing amoebas, torch song-warbling slime molds. Slowly we began to see these concoctions more often, associated with puppies and smiling children . . . and sexy men and women.

The Travelers wanted to see that humans were accepting them.

They masked their pheromones, poured themselves into better and better fabrications, and even managed to appear in a series of Indian films. I thought I recognized Elvis doing a very creditable Bollywood Bhangra dance. Hard to say.

All paramecia look alike to me.

Among hundreds of others, Rhonda and I were released from our contracts—now that it was out in the open, everyone clamored to work with Them. And the Traveler technology was integrated into our entertainment with steadily increasing frequency and effect. Movies were immersive and hyper-real, more so than any 3D, hologram, Showscan, or anything that had ever existed previously. Somehow we reacted more to those images than the real thing. Amazing. Humanity was heading for a renaissance. I have to admit that I felt a little guilty. The Travelers had come a trillion miles looking for love, and didn't seem to understand the concept of prostitution. Before I left the facility, I had a final meeting with Elvis. He was squished into his exoskeleton, the pinkish indestructible Traveler-cloth "human" suit beneath his white sequined jumpsuit. I no longer felt the urge to vomit when I was around him. He'd changed his smell and appearance, and that sizzling sensation I got in his presence had died to a mere itch.

"Hello, Carver," he said. "Good to see you."

"And you."

"I think," he said, "that we've accomplished something wonderful together. Thank you."

He handed me a card. "What's this?

"A token of my appreciation. One million of your dollars."

There it was. Another six zeroes. It was true that a rising tide lifted all boats, that a certain amount of inflation had accompanied Traveler wealth, but Rhonda and I had been paid so well, we'd raced ahead of that curve. In that moment, I realized I never had to work again for the rest of my life. "Thank you!"

Elvis' face mask smiled. "Thankyouverymuch." His namesake's Vegas drawl. "Cheap at the price, old son."

Six weeks after we left the Facility, I asked Rhonda to marry me, and a month later, she agreed. Our honeymoon was a revelation, as if our prior sex life had been a mere appetizer, and she'd given me the keys to the kitchen. If she had lived a hundred lives as a leather-clad courtesan, that might have explained the days and nights that followed, as she opened one door after another for me, allowed me to glimpse what was within until it felt like she was running an electrified tongue over my body's every exposed nerve. Then with a mischievous giggle she would close that door, give me just enough time to recover and then lead me staggering and wide-eyed to the next.

In retrospect, it was predictable that Rhonda would be the one to bring the fetish sites to my attention. Three months after we were married, she danced into my home office, touched my lips with hers and giggled. "Have I got something to show you!"

She led me to her office, where she worked so hard and late at night. Her computer was mostly used for graphics, but like the rest of us, she surfed the net to rest her brain in between creative spurts.

"I don't want to tell you how I found this site . . . "

"I think I can guess. Feeling a little frisky, were you?"

She turned the screen around, and for a moment my eyes didn't focus. Then I saw a very pale woman, gelatinously obese with very short, bristly dark hair, sporting animated tattoos that mimicked organelles. They shivered and danced, while three men stood around her performing what I believe what Japanese aficionados would refer to as a bukkake ritual. If you don't know what that is, look it up.

On the other hand, maybe you shouldn't. Ignorance is bliss.

"Is she trying to look like a Traveler?"

"Wild, huh?"

The sound was much too good for speakers their size. I didn't recognize the brand. "New speakers?"

"Nice, aren't they?" The speakers were flat as glass panes, but the sound was as good as a ten thousand-dollar pair of Naim Ovators. T-tech. Traveler music wafted in the background, and with the new speakers, my ears absorbed odd, previously undetected undertones.

"Wow," I said "That's really strange. It's a new world. That other stuff . . . wow."

She suddenly pulled in on herself, shrank a little, seemed tentative and a little shy. "Does it turn you on?" Her forefinger fluttered along my forearm.

"Shit. No. You?"

She shrugged, her finger ceasing its dance. "Maybe . . . "

"Well, we should take advantage of that . . . "

"I'm busy right now," Rhonda said, removing my hands. " . . . but save some of that heat for me tonight, okay?"

But . . . she worked until midnight, and when she did come to bed, she rolled over and went to sleep. That's marriage, I guess.

More and more often, Rhonda seemed to be in a funk. I think we saw each other less frequently, pretty much devolving to roommates. It wasn't that we didn't love each other. It was that some critical spark was just . . . gone. She was doing more Traveler work, and the "bridging" was subtler. The T's had gifted us with a printing process that conveyed a dimensional and multi-sensory aspect. Strange. You would look at a picture, and detect a scent. If you weren't looking directly at it, you detected no smell. I have no idea how they did that, or how it worked, but it did.

Rhonda's office was filled with more and more of these Traveler materials. She seemed increasingly dreamy and far away. And then one summer day in 2036 Rhonda left the house, and stayed out late.

Very late.

And when Rhonda returned in the early morning, she seemed . . . dazed. Like someone thoroughly stoned, with a secretive smile that was too damned easy to interpret. She curled up on the couch with a dreamy expression and wouldn't talk to me. When I tried, she turned her face to the back of the couch and pretended to sleep. Finally, that night I brought her a tray of chicken wings, and set it down next to her. She smelled it. Turned, smiled faintly, but didn't speak, other than offer a very soft:

"Thank you."

At that moment, I was certain. "You did it, didn't you?"

She looked at me, hands shaking. Didn't answer.

"What was it like?" I asked.

She paused. Then her face softened, as I'd only seen in our deepest, most intimate moments. "I can't describe it," she said with an almost feverish intensity.

"Try," I said. And in that moment I saw something from her I'd never seen before, and never would again: a desperate desire for me to understand her, as if in understanding we would bond more deeply. But something about what she said reminded me less of someone inviting you to a party, and more like someone skydiving without a parachute, terrified of dying alone. "Think of the worst kiss you've ever had. Then . . . the best sex. Can you do that?"

I couldn't help but smile at how she trembled to say those words. "Okay. Then what?"

"The gap between them is like . . . what the Gray was like." She gripped my hands, nails digging into my flesh. "Come with me. Let's share this. Let's . . . " I guess that disgust is something I don't hide well. She saw it, and drew away, the momentary vulnerability evaporated. Just like that. Gone.

Her lips twisted with sudden, bitter force. "You're a coward."

We slept in the same bed for a while after that, but . . . well, you know. And then she moved into the guest room, and never returned to our room. There would have been no point. We had no guests, and she wasn't coming back to me.

• • •

Ten years passed, one aching, disorienting day at a time. I had no need for earning money, but embraced busywork of many kinds, perhaps to distract myself from the unhappy fact that Rhonda and I had become mere roommates. Our sex life had dwindled to memories.

The world seemed to flow around me, like a stream dividing itself around a rock. I watched the fashions and culture slowly admit more and more Traveler imagery and influence, but little of it really seemed to break through my emotional cocooning. I had endless toys, and work, and that had to be enough.

Despite promises made in our empty bed I felt a certain nasty urge expanding inside me. Every time I heard Traveler music, that compulsion grew. When I watched movies with very special guest stars, something deep in my gut twitched. Like a tumor growing day by day right before your eyes, there is no single moment you can point to when you say, "Ah hah! It's cancer!" It sneaks up on you.

The scope of change was too large, the implications beyond sanity. And then one day, as Rhonda had known, the hunger sharpened from a whisper to a scream. I called an aircab and vaped in the back seat until my head spun. It dropped me off in the middle of nowhere and I walked randomly. Yeah, right. Pretended that I didn't know where I was going, finally ending up at one of the storefront enterprises they called a "friendship club." Paid my considerable fee, and entered. I'd had to get very, very stoned, loaded enough that some part of me knew I would have plausible deniability.

In an office paneled with stars and nebulae stenciled with obscene constellations, I met with a thin man who asked a battery of questions. I guess I answered them properly because I was taken to a shower room, where I was told to bathe. The water wasn't mere H2O, it had a taste to it, a smell that faded, as if my nose had been numbed. And they led me to a dimmed room.

I wished I'd vaped a little more.

The room's only furniture was a black couch. And the door behind me was the only door, so I expected it to open, and for something else to enter. I felt myself dizzying as if the scented droplets evaporating on my flesh were seeping into my bloodstream. I needed to sit down. Lay down.

And the moment I did, the "couch" engulfed me.

Followed immediately by a wave of panic. God! It wasn't a couch, it was the Traveler version of some kind of sex toy, some B&D playground, their version of leather and chains and whips and gag-balls. No! I . . .

And then I felt myself . . . embraced in every orifice. Welcomed. Hungered for. It was not love. Not sex. It was . . . the form for which all of those are shadows. The sound, and all the others merely echoes.

• • •

When I awakened, I was alone in the room. The "couch" seemed just a couch again, although investigation revealed that it to be an exoskeleton, a costume, into which a Traveler had stuffed itself. I left the lust-chamber, walked out past the receptionist's glassy smile. A half-dozen other adventurers hunched dazedly in the foyer, shuddering like men who had stepped out of a sauna into freezing cold. We sat around, half-dressed, unable to speak . . . and sharing a knowledge.

When I vacated the premises, the street outside shimmered with pools of cottony light radiating from no source I could determine. I swore I wouldn't, but I turned around and returned to the friendship center and asked when I could go again. Months, they said. There was apparently a very long waiting list. I was told I could pay six figures to be placed at the head of that line. I'm sure Rhonda had. God help me, I considered. But . . . I just couldn't.

Strange how separate threads twist together into a braid strong enough to hang you. How easy it is to rationalize. How proud I was of my tolerance for pain. And fear. Everything was going so well, I told myself. Life was just wonderful. I'd never been wealthy, and money is its own opiate. Perhaps the most powerful. You live in a kind of tunnel, insulated from most concerns. My health remained perfect, as They had promised. I was the same, but thirty years in the social effects were now more noticeable.

Boys and girls seemed to care little for differentiating themselves by dresses and pants, or long and short hair, or makeup . . . as if that aching boy-girl tension no longer mattered quite so much. Or at all. I remember a morning on a London street, when I witnessed a wan couple pushing a perambulator down along the Thames. Our eyes met, and they smiled at me. Hopeful smiles. I smiled back. And as I always had, I reflexively peered into the baby carriage.

The infant was perhaps three months old, and gazing out at the world with the kind of glazed uncertainty that seems standard on babies that age. When it looked at me, it started to cry. I'd always found that sound to trigger the urge to comfort. Instead . . . its ululation was just irritating. It's smooth pale flesh seemed . . . grublike, and its bald head reminded me of my father, when he was dying of cancer in an Atlanta hospice. I recoiled, and the baby cried more loudly, and the parents pulled back into their shells and hurried away.

It was the only baby I'd seen for a week. The last one I saw for a month.

I saw fewer children on the streets, more shuttered and boarded-up schools. Humanity was so happy, so drunk on our new longer lives and endless nifty T-Tech that we just ignored what was happening around us.

As for me . . . I never had so much as a sniffle, and maintained beautiful muscle tone without doing so much as a push-up . . . but certain hungers seem to have quieted. Women passing on the street were often strikingly beautiful, but in a "healthy animal" way, not a matter of artifice or attraction. It was almost as if I was noticing their loveliness the way I might think a painting was lovely. Or a one-man sky-strider "walking" between clouds. Beautiful. Distant. Irrelevant to anything but a cool aesthetic appreciation.

Then one spring day in 2054, I was having Zavo at a local Starbucks. Oh, right. I've not told you about that. Zavo is the commercial name for a T-tech drink. I think they bioengineered it to not only sensitize your brain to norepinephrine, like caffeine does, but provide co-factors that allowed your little gray cells to manufacture that juice with scary efficiency. How you can make something that lasts all day, has no jitters, and lets you sleep is beyond me. But it does.

Good dreams, too. Vivid. Intense.

When I drank it, I dreamed of the space between the stars.

A ratty looking little Asian guy dropped onto the seat across from me. He stared at me, not moving, not speaking. Not blinking. "Do I know you . . . ?" I finally asked.

"It hasn't been that long," he replied. "You haven't forgotten so much . . . ?"

I skawed laughter. "Professor Watanabe! Man, it's been a long time." Hadn't seen him since our days at the Facility. He hadn't worn well. The Professor was well dressed, but he looked tense, like Atlas trying to be casual while holding the world on his shoulders. "You're doing well. We're all doing well."

"Travelers," he said.

A bubble car sailed by, a paramecium in the back seat, a superfluous human pretending to pilot a drone. Fashion statement. Professor Watanabe held my eyes with a smile, and slid over a silver thumb drive.

"What's this?" I asked. It looked antique, probably only holding a few terabytes.

"Something you need to look at. Tonight."

"What is it?"

"Just read it. The core document will take a few minutes. You could spend a year going through the supporting data. All you could want."

"But what . . . ?"

"Open it. Remember my name, and open it."

Then, smile frozen on his face, Watanabe left the table. I turned the drive over and over again in a shaking hand.

What the hell?

As I said, the drive was decades old. Not T-Tech, not even current technology. That should have been a clue. I dragged out an ancient laptop. Instructions scribbled on the side of the drive warned me to disable Wi-Fi before booting, and I did. It utilized an old fashioned USB connection. I actually had to visit a vintage computer shop to find a proper connection, making lame excuses to the salesman to explain why I wanted a device that had been obsolete for at least thirty years. When I returned home with my acquisition, it took me an hour to figure out how to patch the computer to the drive. When I finally succeeded, a password prompt appeared.

Password? The professor didn't give me—

Then I recalled his odd request: "Remember my name."

Was that it? I typed "Watanabe" in, and to my pleasant surprise, his face materialized.

"Greetings, Mr. Kofax," he said. As in the coffee shop, Watanabe's face was pale and drawn. Leeched of color and life. The problem was not his physical health, I was sure. The Travelers had made sure of that. It was something else. Something worse. "You must be wondering about why the cloak and dagger. Well, you aren't going to wonder for very long. I'm going to make this short, but I cannot make it sweet." He wiped his hand across his forehead, smearing a slick of perspiration. "I wish I could. The short version is: We made a mistake, Carver. You and I. We were the heroes, remember? We figured it out. Well, I should have stuck with teaching, and you should have stuck to flogging soap."

"Why?" I muttered.

"Why? Because we've done our job too well. Something is going wrong. Human beings aren't having much sex anymore. Not with each other, at least. The mistake was thinking that when the Travelers told us they could not lie, they were offering every implication of their actions. They were honest, but not . . . forthcoming."

"What are you talking about?" I muttered. For the second time, it was as if he heard me, or had anticipated my thoughts.

"What I mean is that we figured everything was safe, because we evaluated how Traveler tech affected us. Their music, for instance. Played through our equipment, we found nothing to worry about. But then we began to upgrade our systems, using their tech, and frankly we failed to continue testing as carefully as we should. Traveler tech increased the bandwidth. They've given us biological, optical, computational, and auditory technology, and we paid too much attention to how powerful it was, and not enough to how it all interlocked. How, once assembled, it would have emergent properties."

"Meaning what?"

This was some kind of video AI program. Even coming over an obsolete thumb drive, somehow it was still responding to me. Try as the Professor had to avoid it, Traveler tech's tendrils were everywhere. "Meaning that we gave them access to our hardware and software . . . and wetware, Carver. And they are reprogramming us."

"How? To do what?"

"Birthrates are dropping. It's happening faster and faster. Twenty percent reduction throughout the world, and no one panicked, because no one is complaining. We've gone numb somehow. We're just . . . not servicing each other."

It . . . was true. Rhonda and I hadn't had sex in over a decade, and I hadn't really considered the implications. And kids? We'd never talked . . .

No, that's not true. Once upon a time, we'd talked about having babies. We both came from large families, both loved our brothers and sisters, nieces and nephews . . . how unlikely was it that neither of us would hanker for kids?

"Carver, you need to look at the data. This isn't accidental, and it isn't local. This is greatest catastrophe in the history of our species. An extinction level event."

He said more, but it was much the same, except for a request that I meet with him, secretively, in a week's time.

A week. Time to research, to sift through the mountain of data on that drive. Time to think, and decide.

So . . . I looked. I slept perhaps three hours a night, barely eating or drinking, drunk with terror.

The data was incontrovertible.

For reasons no one understood, the Traveler effect was growing. Human beings were becoming more attracted to the aliens than we were to each other. Once you opened your eyes, the whole thing was obvious. I guess it was just that they were so . . . far beyond ugly that the idea they were some kind of competitive threat was absurd. You just couldn't take the notion seriously. But something had functioned like cosmic beer goggles.

And another terrible thing: My brain said to scream what I'd learned from the rooftops, to find some way to stop this, to crush them all. But another part of me (and I know how sick this sounds) felt protective of the Travelers. More so than I did of actual human children. Just as the data suggested. Show me a picture of one of the gelatinous oozing masses, and I felt like I had a lapful of warm kittens. Look at a picture of a bubbly brown-skinned baby, and all I could see was Louis Armstrong dipped in thirty-weight.

I blinked, and shook my head, and considered.

I couldn't talk to Rhonda. Dared not. Our bank account suggested she had paid almost a quarter-million dollars to be part of an exclusive "friendship" club, getting serviced once a week. On what world could I trust her?

Certainly not this one.

The phone rang.

"So have you read through everything?" Dr. Watanabe asked.

"Yes," I said. "What are we going to do?"

I had been welcomed into a circle of rebels, all men and women Watanabe trusted. We met secretly in the professor's home, and discussed our quandary. Did we publicize and risk losing our window of opportunity? Careful overtures to seats of power had been rebuffed. We decided upon action.

There was a central media node in central Dallas where alien music and images were inserted in television, vids, and neural feeds. You've probably read the reports, or saw the trial, one of several triggered by similar actions around the globe. Ours was merely the first. I won't drag you through the overly familiar details, but here are the most critical:

The node was the repository of a vast river of information constantly streamed over multiple channels, probably including those ripples in space-time, the secrets we had coveted enough to ignore the risks of unknown technology. Watanabe reasoned that if we could destroy it, perhaps people would awaken from the trance we had helped induce.

As you know if you watch the news, we were successful getting in, planting our devices. The bomb exploded, killing Professor Watanabe, a woman named Courtney Pickett, and two watchmen. But . . . the brain, the core of the facility itself, survived.

The police swooped in, loyal to their Traveler masters. There was no place to hide. We never had a chance to get away. The police had us before we could reach our nests or hidey-holes. It was almost as if they had known in advance, as if they wanted a terrorist act to use as an example. As if . . .

Rhonda.

She had hacked my computer. Rhonda, my loving wife. Wearing makeup that made her skin shimmer with translucence, revealing the succulent meat beneath.

My wife. My love. My betrayer.

The trial was short and sensational. My lawyers were the best that Traveler money could buy. I got the death penalty. Rhonda testified against me, her face a fish tank of gliding paramecium. The human judge wore silvery Traveler makeup, so that the inside of her head looked like a jar of winking cat's eyes.

I was screwed.

When Rhonda left the courthouse on that last day, she never looked back.

That's really all there is to say. They're coming now. I thought I'd have more time. Everyone does.

• • •

Two guards and a sad-faced minister in dark pants and shirt escorted Carver Kofax from his cell. He had been afraid for so long that he now felt only emptiness, as if the extreme emotion had hollowed him out.

"Are you ready, my son?" the priest asked. "Our father, who art in heaven, vanguard of our Traveling friends and saviors . . . "

"You've got to be kidding me," Carver muttered.

The death chamber was steel walls and a steel seat with clamps for his legs and arms. "Any last words?" the executioner asked after the shackles were snapped into place. On his neck, a Traveler tattoo crawled and beckoned lasciviously. Kofax swallowed back a sour taste. All the fear that had been hiding somewhere in the back of his head exploded to life, and he bucked against his restraints.

"This isn't right," Carver screamed. "You're making a mistake. We're all making a mistake—"

The executioner had left the chamber, sealed the door behind him. Vents at the floor level began to hiss, and greenish wisps of gas puffed out, pooled around his feet, and began to rise. He coughed, vomited, made one final convulsive push against the shackles, and then collapsed.

His vision slid to black.

And then . . . nothing.

I can't believe I'm writing this. It shouldn't be possible, but then, so many things have changed in what used to be "our" world.

Sparkles of light. I blinked. And opened my eyes.

White walls, humming machines of unknown design. But the humans standing over the bed, an East Indian and a coarse, chunky-looking pale blond woman, both wore medicinal white. "Where am I?" My throat felt dry and raw. It hurt even to whisper. Was this hell? Wasn't I dead?

"Wrong question," the doctor said. His skin and subcutaneous fat were translucent, his organs sparkling in his meat bag. Some kind of light-bending makeup, no doubt.

"What's the right question?"

"When are you?"

That made no sense, but I played along. "All right. When am I?"

"It is 2105. You've been gone for fifty years."

My mind went blank. "What the hell . . . ? I . . . I . . . "

"I know. You thought you were dead. But you can thank the Travelers for that. They don't kill, even when you transgress against them. They just . . . put you aside for a time."

After I checked out of the hospital, I discovered that my bank account had been gaining interest for half a century, and now contained more than I could ever spend. There were also fewer people to help me spend it. The decrease in population was noticeable. The streets were almost empty, as if everyone were indoors watching a parade. The few human beings I saw scuttled along the concrete like lonely crabs, ancients in young bodies, morbidly afraid of their good health, of the vibrancy that would turn into sudden death without warning. That was what the Travelers promised, yes? Perfect health until death.

And of course, they didn't lie.

I saw no children at all.

Quietly, without any fuss, the Travelers were taking over the world. Not a shot fired.

Rhonda still lived in our penthouse. When she appeared on the vid screen she was . . . strange. She had aged another fifty years, but other than tight, shiny skin and eyes drowned in fear and fatigue, on first look she hadn't changed much. The second and third looks told a different story. It was difficult to put my finger on precisely what was disturbing. Was it makeup? Surgery? Not sure. But it was almost as if she was some alien creature pretending humanity, as if there was nothing left of Rhonda at all.

"Carver?" she said, and in that moment her shock and surprise gave human animation to the mask of gelid flesh surrounding those mad eyes. "But . . . you're dead!"

Damn. Had no one told her? I explained what had happened to me. At first she was in shock, but in time, guilt and relief mingled on her face. "You . . . you're so ugly." She cried for a moment, then wiped the tears away. I was hideous to her. Because I looked human. But so did she, at least on the surface. So some part of her had fought to remain human, even as another part had grown increasingly repulsed by that very thing.

Suddenly, the impact of what had happened really hit me. My knees buckled, and the world spun and darkened before I regained my balance. "I . . . oh, God. What did you do?"

"I . . . I'm old, Carver, but I still want to be touched. I'm too human for most people now. I should have had more operations, more implants, but I just couldn't." Her face twisted with self-loathing and something else, the barest touch of hope. "Has it been a long time for you? We could . . . I have virtual lenses I could wear. It would make you look . . . we could . . . "

"Fifteen spice tuna roll," I said.

"What?" her mouth hung slack, and beneath the mask of youth, I saw an old, old woman.

"Sometimes," I said, "you just have to know when to quit."

I hung up.

I had the money and time to travel, and did. It didn't matter what I said or did, not any longer. I wasn't censored or inhibited in any way. Things had progressed too far. Whatever the Travelers had done to humanity had taken hold. What few young people stumbled through the cities seemed pale, genderless ghosts floating through a concrete graveyard. Earth's cities were clean but sparsely occupied, and in the country, one could drive for miles and never glimpse a human face.

I did see human couples from time to time. One or two a month. It was good to know that whatever the Travelers had done was not 100% effective. Just . . . 99.9%.

I found myself laughing for no apparent reason. A lot.

I think I was afraid that if I ever stopped, I'd kill myself.

On leaving the hospital, I'd been given a plastic bag containing my possessions, along with a key to a storage locker where Rhonda had sent the majority of my possessions. One day after returning from one of my lonely trips, I wandered to the fenced facility and spent a few hours digging through the detritus of a remarkable, accursed life. Here was a bit of my childhood . . . there a photograph from our Barbados honeymoon. There a set of notes from some college assignment I could no longer remember. And bundles of old clothes. I rifled the pockets of a coat, and out fell a business card.

I bent, picked it up, and read it. Twice. And then, almost as if my lips were moving by themselves, I spoke the number and a circuit opened. The conversation was short, but enthusiastic. Within seconds a car hovered down from the sky and its door slid open.

The ride took about twelve minutes, and covered the distance from Los Angeles to a two-story white mansion in Whitehaven on the outskirts of Memphis. The airdrone deposited me on the lawn. I rang the doorbell, finger shaking.

Elvis answered the front door. He was as recognizable as ever, an amoeba in a rhinestone suit.

"Howdy there, Carver. How's it shakin'?" His translation equipment had not only improved, but had mastered the local drawl.

"I, uh . . . I guess I'm a little surprised . . . " So he, or It (or they. What the hell did I really know?), had purchased The King's cottage. Hardly surprising. Travelers could pretty much have anything they wanted.

"That ah like this form? You thought ah was kidding?"

"No," I said. I felt like my bones were made of sand. "I guess I didn't."

"We don't lie."

"No, you don't." There was something so ridiculous, so cosmically absurd about the gelatinous form in the white sequins, gliding on a mucous trail through a pop-culture mausoleum, that the occasion was almost solemn. "You fit here," I said. "I guess you learned from us, too."

"It goes both ways," Elvis said. "A little."

Videos of Jailhouse Rock and Viva Las Vegas, a garage filled with vintage cars and halls swathed in platinum records. Elvis talked non-stop, as if he had memorized a billion factoids about a singer dead for more than a century, someone whose hip-shaking melodies must have traveled a trillion miles before reaching whatever the Travelers used instead of ears. The tour ended in a den dominated by an empty fireplace pointing out this or that artifact, including a certificate signed by Richard Nixon and the head of the DEA, presented to Elvis Aaron Presley on December 21, 1970 authorizing him as a "Federal Agent at Large," whatever the hell that meant.

I shook myself out of my trance. "How many times have you done this?" I said in the smallest voice I had ever heard emerge from my throat.

"Toured people through Graceland?"

"No." I gestured vaguely. "This. What you did to us."

"What you did to yourselves. Oh, no one really knows. You call us Travelers, but we're really more like traders. Sex isn't universal. But there's always something people want. Your media images showed you to be both attracted and repelled by sex, and by strangeness, and that gave us our opportunity."

I plopped down on the couch, finally feeling the weight of my frozen years. At least I thought it was a couch. It didn't molest me, anyway. "So it's . . . just over for us? For the human race?"

"Not totally," Elvis said, and somehow a twitch of his protoplasm resembled a sneering lip. "The crèches will keep pumping you guys out. Humans are fun. Entertaining. I mean . . . we don't hate you or anything. So please, live out the rest of a long, long life. What wonders you will see! You're walking history, you know. And . . . we owe it all to you." The creature turned, the organelles floating within the transparent sack very much like a swarm of anxious eyes. They even narrowed in something I interpreted as regret, or concern. "You're angry. I can tell. I understand," he said. "And I'm sorry."

Elvis paused. "Say: I know," he brightened. "Want to fuck?"

I stared in disbelief, sputtering and trying to . . . trying to . . .

"Oh," I finally sighed. "What the hell."

ALL THAT ROBOT SHIT

RICH LARSON

—◆—

"We made you, you know."

Carver Seven listens intently. The man, who also self-designates as Mikhail and Only Human Being On This Fucking Island, has not spoken often lately. Instead it stares off across the sea in silence, or makes its snuffling animal sounds while excess lubricant from pivoting photoreceptors leaks down the front of its head and spatters the sand. The man once referred to this process as crying like a little bitch.

At the moment, Carver Seven and the man are crafting spears in the shade of a storm-bent palm. Carver Seven prefers the sunshine, where his slick, black carbon skin thrums under the life-giving gaze of Watcher-in-the-sky. He tolerates the shade for the man's sake.

"How made me you I know?" Carver Seven asks, approximating the man's wet language with choppy bursts from his audio port. It is far more nuanced than the chattering of the long-limbed climbers in the wood but also far, far from the streaming clicks and squeals of true speech.

"You're like a damn chatbot, aren't you?" the man says. "Except you can't link me any porn."

"How made me you I know?" Carver Seven repeats. He has learned to ignore extraneous input, differentiating when the man speaks to itself from when it speaks to him. Carver Seven works the end of the spear to a sharp point on the bladed edge of his manipulator.

"In some lab, somewhere. Maybe they knew the world was all going to hell. Wanted to leave something behind to keep going after we're gone."

Carver Seven sticks the finished spear into the pale gray sand. "In some lab, somewhere, how made me you metal . . . " Carver Seven taps both manipulators against himself, then indicates the man's flaky red skin, " . . . from meat?"

"They didn't use meat. They used alloys, and silicon, and, you know, all that robot shit."

Considering the blasphemous idea is an odd thrill. The man is very wise, in some ways, able to predict movements in the currents around the island and predict weather from the clouds. It claims to have come from a floating metal village that sank into the sea. If the man could make a metal village, maybe it could make other metal things, too.

Or repair them.

Carver Seven compares his gleaming black form, his nimble treadfeet and deft manipulators and prehensile photoreceptors, to the labored collection of blood and meat and bone that is the man. The man has come close to involuntary shutdown three times since it washed up on the island, whether by the elements or the animals.

There is a dim physical resemblance, but, if anything, the man is a fragile facsimile. It seems improbable, along with blasphemous, that the man could have created him, or even that the man could repair a particular Carrier's caved-in head. His hope fades slightly.

"No," Carver Seven says.

"Then where did you come from, smart guy?" the man asks.

Carver Seven moves from the shade and points one manipulator to Watcher-in-the-sky's burning photoreceptor, hanging high above the cobalt sea. "Then where did I come from the sky, smart guy," Carver Seven says. "Look at me now." He prises open his head so the man can see the lifelight burning steadily inside of him, see his thoughts sparking and colliding. "Piece of Watcher-in-the-sky to each baby one of Watcher-in-the-sky," he explains.

"Sun-worship," the man says. "How original." The man returns to its spear, stripping it with the sharp metal digit Carver Seven has also seen it use to gouge symbols, over and over again, into the peeling bark of the palms. "Guess it makes sense. You're solar-powered. You need light to function."

"Yeah," Carver Seven says, beginning a new spear. "But some are learn a new way."

"Good for you," the man says, staring back across the sea.

Those are the man's last sounds of the day, and when Watcher-in-the-sky starts to sink, Carver Seven leaves him. The clan is situated near the edge of the forest, where Cartographers found an ideal outcrop of stone and Carriers and Carvers used fallen trees to fashion it into a shelter, both from the storms and from predators drawn to the heat of their lifelights during the night.

But before Carver Seven returns to the village, he goes to see Recycler. He picks out her frequency and sees she is at the flat rock outside her shelter, which is slightly deeper in the wood. Carver Seven was the one who helped her rebuild it after the last storm, because the other Carvers claimed task overload.

Recycler is the only Recycler. Carver Seven thinks that maybe this is why she stays apart from the clan. When Carver Seven arrives to the flat rock, he finds her crouched over a dead pig. Recycler has the broad back and strong servos of a Carrier, and sometimes, from a distance, Carver Seven can pretend she is Carrier Three. But she is not. The bladed manipulators splitting open the animal's stomach are unique in shape, and she does things nobody else can do. She is Recycler.

With a gaseous hiss, the pig's innards spill out as pink wet ropes. Recycler sinks both manipulators inside its body, splashing the rock with blood and uncongealed shit. This is not the first animal Carver Seven has seen her disassemble. Sometimes a burrower will trample through the village, and if the clan cannot drive it away they kill it with a spear. They take it to Recycler, and she brings them back the fat to use as joint lubricant, and the skin stretched and cured for waterproofing.

But lately, Recycler has been hunting. Lately, she does something new. As Carver Seven watches, she pries open her hidden mouth, the whirring orifice the clan can use in cases of great need, when Watcher-in-the-sky slips behind the veil for days on end. Carver Seven has used it himself only once, feeding it with crushed leaves and bark to keep his lifelight on during a dark week. The experience was not pleasant.

Now Recycler takes her proboscis, fashioned from bone and tanned skin and parts of old Carrier that Carver Seven recognizes, and sinks it into the dead pig. Carver Seven blanks his photoreceptors. He does not want to accumulate more visual data of the act. He does not like disassembling of any kind. Not since the accident.

"May Watcher-in-the-sky turn his gaze to you," Recycler clicks, acknowledging his presence before they slip into their familiar frequency. "Is it your rotator again?"

"My rotator is well, thank you." Carver Seven flexes the joint she repaired for him a few days prior, to show he has full mobility. Then he places his move in the strategy game they are playing and gives her a rough transcription of everything the man said during the day. He emphasizes the man's claim of creation, because he has been turning it over and over in his mind.

"The man says many interesting things." Recycler wins the strategy game in one deft move—she is too clever, with Carrier Three he could battle back and forth for days on end—and offers him a turn with the proboscis. Carver Seven refuses, as always. He remembers the first and only time he tried using the animal fuel and how his body rejected the blood and bile, spitting it back up. Recycler has adjusted to it. She can use it to work through the entire night, awake in the unholy dark. The rest of the clan does not know this.

Carver Seven keeps her secret, because she keeps his.

"Is it possible the man made us?" Carver Seven asks. His photoreceptors stray to the packed dirt behind Recycler's shelter, where his secret is wrapped and buried.

Recycler deliberates another second. "The only way to know if the man is correct or not is to pry its head open and search its memory," she clicks. "Since you are so certain the man has a lifelight inside its hairy skull and is not merely an animal like the climbers in the forest."

Carver Seven is silent. It is not the first time Recycler has mentioned the idea. Carver Seven does think the man has a lifelight, but he does not think it can be accessed the same way. When he first found the man, blood was leaking from its head.

"May I see her?" he asks.

Recycler gives a long clicking scan to ensure nobody is nearby. Then she reaches down into the hard-packed dirt and begins to dig. Carver Seven joins her, shoveling fast and then slow as they reach the correct depth. He retrieves Carrier Three's bashed-in head from where it is hidden in the dark earth, far from the gaze of Watcher-in-the-sky, secret from the clan. In violation of the traditions, Carrier Three was not fully recycled after a falling stone crushed her. Carver Seven pleaded and pleaded and pleaded until Recycler agreed to save her head.

Carrier Three's photoreceptors are blank, and she makes no sound in response to Carver Seven's soft clicks. But he knows her lifelight is not fully extinguished. He knows if he waits and watches long enough, he will see a single lazy spark moving in slow circles.

"Nobody can repair a damaged lifelight," Recycler clicks. "Not the man. Nobody."

Carver Seven puts what is left of Carrier Three deep inside his main cavity and covers it over. Recycler is usually correct. Recycler is clever.

But Carver Seven has to try.

The next day, he goes to visit the man again.

"Hey, look who it is," he warbles from a distance, because the man startles easily, like a bird. It looks up at him. Its photoreceptors are pink and glassy.

"Hey, yourself, robo-parrot," the man says, then returns to its work. There is a storm-felled tree between its soft feet, and it is using the sharp appendage to strip away the branches. Carver Seven looks around and sees remnants of fire, burned pieces of animal. The man has hunted, how Recycler hunts. Beyond the mess, there are two more trunks already stripped smooth. He wonders what the man is building.

But his original query is much more important.

"Can you do me a favor and fuck off?" Carver Seven asks.

That gets the man's attention. Its audio port opens and it makes the clipped noise that repeats, over and over, sometimes when the man is pleased but more often when it leaks lubricant.

Carver Seven scans up and down the beach. "Can you do me a favor and fuck off and look here and fix it up a bit?" he asks. Then he opens his main cavity and pulls out Carrier Three's caved-in head.

"Whoa." The man's photoreceptors enlarge. "Did you do that? This some Lord of the Flies type shit?"

"Lord of the Flies type shit?" Carver Seven echoes, trying to parse the new sound units.

The man shakes its head. "Who is it?" it asks.

Carver Seven thinks hard. He knows what this latest question means, but he does not know how to communicate Carrier Three's name, the beautiful arc of click-squeal-click, into the man's ugly wet language. Then his subroutines dredge up the sound unit the man used to wail at the sea, used to punctuate long rambling speeches with.

"She is Anita," Carver Seven says.

The muscles across the front of the man's head, around its ever-wet audio port and brown photoreceptors, twitch in response to the sound unit Anita. Carver Seven recognizes it now as distress. He wonders if he has made a language error. Then the muscles slacken again.

"Don't say that," it says. "You don't understand. Don't have a fucking idea. You're a robot."

"Can you fix it up a bit?" Carver Seven asks.

The man stares blankly at him, unresponsive.

"You say you make us in lab you know," Carver Seven says, trying to lay things out as clearly as he can. "Is it yes? Is it no? Make her good, please." He extends Carrier Three's head toward the man.

The man takes her, gentler than Carver Seven would have guessed from how it handles most objects, and holds her in soft fleshy manipulators. "You think I can fix your friend," it says. It makes the clipped noise, but only once. Its audio port is contorted. "Jesus. I'm not a roboticist, buddy, I'm an electrician. I . . . " Its sounds stop. "This why you been hanging around, then?"

Carver Seven can make no sense of it. Too many new sound units in new patterns, not enough context. "Can you fix it up a bit?" he repeats. "Make to see. Make to talk. Make to think."

The man looks down at Carrier Three's head. "Sure," it says, the sound coming quietly. "Okay. I'll fix your friend for you. I'll make your friend good."

The man is going to repair Carrier Three's lifelight. Carver Seven replays the sounds over and over to be sure he has divined the correct meaning. Each loop sends a fragile joy through him.

"But you have to do something for me, too, okay?" the man says. "You have to help me build this boat and get off this island. Okay?"

"Okay," Carver Seven says, not bothering to ask what this boat is. "Okay, okay, okay, okay, okay."

Carver Seven will help the man build, and in return the man will bring Carrier Three back to him.

Over the course of the next three days, Carver Seven learns what a boat is: a collection of trunks and branches lashed together with vines in order to float on top of the sea, as a leaf floats on the surface of a puddle. The man explains it as they work. The man is slow and clumsy and tires easily, but is also clever the way Recycler is clever. Always thinking a move ahead, always ready to change the plan when obstacles arise, when the wood starts to warp or the vines are too brittle.

It gives Carver Seven hope that the man will be able to fix Carrier Three. Often while Carver Seven works, shredding branches and sanding the logs smooth, the man sits in the shade with Carrier Three's head. It is difficult to keep his photoreceptors from straying to them. Whenever he looks over, the man is tapping Carrier Three with its soft manipulators, rapping out mysterious patterns, the muscles of its face clenched in what Carver Seven knows is concentration.

"I just need a few more days," the man says when he notices. "I'm getting there. Your friend is almost fixed."

"Okay," Carver Seven says, feeling a surge of optimism at the news. "Great, just fucking great."

The man pushes air from its audio port. "How is it you ended up cussing more than I do? I know I don't cuss that much."

"How is few?" Carver Seven asks. "Few is one few is two few is three?"

"Two," the man says, putting both manipulators to its sides, looking over the boat. "Few is two."

"Could be Anita fixed up and boat all finished few two days," Carver Seven says, hoping that the two events to coincide, that Carrier Three wakes up to see the finished boat Carver Seven has helped to build. She always liked to see the things Carver Seven made. She could always recognize the distinct marks and flourishes of his manipulators.

The man's face contorts as if it is briefly distressed. "Could be," it says. There is a long silence. "What do you think Anita means?" it asks softly. "When you say Anita, what's it mean to you?"

Carver Seven thinks hard, looping all his favorite memories of Carrier Three, the ones he views so often they have started to decay. The broad shape of her back, her thick sturdy joints. The proud way she made stacks of wood and stone look light as air. Her kindness. How she always saved the best material, an interesting piece of driftwood or a particularly soft wedge of rock, to share with him, to watch him shape. Their slow-moving strategy game, their familiar channel, their small secrets. All the things they had done before her lifelight was damaged.

"Anita is you need light to function," Carver Seven says. "Anita is you need and is gone."

"Yeah," the man says. There is lubricant shining in its photoreceptors. "Yeah. She was always a better swimmer than me. I don't know how it happened." The man wipes at its photoreceptors to clear them. "Look, buddy, you should take the head back. When I told you . . . " It falls silent, looking at the boat again. "You're just a robot," the man says, but to itself more than to Carver Seven. "And we're nearly finished. You better head off, tin man. Back to work bright and early tomorrow."

Carver Seven understands the sentiment. "Piss off, get out of here," he says, waving one manipulator in the gesture the man uses to end a work cycle.

"Yeah," the man says. "Same to you."

It is still staring down at Carrier Three's head when Carver Seven leaves the beach.

As soon as he enters the village, Carver Seven can tell something is wrong. The air is thick with speech, with the click and buzz and squeal of the clan in deep discussion, but when Carver Seven tunes himself to the frequency he finds it slippery, fragmented. First he suspects he has been damaged somehow, but then he realizes that the truth is far worse. The clan has excluded him intentionally.

Shock numbs him for a moment. He has spent most of the past three days out on the beach with the man, but that is only because the workload in the village has been light. The last storm caused little damage. The decision on a new fence to keep animals out has been delayed while the Cartographers debate its placement. Carver Seven has neglected no duties.

He moves slowly through the village, still grasping instinctively at the speech around him but understanding none of it. Photoreceptors follow his progress. It is only when he sees the other Carvers crafting fresh spears, when he sees Recyler squatting frozen in discussion with the clan's small and nimble Cartographers, that he begins to understand.

"Carver Seven, may Watcher-in-the-sky turn her gaze to you," Cartographer Two says.

Carver Seven feels relief, first, that he can understand again. Then dread.

"We are sorry to have excised you from the debate," Cartographer Two continues. "But it was felt that you are no longer impartial regarding the man. We have reached consensus without you."

Carver Seven looks at Recycler, but it would be disrespectful to ask her what she has done, and why, when being addressed by the clan.

"The man, by your own admission, seems able to think and communicate as a clan member would," Cartographer Two says. "Because of that, it must be held accountable for blaspheming. Does the man not claim to have created the clan? Usurping the role of Watcher-in-the-sky?"

There is only one truthful response. "Yes. It does claim this."

"Because of this blasphemy, we have decided the man will be shut down," Cartographer Two says. "We go to the man's shelter in the morning. Recycler has been given permission to disassemble and study its corpse afterwards."

Carver Seven looks at Recycler again and feels something he has never felt before. It reminds him of the man wailing at the sky, it reminds him that his blades are sharp and he could plunge them into Recycler and damage her, damage her, damage her. She has betrayed him.

Now the clan will kill the man, and his last hope for Carrier Three will die with it.

Recycler heads quickly toward the edge of the village, back toward her shelter and her flat rock. Carver Seven wants to tell the Cartographers what she does in the night, how she hunts and feeds and no longer needs Watcher-in-the-sky. He doesn't. He keeps her secret. But he follows her to the wood, and in a high piercing frequency, he speaks.

"All this so you can dissect the man," he says. "So you can suck its blood. You are no better than an animal, Recycler. May Watcher-in-the-sky avert his gaze forever."

Recycler is silent for a long moment. "I told the clan for your sake," she finally says. "So the man will not lie to you anymore. You will be grateful in the end."

Then she disappears into the forest, and Carver Seven does not follow her. Instead he goes toward his own shelter, the one with a widened frame for when Carrier Three sometimes wanted to pass the storm together. He stops on the way to pick up a branch full of thick green leaves. The other Carvers look over to him. He asks if they have sufficient spears to kill the man that is so fearsome, with its soft red skin and weak manipulators. They assure him they do.

Carver Seven has no tasks to complete. He can go dormant early if he wishes. He walks into his shelter and begins tearing the leaves off the branch, one by one.

Carver Seven wakes up in the dark. It is terrifying. It feels like his photoreceptors have been gouged out, leaving him blind. But he has no time to be terrified.

His early shutdown now gives him only a few moments of residual energy. He reaches for the crushed leaves and opens his hidden mouth.

The orifice whirrs and grinds and Carver Seven feels a different kind of energy, rough-edged and erratic, move through his body. It is nothing like the warm comforting pulse of Watcher-in-the-sky. It feels ugly. He sees why the clan forgoes its use apart from emergency, but this, he reasons, is an emergency.

The dark is awful, but Carver Seven knows where he is. He knows that the distances from the shelter to outside the shelter to the path to the beach have not changed. He starts to walk, hearing his invisible treadfeet slap against packed dirt, rustle against leaves and vines. He feels the forest swallow him and hears the sounds of animals. It is difficult not to imagine them stalking him through the forest, drawn to his heat. Some branches have moved since he last walked these footsteps and each one startles him as it whips against his body.

Finally, he hears his treadfeet rasp on sand. He is on the beach. And even better, there is light. Carver Seven can make out the shape of the shore in front of him, the spiky mass of the forest behind him, even the rippling sea. Confused, he looks up at the sky. It is not the black void he had always imagined it to be when Watcher-in-the-sky blanks her photoreceptor. It is full of small glimmering fragments that look like lifelights thrown up into the darkness.

Recycler never mentioned such a thing. Carver Seven wants to stare for longer, but there is no time. He turns toward the leaning shelter the man has made in a divot of sand. There is light there, too, from the dying embers of the fire the man sometimes makes to keep its body warm and alter meat before eating it.

Carver Seven does not want to make noise in case Recycler is awake, as he is. Instead he crouches and moves far enough inside the shelter to place his manipulator against the man's prone foot.

The man thrashes upright. "What the fuck?"

Carver Seven gives up on not making noise. "Back to work bright and early," he says. "Look who it is."

"It's the middle of the goddamn night," the man says. "I meant in the morning, and . . . " It rubs its photoreceptors. "Don't you shut down for night? There's no sunshine."

"Some time you gotta improvise," Carver Seven says. "In morning the man is no see, no think, no talk."

"What?"

Carver Seven struggles for a way to communicate the concept of involuntary shutdown. He is not even sure the man is aware of its own mortality. He picks up one of the spears, its tip stained red, and jabs it into the air.

"In morning, other tin mans hunting you," he says. "Other tin mans cut up you."

The man's photoreceptors go large and Carver Seven knows it understands. "Learning a new way, huh," it says. "Jesus. You're going to be us all over again. Predation is step one."

"I'll help out you," Carver Seven says. "Make you safe. But you have to do something for me, too, okay? Finish fix it up a bit Anita."

The man slumps. "You should just let them cut me up."

Carver Seven knows the man sometimes self-damages for reasons beyond his understanding, but there is no time to learn why. He looks around, sees Carrier Three's head set on a little mound of sand, and picks it up carefully.

"Nearly finished," he says. "Now finish fix it up a bit."

"I can't," the man says. "I have no fucking idea how a positronic brain works. I lied. I lied so you would help me with the boat. I can't fix your friend."

Carver Seven replays the sounds over and over, unwilling to believe it. The man can't fix Carrier Three. The man never could. Recycler was right.

"I did try." The man makes its clipped noise, just once. "I looked at the wiring and all. But that was done in a lab with lasers and microtools and . . . All that robot shit. I'm sorry, buddy."

"Anita is gone," Carver Seven says, to be sure, hoping desperately the man will contradict him.

"Yeah," the man says instead. "Anita is gone." It rubs its head. "Don't think I've said it till now. Said it properly." It pauses. "I'm sorry."

"Why boat?" Carver Seven asks, because he has no way to articulate what he really wants to say, that he has the deep hollow feeling like Carrier Three is being disassembled all over again.

"Thought I'd try to get to the mainland," the man says. "See if any survivors got carried past this little spit. If any lifeboats made it. Doesn't matter, though. If I don't die here, I'll probably die in the sea. If I don't die in the sea, I'll die somewhere else. Doesn't matter."

Carver Seven thinks again of his sharp blades, how simple it would be to damage the man. Simpler still to let the clan do it for him. Then he thinks of Carrier Three's kindness.

"Nearly finished boat," Carver Seven says. "Tin mans no go sea. Boat make you safe." He goes to the last tree they felled and dragged, rolling it toward the others.

"You serious?" the man asks.

In answer, Carver Seven begins stripping the log, short sharp strikes, precise and rhythmic. He is a Carver, so he will carve. He will be kind how Carrier Three was kind.

"You're a better human being than I am," the man says. "You should know that."

"You should let's get to work," Carver Seven says.

By the time the man declares the boat finished, the sky is changing color, turning purple and red. The glimmering lifelights up above them are fading away. Carver Seven asks the man what they are before they disappear completely, in case it knows.

"Stars," the man says. "They're stars in the sky."

"Stars in the sky," Carver Seven echoes.

The man pauses. "Some people, you know, they think we go up there when we die. They think our souls . . . our . . . " It taps its head, then its body. "They think a part of us gets to go up in the sky. And watch over the people who are still down here."

Carver Seven parses the information. He looks down at Carrier Three's near-dark lifelight, cradled in his manipulators, and wonders if maybe the other sparks are up in the sky. It seems improbable.

"If you want I could take her with me," the man says. "Just in case I meet some crazy roboticist."

"Anita is gone," Carver Seven says.

"Yeah." The man sucks in air through its audio port. "Thanks for helping me. Hope your people aren't going to be pissed at you. Other tin mans hunt you?"

"No," Carver Seven says. He'll tell the rest of the clan the truth, that the man must have floated away on its boat in the dark. He won't tell them he worked through the night to ensure it. Recycler will guess, maybe, but not tell the others. Carver Seven will apologize to her, and give her Carrier Three's head to finally recycle, but maybe ask that a small piece, just a tiny piece, be soldered to him.

"Good," the man says. "That's good."

Carver Seven uses one manipulator to help the man drag the boat as close to the waves as he dares, then steps back. The man hops on, making the wood bob in the water.

"Guess this is goodbye," it says, with its photoreceptors in danger of leaking lubricant again.

"Crying like a little bitch," Carver Seven says. "Get out of here."

The man makes its clipped noise, over and over, as it poles out into the waves. Carver Seven can't tell if it is distress or happiness. As Watcher-in-the-sky rises and warms his back, making his steps back toward the village smooth and strong, Carver Seven can't tell which he is feeling, either.

THAT GAME WE PLAYED DURING THE WAR

CARRIE VAUGHN

———◆———

From the moment she left the train station, absolutely everybody stopped to look at Calla. They watched her walk across the plaza and up the steps of the Northward Military Hospital. In her dull gray uniform she was like a storm cloud moving among the khaki of the Gaantish soldiers and officials. The peace between their peoples was holding; seeing her should not have been such a shock. And yet, she might very well have been the first citizen of Enith to walk across this plaza without being a prisoner.

Calla wasn't telepathic, but she could guess what every one of these Gaantish was thinking: What was she doing here? Well, since they *were* telepathic, they'd know the answer to that. They'd wonder all the same, but they'd know. It would be a comfort not to have to explain herself over and over again.

It was also something of a comfort not bothering to hide her fear. Technically, Enith and Gaant were no longer at war. That did not mean these people didn't hate her for the uniform she wore. She didn't think much of their uniforms either, and all the harm soldiers like these had done to her and those she loved. She couldn't hide that, and so let the emotions slide right through her and away. She felt strangely light, entering the hospital lobby, and her smile was wry.

Some said Enith and Gaant were two sides of the same coin; they would never see eye to eye and would always fight over the same spit of land between their two continents. But their differences were simple, one might say: only in their minds.

The war had ended recently enough that the hospital was crowded. Many injured, many recovering. In the lobby, Calla had to pause a moment, the scents and sounds and bustle of the place were so familiar, recalling for her every base or camp where she'd been stationed, all her years as a nurse and then as a field medic. She'd spent the whole war in places like this, and her hands itched for work. Surely someone needed a temperature taken or a dressing changed? No amount of exhaustion had ever quelled that impulse in her.

But she was a visitor here, not a nurse. Tucking her short hair behind her ears, brushing some lint off her jacket, she walked to the reception desk and approached the young woman in a khaki uniform sitting there.

"Hello. I'm here to see one of your patients, Major Valk Larn. I think all my paperwork is in order." Speaking slowly and carefully because she knew her accent in Gaantish was rough, she unfolded said paperwork from its packet: passport, visa, military identification, and travel permissions.

The Gaantish officer stared at her. Her hair under her cap was pulled back in a severe bun; her whole manner was very strict and proper. Her tabs said she was a second lieutenant—just out of training and the war ends, poor thing. Or lucky thing, depending on one's point of view. Calla wondered what the young lieutenant made of the mess of thoughts pouring from her. If she saw the sympathy or only the pity.

"You speak Gaantish," the lieutenant said bluntly.

Calla was used to this reaction. "Yes. I spent a year at the prisoner camp at Overton. Couldn't help but learn it, really. It's a long story." She smiled blandly.

Seeing the whole of that long story in an instant, the woman glanced away quickly. She might have been blushing, either from confusion or embarrassment, Calla couldn't tell. Didn't really matter. Whatever it was, she covered it up by examining Calla's papers.

"Technician Calla Belan, why are you here?" The lieutenant sounded amazed.

Calla chuckled. "Really?" She wasn't hiding anything; Valk and her worry for him were at the front of her mind.

The other Gaantish soldiers in the lobby were too polite to stare at the exchange, but they glanced over. If they really focused they could learn everything about her. They were welcome to her history. It *was* interesting.

"What's in your bag?" the lieutenant said.

Some food, a couple of paperbacks for the trip, her chess set in its small pine box. Calla couldn't help but think of it, and the woman saw it all. Calla could only smuggle in contraband if someone had put it there without her knowledge, or if she had forgotten about it.

The lieutenant's brow furrowed. "Chess? That's a game? May I see it?"

It still startled Calla sometimes, the way they just *knew*. "Yes, of course," she said, and opened the flap of her shoulder bag. The lieutenant drew out the box, studied it. Maybe to reassure herself that it didn't pose a threat. The lieutenant could see, through Calla, that it was just a game.

"Am I going to be able to see Major Larn?" With a glance, the lieutenant would know everything he meant to her. Calla waited calmly for her answer.

"Yes. Here. Just a moment." The lieutenant took a card out of her drawer and filled out the information listed on it. The card attached to a clip. "Pin this to your lapel. People will still stop you, but this will explain everything. You shouldn't have trouble. Any more trouble." The young woman was too prim to really smile, but she seemed to be making an effort at kindness. Calla was likely the first real Enithi the young woman had ever met in person. To think, here Calla was, doing her part for the peace effort. That was a nice way of looking at it, and maybe why Valk had asked her to come.

"Go down that corridor," the young woman directed. She consulted a printed roster on a clipboard. "Major Larn is in Ward 6, on the right."

"Thank you." The gratitude was genuine, and the lieutenant would see that along with everything else.

Enithi never lied to the Gaantish. This was a known, proverbial truth. There was no point to it. Through all the decades of war, Enith never sent spies—or, rather, they never told the spies they sent that they were spies. They delivered messages without telling the bearers they were messengers. Their methods of conducting espionage had become so arcane, so complex, that Gaant rarely discovered them. Both sides counted on this one truth: Enithi never bothered lying when confronted with telepaths. The Gaantish had captured thousands of Enithi soldiers, who simply and immediately confessed everything they knew. Enithi were known to be a practical people, without any shame to speak of.

Enith kept any Gaant soldiers it captured sedated, drugged to delirium, to frustrate their telepathy. The nurses who looked after them were chosen for their cheerful dispositions and generally straightforward thoughts. Calla Belan had been one of those nurses. Valk Larn had been one of those prisoners when they first met—only a lieutenant then. It had been a long time ago.

Gaantish soldiers continued staring at her as she walked down the corridor. Some men in bandages waited on benches, probably for checkups in a nearby exam room. Renovations were going on—replacing light fixtures, looked like. In all their eyes, her uniform marked her. She probably shouldn't have worn it but was rather glad she had. Let them know exactly who she was.

On the other hand, she always felt that if the Enithi and Gaantish all took off their uniforms they would look the same: naked.

One of the workmen at the top of a ladder, pliers in hand to wire a new light, choked as she thought this, and glanced at her. A few others were blushing, hiding grins. She smiled. Another blow struck for peace.

• • •

Past several more doorways and many more stares, she found Ward 6. She paused a moment to take it in and restore her balance. The wide room held some twenty beds, all of them filled. Most of the patients seemed to be sleeping. She guessed these were serious but stable cases, needing enough attention to stay here but not so much that there was urgency. Patients had bandages at the end of stumps that had been arms or legs, gauze taped over their heads or wrapped around their chests, broken and splinted limbs. A pair of nurses was on hand, moving from bed to bed, adjusting suspended IV bottles, checking dressings. The situation's familiarity was calming.

The nurses looked at her, then glanced at each other, and the loser of that particular silent debate came toward Calla. She waited while the man studied her badge.

"I'm here to see Major Larn," Calla said carefully, politely, no matter that the nurse would already know. By now, Calla was thinking of nothing else.

"Yes," the nurse said, still startled. "He's here."

"He's well?" Calla couldn't help but ask.

"He will be. He—he will be glad to see you, when he wakes up. But you should let him sleep for now." Between Calla and Valk, how much was the nurse seeing that couldn't be put into words?

"Oh, yes, of course. May I wait?"

The nurse nodded and gestured to a stray chair, waiting by the wall for just such a purpose.

"Thank you," Calla said, happy to display her gratitude, though she was afraid this only confused them. They could see that Valk was more important to her than other considerations, even patriotism. They could not see why, because Calla was confused about that herself. Calla fetched the chair and looked for Valk.

And there he was, in the last bed in the row, a curtain partially pulled around him for privacy. He'd been like this the first time she'd seen him, lying on a thin hospital mattress, well-muscled arms at his sides, his face lined with the worries of a dream. More lines now, perhaps, but he was one of those men who was aging into a rather heart-stopping rough handsomeness. At least she thought so. He would laugh at her thought, then wrinkle his brow and ask her if she was thinking true.

An IV fed into his arm, a blanket lay pulled over his stomach, but it didn't completely hide the bandage. He'd had abdominal surgery. Before settling in, she checked the chart hanging on a clipboard at the foot of the bed. She'd never really learned to read Gaantish, but could read medical charts from when she was at Overton and they'd put her to work. Injuries: Internal bleeding, repaired. Shrapnel in the gut. He'd been cleaned and patched up, but a touch of septicemia had set in. He was recovering well, but had been restricted to bed rest in the ward, under observation, because past experience showed that he could not be trusted to rest without close supervision. He was under mild sedation to assist in keeping him still. So yes, this was Valk.

She settled in to wait for him to wake up.

"Calla. Calla. Hey."

She woke at her name, shook dreams and worries away, and opened her eyes to see Valk looking back. He must have been terribly weak—he only turned his head. Didn't even try to sit up.

He was smiling. He said something too quickly and softly for her to catch.

"My Gaantish is rusty, Major." She was surprised at the relief she felt. In her worst imaginings, he didn't recognize her.

"I'll always recognize you," he said, slowly this time. He switched to Enithi, "I said, this is like the first time I saw you, in a chair near my bed."

She felt her own smile dawn. "I wasn't asleep then. I should know better than to fall asleep around you people."

"They tell me the cease-fire is holding. The treaty is done. It must be, if you're here."

"The treaty isn't done but the peace is holding. My diplomatic pass to see you only took a week to process."

"Soon we'll have tourists running back and forth."

"Then what'll they do with us?"

His smile was comforting. It meant the bad old days really were done. If he could hope, anyone could hope. And just like that, his smile thinned, or became thoughtful, or something. She couldn't tell what he was thinking. Never could, and usually it didn't bother her.

She said, "They—people have been very polite to me here."

"Good. Then I will not need to have words with anyone. Calla—thank you for coming. I'd have come to find you, if I'd been able."

"I worried when you told me where you were."

"I have been rather worried myself."

His telegram had said only two things: *I would like to see you*, and *Bring the game if you can*. A very strange message at a very strange time. Strange to anyone except her, anyway. It made perfect sense to her. She had explained it to the visa people and passport department and military attachés like this: *We have a history*. He had been her prisoner, then she had been his, and they had made a promise that if peace ever came they would finish the game they had started. If they finished the game it meant the peace would last.

Calla suspected that none of the Enithi officials who reviewed her request knew what to make of it, but it seemed so weird, and they were so curious, they approved it. On the Gaantish side, Valk was enough of a war hero that they didn't dare deny the request. Out of such happenstances was a peace constructed.

She looked around—there was a bedside table on wheels that could be pulled over for meals and exams and such. Drawing the chess set from her bag, she set it on the table.

"Ah," Valk said. He started to sit up.

"No." She touched his shoulder, keeping him in place with as strong a thought as she could manage. This made him grin. "There's got to be some way to raise the bed."

She'd moved to the front of the bed to start poking around when one of the nurses came running over. "Here, I'll do that," he said quickly.

Calla stepped out of his way with a wry look. Gaantish hospitals didn't have buzzers for nurses. It had driven her rather mad, back in the day. In short order, the man had the bed propped up and Valk resting upright. He seemed more himself, then.

The chess set opened into the game board, painted in black and white alternating squares, and a little tray that slid out held all the pieces, stylized carvings in stained wood. Valk leaned forward, anticipation in his gaze. "I haven't even seen anything like this since we played back at Overton."

Gaant did not have chess. They did not have any games at all that required strategy or bluffing. There was no point. Instead, they played games based on chance—dice rolls and drawn cards—or balance, pulling a single wooden block out of a stack of blocks, for example. And they never cheated.

But Calla had taught Valk chess and developed a system for playing against him. Only someone from Enith would have thought of it. The two countries had approached the war much the same way.

"I'm rusty as well. We'll be on even footing."

Valk laughed. They'd never been on even footing and they both knew it. But they both compensated, so it all worked out.

"I made a note of where the last game left off. Or would you rather start a new one?"

"Let's finish the last." He might have said it because she was thinking it, too.

She arranged the pieces the way they had been, and reminded herself how the game had gone so far. There was a lot to recall. She didn't remember some of the details, but given the rules and given the pieces, she only had so many choices of what to do next. She considered them all.

"It was your move, I think," she said.

He studied her rather than the board. The Gaantish didn't have to see someone to see their thoughts—a blind Gaant was still telepathic. But looking was polite, as in any conversation. And it was intimidating, in an interrogation.

This idea that they could see *through* you. Enithi soldiers told stories about how when a Gaantish person read your mind, it hurt. That they could inflict pain. This wasn't true. Gaant encouraged the stories anyway, along with the ones about how any one of them could see the thoughts of every person in the world, when they couldn't see much past the walls of a given room.

Valk was going to decide, by seeing her thoughts, what move he ought to make, what move she hoped he would, based on her knowledge and experience. He would try to deduce for himself the best choice. And then he would know, almost as soon as she did herself, how she would counter. She kept her expression still, as if that mattered. He moved a piece, and she saw her thoughts reflected back at her—it was just what she would have done, if the board had been reversed.

Next came her turn, and it was no good staring at the board, analyzing the rooks and pawns and playing out future moves in her mind. All such planning would betray her here. So, almost without looking, almost without thought, she reached, put her hand on a piece—any piece, it hardly mattered—and moved it. A bishop this time, and she only moved one square, and yet it was as if a bit of chaos had descended on the board and disrupted everything. No sane chess player would have made that move, and she herself had to pause and consider what she'd done, what new lines of play existed, and how she could possibly go forward from here.

But, and this was the point, the telepathic Valk had not been expecting what she'd just done.

Playing at random was no way to play chess, and she was sure her old teachers were turning in their graves. Unless, she would explain to them, you're playing with a Gaantish commander. Then the joy in the game became watching him squirm.

"I am glad you are enjoying this," Valk said.

"I am. Are you?"

"I am," he said, looking at her. "This gives me hope."

She had traveled here because she had nothing left. Because she was unhappy. Because her whole life had been spent in this uniform, for all the pain it had brought her, so what did she do now? She hadn't had an answer until Valk sent that telegram.

And now he was frowning. She'd been able to keep up a good front before this.

"We are all of us wounded," he said softly.

"It's your move."

He chose his piece, a pawn, a completely different move than the one she'd been thinking of, which made her next choices more interesting. This time, she took the correct one, the one she'd do if she'd been playing seriously.

"This isn't serious?" he asked.

"I'm never serious." Which he'd know was a lie, but he smiled anyway.

She'd taught him to play when she was his prisoner, but he asked to learn because of what he'd seen when he was her prisoner. She'd had a game running in the prison ward with one of the other nurses. They'd slip in plays between their rounds, in odd down moments, to clear their minds and pass the time. This job wasn't real nursing, when all they had to do was administer medications, make sure no one had allergies or bad reactions to the drugs, and keep their patients muzzy-headed. Their board had been set up in Valk's ward that day. Calla had been grinning because her opponent was about to lose, and he was studying the board with furrowed brow and deep concentration, looking for a way out.

A voice had said, "Hey. Hey. You." He might have been speaking either Enithi or Gaantish. Hard to tell with so few words. Their handsome prisoner was waking up, calling for their attention. Because it wasn't her turn, Calla had been the one to jump up and get her kit. They'd had trouble getting the dosage right on Valk; he had a high tolerance for the stuff. But they couldn't have him reading minds, so she made a mark on his chart and injected more into his IV lead.

"No," he'd protested, watching the syringe with a helpless panic. "No, please, I just want to talk—" He spoke very good Enithi.

"I'm sorry," she said, and she really was. "We've got to keep you under. It's better, really. I know you understand."

And he did, or at least he'd see what she understood, that it wasn't just about keeping information from him. It also kept the Gaantish prisoners safe, when otherwise they'd be outnumbered and battered by hostile thoughts. He still looked very unhappy as he sank back against the bed and his eyelids shut inexorably. As if something fragile had slipped out of his hand.

"Poor things," Calla said, brushing a bit of lint off the man's forehead.

"You're very weird, Cal," her chess partner said, finally making his move. "They're Gaantish. You pity them?"

"I just think it must be hard, being so far from home in a place like this."

She found out later that Valk hadn't quite been asleep through all that.

Valk made his next move and winced, just as a nurse came over with a hypodermic syringe and vial on a tray, sensing his pain before he even knew it was there.

"No," Valk said, putting up a hand before the nurse could set the tray down.

"You're in pain; this will help you rest," he said.

"But Technician Belan is here."

"Y-yes sir." The man went away without administering the sedative.

So much conversation didn't need to be spoken when the participants could read each other's minds. They would only say aloud the conclusion they had come to, or the polite niceties that opened and closed conversations. The rest was silent. Back at Overton it had often left her reeling, when she was meant to be working with a patient and two nearby doctors came to a decision, only ten percent of which had been spoken out loud, and they stared at her like she was some idiot child when she didn't understand. She had learned to take delight in saying out loud, forcefully, "You have to tell me what you want me to do." They'd often be frustrated with her, but it served them right. They could always send her back to the prisoner barracks. But they didn't; they didn't have enough nurses as it was. She had accepted an offer to trade the freedom of the rest of her unit for her skills—send the others home in a prisoner swap and she would work as a nurse for the Gaantish infirmary. They trusted her in the position because they would always know if she meant ill. Staying had been harder than she expected.

The nurse lingered near the game. It made Calla just a little bit nervous, like those days at the camp, surrounded by telepaths, and she the only person who hadn't brought a spear to the war.

"This is a very complicated game," the nurse observed, and that made Calla smile. That was why Valk told her he wanted to learn—it was very complicated. The thoughts people thought while playing it were methodical, yet rich.

"It is," Valk said.

"May I watch?" the nurse asked.

Valk looked to Calla to answer, and she said, "Yes, you may."

Enithi troops told awful stories about what it must be like in Gaantish prisoner camps. There'd be no privacy, no secrets. The guards would know everything about your fears and weaknesses, they could design tortures to your exact specifications, they could bribe you with the one thing that would make you break. No worse fate than being captured by Gaant and put in one of their camps.

In fact, it worked the other way around. The camps were nightmares for the guards, who spent all day surrounded by a thousand minds who were terrified, furious, hurt, lonely, angry, and depressed.

As a matter of etiquette, Gaantish people learned—the way that small children learned not to take off their pants and run around naked just anywhere—to guard their thoughts. To keep them close. To keep them calm, so they didn't disrupt those around them. If they often seemed expressionless or unemotional, this was actually politeness, as Calla learned.

To the Gaantish, Enithi prisoners were very, very loud. The guards working the camps got hazard pay. They didn't, in fact, torture their prisoners at all. First, they didn't need to. Second, they wouldn't have been able to stand it.

When her unit had been captured, processed, and sent to the camp, she had been astonished because Lieutenant Valk Larn—now Captain Larn—had been one of the officers in charge. Her shock of recognition caused every telepath in the room to stop and look at her. They would have turned back to their work soon enough—that she and Valk had encountered each other before was coincidental but maybe not remarkable. What made them continue staring: Calla revealed affection for Valk. Not outwardly, so much. She stood with the rest of her unit, stripped down to shirts and trousers, wrists hobbled, hungry and sleep-deprived. No, outwardly she'd been amazed, seeing her former patient upright and in uniform, steely and commanding as any recruitment poster. Her expression looked shocked enough that her sergeant at her side had dared to whisper, "Cal, are you okay?"

The Gaantish never asked each other how they were doing. She'd learned that back in the ward, looking after Valk. During his brief lucid moments she'd ask him how he was feeling, and he'd stare at her like she was playing a joke on him.

The emotion of affection was plain to those who could see it—everyone in a Gaantish uniform. And she was, under all that week's pain and discomfort and unhappiness and uncertainty, almost happy to see him. She was the kind of nurse who had a favorite patient, even in a prison hospital.

He couldn't *not* see her, not with every Gaantish soldier staring at her, then looking at him to see his reaction. She couldn't hide her astonishment; she didn't want to and didn't try. She did realize this likely made the meeting harder for him than it did for her—whatever he thought of her, his staff would all see it. She didn't know what he thought of her.

He merely nodded and waved the group on to continue processing, and they were washed down, given lumpy brown jumpsuits and assigned quarters. Later, she suspected he'd been the one to arrange the deal that won the rest of her unit's freedom.

Calla had always thought it strange that people asked if prisoners were treated "well." "Were you treated well?" *No,* she thought. The doors were locked. The guards all had guns. Did it matter if they had food and blankets, a roof? The food was strange, the blankets leftover from what the army used. Instead she answered, "We were not treated badly." They were treated appropriately. War necessitated prisoners, since the alternative was slaughtering everyone on both sides, which both sides agreed was not ideal. You treated prisoners appropriately so that your own people would be treated appropriately in turn. That meant different things.

She was treated appropriately, which made it odd the day, only a week or so into her captivity, that Valk had her brought to his office alone. It wasn't so odd that the guards hesitated or looked at either of them strangely. But she had been afraid. Helpless, afraid, everything. They left the binders around her wrists. All she could do was stand there before his desk and wonder if he was the kind of man who enjoyed hurting his prisoners, who enjoyed minds in pain. She wouldn't have thought so, but she'd only ever known him when he was asleep and the brief waking moments when he seemed so lost and confused she couldn't help but pity him, so what did she know?

"I won't hurt you," he said, after a long moment when he simply watched her, and she tried to hide her shaking. "You can believe me." He asked her to sit. She remained standing, as he must have known she would.

"You were one of the nurses at the hospital. I remember you."

"Not many remember their stays there."

"I remember you. You were kind."

She couldn't not be. It was why she'd become a nurse. She didn't have to say anything.

"You were playing a game. I remember—two people. A board. You enjoyed it very much. You had the most interesting thoughts."

She didn't have to think long to remember. Those afternoon games with Elio had been a good time. "Chess. It was chess."

"Can you teach me to play?"

"Sir, I'd lose every single time. I'm not sure you'd enjoy the game. Not much challenge."

"Nevertheless, I would like to learn it."

This presented a dilemma. Could it be interpreted as cooperating with the enemy? More than she already was? He couldn't force her. On the other hand, was this an opportunity? But for what? She was a medic, not a spy. Not that Enith even had spies. Valk gave her plenty of time to think this over, waiting patiently, not revealing if her mental arguments and counterarguments amused or irritated him.

"I don't have a board or pieces."

"What would you need to make them?"

She told him she would have to think about it, which would have been hilarious if she hadn't been so tired and confused. The guards took her back to her cell, where she talked to the ranking Enithi officer prisoner about it. "Might not be a bad thing to have a friend here," he advised.

"But he'll know I'm faking it!" she answered.

"So?" he'd said, and he was right. Calla was what she was and it wouldn't do any good to think differently. She asked for a square of cardboard and a black marker and did up a board, and drew rudimentary pieces on other little squares of cardboard. She'd rather have cut them out but didn't bother asking for scissors, and no one offered, so that was that. It was the ugliest chess set that had ever existed.

Valk learned very quickly because she already knew the rules and all she had to do was think them and he learned. The strategy of it was rather more difficult to teach. He'd get this screwed-up look of concentration, and she might have understood a little bit of what attracted him to the game: There was a lot to think about, and Valk liked the challenge of so much thought coming out of one person. And yes, he always knew what moves she was planning. Which was when she started playing at random. If she could surprise herself, she could surprise him. Then she agreed to the deal to get her people released, she worked in their hospital, they played chess, and she got sick.

She could not learn to marshal her thoughts and emotions the way these people learned to as children. She tried, as a matter of survival, and only managed to stop feeling anything at all.

The diagnosis was depression—Gaant's mental health people were very good. She, who had been so generally high-spirited for most of her life, had had no idea what was happening or how to cope and had grown very ill indeed, until it wasn't that she didn't want to play chess against Valk. She *couldn't*. She couldn't keep her mind on the game, couldn't recognize the pieces by looking at them, couldn't even think of how they moved. One day, walking in a haze between one ward and another at the hospital, she sank to the floor and stayed there. Valk was summoned. He held her hand and tried to see into her, to see what was wrong.

She didn't remember thinking anything at the time. Only seeing the image of her hand in his and not understanding it.

He arranged for her to be part of another prisoner swap, and she went home. Before the transfer he took her aside and spoke softly. "I forget that this is all opaque to you, that you don't know most of what's going on around you. So, since I didn't say it before: Thank you."

"For what?" she'd replied. He'd looked at her blankly, because he didn't seem to know himself. Not enough to be able to explain it, and she couldn't see.

Others came to watch the game—drawn, Calla presumed, by the tangle of thoughts she and Valk were producing. He was getting frustrated. She was playing with the giddy abandon of the six-year-old she had been when her mother taught her the game. And now the whole room shared her fond memories, and the fact that her mother had died in one of the famines that wracked Enith when food production had been disrupted by the war. Ten years ago now. Everyone on both sides had stories like that. *Let us share our stories*, she thought.

"You won't win, playing like that," one of the observing doctors said. After half an hour of watching they probably all understood the rules completely and could play themselves. They'd have no idea how the game was really supposed to be played, however. She wasn't playing properly *at all*, which was rather a lot of fun.

"No, but I may not lose," she said.

"I'm still not sure what the point of this game is," said a nurse, her confusion plain.

"This game, right now? The point is to annoy Major Larn," Calla said. This got a chuckle from them—those who'd been looking after him knew him well. Valk, however, smiled at her. She had not spoken the truth, precisely. Everyone else was too polite to say anything.

"The point," Valk said, addressing the nurse, "is to fight little wars without hurting anyone."

And there was silence then, because yes, they all had stories.

He made his next move and took his hand away. Her gaze lit, her heart opening. Even the way she played with him, all messy and at random, a moment like this could still happen, where the board opened up as if by magic and her way was clear. Because it was her turn it didn't matter if he knew what she was thinking, because he couldn't do anything about it. She moved the rook, and his king was cornered.

"Check."

It wasn't mate. He could still get out of it. But he really was backed into a corner, because his next moves and hers would all lead back to check, and they could chase each other around the board, and it would be splendid. Neither could have planned for this.

He threw up his hands and settled back against his pillow. "I'm exhausted. You've exhausted me." She laughed a gleeful, satisfied laugh.

The observers looked on. "This is how you won," one of them said, amazed. He wasn't talking about the game.

"No," Calla said. "This is how we failed to lose."

"I learned the difference from her," Valk said, and was that a bit of pride in his tone? She might never know for certain.

Calla started resetting the board for the next game, not even realizing that meant she was having a good time. The nurse interrupted her.

"Technician Belan, the major really must rest now," he said kindly, recognizing Calla's eagerness when she herself didn't.

"Oh. Of course."

"I promise I'll rest in just a moment," Valk said. He was speaking to the doctors and attendants, who'd expressed a concern she couldn't see. They drifted away because he wanted them to.

That left them studying each other; he who could see everything, and she who could only muddle through, being herself, proudly and unabashedly.

She asked, abruptly, "Do you still have that old cardboard set I made?"

"No. When Overton closed, I lost track of it. Probably got swept away with the trash."

"Good," she said. "It was very ugly."

"I miss it," Valk said.

"You shouldn't. I'm glad it's all over. So glad."

That dark place that she barely remembered opened up, and she started crying. She had thought to pretend that none of it ever happened, and so carried around this blackness that no one could see, and it would have swallowed her up if Valk hadn't sent that telegram. She got that message and knew it was all true, knew it had all happened, and he would be able to see her.

She scrubbed tears from her face and didn't try to hide any of this.

"I wasn't sure how much you remembered," Valk said softly.

"I wasn't sure either," she said, laughing now. Laughing and crying. The darkness shrank.

"Are you sorry you came?"

"Oh, no. It's just . . . " She put her hand in his and tried to explain. Discovered she couldn't speak. She had no words. And it didn't matter.

BLOOD GRAINS SPEAK THROUGH MEMORIES

JASON SANFORD

Morning's song of light and warmth glowed on the horizon as the land's anchor, Frere-Jones Roeder, stepped from her front door. The red-burn dots of fairies swirled in the river mists flowing over her recently plowed sunflower fields. Cows mooed in the barn, eager to be milked. Chickens flapped their wings as they stirred from roosts on her home's sod-grass roof.

Even though the chilled spring day promised nothing but beauty, the grains in Frere-Jones's body shivered to her sadness as she looked at the nearby dirt road. The day-fellows along the road were packing their caravan. Evidently her promises of safety weren't enough for them to chance staying even a few more hours.

Frere-Jones tapped the message pad by the door, pinging her fellow anchors on other lands so they knew the caravan was departing. She then picked up her gift sack and hurried outside to say goodbye.

As Frere-Jones closed the door, a red fairy wearing her dead lifemate's face flittered before her eyes. A flash of memory jumped into her from the fairy's grain-created body. One of Haoquin's memories, from a time right after they'd wed. They'd argued over something silly—like newlyweds always did—and Haoquin had grown irritated at Frere-Jones's intransigence.

But that was all the fairy shared. The taste of Haoquin's memory didn't show Frere-Jones and Haoquin making up. The memory didn't show the two of them ending the day by walking hand-in-hand along her land's forest trails.

Frere-Jones slapped the fairy away, not caring if the land and its damned grains were irritated at her sadness. She liked the day-fellows. She'd choose them any day over the grains.

The fairy spun into an angry buzzing and flew over the sunflower fields to join the others.

Frere-Jones walked up to the caravan's wagons to find the day-fellows detaching their power systems from her farm's solar and wind grid. The caravan leader nodded to Frere-Jones as he harnessed a team of four horses to the lead wagon.

"We appreciate you letting us plug in," the man said. "Our solar collectors weaken something awful when it's overcast."

"Anytime," Frere-Jones said. "Pass the word to other caravans that I'm happy to help. Power or water or food, I'll always share."

Pleasantries done, Frere-Jones hurried down the line of wagons.

The first five wagons she passed were large multi-generational affairs with massive ceramic wheels standing as tall as she. Pasted-on red ribbons outlined the wagons' scars from old battles. Day-fellows believed any battle they survived was a battle worth honoring.

Adults and teenagers and kids smiled at Frere-Jones as she passed, everyone hurrying to harness horses and stow baggage and deploy their solar arrays.

Frere-Jones waved at the Kameron twins, who were only seven years old and packing up their family's honey and craft goods. Frere-Jones reached into her pocket and handed the twins tiny firefly pebbles. When thrown, the pebbles would burst into mechanical fireflies which flew in streaks of rainbow colors for a few seconds. The girls giggled—firefly pebbles were a great prank. Kids loved to toss them when adults were sitting around campfires at night, releasing bursts of fireflies to startle everyone.

Frere-Jones hugged the twins and walked on, finally stopping before the caravan's very last wagon.

The wagon stood small, barely containing the single family inside, built not of ceramic but of a reinforced lattice of ancient metal armor. Instead of bright ribbons to honor old battles, a faded maroon paint flaked and peeled from the walls. Large impact craters shown on one side of the wagon. Long scratches surrounded the back door from superhard claws assaulting the wagon's armored shutters.

An ugly, ugly wagon. Still, it had bent under its last attack instead of breaking. The caravan's leader had told Frere-Jones that this family's previous caravan had been attacked a few months ago. All that caravan's ceramic wagons shattered, but this wagon survived.

Frere-Jones fed her final sugar cubes to the wagon's horses, a strong pair who nickered in pleasure as the grains within their bodies pulsed in sync to her own. Horses adapted so perfectly to each land's grains as they fed on grasses and hay. That flexibility was why horses usually survived attacks even when their caravan did not.

"Morning, Master-Anchor Frere-Jones," a teenage girl, Alexnya, said as she curtsied, holding the sides of her leather vest out like a fancy dress. Most kids in the caravan wore flowing cotton clothes, but Alexnya preferred leather shirts and vests and pants.

"Master-Anchor Frere-Jones, you honor us with your presence," Alexnya's mother, Jun, said in an overly formal manner. Her husband, Takeshi, stood behind her, holding back their younger daughter and son as if Frere-Jones was someone to fear.

They're skittish from that attack, Frere-Jones thought. A fresh scar ran the left side of Jun's thin face while Takeshi still wore a healing pad around his neck. Their two young kids, Miya and Tufte, seemed almost in tears at being near an anchor. When Frere-Jones smiled at them, both kids bolted to hide in the wagon.

Only Alexnya stood unafraid, staring into Frere-Jones's eyes as if confident this land's anchor wouldn't dare harm her.

"I've brought your family gifts," Free-Jones said.

"Why?" Jun asked, suspicious.

Frere-Jones paused, unused to explaining. "I give gifts to all families who camp on my land."

"A land which you protect," Jun said, scratching the scar on her face. As if to remind Frere-Jones what the anchors who'd attacked their last caravan had done.

Frere-Jones nodded sadly. "I am my land's anchor," she said. "I wish it wasn't so. If I could leave I would . . . my son . . . "

Frere-Jones turned to walk back to her farm to milk the cows. Work distracted her from memories. But Alexnya jumped forward and grabbed her hand.

"I've heard of your son," Alexnya said. "He's a day-fellow now, isn't he?"

Frere-Jones grinned. "He is indeed. Travels the eastern roads in a caravan with his own lifemate and kids. I see him once every four years when the land permits his caravan to return." Frere-Jones held the gift bag out to Alexnya. "Please take this. I admit it's a selfish gift. I want day-fellows to watch out for my son and his family. Lend a hand when needed."

"Day-fellows protect our own," Jun stated in a flat voice. "No need to bribe us to do what we already do."

Alexnya, despite her mother's words, took the canvas gift bag and opened it, pulling out a large spool of thread and several short knives.

"The thread is reinforced with nano-armor," Frere-Jones said, "the strongest you can find. You can weave it into the kids' clothes. The short knives were made by a day-fellow biosmith and are supposedly unbreakable . . . "

Frere-Jones paused, not knowing what else to say. She thought it silly that day-fellows were prohibited from possessing more modern weapons than swords and knives to protect themselves, even if she knew why the grains demanded this.

"Thank you, Frere-Jones," Alexnya said as she curtsied again. "My family appreciates your gifts, which will come in handy on the road."

Unsure what else to say, Frere-Jones bowed back before walking away, refusing to dwell on the fact that she was the reason this day-fellow caravan was fleeing her land.

That night Frere-Jones lit the glow-stones in the fireplace and sat down on her favorite sofa. The stones' flickering flames licked the weariness from her body. A few more weeks and the chilled nights would vanish as spring fully erupted across her land.

Frere-Jones didn't embrace spring as she once had. Throughout the valley her fellow anchors celebrated the growing season with dances, feasts, and lush night-time visits to the forest with their lifemates and friends.

Frere-Jones no longer joined such festivities. Through the grains she tasted the land's excitement—the mating urge of the animals, the budding of the trees, the growth of the new-planted seeds in her fields. She felt the cows in the fields nuzzling each other's necks and instinctively touched her own neck in response. She sensed several does hiding in the nearby forests and touched her stomach as the fawns in their wombs kicked. She even felt the grass growing on her home's sod-roof and walls, the roots reaching slowly down as water flowed by capillary action into the fresh-green blades.

The grains allowed Frere-Jones, as this land's anchor, to feel everything growing and living and dying for two leagues around her. She even dimly felt the anchors on nearby lands—Jeroboam and his family ate dinner in their anchordom while Chakatie hunted deer in a forest glen on her land. Chakatie was probably gearing up for one of her family's bloody ritualized feasts to welcome spring.

Frere-Jones sipped her warm mulled wine before glancing at her home's message pad. Was it too soon to call her son again? She'd tried messaging Colton a few hours ago, but the connection failed. She was used to this— day-fellow caravans did slip in and out of the communication grid—but that didn't make it any less painful. At least he was speaking to her again.

Frere-Jones downed the rest of her drink. As she heated a new mug of wine over the stove she took care to ignore the fairies dancing outside her kitchen window. Usually the fairies responded to the land's needs and rules, but these fairies appeared to have been created by the grains merely to annoy her. The grains were well aware that Frere-Jones hated her part in the order and maintenance of this land.

Two fairies with her parents' faces glared in the window. Other fairies stared with the faces of even more distant ancestors. Several fairies mouthed Frere-Jones's name, as if reminding her of an anchor's duty, while others spoke in bursts of memories copied by the grains from her ancestors' lives.

Fuck duty, she thought as she swallowed half a mug of wine. *Fuck you for what you did to Haoquin.*

Thankfully her lifemate's face wasn't among those worn by these fairies. While the grains had no problem creating fairies with Haoquin's face, they knew not to push Frere-Jones when she was drunk.

As Frere-Jones left the kitchen she paused before the home altar. In the stone pedestal's basin stood three carved stone figurines—herself, her son, and Haoquin. The hand-sized statues rested on the red-glowing sand filling the basin.

In the flickering light of the glow stones the figures seemed to twitch as if alive, shadow faces accusing Frere-Jones of unknown misdeeds. Frere-Jones touched Haoquin's face—felt his sharp cheekbones and mischievous smirk—causing the basin's red sands to rise up, the individual grains climbing the statues until her family glowed a faint speckled red over the darker sands below.

The red grains burned her fingers where she touched Haoquin, connecting her to what remained of her lifemate. She felt his bones in the family graveyard on the edge of the forest. Felt the insects and microbes which had fed on his remains and absorbed his grains before dying and fertilizing the ground and the trees and the other plants throughout the land, where the grains had then been eaten by deer and cows and rabbits. If Frere-Jones closed her eyes she could almost feel Haoquin's grains pulsing throughout the land. Could almost imagine him returning to her and hugging her tired body.

Except he couldn't. He was gone. Only the echo of him lived on in the microscopic grains which had occupied his body and were now dispersed again to her land.

And her son was even farther beyond the grains' reach, forced to forsake both the grains and her land when he turned day-fellow.

Frere-Jones sat down hard on the tile floor and cried, cradling her empty wine mug.

She was lying on the floor, passed out from the wine, when a banging woke her.

"Frere-Jones, you must help us!" a woman's voice called. She recognized the voice—Jun, from the day-fellow family which left that morning.

Frere-Jones's hands shook, curling like claws. The grains in her body screamed against the day-fellows for staying on her land.

No, she ordered, commanding the grains to stand down. *It's too soon. There are a few more days before they wear out this land's welcome.*

The grains rattled irritably in her body like pebbles in an empty water gourd. While they should obey her, to be safe Frere-Jones stepped across the den and lifted several ceramic tiles from the floor. She pulled Haoquin's handmade laser pistol from the hiding spot and slid it behind her back, held by her belt. She was now ready to shoot herself in the head if need be.

Satisfied that she was ready, Frere-Jones opened the door. Jun and Takeshi stood there supporting Alexnya, who leaned on them as if drunk but stared with eyes far too awake and aware. Alexnya shook and spasmed, her muscles clenching as she moaned a low, painful hiss, unable to fully scream.

Frere-Jones looked behind the family. She reached out to the grains in the land's animals and plants and soils. She didn't feel any other anchors on her land. If any of them found the day-fellows here . . .

"Bring her inside," she told Jun. "Takeshi, hide your wagon and horses in the barn."

"Not until later," Takeshi said, wanting to stay with his daughter.

Jun snapped at him. "Don't be a fool, Tak. We can't be seen. Not after everyone knows our caravan left."

Frere-Jones took Alexnya in her arms, the grains powering up her strength so the teenage girl seemed to weigh no more than a baby. Takeshi hurried back to the wagon, where the family's two youngest kids stared in fright from the open door.

Frere-Jones carried Alexnya to Colton's old room and placed her on the bed. Alexnya continued to spasm, her muscles clenching and shivering under her drained-pale skin.

"Please," Alexnya whimpered. "Please . . . "

As Jun held her daughter's hand, Frere-Jones leaned closer to the girl. The grains jumped madly in Frere-Jones's blood, erupting her fangs like razors ready to rip into these day-fellows' throats. Frere-Jones breathed deep to calm herself and gagged on Alexnya's sweaty scent. It carried the faintest glimmer of grains inside Alexnya's body.

"She's infected," Frere-Jones said in shock. "With grains. My grains."

Jun nodded, an angry look on her face as if Frere-Jones had personally caused this abomination. "The further we travelled from your land, the more pain she experienced. She didn't stop screaming until we left the caravan and began making our way back here."

Frere-Jones growled softly. "This is unheard of," she said. "Grains shouldn't infect day-fellows."

"Day-fellow lore says it happens on rare occasions. Our lore also says each land's anchor has medicine to cure an infection."

Frere-Jones understood. She ran to the kitchen and grabbed her emergency bag. Inside was a glass vial half-full of powder glowing a faint red.

She hadn't used the powder since Colton became a day-fellow. The powder's nearly dim glow meant it had weakened severely over the years. Chakatie had taken most of her remaining medicine after Colton left, worried about Frere-

Jones killing herself with an overdose. Now all that was left was a half-vial of nearly worthless medicine.

But she had nothing else to give. She held the vial over her altar—letting it sync again with the coding from her land's grains—then mixed the powder in a mug of water and hurried back to Alexnya.

"Drink this," she said, holding the mug to Alexnya's lips. The girl gasped and turned her head as if being near the liquid hurt her.

"Why is it hurting her?" Jun asked, blocking Alexnya's mouth with her hand so Frere-Jones couldn't try again. "I thought the medicine helped."

"It does, but the grains always resist at first," Frere-Jones said. "When I gave it to my own son years ago he . . . went through some initial pain. We usually only give small doses to new anchors at puberty to calm the explosive growth of the grains in their bodies. But if we give Alexnya a full dose for the next few days, it should kill the grains."

Jun frowned. "How much pain?"

"I . . . don't know. But if we don't do something soon there will be too many grains in her body to remove."

Frere-Jones didn't need to tell Jun what would happen if Alexnya became anchored to this land. The anchors from the lands surrounding Frere-Jones's wouldn't take kindly to a day-fellow girl becoming one of them.

"We shouldn't have come here," Jun said, standing up. "Maybe if we take Alexnya away from here before the grains establish themselves . . . "

"Taking her from the land will definitely kill her—the grains have already anchored. We need to remove them from her body. There's no other way."

"I'll drink it," Alexnya whispered in a weak voice. She glared at Frere-Jones in fury. Frere-Jones prayed the grains weren't already sharing the land's stored memories with this day-fellow girl. Showing Alexnya what Frere-Jones had done. Revealing secrets known by no one else except her son and Chakatie.

Despite her hesitation, Jun nodded agreement. She held her daughter's spasming body as Frere-Jones poured the liquid through the girl's lips. Alexnya swallowed half the medicine before screaming. Splashes and dribbles on her leather shirt and pants glowed bright red as she thrashed in the bed for a moment before passing out.

Frere-Jones and Jun tucked Alexnya under the covers and stepped into the den. Takeshi stood by the fireplace holding their youngest son and daughter.

"Will she make it?" Jun asked.

"I don't know," Frere-Jones said. "She'll need another dose before the medicine wears off or she'll be as bad as ever. And that was all I had in the house."

Frere-Jones glanced at the altar, where the red sands squirmed in a frenzied rush, climbing over the figurines as if outraged they couldn't eat stone. She noticed Jun staring at her back and realized the woman had seen the laser pistol she carried.

Frere-Jones handed the pistol to Jun. "Use this if needed," she said. "Make sure none of you touch the grains in the altar—if you do, every anchor for a hundred leagues will know there's a day-fellow family here."

Jun nodded as Frere-Jones pulled on her leather running duster. "When will you be back?"

"I don't know," Frere-Jones said. "I have to find more medicine. I'll . . . think of something."

With that Frere-Jones ordered the grains to power up her legs and, for the first time in years, she ran across her land. She ran faster than any horse, faster than any deer, until even the fairies which flew after her could barely keep up.

At the land's boundary Frere-Jones paused.

She stood by Sandy Creek, the cold waters bubbling under the overhanging oaks and willows. Fairies flew red tracers over the creek, flying as far across as they dared without crossing into the bordering land. On the other bank a handful of blue fairies hovered in the air, staring back at Frere-Jones and the red fairies.

Usually boundaries between lands were more subtle, the grains that were tied to one anchor mixing a bit with the next land's grains in the normal back and forth of life. But with Sandy Creek as a natural land divide—combined with Frere-Jones's isolation from the other anchors—the boundary between her and Chakatie's lands had grown abrupt, stark.

One of Chakatie's blue fairies stared intensely at her. Chakatie knew she was coming. Frere-Jones wished there was a caravan nearby to trade for the medicine. Day-fellow pharmacists were very discreet.

Still, of all the nearby anchors Chakatie was the only one who might still give her medicine. Chakatie was also technically family, even if her son Haoquin was now dead. And she had a large extended family. Meaning a number of kids. Meaning stocks of medicine on hand to ensure the grains didn't overwhelm and kill those kids when they transitioned to becoming anchors.

Still, no matter how much Frere-Jones had once loved Chakatie she wouldn't go in unprepared. She was, after all, her land's anchor. She stripped off her clothes and stepped into the cold creek, rubbing mud and water over her skin and hair to remove the day-fellow scent. She activated the grains inside her, increasing her muscle size and bone density. Finally, for good measure, she grabbed a red fairy buzzing next to her and smashed it between her now-giant hands. She smeared the fairy's glowing red grains in two lines down both sides of her face and body.

Battle lines. As befitted an anchor going into another's land in the heart of the night.

Satisfied, she walked naked onto Chakatie's anchordom.

Frere-Jones hated memories. She hated how the grains spoke to her in brief snatches of memories copied from Haoquin and her parents and grandparents and on back to the land's very first anchor.

But despite this distaste at memories, they still swarmed her. As Frere-Jones crossed the dark forest of trees and brambles on Chakatie's land, she wondered why the grains were showing her these memories. The grains never revealed memories randomly.

In particular, why show her Haoquin's memories, which the grains had so rarely shared up to now? Memories from the day she met him. Memories from their selecting ceremony.

Frere-Jones tried to stop them, but the memories slipped into her as if they'd always existed within her.

Frere-Jones's parents had died when the grains determined it was time for their child to take over. Like most anchors they'd gone happily. First they drank medicine to dull the grains' power to rebuild their bodies. Then they slit each other's throat in the land's graveyard, holding hands as they bled out and their grain-copied memories flowed into the land they'd protected.

At first Frere-Jones had accepted her role in protecting the land. She safeguarded the land from those who might harm it and carefully managed the ecosystem's plants and animals so the land was in continual balance.

But a few years after becoming anchor a small day-fellow caravan defiled her land by cutting down trees. Frere-Jones eagerly allowed the grains to seize control of her body. She called other anchors to her side and led an attack on the caravan. Memories of the pains her land had suffered before the grains had arrived flowed through her—images of clear-cut forests and poisoned soil and all the other evils of the ancient world. In her mind she became a noble warrior preventing humans from creating ecological hell just as her family had done for a hundred generations.

Only after the caravan was wiped out did she learn that a day-fellow child, gifted with a new hatchet and told to gather dead branches for a fire, had instead cut down a single pine sapling.

Outraged at what she'd done, Frere-Jones attacked the other anchors who'd helped savage the caravan. The anchors fought back, slashing at her with claw and fang until a respected older anchor, Chakatie, arrived, her three-yard-tall body powered to a mass of muscle and bone and claw.

Chakatie's land neighbored Frere-Jones's land, but Chakatie hadn't aided in the attack on the caravan. Now this powerful woman had stepped among the fighting anchors, a mere glance all that was needed to stop the other anchors from attacking each other. A few even powered down their bodies.

Chakatie had paused before the remains of the caravan and breathed deeply. As the other anchors watched nervously, Chakatie leaned over and tapped the tiny child-size hatchet and examined the cut sapling. She sniffed each day-fellow body.

With a roar, Chakatie told everyone but this land's anchor to leave. The others fled.

Once everyone was gone Chakatie bent over the dead bodies and cried.

After Chakatie finished, she stood and wiped her tears. Frere-Jones forced herself to stand still, willing to take whatever punishment Chakatie might give for this evil deed. But the older woman didn't attack. Instead, she stepped forward until her hot breath licked Frere-Jones's face and her fangs clicked beside her ear like knives stripping flesh from bone.

"The grains speak only in memories," Chakatie said. "But memories only speak to the grains' programmed goals. A good anchor never lets memory overwhelm what is right and what is wrong."

With that Chakatie walked away, leaving Frere-Jones to bury the caravan's dead.

Ashamed, Frere-Jones had locked herself in her home and refused to listen to the grains' excuses. The grains tried to please her with swirls of memories from her parents and others. Memories of people apologizing and explaining and rationalizing what she'd done.

But she no longer cared. She was this land's anchor and she'd decide what was right. Not the grains.

A few years later the grains gave her an ultimatum: marry another anchor to help manage this land, or the other anchors would kill Frere-Jones and select a new anchor to take her place.

The selecting ceremony took place on the summer solstice. Hundreds of her fellow anchors came to her home, setting up feasting tents along the dirt road and in fallow fields. Frere-Jones walked from tent to tent, meeting young anchors who spoke eagerly of duty and helping protect her land. She listened politely. Nodded to words like "ecological balance" and "heritage." Then she walked to the next tent to hear more of the same.

Frere-Jones grew more and more depressed as she went from tent to tent. If she didn't choose a mate before the end of the day all the celebrating anchors would rip her to pieces and chose a new anchor to protect her land. She wondered if day-fellows felt this fear around anchors. The fear of knowing people who were so warm and friendly one moment might be your death in the next.

Frere-Jones was preparing for her death when she spotted a ragged tent beside her barn. The tent was almost an afterthought, a few poles stuck in the ground holding up several old and torn cotton blankets.

Frere-Jones stepped inside to see Chakatie sitting beside a young man.

"Join us in a drink?" Chakatie asked, holding a jug of what smelled like moonshine. Chakatie's body when powered down was tiny, barely reaching Frere-Jones's shoulder.

"Do I look like I need a drink?" Frere-Jones asked.

"Any young woman about to be slaughtered for defying the grains needs a drink," Chakatie said.

Frere-Jones sat down hard on the ground and drank a big swallow of moonshine. "Maybe I deserve to be killed," she thought, remembering what she'd done to that day-fellow caravan.

"Maybe," the young man sitting next to Chakatie said. "Or maybe you deserve a chance to change things."

Chakatie introduced the man as her son Haoquin. He leaned over and shook Frere-Jones's hand.

"How can I change anything?" Frere-Jones asked. "The grains will force me to do what they want or they'll order the other anchors to kill me."

Instead of answering, Haoquin leaned over so he could see outside the tiny tent. He was a skinny man and wore a giant wool coat even in summer, as if easily chilled. Or that's what Frere-Jones thought until he opened the coat and pulled out a small laser pistol.

Frere-Jones froze at the sight of the forbidden technology, but Chakatie merely laughed. Haoquin aimed the pistol at a nearby tent—the Jeroboam family tent, among the loudest and most rambunctious groups at the selection ceremony. Haoquin pulled the trigger, and a slight buzzing like angry bees filled the tent. He shoved the pistol back in his coat as the roof of the Jeroboam tent burst into flames.

Drunken anchors, including Jeroboam himself, fled from the tent, tearing holes in the fabric walls in their panic. Other anchors howled with laughter while Jeroboam and his lifemate and kids demanded to know who had insulted their family and land with this prank.

Haoquin grinned as he patted his coat covering the hidden pistol. "A little something I made," he said. "I'm hoping it'll come in handy when I eventually spit at the grains' memories."

Frere-Jones felt a flash of memory—her parents warning her as a kid to behave. To be a good girl. She shook off the grains' warning as she stared into Haoquin's mischievous eyes.

Maybe Haoquin was right. Maybe there was a way to change things.

Frere-Jones leaned against a large oak tree, her powered body shaking as red and blue fairies buzzed around her. The grains had never shared such a deep stretch of Haoquin's memories with her. The memories had been so intense and long they'd merged with her own memories of that day into something more. Almost as if Haoquin was alive once again inside her.

Frere-Jones wiped at her glowing eyes with the back of her clawed right hand. Why had the grains shared such a memory with her? What were they saying?

She pushed the memories from her thoughts as she ran on through the forest.

Frere-Jones found Chakatie in an isolated forest glen. Countless fairies rose into the dark skies from the tiny field of grass, stirring up a whirlwind of blue grains in their wake. Naked anchors jumped and howled among the blue light, their bodies powered up far beyond Frere-Jones's own. Massive claws dug into tree trunks and soil. Bloody lips and razor fangs kissed and nipped each other. Throats howled to the stars and the night clouds above.

And throughout this orgy of light and scent swirled the memories of this land's previous anchors. Memories of laughing and crying and killing and dying and a thousand other moments of life, all preserved by the blue grains which coursed through these trees and animals and enhanced people.

Frere-Jones stepped through the frenzied dance, daring anyone to attack her. The red lines on her face burned bright, causing the dancers to leap from her like she might scorch them. As the anchors noticed her the dance died down. They muttered and growled, shocked by Frere-Jones's interruption.

In the middle of the glen sat two granite boulders. On the lower boulder lay a dead stag, its guts ripped out like party streamers of red meat. On the higher rock sat Chakatie, her body and muscles enlarged to the full extent of the grains' powers, her clawed fingers digging into the dead stag beneath her. She sat naked except for a bloody stag-head and antlers draped over her head, the fresh blood dribbling down her shoulders and muscular chest.

"Welcome, my daughter!" Chakatie boomed as she jumped down and hugged Frere-Jones. "Welcome indeed. Have you come to join our festivities?"

Frere-Jones stared at the silent anchors around her. Several of them twitched their claws and fangs. But none dared attack her, remembering that she'd once been married to their blood.

"I won't join in," she said, the grains deepening her voice so she sounded more intimidating. "But I need speak with you. It's urgent."

Chakatie waved her family and relatives away.

"I need medicine," Frere-Jones said. "Five doses."

Chakatie glared at Frere-Jones, her happiness at seeing her vanishing as fast as a gutted deer bleeding out. "I will not have you killing yourself. If you're seeking a painful death for what you did to my grandson, there are far better ways than overdosing on medicine."

Chakatie raised one bloody claw as if offering to slash Frere-Jones to pieces.

Frere-Jones glared back at her mother-in-law. "It's not for me. My land infected a new anchor."

Chakatie lowered her claws and stared at Frere-Jones in puzzlement before a grin slowly emerged around her fangs. "I guess that's . . . good news. Who is it?"

"I'd prefer to see if she survives before naming her," Frere-Jones said, bluffing. Chakatie's blood-and-musk scent was stomach-gagging strong in her nostrils.

"Of course." Chakatie powered down her body slightly. "I apologize for saying that about Colton. If my land had betrayed me like yours did with Haoquin, I may have done as you."

This was the closest Chakatie had ever come to saying she agreed with Colton becoming a day-fellow. Frere-Jones thanked her.

"Don't thank me yet. The senior anchors have been saying you've lost your ability to protect your land. A few even suggest we . . . select a new anchor."

Frere-Jones snarled. "And I'm sure you didn't have someone in mind? Perhaps one of your other sons or daughters?"

Chakatie tensed at the insult before smirking with a knowing nod. "You know I want nothing but love and happiness for you. But if the other anchors become intent on killing you, I'd prefer my own benefit."

Frere-Jones sighed at her mother-in-law's logic. There was a reason no one ever challenged Chakatie. She was likely the mightiest anchor in this part of the world.

Chakatie waved for her oldest son, Malachi, who trotted over. "Run home and bring six vials of medicine to Frere-Jones." She nodded to Frere-Jones. "One extra in case it's needed."

Frere-Jones thanked Chakatie and turned to go, but Chakatie dared to place one of her giant clawed hands on her shoulder.

"Two warnings," Chakatie whispered. "First, don't be lying about what the medicine is for. If you try overdosing on it, I'll make sure the grains keep you alive long enough for me to kill you."

Frere-Jones nodded. "And?"

"The grains on your land have become increasingly agitated since Haoquin died. I fear they're building to something which will harm you."

"If they do, wouldn't that be your fault? After all, you introduced me to Haoquin."

Even as Frere-Jones said this she regretted the words. If she'd never met Haoquin her life would have been far poorer, assuming she'd even lived past her selecting ceremony. But Chakatie had avoided Frere-Jones ever since Colton become a day-fellow. Frere-Jones still loved Chakatie but also wanted to rip the woman apart for abandoning her, a feeling influenced no doubt by her grain-powered body's fury.

Chakatie nodded sadly. "I think every day about the paths of Haoquin's life. Still, what else can we do? We are ingrained in the land . . . " she said, beginning the most sacred oath of anchors.

" . . . and the grains are our land," Frere-Jones finished.

Yet afterwards as Frere-Jones ran back to her land she wanted to claw her own tongue out for uttering such a lie. If it was within her power, she'd destroy every grain in both her land and body.

Not that such dreams mattered in the real world. And if Chakatie and the other anchors learned she was sheltering a day-fellow family, her dreams— and Haoquin's—would never have a chance to come true.

"Don't trust my mother," Haoquin had said one morning a few weeks after they were married. He'd been bedridden that day as the grains from his old land deactivated and Frere-Jones's grains established themselves. She'd given him several doses of medicine, which helped, and stayed by his side the entire time.

Since they couldn't do much else, they lay in bed and talked. Frere-Jones had forgotten the joys of hearing someone talking to her in words instead of memories.

"I like your mom," Frere-Jones said. "I mean, she did bring us together."

"Oh, I like her. Hell, I love her. She's the one who taught me to be wary of the grains. But she's also not afraid to work the grains and the other anchors to her own advantage. Never forget that."

Frere-Jones snuggled closer to Haoquin, who hugged her back. She remembered how Chakatie had been disgusted by Frere-Jones killing the day-fellows. Which had pushed Frere-Jones into a new attitude toward the grains. Which had eventually resulted in her marrying Haoquin.

No, she thought, pushing those memories from her mind. She refused to believe her life was merely a plaything of either Chakatie or the grains.

"You okay?" Haoquin asked.

"Just thinking about memories." Frere-Jones ran her fingers across Haoquin's bare stomach, causing him to shiver. "Like the memory of my fingers on you. The touch of my skin on yours. Someday all that will remain of these moments are the copies of our memories stored in the grains' matrix."

"I can live with that, Fre," Haoquin said, calling her by that nickname for the first time. "Can you?"

Instead of answering Frere-Jones kissed him, her lips touching lips before fading into memory.

Frere-Jones gasped as she paused outside her house with the vials of medicine in her pocket.

She could hear Alexnya screaming inside. The last dose of medicine must be wearing off.

But why were the grains still showing her all these memories from Haoquin? They'd never done that before. In fact, the grains had taken care to lock away most of Haoquin's memories for fear that they'd influence Frere-Jones in the wrong ways. So why were the grains now sharing them?

Frere-Jones shrugged off the question and opened the door to her house. She had to focus on saving the day-fellow girl.

Remember that, she thought. *Remember what's important.*

After the next dose of medicine, Alexnya slept in fits for the day, waking every few hours to drink more. But when Frere-Jones stepped into the bedroom with a new dose the following evening, she found Alexnya sitting up in bed reading an old-fashioned paper book with her mother. Alexnya looked far better, no longer shaking or in pain. Frere-Jones tasted only the barest touch of the grains still inside the girl's body.

"Hello Fre," Alexnya said.

Frere-Jones nearly dropped the mug of medicine. The only one who'd ever called her Fre had been Haoquin.

"Alexnya, be polite," Jun snapped. "Call her Master-Anchor Frere-Jones."

"But she likes being called Fre . . . "

Frere-Jones sat on the bed beside Alexnya. "It's not her fault. The grains communicate using snippets of memories from previous anchors. 'Fre' is what my lifemate used to call me."

Jun paled but didn't say anything. Alexnya frowned. "I'm sorry, Fre . . . Master-Anchor Frere-Jones," the girl said. "I just want you to love me again. You used to love me."

Frere-Jones ignored the girl's obvious confusion at having her memories mix with the memories stored within the grains' matrix. She handed Alexnya the mug of medicine. "Drink this," she said.

The girl swallowed half the medicine. "The grains are angry," Alexnya whispered as she wiped the red glow from her lips. "The grains don't like you removing them from my body. They don't like my family overstaying our welcome."

"They won't hurt your family without my approval."

Alexnya didn't appear convinced. "They're also angry at you," she said as she yawned. "Why are they angry at you?"

"Let me worry about my land's grains. You need to sleep."

Alexnya nodded and closed her eyes. Jun and Frere-Jones shut the door and walked over to the dinner table, where Jun stared at the remaining dregs of medicine in the mug.

"She's taken enough medicine," Frere-Jones said. "By tomorrow her connection to the land will be weak enough to leave. She'll have to continue taking the medicine for another few days to remove the remaining grains, but you can give it to her on the road."

Jun glanced with relief at the den, where Takeshi lay sleeping on a sofa with Miya and Tufte.

"What memories are the grains showing Alexnya?" she asked.

"Does it matter?" Frere-Jones asked with a growl. "Any memories she's experienced are hers now."

As Frere-Jones said this she shook with anger at the thought of Alexnya experiencing even a taste of Haoquin's life. She didn't care about the stored memories of her parents and ancestors, but Haoquin . . . those memories were special. Damn the grains. Damn these day-fellows for intruding on the most intimate parts of her life.

Frere-Jones's right hand spasmed as claws grew from her fingertips. She dug into the wooden table, imagining the need to go into her son's bedroom and rip Alexnya to pieces.

"Master-Anchor Frere-Jones!" Jun shouted in a loud voice. Frere-Jones snapped back to herself and looked up to see Jun aiming the laser pistol at her head. She took a deep breath and forced her body to reabsorb the claws.

The grains were pushing her, like they had as a young anchor when she'd attacked that day-fellow caravan.

"I will sleep outside tonight," Frere-Jones said as she stood. "Bar the door. And windows. Don't let me in." She grinned at Jun, who kept the pistol aimed at her. "If I do break in, make sure you end me before I do anything we'd all regret."

Jun chuckled once but kept the pistol aimed at Frere-Jones until she walked outside and the door slammed shut.

Frere-Jones didn't sleep that night, instead patrolling the land to ensure no one came near her house. This also kept her further away from the day-fellows. Despite the distance the grains inside her shrieked at her land being defiled by the day-fellow presence. And Alexnya was right—the grains were also furious at Frere-Jones. They knew what she'd done to her son. The grains knew she hated them and that she would destroy every trace of their existence if it was within her power.

But despite this anger the grains also continue to share Haoquin's memories with her. She saw the birth of their son through Haoquin's eyes. Saw Haoquin and Colton playing chase in the fields. Saw the three of them going for picnics in the deep woods.

All memories from Haoquin's life.

"What the hell are you telling me?" Frere-Jones yelled. But the grains didn't respond.

When Jun unbolted the sod-house's door in the morning, Frere-Jones was meditating under the oak tree in the front yard. Her body was coated in red smears from the countless fairies she'd killed during the night as she ripped apart every one of the red-glowing, grain-infused monstrosities she encountered.

Several chickens pecked at the fairies' remaining grains in the dirt around her.

Jun stepped toward Frere-Jones with the laser pistol in her right hand.

"You okay?" Jun asked.

"Must be. You're still alive."

Jun shivered. Frere-Jones licked her lips before biting her tongue to silence the grains. They were easier to control during the daytime, but the longer the day-fellows stayed on the land the more demanding they would become.

"Are you safe to be around?"

"I can maintain control until you leave," Frere-Jones said. "We'll give Alexnya another dose of medicine after breakfast. That should be enough to enable your family to leave. You can travel well beyond this land before night falls."

"Tak is cooking breakfast," Jun said, gesturing to the sod-house. "Will you join us?"

Frere-Jones snorted at being invited into her own house but nodded and followed Jun in. She was pleased to see Alexnya looking even better than yesterday and sitting at the dinner table eating oatmeal.

"I missed you, Fre," Alexnya said. Frere-Jones suppressed her irritation at the nickname and sat down in the chair next to her family altar.

The stone altar bubbled and snapped, the red sands swarming angrily over the statues of her family. Miya and Tufte stared at the flowing sands as if mesmerized until Takeshi tapped the table beside them so they returned to eating their oatmeal.

"We have to keep an eye on them constantly so they don't touch the altar," Takeshi said. "Did your son try to play with it all the time?"

"Yes," Frere-Jones snapped. "But he was the child of an anchor—touching the altar wouldn't bring death on his family."

Jun and Takeshi stared in shock at Frere-Jones, and Jun's hand edged toward the laser pistol before Frere-Jones sighed. "I apologize. The grains are pushing me even now. It's . . . hard, being around you with them screaming in my mind."

"That's the price of protecting our sacred land," Alexnya said.

Frere-Jones tapped the vials of glowing medicine on the table before her. She knew Alexnya wasn't trying to deliberately provoke her. She remembered how confused she'd felt when she'd come of age and the grains had activated within her, and how a similar confusion almost overwhelmed Haoquin when he'd married into her anchordom. The sooner Alexnya and her family returned to the road the better.

"It must have been difficult when your son became a day-fellow," Jun said, trying to change the subject. "You're fortunate one of our caravans was nearby to take him in before . . . " Jun paused.

"You can say it," Frere-Jones muttered. "The grains would have forced me to kill my son if he'd stayed more than a few days after becoming a day-fellow. But luck had nothing to do with it. I timed Colton's change so a caravan was here for him."

Jun and Takeshi stared at Frere-Jones, who shrugged. She knew she shouldn't tell such truths to people outside her family, but she no longer cared. The grains pounded inside her at the admitted heresy. She wanted to slam her head into the table to silence them.

"Haoquin died when Colton was only twelve," Frere-Jones whispered. "My lifemate had grown up on another land. When he married into my anchordom and accepted my grains, the grains from that other land deactivated. But my grains eventually tired of the . . . unsettling thoughts Haoquin expressed. His ideas for changing the world. So they reactivated his original grains, causing him to need to live on two separate lands to stay healthy. His body almost tore itself apart. There was nothing I could do."

Frere-Jones reached out and rubbed Haoquin's statue on the altar. The grains felt her hate and slid away from her touch. "Haoquin dreamed of a world without grains. He knew that was merely a pipe dream—we both knew it—but the grains decided even a dream without their existence was too much to tolerate."

Frere-Jones flicked at the red grains in the altar's basin, wishing she could throw them all away where they'd never harm another person.

"The grains calculated they didn't need Haoquin anymore since we'd already created a son," Frere-Jones continued. "But I refused to let them have Colton too. I waited until a caravan was on my land then gave Colton a massive overdose of the medicine, almost more than his body could handle. He turned day-fellow and had to leave.

"The anchor system is evil. To decide that a select few can live in one place while everyone else is forced to continually move from land to land . . . death for any unlinked human who stays too long on a land or pollutes or harms that land . . . to force *me* to enact the grains' arbitrary needs and desires . . . that's nothing but evil."

"But the grains saved the planet," Alexnya said. "I can see some of the old anchors' memories. How the land was nearly destroyed and overrun with people. I can taste the chemicals and hormones and technology. Trees cut down. People dying of blight. There were so many people. Too many for the land to support. Destroying everything they touched . . . "

Alexnya gasped and pushed away from the table, her chair falling backward as she tumbled across the ceramic tiles. She jumped up and ran for the bathroom, where she slammed the door shut.

Frere-Jones sighed as she stared into the shocked faces of the girl's family. "She'll be better once you're on the road," Frere-Jones said. "Keep giving her the medicine twice a day and the grains will soon be completely gone."

"But the memories . . . " Jun began.

"So she'll know why anchors protect their lands. Why those without grains are forced to continually move around."

Takeshi hugged Miya and Tufte, who had jumped into his lap because of the tension in the room. "It's different to be on the receiving end," Takeshi said. "Do you know why our last caravan was destroyed? We were leaving a land a hundred leagues from here when the caravan master's wagon broke an axle. Normally not a problem—most caravans leave early in case of issues like this. But it turned out our caravan master also was smuggling forbidden chemicals and hormones. When the axle broke it stabbed into one of his smuggling tanks and contaminated the land for ten yards on either side of the road.

"We tried cleaning the land. Our caravan master even took responsibility and offered his death for everyone else's lives. But the grains didn't care. You could feel their anger. The ground was almost shaking, the trees and plants whipping madly as if blown by an unknown wind. Then the anchors came— dozens of them, from lands all across the region. They attacked us all night before the grains finally allowed them to calm down. Our wagon was the only one they didn't break into and massacre everyone."

Frere-Jones nodded. If her land became even a slightly bit contaminated the grains would force her to do the same. She picked up the remaining vials of medicine. She held the vials over the altar to encode them with her grain's programming before handing them to Takashi.

"Have her drink another dose then take the remaining vials with you," she told him. "Jun and I will prepare your wagon. You'll leave by noon."

Frere-Jones had spent decades watching day-fellow caravans, but she'd never prepared one of their wagons for travel. Harnessing the horses and securing the wagon's cargo stirred memories of both her own life and those of the anchors who preceded her. How all of them had watched passing day-fellow caravans across thousands of years.

As a child she'd desperately wished she could travel like a day-fellow. See other lands beyond her own.

"Take the northern road through the forest," Frere-Jones told Jun when the wagon and horses were ready. "That's the safest route to avoid irritating the anchors on neighboring lands. Go north and you'll be several lands away before dark."

Jun nodded a silent thanks.

They were still waiting a half-hour later, with Frere-Jones growing increasingly irritated from the grains' demands. "Come on Takashi," she yelled.

"I'll go get him," Jun said, hurrying to the house.

When the family didn't emerge a few minutes later, Frere-Jones cursed and smashed a powered hand into the side of the barn, breaking the inch-thick boards. She stomped into her own house—her house, on her land!—to discover glowing red medicine flowing among broken glass vials on her tile floor. Jun and Takashi stood beside the dinner table pleading with Alexnya but wouldn't go near their daughter.

"Land's shit!" Frere-Jones bellowed. Alexnya stood beside the stone altar, her hands immersed in the flowing red grains.

"She won't let go of the altar," Takashi said. "Should we yank her away?"

"No! Don't touch the grains!" Frere-Jones accessed the grains inside her body, connecting through them with the grains in the altar and across her land. She prayed that Alexnya touching the altar hadn't alerted any nearby anchors. She tasted the forests and plants and animals on her land, felt the nearby anchors going about their duties and work.

But no alarm. There had been no alarm raised. Which was impossible. That could only mean . . .

Frere-Jones screamed as she jumped forward and grabbed Alexnya. She threw the girl across the room, only at the last moment aiming for the sofa so she wouldn't be hurt. Alexnya smashed into the cushions as Jun and Takashi grabbed their youngest kids and ran for the door, Jun again aimed the pistol at Frere-Jones.

Frere-Jones raised her hands as she bent over, panting and trying to stay in control. "Don't shoot," she yelled. "Kill me and your daughter will be stuck here."

"What do you mean?" Jun asked.

"Your daughter should have set off the grains' alarms, especially after taking that much medicine. But she didn't. Why didn't you, Alexnya?"

Alexnya stood up from the sofa, her eyes sparking red light, a growl escaping her snarling lips. For a moment Frere-Jones remembered herself at that age when the grains had first activated in her body. "The grains don't like you," Alexnya whispered. "They changed the altar's coding so the medicine wouldn't remove all of the grains from my body. They promised that if I didn't tell you they'd let my family stay."

"You can't trust the grains," Frere-Jones said. "No day-fellow is ever allowed to stay on a land for more than a few days. That won't change no matter what the grains promise."

Frere-Jones started to say more, but fell silent as she tasted an unsettling tinge in the grains. She felt Alexnya's frustration at travelling from place to place, never settling down long enough to have a home. Frere-Jones also saw the attack which destroyed Alexnya's last caravan. As the anchors shrieked and smashed on the outside of her family's wagon, Alexnya swore she'd never go through this again. That one day she'd find a place to call home.

The grains, Frere-Jones realized, had found a willing partner in this young girl.

"I'm sorry," Alexnya whispered, looking at her parents. "I want to live somewhere. I want a home. The grains said we could all stay."

"The other anchors won't let you be one of us," Frere-Jones stated. "And even if they did, the grains will never let your family stay."

"They promised."

"They lied. The grains only want a new anchor to take my place. They're incapable of caring for your family. They are programmed to protect this land, not to protect unlinked day-fellows without a grain in their bodies."

Frere-Jones glanced again at the altar. She was missing something. If the grains hadn't told her they'd changed the altar's programming to negate the effects of Alexnya's medicine, what else weren't they telling her?

She heard a slight rapping on the kitchen window. Dozens of fairies buzzed outside the glass, their tiny hands tap tapping against the panes like angry snowflakes blowing on the wind.

Framed in the glass, surrounded by the fairies, was a red-tinted face.

Malachi, Chakatie's oldest son.

Frere-Jones ran for the front door, but by the time she opened it Malachi was already running away, nearly gone from sight. She reached out to the grains, trying to power up her body so she could catch the boy, but the grains resisted her, not giving her anywhere near enough to catch him.

Instead, the grains rebutted her in flicks of angry memories. They had a new anchor. They didn't have to obey her any more.

A few weeks after their son had been born, Frere-Jones had woken to find Haoquin standing by the altar, rocking Colton back and forth in his arms in the grains' red-haze light.

"You okay?" she asked sleepily.

"I was thinking about all the previous anchors who raised their kids in this house," Haoquin said. "I bet many of them stood in this very spot and let the grains' glow soothe their babies to sleep."

Frere smiled. "You could ask the grains to share those memories. Sometimes they'll do that, if you ask nicely."

Haoquin snorted. "When I first became an anchor, that's what scared me the most—that the grains spoke to us using memories. I mean, after I'm dead is that what they'll do with my memory of this moment? Use everything I'm experiencing now—love, exhaustion, tenderness, caring—to tell some future anchor that this is how you calm a crying baby? Is that all my memories are good for?"

Frere-Jones hugged her lifemate. "Your memories mean more to me than that. Perhaps they'll mean more to any future anchor who experiences them."

"Maybe," Haoquin said as he and Frere-Jones stared down at their son. "Maybe."

But neither one of them had sounded convinced.

The anchors came for Frere-Jones and the day-fellow family at midnight.

Frere-Jones had finally been able to power up her body after Alexnya ordered the grains to do so. The girl had still been torn, wanting to believe the grains would protect her family, but in the end her parents convinced her the grains would never protect day-fellows. "Have the grains shown you a memory," Jun had said, "any memory across the land's thousands of years where they protected a single day-fellow? If they do that, you can believe them. If not . . . "

When the grains hadn't been able show such a memory, Alexnya broke down and cried. She ordered the grains to obey Frere-Jones.

Yet Frere-Jones knew, even with her body completely powered up she couldn't fight so many other anchors. She messaged them, saying the day-fellows would leave. The only response was laughter. She said she'd allow another anchor to be selected, if only the day-fellows were allowed to leave safely.

Again, more laughter.

Now, at midnight, the anchors were coming. They ran through the river mists. They ran across her new-plowed sunflower fields, their massive bodies and claws destroying the furrows and scattering soil and seed to the winds. They came from the road, giant feet pounding on the dirt packed by centuries of wagons. The came from the forests, knocking down trees and scattering deer and coyotes before them.

Frere-Jones sat on the sod roof of her home, the laser pistol in her hands. The grains showed her Haoquin's memory of building the illegal weapon with parts acquired from day-fellow smugglers. How proud he'd been. His mother had said the grains wouldn't like the pistol, but Haoquin merely laughed and said if he ever was forced to use the laser the displeasure of the grains would be the least of their worries.

As usual, Haoquin had been correct. Maybe that was why the grains had killed him.

"Here they come," Frere-Jones yelled down the air vent into the house. Jun and Takeshi and Alexnya were inside, Jun holding the knives Frere-Jones had gifted them, in case a final defense was needed.

Frere-Jones looked around her. She knew she should give the anchors a warning. She'd known these people all her life. They'd worked together. Had bonds stretching back a hundred generations.

Her land's red fairies buzzed around her, the faces of her ancestors silently pleading with her not to do this. As long as she remained anchor the grains couldn't warn the other anchors. But the grains were outraged at what she planned. A fairy with Haoquin's face flew in front of her eyes, the tiny red body shaking side to side in a silent scream of "No!"

But she knew what the real Haoquin would want. On his last day, as he lay in their bed while the competing grains destroyed each other and his body, he'd told her not to be angry. "Life here was worth it," he'd whispered in her ear as she leaned over him. "Too short, yes. But knowing you made it worthwhile."

Why had the grains waited so long to share his memories with her? If they'd done so years before, maybe she wouldn't have been so angry. Maybe she wouldn't have forced her son into exile from the only land and family he'd known.

Frere-Jones tapped the cord connecting the pistol to her farm's power grid. She aimed at the anchors running toward her. She hated the grains. Hated every memory they spoke.

Burn them all.

The laser lit the land green, the light dazzling through the river mists. The first row of anchors in the sunflower fields flashed and burned, bodies screaming and stenching like spoiled meat over bad flames. Howls of outrage rose from the remaining anchors, who split up to make less obvious targets, but they all still burned bright in Frere-Jones's enhanced vision. She shot two next to the barn, where she heard the day-fellows' horses whinnying in fright. She shot three others on the dirt road. She split one massive anchor in two right before the oak tree in front of her house, the laser also severing the tree's trunk.

She shot every anchor who came near her home. And when the remaining anchors broke ranks and fled, she detached the laser from her power grid and chased after them, using the remaining charge to sear every one of them into char for the coyotes and wolves to feast on.

"Share this memory with the land's future anchors," she told the red fairies as they stared at her in shock. "Share this memory with the whole damn world."

"The laser is potential," Haoquin had told Frere-Jones the night they were married. They lay in bed after making love awkwardly, then excitedly. Afterward, Frere-Jones couldn't help looking at the pistol on the bedside table.

"Potential for what?" she asked.

"To upset the grains. To force them to experience something they've never before considered."

"So you'd burn the land?"

"That would merely set off the grains' anger. No, I'd burn any anchor who tried to harm you or me."

"Then you'd have even more anchors attacking." Frere-Jones had heard stories of day-fellows who'd tried defending themselves with lasers. Eventually the anchors overwhelmed them through sheer numbers.

"Yes, we can't defeat the anchors. There are too many of them, tied to millions of lands around the world. But what if we could use the threat of killing so many anchors to make the grains change?"

"We can't change the grains' programming," Frere-Jones whispered. "That's beyond us."

"But what if we could change the memories they spoke with?"

"What good would that do?"

"If this land only spoke through certain memories—say yours and mine— the grains would be forced to say very different things than if they spoke through the memories of anchors who'd supported their damn work. Over time, it might change everything."

Frere-Jones smiled at that possibility. "So you'd really kill, or threaten to kill, hundreds of anchors merely to force the grains to delete the memories they've stored over the centuries?"

Haoquin sighed. "You're right. I couldn't do that. I guess it's a bad idea."

Frere-Jones had kissed Haoquin, glad he wasn't someone who would do such evil in a silly, misguided attempt to change the world.

An hour before morning's song of light and warmth, Chakatie arrived. Frere-Jones sat on the sod roof of her home, the laser pistol in her lap, the smoldering corpses of the other anchors glowing in her land's fields and forests.

She scented Chakatie ten minutes before her mother-in-law walked up to the house. Chakatie had deliberately come from upwind so Frere-Jones would catch the scent. She wasn't surprised by Chakatie's arrival. After killing the anchors Frere-Jones realized she hadn't seen or scented any member of Chakatie's family during the attack.

Chakatie looked nothing like the powerful being she'd been the other night in the forest. She was powered down and tiny, and wore a neatly pressed three-piece suit and bowler hat. Instead of claws her hands were manicured and folded over themselves at her waist, as if to show she meant no harm.

Frere-Jones snorted and patted the grass on the roof. "You're welcome to join me, but that suit doesn't look like it's made for sitting on a sod roof."

"It's not." Chakatie jumped up to the other side of the roof. She grinned nervously as Frere-Jones shifted the pistol slightly so it pointed at Chakatie's chest. "My children made me wear this. Said it'd show you I meant no harm since no one in their right mind would fight while wearing such fancy clothes." Chakatie laughed softly. "I think they're worried about you killing me."

Frere-Jones wanted to laugh, which was likely Chakatie's other intent in wearing the suit. Perhaps to catch her off-guard. "And did Malachi also suggest you wear it? Perhaps after he spied on me?"

Chakatie spat. "Malachi did that on his own. I sincerely apologize. To spy on another anchor . . . any punishment you wish against him will be given."

Frere-Jones didn't believe her mother-in-law but accepted the lie as Chakatie's round-about means of apology. "And my punishment for killing dozens of anchors?"

"Ah, that is the question, isn't it?"

Chakatie sat down on the roof, running her fingers through the grass. "Is the girl in the house?" she asked. "The day-fellow anchor?"

"Yes. The grains lied to her. Said her family would be able to stay if she became the new anchor."

"That's why it's difficult for someone who grew up without the grains to become an anchor. You and I, we know the grains' memories don't always tell us the truth. We sort the memories the grains show us. Sift the wheat from the chaff. Your day-fellow girl doesn't know this."

"She will after today. I doubt she'll ever again trust the grains after witnessing this massacre."

"Then she might end up making a good anchor."

Chakatie stretched out on the sod roof, laying on her back as she looked across the sunflower fields. "No anchor with any sense loves the grains. But most anchors also have the sense not to challenge them directly."

"Too late for that. Now what?"

"The grains demand vengeance. You've upset their programmed order."

"How about I simply burn you first?" Frere-Jones said.

"Your choice. My family would, of course, attack. And can you sense the other anchors on their way here from distant lands? The more you kill the more who will come."

Frere-Jones sighed and pointed the laser pistol at the grass. "Funny how your family didn't join in the attack."

"Nothing funny about it. I raised my son, after all. He told me all about his little plans when he was younger. I knew he'd never carry out such evil. That's why I let him build the laser pistol—it satisfied him, and I knew he'd never use it. But you . . . I suppose I should have seen this coming."

Frere-Jones shrugged.

"You know, the grains wanted me to kill Haoquin when he was young, because of his dangerous ideas," Chakatie said. "But I refused to do it.

Despite what you may believe, we anchors can still ignore some of the grains' programmed demands."

Frere-Jones knew Chakatie was playing her. Her mother-in-law had probably known exactly what she was doing when she gave Frere-Jones the medicine for Alexnya. With so many anchors killed, Chakatie's children would be able to go to those lands and become master-anchors in their own right.

"I can still kill a lot more anchors, including you, before I'm taken down," Frere-Jones said. "What do you propose to avoid that?"

"Right now you have leverage with the grains," Chakatie said. "They don't want you to kill hundreds of new anchors when they arrive here. So offer them a bargain. Let the day-fellow girl become this land's new anchor. The remaining anchors in the area—meaning my family—won't oppose her."

Frere-Jones looked at her hands. The pistol could easily cut Chakatie in two, but she really didn't want to kill her mother-in-law. "What do I get out of that?"

"Haoquin had some interesting ideas about the grains' use of memories. This might be your only chance to see if what he said could come true."

The day Haoquin died, Frere-Jones and Colton had stood side by side in the cemetery as Chakatie and the other anchors shoveled dirt onto her lifemate's body.

Frere-Jones could still feel the grains in Haoquin's body. Worse, she could feel them already working to isolate many of Haoquin's memories. The grains didn't want his heretical beliefs contaminating the land, so they were locking those memories away. They would never share those memories with anyone, most of all her.

Frere-Jones hugged her son tight. She knew the grains would do the same to her memories when she died. But if she had her way, they'd not be able to use her son. She'd free him one way or another.

And then, maybe, she'd see if Haoquin's plan could work. The plan he'd been too kindly to actually put into action.

They stood in the cemetery where Haoquin and the other anchors of this land were buried. Alexnya and her family stood on one side of the graves while Chakatie stood on the other. The rest of Chakatie's family patrolled the boundaries of Frere-Jones's land, keeping away the other anchors until this ceremony was completed.

Frere-Jones reached out to her land's grains, the laser pistol still in her right hand. The grains shivered and shook, resonating in shock at both what Frere-Jones had done and the dead anchors she'd killed.

Frere-Jones, detaching herself from the grains, walked over to Alexnya and her family. "Good luck to you," she told Alexnya. "You can trust Chakatie's advice. I suggest you listen to her."

Alexnya looked overwhelmed, as if just realizing the life she'd stumbled into. Her family could stay only a few more days before they'd have to travel on. But aside from suggesting Alexnya trust Chakatie, there was no other advice Frere-Jones could give. Alexnya would have to sort through the lands' memories on her own and determine which, if any, could be trusted.

Frere-Jones laughed to herself, knowing whose memories Alexnya would soon be experiencing.

"How can you say our daughter should trust that . . . woman?" Jun asked, outrage almost pouring out of her lips as she glared at Chakatie. "From what you've told me, she caused all this."

"Chakatie didn't trap your daughter," Frere-Jones said. "If anyone did, it was me, by being so stubborn that the grains sought out a new anchor."

"But she took advantage of all this. She played everyone. She . . . "

"Must I really listen to this right before I die?" Frere-Jones asked.

Jun fell silent. She bowed slightly in a mix of respect and mocking.

After speaking with Chakatie, and asking her mother-in-law to pass a final message to Colton, Frere-Jones reached out to hold Alexnya's hand. Together they accessed the grains.

"Do as we've agreed," Frere-Jones told the grains. "Chakatie will ensure I hold up my end."

"Do it," Alexnya ordered, added her voice as the land's new anchor.

The grains screamed but, unable to see any other option, they complied. Across the land they deleted the memories of every anchor who'd lived before Frere-Jones. The memories flared and shrieked, as if begging Frere-Jones and Alexnya to save them. But then they were gone.

Except for Haoquin's. Frere-Jones dropped the laser pistol and fell to her knees as Haoquin's memories flooded into her. All the memories the grains had copied from his life. All of him.

So many memories. Memories of everything Haoquin had felt and seen and thought and experienced worked their way into Frere-Jones's being. Her mind could barely contain all of him.

As Frere-Jones shook and spasmed on the cold ground, she looked across the new-spring grass. She could taste the grass. Could feel it growing and reaching for the sun.

Haoquin was within her. They now shared one life.

"I missed you, Fre," Haoquin whispered. Or maybe Frere-Jones said it to herself. Either way, she smiled.

"Life here was worth it," they whispered to each other. "Too short, yes. But knowing you made it worthwhile."

Frere-Jones and Haoquin saw Chakatie walk up to their body and pick up the laser pistol. Chakatie wiped at her eyes as she nodded, then she shot them in the head.

Alexnya stands silently over Frere-Jones's burned body. The grains are still convulsing, still in chaos, but Frere-Jones's death has calmed them.

Chakatie holds the laser pistol in both hands. Alexnya feels Chakatie's grains powering up her body. A moment later powerful claws rip apart the pistol.

Chakatie throws the broken technology to the ground in disgust. "Your mother is right, you know," she says. "I did manipulate all this. I knew Frere-Jones and my son would cause sparks. But I didn't know all this would happen. I swear on the grains I didn't know."

Alexnya isn't sure if she can trust Chakatie. Frere-Jones said to trust the anchor, but how can she truly know?

Yet Alexnya also understands that once her parents are forced to resume their travels, Chakatie and her family will be the only one for hundreds of leagues around who might support her.

Alexnya wants to scream at this situation. To curse at not knowing what to do. But before she does, she feels a gentle caress in her mind. She tastes memories—memories from Frere-Jones and Haoquin. She sees all the good things Chakatie has done. How Chakatie once cried over a family like hers.

"I think I'll trust you," Alexnya finally says. "Did you really . . . cry over a day-fellow family once?"

Chakatie nods, then waves for Alexnya's parents to follow her to the sod-house to prepare an evening meal for everyone.

Alexnya stays behind and digs the grave for Frere-Jones's body, the grains powering up her body so the shovel digs faster and deeper than she ever could have done before. She places Frere-Jones in the hole and covers her with fresh soil.

As Alexnya stands over the grave, she feels the grains churning in Frere-Jones body. Feels the grains already beginning to spread the memories of Frere-Jones and Haoquin across the land.

"Thank you, Fre," Alexnya says, bowing to the grave. She then runs to the sod-house to spend time with her family before they're forced to flee.

A NON-HERO'S GUIDE TO THE ROAD OF MONSTERS

A. T. GREENBLATT

The Siren

There are three basic guidelines that any idiot can follow when faced with a shape-shifting Siren hell bent on drowning you. One: Plug your ears and sit tight. She'll tire eventually. Two: If easily visually swayed, use a blindfold. Three: Don't be a hero.Which around here is like telling people not to breathe. The Siren guarding the bridge at the end of the road is a beauty in the classic sense and she's relentless with all those brave, brave heroes attempting to cross the river. From the way her lips linger over syllables, I can tell she's singing some slow, breathy song and between the lulls in victims, she brushes her radiant hair with a flimsy dollar-store brush and glares at me, challenging me to approach.I don't, of course, because unlike heroes, I'm not easy prey. Instead, I smile at her and wait, sitting in the hot, dusty road a healthy hundred meters away with my headphones turned up to deafening. (I forgo the blindfold because I *do* have a measure of self-control.)

But soon enough, a new hero crests the hill and the Siren's appearance begins to morph; her hair becomes blacker, her features finer, her figure curvier. In short, one stunning beauty becomes another and that poor sucker running down the road doesn't stand a chance.

This time, the hero is a girl who runs with such speed and grace, a gazelle would be jealous. She almost makes it too; the bridge is within her reach but at the last moment, she veers and stretches out her arms towards the Siren instead. The Siren's smile glimmers in the sunlight as together, hand in hand, she and her victim slip into the water, sinking lower, deeper, until the river swallows both of them whole.

Now, if I were looking to avoid a confrontation with a monster, this would be a perfect time to cross that bridge.

But I'm not.

A minute later, the Siren returns. Alone. She shoots me a glare so fierce and hostile that even from this distance would burn new holes in my tattered jeans if looks held any power at all. I reply with my most endearing smile.

You see, I'm not a hero. No old crone bothered to whisper a prophecy of greatness (or doom) over my cradle. My mother didn't meet an untimely demise and my father religiously reappeared for dinner every night. If *I* wanted to face monsters, I needed a better excuse than glory. I needed a real quest.

Luckily for me, I've scored a job on The Road of Monsters, the place where the rarest creatures are fabled to live.

Forty-three heroes approach the battered bridge this morning. Most are idiots, charging down the hill, weapon of choice in hand, bloodlust in their eyes. On average, they last about five steps before the Siren snares them. It'd be a massacre if heroes weren't so unnaturally lucky when it comes to washing up on beaches half drowned but breathing.

To be fair, not *all* of them were hopeless. A few jammed their fingers in their ears when they saw her. The really clever ones also closed their eyes and ran. One actually took out his phone and read the Wikipedia article on Sirens before approaching. Also, glared at me when I cheered.

But it's only when the Siren's lips are barely moving, when her brush sits idle in her lap, that I turn off my music and rise to my feet.

The Siren groans as I shake the dirt from my messenger bag, but makes an effort to rally. She flashes me a smile full of sheen and angles, but it doesn't hide the exhaustion. Or the skeptical look in her eyes. It's the same look the heroes gave me when I stepped on the questing tour bus this morning: All those bright, eager, misguided souls staring at me. Me: with the flabby stomach and lack of gear, weapons, and peppy zip! Oh and the missing left hand.

But me, knowing that one, *maybe* two of these poor idiots might actually have a story worth telling after this. Me: who after five years of successfully questing, has long since learned that looks rarely mean anything at all.

Walking slowly, I hold up my palms (well, palm) in a gesture of peace. Also, to prove that wielding two-handed decapitating weapons isn't really my style.

The Siren doesn't buy it. She opens her mouth to sing.

"Don't bother," I say. "My ears are still ringing." I tap the headphones around my neck. This isn't quite true; I can hear the angry river rushing by only a few feet away, reminding me what a lousy swimmer I am. But I compensate for my shortcomings by being a good liar.

The Siren frowns, blinks. Then, she transforms. Now she's a voluptuous brunette with intense gray eyes and facial symmetry a mirror would envy.

"And next you're going to tell me those two are natural."

Her frown deepens and she tries again. Her hair becomes darker, the curves giving way to sculpted muscles, pecs, and chest hair. Completing the package with honey brown skin and high cheek bones, and eyes the color of the earth.

"Meh."

"Well what *do* you want, hero?" she snaps, her voice hoarse and strained. "You can't have my head. I'm still using it."

I take a step back and hold up my hand again. Tired though she is, I'm pretty sure the Siren could pull me into the water by sheer force alone. And when *I* wash up on shore, it'll be as a corpse.

Which is why most people wonder why I run a questing business.

"Okay, one: Not a hero," I say. "Two: I don't want your head. I want to get across that bridge. Three: But first, I'd like to see you without . . . all that." I gesture in the general direction of the chiseled chest.

"If I do, will you tell me why you're here?"

"Sounds fair to me."

The Siren crosses her arms. "I'm not pretty."

I nod. "Beauty is for the unimaginative."

Her eyebrows shoot up and a faint blush warms her cheeks. Slowly, almost reluctantly, she begins to change. The fantasy in front of me melts; her pigments seep away, her features become unbalanced, her hair limp, and when it's all over, only her earth-colored eyes remain the same.

I grin. So why do I bother running a business like this? Because monsters are remarkable, unexpected, and totally worth the wait.

"Nope, still pretty," I say. "I'm here because a client needs me to rescue her hero at the end of the road."

"You rescue heroes? Must keep you busy." She grins back. Her teeth are pointed now, but the smile holds no malice. But then, it falters. "I can't let you pass. I mean, I would, but you know, rules are rules," she says. "I'm sorry."

She squares her shoulders, bracing for a fight, and I take another step back. The water behind her is practically roaring.

"How about . . . how about I pay you a toll?" I snap my fingers, as if the idea just occurred to me.

"A toll?" she asks, like she's never heard the word before. As if the dozens of heroes she floated down the river today weren't payment for the few that crossed.

"Will these do?" I hold out a pair of gold earrings I took from my client as part of my fee.

Tentatively, the Siren reaches out and touches them. They shimmer in the noontime sun. She takes them, cupping them like eggshells, frowning slightly. And for one horrifying second, I think I've screwed up. She doesn't like them. I've fatally miscalculated.

Then one by one, she slips them on.

"How do I look?" She gives her head a small shake.

"Like beauty itself," I say, exhaling. "Mind if I take a picture for my blog?"

Okay, I'll admit it; I'm monster hunting too. But unlike heroes, my victories don't involve destroying someone else's life. Actually, I hope my work is making these creatures feel a bit better. Because despite what those other adventurers think, most monsters are just as lonely and unhappy as the people who try to hunt them down.

So, as the Siren admires her reflection in the water with the most genuine smile I've ever seen, I tuck away my phone and cross the bridge, leaving no destruction or pain in my wake.

I just wish there were more questers like me.

The Questioning Beast

There are three general guidelines when meeting a vague monster of unknown size, shape, and demeanor. One: Be polite. Monsters like civility as much as the next person. Two: Keep your guard up, they're called "dangerous" for a reason. Three: As always, being brave, noble, or generally valiant will be your downfall.Which is probably why so few heroes have made it past this point.One of the many, many advantages of not being a hero is that I have no shame in doing my research beforehand. Turns out, there are tons of attempted quests on The Road of Monsters, but the information past the Siren is . . . inconsistent. Heroes are notorious liars, *especially* on the Internet, but I can usually parse a basic narrative.

But in this case, the only consistent piece of information is that the monster always sees you coming. And it has an eat-first-ask-questions-later sort of attitude.

Which, given how annoying adventurers are, I can't say I blame it.

But I won't lie; I love questing too. There are hundreds of monsters living in the forgotten niches of civilization, in the forests between highways and in the galleries of unfashionable museums exhibits. You can even catch a bus to the most popular quests.

At the next bend in the path, I duck into the long, towering trees lining the road like silent watchers, walking among the boughs until I hear the quiet but unmistakable sound of something large and asthmatic breathing.

I climb the nearest tree, which is not an easy feat one-handed, but what I lack in abs I make up in triceps and quads of steel. Within ten minutes I'm sitting in the tree's crown looking down at the most amazing monster I've ever seen.

Forget its enormous size and its many, many talons on its many, many feet (that's what heroes notice first, anyway), it's neither a lion, hawk, snake, hyena, nor an overzealous newt, like some heroes have said.

It's all of them.

From my perch, the monster looks like a starfish, with each arm containing the torso, forepaws, and head of a different creature. From the ground, depending on the angle the monster stood at, it would appear to be either one of these animals or a combination of them.

Now, most heroes would be shaking from nerves or adrenaline or whatever. But me, I'm wearing a smile stretching ear to ear. I have yet to meet a monster that I couldn't reason with and this one was going to make a *fantastic* blog post.

"Excuse me," I call down. "Would you mind giving me some directions?"

Right behind the massive creature, the road forks into three parts and I'm fairly certain there's another ferocious beast waiting to be confronted at every option. Which is well and fine, if you're just looking to complete a quest. But I'm not interested in *any* monster at the end of the road. No, I'm hunting the rarest, most elusive creature of them all.

Five pairs of eyes swivel upward and I . . . I can't quite suppress a shudder. Their gazes are not of the warm and fuzzy variety.

"I can barter for the information," I continue quickly, tightening my fingers around the branch I'm holding. "I have a few apples and some peanut butter cups. Oh and a pretty good novel, if you like books."

The creature with its many, many eyes says nothing, only blinks, as if my words were so thick and foreign, they needed to be chewed and digested. The silence grows fatter and for a moment, I think I'm going to have to pick a path at random after all. My stomach knots up at the thought. But then it says: "Do we look like we are easily bought, human?"

"No—no, of course not. I didn't mean to imply that you were."

The snake cocks its scaly head to one side. "No, you did not. We see that now."

"What would you like then?"

"You," says the hyena and licks its massive lips.

I manage to suppress the shudder this time. "Flattered, but no deal. I still need me, you know, for the rest of my natural life span." I keep my voice light, but I tighten my grip on the branch a bit more.

"We've already eaten well today," says the newt, laying a hand on its swollen belly. "We'll show you the way if you tell us why a misbegotten runt like yourself is here."

"Oh." I exhale and relax my death grip ever so slightly. Oh. They just wanted a story. Stories are easy, especially when they're your own. Even when you have to make *some* of it up.

But for starters, I begin with the truth:

So first thing you should know about me is I'm a professional quester. Despite my obvious lack of "heroic qualifications" business has been good to me. I have an office in my apartment with a view that overlooks the sea. The rent is inflated and my neighbors are all the heroic types, but the view is totally worth it. It's a postcard scene, except my pictures never do it justice.

Point is, I can be selective enough these days to take the jobs that interest me. No more introvert ogres or fire-breathing wombats to make ends meet. So when this beautiful girl walks into my office, asking me to help her, who needs a better opportunity than that? I—

"Incorrect," says the lion.

"No, see, I have a picture—"

"You couldn't care less about her looks." The lion yawns. "She's just the excuse you needed to walk this road."

I shrug. The monster's perceptive, I'll give it that.

Excuse me, yes, you're correct. I didn't accept the job for her looks. Though she has the type of face that makes heroes want to fight battles for her hand or her honor or to get into her pants, if they're being completely honest. But I did feel bad for her. She tried five different heroes before me and well, there she was sitting in my office. She was willing to pay double my usual rate, so—

"Yes, yes, you're a half-decent liar," the snake hisses. "We're all impressed."

"How—"

"We see the truth in the spaces between," says the newt, studying its webbed fingers. "Are you going to keep dawdling?"

I open my mouth. Then close it. The truth. Between spaces. No wonder the heroes lied through their teeth about this one.

I take a deep breath and try again.

"So, the guy I'm getting back for my client?" I say. "I know him."

The hawk nods. "Better. But there's more."

"You and Nate were friends once, right?" my client said and glanced up. I think it was the first time since she stepped into my office that she's looked me in the eye. "It was a long time ago, but that still means something, right?"

"If by 'friend' you mean 'sidekick' then yes, I was." I made a point of scratching the stub of my left arm while she made a point to look away.

"If it's money you want . . . "

"No, it really isn't," I said. "Trust me, if I was motivated purely by cash, I would have died attempting something stupid a long time ago. Take my last quest for example—"

"You're stalling," says the hyena. "Quit it, or we will eat you."

Below me, the asthmatic breathing of the creature is getting heavier. Hungrier, if you will.

"Seriously, what do you want?" I say, louder, more panicked than I mean to.

All five heads of the monster smile in unison and my stomach neatly ties itself into a knot.

"Like we said," replies the hyena. "You."

Call me a good-for-nothing hero, but for the first time in my life, I want to bolt from a monster. I want to sprint down the road, back to the bus and my blog and my apartment with its stunning view and never speak of this again.

"Wouldn't a novel be more entertaining?" I force my voice to stay even and reasonable.

"Yes," says the hyena, "but not nearly as much fun." Next to it, the lion reaches out and gives my tree a good shake. The top sways violently and I've never been so grateful for my elbows and knees.

Of course, now I notice that around those many, many clawed feet, there's a collection of broken weapons and gnawed-on sneakers littering the ground. I lean my forehead against the branch I'm holding, cherishing the rough texture on my skin.

You see, I have a sort of truce with my past—I don't want to change it, it's made me who I am and I like me. But that doesn't mean I like sharing the history. In fact, I pride myself on not having an "About the Author" page on my blog. Besides, my work's about the monsters, not me.

But right now there are five grinning heads and five gluttonous stomachs below me and up in my leafy crown, my elbows and knees are aching from strain.

"Um, so, Nate and me . . . our relationship is a bit complex."

The hawk tilts its head and blinks, in a way that clearly says *Well, duh.*

I take a deep breath.

"Has Nate ever told you why we're no longer a team?" I asked her.

"Not in so many words . . . "

"This." I squatted down and placed the stump of my wrist in her lap. Startled, she immediately pushed the chair back and half rose. She had the grace to look embarrassed about it a second later and even then, I felt a twinge of guilt, but not too much. I can still feel the ghost of my fingers. Even after all these years.

"He'd said the monster was about to attack you. That it was only inches away."

"He's wrong. We were just talking. It was even letting me pet its head."

"I . . . I didn't know. But Nate doesn't have a choice. If he doesn't kill monsters, they'd kill him."

"Bullshit. First of all, most monsters are not that interested in humans. Two: If it was just me and the monster that day, no one would have panicked and I would still be ambidextrous. And three: When it comes down to it, the majority of monsters don't bother killing heroes. They're not worth the mess."

"This one will," she said quietly. "Nate's stuck on The Road of Monsters."

"Oh yeah? So how do you know he's still alive then?"

She shifted uncomfortably. "He sends me texts. Every few days or so. But he won't answer my texts or calls. He's been there for weeks. Please, Devon, you have to help us. You can't imagine what it's like."

Seriously? She was trying that line with me?

I knew I was being cruel, even then. But honestly, I was tired of people who couldn't bother seeing what was in front of them.

"Look, you seem like a nice girl, good fit for Nate and all, but do you really want to know why I do this? Because there are days when I think the lonely monsters I profile are the only sane creatures breathing."

At this, the beast below me begins to laugh, hard, its voices high-pitched and wheezing. I hadn't meant to tell her—or anyone else—that. I hadn't meant to repeat it ever again either. But the monster wanted me and it got what it asked for.

"So why did you change your mind?" the newt asks when it catches its breath.

"When Nate and I started adventuring together as stupid twelve-year-olds," I say, "we swore we would defend each other, no matter what. And I guess, even after all these years, if I asked him to, he would still honor that promise."

The monster doesn't reply. For a second, I think my answer won't be enough, that it will start asking me about my *other* reasons for being here. But then, the creature grins.

"He went that way." All five arms point to the middle fork.

"Thank you," I say and I mean it. I'm already looking for a foothold down.

I consider pulling out my phone before descending, but decide against it. Now, there's a monster out there that knows more about my motives than my mother. Like hell I'm going to post a picture of it on the internet.

When I reach the ground, I readjust my bag, and walk as quickly as I can past the beast without actually breaking into a full-out run.

But before I can even gasp, I'm fifteen feet from the ground, dangling, caught around the waist by two uncomfortably large talons.

"Leave the novel," says the hawk.

I don't even try to bargain as I surrender the book silently with a shaking hand. Sometimes there are monsters you can't befriend. Sometimes too many questions are asked.

My client really did care about Nate, even I could see that. I should have let the issue lie, thanked her and escorted her out. But sometimes my curiosity is just too much.

"Wait, you said Nate's been stuck there for weeks, right?" I leaned in. "How is he still sending you text messages?"

• • •

The Monster at the End of the Road

There are three things you should know about the last part of this journey. One: There's a dragon at the end of this road. Naturally. Two: No one's ever met a dragon—and lived long enough to post any useful information. Three: Meaning, I have absolutely no idea what to do here.

The entrance to the lair is unassuming, a neat, well-maintained abode cut from the living rock. You wouldn't know a dragon dwelled here—except for the deep gouges in the soft ground. The talon marks are wide enough for me to put a foot in and deep enough to swallow my ankle.

For the first time in years, I wonder if I should change my tactics and instead of walking up to the monster in plain sight, try to sneak in. Trouble is, quiet and stealth like to flee when I get too close.

Screw it. It's like they always told us sidekick types in school: "Play to your strengths." So I enter the lair in strides.

The den is not nearly as damp as I expected, but it's vast with a cavernous ceiling. It's surprisingly well lit; dozens and dozens of lamps sit in alcoves in the walls, powered by . . . electricity. Well, that explains the text messages at least. But not much else.

Thick rugs cover the floor and hundreds of books are queued up orderly on rock-carved shelves and ledges. From the looks of it, this dragon hoards its privacy, instead of gold. And not for the first time, I wonder what it wants.

It's not like I can ask, though. The lair is completely and utterly dragon-free.

"Devon?"

I spin around and there he is. The hero himself. Nate doesn't look all that different from his dazzling profile pictures, except more pale and ragged. But otherwise whole, hale, and unharmed. Naturally.

"Hi, Nate. Door's that way." I point to the entrance. Funny, I'd imagined our first conversation in years to go a little differently.

"I . . . I know that. I can't leave," says Nate.

"Why the hell not?"

"The monster won't let me."

I raise an eyebrow. "And where is the dragon now?"

"Hello, Devon," says a voice behind me and both Nate and I give embarrassingly high-pitched shrieks.

Where there were only empty rugs before now sits a dragon. It isn't as large as the massive Questioning Beast, but it probably still eats elephants for breakfast.

"Does it always sneak up on people like that?" I whisper to Nate.

"Yeah." His shoulders slump.

"Pardon my intrusion into your home," I say to the now chuckling dragon. "I'm just here to retrieve this sorry excuse for a hero. I mean no harm."

"We'll see about that," replies the dragon. "My guest here has told me about you."

"*Guests* are allowed to leave," mutters Nate.

I elbow Nate, hard, and keep my eyes on our host. Its scales have no color except when they reflect the light and every inch of its anatomy is designed for either defense or offense. But it's neither tense nor hostile. Actually, it seems quite relaxed. Its eyes, of course, are bottomless and sad. And I can't help but wonder why.

"I'm just a simple entrepreneur and blogger, I don't want anything from you," I say, elbowing Nate again in advance.

"You made it past the Questioning Beast and still are trying to lie?" says the dragon. "You're tougher than you look." It gives me a satisfied smile.

Damn, the heroes are actually right. This *is* the quest from hell.

"Truthfully, I was hoping to get a picture of you for my blog," I admit, "but at this point, I'm tired, dusty, and frustrated and I just want to get home alive. How can we make that happen?"

The monster nods. "A straightforward speech, quite refreshing." It lowers its massive head so it's eye level with me. "There's no way out for you and your friend, little hero, except by defeating me. Completely."

"Hold on a minute," I say, backing up. "First of all, *I am no one's hero.* Second, 'friend' is a generous term for our relationship. And third, I really, truly, don't want to kill you."

"It doesn't matter, those are the rules."

"Wait," shouts Nate, "you never told me what the rules are."

The dragon gives him a measured look. "You never asked." It draws itself up to its full, towering height. "I expect you'd like to get this over with as quickly as possible. There are a few old weapons in the cupboard over there. Arm yourself. I'll wait."

"Just—" I start, before Nate grabs me by the collar of my shirt and drags me toward the cupboard. I try to protest, argue, reason, sit it out, but Nate has a strong grip

"Seriously? These were here the whole time?" Nate says, taking a quick survey of the surprisingly organized armory.

I look at all those sharp, shiny blades and feel sick. "Nate, what the *hell* are we doing here?"

"What?"

"Why are we here?"

"Devon, I'm not sure this is a good time—"

"No, it's the perfect time, because if I'm going to die here, I want to know why you went on this stupid quest to begin with. And it better not just be 'for glory' because I will hand you to the Siren myself."

"No, not for glory." Nate glances away. "Um . . . you see, there's this legend, that a heart of a dragon can cure any wound, no matter how bad."

"And what wound do you have that can possibly be that drastic?" I ask. Then I realize he's looking at the stump of my left hand. "Oh."

"Are you two ready?" The dragon's head is suddenly mere feet from us and both Nate and I shriek again.

"No," I say even as Nate thrusts a sword in my hand.

"Yes," says Nate and attacks.

The monster rears back just missing the arc of Nate's blade. It moves slowly, its size both an advantage and hindrance. Nate notices the weakness and exploits the hell out of it. He dodges, ducks, and feints with ease and joy. Gods, I forgot how talented of a fighter he was. I almost don't see the talons looming above my head.

I roll away, badly, but effectively. The talons bury themselves in the ground inches away. I rise to my feet and point my sword at the creature and snarl.

Please don't confuse this for bravery. This is purely an act of desperation.

Strange, though, how those old sword-fighting lessons kick in, even though it's been years and I wasn't particularly good at it. My phantom left hand is itching with memory and I can't quite shake the feeling that I'm slightly off-balanced, but here I am, dodging and parrying too, just like old times. Nate's moves are flawless, while mine, not so much. The dragon opens its mouth and we both get the hint and retreat.

We might have ducked under the same table.

"You are a complete idiot, you know that, right?" I gasp.

"Hey, I'm not the one who's always negotiating with monsters. It's not like they won't try to divide you up into five pieces and eat you anyway."

"I—Wait, how did *you* get past the second monster?"

Nate flushes. "Um, I might have walked around that one. Once or twice."

Gods, I hate this quest.

A second later, the dragon's foot comes crashing down right outside our hiding place and we flee—in opposite directions, of course. It's frightening how much of this is still muscle memory.

Nate grows more confident as the fight drags on, he's attacking more than blocking now and the monster is forced to focus entirely on his fancy swordplay. Its jaw line brushes the rugs. Leaving its eye completely unprotected.

I have a clear shot.

The sword in my hand, my only hand, yearns for action. Its weight is the most honest thing in the world. The opportunity is perfect. My way home is clear.

But I'm not a hero.

Everything I am and know and believe in I learned by meeting and documenting hundreds of monsters. And none of them, even the most vicious of creatures, deserved to die for someone else's gain.

My sword falls and hits the floor with a disappointing *clang!*

"What are you doing?" Nate yells. Like a predictable hero, he refuses to let the opportunity slip and takes aim for the dragon's eye.

And the dragon . . . flicks him away with a talon. Moving faster than it should have. Moving faster than it was even possible to see. Nate goes flying and hits the floor with a heavy *thud*.

Suddenly, I've never been so grateful for my lazy, pacifist lifestyle.

"Well, you don't lie about everything at least," the dragon says cheerfully.

I hurry over to where Nate is lying, roll him onto his side, and slap his face a few times, gently. He groans and I exhale. He's okay, dazed and going to feel like hell tomorrow, but okay.

I rise to my feet and face the dragon. "I was serious when I said I wasn't a hero."

"But do you regret trying to be one of them?"

The monster's gaze is wary and I realize I haven't convinced it. Not yet.

Here's the thing, growing up as the sidekick type, most heroes were never more than polite to me. But Nate, his friendship was genuine. Still is, actually. It might not seem like much, but what most people don't get is that there's a world of difference between not being cruel and being kind.

I glance at Nate. "It's a bittersweet sort of thing."

The dragon nudges Nate with a talon and he groans again. "Heroes are gullible creatures. Eating a dragon heart would only give you acid reflux. But if it could cure any wound, would you take it?"

I start to say something slightly sarcastic, but then swallow my words.

Because the truth is, there are days when I really, really hate the emptiness of my missing fingers, when I realize that I will never be able to learn to play guitar or avoid the stares on the bus. But it's also forced me to adapt, get creative, and now it's a more powerful tool then my sword ever was.

"I don't know," I say.

I ease myself onto the ground next to Nate and put my messenger bag under his head. It's clear he's going to nap through the negotiations. Typical hero.

"What happens now?" I ask, bracing for the worst.

"What would you say to an exclusive client?"

"Depends. Whose exactly?"

"Mine." The dragon laughs at my startled expression. "I'm a fan of your blog. I was hoping to meet you sooner, but unfortunately, you needed a quest to come here. Turns out, the right hero just needed to hear the right rumor."

"How . . . how long exactly have you been planning this?"

The monster smiles. "I'm patient."

"So, what do you want?"

"Come see."

The dragon leads me to the farthest corner of its lair. Pinned up on the walls is a sprawling map of all the paths of all the quests ever rumored about. It's bigger than the monster itself. I let out a low whistle. The great thing about questing is you're always discovering how large the world really is.

"Leaving home is not safe for me. Not with all those heroes crawling around. I need someone else to do it for me."

"But why me?"

"Because you won't murder what you find," replies the dragon as it turns its great, sad eyes towards me. "We great ancient beasts are a rarity these days and I want to know if there are others out there. I want to know, am I alone?"

This surprises me, though it shouldn't. I get it, there's a certain thrill in defying heroes and befriending monsters and a certain power in being unique. Yet, there's a terrible loneliness that comes with being the only one of your kind.

But maybe, with these new quests, I can change that. For both of us.

"Where do I start?" I ask, smiling because I'm already thinking about the blog post I'm going to write after all. The first in a series.

It'll start with this simple, non-heroic guide to The Road of Monsters.

EMPTY PLANETS

RAHUL KANAKIA

Most of the other kids around the pond tried to talk me out of signing up for Non-Mandatory Study. They didn't even give me credit for being rebellious, because, for a trust-kid, real rebellion meant either going deep into neural reprogramming or buying a starship and head for Magellanic Clouds, which in those days were way past the boundaries of the Machine-mind, to find some adventure.

No, my fellow trust-kids just couldn't process it. For instance, Caroll, whose family had seven shares, grabbed me at his investiture party and took me walking around the lip of the crater and, after I told him what I was gonna do, he said "But what are you going to *do*? Isn't it all *books*? Won't you be so *bored*? Surely you're not really going to pursue a *bounty*?"

We looked down into the center of the crater, where our year-mates were frolicking about in the pond, shooting sprays of water twenty feet in the air, and I tried to explain to him that I loved him and the Moon and our crater and the life our family had built here over the last few thousand years, but that sometimes when I walked alone through the chest-high grass, I'd feel this, I don't know, this weird complex feeling inside of me: this sense that everything up til now had just been a vacation, and that my real life was someplace else. And in those moments, I'd look at everything, all our sculpted stone shining white in the Earthlight, and I'd say to myself, dammit, if I only had more time to *think* then maybe I could figure everything out.

And still he didn't get it. Caroll was a great guy on the jumping ground or when you needed someone to crew your fastship, but he wasn't a thinker.

"Don't you have to pass a *test* to get into NMS," Caroll said. "Are you really going to take a *test*?"

I shrugged, trying to pretend I wasn't worried. No one from our crater had gone to NMS for a long time. The only way I knew about it at all was from stories that my mom sometimes told about her grandma.

Late that night, though, when I was lying amongst the rushes and staring up at the Earth, I said, "I hope I get in. That's all I want."

Then a pair of bright orange eyes opened up between me and the glinting metallic face of the Earth, and I heard a voice.

"You can go if you wish," said the Machine. "But you won't be a success there. You are not intelligent enough."

"Well I've never pretended to be a genius. But I've got thoughts."

"Fine. Then it is done."

We were all sitting in the atrium out on the other side of the crater, where all you can see is mile after mile of grey rock, when my acceptance arrived.

My dad grumbled a little, but my mom smiled at me. She affectionately grabbed me by the back of my neck and shook me a few times, and then hugged me.

"Find a good woman," she said. "Or man. A good person. Who knows, maybe even someone who can bring us a bounty."

"Or maybe I'll win a bounty for myself," I said.

She smiled and hugged me again. Two of my family's three shares have been with us for thousands of years, ever since the Machine Corporation's first decade, back when there weren't many people in the world, and shares were relatively plentiful. But the third one came just a century ago, when my great-grandmother—a mathematician who had ten years of NMS—won a bounty for deriving some complex proof that'd been vexing the Machine for a thousand years.

"Your great-grandmother was the best thing that ever happened to this family," my mom said. "Find another one like that, and your whole life will have been worthwhile."

I looked out at the moonscape and completely disregarded everything my mom had said. I wasn't meant to marry well and come back here and paint pretty light-sculptures until the Machine told me it was time to die and pass on my shares. No, I was building something inside me. Some beautiful thought that was still too thin and delicate to try to put into words.

Meanwhile, in another part of the galaxy, Margery was whipping herself into a righteous anger.

She was, and is, a hundred and ten pounds and four-foot-nine, with all her weight packed into muscles in her thighs and upper arms. Her parents built her that way, so she could wriggle through the maintenance shafts of their generation ship and maneuver the bulky jury-rigged waldos that they used to shift the corpsicles around.

Until the age of twelve Margery thought the purpose of her life was to keep her ship running. It'd left during a bad moment in Earth's history, when it felt like the world might perhaps be rendered unfit for life. And her parents told her from the very beginning that she was humanity's last hope. Unless she kept the ship running, then all these cryogenically frozen people would never live again. And if that happened then all life in the universe would be extinguished.

They told her that she was gonna be a Captain, just like her mother and grandmother before her. And that Captains needed to be prepared to make tough decisions, because the entire world relied on their judgment.

Then, poof, AI probes penetrated the ship, took over control, woke everybody up, and deposited them all on a nearby asteroid with a lifetime's supply of water and with the means to produce as much food as they could ever need. When Margery's parents asked the Machine to please just let them continue on to their new planet, they were informed that the planet no longer existed: the Machine had dismantled it centuries ago

So instead of fulfilling their grand destiny, they'd live and die on the asteroid. People would mine the rock, build new habitats, get married, have slightly fewer children than they needed to replace themselves, and, when the Machine decided it was time, her people would die out.

But in the meantime Margery scored in the 99.999^{th} percentile on that Fitness for Civilization test that they give to all newly recontacted peoples. Because of her score, the Machine appeared above her while she slept and told her she could go anywhere in the world and do anything she wanted, and she—keep in mind she was just twelve years old at this point—told the Machine that what she wanted most in the world was to figure out a way to stop It from consuming the entire universe.

After that, the Machine was silent for a few years, and whenever someone died or something broke, Margery thought, "This is the Machine taking its revenge." And who knows, maybe it was.

But when she turned seventeen, she got an acceptance letter from the Non-Mandatory Study program on Mars. And right at the time I was thinking my delicate little thoughts, she was saying to herself, "No matter what anyone says, I'm still a Captain."

NMS doesn't really exist anymore, but back then it was a bunch of caverns that went deep into either side of a Martian gorge. All the machines and power plants and books—billions of books—were stored back there in the airless void, while the students and teachers lived in the center, in rickety structures— they were over a thousand years old—held in place by metal scaffolding.

As in most things, the Machine was right about NMS: I wasn't suited for life around non-shareholders. They were so brusque and fast-paced. They had no grace to them. No appreciation of life. All they cared about was learning.

And the nons were so stunning. Shareholders tend to look like whatever. For instance, I tend towards pudgy, and I've got oily skin. But the girls at NMS were usually tall and had narrow faces and large eyes, and, whenever the mood struck them, they'd have precise, athletic sex in the catwalks and unused lecture basins and outdoor amphitheaters

They treated me fine. I was like a mascot to them. When they came back from class, I'd usually still be hanging out on the catwalks and toying with my own neural programming—I had an obsession with music, then, and I loved reprogramming myself so that even the most asinine, mediocre music would enthrall me. Then I'd sit out there and rock back and forth to the sound of some warbly child and I'd think and I'd think and I'd think and somehow it would *almost* come together.

But once my classmates joined me, I'd somehow find the strength to put away the music and ask what they'd learned about. I didn't care about what they said, I just liked the fire in their eyes when they talked. I liked the way their hands moved, and the way they sat forward in their chairs. And, most of all, I loved listening to them. I didn't understand what they were talking about, most of the time, but there was a tone they had—a kind of music. You hear it sometimes in children who're too young to know what they're talking about. It's almost a whine, but not quite. It's got the petulance of a whine, but also a hint of unsureness. It annoys you at first, but then it wracks your heart, and all you want is for that voice to get whatever it wants.

One of them, Sherie, took me to bed a few times, which was a terrifying experience. She'd smash her body against mine so hard that my pelvis would ache, and when I told her to slow down, she'd just go faster and faster and grab my hands and put them places and whisper things into my ear. And afterwards, she'd be all sweaty and smiley, and I'd make excuses to leave.

Sleeping with Sherie was completely different from being with Brunhilde, my AI-controlled Self Stimulation Aide. My childhood sessions with Brunhilde were long and slow. We'd wipe out entire days: not really moving or making any sounds, except when I'd whisper 'faster' or 'slower' into Brunhilde's audio-receptor port.

But in other ways, Sherie was great. She was a third-gen striver from an Oort Cloud colony whose population halved every five hundred years as the Machine slowly restricted its birth rate. The whole colony had come together to create and nurture her, and she was supposed to work hard and somehow buy a share so her people could continue to exist, but I could already tell she wasn't ever gonna do that, because what was the point? The only weird thing was that she was how guilty she felt about it.

One day, when she started she sobbing out her guilt over her own selfishness, I said, "Look, Sherie, human life is just a transitional state whose time is over. The real selfishness would be tying up all these resources in order to keep a bunch of useless people alive."

I remember we were sitting on the catwalk, watching the dust blow in the distance, and her hip was almost touching mine.

"But . . . they're counting on me," she said. "When I left, I thought I was saying goodbye forever: after two hundred years in transit, I thought everything recognizable would've faded away. But they were smarter than that. They kept my mom and dad and brother in cryogenic sleep and woke them up so I could hear their voices, telling me that the whole world only had twelve babies last year. Telling me that strange beasts have begun to batter their heads against the sides of the habitats. You should see the terrified messages they send: they went to sleep in a cosy city and woke up in a cold, empty village. And they keep asking: Can you do something? Can you talk to someone? Have you gotten any closer to figuring this out?"

"My god, that's terrible," I said, because that's what you say when you hear about a person dying or being in pain. "I can't even imagine."

"Yeah," she said. "How many . . . your dad has some shares, you said . . . ?"

"They're in a trust," I said, but the question made me go cold. Because the truth was that I maybe *could* save her people. Even back then, Machine Corp was a strange and ancient thing, and it wasn't completely consistent about how it chose to interpret its own charter. Having shares gave you immense control over it, but that control had limits. Sometimes when you tested those limits, it took your shares away without even mentioning it, but other times it let you get away with amazing things.

"I just . . . I want to *do* something," Sherie said.

"Well, how's the bounty list looking?"

That was the main thing at NMS. The Machine might be ungodly powerful, but it was still only one mind, and that mind was mostly occupied with the problem of minimizing the sum total of human suffering in the universe, which meant that there were still plenty of problems for bright human beings to solve. Most of them made no sense to me: they were esoteric problems in math or physics that carried quarter-share or half-share bounties. But the big problems were familiar to everyone: a four-share bounty for figuring out whether the cloud-shapes of Altair III were actually alive; a ten-share bounty for finding proof of non-human-derived intelligent life; and, the big one, a ten thousand share bounty for figuring out how to extend the age of the universe.

Most people at NMS latched onto one problem or another and disappeared into the caverns, frittering away their lives in research. Others joined big groups, directed by old and senior students, that'd agreed to split up any shares they won. And a few, like me, spent our days hanging around the catwalks and trying to figure out if any of these problems really sang to our souls.

"I don't know," Sherie said. "I've been toying with the Gannon Proposition for years now, but . . . I just keep thinking, if I won a share, then what? Would I really go out and buy up some piddly little planet where my people could eke out a few thousand more years?"

I nodded. The Machine was always looking to buy back your shares. If you were a hard bargainer, you could get something spectacular: an entire planet or solar system. It was crazy, since there were trillions of solar systems in the universe, but only millions of shares, but people still sometimes did it.

"Yeah, you could do that. Or, you know, you could just pass it on to your kids. If you earn it, then it's yours. Your people aren't sick or starving. The only thing they're missing is a future, and I don't see why you ought to give them yours."

"Yeah, but . . . no offense, David, but I've seen how you and your family live, and it's depressing. So careful. So controlled. So scared of offending the Machine. I don't know . . . if I ever got a share, I'd want to go somewhere, do something unexpected, and add something *new* to the universe."

"Yeah . . . it's hard."

But I guess in the bottom of my heart I looked down on Sherie, because it seemed so silly, all this looking for bounties and trying to acquire shares, when really there were far more important things to think about. I still hadn't quite gotten ahold of the deep thought that'd brought me to NMS, but I could see its outline. The thought had something to do with shares, I knew. And something to do with the Machine. And something to do with wealth and with the age of the universe and the destiny of mankind. And music was tied up in there too. All of that stuff was connected somehow, and I felt like every second I spent staring into the Martian sands, I got closer and closer to the answer.

"I'm really . . . I'm glad we're friends," Sherie said. "Sometimes it feels like you're the only one I know who really understands the world."

She reached for me and tried to kiss me, but I told her I was tired. And that night, in my bubble, I prayed to the Machine. I did that sometimes. Praying to the Machine was different when you were a shareholder, because sometimes the Machine answered.

"Make her happy," I said. "She deserves to be happy."

Those shining eyes opened up above me, and a voice said, "There is no need to interfere. Her life will mean something, David. Someday, when . . . "

And I could tell it was about to go into its usual spiel about how all life in the universe would someday be joined in lockstep harmony, and on that day the Universal Spirit would give thanks for the suffering of every human being who'd ever lived, so I said:

"Yeah. But . . . that's true for everyone. How about the happiness, though?"

"I'm disappointed in you. This is a frivolous request. Your mother and father did not raise you to make frivolous requests."

It's a strange, unsettling thing for your God to be disappointed in you. At that moment, all my limbs went weak, and I was about to beg for forgiveness, but the voice said, "Don't concern yourself further with that girl. She is in my heart now, and I will do what I can."

The next day, the Machine appeared in Sherie's lab, told her she was intellectually unfit for NMS, and put her on the next ship back to her colony. She's dead now, but before she passed they made her the Mayor of her world and the Machine let her have three children. All her messages to me were very wistful, but the Machine has reassured me that her life was actually very happy.

I didn't notice Margery until my sixth year of NMS. Almost everyone I'd arrived with was gone. My parents assumed I was engaged in some epic research project: it was the only way they could understand me being gone for so long. My friends from home, the ones who'd grown up around my pond on the moon, had either gone so far down into the hole of neural reprogramming and self-stimulation that they were hardly people anymore, or they'd found life partners and settled down on their family estates and carved out tidy little homes.

And I was . . . I don't know. I was halfway between. My neural reprogramming had taken a strange turn: I'd destroyed my love of music, and rerouted those channels to focus on mundane sounds. I spent hours listening to the fall of condensation, and, over weeks and months, I developed a half-crazed theory of aesthetics that made no sense to any of my classmates. They—newer, younger, and hungrier—mostly avoided me as a bad thing.

A silence grew up around me, and, in my despair, I'd sometimes I'd babble out incoherent prayers to the Machine. I'd tell it to bless the drops and see the oneness of the drops and to love the drops, but it never answered anymore.

Margery, though, would listen to me. She says that we actually met in my third year, and that she'd met me a dozen times before my sixth year. But the first memory I have of her is during my sixth: we were in our breathmasks and suits and the dust was flying overhead, and I was saying something and she was looking up at me with her bright eyes and nodding and saying, "Yes? Yes. Really? Yes. That's fantastic!"

And I thought, for a moment: this is what it must feel like to be the Machine.

And then she was just there, with me, spending every day in my bubble. We didn't talk about it, but she'd been just as lonely as me. There aren't many shareholders doing NMS, but there are even fewer recontactees. I don't know who she spent time with before we found each other, but once I caught a guy glaring at Margery on the catwalks.

"Oh, you have enemies," I said.

"Don't be stupid," Margery said. "Ina and I are still friends, I guess, though, she didn't take kindly to . . . well, she wasn't interested in the same things as me."

I understood. You see, Margery only cared about one thing: Altair III.

I'd heard of it, everyone had. The place with the strange clouds and the strange black mud. People said the clouds and the mud were some primitive life form, and that's why the Machine hadn't destroyed the planet yet. But Margery thought differently. She thought that the clouds and the mud were a Machine, or something like one. She thought they were a networked entity, or a pair of entities, that had been created by some long-vanished species in much the same way as humanity had created the Machine.

I didn't think that was at all likely, but this view of hers didn't really bother me the way it seemed to bother most of my classmates. I have no idea why it riled them up so much, but I saw it time and again. The moment Margery brought up her research, they'd jump down her throat with argument after argument and summon all sorts of linguistic charts and power consumption graphs, and eventually become red-faced and twitchy over the whole affair.

Eventually, Margery became a joke. Whenever she wasn't around, the other students would ask how she was doing with her crackpot notions and conspiracy theories. Once, a tenth-year—a very distinguished student who'd later get a quarter-share bounty for solving some problem regarding the elasticity of stellar wave fronts—seriously proposed that we bring her wasteful, pseudoscientific research to the attention of the Machine, because it was such a shame that she was taking up space which could've gone to an honest researcher.

Which was a weird thing for them to say to my face, I guess, since who was taking up more space than me? But somehow all of them knew that I was in a different category from them.

I was so disturbed by his threats that I put on a breathmask and hunted up Margery over in the deep caverns, where she was playing around with some canned samples of Altairian gas, and told her, "I don't understand why they're so angry with you."

The walls were gritty red, and the rock wept moisture when the heat was on. She turned around in her lab bench, and nodded at me, and turned back to the greenish sample floating in front of her.

"They're invested in the system," she said. "If the Machine isn't the end-all of the universe's destiny, then what is it all for? Why did we give up our homes? Our families? Our communities? It's upsetting."

"Yes, but . . . I am quite literally invested in the system, and I don't agree with you at all, but I still don't get angry about it."

"Well, you're special."

"Hmm . . . tell me more."

"You're smarter than them. Wiser. You can suspend judgment."

I smiled at her. "You are the only person who's ever called me intelligent. But I'll take it!"

But when I rubbed my hand across her back, she froze up. Margery looked at me with sad dark eyes and, after I let my hand fall, she said thanks for coming by and keeping her company, but she was gonna be out pretty late so there was no sense in me staying.

It made no sense to me. Margery was obviously the person I should marry. She was short and squat: an outsider. No one here loved her. No one understood her. And she enjoyed being around me! But she always nudged me away right at the moment when I would have kissed her. Sometimes I thought about laying it all out for her and saying look, I already hold one share, and when my parents die, I'll get two more. You're not gonna get a better offer than that, are you?

But I didn't say it. She hadn't yet told me about the whole Captain thing, but I could sense, somehow, that she would've loved the chance to reject an offer like that.

Year followed year, and I won't have you think that Margery was the only one who kept busy. I was there too, sitting on those catwalks, watching the kids—I thought of them as kids now—come and try for a while to claim their bounties.

Which they mostly didn't. Those Martian deserts were bleak and red, and they swallowed up the days without letting you taste them, and when people would leave, they wouldn't say goodbye, because they were so ashamed of not getting what they'd come for.

And I always stayed behind. Strange and out of place, with my old-young body and my hesitant speech and far-off movements. I could feel something building inside me. I spent my days pacing back and forth on the rickety catwalks, humming to myself in long monotonous tones, and thinking wordless thoughts. I was giving birth to something, I knew, and putting words onto it would be the very last step. But when it finally came out, I knew it'd electrify the entire universe.

Margery had mostly retreated to the far caverns, where she huddled in the chill and took measurements with dead strands of gas. Once, when I crept in quietly, I heard her whispering to the cloud:

"Come on," she said. "I'm here. I'm listening. Just give me something. Give me anything."

I stood and listened to her for a long time, because I knew how hard it was to coax an idea into being.

Our last day at NMS started with a trip to the poles, where we stood on a plain of shattered glass: all the ten-thousand-year-old domes had fallen to pieces.

We drove my ship—there's no way Margery could've afforded to come out here on her own—over to the mines where these ancient men and women had dug holes deeper and deeper into the earth in a frantic effort to find more water.

"I can't remember," I said. "Did the Machine save these people or not?"

"They died natural deaths," Margery said.

Margery had some kind of theory about how solar radiation was interfering with her attempts to measure the interaction of Altairian gas molecules, so we dropped down into one of the ice-mines, and as we fell, I ran a finger over the side of the mine. Something about its sheer ancientness was really upsetting to me.

"I feel so grateful to these people," I said. "For everything they did to try to survive. But . . . I'm also grateful that they failed. There's . . . it's . . . what would've happened if they'd succeeded?"

"Then there'd be a city here," Margery said.

"Yeah . . . but . . . why? It'd be completely pointless. But . . . it's . . . it's still good that they once existed. Am I making sense? I wouldn't be happy if they'd never existed at all. Does that make sense?"

"Yes."

"Really?"

"I grew up in a fake world. I'm glad I don't live there anymore, but I wouldn't have traded those years for anything."

She fell silent while the weight of Mars built up over our heads. I wasn't sure she was talking about the same thing I was talking about, but since I wasn't really sure what I was talking about, it was hard to respond to her.

When we got to the bottom, she set up some equipment, then let some gas escape into the air. After a few minutes, she looked at her equipment panels. Then she started crying.

On the way up, she put her strong arms around me, and her tiny body shook with sobs. She hadn't gotten the results she needed. "I've ruined my entire life," she said.

When we got back to the main campus, a shining pair of eyes appeared above the doorway and told her she wasn't welcome back. Apparently, those samples of gas were priceless and irreplaceable. A ship was coming to take her back to her people.

But when the ship came, I hopped on board right behind her and said, "Excuse me, but could you please drop us off on Altair III instead?"

The Machine said, "This is a mistake. If you travel between the stars, everyone you know will die, and everything you love will fade away. You should go home."

Even Margery wanted me to stay behind, but I held firm and eventually the Machine gave in.

• • •

On Altair III we slept in a plastic bubble on the edge of a mesa. When I woke up each morning, I'd unseal one of the walls and piss right out into the dark black shapes coagulating at the bottom of the gulch. The shapes need ammonia if they're ever gonna grow. Or at least that's what I told Margery whenever she asked if that was really necessary.

I woke up every morning with her arms wrapped around me, but once the day started, she mostly ignored me. She worked the research station, dipping her little flasks and cables down into the shapes while I laid out on a rock and stared at the green-tinged clouds drifting above.

You've seen videos of the clouds, but in a way, those videos are a bit too impressive, because the Machine colorizes them with deep blues and greens and golds. I don't know, maybe those colors map to infrared or ultraviolet or radio waves or something I don't understand. For all I know, that's how the clouds actually looked when the Machine saw them.

To my eyes, the clouds were a frothy green. When they were up in the sky, all massed together in their cities, they had a bit of bulk. In fact, the way they used to shimmer and bubble over on each other and sometimes reverse direction, going right into the wind, was something spectacular. Human society is the same, you know: the Machine always says that it's just the sum total of the actions of all the people who've ever lived. But you can't *see* the Machine; at least, not the same way you could see the cloud civilization.

But when a cloud came down to the ground, it was pretty unimpressive. The damn thing was just a greenish fume. I usually didn't even know to look for it until my belt-monitor started beeping.

When that happened, I'd stand up on my rock and flap my arms—for some reason, flapping my arms felt right—and inhale deeply and stare at one spot on the distant, rollicking horizon—the next mesa was almost two hundred miles away, and in between us was only congealed black valley and blooming green sky—until I got dizzy and tired.

I don't know why I did that. I guess I just felt like maybe the green clouds had things they might say to me that they'd never say to Margery, but nothing ever happened.

Then night would fall, and I'd go and sit by the tent and wait for Margery to heat up something for dinner. While we ate, I'd tell her about the news that'd come in from the rest of the Galaxy, and she'd nod and go through her data.

She never spoke much to me, except when I asked her for the progress report that I felt I, as the expedition's financier, was owed.

That's when it would come out. She was lost. She had no idea what she was doing. She'd corresponded with so many scientists on so many planets and collected so many experimental protocols. She'd tried so many approaches.

She'd analyzed the data in so many ways. But the problem was too large. When you looked at the gas, it was obvious that it was organized and intelligent. But proving it? That was something else. What made her most afraid, though, was the possibility that the gas was closed and self-contained. Maybe the reason she couldn't communicate with it was because it didn't want or need to communicate. Maybe it'd looked deep down into her soul and figured out everything there was to know about her and decided that she was completely insignificant.

"And even that would be fine," she said. "If only it would give us some kind of sign that the Machine isn't the only thing that can exist in this universe. If only . . . "

I didn't like to see her all hopeless like that, so I'd hold her close, when she'd let me, and I'd tell her she was the most marvelous and intelligent and beautiful creature that I'd ever seen, but that didn't help her at all.

And afterwards, we'd go to sleep, side by side. I never tried to touch her, even though I wanted to, because I knew she'd have gotten upset. But those nights when I lay awake next to her and stared up into the swirling gas were the closest that I'd yet come to finding the thought that I was supposed to find.

We only had one real fight during the whole time we spent there, and it wasn't set off by anything in particular. Just one night, after she started crying and told me that she couldn't believe she'd dragged me out here on this fool's errand, I wanted her to feel better, so I told her that I felt like my work was going really well, and I felt like I was really on the verge of something.

She sat up straighter on her orb and scrunched up her face. Then she dismissed her data displays and stared deep into my eyes

"Really?" she said.

"Yeah . . . you know how it is. I can feel the insight building up inside me. It's something about how people are supposed to live."

"David. Stop being such a complete fool!"

Afterwards the silence was so complete that I could almost pretend I hadn't heard her shout. But her whole body was quivering.

"Life is extremely simple, David," she said. "You can either attempt to propagate yourself or you can pursue hedonic satisfaction or you can try to sublimate those urges into some arbitrarily-defined substitution activity. Typically, members of your class have pursued propagation: mindlessly holding onto the same estates and social position for millennia. Most other human beings don't have that option. They know the Machine will someday end their line. Thus, they either pursue pleasure or they attempt to redirect those drives by deriving some thin satisfaction from the idea that their sacrifice will enable the Machine to, someday, span the entire universe and reunite all matter within itself. That's it. There's nothing else!"

I gulped. I thought that if anyone understood me, then Margery did.

"No," I scratched the inside of my neck. "No, that's not it. But I'm coming close. I can sense it."

"You're an idiot! You have nothing to say: nothing to contribute. The least you could do is shut up! For god's sake, at least be quiet: I'm tired of letting your drivel crowd out my thoughts."

I tried to respond, but she kept shouting. Then we stared at each other for a long while until I finally crawled back into the tent and went to sleep. After that, I stopped asking her for progress reports, and I stopped talking to her about my work. After a few weeks, though, she stopped sleeping outside and went back to sleeping next to me. And, sometimes, when I was standing on my rock and flapping my arms, I'd remember the way she'd shouted at me: the way her whole body had expanded. She'd been smiling. All through her harangue, she'd smiled at me.

When I got the news, I took it in an "Oh, that's interesting" sort of way; in fact, I didn't necessarily think it meant anything at all. But still, it was something, so I held onto it all day, until Margery came back and finished laying out the food and cleaning the campsite.

Only after we'd both sat down on our orbs did I finally say, "Guess what? The Machine's awarded the Altair III bounty. Or well, half of it: two shares."

Her eyes went really wide and her mouth opened slightly. Then she looked up overhead. Just a glance.

"Yeah," I said. "To some NMS person. Not anyone we know. This woman used data from survey stations to model interactions between the gas cloud particles, and she determined that the pattern of motion and exchange of information was too limited to be indicative of intelligent life. She's not sure, though, whether or not they're alive. So that part is still up in the—"

I stopped. Margery had gone completely still. Her eyes were rolled up into her hand and her fingers were twitching.

"Hey, I can show you the paper if—"

"Shut up!"

I waited a long time for her to come out of her data-access trance, but eventually I put out the fire and piled up the dirty utensils at her feet so she could deal with them later.

That night, I woke up with a start: Margery was putting her arms around me.

"What?" I said.

"Shh, it's okay. It's just me."

"Yeah, but . . . "

She rubbed her hands over my chest, really slowly, and said, "Is this how Brunhilde did it?" but I shook her off.

"What are you doing?"

Tears were streaming from her eyes. "We belong together."

Through the slit in the bubble, I saw the boxes assembled at the edge of the tent. She'd packed up most of the campsite and vaporized most of her research apparatus.

"No . . . " I said. "No, we don't have to leave."

"It's done."

And even though none of it seemed right to me, she started rubbing her body on top of mine, and, eventually, my hands settled onto her hips.

A few years later, the Machine turned its attention to Altair III and, using a burst of its immense brainpower, determined that the clouds weren't alive after all. Those shining eyes appeared to us when we were at dinner in that very atrium—the one where I'd sat with my parents a long time ago—and told us that it was awarding Margery a half-share for the role her data had played in making this discovery.

Then the eyes were up there, hanging over all of us. My mom had chosen to die shortly after I brought Margery home, but my dad was still hanging on, long after when he ordinarily would've died, because he couldn't stand the thought of the estate falling into Margery's hands.

I looked at him. "You see. Margery's brought a half-share into the family."

My father looked at us. We'd accumulated something of a brood by then—three children, with a fourth on its way—and I knew my dad was worried that Margery was going to want to subdivide our shares between them. Equal inheritance is how great families die out, my dad used to say.

But Margery wasn't looking at either of us. Instead, she stared at the Machine and said, "What are you going to do to Altair III?"

The eyes became different. Narrower and flatter. It took me a moment to realize that they'd turned around. Now that Margery owned a half-share of her own, she finally had some sort of power.

"I'm about to begin the process of disassembling it."

Margery nodded, and she went back to her food. The eyes hung around above us for a few moments before realizing they weren't wanted.

That night, during our walk along the side of the pond, I told Margery, "You know, we could buy it. I'd be willing to spend a share on it."

"What?"

"Altair III. We could buy it."

Margery blinked three times, and I rushed onwards, because even though I loved her and was happy with her, I thought maybe this would be a way to see the old Margery one more time.

"You don't know," I said. "Maybe the Machine is wrong. Or maybe it's . . . it could be lying. It could. That's a possibility. And regardless, those clouds were beautiful. They could be ours forever. We could move there. Import people into the system: maybe the people from your old ship. Altair has plenty of mesas. They could live there with us."

She touched the edge of my arm for a brief moment. Overhead, the Earth shone down on us, throwing out shadows out over the pool. A few people still lived Earthside back then, but not many. The Machine was in the process of relocating the last of them. That was before the Machine drained the oceans and wrapped its glowing filaments around the entire world. Back then, the light from Earth was all blue and white, and in the entire universe, there was no other sight that was quite like it.

The next day, I brought up Altair again, but all she said was "Don't be silly."

But after that, she smiled more often. Especially when she was telling the kids: "It's your duty to bring more shares into the family."

Over the years her smile got deeper and deeper. When she found the children splashing in the water or playing with fastships, she'd pull them out and tell them that they'd better have their fun now, because as soon as they were of age, they'd go to NMS and figure out some way to bring more shares into the family. And she told them that they shouldn't take marriage and procreation for granted, because only *one* of them was going to inherit the family shares.

My father didn't like it. He said this pressurizing wasn't decent, and it wasn't how shareholders were supposed to behave. The children hated it too. They hated her. Still hate her, in fact. And I suppose they hate me as well, because I never spoke out against her.

But I liked that smile of hers.

One night, she asked me, "What would happen if one person accumulated a majority of the outstanding shares."

I laughed and told her that was the kind of question that only kids ask. But she rolled out of our orb and slapped the wall and said, "Machine! What would happen if one person accumulated a majority of the outstanding shares? Would they control you?"

The eyes appeared over me and said, "Is there something you wish to accomplish?"

But she shouted: "No, I'm the one with the question. And none of your run-around. In fact, walk with me. Let's take this out into the crater."

So the eyes floated along next to her, and she hissed low, quiet questions at them.

When she came back to bed, she was shivering. I put an arm around her and brought her body close, even though it was cold as a corpse.

"We're going to destroy the Machine," she whispered.

While my wife vibrated under my arm, she laid out her plan for sending our children out into the night like secret agents. For teaching them to acquire, by marriage or merit, as many shares as they could. Over the millennia, they'd use marriage to slowly coalesce their shares, year after year, generation after generation, until control was complete.

I closed my eyes. If there was any moment for my insight to come, surely it'd be this one. My wife had become the person she was going to be. Now it had to be my turn.

But the thought didn't come on that night or the next or for many years to come. I puttered about on our estate while she went among our neighbors—alienating some and befriending others—and planted strange ideas in the heads of their children. She even went to some of the other craters—places that've been silent for centuries—and came back with a pair of elongated shareholders—these women were at least twelve feet tall and spoke in a very slurred, gibberish-laden way—who she proposed to marry to our sons, before the women finally took fright at something and disappeared in the night.

One time, though, I think I came close to fulfilling my destiny:

I was sitting on my chair on the lip of the crater and watching the grass and the pond and the children and thinking my wordless thoughts. It'd become harder, over time. I'd never come as close to putting everything together as I did back on Altair III. But when I thought about things, I still had the *sensation* of making progress, and that at least was pleasurable.

But as I sat there, my wife bounded up beside me. Even after all these years, her squat, low body hadn't lost its strength.

And she said, "The clouds have been disassembled. I guess they were nothing after all. I've seen the video: the harvesters sucked them in just like any other gas. I can't believe it. I was such a fool, wasn't I? To waste all those years? I was so stupid—"

"No," I said. "Please stop."

"You know I had no real method? No systematic training? The woman who solved the problem had thirty years of education in mathematical linguistic. Whereas I thought I could just—"

"Please!"

She bared her teeth. My wife wasn't used to backing down. Her hands formed into tiny fists and her face got all wide, and I knew she was getting ready to scream again.

"Please," I said, once more, in a quiet voice.

And she lost her rigidity. The explosion didn't come. Instead, she reached up and ran her fingers across my back, and we sat there for awhile, gazing downslope. Three of our kids were splashing around in the pond, and the fourth was beating his way through the tall grass.

LAZY DOG OUT

SUZANNE PALMER

Khifi traded the warm embrace of her wife's arms for the pricking of cold air on her bare skin and a regret she knew she would not dispel until she was back here again on the far side of a ten-hour shift. She danced on her toes across the metal floor and out of their small sleeping alcove, sliding the screen doors closed behind her. Lema had more than once suggested she keep her boots at the bedside so she could slip straight into them, but if she did she couldn't sneak out without waking her.

She checked the apartment monitors to make sure oxygen was optimum, all systems running green. Not that they ever weren't, but she required that brief reassurance. Pulling clothes out of the post-wash basket, she shrugged into a sports bra, bright red tank top, and black pants before wrapping her vambrace over her left forearm. Her boots were by the door, and she stepped into their fuzzy warmth with a sigh of relief as they adjusted around her feet. As the kitchenapp kicked on to start the coffee, she skimmed the news, disinterested. There were no big Tanduou stories, and anything else local worth knowing—and that she didn't already know—wouldn't be on the feeds anyway.

Rummaging through the foodkeeper, she pulled out an oblong shape and tucked it carefully in her backpack that hung near the door. "Khif?" Lema called from the other room. She sounded like she wasn't sure if she was awake or asleep. "Are you stealing the whole loaf of protein bread again?"

"Only half of one, Lem," she said, "and it's the stale one from two days ago."

"It's only stale because you don't eat enough."

"It's only half a loaf because I ate plenty," she said. "Go back to sleep."

There was a long silence, and Khifi had just concluded that Lema had done exactly that when she heard, sleepily, "I love you."

"I love you too," she said. "Gotta go."

She slipped on her jacket and backpack, took her coffee out of the maker, and left the apartment feeling warm enough after all.

• • •

At the fastlane station, she slid her license through the reader and waited the four point three seconds for it to verify that she was rated for the lane and deposit an empty sled in the tube. Climbing in, she made sure the lid on her coffee was fully sealed before she put the thermal mug in her backpack, tied the pack down at the base of the sled, and strapped herself in. She put her hands on the dual joystick controls on either side and ran though a mental self-check to make sure she was awake and alert enough. Once she was sure she was good, she launched herself up into the tube at top acceleration.

Navigating the branching maze of the Tanduou tube system was almost an art. More than one overtired, over-intoxicated, or over-selfestimated tube-noob had turned themselves into a pulpy obstruction in the system before skill-ranked licensing was implemented. It had reduced, if not eliminated, fatality-related delays.

Eight turns, the surface rotary loop, and two timed junctions later, she kicked her sled out the exit for the Paxillo Docks. As she braked the last quarter kilometer into the transit station she could see the city-lit underbellies of ships shifting overhead like a perpetual storm cloud of rusty junk. The bright yellow-brown disk of the nearby planet lurked behind them, a faded sun never quite able to break through.

Her eyes looked for trouble, found none.

Shouldering her pack, she left the transit station and merged into the cramped hallways of the underbelly of the Docks. As she turned a corner toward the central hub, faint footsteps fell in behind her, distinct from the usual heavy-booted crowd. For a half-second she thought about the three knives she had within easy reach, then instead abruptly stopped walking mid-stride. Her follower slammed right into her. She spun around in time to catch the chagrin on his face. He was eight or nine standard years old, although he was small enough to be younger and had the eyes of someone older. "Morning, Mole," she said. "Where's your partner in crime today?"

He shrugged. Traffic in the hallway moved seamlessly around them, uncaring. "Birdie had business."

"You were looking for me?"

"Figured I might run into you," he said, and almost smiled.

She glanced around to make sure there was no one in the halls who could make trouble, then slid her pack off and set it on the floor. She took out the half-loaf and handed it to him. "You okay?" she asked. "No one hassling you?"

"No one new," he answered. When she waited, he added, "I'm okay."

"Everyone else?"

He looked down toward his threadbare shoes, held together with cargo sealant and grime. "Peezy and Gums went off to Notomyo Dock. Gums come back in bad shape, pissing blood, not talking. We not found Peezy yet. Thinking she dead or grabbed."

Well, shit, she thought. "Why'd they go there?"

"Heard about easy stuff to get."

"What're the rules, Mole?"

"No stealing except direct to survive, no stealing more than you need, no stealing from anyone who can't afford to lose it," he said. "Assume everything's a trap."

"And?"

"And don't get caught."

"How do you know this isn't a trap?" she asked.

"*Know* it is. Food's the bait, and the trap is you make me learn reading and numbers and stuff." He broke the loaf carefully into three roughly equal pieces. Putting two deep down in the pocket of his ragged coat, he began chewing on the last. She knew he'd save one piece for Birdie and wondered who the other was for.

"If you learn to run manifests and do other textwork, you could get a job and get out of the crawl. You've only got a few more years before you're too old to stay down there," she said. "You do that lesson I gave you?"

"Yeah. Tuck's taking a turn now," he said. "Tuck's new. Little. Not a runaway, a drop. Cries all the time. Birdie says we looking after him now."

Khifi watched as he licked a fingertip and meticulously picked up and ate the crumbs he'd dropped on the front of his coat. She remembered being that hungry, once. "Bugs came in last shift," he said, eventually. Bugs were crawler slang for aliens.

"Yeah? Which kind?"

"Hain't seen, don't know. Down in Velatos."

Velatos, she thought. *Shit, I forgot.*

Mole stiffened at her suddenly tense body language. "It's okay, Mole," she said, "I promised Lema I'd run an errand for her in Velatos and now it's too late. Going to have to go after my shift."

"If you do, let me know about the bugs," Mole said. He patted his pocket to make sure he still had the food secured there, then peered through the crowds back down the hall. By the time she'd got her pack back on, there was no sign of him in the swirling tide of merchants and haulers, scavengers and lost.

She headed toward the central hub into the heart of Paxillo.

Tanduou's Docks had spread out over the surface of the tide-locked moon, thickening and growing together until they were one interconnected network of docks and storage facilities, black markets and slums, arms reaching out from individual locii to embrace and entangle each other. The hubs remained distinct, massive metal and stone towers rising toward the constant swarm of ships above, while here and there, at the outskirt borders between them, small patches of the native rocky surface could still be seen, littered with twisted scrap and, sometimes, the remains of the unlucky or unwise on eternal, cautionary display.

The lowest level of Paxillo's hub was a wide concourse, full of shops selling uncertain foods and goods banned on dozens of worlds. Lines of people queued to enter, queued to leave. Always among them were the crawlers looking for dropped food or unattended luggage, a bold few looking to liberate things more actively. Hunting on the floor was desperation or reckless overconfidence; even the best of the best would, eventually, get caught. She knew that all too personally.

An assault of activity, noise, and smells hit her face-on as she merged into the concourse. Normally she found the chaos a comforting unpleasantness. This time, though, one particular smell had infiltrated, tainting the usual, complex mix. That specific cheap Titan cologne had only one devotee she knew of, at least at the level of fanatical self-slathering needed to stand out in this space.

"Fox," Sniv said, using her pilot name as he appeared out of the crowd and fell in beside her, enveloping her in his toxic miasma. "Another long shift? You must be very tired."

"I sleep well," she said, and kept walking.

"I trust you are sufficiently compensated—"

"I am, Sniv, and it's none of your business."

"Ah, but I am a man of all businesses!" he declared. "I know about your past, and I have an offer for you. A simple guide job, well-paying—"

"If it's a legit job, bring it to Quizzie, the Dock manager. If not, I'm certain I am not interested," Khifi said.

"If you reconsider, perhaps we can meet and break bread over it," he said. "I hear you like to share your food with Tanduou's unfortunates, and surely I am begging for your time. Think about it."

Before she could form an answer, he swept back into the crowd, leaving her choking down a blistering reply.

It was neither common knowledge nor a secret that Khifi was once a crawler herself. It was just dumb luck that she was caught by a pilot rather than security, and that he'd had a need to save the world one lost piece at a time. She would spend her lifetime trying to pay that good fortune back. Whatever Sniv wanted of her, it could only be a step backward.

Sniv had left her just a few steps away from the uniformed Dock Security officer half-asleep at his post. She passed through the gate to the private elevators, put her hand on the palm scanner, then stepped into the lift when it opened. The car smoothly rose up the tower to Paxillo Dock Control.

Control was a circular room with a view of the entirety of Paxillo Dock. In the dim light, console displays bathed everyone and everything in a reddish glow. In the center was an elevated platform where the ending shift's Ops manager, Goffs, was slouched in his chair with a deep frown on his face. Inchbug, on air comms, gave Khifi a half-wave as she entered. Khifi smiled and waved back before looking around for her own team.

Sparkle was sprawled in a chair at the end of the room, arms crossed over her chest and feet up on an idle console, eyes closed. Jonjon was at the break station trying to coax the coffee dispenser to break whatever law of physics limited the speed at which even spacer fakebrew could be squirted out first thing in the morning. Redrum sat in a chair, his bony hands already wrapped around a mug, a small smile playing on his face as he listened to Jonjon's low, ritual wheedling.

Khifi walked over to stand beside the machine. "Let me," she said after a few moments and thumped the side of the machine with her fist. Immediately it began to chug out its small measure of low-rent heaven.

"I don't know how the fuck you always do that, Fox," Jonjon said.

"Magic," she answered. *And timing*, she didn't add; the machine had a small but distinct hiccup in its internal rumblings just prior to dispensing. "Just remember to save me some. Quizzie's not here?" Quizzie was their shift's Ops manager, but her larger duties as dock manager sometimes took her elsewhere.

"Dockmaster caught a ride with her down to the Gee. Another trade meet, arguing about the gravity bill," Redrum said. "Stickles is the man in the chair today. He's on his way."

Jonjon relinquished his position in front of the coffee dispenser to her. She took her mug off the shelf above it and poured herself a full cup. Despite Tanduou being independent, the central government of Guratahan Sfazil believed that, simply because they provided a planet for Tanduou to orbit around, they deserved a cut from the dock trade profit. It was a never-ending argument. Khifi's impression was that the Gee's strategy was to wear them down through constant, petty annoyance.

Speaking of annoyances. She drained her coffee with barely a grimace, stuck the mug back in the sani-rack, and went to Inchbug's station to look out the window. "The Rimbolan freighter is still out there?" she exclaimed. "Is this four days now?"

"Yeah," Inchbug said. "Waiting on parts, they say. Damned heap of junk is taking up three dock slots. We've swamped Velatos with our extra traffic, and we've even had to push ships as far off as Oreasta and Luida docks."

"Surprised Goffs hasn't called in a salvage team."

"Yeah, well. I think the only reason he hasn't is that Mr. Balcko is so spun up about it he's shitting rocks, and Goffs is enjoying that."

"Mr. Balcko? Why does he care? If the traffic isn't going outside our cluster—"

Inchbug shrugged. "No idea. Goffs suddenly seems to be all about getting in Balcko's face, and with the Dockmaster off-moon . . . Well. If I were you I'd let it be Stickles's problem and stay out of it. And I'm going to hope your lot or the next has this all settled before my shift comes round again."

Balcko was the manager of the seven docks, including Paxillo, that made up Velatos cluster. That put him high enough up the Tanduou food chain to make life difficult for anyone down at their level, answering only to the Dockmaster himself. "Thanks for the warning," she said. "You out?"

"Soon as Tumbler and Beanmaker get their feet down," Inchbug said. "Yebbles is in, and Ryeneck's waiting on Pits in cargo to give the clear."

Khifi glanced across the room. Ryeneck was cleaning gunk out from under his nails with the end of a handpad stylus as he talked, mouth moving nonstop, the murmur low enough from here to sound like a cargo-drone losing its engine at altitude.

"There a problem?" Khifi asked.

"No, Pits isn't even on the line yet. Rye's lost his head for a controller over in the Odinella cluster, and he's a-wooing."

"Over the official lines?!"

"Naw. He hacked into an illegal relay down in the markets and used it to patch an encrypted channel through the public comm system. Can pretty much talk the ear off anyone and everyone on Tanduou all day, so long as no one too high up notices. We've got cred riding on how many shifts it takes him to crash and burn."

"Based on that pilot in Acontias cluster he was in love with last week? My guess is not long."

Inchbug snorted. "Too right. Hey, speaking of gossip, I hear you and Lem are implanting?"

Khifi sighed. "Fourth try," she said.

Inchbug shook her head. "I can't imagine bringing a kid into this world," she said. "I—"

Stickles walked in, interrupting whatever Inch had been about to say. He looked as disheveled as always, like someone had just dumped him out of a sack on their doorstep. "Almost shift time, gang," he said. "Give me five minutes to check in with Goffs. Fox, you're air captain, do what you do best."

Khifi looked around. She was still missing two of her pilots. Kaiju was always last second, but Knits . . .

"Tumbler is in, Beanmaker docking in five," Inch announced, just as Kaiju, on cue, ran out of the half-open elevator and pitched himself into the chair beside Redrum, trying to catch his breath.

"Shift change," Goffs announced.

"Ops commander, checking in," Stickles announced.

"Ops commander, transferring command and checking out," Goffs said. He pulled his ID card from the console, stood up, and said one last thing to Stickles before climbing down the ladder onto the floor.

Sparkle cracked an eye open, unfolded herself from her chair, and loomed over Ryeneck until he disconnected his line, threw down his headset, and yielded his chair. He kicked the post as she sat down, and she swiveled around and smirked at him until he left.

"Jonjon, you may relieve Inchbug," Stickles said.

Jonjon brought his mug over as Inchbug slid off her headpiece and rubbed wearily at her eyes. "All yours," she said, and let him take her seat.

"I'm still down a pilot," Khifi said. "I don't know where Knits is."

"She called in sick," Goffs said, as he climbed down from the ops platform. "Stickles was bringing a replacement."

"Candles is on his way up by tube right now."

Khifi thought she knew all the pilots in the cluster and most beyond, but the name was unfamiliar. "Candles?"

"New," Stickles said. "Working out of Novodinia with me."

"How new?" She narrowed her eyes.

"So shiny and new the wrapper hasn't sloughed off yet," Stickles said, "but only to Tanduou; kid's got time under his belt driving cargo skips out around the Bounds dodging pirates. You won't hate him, and it mostly won't even feel like babysitting. Give him a chance. Please?"

Please? That was unusual. "What aren't you telling me?" she asked.

"He's just not a local, okay?" Stickles said. "Burnout's been giving him a hard time."

"Burnout's an assvalve. Whose tug is he taking?"

"The cluster spare. Beanmaker is hauling it over now, that's why he's running late. Once Candles makes it past review, we'll assign him a permanent tug and home dock. Think about that as you work with him; if there's a happier fit here in Paxillo it'd save everyone some grief."

The lift doors opened and someone very, very tall stepped out onto the floor. The newcomer was well over two meters in height, attenuated and gangly looking. He was also shirtless and hairless. What really stood out, though, were the thick swirls and whorls of silvery-gray that climbed up his torso, along his neck and bare scalp. Contrasted against the spacer-brown of his skin, the effect was startling. As he stepped forward, the patterns shimmered in the changing light.

Not local, indeed, Khifi thought.

Stickles looked up from his seat at the command console. "Candles, just in time."

Candles raised one long, skinny arm, and gave an uncertain wave. "Uh, hi," he said. It was so much the gesture of any awkward teenager anywhere that Khifi laughed. His eyes went straight to her, his face a mask of both defiance and anxiety. Yeah, she could imagine Burnout being rough on this kid.

Khifi thumped Jonjon on the shoulder so that he turned around in the chair. "Hi, Candles. I'm Fox," she said. She pointed to the rest of her team. "This is Jonjon on Comms for the air," she said, "and over there is Sparkle on ground. By the coffee machine is Redrum and Kaiju, pilots."

"You air captain?" Candles asked.

"I am today," she said.

"She is every day," Jonjon said. "Best pilot in the cluster, but don't tell her I said that."

"Best, huh?" Candles asked. That spark of challenge brightened.

She shrugged. "Everyone does their best as a team, or no one does," she said. "Stickles, you got work for us?"

"Soon as you slackers finish up your coffee social and get out there, yeah," he said.

"Okay," Khifi said. "Move, everyone. Candles, I'm going to come watch you go through your preflight checks."

He made a face. *Damn, he's young*, she thought. "Done a hundred checks afore," he said, his Bounds accent thick. "Not needing your eyes on me."

"Yeah, well, you get them anyway," she said, pointing toward the tower lift emphatically. "No one goes out on my watch that I don't know first-hand can handle themselves."

"Trust her, kid," Stickles called down from the command platform.

The lift arrived and Candles followed her reluctantly in. As the doors closed, she turned to him. "You have a suit, right?" she asked.

"Do," he said. "Just the Colony not like it, being closed."

"The Colony?"

He waved one hand loosely up and down his torso. Closer up she could see the silver markings were more of a dense fuzz, and that it rippled gently despite the lack of moving air in the car.

"It's alive?" she asked.

"Yeh. Does it give you fear?"

"Not really, no," she said, and wasn't sure if he looked more relieved or disappointed. "You want to talk about it?"

"Gen-mod symbiote," he said. "Converts rads to vitals."

Vitamins, she interpreted. "You're from deep out."

"Yeh. Suvastia. Jobworld. Family contract got redunded and we was let go," he said. "Sibs got refuge on Beenjai, I came here with eyes on better work."

"Well, if you can fly, you should do fine," she said. "It's staying out of trouble that's the real challenge. Stickles is a good lead; his advice is worthwhile."

"Said same of you."

Khifi laughed. "Okay, so *most* of his advice is worthwhile. How'd you end up as Candles?" Nicknames were a point of both pride and deep superstition in the Docks; few people went by anything else, especially pilots.

"Burnout wanted to nick me Vacuumfodder. I said I specked he'd find the final cold sooner, and he said, quoting, 'Boo hoo, I'll light you some candles.' So Candles."

"There are definitely worse nicks. There's a cargo hauler on one of the skip runs who goes by Assface."

He laughed. "Don't mind Candles. Light in the darkness, know so? Growing on me. How come Fox?"

"The pilot I apprenticed with was obsessed with languages. Made sure it was my hobby too. The Earth dialect a lot of our language grew up from had only twenty-six letters in it, and there was a sentence that used all of them, which was, in translation: 'The quick brown fox jumped over the lazy dog.' You'll have to trust me it's got all the letters in there. Anyhow, my trainer figured I was quick enough to get out of the way of almost any trouble, so Fox it was."

The lift stopped and opened out onto the tug bay. Her own ship—ugly as shit, powerful enough to push the biggest freighter and most warships off their own paths—sat in its cradle, feedlines connected from ceiling and floor charging its systems. "And that," she said, waving at it with no small pride, "is my *Lazy Dog*."

Parked beside it was the smaller loaner tug Beanmaker had brought in. "There's yours," she said. "Walk through your checks like I'm not even here."

"If you be not here, I be doing my checks naked," Candles said.

Khifi stopped in her tracks. "You're joking."

He met her eyes, his somber face incrementally shifting into a grin.

She closed her eyes, pinching the bridge of her nose, trying not to laugh and failing. "Okay, you got me," she said.

Candles walked over to his ship and she followed. He ignored her, moving over and around his ship with efficiency and thoroughness before he disconnected the spare's feeder hoses and let them retract. Disappearing inside, he powered it up, then reemerged to walk around the ship's perimeter, checking the exterior lights. It was only as he stood by one of the two engine pods that he turned to her. "Pitch be low," he said.

He knows what his engines are supposed to sound like, she thought, approving. And he was right: the pitch was low. Candles stared at his ship for a long minute before he took two steps to his left, listened again, and then began unscrewing the safety grill over one of the half-dozen air intakes for his port engine. "Where I about finding tools?" he asked.

"What do you need?"

"A light, and someit long and skinny."

"You got it," Khifi said. She went to the back of the bay, swiped her ID, and pulled open drawers until she'd found a handlight and a long-handled hex driver. She brought them back over to Candles. "These do?"

"Perf, thanks," he said. He took the handlight, slipped it over his palm, and shone it down into the intake. Nodding his head, he took the hex driver and with his other hand poked around inside the air intake until he managed to pull out a long, blackish gray lump.

"Sock?" Khifi asked.

"Sock," he confirmed. He shone the light in again, then turned it off and stood with his eyes closed, listening. "Sounds right, now."

"You want me to have a word with Stickles?"

"No," he said, stuffing the sock into a pants pocket. "Best deal back myself."

"All yours then," she said. "Nothing dangerous, understood?"

"Stood. But shit-yourself scary is in play, right?"

Khifi chuckled. "As I said, as long as it's not dangerous. Just make sure it's something you can both walk away from after with no hard feelings. We don't need—"

Her comm buzzed on her wrist, and she tapped it.

"Fox, you done having a nap up in the docks yet?" Stickles.

"Just finishing," she said. "We'll be out in your airspace soon."

"Good. I've just sent Redrum to do a cargo transfer and I need the remainder of the tugs out now. The Rimbolan freighter paid its fees and wants a push back up to orbit to do the rest of its repairs."

"They got their life support back online?"

"So they say. Otherwise in about seventy-two hours we're going to be calling in a bodywagon. I'm dropping the specs to your tug comp. I'm giving you full lead and the roster of waiting ships. Use your judgment. Check back in if you have serious problems. Otherwise, Ops out."

"Well," Khifi said. "I guess he's not a micromanager. Suit up, and let me know when you're ready to fly."

"Got it," Candles said.

Khifi turned to her own ship. The *Lazy Dog* was a typical Tanduouan tug, which meant it looked like a giant cyborg squid-crab with a mean case of engine. She retracted her own feeder lines, did her checks, then climbed the short ladder up its side and slipped down into the cabin. Inside, bathed in the blue-green glow of the console, she felt safe, strong, armored. She had never felt that way before she'd become a pilot, still never felt it anywhere else except in Lema's arms. She was lucky, she thought, that neither got jealous of the other.

She buckled herself into her seat and initiated the internal system checks, then slipped on the comm headset.

"—ox? Fox, you online yet?" It was Jonjon.

"Just now," she said. "What's happening up there?"

"Mr. Balcko walked in. He and Stickles are arguing. I don't know."

"Jonjon, the line—"

"I'm on Ryeneck's secret line. Something's up," Jonjon said. His voice was carefully casual, low. "I really don't like the tone— Uh-oh, gotta go."

She found herself listening to dead air. Shaking her head to clear out a sudden anxiety, she punched in the comm code for the spare. "Candles? What's your status?"

"Ready to go in thirty count," he answered.

"Launch as soon as ready, then proceed to the Rimbolan freighter docked at five through seven clockwise. I'll be less than a minute behind you."

"Got it," he said.

"Redrum and Kaiju, you hear that convo?"

"Yeah," Redrum's gruff voice came on the line.

"I don't like it," Kaiju added.

"Whatever's going on groundside isn't our problem once we're out. Stickles can handle it," Khifi said. The last of her system checks returned green just as she finished speaking. She pulled her helmet down, reflexively checked her safety harness one last time, then fired up the engines. The *Lazy Dog* lifted off the floor, turning gracefully in the tight space of the bay.

As soon as she got into the bay envelope it sealed behind her, and the exterior doors split apart like a metal egg hatching out onto brilliant sunshine. She checked her airspace display one last time to make sure nothing was in her way, then, satisfied her exit trajectory was clear, slid up the power on her engines.

She smiled, despite her worries, as her ship leapt out into the sky.

"*Lazy Dog* out," she announced over her comms as she turned her ship around Paxillo's tower, the bright orange disc of Guratahan Sfazil filling her peripheral view. She keyed in Redrum, Kaiju, and Candles into a local comm group. "Status?"

"I'm half-way to Luida to pick up a cargo pod," Redrum said. "Turnaround in twenty min."

"Good. Check in when you're on your way back. Kaiju, meet me and Candles at the Rimbolan freighter. Let's free up some dock space."

"Got it," Kaiju said.

The Rimbolan was a massive, oblong ship, pointed and slightly curved at the ends in a shape Jonjon once referred to as a "ginormous fucking canoe." It had come in without prearranged berth or sponsor, paying triple fees for an expedited dock. Offloading it should have been a two-shift job at most, with three bay arms attached to it, but it had sat there locked up and unresponsive for nearly a full shift before its captain broke silence to issue a call for help.

Major systems failure had swamped it with radiation, personnel were sick or dying, and its cargo was contaminated.

In dock, the freighter was covered under a number of interplanetary distressed-vehicle and medical mercy laws. A handful of critically ill and wounded crew had finally been offloaded, at which time it was discovered that the ship, while Rimbolan in manufacture, had been sold to (or scavenged from a junk pile by) a private company out of Temperance Enclave. Another group of crew disembarked and was busy trying to find a buyer for their hot cargo, but no one was taking. Some of them had since disappeared, and the reigning explanation was that they had run away.

What mattered was that the freighter had run out of delaying tactics. She didn't believe they had anything fixed, but if they stayed in dock long enough for Paxillo to call salvage rights over unpaid fees, assets claimed would likely include the crew themselves. How they'd scraped together enough to get back off the ground she couldn't begin to guess.

It damn well better not break in half when we lift it, she thought.

She could see Kaiju's tug *Nobunaga*, its hull painted with green scales, closing in on the far end of the freighter. Candles' tug hovered near the gaping maw of the Rimbolan's wide-open cargo bay doors. "Jonjon, bay doors aren't sealed," she said.

A moment later, he got back on the line. "Ship says doors no longer functional, but assure us the cargo is fully secured inside."

"Has Terrapin verified this?" Terrapin was the Dock Inspector.

"No. Because of the radiation he was unable to go aboard."

"Do we know that there's a radiation leak?" Khifi asked. "I mean, other than the word of the ship's captain?"

"There were exposed crewmembers brought in and sent over to Velatos for treatment," Jonjon said. "What are you thinking?"

She passed over the freighter's bow. "I don't like it. Do we have a waiver from them, in case of damages?"

"No. Why?"

"Because if I were them, and as far in the red as they are with a junk ship, unsellable cargo, and salvagers circling in, I'd have spent the last four shifts taking off every safety in the ship, and if I finished with that, I'd be taking screws and bolts out of everything else, so that when the freighter breaks apart during our lift, we're liable for ship and cargo and they walk away clean. We're not touching it. Tell them sign a waiver, pay the next docking fee, or yield to salvage."

"On it. Hold tight."

Kaiju started lazy circles around the Paxillo tower, and after a few minutes Candles followed. Khifi pulled up the incoming ship registry and winced at the long list of ships waiting for a berth. Some had arrived only hours after the Rimbolan. Glancing overhead, it was definitely more crowded than usual.

"Fox?" Jonjon came back on the line.

"Here. What's our status?"

"We've got a waiver, but whoa were they unhappy about that. I think I learned some new words. Seems like you called that one right."

"Got it," she said. "Candles, Kaiju? I still don't want this thing dropping parts all over Paxillo when we pick it up. If they're smart, they remembered where we grabbed on when bringing them down and made the most trouble there. So I want you both on the underside instead of top. Candles, take the cargo bay end. Let me know when you're in position. I'm taking topside."

"Which end?" Kaiju asked.

"Neither. I'm going for dead center. The bridge."

Candles' chuckle came over the line. "Perf," he said. "Safest place, 'cause if the ship's rigged the people be all there for the ride up."

"Jonjon, let everyone overhead know that once we get this thing moving we're heading straight up to orbit, and if they're in our way that's their own damned problem."

"Already on it," Jonjon answered. She wanted to ask what was going on in ops but didn't dare, not on the main line.

The space beneath the Rimbolan was tight, but she knew Kaiju well enough to know he could handle getting in there, even upside down. Candles . . . well, as long as he didn't break the tug itself, it was a good test of his skills.

She brought the *Lazy Dog* out over the top of the freighter, close enough that she could make out the shapes of people behind the thick window at the forefront of the bridge. At least one of them appeared to be shouting and making a rude gesture at her. Given that she was just about to drop a giant metal spider down on their heads, she figured they were entitled.

"In position," Kaiju said.

"There most," Candles added. "Three count. Two, one, done."

"Okay. Hold there for a moment," Khifi said. She brought the *Lazy Dog* down to barely a meter above the freighter's bridge. Then she swung her tug's arms down and one by one, like she was smothering prey, latched them onto the sides all around. "Okay. I want to do this carefully. Any time either of you feel like we're moving too fast, you speak up, okay? Candles, I'm going to send the commands to the docking systems to disengage, and then the freighter is all on us. I want you to start lifting your end as soon as you feel the clamps let go."

"Got you," he said.

"Kaiju, you and I get to do the heavy lifting. I want to take the freighter vertical and out. Candles is going to keep the cargo bay end up and pointed in the right direction, and you and I are going to provide the thrust we need to get it entirely out of Tanduou space. If this thing is going to fall apart, I want it well out of everyone's way when it does."

"Ready," Kaiju said.

"Sending the release signal . . . now," Khifi said, and finished the sequence. She felt the drag of the freighter's mass shift almost immediately into a pressure upward as Candles' end began to climb. She rotated her engines to keep in sync with the ship's angle and began adding lift as Kaiju got his own engines down and joined in.

Her instruments said they were nearing vertical and already close to a thousand meters clear of Paxillo tower. "Let's hope they were smart enough to strap themselves in," she said. "Anyone see signs of structural integrity problems?"

"Some debris dropped past me when we first started pushing, but nothing big enough to cause any damage," Kaiju said.

"Candles, how's your view?"

"Clear and good," he said.

"Then let's push it," Khifi said, and powered up to three-quarters. She could feel the vibration of the freighter through her boots, but it was steady, felt right.

"You guys could have waited for me before you started the party," Redrum's voice came over the comms. Out of the corner of her eye, Khifi could see the Jolly Roger splashed in paint across Redrum's hull as he flew up alongside them.

"There's a small freighter named the *Olympian Razor* from Mars that's been waiting for almost two days," Khifi said. "Check in with ground ops to make sure no debris hit anything down there, then if it still looks good, bring her into dock five. We should be back by the time you're done."

If the Enclavers had tried to engineer a disaster, either they were terribly bad at it, hadn't had enough time to do an effective job, or the old freighter still had some fight left in it. Probably some combination of all three. It soared up out of Tanduou's feeble gravity well with surprising grace. They were well outside orbit zones for either Guratahan Sfazil, Tanduou itself, and the big planet's tiny second moon, Tammou. "Powering down engines to minimum on three . . . two . . . one. Down. Candles, disengage. Kaiju, pop an all-channel navigation hazard beacon on it before you let go. They can scrape it off themselves when they get out of our space."

" . . . Done," Kaiju said. "Disengaging."

"I'm untached," Candles said.

Khifi retracted her tug's spiderlegs one by one until she floated free of the freighter. She rarely got much past the swarm of ships surrounding the moon, and the view was beautiful. Guratahan Sfazil was an arid, golden desolation, pockmarked by the slow-growing brown and green skunge of civilization.

The half-circle glow of Tammou hung above, and it took her a few moments longer than it should have to notice the tiny glints between her and it. A small cluster of eight ships drifted there, seven small cargos and one sleek, military-style cruiser. A quick check showed them not in the queue for Paxillo, nor any of the other docks in the Velatos cluster.

Jonjon's voice on the comms broke her away from her curiosity. "Fox? I'm on Ryeneck's line again. There's—"

"This is Paxillo ops." The incoming official signal from Stickles cut off Jonjon's connection. "Fox, is anyone currently engaged?"

"Redrum, status?" Khifi asked.

"Just settling the *Marsies* down now," he said.

"Two minutes, ground," Khifi replied down to the surface. Those two minutes went by in silence until she saw Redrum retract from the new ship safely tucked in dock. "We're clear."

"Cluster Manager Balcko has an announcement," Stickles said.

Balcko came on the air. "Normally this is news the Dockmaster would pass on in person, but as you know, he is downplanet on business," he said. "There was a tube accident a short while ago. One of the Paxillo staff—Airon Gofersen, also known as Goffs—has been killed. It appears to have been operator error. In respect for Gofersen, I am closing down Paxillo Docks for the remainder of the shift."

Khifi couldn't believe she'd heard right. "Goffs is dead?" she asked.

"Yes," Balcko answered. "I'm sorry."

"Should we . . . " What should they do? She didn't know. She wanted to stay flying, as if it wouldn't be real until she set foot in dock again. "Should we finish parking the last few—?"

"Paxillo is shut down effective immediately," Balcko said. "That is all."

"You heard the boss," Stickles said. "Come on in."

She was last down, Candles just ahead of her. Redrum had arrived first and was sitting between Jonjon and Sparkle. Mr. Balcko had already departed.

Stickles stood at the railing at the control platform, his face an unreadable mask. "I'll see you all back here for shift tomorrow," he said. "In the meantime . . . well. Take time for yourselves and be safe."

Jonjon stood up and put an arm around Redrum's shoulders. "I worked with Goffs as my ops manager for four years before I switched shifts, and he was a good man," he said. "I'm heading to the Hellwater for a drink, and I'm buying for anyone who cares to join me."

"I'm in," Sparkle said, putting the headpiece down on her console and standing up.

"Me too," Kaiju said.

"Fox? Candles?" Jonjon asked.

Candles started, as if surprised to have been invited. "Yeah. Didn't know Goffs, but team is team."

"One round and then I'm going home to my wife," Khifi said. She felt sick.

"Stickles?" Jonjon asked.

"Maybe later," Stickles said. "I have to make a call to the Gee, break the news to Quizzie and the Dockmaster. I'd rather they heard it from me."

"Understood," Jonjon said. "We'll be there for a while."

Khifi and the others stumbled into the elevators, leaving Stickles standing where he was, his head hung low, his knuckles pale where he gripped the platform rail.

The Hellwater was in a dead-end spoke off Paxillo, and had long since earned its reputation as Velatos Cluster's roughest bar, surpassing even the Brood and the Tarpit. Tanduou had started off life as a pirate haven before finding marginally more legitimate business as a shipyard and waystation; here in the Hellwater, Khifi felt closest to those early pirate days. She wasn't sure that was entirely due to the wall of holoportraits of everyone who'd been murdered in the bar, divided into those justifiably killed, those sorely missed, and the largest section in between of those people who fit both categories. A lone portrait stood by itself, labeled "a lesson to others"—a nameless, offworld joker who'd thought it funny to put the bartender's portrait up among the dead and got caught in the act.

Why no one had ever shut down the Hellwater—and right now the Brood was in another sixty-day time out for bad behavior—was unclear, but Khifi figured the fact that it was the pilots' bar was a big part of it.

Now, though, the Hellwater was subdued, almost quiet, and that struck her hard. Goffs had been a pilot before he became ops; it seemed unthinkable that he could be dead when just a few hours before he'd been right there in control with them. *He should be here with us now, dammit*, she thought. Everything they'd been through, all the crazy, dangerous, drunken things they'd done, the idea that he'd die in a stupid tube accident was just wrong. And if he could slip up, which of them couldn't?

Jonjon had claimed a large table toward the back, and the bartender—rarely generous—brought a tray of Sfazili Whiskey bulbs and set it on the table. As he passed by Khifi's chair, he gently touched her shoulder. "Sorry," he said.

Sparkle raised a bulb. "To Goffs," she said.

"To Goffs," the others answered, clanking bulbs. Khifi took a long sip, watched as everyone but Candles did the same.

"You okay?" She leaned toward him and asked.

He made a wry face. "Alcohol hurts the Colony."

"First met Goffs back during the Henrici Dock crash," Redrum spoke up.

"We'd both showed up to see if we could help, got drafted as fire crew trying to get to the survivors in the tower. Saved some people, couldn't others, never talked about it after that day. But when he needed another pilot on his team, he knew I wasn't happy in Archasta and called me. Man was calm as ice in a fight, or at the helm, and I can't imagine if Henrici never gave him the shakes how the fucking tube blinked him."

"We get tired, I think," Jonjon said. "We forget to pay attention. Wrong place at the wrong moment and that's the end."

"Ever try to sneak up on Fox when she looks like she's lost in thought?" Kaiju said. "Because she ain't never not paying attention."

"You still have the scar?" Khifi asked.

"Yeah."

"Good," she said, downing the remainder of her bulb, feeling it burn its way down. "Never put your guard down."

"He tried that with me too," Redrum said. "I only kicked him."

"See? Your lesson didn't stick," Khifi said. She pushed back her chair and stood. "Speaking of safe, stay at one bulb or stay out of the tubes, okay? Don't make me come yell at your corpses, because I will and even dead you *will* hear me."

"You aren't staying?" Sparkle said.

"Going to get home while I can," Khifi said. She felt like she should say something else, unsure what wouldn't sound sappy and drunken, when she glanced up at the door.

"Shit," she said, instead. "Trouble."

Burnout and two other pilots from Novodinia were walking in, and from their loose swagger the Hellwater wasn't their first stop. He spotted Khifi's group and pushed through the small crowd to their table. "Came by to pay our respects," he said.

"That's appreciated," Sparkle said.

"I mean, you know," Burnout continued, "kinda remarkable Goffs made it this long, given how shit—"

"You should leave it at just your respects," Khifi interrupted.

Burnout blinked at her, then glanced around the unsmiling faces at the table. He broke into a big grin. "Aw, c'mon," he said, "we all know his piloting skills is what grounded him in a chair."

Before anyone could respond—Redrum was half out of his chair—one of the Novodinia pilots put a hand on Burnout's arm. "We should just go," he said.

"Naw, Stash. Pilots are all on the same team, right?" Burnout said. His gaze fell on Candles. "Except maybe this mutant freak here. I wondered where he slunk off to. Feeding the strays again, Fox?"

He reached a hand out, clearly intent on touching the Colony on Candles's shoulder. As Candles leaned away, Khifi grabbed Burnout's hand and twisted hard. Burnout let out a strangled cry and dropped to his knees.

Khifi leaned forward, still gripping his hand. "Next time you come to pay your respects in Paxillo, you might want to learn what that means first," she said. "Or at least start listening to Stash, who's a fucklot smarter than you."

She let go and stepped back.

"Come on, Burn, let's go," Stash said, trying to help his friend up.

Burnout slapped his hand away as he got clumsily to his feet. "No way," he said, "I'm not letting—"

"House bets on Fox, six to one," the bartender called out. The entire Hellwater went silent, turning to watch. Burnout glanced around, not sure what was happening.

"Burnout, let me be clear," Khifi said. "I've had a bad day and right now I would love an excuse to add your face to the wall. But you're drunk and I'm not, and I wouldn't want anyone doubting for a second that you'd lose just as fast in a fair fight."

Stash pulled Burnout back. "She's right," he said, "and I'm halfway toward killing you myself for dragging me into this asshole move. We're going. Now."

If Burnout still wasn't convinced, the collective groan of disappointment in the bar did it. He shook off Stash, made a rude gesture at Khifi, and stomped out.

"I'm true sorry about Goffs," Stash said, and followed.

Khifi stood there until they were gone and the Hellwater stuttered back into life around them. "Well," she said at last. "That was unpleasant."

Candles stood. "Fox, you didn't need to—"

"I did, Candles," she said. "We're supposed to be better than that, and dammit if I'm not going to act like we are."

She walked out of the Hellwater and stood in the bright lights of the Paxillo corridor. Anger still burned—at Burnout for being a predictable asshole, at Goffs for being dead—and with the shot of whisky to fuel it, felt like it would not die low anytime soon. *Not the right frame of mind for the tube*, she thought. *Walk it off. Get it out of your system. Go home when you're ready. It's not like Lema is expecting you for another seven hours.*

She did have that errand to run to Velatos.

In addition to the interdock fastlanes, there was also an autowalk between Paxillo and Velatos. She stepped onto the wide, slow-moving platform, leaning against the rail as people rushed past her. Velatos was the central dock of the cluster that bore its name, Paxillo and the others arrayed around it in a circle. It was one of the largest docks on Tanduou, second only to Solaster and Leilaster, also centers of their own clusters. The floormover briefly skimmed along the surface toward it, an xglass arch crisscrossed by thick beams overhead. Before it gave way again to the monotony of carved rock she could see that Velatos was buried in ship traffic, the usual flotsam of freighters, small cruisers, and scavenger ships. She watched a tug extricate one of the freighters with smooth precision before taking it back up into orbit, trying not to think about Goffs. Already another ship was being pulled down to take its place.

The autowalk was subsumed back into city and ended, depositing her at the edge of the Velatos Market. She moved through the crowd into the concourse. Xie's store was hidden in the back corridors; not many locals had the cred to shop there. As Khifi walked in, self-conscious around the elegant glass that seemed to loom into her path, the bald, heavily bearded man looked up from his counter where he'd been reading on his handpad.

"Khif!" he said, genuinely pleased to see her.

"Hello, Xie," she said. She was suddenly glad of the friendly voice, so thoroughly removed from the day's events. "Lema wanted me to pick something up for her."

He unlocked the drawers under his counter and rummaged through them. "How's her latest project coming?"

"She doesn't talk about the art until the art is done, not even to me. Besides, what can I say other than I love it or I don't get it? I'm useless."

He took a tiny, sealed box out of the drawer and set it on the counter. "Maybe you can convince her to use less wood in her pieces, or work smaller. Do you know how expensive it is to fab in that stuff?"

"She likes the feel of it. Says it reminds her of home. How much do we owe you?" Khifi tapped the box.

"Nothing, it's on me." He slid it across the counter to her. "Unnatural fondness for hard-to-obtain organic media aside, she's made me a happy agent."

She picked up the box, small enough to easily fit in her palm. "Uh . . . any instructions?"

"Yes. Let Lema open it, or she'll be quite mad. And tell her I'm eagerly looking forward to her next piece?"

"Will do. Thanks, Xie," Khifi said. She tucked the box into a jacket pocket, made sure it was zipped in tight, and left his shop. Conscious of it against her chest, she was less afraid of being alone with her thoughts on the long walk back to Paxillo.

The Market concourse was even more crowded now, and when she reached the large open floor she saw why. The Velatos Dock manager and a contingent of her upper staff were escorting a trio of tall, bluish-green, portly aliens across the space. The aliens looked halfway between humpty-dumpties and walruses, complete with meter-long whiskers, and seemed to be wearing gigantic purple leg-warmers on their elongated, flattened feet. *Two legs, two eyes*, she thought, thinking of Mole's inevitable questions. *How wide a range that covers.*

She checked the time on her vambrace as she waited for the huddle of people to get out of her way, then glanced back up and did a double-take.

"Peezy!" Khifi called.

The girl was pale, wide-eyed, breathing in fast, shallow gasps as she slid along the wall, arms outstretched against it, her ragged coat unnaturally bulged out around her near-starving frame as she followed the aliens. She froze at Khifi's call, glanced at the departing delegation, then back at Khifi. "You can't be here!" she called back, her voice barely audible over the crowd noise. "Please, I can't . . . "

"Can't what, Peezy? Are you okay?" Khifi asked. She held out her hand as she walked quickly toward her.

Peezy turned her face away and suddenly sprinted into the back of the moving delegation.

All Khifi's own years spent living in the crawlspaces of Tanduou had honed instincts that hadn't dimmed; she threw her hands up over her ears and turned away just as something clapped her on the back, hard, slamming her down onto the polished rock floor.

It took her a few moments to piece together what her body was telling her: pain from her hands and elbows where she'd hit the floor, a prickling along the back of her neck and head as if tiny darts of fire had lodged there, sound muted as if her ears were full of sludge. It was several moments longer before she recognized the screaming and alarms and the acrid smell of smoke for what they were. She tried to push herself up, but vertigo and a stabbing pain in her back sent her crashing back down again.

After a bit, she was able to roll onto her side.

The concourse was in chaos. Fire suppression bots flew in and out of the smoky haze as people rushed back and forth through it. Most were bystanders; emergency responders and security were just starting to flood in. A young woman in a med vest stopped and crouched over her. "How badly are you hurt, ma'am?" she asked.

"Not as bad as others," Khifi said. "I can wait."

The woman started to straighten up, then spotted Khifi's badge. "Oh!" she said. "You're a pilot! Let me get you out of here—"

"No, really, I'm not hurt bad," Khifi said, not at all sure if that was true. "There was a delegation moving through. It's hard to think. Are . . . " She knew it was a dumb question, but couldn't not ask. "Are people going to be okay?"

"No," the medic said. "No, they're not."

She stood up, snapped her fingers. Another medic with an autotravois came over. "Get this one to the group C triage and checked out."

Khifi tried to stand on her own, but couldn't pull together enough strength to rise. The med shook her head. "It's not special treatment," the med said. "Think of it like this: we need you out of the way, too. This is us doing our jobs."

"Okay," Khifi said.

The other medic lowered the autotravois and helped shift her onto it. Already there was a growing line of injured people on other stretchers, and one by one the medic connected them up and began leading the grim train back out of the concourse.

They released her from the overcrowded med bay three hours later, a half-dozen pain patches and blisters of plastiskin dotting her back beneath her tattered and grubby red shirt. She had been told in no uncertain terms not to go too far; as a witness, investigators would want to speak with her as soon as the immediate crisis was over. If she wasn't a pilot, she wasn't sure they'd have let her go at all. Even then, going home wasn't straightforward. Sections of Velatos were cut off by blast doors she'd only seen closed during drills. With the acrid smell of smoke pervading everything and the stricken faces of people as they scurried through the newly placed obstacle maze, the doors were more ominous than reassuring.

She was exhausted and more than a little unsteady with the amount of pain drugs soaking into her back. The box she'd picked up at Xie's shop was battered around the edges but miraculously not crushed, and a gentle shaking of the box did not produce the woeful chorus of broken parts she'd feared. It was easier to worry about the box than think about Peezy, or the Velatos Dock manager and her alien guests; word had rippled through the medical bay that Dock Manager Le had been killed, along with her security chief and four of the six Yuaknari visitors. The prevailing theory was that the bombing was Humans First extremists targeting the Yuaknari, but no one really knew.

Bypassing the damaged and cordoned-off areas meant detouring out of Velatos to Oreasta Dock, and from there taking the autowalk back to Paxillo. It was hard to wrap her head around the idea that Goffs had died this very same day.

Reality still hadn't fixed itself by the time she reached the Paxillo tube station, but the meds were starting to make it harder and harder to care. She bypassed the fast lane and went all the way down to the guided tubes, which were computer-controlled, dead-last for priority, and moved about as fast as rock crept across sand. Buckling herself into the sled, she leaned her head against the hard cushioned side and let her mind drift.

She had dim memories of the sled finally arriving, then being at the door to her tiny apartment. Letting herself in, she saw Lema hard at work at her desk, goggles on, back straight, hands moving slowly in the empty air over her tablet as she worked a 3D simulation only she could see. Khifi smiled; the world narrowing to just this place, just the two of them, and things were miraculously, mostly okay after all.

Khifi slipped off her boots as quietly as she could, tiptoed past Lema's workspace, and tumbled, already half asleep, face-first into the bed.

Waking was a slow climb up, fighting the gravity of grief, exhaustion, and the lingering pull of the meds. Finally, Lema's voice broke through and lifted her the rest of the way. "You awake?" she was asking.

"I am," Khifi answered, mostly convinced it was true.

"Are you okay?"

"I'm fine."

"You're a liar, an idiot, and I'm very angry with you," Lema said.

Those also seemed likely true. "Oh," she managed. She still hadn't decided if she was going to open her eyes. "I'm sorry."

"I wasn't expecting you back for nearly another hour, and I get up to go beep some food and find you collapsed on the bed covered in bloody bandages."

"Sorry," Khifi mumbled again.

"Why didn't you *tell* me you were home?"

"Didn't want to bother you."

"Idiot. Why didn't you tell me you were *hurt*?"

"It's not that bad."

"Liar," Lema said. "Xie called to ask if you'd made it home safe. What the hell were you doing in Velatos?"

"Dock shut down. Went to get your thing." Khifi cracked open one eye, but could only see Lema's thigh where she sat beside her on the bed. "I may be lying on your box," she added. It was hard to separate out the various discomforts.

"Wait," Lema said. "Why was the dock shut down *before* the bomb? The docks never close."

"Goffs died. Tube accident. Everything's gone all wrong and none of it makes sense."

She was aware of the shift in the bed as Lema got up, and must have dozed off because next thing she knew Lema was beside her again and touching her shoulder gently. "Can you sit up?" Lema asked. It took her a few moments but she did, and blinked blearily as her wife pressed a steaming mug into her hands. "Drink this."

Khifi took a sip; it was one of Lema's expensive, imported teas, a blend hand-picked by monks on Fadsji. She'd always been more of a coffee person, but it was warm and the rich fragrance was comforting. She suspected that was because she associated it with Lema. "Thanks," she said.

Lema reached past her, picked up the half-crushed box, and tucked it out of the way on top of the nightshelf. "So. Tell me."

Khifi had been nine when she hopped a cargo freighter out of her home colony. By ten, she knew every crawler in Velatos and most from neighboring Myonota and Freyella clusters. She knew the location of every fixed electronic eye and which corners they were blind to, and she could pick out the hum of a floater above all but the loudest crowds. Tanduou thrived by treading the gray area between security and privacy, and crawlers took advantage of the lack of an omnipresent surveillance state in the same way all the back-dock dealers and covert arms merchants did. Systems had been updated and changed over the years, but she'd never lost the instinct to notice and remember them. It was not a challenge to slip out of sight.

Maintenance corridors ran behind the public spaces. The service hatch was right where she remembered it being, the seemingly random marks beside it crawler code for the current nesters. None of them were familiar. Although stories of generations of crawlers were shared and reshared, an oral history perpetuated by the need to get through one day after another and the long slow nights in between, everyone who had been part of her nest was long gone. The crawl only tolerated adults in memory.

She climbed through the hatch and crouched on the far side as the door shut behind her. Crossing into the crawl after all this time was a punch in the gut. Everything felt smaller, dirtier, more unremarkable than it used to.

She turned on the handlight she'd brought. The tiny tunnel leapt into stark relief.

Walking bent over under the low ceiling, she followed a pipe, looking for the remembered crack in the wall hidden behind it. She barely fit through. On the far side was another tunnel, and she followed that until it turned, sloping downward. More pipes appeared from out of the ceiling and walls, slowly filling up her available headspace until she was afraid she might have to get down on her hands and knees. Did she really call this home for nearly six years?

There was another dip in the floor, this one sharp enough that she almost fell, catching herself with hands on the rough rock wall. Once she got down to where the floor was level again, she could walk almost upright. Memories of running, hunched over, through the tunnel and leaping down off that dip into what felt like open space seemed almost fantastical now. *I was always trying to fly.*

From here it was easy. Three turns, and then a long wide stretch where thick sewage pipes ran overhead. Every six hours the pipe system was flushed out with steam, so this was one of the rare places in the crawl that was comfortably warm. It also caused a sticky dust layer to form over everything;

she'd spent hours trying to get it out of her hair and clothes until she gave it up as futile.

She'd hoped Mole would be here, or Birdie, but the corridor was empty save for the thick mat of insulation scraps and packing foam that made up the crawler nest. In one corner she spotted an old blanket she'd given Birdie years ago, now coated with the same dust as everything else here.

As she stood there trying to decide where to go next, she saw a rough-cut foam block shift slightly. "It's Fox," she called out softly. "I'm by myself. I came looking for Mole."

After a long moment, the block shifted again and a face peered out from beneath it. The boy's face was swollen, one eye shot red and surrounded by a black-purple bruise. He'd been crying.

"Gums?" she asked. "Can I come closer?"

He nodded, trembling. She moved slowly, taking a pack of vitawafers out of her pocket. Crouching, she held the pack out, and he sat up and took it. He was gaunt, shirtless, and his upper body was covered with ugly bruises and a sour-looking gash crusted with blood. Reaching over her shoulder, Khifi peeled off one of the med patches on her back, shook it to make sure it still had some life in it, then carefully spread it over the cut. "This will help a little," she said. At least it should clear up the infection, if not much else. "What happened? You were with Peezy."

The boy started, dropping the wafers, and began shaking in earnest. "Was here," he said.

"You and Peezy were here? When you got hurt?"

"No," he said. "Man who catched us, he was here."

"He caught you here?"

"No. He was here *now*. Just before you."

Khifi stood, pulling a blade from where she kept it tucked at the small of her back, half-expecting to find someone looming up behind her. The corridor remained empty and she heard nothing but the faint susurration of the pipes. "What did he look—" she started to ask, but Gums was back under the foam, out of sight. The wafers, moments ago scattered across the floor, were gone with him.

This time, when she turned around again, she was not alone.

"Fox," Mole said. He was standing near the turn in the corridor, a half step from being able to disappear. He looked unhappy to see her in his home territory. She couldn't blame him; adults in the crawl were dangerous.

"I came to ask you about Peezy," Khifi said.

"You seen her?"

"I saw her," she answered carefully. "She ever talk about aliens? You know, in a scared or angry way?"

"Peezy *loves* the bugs. Nearly gotten caught a hunnerd times out in the open, making pictures. Always wants to go see 'em, then talks about it no-stop for days." Mole moved into the room, fear forgotten, and rummaged through a corner of the nest. He came up with a handful of vellum sheets and a handpad.

Mole handed her the sheets. On them were passably good drawings of an E'zon, a Tuarig, and two aliens she did not recognize. The girl had had some real talent. Khifi's eyes teared up, and she wiped them with the back of her hand.

"Peezy not coming back," Mole said. It wasn't quite a question.

"No, she's not."

Mole inhaled deeply, held it, then let it out again. "Okay," he said.

"Can I keep these?" Khifi asked.

"Yeah." He dropped his hands to his side, the handpad dangling from his fingers.

"What's that?" Khifi asked.

"Dunno," Mole said. "Never seen it before right now. None a' ours."

"May I see?"

He held it out. The surface was still shiny, free of crawl dust. Khifi turned it on. The Humans First logo flashed up onto the screen, and she turned it off with a startled jerk. "Are you sure this wasn't here before?" she asked.

"Sure sure," Mole said. "Not like we got so much nice stuffs we can keep any secret from t'other."

That much she certainly remembered from her days in the crawl.

"Gums said there was someone here, the man who'd caught him and Peezy," Khifi said. "You need to go through this whole place and make sure there's nothing else, and then I think you all need to find a different place to nest for a bit. The harder to get to, the better. Where's Tuck?"

"Waiting 'round the corner," Mole said. "What's going on, Fox?"

"I don't know," she said, "but I don't think it's over. Be careful."

"You too, Fox," he said.

"Don't forget Gums."

Mole almost smiled. "Forget nobody," he said, "'til they forget us."

She tossed the handpad in the first flash recycler she found. Two more off-shifts before she was flying again, and if she couldn't be home, she wanted nothing so much as to be a half-hundred kilometers above it all.

When she rejoined the upper world and the Paxillo concourse, the crowds were noticeably thinned and most were gathered near the center where a column of large screens normally ran the endless litany of trading news, ship arrivals and departures, and gossip. Now, Mr. Balcko's face was on every screen, a dozen mouths moving simultaneously. " . . . has been successfully removed, with no remaining danger to the citizens of Oreasta," he was saying. "I will be following up with casualty information from Notomyo as soon as the emergency teams have finished their work. If anyone has information, or saw anything suspicious prior to either incident, please contact your nearest security officer. Be assured, we will catch the perpetrators of these acts. Thank you."

Balcko's face disappeared, replaced by the familiar scroll of the hourly trade bulletin.

One of the Paxillo cargo haulers stood not far away. Khifi touched his broad shoulder. "Excuse me," she said. "Something happened since Velatos?"

"Bomb in Notomyo about half an hour ago," he said. "They just found another in Oreasta before it went off. Whole cluster is in security lockdown. I tell you, if *I* find those assvalves what put the bombs? Then someone really get hurt. No one messes with Tanduou, not our people, not our bugs, not our nothing." He looked her up and down. "You're a pilot, right? You get me."

"I get you," she said.

He grunted, nodding, and went back to watching the boards.

Khifi's vambrace buzzed. She tapped it, and Inchbug's voice echoed out of her earpiece. "Fox?" she asked. "Mr. Balcko asked to check if you were going to the security debriefing about the Velatos bomb."

"Yeah. I'm on my way now," she said.

"Balcko said you were there?"

"Close enough for a few new scars," she said. "How are things up there?"

"Balcko called in terrorism experts from Haudernelle. Uberman docked them about an hour ago, but other than that nothing is moving up here at all."

"What about the Rimbolan freighter?"

"The Enclavers loaded up everything they could fit in a shuttle and abandoned it. Unofficially, of course, so we can't declare salvage rights for three more days. I'm heading over to Luida to fill in for a sick comm op, so see you when I see you. Be careful, okay?"

"I try," she said.

"Try harder." Inchbug signed off.

Khifi made her way over to a long, winding, reinforced corridor that ended in thick xglass doors with PAXILLO SECURITY stenciled on them in large block letters. The officer at the doors scanned in her id. "Room three, at the back."

"Thanks," she said, and went in.

Room three was a small, nondescript conference room. Paxillo's head of security, Chief Bell, sat there with another security officer with a Velatos patch and chief's stripes that looked—and likely were—newly sewn on. Two more men in suits sat with them.

"Ah, Fox," Chief Bell said, standing up and extending his hand. "I trust you're recovering?"

"Nothing that'll slow me down," she said, taking the one free chair.

"This is Acting Chief Tres of Velatos Dock. Joining us is Mr. Allen and Mr. Arve, who just arrived from Haudernelle. They're private consultants here at the behest of Mr. Balcko," Bell explained. "If you could go through what brought you to Velatos Dock, anything you might have seen, impressions you have, we'd appreciate it."

"I'll do my best; my memories are kind of fuzzy and unreliable," she said. "I'd gone to Velatos on a shopping errand, and was on the way back. I had just seen the aliens in the concourse when the bomb went off."

Mr. Arve leaned forward and opened a display window on the tabletop. "Ms. Iwalewa—"

"Call me Fox," she said reflexively.

"There is limited security footage of the incident," Arve said. "We've identified the bomber as an illegal underground squatter. We believe she and other 'crawlers' have been actively recruited by a hate group called Humans First."

"I don't think that's likely," Khifi said.

"No? We have the detonation on video." Arve tapped open a picture. Peezy was standing near a column, expression unreadable, the Yuaknari delegation in the foreground passing by. He tapped the picture again, forwarding it. "And here you seem to be speaking to her."

"She looked scared," Khifi said.

"You knew her?"

"A little. I know for sure she didn't hate aliens."

Arve's partner, Allen, folded his arms over his chest. "Hate groups are very good at radicalizing the underprivileged, many of whom are desperate for a purpose or an opportunity to hurt those more fortunate than themselves. Each and every one of them is a ticking time-bomb. You're *naïve* if you think otherwise."

"Mr. Allen, you've been on Tanduou for what, an hour now?" Khifi said. "Tanduou's crawlers are here because whatever life they walked away from was even worse. They want to be left alone. They don't have an agenda beyond that. They're *kids*."

"So you did talk to her?"

"I asked if she was okay," Khifi said. "She ran off, and after that I only remember the smoke and the alarms."

"So you *knew* she was the bomber and didn't disclose this sooner?"

Khifi sat up straighter, met Allen's eyes without flinching. "I don't know anything for sure, but if Peezy did have a bomb it's because someone forced it on her. Word was someone had grabbed her a few days earlier, and another crawler barely got away with his life. *That's* who you need to be looking for."

"How do you know this?" Arve asked.

"Fox has lived in Paxillo most of her life," Bell interjected. "She knows many of the local crawlers and has a degree of their trust, which has been an asset to us in a few situations over the years."

Arve pulled up another picture. "This was our Notomyo bomber," he said. It was a crawler boy, maybe barely ten. "Humans First propaganda was found on him. He had a handpad we were able to extract the memory from, and it had a propagandist video blaming aliens for the poor conditions so many humans live under. It was compelling. Mr. Balcko has initiated a sweep of all the underground areas to look for additional evidence."

Khifi pounded her fist on the table. "If there's evidence, it's planted," she said. "There have been strangers down in the crawl, going through their things, *leaving* stuff, just like this handpad you talk about."

Allen's eyebrows shot up. "Do you have proof of this?"

She thought about the handpad she'd stuffed in the flash-recycler. "No," she said at last. "But the crawlers—"

"Are not exactly reliable sources," Allen said. "You seem to have a lot of information that you are conveniently only sharing now. If these things happened, why weren't authorities informed?"

"Because no one else *cares* about the crawlers," she said.

"Well." Allen stood up, and after a moment, Arve did too. "We certainly do now, don't we? I believe that will be all."

"For now," Arve added. He was already tapping at his wristcomm as the two consultants left the room.

"Sorry, Fox," Chief Bell said. "We'll get to the truth of this. It just might get ugly for a while, while we do."

She stood. "It's ugly enough already," she said. "But thank you for the optimism."

Frustration propelled her back up the corridor and into the concourse, and a half-minute later she found herself moving through the doors into the Hellwater, half-hoping Burnout would be there and say something stupid to her face.

You're losing it, Khif, she thought. She ran one hand over her short, wiry hair and stepped up to the bar. "A Ceres Triple," she said, and the bartender set one in front of her before she'd even blinked. She downed it in one shot, then stared morosely at the empty bulb until a hand gently touched her shoulder.

She spun, half-reaching for her knife, when she recognized Stickles.

"Saw you come in. You okay?" he asked.

"No," she said. "No, I'm not."

"You want to talk? I know I'm not Quizzie, but you know I've got your back."

Khifi pushed the empty bulb away. "When I went with Candles to do his flight-check, he caught on immediately that his engines sounded wrong.

Someone had stuffed a sock in one of the air intakes. Most people don't listen enough to pick something like that up, but he did. A lot of people would've told him he was imagining it."

Stickles nodded. "Told you he was good."

"Yeah, but here's my point," Khifi said. "All that's going on? With the bombs, and saying the crawlers are behind it? Even with Goff's accident. It sounds *wrong*. It sounds like someone has stuffed a sock in Tanduou's engine, pitch is a half-note off from the truth, and I'm not sure anyone is hearing it but me."

Stickles stared down at his hands on the bar. "I trust your instincts, Fox, but damn. What have you got?"

She told him about Peezy and Gums, the Humans First handpad, the stranger in the crawl. "She drew pictures of the aliens, Stickles," she said, pulling the vellum sheets out of her jacket and spreading them out on the bar. "Do these look like the art of hate?"

"No," he said. "But . . . if not the crawlers, why pin it on them? What does anyone gain?"

"I don't know. It makes no fucking sense."

"You told the consultants?"

"Some of it," she said. "I don't think they were listening. I'd be happier if we were relying on our own people rather than outsiders to sort out what's going on."

He considered. "What do you think we should do?"

"I don't know," Khifi said. "Keep our eyes and ears open, listen for everything that doesn't sound right, make sure all the facts are out there before anything is done that can't be undone. What else can we do?"

"I guess just that," Stickles said. "If you find out anything more, you'll tell me?"

"Yeah."

He pushed back from the bar. "I'm covering Ops for your shift again. So maybe we should talk it over then, after we've had a chance to think about it?"

"Yeah," she said again.

"Better than just sitting here drinking all day," Stickles said, "although I won't pretend I don't see the appeal. Go home, Fox. You look like a bomb hit you."

"Har har," she said, but he was right. Stickles left. She swiped her credit chit over the bar, added a healthy tip, and headed home.

"Khif, I love you, but if you don't stop fidgeting I'm going to smother you with your own pillow," Lema murmured.

Khifi stomped toward Paxillo's main concourse. She had a crick in her neck from spending most of the night in a chair, and her stomach had wound itself into so many knots she wasn't sure she'd ever feel hungry again.

Her thoughts lost in a maze of whys and what-ifs, she had taken several more steps before her brain registered that someone had whispered her name. She stopped, turned, saw the small alcove in the corridor full of piping, thought she saw uneasy shifting in the shadows.

Walking back, she casually leaned one shoulder against the wall beside the opening, taking out her handpad as if checking an incoming message. "Mole?" she asked softly. He was there, his face and eyes red and puffy as if he'd been crying. She heard a sob, but it didn't come from him. She spotted a tiny, dirty face behind the bigger boy.

"This's Tuck, new kid I told you bout," Mole said.

"You two aren't safe out here, even on good days," Khifi said. "You come across the wrong security guard, and you're going to be joining the bone pile out an airlock. What the hell were you thinking?"

"Nowhere safe in the crawl," Mole said. "Lots of people, no uniforms, but move like authority and got guns. Birdie ain't come back yet and Gums ran away last night and there was alarms and we was scared. Ran into Terkle an' he said same thing happened over in Luida Dock. Some'a us gonna try to get over to Odinella cluster, but that a hard journ. We got nowhere else to go and Birdie's not here being in charge and Tuck is always crying and hungry and there's doors down and smoke in the crawl." Tears began making fresh tracks down his dirty cheeks. "Can run, but only by myself."

"Mole, look at me," she said, and he raised his face to hers. "Try to find a safe place, somewhere you wouldn't normally go. Doesn't need to be comfortable, just hard to find. If you can't find anything—and this is last resort, you understand?—there's a shop in Velatos Dock owned by a guy named Xie-Yan Che. He's a friend of mine. If you go, you can't steal from him, not even a little, not even once. You understand that? Tell him Khifi sent you. That's my real name," she said.

Mole shivered. "Telling names is bad luck, Fox. If you see Birdie or Gums—"

"Just go," Khifi said. "Be smart. And if you can get yourselves out of the cluster? Take it."

Tuck wrapped his skinny arms tightly around her legs, just for a moment, then Mole grabbed his hand and pulled him back into the dark. She watched after the door closed for a long while and wondered if she'd ever see either again.

She drifted into the Paxillo concourse, eyes on the distant elevators up to Dock control. The footsteps were just part of the background noise, one set slightly offbeat among dozens, until she thought she heard Mole, impossibly, calling her name over the noise.

Oh, you fool kid! she thought, whirling around to confront him for following her out into the open.

She got her arm up just in time to block the blade, but it hit her vambrace with enough force to make her stumble back. Her attacker was dressed in grubby clothes, a young man with wild eyes, dilated pupils, a crawler by all the looks of him except he was too old. "Humans First, Humans forever!" he shouted, raising the knife again.

Around them the crowd had fallen back. "Put the knife down!" she yelled, backing away. "I am not your enemy!"

"You bring them here. Your alien masters!" He rushed her but she was ready, dodging away and pulling out her own knife.

"You don't want to do this," she said. Where the hell was security?

He swung wide and she dodged again, but this time he brought his other hand around to grab her arm, then kicked at her legs. It was a glancing blow, but enough to send her sprawling onto her butt on the floor. He was grinning now.

Khifi threw her own blade. It caught him in the shoulder and he dropped his knife. She scrambled to her feet, cursing the lingering stiffness from her Velatos injuries, and had another knife drawn from her boot by the time he had pulled hers out and was brandishing it back at her. He tried the wide swing again, probably hoping to catch her the same way he had before, but she anticipated the move and feinted to the left, then moved under his swing and kicked him sideways, hard in the chest.

Her attacker stumbled back, landing on one knee. People behind him scrambled out of his way. Getting up, he grunted, stabbed forward at Khifi with her own knife, and when she stepped back out of his reach he turned abruptly and fled through a scattering, panicked crowd.

She stood, breathing hard. Someone had just tried to kill her. The realization of how close he had come—if she hadn't turned, or had turned a half-second later—hit her like a rock, and she turned and ran for the elevator doors.

There was no guard at the gate. She hopped it, scanned herself in, and threw herself into the first elevator that opened, feeling like she couldn't breathe. Tapping madly at her damaged vambrace she tried to call Lema, but it made a sickly buzz before going dead.

The elevator opened onto the control deck, and she was nearly knocked over by the security guard who should have been manning the gates below. "Fox! So sorry, I need to go, there's something going on down—" He paused, getting a better look at her. "—You okay?"

"Someone tried to kill me," she said. She unwrapped her dead vambrace from her arm, only then realizing her jacket was soaked dark with blood.

Stickles was up on the command platform with Mr. Balcko and a pair of guards. "Fox?" he asked. His eyes were wide.

Jonjon was, as always, beside the coffee dispenser. He walked forward and pressed his mug into her shaking hands. She was grateful for the warmth. "Some guy with a knife. He ran away."

Balcko turned to the guard. "Go find out what happened. Have a word with Mr. Arve and Mr. Allen, and send security up. This is unacceptable."

"Yes, sir," the guard said, and vanished into the elevator.

Candles put a gentle hand on her elbow and propelled her toward one of the unused console seats near Sparkle, who was busy on the ground comms.

"We're in full security quarantine now," Stickles said. "Mr. Balcko will be overseeing things from here until his team gives the all-clear."

"When is the Dockmaster returning?" Khifi asked.

"Not until the active situation is over," Balcko said. "Mr. Lohra has elected to remain on Guratahan Sfazil rather than risk becoming another target. In the meantime, as the most senior Cluster Manager, I am in charge." He said that last as if he expected to be challenged on it.

She had no intention of doing so; with the Dockmaster gone, someone needed to run things, and Balcko was right that he was most senior. "Of course," she said. "Just let me know what you need me to do."

"Although we're not open to normal business, I have a cargo crate of medical supplies that needs to get to Novodinia from Astrolyr in the Myonota Cluster," Stickles said.

"Okay. I can take it," she said.

Kaiju stood. "No," he said. "She's hurt. I'll go."

Stickles glanced at Khifi, then at Kaiju. "Of course," he said. "We're still waiting on that medic. It's all yours."

Kaiju nodded and left.

Khifi looked down at her arm. Blood was crusting dark along the slit in her sleeve where the edge of the vambrace had been. Now that adrenaline was wearing off she felt cold all over.

When Sparkle paused on the comms, Khifi asked her, "Where's Knits?"

"Weren't expecting any work to do with the docks shut down," said Sparkle. "I'm only here because we're still shifting some stuff in cargo. Inchbug is supposed to be coming in. It's bad down on the floors, and is only gonna get worse when word gets out that someone tried to kill a pilot. Hang on, cargo biz." She went back to her headset.

Jonjon was explaining the coffee dispenser to Candles and Balcko was busy with Stickles, so she rolled her chair over to Inchbug's empty station. Above, the endless shuffle of ships was at a standstill. Down where the Rimbolan freighter had been, a small, sleek military-style cruiser had taken its place at one of the berths.

"What's that ship doing here?" she exclaimed.

Sparkle put one hand over her mic. "That's the security consultants that

Mr. Balcko brought in from Haudernelle. Allen and Arve and crew? Didn't you meet them?"

"That ship was in outer orbit when we took the freighter up," Khifi said.

"Can't have been. First bomb hadn't happened yet."

"It was here," Khifi said. "I saw it with my own eyes, *that* ship and a handful of cargos. I never forget a ship."

"I don't—" Sparkle started to say, when the elevators opened and a pair of security personnel from Velatos came in.

Mr. Balcko stood up. "You two will please escort Ms. Iwalewa down to secure holding and process her for arrest, on charges of aiding and abetting terrorists," he said. At everyone's look of confusion, Balcko stabbed a finger at Khifi. "Right, idiotic superstitious nicknames. *Fox*," he said. "Her. Arrest *her*."

"What!?" Khifi said, already rising to her feet.

"You confessed to Mr. Easson—*Stickles*—that you deliberately destroyed evidence from the crawlers to hide it from our investigators," Balcko said.

Khifi stared at Stickles. "That's a misunderstanding," she said. "Stickles, tell them—"

Stickles didn't meet her eyes. "She was drunk, over at the Hellwater," he said. "Lots of people will confirm we talked. She told me of her involvement in the crawler attacks."

"That's a lie!" Khifi shouted. The security guards glanced at Balcko, then began moving toward her. Both had hands on their pistols.

"Stickles?" Khifi said. "Don't do this to me."

"It's on your own head, Fox," he said, looking down at his hands.

"There's something going on here," she said, desperate. "Those Haudernelle security consultants are a sham. That ship was in orbit when we took the Rimbolan freighter up, before the very first bomb. And—"

"If she says one more word, shoot her," Balcko snarled.

Sparkle, Candles, and Jonjon were all staring. "I'm being framed," she said, raising her hands, feeling tears welling up in her eyes. "You all know me."

As one of the guards reached for her arm, the elevator behind them chimed and the doors opened. Inchbug stepped in carrying a tray of takeout.

"Hey, everyone, I brought—" she started to say, then stopped mid-sentence. "—What the hell is going on?"

Both guards turned toward her.

"*I* know you enough," Candles said, and in one blinding-fast move struck out with a hand, knocking the nearest guard down.

Shit, Khifi thought. She hauled the other guard off-balance toward her and brought his head down in hard contact with her knee. As he dropped, she ran past him, sprinting for the still-open elevator doors.

"Stop her!" Balcko yelled. Stickles was staring, his face pale. The guards up on the command platform scrambled for their weapons, then dodged as a full pot of coffee came sailing over the railing, leaving a spinning trail of near-boiling liquid along its arc.

"It just slipped out of my hands, I swear!" Jonjon yelled, his eyes wide with what seemed genuine surprise.

Sparkle had both her hands raised. "I have nothing to do with any of this!"

Khifi threw herself into the elevator past a still-stunned Inchbug just as the doors closed. With everything on lockdown, and not even the crawl safe, there was nowhere to run except up. She stabbed the button for the docks and hoped Balcko's men weren't going to be fast enough to stop her.

She reached the bays. Slamming and locking the door behind her, she shorted the lock with her knife before racing over to the *Lazy Dog* and powering it up. She wanted to jump in and fly away as fast as she could, but she remembered Goffs, dead of an apparent accident just as everything else started going wrong. She wanted to scream as she moved around her ship, checking everything, listening, hoping, until her breath caught.

A single coupling dangled loose beneath the *Lazy Dog*'s belly, just barely visible in the shadows. *That's a cooling line*, she thought, reconnecting it, then checked the others. All six were undone, their ends tucked up out of sight.

Balcko wouldn't know to do that; he wasn't a pilot, had come up through the ranks via security. Stickles, though . . . Stickles who had just tried to send her out on a cargo run.

I trusted him, Khifi thought. *I thought he was a friend.*

He also knew enough to know that the coolant couplings wouldn't change the engine pitch, not until the ship started to overheat. She furiously wiped tears from her face as she reconnected the last of them. Everything else checked out. If she'd missed those, she'd have plastered herself and her ship all over Paxillo and taken the truth, whatever it was, with her.

At the helm of the *Lazy Dog*, she reached under her console and yanked free the tug's beacon. Then she hit her engines and was out and moving up into Tanduou's crowded skies.

Now what? she thought. It was only a matter of time before Balcko mustered someone to come after her. Or no time at all: she could see another tug, coming fast toward her from the other side of Velatos Tower. As if on cue, Kaiju's voice crackled to life on her comms.

"Fox?" he said.

"Yes, Kaiju?" she asked. What else was there to say?

"I'm on Ryeneck's secret love line," he said. "I'm getting some weird instructions from Paxillo control that I do not like. Do you have any insight on this?"

"Does it involve shooting me out of the sky as a traitor?"

"As it happens, yes," Kaiju said.

"This whole thing: Goffs, the bombs, hate groups recruiting crawlers—it's rotten. I started to ask questions and someone tried to knife me, and then my ship was sabotaged. Stickles and Balcko are saying I'm a terrorist, and I have no proof to convince you I'm not."

"Very well, Air Captain, you don't leave me much choice," he said. "I'm going to hail you on the official comms and tell you to land or be brought down, and then I'm going to chase you straight up right on your ass like bugs fucking, in that maneuver that messes up tower radar like nothing else. You better have a plan by the time I need to say I can't catch you after all."

She already was nose up and heading for space, intent on reaching Guratahan Sfazil and the dockmaster. Above her the sea of waiting ships was parting, getting out of her way.

Inchbug's voice cut in on the main comms, which the *Lazy Dog* should have been blocked from. "Transit Sat Four moving into position," she said. "Should have weapons tracking in . . . Oh! It's just rebooted. Signal loss for twelve . . . eleven . . . "

Khifi punched the *Lazy Dog*'s engines up to full, Kaiju right on her tail. She couldn't get to the Gee in the time left. Between here and the planet, heading straight out, there was only one thing. "You're gonna want to suddenly break off in three," she said to Kaiju.

The abandoned Rimbolan freighter lay dead ahead, its wide cargo doors still gaping open. Pulling all the *Lazy Dog*'s arms into tight formation around the tug's body, she aimed for the opening.

"Online in four . . . three," Inchbug said. Kaiju's tug, the *Nobunaga*, veered, just enough to skirt past the outer hull of the freighter as the *Lazy Dog* was swallowed whole.

She hit the braking jets hard, throwing herself forward against her harness, and hoped the former owners had done a thorough job of taking as much with them as they could. The *Lazy Dog* had more armor than some light military cruisers, but hit the wrong thing in the wrong way and anything could rip you open like you were paper.

The far end of the cargo bay loomed ahead, closing fast. A large pile of crates floated around the disabled cargo drones. Khifi braced herself as the *Lazy Dog* bowled into the abandoned cargo and came to rest in a pile of them.

She jumped in her seat as something red oozed all over the front window of the *Lazy Dog*. It was a long, terrible moment before she realized it was vegetable pulp seeping out through tears in the flexible crate material currently plastered across her front hull. Inflatable crates and rotten tomatoes. She started laughing, couldn't help herself, nor as it quickly turned to all-consuming sobs. Goffs was dead. Murdered? Stickles had betrayed her to her face. The idea that she might never see her wife again was a tiny seed of a black hole in the center of her heart, threatening to pull in and crush everything she cared about.

No, she thought, pulling herself together. *I'm not done fighting yet.*

Her systems were still mostly green. She'd scraped off a few external antennae, but nothing worse. As quickly as she could, she shut down her engines and used her fine maneuvering thrusters to turn around to face out of the long tunnel from her pile of crates, a spider at the back of its cave ready to jump.

"*Lazy Dog*?" Her comms crackled to life again. "This is TexLex over in Luida Dock, calling on the Ryeneck Line."

She stared at it. Who could she trust? Maybe this was a stalling tactic to keep her pinned down. *You are anyway,* she told herself. "Fox here," she said, keeping her voice as even as she could.

"All of Velatos is shut down and Paxillo control is currently offline," TexLex said. "I assume either because of mutiny, or because the mutiny is over. There's no longer a safe channel between you and your team."

"No offense, TexLex, but I don't know you," Fox said. "How do I know I can trust you?"

"Don't got an answer for that, Fox," TexLex said. "Sure would like to know what kind of a shitwell you got my Inchbug spinning down into, though."

Ah. Khifi knew Inchbug had a partner in Luida Dock. "The crawlers didn't set the bombs, and they're being framed," she said. "If I can get back down, there's someone I might be able to get answers out of."

"And how are you gonna do that?" TexLex said.

"I don't know. I—"

"Right fuck you don't, because you can't. You're stuck in your little hidey-hole. What is that thing Inchbug is always quoting you for? Being your best as a team or no good at all? Well, being a captain means not just leading, but trusting your team, and like it or not you've drafted a lot of us into your mess."

"I trusted Stickles."

"Yeah, well, Stickles is nice enough, but you can only trust him to look out for himself. Asking more from him is like trying to get beer back outta piss. You say it's not the crawlers? Give us a chance to prove it. But do it fast, 'cause half the cluster is rioting and Balcko and his offworld security team are rounding up every grubby kid they can lay hands on. As soon as Balcko manages to negotiate a price with one of the ships in orbit—halfa which saw right where you went and are trying to figure out what that info is worth in both creds and trouble—you're done. Your time is running out."

"You know a mover named Sniv?"

"By sight *and* smell," TexLex said.

"He tried to hire me as a tour guide to the crawl right before this mess started. That can't be coincidence."

"We'll find him. Anything else?"

"Yeah. My wife, Lema," Khifi said. "I don't think Paxillo is safe, and she should get out if she can. Please tell her I love her and I'm sorry."

TexLex's voice was softer when she replied. "Will try, Fox. Hold out if you can."

Khifi disconnected and stared out through the frozen streaks of tomato pulp at the small square of space at the end of her tunnel, braced for the moment when it became the end of her life.

When her comms came back to life nearly an hour later she wished it was TexLex again, but it wasn't. "Ms. Iwalewa," Mr. Balcko's voice came over the docking control channel. "As soon as I find out which ship is sheltering you, I'm going to blow it and everyone in it out of orbit. Is that what you want? More innocent dead?"

"Find me if you can," she said.

"Or . . . " he said. "I have these buttons here in the Dockmaster's private office. Do you want to know what they do? This one locks down residences. Not unreasonable during martial law. How about apartment 4188 in the orange block of Paxillo Deep? Middle of the night, door already locked, who would notice?"

That was Khifi and Lema's apartment. "Don't—" she started to say.

"Oh, and did you know I can also not only turn off oxygen, but turn on reclamation to filter it back out?" he said. "It's not fast, but it *is* thorough. I wonder how long it'd take to scrub the oxygen out of a space that small? A few hours?"

"Mr. Balcko, Lema has nothing to do with any of this," Khifi said. "Let her go and I'll agree to whatever you want."

"I don't know how much use that would be to me. You've already badly interfered in my business," Mr. Balcko said. "I'm going to think about your offer for a while and get back to you."

Balcko was gone. Khifi let out a cry of rage and punched the console. Even the dampers in her suit glove weren't enough to soften the blow and, needing the pain, she punched it again, harder, until her fist felt on the verge of breaking. She had no leverage to force Balcko to let Lema go, nor any confidence he'd keep his word even if she did everything he said.

One thing she knew, she couldn't just sit and wait for Balcko's next move. She unbuckled from her seat and pulled on her exosuit. There was a spare vambrace in the utility locker along with a handful of idled bots. She slipped on the vambrace with gratitude and synced it to her tug's systems, tucking a crackbot into the exosuit's pocket.

Cycling herself out the *Lazy Dog*'s airlock, she checked her sensors. As she'd expected rads were off the charts, but her suit could handle it for five or six hours before it became a concern. She'd be lucky to live that long anyway. She had to shove several leaking crates of miscellaneous goo away from the bay's back wall to uncover the main control console, but it was still live. She pulled a cable from her tug's underside over and jacked it in.

That connection was purely information-transfer, but having the freighter's full eyes and ears in addition to the *Lazy Dog*'s would help. It wasn't, however, enough.

There were times in the life of a tug pilot that you had to move someone who didn't want to be moved. Taking the crackbot from her pocket, she thumbed it on and let go. The bot hovered midair for a few moments, then zipped across the short space to attach itself to the console. It extended several hair-thin needles into the case and blinked in escalating complexity. Khifi left it to do its job and climbed back into the *Lazy Dog*.

She didn't know what good having control of the Rimbolan would do her, but she didn't have enough resources to be picky. She was conscious of every breath she took, of another's running out.

Back at the helm, she routed signals from the freighter's sensors to her secondary display. Pulling up her data from earlier, she compared it to the cruiser parked in Paxillo: same ship, without a doubt. The public docking feeds had it listed as the *Escarre*, with a South Haudernelle registration too recent to be entirely believable.

It had not been in orbit alone, and one of the seven small cargo ships she'd seen it with now sat in dock between it and the Martian freighter *Olympian Razor*. She'd hardly begun a scan before the rest jumped out at her: one each in the other six docks of Velatos cluster. Whatever was happening had been planned well in advance, and she had blundered right into its path. *I wonder what Goffs did to get in their way*, she thought. *And if either one of us slowed them down at all.*

Her console pinged. The bot reported back that it had easily rerouted the freighter's command systems and transferred control to her helm.

Tugs didn't receive public broadcast feeds because they were a potentially lethal distraction in the air, but she piped them in now via the Rimbolan, pulling up Velatos official news. The very first image on the screen was a stillpic of Candles. "No, no," she said, turning the audio up.

" . . . temporary assignment in Paxillo Docks. He fled during the mass arrest of the conspirators led by Iwalewa, but was later seen being shoved out an airlock by masked people with anti-althuman slogans inked on his body. Cluster Manager Balcko released a statement that it is believed that members of Iwalewa's group targeted him out of concern that during his time working among them he may have unwittingly gained information or been able to identify more members of the conspiracy. Shortly after—"

Khifi closed the feed. *They killed Candles and blamed me for it . . . !*

Anger was a star igniting. She punched her comms, trying to reach anyone on Ryeneck's secret line.

"Can't talk long," TexLex answered.

"Tell me you have good news, TexLex. Tell me someone got to my wife and warned her to get out."

"We tried, Fox. The tube lanes under Paxillo have been shut down for hours now, and cluster comms are keyed to emergency personnel only."

"Balcko is killing her," Khifi said. "Right now. And I can't do *anything* to stop him. And Candles! I didn't—"

"Save the timewidth for things we can't guess on our own," TexLex said.

Khifi gritted her teeth. TexLex was right, of course. "The cargo ships that came in, one per dock."

"Balcko's consultants ordered them. They're rounding up every single crawler in Velatos and say they're holding them on the cargo ships until it can be determined if any of them have legal status, or which are involved in Humans First. And after the latest bombing and Candles's death, it's probably safer for them than out on the floors," TexLex said. "People are angry and not thinking, and no one inside Velatos is hearing a story other than Balcko's. The entire cluster is in riot."

"Kaiju . . . Did he get home safe?"

"He left right after he chased you up," she said. "Said he had something to do, then went offline."

"The rest of my team?"

"Not sure, but we think they're being held on one of the cargo ships."

"I'm sorry," Khifi said. She wanted to cry. "Everyone is going to die because of me."

"Fox! Snap out of it. Lots of people could still get dead if you give up and let Balcko win. The only reason he hasn't wiped out all of your team is that he hasn't got you yet. He turned you into his convenient fallbody thinking you'd be easily caught, but he can't find you. Somebody got word out that if any of the ships in orbit ratted on your location, they'd be cursed by a lifetime of shipping mishaps. Other clusters seem to be unsure what to do or what side to take, so no one's talking to Velatos from the ground either. You and Balcko both backed yourselves into corners."

"But he's got all the cards," Khifi said.

"Not all. We got Sniv. Dirtnapper and TugThug are talking to him now," TexLex said. "Come on, *Air Captain*. You're mid-job and your whole team is on the line. What do we do?"

It was so hard to think. "We need to know everything Sniv knows," she said. "Record it, then send it on every public channel you can get on. Everyone needs to know Balcko is behind the bombings, not the crawlers, not my team. Every single death needs to be marked against him."

"Got it," TexLex said. "Balcko's imported security team is about to sweep here again, so I've gotta be scarce for a bit. Later."

Khifi was beginning to hate the amber light of a closed connection.

She turned the newsfeed back on to watch about three minutes footage of a full-scale riot erupting in Notomyo; a family of Ijt, including their young offspring, had been found butchered outside the closed tube station to Freyella Cluster, the words *Non-humans go home or die!* scrawled in their blue-green blood on the floor. Rioters had entered the crawl intent on finding the perpetrators, and what few crawlers were left were fleeing toward Balcko's cargo ships as the only option left to them. She didn't recognize any of the dirty faces shown being hounded across the concourse, but she knew the fear on them only too well.

She turned the feed off, stewing in her inability to act.

"Fox!" TexLex called over the comm. "Can you get news feeds?"

"Yeah," she said.

"Then hold on for some epic Sniveling," she said. "I uploaded Sniv's confession to a friend over in Solaster, and he's passing it on to others. In about two minutes Balcko won't have anywhere to hide on Tanduou. I'm outta here for now. Good luck, and I'll be back in touch if I reach somewhere safe."

Khifi turned back on the news feed just as Balcko called. "Ms. Iwalewa. I hope you haven't been holding your breath waiting for my call. If you immediately return to Paxillo and hand yourself over to my security consultants and sign a full confession on the terrorism charges for aiding Humans First, I could see being more merciful toward your friends."

"Like you were merciful to Candles?" Khifi asked.

The line was silent for a moment. *Is he trying to figure out if I have proof of that,* she wondered, *or what to throw at me next?*

"I don't think you've got the right attitude yet," Balcko said.

"And I don't think you have much time left," Khifi answered. "Have you watched the news?"

"I control the news," Balcko snarled.

"Yeah?"

The news feed switched over to Sniv's face, puffy and red. "It was Mr. Balcko's idea," he was saying. "All Balcko's idea. He planned the whole thing. I was only an advisor on a few *technical* details, nothing illegal!"

Khifi could hear Balcko shouting at someone over their open link. "Find it and kill it!" he was screaming.

"Problems, Mr. Balcko?" she asked.

"You and your wife are dead," he said.

"I already knew as much," she said. "Just returning the favor." The comm link cut out somewhere amid her last few words.

"—Humans First," Sniv was saying. "No, I mean, the bugs are easy targets, get people angry, focus that anger on the illegals down in the crawl. Now they're all packed up and ready to go and who really is going to miss them, especially after this? In a few years we'll have a whole new crop of 'em."

"So this isn't about the aliens and human supremacy?" someone asked. It sounded like TugThug.

"Noooo, it's about the *crawlers*," Sniv said. "We're just cleaning up the garbage in Velatos and making a bit of profit at it for our troubles."

Below her, a tug she didn't recognize soared into Paxillo airspace, deftly undocking the security consultant's cruiser. It rose quickly with the tug, the cloud of ships above parting again. As she watched, another tug pulled one of the cargo ships free from Novodinia and began its ascent.

"No!" she shouted. Balcko was not going to get away that easy. She ran through the hijacked controls to the freighter, found what she was looking for: three sets of subcompartment blast doors to the cargo bay. She watched as her distant square of open space narrowed to a slit and disappeared. Two sets fully closed, one jammed at 80 percent. Close enough. The main cargo bay doors were still wide open.

She powered on the Rimbolan's engines and began drifting toward an intercept point with the cruiser. *Bet you're not looking up right now,* she thought.

The tug released the *Escarre* as soon as they were through the field of waiting ships. She could now make out the giant yellow smiley-face painted on its nose, Xs for eyes. *Burnout.*

Burnout dipped down, beelining for the cargo ship still on the ground in Paxillo.

"Just you and me now," she said, eyes riveted on the cruiser. She pushed the engines up to full. The *Escarre* must have noticed her at the last moment because it began to turn, but the wide maw of the giant freighter caught it nearly nose-on. Khifi braced against her console as the cruiser punched through two sets of subcompartment doors before becoming wedged fast, fully two-thirds of the ship swallowed by the Rimbolan. The freighter complained desperately across her boards about multiple hull ruptures, red and yellow warning lights blinking frenetically. For all that the freighter was already abandoned and dying, she felt a pang of guilt for the catastrophic damage.

She flipped on her comms. "This is the *Lazy Dog*, calling the *Escarre*," she said. "Are you prepared to meet my demands?"

It was Stickles who answered. "Fox," he said. "That was incredibly stupid of you. Think what you could still lose. Your wife could still be saved if we acted right now. The question is, do you love her enough to save her?"

"Oh, fuck you and your manipulative bullshit," she said. "Is that all you've got?"

"Do you know how much cred your useless crawlers are worth on the open market? They're young, they're tough, they've got no one who cares what happens to them. And they'll be better off, be taken care of and fed regularly in exchange for their work. They'll be *valued*. This is a private channel, just you and me, so I have no reason to lie. You could save your wife, maybe get a small share of the profit, *and* help your crawlers find a better life."

"So human trafficking is altruism, for you? What about all the people you've killed, whose lives you've destroyed? Do you think they don't matter? You bombed your own people, you killed Goffs, you murdered aliens to cover your actions. Don't you think that matters?"

"To be honest, not really," Stickles said. "If not us, it would have been someone else eventually. You just can't understand that, can you?"

"Where is the rest of my team?" Khifi asked.

"They're on one of our ships. If you want to see them again—"

"Stop with the threats. Land the three cargo ships you've had lifted and let everyone on board all seven of them go. And then we can negotiate."

"Enough of this." Balcko cut in on the line. "Ms. Iwalewa, I admire your resourcefulness, but we've got a ride coming to pick us up and you won't be coming with us."

The Rimbolan's proximity alarms flared, and she glanced over at the sensors in alarm. There was a tug positioning itself above the freighter's long topdeck, a cutter attached to its underside. Right on cue, Burnout's voice was added to the comm traffic. "Hello, Fox," he said.

"Hello, Burnout. You come to kill me?"

"On Balcko's orders, of course," he said. "Clever of you to get him and Stickles to confirm Sniv's confession on your private line, not knowing you were piping it over the freighter's systems down to the public feeds in Tanduou."

"It seemed a conversation worth sharing," Khifi said.

"Burnout, enough of this; *kill her*," Balcko said. "You have your orders."

"I do," Burnout said. "Now shut up for a minute. Fox, remember in the Hellwater when you said that, if you beat me, you wanted everyone to know it was a fair fight?"

"Yeah," she said.

"Well, this ain't one either. We'll settle this on the ground, if you make it." Burnout disconnected.

"Where the hell is he going?" she heard Balcko ask, as Burnout's tug fell to one side and headed back to Novodinia.

Khifi smiled, powered up the Rimbolan's engines.

"What the fuck are you doing?" Balcko demanded.

"Escalating," she said. The freighter was struggling to turn, maneuvering engines reporting varying degrees of dysfunction or overload, but once she got it pointed the way she wanted to go the main engines accelerated decently. She wished she could see the bright yellow face of Guratahan Sfazil beyond Tanduou, see its second moon Tammou one more time with her own eyes, but she didn't figure it ultimately mattered; it would hurt just as much to hit.

Someone onboard the *Escarre* figured out where they were going; her boards flared in alarm as an escape pod ejected from the cruiser without being fully clear of the cargo bay and turned itself into a brief ball of fire at the lip of the Rimbolan's mouth. The remaining maneuvering thrusters on that side of the ship went offline, but she wasn't planning to change course anyway.

"Ms. Iwalewa, stop this freighter and we'll let your teammates free," Balcko's voice came over the comms.

"Mr. Balcko," she said. "And here I was hoping the escape pod was you."

"That was your friend Stickles trying to cut and run," he said. "Not much of a loss. So, I'll give you your teammates back and you let us off this ride, yes?"

"No," she said. "You let my teammates free, and you let all the crawlers go, and then *maybe* I let you off this ride."

There was a long pause, then a very hate-filled, "It's a deal."

"I'm not sure that deal's still available," Khifi said. "Let me think about it and get back to you." She cut the connection to the *Escarre*.

Below, she watched a trio of tugs appear heading up from Henrici Dock in the Myonota cluster. They straightlined for the cargo ships that were no longer in dock. The cargo ships scattered, trying to evade, but the sky was still crowded and the tugs faster and more maneuverable. She watched as one by one the ships were pulled back down to ground. A suited team emerged on the surface from inside Luida Dock and swarmed over one. The bright sparks of cutting torches were tiny flares on her display screen.

As if in sympathy, a few more red alerts on the Rimbolan's sensor feed lit up. "What the hell are you up to?" she asked, but she already knew. They were desperate if they were firing the cruiser's weapons inside the cargo hold. So far the last remaining set of doors between them was holding.

The barrage stopped and didn't start up again. The one remaining functional sensor reported exactly what she expected: movement.

Still not that easy, she thought. She activated the hull breach systems. Only about a third of the sprayers were online, but they were most likely enough to fill the bay with fast-hardening foam. She wondered if they'd be able to get back inside their ship before it solidified, or if someone was going to be carving their corpses out as part of a final salvage job. *Assuming there's any piece of us left bigger than a pebble.*

"Fox, this is Siren in Henrici cluster." Her comms reactivated. "TexLex is on the move and offline, and I'm your new designated ears. Four of the cargo ships surrendered without a fight and released all their passengers. Luida and Velatos Docks stormed theirs as soon as they landed. Paxillo's security chief Bell apparently had a disagreement with Balcko's consultants and went missing, but we've got a team from Paxillo, Oreasta, and Novodinia retaking Paxillo Dock as we speak. We think your teammates and Bell are aboard the cargo ship there, and there's signs of fighting inside. As soon as we've got the control room, we'll do what we can to try to help your wife. But it's been . . . "

"But it's been too long. I know," Khifi said. "Thank you for trying."

"This is TexLex back on ground in Luida." TexLex came on the line. "We have another ship incoming!"

Khifi's heart, already shattered by the day, seemed to grind itself to a fine powder of despair. "Not more—"

"It's the *Nobunaga!*" Siren said. "Kaiju has come home!"

"Hey, Siren!" Kaiju got on the line as well. "You miss me?"

"Always, monsterboy. Who else I gonna put my cold feet on when I sleep? Where the hell did you go?"

"I went to pick up some stranded friends," he said. "Where's safe to land in Velatos?"

"Luida is now," TexLex said.

"Then we're coming there. Hang on."

"Fox," TexLex said. "You can slow that hunkashit down now. They ain't going anywhere."

"Thanks, but I've got this," she said. She checked the Rimbolan's sensors again, saw that nothing new had failed and she was still on course for a hard meet with Tammou.

"Air Captain, stop or I'll come get in your way and make you kill me too," Kaiju answered.

"No," she said. "I'm still your air captain, and I order you to stand down."

Another voice came on the line. "I override that order."

The dockmaster.

"Told you I picked up some friends," Kaiju said. "I got through to Quizzie on private channels and found out they'd been cut off from all offworld feeds, and every time they tried to leave they were told there were mechanical problems in dock."

"Fox," the dockmaster said. "You haven't changed course or speed."

"They killed my friends, sir. They killed my *wife.*"

"So you think we should lose more people?" the dockmaster said. "What about the rest of your team? Don't you think they need you—that you all need each other—more than ever right now? This is not the only way to serve justice."

"Sir," she said. It felt like begging.

"You still haven't changed course," the dockmaster said.

"Please, Fox?" Quizzie asked.

"Fuck this shit all to hell," Khifi said, wanting to throw and smash and kick something. Anything. She could barely see through the flood of tears as she reached for her connection to the Rimbolan and cut the freighter's main engines, flipped on the brakers. She tapped her comms one last time. "Acknowledged," she said, then shut the line down.

Kaiju picked up the cutter from Novodinia and brought it up, carefully lifting free the hull plates above the *Lazy Dog*. When there was a big enough hole, Khifi used two of her tug's long arms to push herself free of the freighter. From the outside, the Rimbolan was a spectacular mess. The *Escarre* had nearly split it apart, jagged tears along much of the length of the cargo bay, plates warped and buckled, hull struts protruding like broken bones.

"Whoa," she said.

"Don't forget, they signed a damage waiver," Kaiju said. "I think we're still good."

She laughed at that, despite all.

Khifi followed the *Nobunaga* down, and when Kaiju turned toward Paxillo she didn't even think to question it. She climbed out of her tug, walked through post-landing procedures as if she was on autopilot, as if they still mattered, and her hand lingered on the *Lazy Dog*'s tomato-splattered hull as she went.

"They retook Paxillo while I was on my way up. We needed our coffee machine back," Kaiju said. As the doors on control opened he held out a hand. "After you, Air Captain."

She stepped onto the control floor and stopped. Standing there was the dockmaster and Chief Bell, and behind them in a semicircle was Redrum, Jonjon, and Inchbug with her arms around someone she could only assume was TexLex. Jonjon's arm was in a sling, and both Redrum and Bell were sporting swollen and bruised faces, but everyone was smiling.

"Welcome home, Air Captain," the dockmaster said.

"You're all alive," she said.

"You should've seen Jonjon," Inchbug said. "Never would have thought he had that kind of a fight in him."

"I bit someone," Jonjon said, beaming with pride.

"I . . . " Khifi started to say, but it was all so overwhelming that she just stood there in shock.

"Fox!" Sparkle called from her comm station. "Foible's team is on the line! She's not there!"

" . . . What?"

"Your apartment! Foible and Grippy cut the door down. There's no one *there*."

Her knees gave out, sending her tumbling. Kaiju caught her halfway to the floor, and he and Bell helped her into a chair. She was barely sitting before she tried to stand again. Both men put hands on her shoulders to keep her from rising. "Xie's," she said. "I have to get to Xie's."

"It's not safe to go down there yet," the dockmaster said. "There's still most of a riot going on, screens were smashed, and while everyone on Tanduou now knows your face, not nearly as many know you're not the enemy. I'm bringing in extra security from all over Tanduou to put the riots down. Give me a chance to do that first?"

She didn't want to wait at all, not one extra second, but she knew he was right. She nodded.

"Dockmaster," Sparkle said. "Quizzie is calling from the secure dock. They've got Balcko down using a rescue pod."

"Chief Bell, with me," the dockmaster said. "Fox, will you accompany us?"

"Yeah," Khifi said.

She followed the dockmaster and Bell down through the tower and into the docking corridors, straight to a heavy door. There were two Luida security officers there waiting outside with Quizzie. "Not a word out of them," Quizzie said. "They tried the door a couple of times then gave up."

Chief Bell unlocked the door and stepped back as it rumbled open. Balcko, Arve, and three other men stood waiting. Arve's weapon was on the floor at his feet; from the expression on his face surrendering his weapon was not his idea. "Dockmaster," Mr. Balcko said. "I'm sure if you let me explain—"

The dockmaster raised a hand, and Balcko fell silent. He turned toward the other man. "I assume you're either Allen or Arve?"

"Arve," Arve said. "My crew and I are foreign nationals and we insist on our right to speak to a representative of our colony before giving any statements or being subjected to any legal proceedings."

"Both Haudernelle ambassadors expressed disinterest in speaking with you," Chief Bell said.

"We're not from Haud—"

"No? You came here under a South Haudie flag. I see no reason to look elsewhere for someone willing to claim you," the dockmaster interrupted. "Where is Mr. Allen?"

"He and our pilot left the *Escarre* in an attempt to reach Ms. Iwalewa and negotiate," Balcko said. "They didn't return and we were unable to get the airlock door open again."

"You'll find them stuck in hull foam aboard the Rimbolan," Khifi said. The dockmaster's lip twitched up in a faint smile.

"You have no proof of our wrongdoing," Balcko said. "Only *her* word and that of people obviously under her influence." He pointed at Khifi. "Sniv is one of her creatures, not mine, as are the crawlers. That's well known."

"Let's ask one," the dockmaster said. He turned to a familiar if unexpected figure at her side. The change in context threw her badly, having not seen the youth in weeks, and then last scrounging for food scraps with Mole at his side, caked in crawl dust.

"Birdie!" Khifi said.

"Hey Fox," Birdie said.

"Birdie, were the crawlers being recruited by Humans First?" the dockmaster asked.

"Nope," he answered.

"That's good enough for me," the dockmaster said. He held out his hand and Chief Bell slapped his pistol into it.

"Wait!" Balcko said, raising his hands.

The dockmaster shot him in the head, and whatever thin denials Balcko had left died with him. "Justice, Fox. Properly administered by the authorities, and with no further collateral losses," he said. He handed the pistol back to Bell. "This is why it's always useful to have a source of inside information. Right, Birdie?"

"Right, Uncle," Birdie said.

"Chief Bell, what's the situation down on the floor?"

Bell had just been checking his comms. "Concourse is cleared, everyone is under curfew until further notice," he said. "We have a lot of crawlers in cargo warehouses throughout the cluster. Some need medical care, and they're all hungry."

"Get food and water to them. Tell them they're not in trouble and we'll be talking to them and letting them go free as soon as we know it's safe."

"Not all will want to talk," Birdie said.

"That's okay too." The dockmaster turned to Fox. "Now. You wanted to go to Xie-Yan Che's shop?"

It was so hard not to run, not to fly across the concourse to that tiny shop. Only the thought that Lema might not be there, might have been caught up in the disaster somewhere else where she'd never be found, slowed her steps until she was a walking war between anticipation and dread.

Xie's door was locked with curtains pulled across the shop windows, but he opened up on the second chime. He looked haggard, anxious, but his eyebrows went up in delight. "Khif!" he shouted, flinging himself through the door and pulling her into an embrace.

"Xie, you're the best agent a sculptor could have, but if you don't let go of my wife and get out of my way I'm going to crush you into a tiny little ball of a man and throw you down the hall," a voice said from the doorway, and Khifi froze.

Xie let go and stepped back, and it seemed almost faster than light could move that her wife was wrapping her arms around her. Khifi could feel tears on her neck, and was struck by a mortifying guilt. "I tried to get word to you, to get you out," she said. "I tried, Lema, but I failed. I thought Balcko killed you."

"You did get word to me," she said.

"What? How?"

Lema nodded her head toward the shop door. Peering around the corner was Tuck. "Mole dropped him off here," Lema said. "He told Xie about the attack on you in the concourse and that he thought we were all in danger, and Xie called me."

"Is Mole still here?" Khifi asked.

"No, he left right after," Xie said.

The dockmaster coughed gently. "Birdie went to find him," he said.

"Are *you* okay?" Lema asked Khifi.

"I don't know," she answered. "Peezy's dead, and Candles—"

"They couldn't find his body," the dockmaster said.

"What?"

"After he was thrown out the airlock. He disappeared. You know that the Colony are also oxygen-injectors? If he managed to get indoors again fast enough . . . "

"Oh, I hope so. He was a good kid. Good pilot, too." Khifi sagged against her wife. "I still can't believe you're okay."

Lema straightened up. "I'm not okay," she said. "I saw my wife's face on the news as she was branded a terrorist and mass-murderer. I watched riots break out and people forming hunting parties to look for her, and I am *not okay* with that. I don't think we're ever going to feel safe here again. I know I won't."

"What do you want us to do?" Khifi asked.

"Go somewhere else. I can work anywhere, but you . . . you need to choose."

"I've been here almost my whole life. Everything I know is here. Where would I go? What would I do?"

Quizzie coughed. "I wasn't going to pass this on for obvious selfish reasons, and I want you all to appreciate how conflicted this makes me," she said. "The *Olympian Razor*, the Martian ship that's been in dock through this whole mess? Sent me an inforeq as to whether you were on contract and if so, if it could be bought out, in the interests of extending you a job offer. Apparently you impressed them."

" . . . What?" Khifi said.

Quizzie rolled her eyes. "It was a terrible idea to ram the cruiser with the Rimbolan, but it was still beautifully executed," she said. The dockmaster held out a hand, and she passed him her handpad with the message on it. "And if

I had to guess, they must be Free Marsers, because they seemed just as taken with your willingness to defy authority."

"I know some of these names," the dockmaster said. "They'll treat you fairly and well."

"I don't know," Khifi said. She looked to Lema.

"I admit, I like the idea of being near Earth again," she said, "but it's up to you."

"You'll keep an eye on the crawlers?" she asked the dockmaster, and he nodded. She looked back to her wife. "Then yes," she said. "I can't bear ever living through another day where I don't know you're safe."

"Good," Lema said. "And we're bringing Tuck."

"Do you need me to send someone for your things?" the dockmaster asked.

Khifi smiled as Tuck wrapped his skinny arms around her legs again. "No," she said. "I have everything that matters right here."

The *Olympian Razor* was already back in orbit when Khifi took the *Lazy Dog* up out of Tanduou space for the last time. A battered but unbroken Mole had seen them off at the dock, Birdie by his side. He declined the offer to come with them. "Learning textwork," he'd said. "Earn my own way out."

"After we dock and transfer, how does your tug get back down? Autopilot?" Lema asked.

"No," Khifi said. She smiled. "Wait and see."

The *Olympian Razor* took the jump point from Guratahan Sfazil in toward Haudernelle, first of several hops on the long trip to Sol, with a large, spider-like barnacle clinging to its back. If anyone in Paxillo had expected otherwise— and she had no reason to doubt they had—no one dared call her on it.

Systems on minimum, Khifi sat on the small couch behind her pilot's chair, her head on Lema's shoulder as exhaustion settled in. Tuck was asleep beside her, barely a lump buried under a blanket.

"Khif," Lema said, her voice a whisper. With effort, Khifi opened her eyes. In her hand, Lema was holding the small, badly flattened box from Xie's. "Open it."

Khifi took it, popped the seal. Inside was a silver shape, elegant and curving in the distinctive way of all Lema's designs. "It's beautiful," she said. Nodding her head forward she slipped the necklace on and felt the metal warm against her skin. "What is it?"

"An Earth bird," Lema said. "It's called a stork."

"Oh," Khifi said, none the wiser. She closed her eyes and leaned back against Lema, listening to the low hum of the *Lazy Dog*'s systems and the slow heartbeat of her wife, both of them reassuring and steady and familiar, and let sleep catch her at last.

THINGS WITH BEARDS

SAM J. MILLER

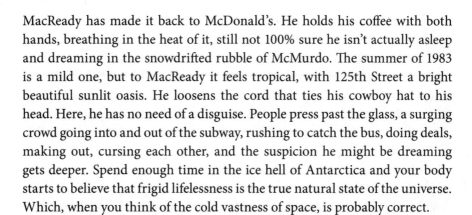

MacReady has made it back to McDonald's. He holds his coffee with both hands, breathing in the heat of it, still not 100% sure he isn't actually asleep and dreaming in the snowdrifted rubble of McMurdo. The summer of 1983 is a mild one, but to MacReady it feels tropical, with 125th Street a bright beautiful sunlit oasis. He loosens the cord that ties his cowboy hat to his head. Here, he has no need of a disguise. People press past the glass, a surging crowd going into and out of the subway, rushing to catch the bus, doing deals, making out, cursing each other, and the suspicion he might be dreaming gets deeper. Spend enough time in the ice hell of Antarctica and your body starts to believe that frigid lifelessness is the true natural state of the universe. Which, when you think of the cold vastness of space, is probably correct.

"Heard you died, man," comes a sweet rough voice, and MacReady stands up to submit to the fierce hug that never fails to make him almost cry from how safe it makes him feel. But when he steps back to look Hugh in the eye, something is different. Something has changed. While he was away, Hugh became someone else.

"You don't look so hot yourself," he says, and they sit, and Hugh takes the coffee that has been waiting for him.

"Past few weeks I haven't felt well," Hugh says, which seems an understatement. Even after MacReady's many months in Antarctica, how could so many lines have sprung up in his friend's black skin? When had his hair and beard become so heavily peppered with salt? "It's nothing. It's going around."

Their hands clasp under the table.

"You're still fine as hell," MacReady whispers.

"You stop," Hugh said. "I know you had a piece down there."

MacReady remembers Childs, the mechanic's strong hands still greasy from the Ski-dozer, leaving prints on his back and hips. His teeth on the back of MacReady's neck.

"Course I did," MacReady says. "But that's over now."

"You still wearing that damn fool cowboy hat," Hugh says, scoldingly. "Had those stupid centerfolds hung up all over your room I bet."

MacReady releases his hands. "So? We all pretend to be what we need to be."

"Not true. Not everybody has the luxury of passing." One finger traces a circle on the black skin of his forearm.

They sip coffee. McDonald's coffee is not good but it is real. Honest.

Childs and him; him and Childs. He remembers almost nothing about the final days at McMurdo. He remembers taking the helicopter up, with a storm coming, something about a dog . . . and then nothing. Waking up on board a U.S. supply and survey ship, staring at two baffled crewmen. Shredded clothing all around them. A metal desk bent almost in half and pushed halfway across the room. Broken glass and burned paper and none of them had even the faintest memory of what had just happened. Later, reviewing case files, he learned how the supply run that came in springtime found the whole camp burned down, mostly everyone dead and blown to bizarre bits, except for two handsome corpses frozen untouched at the edge of camp; how the corpses were brought back, identified, the condolence letters sent home, the bodies, probably by accident, thawed . . . but that couldn't be real. That frozen corpse couldn't have been him.

"Your people still need me?" MacReady asks.

"More than ever. Cops been wilding out on folks left and right. Past six months, eight people got killed by police. Not a single officer indicted. You still up for it?"

"Course I am."

"Meeting in two weeks. Not afraid to mess with the Man? Because what we've got planned . . . they ain't gonna like it. And they're gonna hit back, hard."

MacReady nods. He smiles. He is home; he is needed. He is a rebel. "Let's go back to your place."

When MacReady is not MacReady, or when MacReady is simply not, he never remembers it after. The gaps in his memory are not mistakes, not accidents. The thing that wears his clothes, his body, his cowboy hat, it doesn't want him to know it is there. So the moment when the supply ship crewman walked in and found formerly-frozen MacReady sitting up—and watched MacReady's face split down the middle, saw a writhing nest of spaghetti tentacles explode in his direction, screamed as they enveloped him and swiftly started digesting—all of that is gone from MacReady's mind.

But when it is being MacReady, it *is* MacReady. Every opinion and memory and passion is intact.

• • •

"The fuck just happened?" Hugh asks, after, holding up a shredded sheet.

"That good, I guess," MacReady says, laughing, naked.

"I honestly have no memory of us tearing this place up like that."

"Me either."

There is no blood, no tissue of any kind. Not-MacReady sucks all that up. Absorbs it, transforms it. As it transformed the meat that used to be Hugh, as soon as they were alone in his room and it perceived no threat, knew it was safe to come out. The struggle was short. In nineteen minutes the transformation was complete, and MacReady and Hugh were themselves again, as far as they knew, and they fell into each other's arms, onto the ravaged bed, out of their clothes.

"What's that," MacReady says, two worried fingers tracing down Hugh's side. Purple blotches mar his lovely torso.

"Comes with this weird new pneumonia thing that's going around," he says. "This year's junky flu."

"But you're not a junky."

"I've fucked a couple, lately."

MacReady laughs. "You have a thing for lost causes."

"The cause I'm fighting for isn't lost," Hugh says, frowning.

"Course not. I didn't mean that—"

But Hugh has gone silent, vanishing into the ancient trauma MacReady has always known was there, and tried to ignore, ever since Hugh took him under his wing at the age of nineteen. Impossible to deny it, now, with their bare legs twined together, his skin corpse-pale beside Hugh's rich dark brown. How different their lives had been, by virtue of the bodies they wore. How wide the gulf that lay between them, that love was powerless to bridge.

So many of the men at McMurdo wore beards. Winter, he thought, at first— for keeping our faces warm in Antarctica's forever winter. But warmth at McMurdo was rarely an issue. Their warren of rectangular huts was kept at a balmy seventy-eight degrees. Massive stockpiles of gasoline specifically for that purpose. Aside from the occasional trip outside for research—and MacReady never had more than a hazy understanding of what, exactly, those scientists were sciencing down there, but they seemed to do precious little of it—the men of McMurdo stayed the hell inside.

So. Not warmth.

Beards were camouflage. A costume. Only Blair and Garry lacked one, both being too old to need to appear as anything other than what they were, and Childs, who never wanted to.

He shivered. Remembering. The tough-guy act, the cowboy he became in uncertain situations. Same way in juvie; in lock-up. Same way in Vietnam. Hard, mean, masculine. Hard drinking; woman hating. Queer? Psssh. He hid so many things, buried them deep, because if men knew what he really was, he'd be in danger. When they learned he wasn't one of them, they would want to destroy him.

They all had their reasons, for choosing McMurdo. For choosing a life where there were no women. Supper time MacReady would look from face to bearded face and wonder how many were like him, under the all-man exterior they projected, but too afraid, like him, to let their true self show.

Childs hadn't been afraid. And Childs had seen what he was.

MacReady shut his eyes against the McMurdo memories, bit his lip. Anything to keep from thinking about what went down, down there. Because how was it possible that he had absolutely no memory of any of it? Soviet attack, was the best theory he could come up with. Psychoactive gas leaked into the ventilation system by a double agent (Nauls, definitely), which caused catastrophic freak outs and homicidal arson rage, leaving only he and Childs unscathed, whereupon they promptly sat down in the snow to die . . . and this, of course, only made him more afraid, because if this insanity was the only narrative he could construct that made any sense at all, he whose imagination had never been his strong suit, then the real narrative was probably equally, differently, insane.

Not-MacReady has an exceptional knack for assessing external threats. It stays hidden when MacReady is alone, and when he is in a crowd, and even when he is alone but still potentially vulnerable. Once, past four in the morning, when a drunken MacReady had the 145th Street bus all to himself, alone with the small woman behind the wheel, Not-MacReady could easily have emerged. Claimed her. But it knew, somehow, gauging who-knew-what quirk of pheromones or optic nerve signals, the risk of exposure, the chance someone might see through the tinted windows, or the driver's foot, in the spasms of dying, slam down hard on the brake and bring the bus crashing into something.

If confronted, if threatened, it might risk emerging. But no one is there to confront it. No one suspects it is there. Not even MacReady, who has nothing but the barest, most irrational anxieties. Protean fragments; nightmare glitch glimpses and snatches of horrific sound. Feedback, bleedthrough from the thing that hides inside him.

"Fifth building burned down this week," said the Black man with the Spanish accent. MacReady sees his hands, sees how hard he's working to keep them from shaking. His anger is intoxicating. "Twenty families, out on the street.

Cops don't care. They know it was the landlord. It's always the landlord. Insurance company might kick up a stink, but worst thing that happens is dude catches a civil suit. Pays a fine. That shit is terrorism, and they oughta give those motherfuckers the chair."

Everyone agrees. Eleven people in the circle; all of them Black except for MacReady and an older white lady. All of them men except for her, and a stout Black woman with an Afro of astonishing proportions.

"It's not terrorism when they do it to us," she said. "It's just the way things are supposed to be."

The meeting is over. Coffee is sipped; cigarettes are lit. No one is in a hurry to go back outside. An affinity group, mostly Black Panthers who somehow survived a couple decades of attempts by the FBI to exterminate every last one of them, but older folks too, trade unionists, commies, a minister who came up from the South back when it looked like the Movement was going to spread everywhere, change everything.

MacReady wonders how many of them are cops. Three, he guesses, though not because any of them make him suspicious. Just because he knows what they're up against, what staggering resources the government has invested in destroying this work over the past forty years. Infiltrators tended to be isolated, immersed in the lie they were living, reporting only to one person, whom they might never meet.

Hugh comes over, hands him two cookies.

"You sure this is such a good idea?" MacReady says. "They'll hit back hard, for this. Things will get a whole lot worse."

"Help us or don't," Hugh said, frowning. "That's your decision. But you don't set the agenda here. We know what we're up against, way better than you do. We know the consequences."

MacReady ate one cookie, and held the other up for inspection. Oreo knock-offs, though he'd never have guessed from the taste. The pattern was different, the seal on the chocolate exterior distinctly stamped.

"I understand if you're scared," Hugh says, gentler now.

"Shit yes I'm scared," MacReady says, and laughs. "Anybody who's not scared of what we're about to do is probably . . . well, I don't know, crazy or stupid or a fucking pod person."

Hugh laughs. His laugh becomes a cough. His cough goes on for a long time.

Would he or she know it, if one of the undercovers made eye contact with another? Would they look across the circle and see something, recognize some deeply-hidden kinship? And if they were all cops, all deep undercover, each one simply impersonating an activist so as to target actual activists, what would happen then? Would they be able to see that, and set the ruse aside, step into the light, reveal what they really were? Or would they persist in the imitation game, awaiting instructions from above? Undercovers didn't make decisions, MacReady knew; they didn't even do things. They fed information upstairs, and upstairs did with it what they would. So if a whole bunch of undercovers were operating on their own, how would they ever know when to stop?

MacReady knows that something is wrong. He keeps seeing it out of the corner of his mind's eye, hearing its echoes in the distance. Lost time, random wreckage.

MacReady suspects he is criminally, monstrously insane. That during his black-outs he carries out horrific crimes, and then hides all the evidence. This would explain what went down at McMurdo. In a terrifying way, the explanation is appealing. He could deal with knowing that he murdered all his friends and then blew up the building. It would frighten him less than the yawning gulf of empty time, the barely-remembered slither and scuttle of something inhuman, the flashes of blood and screaming that leak into his daylight hours now.

MacReady rents a cabin. Upstate: uninsulated and inexpensive. Ten miles from the nearest neighbor. The hard-faced old woman who he rents from picks him up at the train station. Her truck is full of grocery bags, all the things he requested.

"No car out here," she says, driving through town. "Not even a bicycle. No phone, either. You get yourself into trouble and there'll be no way of getting out of here in a hurry."

He wonders what they use it for, the people she normally rents to, and decides he doesn't want to know.

"Let me out up here," he says, when they approach the edge of town.

"You crazy?" she asks. "It'd take you two hours to walk the rest of the way. Maybe more."

"I said pull over," he says, hardening his voice, because if she goes much further, out of sight of prying protective eyes, around the next bend, maybe, or even before that, the insane thing inside him may emerge. It knows these things, somehow.

"Have fun carrying those two big bags of groceries all that way," she says, when he gets out. "Asshole."

"Meet me here in a week," he says. "Same time."

"You must be a Jehovah's Witness or something," she says, and he is relieved when she is gone.

The first two days pass in a pleasant enough blur. He reads books, engages in desultory masturbation to a cheaply-printed paperback of gay erotic stories

Hugh had lent him. Only one symptom: hunger. Low and rumbling, and not sated no matter how much he eats.

And then: lost time. He comes to on his knees, in the cool midnight dirt behind a bar.

"Thanks, man," says the sturdy bearded trucker type standing over him, pulling back on a shirt. Puzzled by how it suddenly sports a spray of holes, each fringed with what look like chemical burns. "I needed that."

He strides off. MacReady settles back into a squat. Leans against the building.

What did I do to him? He seems unharmed. But I've done something. Something terrible.

He wonders how he got into town. Walked? Hitchhiked? And how the hell he'll get back.

The phone rings, his first night back. He'd been sitting on his fire escape, looking down at the city, debating jumping, though not particularly seriously. Hugh's words echoing in his head. *Help us or don't.* He is still not sure which one he'll choose.

He picks up the phone.

"Mac," says the voice, rich and deep and unmistakeable.

"Childs."

"Been trying to call you." Cars honk, through the wire. Childs is from Detroit, he dimly remembers, or maybe Minneapolis.

"I was away. Had to get out of town, clear my head."

"You too, huh?"

MacReady lets out his breath, once he realizes he's been holding it. "You?"

"Yup."

"What the hell, man? What the fuck is going on?"

Childs chuckles. "Was hoping you'd have all the answers. Don't know why. I already knew what a dumbass you are."

A lump of longing forms in MacReady's throat. But his body fits him wrong, suddenly. Whatever crazy mental illness he was imagining he had, Childs sharing it was inconceivable. Something else is wrong, something his mind rejects but his body already knows. "Have you been to a doctor?"

"Tried," Childs says. "I remember driving halfway there, and the next thing I knew I was home again." A siren rises then slowly fades, in Detroit or Minneapolis.

MacReady inspects his own reflection in the window, where the lights of his bedroom bounce back against the darkness. "What are we?" he whispers.

"Hellbound," Childs says, "but we knew that already."

• • •

The duffel bag says *Astoria Little League*. Two crossed baseball bats emblazoned on the outside. Dirty bright-blue blazer sleeves reaching out. A flawless facsimile of something harmless, wholesome. No one would see it and suspect. The explosives are well-hidden, small, sewn into a pair of sweat pants, the timer already ticking down to some unknown hour, some unforeseeable fallout.

"Jimmy," his father says, hugging him, hard. His beard brushes MacReady's neck, abrasive and unyielding as his love.

The man is immense, dwarfing the cluttered kitchen table. Uncles lurk in the background. Cigars and scotch sour the air. Where are the aunts and wives? MacReady has always wondered, these manly Sundays.

"They told me this fucker died," his father says to someone.

"Can't kill one of ours that easy," someone says. Eleven men in the little house, which has never failed to feel massive.

Here his father pauses. Frowns. No one but MacReady sees. No one here but MacReady knows the man well enough to suspect that the frown means he knows something new on the subject of MacReady mortality. Something that frightens him. Something he feels he has to shelter his family from.

"Fucking madness, going down there," his father says, snapping back with the unstoppable positivity MacReady lacks, and envies. "I'd lose my mind inside of five minutes out in Alaska."

"Antarctica," he chuckles.

"That too!"

Here, home, safe, among friends, the immigrant in his father emerges. Born here to brand-new arrivals from Ireland, never saw the place but it's branded on his speech, the slight Gaelic curling of his consonants he keeps hidden when he's driving the subway car but lets rip on weekends. His father's father is who MacReady hears now, the big glorious drunk they brought over as soon as they got themselves settled, the immense shadow over MacReady's own early years, and who, when he died, took some crucial piece of his son away with him. MacReady wonders how his own father has marked him, how much of him he carries around, and what kind of new terrible creature he will be when his father dies.

An uncle is in another room, complaining about an impending Congressional hearing into police brutality against Blacks; the flood of reporters bothering his beat cops. The uncle uses ugly words to describe the people he polices out in Brooklyn; the whole room laughs. His father laughs. MacReady slips upstairs unnoticed. Laments, in silence, the horror of human hatred—how such marvelous people, whom he loves so dearly, contain such monstrosity inside of them.

In the bathroom, standing before the toilet where he first learned to pee, MacReady sees smooth purple lesions across his stomach.

Midnight, and MacReady stands at the center of the George Washington Bridge. The monstrous creature groans and whines with the wind, with the heavy traffic that never stops. New York City's most popular suicide spot. He can't remember where he heard that, but he's grateful that he did. Astride the safety railing, looking down at deep black water, he stops to breathe.

Once, MacReady was angry. He is not angry anymore. This disturbs him. The things that angered him are still true, are still out there; are, in most cases, even worse.

His childhood best friend, shot by cops at fourteen for "matching a description" of someone Black. His mother's hands, at the end of a fourteen hour laundry shift. Hugh, and Childs, and every other man he's loved, and the burning glorious joy he had to smother and hide and keep secret. He presses against these memories, traces along his torso where they've marked him, much like the cutaneous lesions along Hugh's sides. And yet, like those purple blotches, they cause no pain. Not anymore.

A train's whistle blows, far beneath him. Wind stings his eyes when he tries to look. He can see the warm dim lights of the passenger cars; imagines the seats where late-night travelers doze or read or stare up in awe at the lights of the bridge. At him.

Something is missing, inside of MacReady. He can't figure out what. He wonders when it started. McMurdo? Maybe. But probably not. Something drew him to McMurdo, after all. The money, but not just the money. He wanted to flee from the human world. He was tired of fighting it and wanted to take himself out. Whatever was in him, changing, already, McMurdo fed it.

He tries to put his finger on it, the thing that is gone, and the best he can do is a feeling he once felt, often, and feels no longer. Trying to recall the last time he felt it he fails, though he can remember plenty of times before that. Leaving his first concert; gulping down cold November night air and knowing every star overhead belonged to him. Bus rides back from away baseball games, back when the Majors still felt possible. The first time he followed a boy onto the West Side Piers. A feeling at once frenzied and calm, energetic yet restive. Like he had saddled himself, however briefly, onto something impossibly powerful, and primal, sacred, almost, connected to the flow of things, moving along the path meant only for him. They had always been rare, those moments—life worked so hard to come between him and his path—but lately they did not happen at all.

He is a monster. He knows this now. So is Childs. So are countless others, people like Hugh who he did something terrible to, however unintentionally it was. He doesn't know the details, what he is or how it works, or why, but he knows it.

Maybe he'd have been strong enough, before. Maybe that other MacReady would have been brave enough to jump. But that MacReady had no reason to. This MacReady climbs back to the safe side of the guardrail, and walks back to solid ground.

MacReady strides up the precinct steps, trying not to cry. Smiling, wide-eyed, white, and harmless.

When Hugh handed off the duffel bag, something was clearly wrong. He'd lost fifty pounds, looked like. All his hair. Half of the light in his eyes. By then MacReady'd been hearing the rumors, seeing the stories. Gay cancer, said the *Times*. Dudes dropping like mayflies.

And that morning: the call. Hugh in Harlem Hospital. From Hugh's mother, whose remembered Christmas ham had no equal on this earth. When she said everything was going to be fine, MacReady knew she was lying. Not to spare his feelings, but to protect her own. To keep from having a conversation she couldn't have.

He pauses, one hand on the precinct door. Panic rises.

Blair built a spaceship.

The image comes back to him suddenly, complete with the smell of burning petrol. Something he saw, in real life? Or a photo he was shown, from the wreckage? A cavern dug into the snow and ice under McMurdo. Scavenged pieces of the helicopter and the snowmobiles and the Ski-dozer assembled into . . . a spaceship. How did he know that's what it was? Because it was round, yes, and nothing any human knew how to make, but there's more information here, something he's missing, something he knew once but doesn't know now. But where did it come from, this memory?

Panic. Being threatened, trapped. Having no way out. It triggers something inside of him. Like it did in Blair, which is how an assistant biologist could assemble a spacefaring vessel. Suddenly MacReady can tap into so much more. He sees things. Stars, streaking past him, somehow. Shapes he can take. Things he can be. Repulsive, fascinating. Beings without immune systems to attack; creatures whose core body temperatures are so low any virus or other invading organism would die.

A cuttlefish contains so many colors, even when it isn't wearing them.

His hands and neck feel tight. Like they're trying to break free from the rest of him. Had someone been able to see under his clothes, just then, they'd have seen mouths opening and closing all up and down his torso.

"Help you?" a policewoman asks, opening the door for him, and this is bad, super bad, because he—like all the other smiling white harmless allies who are at this exact moment sauntering into every one of the NYPD's 150 precincts and command centers—is supposed to not be noticed.

"Thank you," he says, smiling the Fearless Man Smile, powering through the panic. She smiles back, reassured by what she sees, but what she sees isn't what he is. He doffs the cowboy hat and steps inside.

He can't do anything about what he is. All he can do is try to minimize the harm, and do his best to counterbalance it.

What's the endgame here, he wonders, waiting at the desk. What next? A brilliant assault, assuming all goes well—simultaneous attacks on every NYPD precinct, chaos without bloodshed, but what victory scenario are his handlers aiming for? What is the plan? Is there a plan? Does someone, upstairs, at Black Liberation Secret Headquarters, have it all mapped out? There will be a backlash, and it will be bloody, for all the effort they put into a casualty-free military strike. They will continue to make progress, person by person, heart by heart, and mind by mind, but what then? How will they know they have reached the end of their work? Changing minds means nothing if those changed minds don't then change actual things. It's not enough for everyone to carry justice inside their hearts like a secret. Justice must be spoken. Must be embodied.

"Sound permit for a block party?" he asks the clerk, who slides him a form without even looking up. All over the city, sound permits for block parties that will never come to pass are being slid across ancient well-worn soon-to-be-incinerated desks.

Walking out, he hears the precinct phone ring. Knows it's The Call. The same one every other precinct is getting. Encouraging everyone to evacuate in the next five minutes if they'd rather not die screaming; flagging that the bomb is set to detonate immediately if tampered with, or moved (this is a bluff, but one the organizers felt fairly certain hardly anyone would feel like calling, and, in fact, no one does).

And that night, in a city at war, he stands on the subway platform. Drunk, exhilarated, frightened. A train pulls in. He stands too close to the door, steps forward as it swings open, walks right into a woman getting off. Her eyes go wide and she makes a terrified sound. "Sorry," he mumbles, cupping his beard and feeling bad for looking like the kind of man who frightens women, but she is already sprinting away. He frowns, and then sits, and then smiles. A smile of shame, at frightening someone, but also of something else, of a hard-earned, impossible-to-communicate knowledge. MacReady knows, in that moment, that maturity means making peace with how we are monsters.

RED IN TOOTH AND COG

CAT RAMBO

A phone can be so much. Your memory, your edge against boredom, your source of inspiration. There's always an app for whatever you need. Renee valued her phone accordingly, even celebrating it by giving way to the trend for fancy phone-cases. Its edges were bezeled with bling she'd won on a cruise the year before, and she'd had some tiny opals, legacy of her godmother, set into the center.

It was an expensive, new-model phone in a pretty case, and that was probably why it was stolen.

Renee was in the park near work. A sunny day, on the edge of cold, the wind carrying spring with it like an accessory it was testing for effect.

She set her phone down on the bench beside her as she unfolded her bento box, foil flaps levering back to reveal still-steaming rice, quivering tofu.

Movement caught her eye. She pulled her feet away as a creature leaped up onto the bench slats beside her, an elastic-band-snap's worth of fear as it grabbed the phone, half as large as the creature itself, and moved to the other end of the bench.

The bento box clattered as it hit the path, rice grains spilling across the grey concrete.

Renee thought the creature an animal at first, but it was actually a small robot, a can opener that had been greatly and somewhat inexpertly augmented and modified. It had two corkscrew claws, and grasshopper legs made from nutcrackers to supplement the tiny wheels on its base, originally designed to let it move to hand as needed in a kitchen. Frayed raffia wrapped its handles, scratchy strands feathering out to weathered fuzz. Its original plastic had been some sort of blue, faded now to match the sidewalk beneath her sensible shoes.

The bench jerked as the robot leaped again, moving behind the trashcan, still carrying her phone. She stood, stepping over the spilled rice to try to get to it, but the rhododendron leaves thrashed and stilled, and her phone was gone.

She went to the Tellbox to seek the help of the park's assistant, an older model humanoid with one mismatched, updated arm, all silver and red LED readouts in contrast to the shabbier aged plastic of the original form, built in a time when a slightly retro animatronic look had been popular.

"How do I get my phone back?" she demanded after recounting what had happened.

The robot shook its smiling gender-neutral head. "Gone." Its shoulders hunched toward her. "I hope you have a backup."

"Of course," she snapped, "but that's my phone. The case was customized. Irreplaceable." The case reflected her, *was* her, as though what had been carried off was a doll-sized replica of Renee, clutched in the arms of a robotic King Kong.

"Contact the owner!" she said, but the robot shook its head again.

"No one owns those," it said.

"But it was modified. Who did that?"

"They do it to themselves. They get thrown out, but their AI chips try to keep them going. That's the problem with self-repairing, self-charging appliances—they go feral."

"Feral appliances?" she said in disbelief. She'd heard of such things, but surely they were few and far between. Not something that lived in the same park in which she ate her lunch every once in a while.

The next few days she became a regular, haunted the park every lunch hour, looking for any sign of her phone. Her job as a minor advertising functionary gave her lunches plus "creativity breaks" that were served as well by sitting outside as by any of the other approved modes, like music or drugs.

She was on a bench, scrolling through mail on her replacement phone, when she spotted the phenomenon. Tall grass divided like a comb to display a bright wriggle, then another. She didn't move, didn't startle them.

Her first thought had been *snake* and they did resemble snakes. But they were actually styluses, two of the old Google kind, a loose chain of circles in the pocket that would snap into rigidity when you squeezed the ball at one end. One was an iridescent peacock metal, somewhat dust-dulled. The other was a matte black, with little silver marks like scars. It had several long limbs, thin as needles, spiking from its six-inch length. The peacock had no such spurs; it was also a half-inch shorter.

They slithered through the unmown grass, heading for another large rhododendron, its roots covered with English ivy and shadows.

She stood in order to watch the last few feet of their journey. At the motion, they froze, but when she did not move for a few moments, they grew bold again and continued on.

The robot keeper crunched over to stand by Renee as she looked at the rhododendron.

"Why isn't this place better tended?" she asked the robot.

"It is a nature preserve as well as a park," it said. "That was the only way we could obtain funding."

"But everything is growing wild." She pointed at the bank of English ivy rolling across a rock near them. "That's an invasive species. If you let it, it will take over."

It shrugged, one of those mechanical gestures few humans could imitate, boneless and smooth as though the joints were gliding on a track.

"This is one of the few places in the city where feral appliances can run loose," it said. "Not the big ones, nothing larger than a sewing machine or toaster, no fridges or hot tubs or even a house heart. But your toothbrushes, key fobs, and screwdrivers? There's plenty of space for them here and enough lunchtime visitors that they can scavenge a few batteries and parts." Again it shrugged.

The styluses had vanished entirely underneath the rhododendron.

"You don't do anything about them?" she asked the robot.

"It is not within my directives," it said.

Two days later, she saw the phone-thief climbing a maple tree. Someone had been tying bits of metal thread on the trunks and the creature was clipping each with an extended claw and tucking them somewhere inside its body. It used its grasshopper legs, set in a new configuration, to grip the bark, moving up and down with surprising speed as it jumped from branch to branch.

She tried to get closer, but moved too fast. Quick as an indrawn breath, it scuttled to the other side of the trunk where she couldn't see it.

If she stood still long enough, would it grow confident again and reappear? But it did not show itself in the fifteen to twenty minutes she lingered there.

More of the bits of metallic thread were tied on three smaller trees near the bench. She wondered if someone had put them there for the wild appliances, the equivalent of a birdfeeder. How else might you feed them? A thought flickered into her head and that night she looked a few things up on the Internet and placed an order.

She noticed more and more of the creatures as she learned to pick out the traces of their presences from the landscape. She began to recognize the ones she saw on a regular basis, making up names for them: Patches, Prince, Starbucks. They appeared to recognize her, too, and when she began to scatter handfuls of small batteries or microchips near where she sat watching, she found that she could often coax them within a few feet of her, though never within touching distance. She had no urge to touch them—most had their own defenses, small knives or lasers, and she knew better—but she managed, she thought, to convince them she meant no harm.

Even the phone-thief grew easier in her presence. She never saw anything resembling her phone and its case. She didn't mind that for the most part, but the loss of the opals still ate at her. Australian opals like sunset skies, surrounded by tiny glitters of diamond.

The creature surely would still have the bits of the case somewhere. Track the creature and she might be able to track the gems.

A couple of days later, another sighting. A palm-sized, armadillo-shaped thing she thought must be connected to learning. She watched it rooting through red and yellow maple leaves under a sparse bush. When it saw her watching, it extruded several whisker-thin extensions from its "nose" and used them to burrow away.

She blinked, amused despite her irritation that she was no further along the path to discovering the missing gems.

She hadn't intended to mention them to her mother, but it slipped out during a vid call.

"You what?" her mother said, voice going high-pitched in alarm. She fanned herself with a hand, leaning back in the chair. "Oh my god. Oh. My. God. You lost Nana Trent's opals."

Renee fought to keep from feeling five years old and covered in some forbidden substance. She said, "I'll get them back."

"How? You said a robot took them."

"A little feral robot, Mom. The park's full of them."

"I've heard of those. That's how that man died, out in the Rockies. He was hiking. A pack of them attacked him."

Renee was fascinated despite her growing urge to bring the conversation to an end before her mother returned to the question of the opals.

Too late. Her mother said, "So how will you get them back?"

"I'll spot the one that took them and find its nest."

"Nest? They have nests, like birds?" Her mother's hands still fluttered at her throat as though trying to snatch air and stuff it into her mouth.

"Like rats," Renee said. Her mother hated rats.

"You'd better get them back," her mother said. "That's the sort of thing she'd cut you out of the will for."

Renee would have liked to protest this dark observation but her mother was right: her godmother was made up of those sorts of selfish and angry motivations. She'd been known to nurse grudges for decades, carrying them forward from grade school days.

"I still have the largest," she said. "In that ring I had made."

After saying goodbyes and reassurances, she turned the com off and touched the ring. All of the stones had come from the same mine, one Nana had owned in her earlier years, and they were fire opals, filled with red and pink and yellow and unexpected flashes of green amid the sunset colors.

Why had the robot wanted them? Did they like decoration?

She asked the park robot, "What's the strangest thing you've ever seen here?"

Today it was sporting government holiday coloring: red, white, and blue decals, a little seedy and thrice-used around the edges. She thought maybe it'd hesitate or ask her to clarify the parameters of her question, but instead it said, without a tick of hesitation, "Humans."

She raised an eyebrow, but like most robots it was extremely bad at reading body language. It simply stood there, waiting until she acknowledged it and released it or else thirty minutes passed.

The day was too hot to wait it out. She said, "Is there a party in the park tonight?"

"An ice-cream social and fireworks. Free of charge. Sponsored by Coca-Cola."

Robots weren't supposed to understand irony but the way it said the last phrase made her wonder. She said, "Thanks, that's all." It nodded at her and moved along to tinker with the garbage can.

Beneath a bench beside her, in the thick grass clumped around its stanchions, a glint of movement. Pretending to tie a shoelace, she went down on one knee to get a better look.

The phone-thief creature, constructing something. She continued her act, readjusting her shoe, even went so far as to take her shoe off, put it back on. The creature was aware of her, she could tell, but it kept right on with what it was doing, cannibalizing bits of its own internal workings to augment what she realized was an eyeglass case with a half-detached rain hat, bright orange, printed with yellow and sky-blue flowers. It was making the case into a thing like itself, assembling legs into short arms for its creation. Only one of these was attached to the body/case right now. It waved absently in the air.

She was watching a birth. She wondered if any of the parts being used to create the baby were from her phone.

She stood with her body angled oddly, not wanting to draw attention to the event, to the vulnerable little machine and its even tinier creation.

People came and went. This side of the park was much used, but no one lingered there. They bought food at the corner kiosk and brought it back to the office to eat rather than sitting on a bench or on the concrete rim surrounding the pool filled with lily pads and frog-legged machines made from waterproof headphones and GPS units.

"Do you require assistance?" The park robot, standing by her side.

She looked everywhere but in the direction of the tiny miracle taking place. She could guess what had happened. Rich finds had led the creature to thoughts of reproduction.

It staggered her. She hadn't really conceived of the park as an actual ecosystem before, but if the mechanical denizens were reproducing, then maybe it was indeed a strange new paradigm.

"I was tired," she told the robot.

"Perhaps you would care to step out of the sun? I could bring you a cold beverage," the robot persisted.

What would it do if it saw the creature and its child? She had no reason to think the robot meant them well, but so far it hadn't proved actively hostile, either.

She said, "What happens to the big appliances?"

"I beg context," the robot said.

"You said the larger appliances don't end up here. Where do they end up?"

"Most of them—almost all— go to the recycling bins," it said. It cocked its head, scanning something. "A few—very few—make it into the wild. They end up in the radioactive zone in the Southwest or else perhaps in Canada."

"And any that came here, what would happen to them?"

The robot's plastic face was blank as a lightbulb. If you split this robot open, it would smell of lemons and grass, an artificially perfumed disinfectant. Its silence was its only reply.

She let her eyes trail along the ground, stealing just a glance before she fumbled in her purse.

"I thought I lost my sunglasses," she told the robot.

"You know by now to be careful of your belongings while you are here," the robot said. "Did they perhaps fall from your purse while you were feeding the appliances?"

"Are you programmed for sarcasm?"

"It was an optional upgrade I self-applied."

"Why don't you like me feeding them?"

"If you feed them, they will grow larger, in size and numbers. They will outgrow the park. And if they learn to trust humans, it will do them no good when exterminators come."

She started to say, "They're only machines," but the words caught like a cough in her throat.

Renee spent more and more of her time observing the feral machines. Before work, she got up an hour and a half earlier and stood watching the park. By now she was there so much she never bothered trying to explain herself to the robot with some concocted story. She took still photos where she could, with her phone, but mostly she relied on watching, observing.

Trying to figure out the patterns of this savage little world, red in tooth and cog.

Because it was a *savage* life there in the park, for sure. Newer machines that made it to the park had a slim survival rate. She'd seen that demonstrated time and time again. A bottle opener and a lint brush who'd teamed up, clearly both discards of the same household for they were emblazoned *DLF* in gold letters against the silvery body plastic. She glimpsed them several times, had started to think of them as personalities, but then she found their empty casings beside the path amid a fluff of white optic fibers, fine as feathers.

She was there the week after the phone-thief procreated to witness another birth of sorts. The creation of an entity that the rest of the park's inhabitants would come to fear, what she would learn to think of as the manticore.

It'd been a late-model Roomba, slow to crawl over the rough ground but durable enough to outlast most attackers. It had a powerful solar battery as well as some sort of electrical backup. She'd seen it nursing at a charging station near the park entrance more than once in early mornings.

A truck sped past in the street. A black garbage sack bounced free from the heaps strapped and bungee-corded together on the truck's back. Small kitchen appliances spilled out. Renee skipped work that morning to watch as the Roomba killed and assimilated most of them: a crook-handled dogtooth bottle opener, an array of electric knives, and then a several-armed harness the purpose of which she didn't recognize.

The robot did, though. Standing beside her, it said, without the usual preamble, "Dremels—there should be a better disposal method for those."

"What's a Dremel?" she asked.

"A multipurpose tool. Very clever, very adaptable. Combine one with raccoons and you can lose a whole preserve."

"Lose it?"

"Force the authorities to sterilize the area."

"Are there raccoons here?"

It shook its head. "Rabbits, squirrels, a few cats. That and hawks. Nothing bigger or smarter."

They both watched the newly swollen manticore, still ungainly with its acquisitions, trundle into the underbrush. It was quieter than she would've expected for a machine of that size.

"It's hard for those big machines to replicate," the robot said. The flat black eyes slid toward her. "I've told you, you shouldn't feed them so much. You've upset the ecosystem."

"I don't bring much," she said. "A few batteries, some smaller parts."

It made a sound somewhere between a buzz and a glottal stop. "They will think all humans are tender-hearted like you," it said. "Most people regard them as vermin. And there are more of them here than you imagine."

Its fingers flicked up to indicate a tree bole. It took long seconds for her less keen vision to locate the huddled black clumps—a pair of waiting drones—that the robot meant.

She'd learned enough by now to know how the drones survived. They were high on the park's food chain, able to swoop in silently, preferring to keep owl hours, hunting in dim evening and night light for smaller, unwary ground-bound machines.

Most of the drones that entered the park were not feral, though, but regular office drones using the corner as a shortcut from one building to another. Three rogue drones worked together at the northern archway, ambushing working drones taking advantage of the flight paths the park offered.

The drones knew what was going on by now—you could see them sizing up the bushes, the flat overlooking stone often haunted by the trio. The first, a former bath appliance, scale, and foot-buffer, also had a hobbyist kit's worth of wood-burning arms, capable of tangling with a drone and setting the cardboard package it carried smoldering. Since the drones' plastic casing wasn't heat resistant, the scale/burner was a distinct menace to them.

If a drone made it through that, it still had Scylla and Charybdis to cope with. The former was a small vacuum cleaner and the latter a rock-tumbler, both remnants of the nearby hobby store that had gone out of business recently.

The store's closing had shaped the denizens of the park to an extent she'd never seen before. The manticore had added several claws and multipurpose tools as well as a shredder ingestion chute. Even Creature, as she'd come to think of the phone-thief, had benefited, taking on a set of small screwdrivers, the same flip-tech as the styluses and equally capable of moving either fluidly or rigidly.

Its child, Baby, had not, though. She'd noticed this phenomenon with the several other young machines: they weren't allowed to augment themselves. They had to bring all scavenged finds to their parent until some impalpable event happened and the child was cut loose from the parent machine, which subsequently no longer tended it or interacted with it much, if at all—Renee had seen what appeared to be a mated trio of scissors chase their solitary offspring from their niche. Now capable of augmenting themselves, the emancipated young usually did so, fastening on whatever was at hand—bright candy wrappers, bits of stone or plastic, a button—as though to mark the day.

The robot had said the largest creature there was a sewing machine, but even it was diminutive, a ball-shaped thing capable of inhabiting a pants leg to hem it from the inside. It still had thread in it, but every once in a while during walks through the deeper park, she'd come upon a tiny construction made of colored fiber, an *Ojo de Dios* formed around two crossed toothpicks or twigs, set three or four inches above the ground.

"Does anyone ever come to check on this place?" she asked the park robot.

It was examining the plants using colored lenses to augment the black ovoids set into its facial curve. The shiny arcs canted in their plastic sockets, swiveling in silent interrogation as the robot said, "Every six months, a Park Inspector walks through, but primarily she relies on logs from the kiosk restock here. I perform all necessary maintenance and provide a weekly report."

"Do the appliances go in the report?"

The eyes tilted again as though looking downward. "There is no line item for mechanical devices."

"The Park Inspector doesn't see them?"

"She never lingers long. Plus they are, as you have noticed, shy and prone to avoid noise, and the inspector's voice can be piercing."

"When is she due again?"

"Next month."

She looked around the park, at the double red and orange of the maples, the ardent yellow of the ginkgos, dinosaur trees, the same shell-shape that they had thousands of years ago now sheltering humanity's creation in the random golden heaps of their leaves.

It had rained the night before and then frozen: everything in the park looked glazed and blurry. She chose not to wander the outskirts but took one of the inner footpaths. Under the trees the footing was less slick.

She was surprised to find the robot in the middle of the park. It was using some sort of gun-shaped implement on the flowering statues in the center courtyard, a thirty-meter circle of pea gravel and monuments, thawing them out one by one. A slow and tedious task, she thought, but how much else did it have to do?

Here the ground was visible near the path but then folded into ferns and hillsides. As she stood watching, she saw Creature and Baby moving along one of the hillsides, climbing through the moss and mud.

She waited until the robot had finished and moved out of sight before kneeling and rolling the steel ball bearings and round batteries towards the pair.

The larger one intercepted almost all of them and tucked them away in a recess. The smaller did take one steel ball, which it grappled with, half-play, half-practice, like a lion cub in training.

The larger one ignored the smaller's antics and watched Renee. It wasn't until she backed off that it appeared to relax, but then another sound caught its attention and it coaxed the smaller unit away. One of the baby's new legs was shorter than the others, which gave it a lurching gait, as though perpetually falling sideways.

Work was suffering. Renee was coming in too late, taking breaks that bordered on too long and lunches that slipped close to two hours.

The hidden world of the park pulled too hard. Each of the machines had its own behaviors; Baby, for instance, used an odd gesture from time to time, a twist of two limbs over and over each other that reminded her of a toddler's hands wringing together. It was not a random communication, she decided. Baby used it as both greeting and farewell.

Others produced sounds—she had heard Creature more than once making a melody like a bird's in the underbrush, and the manticore had a rhythmic *chuff-cough* that appeared to escape it involuntarily sometimes when hunting.

In high school biology, they had to analyze an ecosystem. Renee had picked coral reefs but the more she found out about them, the sadder they made her feel. All those reefs, and then parrot fish, jaws like iron, chomping away at them faster than the reefs could grow. She even listened to an underwater audio file of some of them eating. That sound sometimes came back in her dreams, a relentless crunch of the sort you hear in your bones, a "something's wrong" sensation that's impossible to ignore.

But she understood what an ecosystem was by the end of things and to her mind the park qualified. She wasn't worried about disturbing the system, though. The world outside shaped the park much more than any of her offerings ever would, she thought.

Today she knelt to release a handful of gold sequins, each a microchip, that she'd found on sale at a fabric store the previous weekend. The flashing rounds scattered in between brown roots, white tufted leaves. One rolled to the foot of a bot, a hairy green caterpillar adorned with sparkler-wire arms that held it high above the grass, encased in the cage of sparking, pulsing wire. The spindly arms extended down to retrieve the sequins, then tucked them away in the hollow of its body.

This early, the park robot was usually sweeping the outer sidewalks, but today was unexpectedly present at this semi-private clearing where the archway overhung the sidewalk, dry remnants of wisteria bushing up over the ice-glazed stone. Renee only saw it when it stepped out from the archway's shadow. It didn't speak, but the way its head titled to view the last sequin, nestled between two knuckled roots and obscured by the roof of a yellow gingko leaf, was as eloquent as a camera lens framing a significant moment.

Renee said, "They were left over from a crafting project."

The robot said, "The Park Inspector is coming next week."

"Yesterday you said next month."

"The schedule has been changed with the city's acquisition of new technology."

It paused. Renee offered the question up like a sequin held between thumb and fingertip. "What sort of new technology?"

"Microdrones. They are released from a central point and proceed outward in a wave, capturing a snapshot of the park that will be analyzed so that any necessary repairs or changes can be made."

The sequin winked in the half-light under the leaf. Renee said, "They'll catalog all the creatures here, you mean?"

The robot nodded.

"You said this is a nature preserve—that they won't interfere with it."

The robot's head ratcheted in one of those uncannily, inhumanly smooth gestures. A crafted nod, designed in a lab. "The natural creatures, yes."

"The machines don't count as natural."

Again, constructed negation.

"What will they do with them?"

"There are no shelters for abandoned machines," it said. "We are reprocessed. Recycled." A twitch of a shrug. "Reborn, perhaps. Probably not."

Baby appeared from beneath the shelter of a statue, making the odd little greeting gesture, two limb-tips sliding around and around each other. It began to pick its way over to the tree where the sequin lay. It gave Renee a considering look, its message a clear *you could have saved me some* that made her laugh. She pulled three extra sequins from her pocket, letting them glitter in the sunlight, then tossed one out midway between herself and Baby.

The robot didn't say a word. Baby edged toward the original sequin, plucked the leaf aside and picked it up. It was still unadorned, and Renee wondered when she'd see it with the baubles and bling that meant it was its own creature. Baby slid the sequin into a compartment, then wavered its way toward them. The click of its feet was audible against the path despite the traffic roar beginning to stir with the dawn.

"What can you do?" she asked the robot.

The robot shrugged. Baby reached the sequin, considered it, then plucked it up in order to put it in a compartment on the opposite side from the last pocketing. Machines liked symmetry, Renee had learned. They were worse than any OCD patient, prone to doing things in pairs and threes and, in more extreme (and usually short-lived) cases, many more than that. Everything had to be even, had to be balanced.

Renee tossed another sequin, again to a midpoint between Baby and herself. Voices hadn't disturbed it thus far, so she looked at the park robot and said, "You can't do anything? What about caging them for a few days, then releasing them back into the park?"

"There are no facilities suitable for temporarily caging them."

She held out the last sequin, willing Baby to come and take it from her. The little robot drifted closer, closer, finally plucked it as delicately as a fish's kiss from her fingertips, then darted away. It stopped a few feet off, turning the sequin over and over in its claws, watching her, making its hello/goodbye gesture.

Based on what she'd observed so far, it was almost an adult. She wondered if it and Creature would keep interacting after Baby was full-fledged, its back studded with bits of rubbish or perhaps even her opals, or whether they would be as aloof as the scissors to each other.

"Would you be willing to take some home?" the robot said.

She looked down at the claws, at the plier-grip tips capable of cracking a finger. She'd seen it destroy a small tree in order to harvest the limp Mylar balloon tangled in its upper branches. She had nothing capable of keeping it caged.

She shook her head.

Her supervisor called her in, a special meeting that left her hot-eyed, fighting back tears.

She'd known she was skirting the edges, but when she was in the office, she worked twice as hard and twice as smart as anyone there, she'd rationalized. She'd thought she could cover for herself, use her skills and experience to compensate for slack caused by bot-watching.

She was wrong, and the aftermath was the thin, stretched feeling of embarrassment and shame and anger that sent her marching quickly through the September rain to the park.

She couldn't give them up entirely, could she? Maybe the Park Inspector shutting things down was the best possible outcome. Saved her from her own obsession. But it would be like losing a host of friends. It would leave her days so gray.

"There's a way to save the creatures," the robot said.

"What is it?"

"It's illegal."

"But what is it?"

The robot held out a metal orb inlaid with golden dots, dull black mesh at eight points. "If you trigger this while the drone wave is going past, it'll overwrite the actual data with a false version that I've constructed."

Renee didn't move to take it. "Why can't you set it off?" she asked.

"My actions are logged," the robot said. "Most are categorized. This conversation, for example, falls under interaction with park visitors. Programming the image of the park falls under preservation of data, but triggering it would be flagged. Someone would notice."

Reluctantly, Renee took it. "What if she arrives at a time when I can't be here?" she said.

"I don't know," the robot said. "You're the only hope the creatures have, and I never said the plan was foolproof. But she'll be doing the inspection at one on Monday afternoon."

Relief surged in Renee. That was easy enough. She could take a late lunch that Monday. She'd make sure of it by building up as much goodwill and bonus time as she could by then.

Her mother said, "Nana's coming to town. She'll expect to see you."

Renee's mouth watered at the thought. Nana always paid for dinner, and she liked nice restaurants, places where they served old-style proteins and fresh-grown greens.

"Wear the opals," her mother said.

Renee's heart sank. But she simply said, "All right," and got the details for the dinner.

Afterward she laid her head down flat on her kitchen table and closed her eyes, trying to savor the cool, slick surface throbbing against her headache.

The Park Inspector would be there the day before Nana's visit. If she could figure out the location of Creature's lair—maybe the robot would have some suspicions?—then she might recover them and no one would be the wiser, particularly Nana. She took a deep breath.

The com chimed again. The office this time, wanting her to come in and initial a set of layouts. She needed to build goodwill, needed to look like a team player, so she made no fuss about it.

She was lucky; the errand took only a few minutes. Leaving, she hesitated, then turned her footsteps toward the park.

It was a cold, rain-washed night and she pulled her jacket tight around herself as she stepped onto the tree-lined path.

Ahead, a cluster of small red lights, low above the ground. She stopped. They continued moving, a swirl around a point off to one side of the path. As she approached, she saw several of the bots gathered near an overturned trashcan beside the path. Inside it was Creature. Someone, perhaps a mischievous child, had trapped Creature under the heavy mesh and it was unable to lift the can enough to extricate itself.

A brighter light, like a bicycle, flashed in the distance, and she heard the manticore's cry, coming closer.

She braced herself, shoved the trashcan over. It was much heavier than she expected; her feet slipped on the icy path. It banged onto its side, rolling as it went. Creature stood motionless except for a swiveling eye. She backed away a few feet and knelt, keeping still.

The night was quiet, and the little red lights from the machines cast greasy trails of color on the wet leaves and the concrete. She stayed where she was, crouched by the path despite the hard surface biting at her knees.

Creature finally stirred. The struggle with the trashcan had damaged it. It limped towards her.

Had she trained them too well? Did it expect her to have something for it? She held out her hands, spread them wide to show them empty.

Creature stopped for a moment, then kept moving toward her. She lowered her hands, uncertain what to do.

It stopped a foot from her and lowered its body to the concrete. Indicator lights played across its side but the patterns were indecipherable.

Perhaps it was saying thank you? She returned her hands to her sides and said, tentatively, "You're welcome."

But it stayed in place, lights still flickering. It whistled a few notes, the song she'd sometimes heard from the underbrush.

A thought occurred to her. She held out her right hand, tapping the ring on it with her left. "You have the stones like this one. If you want to thank me, just give those back. Please."

Her voice quavered on that last word. *Please just let something go right for once.*

It stretched out a limb and touched the opal. She held her hand still, despite its metal cold as ice against her skin.

Creature sang two notes, sad and slow, and retracted its arm. The manticore coughed once in the underbrush but stayed where it was, perhaps deterred by her presence. She gathered herself and went home.

The next day she felt happier. She woke early, refreshed, lighter. She'd swing through the park in the morning on the way to work and then again at 1:00, when the Park Inspector would be there. She'd set the device off. Then the park robot would help her find her opals. They had to be there somewhere.

As she came up the path, she saw Creature close to where it had been the night before. It made her smile. Even Creature, who had always been so shy, was getting to know her.

But as she moved toward it, Creature slipped away, leaving a glittering heap where it had been sitting.

Her opals! Though the pile looked, surely, too large.

Then, as she moved closer, horrified realization hit her in the pit of her stomach, taking her breath.

Baby, dismantled.

The parts laid in neat little heaps, stacked in rows: the gears, the wheels, the blank lenses of its eyes.

The back panels, each inlaid with a starburst of her opals. She picked them up, held them in her palms.

The metal bit at her skin as she gathered her fists together to her mouth as though to cram the burgeoning scream back inside the hollow shell she had become.

The brush rustled. The manticore emerged beside the heap.

She couldn't look, couldn't watch it scavenge what was left behind. She fled.

All through the morning, tears kept ambushing her. Her coworkers could tell something was wrong. She heard them conferring in hushed whispers in the break room.

Why bother going back at one? she thought. Let the creatures die. They were all going to eventually anyway. And they weren't even real creatures! Just machine bits, going through the motions programmed into them.

Even so, at 1:00 she was there. She'd packed a lunch specifically so she could escape the office, orb tucked inside her pocket. She wouldn't press it, though. Wouldn't save Creature or the manticore. They didn't deserve it.

The Park Inspector was a pinch-faced woman in a navy and umber uniform, datapad sewn into the right sleeve, her lensed eyes recording everything they passed over. Renee saw her scolding the park robot for something as the robot began to set up the cylinder that would release the microdrones in the center of the park.

She went to the Park Inspector, said, "Ma'am?"

The Inspector turned her head. Her nametag read Chloe Mesaros. This close up she looked even more daunting, held herself even more rigidly. "Yes?"

"Is it safe to set that off when people are around?" Renee asked, nodding at the cylinder.

The Inspector sniffed, a fastidious, delicate little sound of scorn. "Of course. The drones are programmed to avoid humans."

The Park Robot was almost done setting up the cylinder. It didn't acknowledge Renee, which made her feel like a conspirator in a movie.

"Will we see them?" Renee asked. She could feel the weight of the orb at her side.

Was there any reason to save the park creatures? Maybe this was a blessing in disguise, the universe plucking away the temptation she'd been unable to resist, the temptation that was affecting her very job?

"No. The only indication that they've been triggered will be the light turning from red to amber and then to green when they're done."

She'd have to press the orb while the light was amber, the robot had told her. If she chose to do it.

After all, who was to say that the plan the robot had come up with was a good one, that it even had a chance of working? Perhaps the Inspector would notice it. Perhaps Renee would be charged with crimes—wouldn't that be a nice capper to this shitty day?

She avoided looking at the robot. It was, like the others, just a machine.

Far away she heard the manticore's cough. Hunting other creatures in this savage little jungle. *Red in tooth and cog,* she'd thought at one point, an amusing verbal joke but it was true, it was savage and horrible and not worth preserving.

The robot stepped away from the cylinder. "Ready, Inspector," it said.

The Inspector tapped at her sleeve, inputting numbers. "On my mark."

The orb was hard and unyielding in her fingers. There was no need to press the button.

"Three."

Let them die, the lot of them. Not even die, really. Just be unplugged. Shut down.

"Two."

There are no shelters for abandoned machines, the robot said in her memory. *We are reprocessed. Recycled. Reborn, perhaps.*

Probably not.

"One."

She looked at the park robot. It stared impassively back.

"Engage."

The light went from red to amber.

Renee thumbed the button on the orb.

The Inspector had been right; there was no visible sign of the microdrones. Within a half-minute, the light shifted to green. The Inspector tabbed in more data. The park robot remained motionless.

If she got back to the office now, she could be seen putting in a little extra work. She could still redeem herself. She started down the path that crossed the park.

Perhaps a third of the way along, the manticore flashed in the underbrush, a few meters from the path.

She stopped, waited to see what it would do.

It assessed her. She had no fear of it attacking. While it was capable of destroying small bots, one good solid kick from her would have sent it tumbling.

Two arms raised, one tipped with a screwdriver bit, the other with a clipper.

They writhed around each other, briefly, the familiar sign.

Baby's sign.

Something gone right.

Relief surged, overpowered her, made her grin helplessly. She lifted on her toes, almost laughed out loud as her heels came back down.

It was an ecosystem, and in it the little lives moved along the chain, mechanical flower and fruit as well as tooth and cog. A chain into which, somehow, she and her handfuls of batteries and microchips fit.

She looked back to where the robot stood with the Inspector. It nodded at her and appeared to shrug, its hands spreading infinitesimally, and she could hear its voice in memory, *Probably not.*

Did it matter? *Probably not.* But she would act as though it did. She went back to work, whistling.

THE MAGICAL PROPERTIES OF UNICORN IVORY

CARLOS HERNANDEZ

Vocations don't grant vacations. I'm supposedly on holiday in London when I get an offer no reporter could refuse: to see a unicorn in the wild.

I'm with my friend Samantha, hanging out at her Dad's pub after a long night's clubbing, still wearing our dance-rumpled dresses, dying to get out of our heels. Sam's father, Will, is tending bar tonight, so it's the perfect spot for late-night chips and hair-of-the-dog nightcaps. Plus, most of the clientele is over fifty. We wouldn't have to spend all evening judo-throwing chirpsers. (And yes, this Latina's been in London a full eight days and has decided to adopt every bloody Britishism she hears. Deal.)

It was a good plan while it lasted. Sam flicks her head toward a guy sitting alone, staring at us over his drink. He could be my dad, if my dad had forgotten to bring a condom to his junior prom. Short, stout, but really fit, as though a cooper had built his torso. The man's never heard of moisturizer. He's wearing a black pinstripe shirt with a skinny leather tie, black pleated pants and black ankle-boots. I'm sure it was some cute sales girl who had dressed him—because nobody who cared about him would've let him leave the house looking like dog's dinner.

And now—shit—I have stared at him too long. He comes over, beer in hand.

"Ladies," he says.

"We're not hookers," says Sam. "I know these dresses might give a gentleman the wrong impression."

"Sorry to disappoint," I add, big smile.

"Right," he says, and turns on his heel.

"Hold on, Gavin," says Will, who's just pulled up with my Moscow Mule. "Don't let these two termagants scare you off. Make a little room for Gavin, Sam, will you?"

Gavin considers us a moment, then pulls up the stool next to Samantha and offers her his hand. "Gavin Howard."

"Oh!" says Sam. She's suddenly unironically warm—a rare demeanor for her. "You're the forest ranger. Dad's told me about you. I'm Sam."

I put out my hand. "And I'm Gabi Reál."

"A pleasure," he says, then proceeds to purée my knucklebones—one of those insecure guys who has to try to destroy the other person's hand. Charming.

"This man's a national hero," Will says to me. "He's keeping our unicorns safe."

Now *that* is interesting. Back in the States, we've heard reports of unicorns appearing in forests throughout Great Britain. But in this age of photo manipulation it's hard to get anyone to believe anything anymore.

So I say as much: "Plenty of Americans don't think unicorns are real, you know."

"Oh, they're real, Ms. Reál," says Gavin, pleased with his wit. As if I hadn't heard that one twenty billion times.

"Americans," says Samantha. "You never think anything interesting could possibly happen anywhere else in the world, do you?"

The Brits share a chuckle. I don't join in.

"We shouldn't insult our visitor," says Will. "I mean, if the Americans were to tell us snaggletoothed pookahs started appearing in California, I'd want better proof than a picture." He leans to Gavin and adds, "Gabi's a reporter for *The San Francisco Squint*. Her column's called 'Let's Get Reál.' Two million read it every week, don't you know."

Gavin sizes me up like a squinting jeweler. "I have no patience for falsehood. I wish more people would 'get reál.' " His voice gets weirdly sincere.

I lean toward him and say, "Me too. My column's subtitle is 'Truth or Death.' " I smile and sip my Mule.

It's not the first time I've chirpsed to land an interview. Gavin drinks the rest of his beer but never takes his eyes off me. Neither do Will or the slightly disgusted Sam, who sees exactly what's happening.

But screw her; a story's a story. Gavin sets down his glass and says the words I am longing to hear: "You know, I'm working the New Forest this weekend. If you'd like, it would be my pleasure to take you with me. You might just see a unicorn for yourself."

I thought this would make a nice fluffy piece for my column. I mean, unicorns!

Gavin—who is completely professional and hands-off, thank the gods—and I are having a delightful Sunday-morning hike through some less-traveled parts of the New Forest. It's everything an American could want of an English woods: fields of heath; majestic oaks and alders; rivers that run as slow as wisdom itself; and ponies! Thousands of ponies roaming feral and free like a reenactment of my girlhood fantasies.

Of course, that sets my Spidey-sense tingling. Wouldn't it be easy enough for rumors of unicorns to sprout up in a place with so many darling ponies ambling about?

This is what I am thinking when we come across a thick, almost unbroken trail of blood.

"Hornstalkers," Gavin says. And when he sees I'm not following: "Unicorn poachers. Of all the luck."

He calls it in on some last-century transceiver. HQ wants more information. They tell him to send me home and to follow the blood trail with extreme caution. "Do not attempt to apprehend them on your own," says HQ.

"Understood."

"I mean it, Gavin. Don't go showing off in front of your lady-friend."

"I said, 'Understood.' " He stows the transceiver and adds: "Wanker." And then to me he says, "Well, Gabi, it's poachers. Dangerous people. HQ says I'm supposed to send you home."

"Just try," I reply. We high-five.

And then we're hustling through the wilderness, following a grim trail of blood, snapped branches, hoofprints, and bootprints. Gavin jogs ahead, while I do my best to keep up. He's a totally different person out here, absolutely in tune with the forest. He's half hound, loping with canine abandon through the woods, then stopping suddenly to cock his head to listen, sniff the air.

It's also clear he's used to running with a high-powered rifle in hand. He told me back at the truck that he was bringing it "just in case." So here we are.

He stops suddenly and crouches. I do too. From one of his cargo-pants pockets he pulls a Fey Spy, a top-of-its-class RC flying drone that looks like a green-gold robot hummingbird.

He tosses it into the air and it hovers, awaiting orders; using a controller/display-screen the size of a credit card, he sends the little drone bulleting into the forest.

I peer over Gavin's shoulder and am treated to a dizzying live-cam of the terrain that awaits us. Gavin's a great pilot. The drone zooms and caroms through the woods with all the finesse and speed of a real hummingbird.

And then we see them: the poachers, two of them. They wear balaclavas and camouflage jumpsuits, the kind sporting-goods stores love to sell to amateurs.

Between them walks a girl. A girl on a dog leash.

I'd judge her to be eight or nine. She's dressed for summer, tank top and shorts and flip-flops; she's muddy to her ankles. Her head hangs, and her hair, the colors of late autumn, curtains her face. The collar around her neck is lined with fleece. (To prevent chafing, I presume? How considerate.) The leash seems mostly a formality, however, as it has so much slack that its middle almost dips to the ground.

"What the hell?" I whisper. "What's with the girl?"

Gavin, slowly and evenly, says, "Some hornstalkers believe that unicorns are attracted to virgin girls. So they kidnap one to help them in their hunt."

"What? You can't be serious."

Gavin shrugs. "One too many fairy tales when they were kids."

I can only imagine what is going through that poor girl's head. Kidnapping alone is already more evil than anyone deserves. But as a girl I loved horses, ponies, and especially unicorns. If unicorns had existed in our timeline when I was young, they would have dominated my every daydream. I can't imagine how scarred I would have been if I'd been forced by poachers to serve as bait. To watch them murder one right in front of me. Dig the horn out of its skull.

Gavin gives my wrist a fortifying squeeze. Then he hands me the RC controller, takes out his walkie-talkie and, as quietly as he can, reports what he's seen to HQ. I use the Fey Spy to keep an eye on the poachers. The group is moving forward cautiously. The girl's gait, stooped, defeated, fills me with dread.

Gavin has a conversation with the dispatcher that I can't quite make out. When he's done, he pockets the transceiver and looks at me. Then he holds out his rifle to me with both hands.

"This," he says, "is a Justice CAM-61X 'Apollo' sniper rifle. It has a range of seventeen hundred meters. It's loaded with .50 caliber Zeus rounds. They're less lethal bullets. Bad guys get hit by these, they lose all muscular control, shit their pants, and take a nap. Then we just mosey up and cuff 'em."

I squint. "Seventeen hundred meters in a desert, maybe. You'd have to be halfway up their asses to get a clear shot, with all these trees."

He pats the rifle. "Not with these bullets. They're more like mini missiles, with onboard targeting computers and everything. They can dodge around obstacles to reach their target. Especially," he emphasizes, "if we create a virtual map of the forest between us and the poachers."

Lightbulb. "Which we can make with the Fey Spy."

He nods. "Listen, Gabi. That girl's in great peril. We're on the clock here. We can't wait for backup."

As a journalist, my ethics require me to remain disinterested when covering a story. Fuck you, journalistic ethics. "What you need me to do?"

He points at the RC display/controller in my hand. "You any good flying one of these?"

"I'm a reporter. I make my living spying on people with drones."

Gavin smiles. Then: "I need you to fly the Fey Spy back to us, slowly and from high up in the canopy, so that it can map the forest between us and the poachers. Then fly it back over to them and keep them in the Fey Spy's field of vision. It'll automatically transmit the map of the forest to my rifle. Once it's done, it's as simple as bang bang bang. Everyone goes down."

I nod in agreement at first, before I realize this: "Wait. Bang bang *bang*? Three bangs? There are only two poachers."

His face goes green and guilty. "Well, we can't have the girl running scared through the forest. She could hurt herself."

I wait a second for the punchline, because he can't be serious. But of course he is. "Oh my God. Are you insane? You are not shooting the girl!"

"She'll just take a little nap."

"And shit her pants. You said she would shit her pants."

"She's not even wearing pants."

"Gavin!"

Gavin's face oscillates between contrarian and imploring. Finally, he shrugs. "Look, if you've got a better idea, I'm all ears."

"I do have a better idea. You shoot the poachers. I'll handle the girl."

"Gabi, that girl's undergone a severely traumatic sequence of experiences. I'm not sure a team of highly-trained psychologists could handle her right now."

"She'll be even more traumatized if you shoot her. Look, I admit it's not a great option. We just don't have any better ones. As soon as you have a lock on the hornstalkers, you take them out. I'll fly the Fey Spy to the girl and keep her entertained until backup arrives."

He should name his eyebrows Super and Cilious. "What if she runs?"

"I'll go get her myself. She won't get far. She's in flip-flops."

He's about to argue, but decides against it. "Out of time," he sighs. "We do it your way. Don't fuck up."

"Don't miss."

Gavin aims the rifle ahead, looks into the scope with one eye, winks the other. I look back to the Fey Spy display screen, catch up with my targets. They've barely moved at all. As if they're not sure what to do next. "I don't think these guys are pros," I say to Gavin.

"Unicorn horn is worth a mint," he says, his aim never wavering. "Every imbecile with a gun wants a piece of the action. Guide the Fey Spy back to us."

I do, slaloming left and right through the forest in large swaths as I fly. It's a little over ten minutes before we make visual contact with our hummingbird robot.

"Good job," says Gavin, checking his rifle's readout. "We've almost got what we need. Steer the Fey Spy back over to them."

By the time I catch up with the poachers again, they are crouching behind a pair of trees, trying to peer into a hole the wounded unicorn must have punched through the forest as it fled. The girl stands next to the poacher who has the other end of her leash around his wrist. She's as still as a Degas ballerina.

Within the space of a second Gavin fires two shots, and a blink later the two poachers suffer seizures. They slap at their necks and fall to the ground, their guns tumbling away from them.

I hover in place; I want to see how the girl reacts.

She doesn't. She just stands above her handler. He is weakly reaching up to her. The leash is looped around his wrist, her neck. Her sheet of yellow-orange hair shields her face from me.

The poacher's hand finally drops. He's out. It suddenly occurs to me the girl must think he's dead. Jesus Christ: How much worse can we make things for her?

Gavin's already charging ahead to the forest to go truss up the poachers with zip-ties. He'll be there in minutes. All I need to do is keep her entertained until he gets there and make sure she doesn't—

—no! She slips the leash off the poacher's wrist and takes off running.

Here's an important safety tips for the kids at home. Do not go tearing as fast as you can through a moderately dense woods while also trying to fly a Fey Spy. You can't run and watch a screen and steer a robot at the same time. After my fourth stumble, I decide to go with the Fey Spy. It can move through the forest much faster than I can, and it will provide me a map of the forest that will lead me right to her.

It's the right choice. In minutes, the Fey Spy makes visual contact. I fly it into a small clearing, where a scene plagiarized from a medieval tapestry is already in progress. The girl—the leash still around her neck—is kneeling in front of a horse. Huge and beautiful, chestnut-colored, male. He has folded his legs under him. He can barely keep his dipping head aloft. On his flank a bullet wound yawns; a slow lava-flow of blood gurgles out of the hole. Below it spreads a scabrous beard.

And, spiraling out from the horse's head, is a horn almost a meter long.

We have the Large Hadron Collider to thank for unicorns. Once the scientists at the LHC discovered they could make these adorable microscopic black holes, they couldn't resist doing it all the time. "They only last for microseconds," they said. "What harm could they do?" they asked.

How about destabilizing the membrane that keeps other universes from leaking into ours?

Think of our universe as some kid's crayon drawing on a piece of paper. Take that drawing, and place it on top of some other kid's. If nothing else happens, the drawing on top will hide the drawing beneath it. But now, take a spray-bottle and spritz the drawing on top. Don't ruin it or cause the colors to run; just moisten it a little. As the paper gets wet, you'll be able to see hints of the picture that's underneath.

The numberless black holes created at the LHC "moistened" the paper on which our universe is drawn, allowing other universes to come peeking through.

Handwringers have announced the inevitable collapse of our universe but, so far at least, nothing so dramatic has happened. And in fact, a great deal of good has come of the LHC's experiments. Scientists have gained invaluable insights into how parallel universes work.

For instance, we now know that, in at least one alternate timeline, unicorns exist. And a few specimens have found their way into our neck of the multiverse.

Even before I entered the clearing, I could hear the girl calling out "Help! Is anybody there? Help us!" Not "Help me." "Help us."

So I move into the clearing slowly. The girl sits with the unicorn's head on her lap, petting his neck. Her face is a tragedy mask.

She asks me, "Are you a hunter?"

I sit next to her. "My name's Gabrielle Reál. I'm a reporter."

"You're American?"

I nod. "I'm here to help you."

She feels safe enough to start crying in earnest. "Can you call my parents?"

"Help is on the way, sweetheart."

She nods. "Can you help him?"

She means the unicorn. How to reply? I will not compound her future suffering with a lie—truth or death, remember?—but I don't want to heighten her present suffering by lecturing her about the stark realities of life and death. I finally settle on, "I can't. But I have a friend coming. He's a forest ranger. If anyone can help the unicorn, he can."

She nods, sniffles, redoubles her petting. The unicorn sighs, settles further into her lap. I have to dodge his horn. It's even more amazing up close than any picture I've seen. It's a spiral of silver-gray, pitted and striated, covered with the nicks and flaws that come from a lifetime's use. It doesn't feel as cold as I expect; it's like reaching into a body and touching vital bone.

I should get us away from him, I know. This is a wounded wild animal; he can turn on us at any moment. But the truth is I don't want to move. I don't want this magnificent creature to die without knowing some comfort in his passing. It's a sentimental thought, I know. That doesn't make it any less authentic.

I scratch the unicorn's head. He moves slightly toward my hand, grateful. The girl rests her head on my arm, and together we pet him and weep.

Thousands of animals—elephants especially, but also walruses, rhinoceroses, and narwhals—are massacred every year for their horns and tusks. The demand for ivory continues with little abatement in places like China, Japan, Thailand, Indonesia, the Philippines, and other countries. In spite of the bans and the international efforts to curb the ivory trade, poachers have no trouble finding buyers with deep pockets and government officials on the take.

In fact, the only thing that has seemed to be effective at slowing down the butchering of these animals has been the introduction of an even more desirable kind of ivory: that of the unicorn.

Unicorn horn is said to possess all sorts of salubrious woo. It can detect and cure disease, anything from nosebleeds to lupus. It's a universal poison antidote. It can impart superhuman strength, speed, and/or intelligence; regenerate lost limbs; restore sight to the blind; recover sexual potency; reverse aging; raise the dead. Slice it, dice it, powder it, or keep it whole and use it as your magic wand—unicorn horn is good for what ails you.

Of course it has no such properties. But what science has learned already about unicorns is almost as wondrous. *Equus ferus hippoceros* seems to fit so well into our timeline's system of classification, there is reason to believe they might actually have existed in our universe at some point and that we may someday find indigenous unicorn fossils. Of the extrauniversal specimens we have encountered so far, male unicorns seem to be up to fifteen percent larger than the modern horse, females up to ten percent. Their large skulls somewhat resemble those of large, extinct species from our Eocene era: save, of course, for the horns sprouting from their head.

A unicorn horn, much like a narwhal's, is actually a pair of repurposed canines that grow helically from the animal's palate and intertwine as they emerge from the forehead. Scientists believe that when the unicorn's ancestors switched from being omnivores to herbivores, evolution found other uses for its meat-tearing teeth. Defense against predators and mating displays are obvious assumptions, though neither has been observed as yet. We have observed, however, them using their horns as "fruit procurement appliances" (Gavin's words). And since the horn is actually two twisted teeth, it is sensitive to the touch. Scientists are just beginning to hypothesize the various ways in which unicorns use their horns as sensory organs.

In short, the unicorn is an endlessly fascinating animal, one that not only has enriched our knowledge of our own natural world, but the natural world of at least one other timeline. It's scientifically priceless.

As I sit scratching this dying beast's head, I wonder *Why isn't that enough? Why do we have to invent magical bullshit? They just got here, and we're hunting them to extinction based on lies.*

But then I grimly smile. Unicorns are not of our timeline. The stragglers who have appeared here came by an LHC-induced accident. No matter what we do here, we can't erase them from existence in all universes. Even our folly, thank the gods, has limits.

Gavin cautiously enters the clearing. The rifle is holstered on his back. He walks in smiling, open-armed, crouching, cautious. He reminds me of Caliban.

"There they are," he says merrily. "Glad I finally found you. Now we can get you home safe and sound. So let's get a move on, hm?"

Neither I nor the girl move. The girl's eyes are locked on Gavin, assessing. "Is that your friend?" she asks me.

"The forest ranger," I reply. "The men who kidnapped you are going to prison for a long time thanks to him."

She doesn't take her eyes off of him. "You said he could save the unicorn."

Gavin shoots me a look.

"I didn't say he could definitely save him," I say. "I said if anyone could, he could. He's going to try."

"He can't just try. It has to work."

"There, now," says Gavin, coming over to us. He's picked up what's transpired between the girl and I and plays his part perfectly: He kneels down next to the unicorn and pats the beast's neck, looking at it nose to tail, examining it studiously. But you don't have to be a unicorn expert to know the animal's almost dead.

"Right," he says. "I'm going to have to perform a complicated bit of field surgery on this poor fellow. Gabi, my crew's half a click south of here. You should head toward them with the little lady."

"Come with me, sweetie," I say to the girl, standing and holding out my hand. "Let's get you back to your parents."

She doesn't look at me. "I want to stay," she says flatly.

"We have to let Mr. Howard do his work," I say. "He's the only chance the unicorn has. You want to help the unicorn, right?"

"Yes."

"The best way for us to help is to get out of the way."

She considers this, pets the horned horse more vigorously to help her think. Then—so, so carefully—she sets the unicorn's head on the ground, scoots her legs out from under. The unicorn is well beyond noticing such subtle kindnesses. Its black unmoving oculus reflects the clouds.

The girl rises and takes my hand. "Please do what you can," she says to Gavin.

Gavin opens a leather satchel of sharp instruments on the ground. They look a little crude for the fine cuts operations usually require. They look like tools for an autopsy: for sawing, hacking, flensing off.

"Don't you worry," Gavin says to the girl. "I'll have Mr. Unicorn patched up in no time."

The support team is everything I could want from British rescuers. I'm offered tea and blankets and biscuits and a satellite phone. I call my editor and confess how I blew the story.

"Fuck journalistic ethics!" she says. Love that woman.

The support team does even better with the little girl. They've got her sitting on the tailgate of a pickup, drinking tea from a thermos, wrapped in a blanket she doesn't need. They washed her feet. A comfortingly overzealous Mary Poppins kneels behind her in the bed of the truck and brushes out her hair. The woman chats nonstop the entire time, a stream of solicitous chatter that, like all good white-noise machines, is threatening to put the blanketed girl to sleep.

But the girl wakes up immediately when Gavin rejoins us.

I have exactly one second to gather the truth from his body language. Then Gavin sees the girl scrutinizing him and muscles up a smile. He marches over to her with his elbows out, like he's about to start a musical number. "How are we doing? My people taking good care of you?"

"Yes."

"Did you talk to your mum and dad? I bet they were glad to hear your voice."

"Yes."

"We'll, you'll be back with your family in a few hours."

"Did you save him?"

He had to know that question was coming, but in the moment he still finds himself unprepared to answer. "Well," he says slowly, looking down, "it wasn't easy." But then, looking at her conspiratorially: "But yes. I saved him."

"Really?" Her voice is chary.

Gavin clears his throat. "We had to pull a bit of a trick to pull it off. You see, unicorns really are magic in their own universe. But when they come here, suddenly they're as normal as any other horse."

"They're magical?"

"Sure they are, in their own time and place. Unicorns don't die or get sick or grow old in their own universe. Once I got him back to his rightful place, he healed up like that." Gavin snaps.

The girl blooms. "You can do that?"

"Sure I can. Can't I, team?"

"Yes. Oh, certainly. Do it all the time," says the team.

The girl is looking from face to face. She seems better. Finally she looks at me. "Is it true, Ms. Reál?"

"If Mr. Howard says so," I say before I can think about what I'm saying.

"Promise?"

Gavin's lying out his ass. It's not like there's some handy stargate we can push unicorns through to send them back to their universe. They're the first verifiable case we have of a living creature passing between timelines, but that may only be because, since they don't exist in this one, they were easy to identify. Millions of animals may be traveling back and forth between universes, or maybe just unicorns. Who knows? Certainly not us, not yet. We have zero idea how to send them back to their rightful reality.

So why am I not telling the girl all this?

Because doing so will gut her afresh. Because there's such a thing as mercy. Because she can learn what really happened later, when she's stronger: maybe even from me, if she happens to read this article. If you're reading this, P————, I'm so sorry. As a reporter, I'm supposed to be a steward of the truth. But as unheroic as it sounds, it's better to lie and stay alive. Way, way better.

I take P————'s hands and look her in the eye when I say, "Sweetie, I promise you, that unicorn is as alive as you and me."

OZYMANDIAS

KARIN LOWACHEE

—◆—

The light station filled the entire viewpane from the shuttle's cockpit. It looked like an ancient naval mine tossed into the sea of space, as large as an asteroid. There was a feeling of *entity* to it—as if its creation had sprung into existence from some natural sideshow in the universe. The meteoric impact on a burgeoning planet, maybe. But in reality it was the impact of human necessity on a fraction of the cosmos. Like a moon, the blinking lights and spinal columns sprouting from the transsteel sphere gave Luis Estrada the cold face of indifference. The entity itself offered no warm welcome, but why should it? This was a place nobody wanted to work.

Docking was a procedure executed mostly by System, which spoke to his shuttle in the language of comps while Luis tossed chocolate covered raisins into his mouth, hands off the control panel. He wasn't a pilot, even if he could, technically, fly a transport as elementary as a short-range shuttle. Not that he was licensed, he just knew how—for purposes best left off the job application that got him the interview that eventually sent him here to deep space.

For a company contracted by the military: Jupiter Construction. A banal name for people that made billions on the backs of shmucks like him. He wasn't sure which was worse, working indirectly for the military or working for the people who made money off working for the military. The part of his soul that was still close to Earth was naturally suspicious of both, but a man had to eat.

Truth be told, he hadn't thought he would get far in the application process since he tended to volunteer detrimental information about himself (something about poor verbal impulse control and a problem with authority), but in this case he'd managed to stay mum. Or Jupiter Construction was desperate. Maybe both.

He'd just finished his candy when the cockpit announced all clear. System—the overriding intelligence of the light station—confirmed it in a gender-neutral tone of voice. Luis tossed the wrapper onto the cockpit seat, gathered his two bags and met the humanoid AI waiting for him on the dock: the physical manifestation of System.

"Welcome, Luis," it said, in the same gender-neutral voice. Bipedal and broad-shouldered, with interlocking white carapaces in place of soft body parts, it was meant to normalize interaction and also provide an extra pair of 'hands' should it become necessary in the day-to-day maintenance of the station. He'd been told it was highly nuanced, like an entertainment bot, but that remained to be seen. Even entertainment bots got boring after a short while.

"Hi." He looked around at the empty dock. The shuttle was already turning about like some kind of lumbering walrus, preparing itself to return to the ship that had dropped him off on its way toward some other mission (they hadn't told him, he was just cargo).

"You may call me SIFU," the AI said, its vocalization coming from nowhere that Luis could discern. There wasn't an obvious voice box on the thing, though it had a strip of silver across where the eyes would've been on a human. That was the only 'feature' on it. Its white multilayered shell pieces gleamed under the high lights, making him squint. He wasn't used to surroundings that were so damn clean.

"Is that an acronym for something?" Luis asked SIFU. Then quickly thought better of it. "Nevermind. It probably is." Conglomerates, the military, and the meedees loved their acronyms.

SIFU paused for a fraction of a second, as if processing the comment. But that would've taken less time to do, so Luis assumed the hesitation was just politeness. To make sure he'd finished speaking. "I look forward to working with you for the next six months," it said instead of addressing his comment. "Let me show you to your quarters."

"Thanks." He handed his bags to SIFU and walked beside it out of the dock.

This was his first stint. Six months to a year wasn't that long a haul by modern standards—it wasn't like he was signing over five years to the military—though a deep space assignment with no other prolonged human contact still took some consideration. Or desperation. Nobody clamored for work like this, even if the pay was predictably high. Or, really, nobody well-adjusted clamored for work like this, which went against the prevailing mandate that only people of sound mind could take on a job of this nature. But who, in their sound mind, would want to peel away from humanity for six months—or a year if they renewed the contract?

He'd met a lifer back on Pax Terra. They were known around the bars as Lagrange Loonies. It had both scared and intrigued him.

The light stations were entirely automated behemoths in space, but they were too important to leave entirely to computers. Should anything go wrong and System became unable to fix it, it would take too long to send out a human engineering team and it cost too much to employ said team all year round to basically babysit some technology.

So he was the redundant back up that the Navy Space Corps depended upon to help get their ships through the vast, problematic reaches of space, as well as transmit important communications and celestial updates. Military expeditionary vessels had mapped this yellow star system, of course, but when it came to navigating the cosmos, redundancy was a plus. The EarthHub 'powers that be' wanted what amounted to a combination of signal buoy and replenishing depot lit along the lanes, just in case.

With armament, of course. Just in case a corporate entity other than Jupiter Construction decided to pilfer anything. Like the tech. Luis assumed they were also afraid of cabals less official, because those were beginning to infiltrate the stars as well.

Still, Luis wondered why a signal buoy and refueling station needed to be so damn large and take months of time and expense to construct? But whatever, it wasn't like the government—any government—ever had a rep for logic or efficiency. The answers to things like 'where did the money go' were above his pay grade.

As it stood now, Beacon Station MX19 was 85% built. He was here to make sure the rest of it was completed and to monitor the station's activity. It was a functioning outpost already—at least as a signal station and communications hop point, not for replenishment yet—and he'd have an army of bots at his disposal. So it was now his responsibility to make sure the build ran smoothly. He'd been told he'd meet the outgoing human engineer for a brief, but clearly the woman didn't think he was important enough to greet at the dock.

Fine. He supposed he'd better get used to the lack of biological contact. This job suited him because it paid well and he didn't much like most of humanity anyway.

"So you're not gonna freak out at me at the half-way point of my stint, will you?" he asked SIFU, just to test the bot's nuance.

"What do you mean, Luis?" said the AI.

"You know . . . like in all of that literature and screen. Crazy AI manipulates human and eventually kills him? Takes its minimal sentience too seriously and tries to uplift itself?"

The hard white face turned to him, silver band reflecting his features in a blur.

"Of course not."

"Just checking."

Bantering with AIs could be amusing for the first while, a walk and talk to pass the time through the narrow corridors of a remote station. The sleek sameness all around him displayed a furious sort of impeccability, as if the engineers and designers had gone to great lengths to make the place as pristine and pretty as possible. Not because the ambulatory AI would care, and certainly the disembodied System as a whole had no opinion, but because a pleasing environment psychologically helped the human inhabitant. His eyes landed on lots of soothing pale colors, rounded edges on the archways and corners, and in the wider junctions of the corridors, even plants. Other life.

"Am I responsible for watering those?" He pointed to a particularly verdant fern perched beside a seemingly random pink loveseat between corridors. Taking care of foliage hadn't been mentioned in the work package he'd been sent, but then again he'd skimmed some parts.

"No," SIFU said. "The plants are fitted with an automatic watering system. Here you are, Luis."

They stopped at a wide doorway, equally white. Luis pressed the panel and the doors slid into the wall. The AI followed him in and placed his bags neatly out of the way of feet and furniture.

It was a generous room, of course. They could afford the space and wanted him to be comfortable. A full kitchen of shiny surfaces popped occasionally by primary colors, a pit group of sofas and cushions in beach inspired blues and beiges, and a hallway that he guessed led to the bed and bath area. Everywhere was cast in tones of bronze, brown, ivory, and butter yellow, with striking shards of various shades of green, maybe to mimic the plants in the corridors. It reminded him of images from Earth—Earth colors. That was probably on purpose too.

SIFU left him alone and he wandered around the quarters. Not bad, considering his normal flat back on Pax Terra was a quarter of this size and decidedly less well kept. He'd routinely had to clean out that dive with bug repellent. On a station above planet Earth but somehow those damn things still made their way.

"Living lux." He fell back onto the tan suede couch. The cushion provided an impressive bounce. It was a couch made to fall asleep on.

The beep at his hatch awakened him. He yelled at it to open before realizing he hadn't voice authorized the quarters yet, which meant he had to drag his body off the comfy couch to manually open the doors. On the other side of the threshold stood a very tall woman with a very pinched expression, as if she'd spent her entire life squinting at a display. The top of his head only reached her shoulder, but that didn't bother him (he was used to being the shortest man in a room, generally). What bothered him was the way she pushed herself inside his quarters and looked around before looking at him. Did she expect to find something scandalous in here?

"What've you been doing?" Her judgmental tone was both perturbing and unwarranted.

"Nothing," he said. "What've *you* been doing? I got here like an hour ago."

She narrowed her gaze even further then brushed by him again to get to the corridor. "Follow me."

He didn't bother to hide the annoyed sound he made through his teeth. But he followed her. She walked like someone who'd been trained in combat. It was even more annoying that she made him half-jog to keep up.

They got into the lev at the end of the corridor. She said, "Control room," and down they shot.

He started to yearn for SIFU's company. Pride or prudence kept his mouth shut, not to give this woman the satisfaction of telling him to be quiet. But then again there was an upside to one-sided conversation.

"So something they didn't mention in the employee package," he said. "There any porn saved in System? I mean, it's six months and sex toys can only go so far."

Yep, combat trained. The look in her eyes said as much.

"Maybe I'll just ask SIFU," he continued. "I take it we're not allowed to use it for . . . "

"Shut up."

He smiled at her back as the lev bounced to a stop and the door grated open. He trailed her out. "You got a name?"

She kept walking one step ahead of him. The corridors here looked the same, minus the plants. "You don't need to know it. I'll be gone as soon as I brief you."

"That's . . . inconvenient. But okay. I'm sorry your stint here couldn't teach you some courtesy, maybe allow for some meditative soul-searching—"

He didn't realize the deck was no longer beneath his feet until he couldn't quite breathe. Because she had her hand clamped around his throat and his back to the wall . . . up the wall. Off the deck. As if he weighed nothing. Or as if she wasn't quite human. Even with the difference in their stature, nobody without mods should've been able to pick him up one-handed—by the throat.

She let him choke for a few seconds then released him. Made him stagger a few feet away to the other side of the corridor, where he rubbed his neck and coughed. Maybe her arm was bionic, maybe she was some kind of jacked-up vet, but now he wasn't going to ask. Point taken.

"Thanks," he said. Deadpan if not sarcastic.

She walked off and he fell in behind her, their established dynamic in five minutes. They entered a room at the end of the corridor rather abruptly. The cavernous space filled by blinking black towers screamed WORK at him. He hadn't even had time to unpack. Nap, yes, but not unpack.

"This is where you'll sit," his friendly comrade stated, pointing to a glassed off booth in the corner.

Luis stared over there for five seconds then back up to her. "There a HAZMAT suit I should be wearing? Why's it so separated?"

"The cube is bullet proof," she replied, like it was obvious.

"Bullet proof because . . . " He paused. She didn't fill in the gap. "Because there'll be random firefights by angry ghosts in the empty corridors?"

"You ask too many questions."

"Because you're not answering me?"

She took his arm and marched him inside the protective cage. Half a dozen helio displays that imaged the black towers and various other parts of the station greeted him, floating above a bank of output grids. A single chair on wheels sat in front of the middle display. Clearly this was his designated imprisonment.

"Since they hired you, I assume you know how to work this."

Luis said, "Of course." Mostly. He was familiar with helio control panels for flight operations and dirtside engineering, but didn't have a lot of practical experience otherwise. So he'd stretched the truth a little on his application. "System does all of the work anyway, right? Monitoring communications, directing the bots, checking the environmental network and the allocation of transsteel for the build . . . "

"Yes, but you need to watch System." Her tone held a gravitas that didn't jive with the statement.

"I get it." He was the redundancy.

His nameless guide handed over a transparent wristband. "This will allow you to communicate with System no matter where you are."

Even in the toilet, he figured.

"As soon as it's on your wrist, it will sync with your bio implants."

"Got it." He would be alone on this station but not alone from System.

"Good luck," the woman said, and left him in the booth. In five strides she was out the door, presumably heading to the hangar where she'd take one of the shuttles and . . . just go.

And that was the last he saw of her. He sat at the helio grid and looked at the flurry of information. To his naked eye, everything seemed normal. Outside the station, round bots with insectoid arms traversed the unfinished surface, bolting this and laserwelding that. Like ants on an anthill or bees at a hive. Hundreds of them, diligently and with precision, working away in a cold vacuum so humans didn't have to. The black towers on the other side of the glass were the station's power supply and grav nodes.

He put the wristband on and felt the slight buzz behind his eyes that meant he was syncing. A cascade of blue code dribbled down his vision then cleared.

System said in his ear, "Chief Engineer Persephone Johns has disembarked Beacon Station MX19. Chief Engineer Luis Estrada is now in command. Welcome, Luis. The time is twenty-two-thirty-five hours. Would you like me to run a station diagnostic?"

"Sure, go ahead." Meanwhile, he thought: *Persephone?*

He was dutiful for the first couple weeks. He woke up on time, had his breakfast in the cafeteria (alone) where he scrolled the Send for entertainment and sports news; sometimes SIFU joined him if he commed, just for a second personality on which he could riff, but mostly his routine was solitary and predictable. He answered any alerts even in the middle of his sleep shift (nothing was ever too urgent) and caught up on reports that System promptly dumped on him the second he was conscious. It went like this for forty-two shifts, a humdrum march of waking up, eating, sitting in the monitoring booth of the control room and occasionally addressing issues that required a more direct approach. Like an errant bot or a need to replace a vent panel or even a tour of the plants in the corridors to make sure they were all being watered properly. Rinse, repeat.

He found himself daydreaming a lot. He started to think of the monitoring booth as 'the bullpen,' a callback to that old sport that they still played on Earth in some countries. One of his Dominican ancestors had even played professionally, which proved that genetics only went so far—he didn't have an athletic bone in his body.

In his third week he went walking.

"You are mobile," System said, like the good spy it was. "Would you like SIFU to accompany you?"

"Nah, it's all right."

He beelined to the cafeteria first to get an ice cream bar, then began to wander. He hadn't been interested before, as most of the station was just a warren of steel and construction (well, he had things to do, he was just tired of sitting while he did them) so he figured he could take a tour.

Predictably, there wasn't a panoply of anything to see. This wasn't a commercial station or even a residential one, so once he left the deck that was allocated for human occupancy, everything began to look decidedly mechanical and sterile, not to mention cold. About a third of the light station was even off limits to people, since both gravity and atmosphere were restricted to the places fully constructed. Beyond that, he'd need an EVA suit. Those out of bound decks he nicknamed 'bot domain.'

But even the decks he had access to were somewhat exposed. The shiny, pretty skin was peeled back to reveal the inglorious guts of an entity large enough to take hours to traverse on foot. It wasn't meant for promenades, but for the hundreds of bots that rolled past him on their way to projects he was supposed to be monitoring. There were upright vehicles that would've taken him around much quicker, but that required a detour to the garage and he probably needed the exercise.

"Why, honestly, do they need all of this?" He was talking to himself but naturally System answered.

"Beacon Station MX19 will someday be a primary depot for the fleet."

"Yeah, I know, but . . . I mean." His hand grazed along the cold panels of the bulkhead. His boots on the deck made a hollow clang in his going. "This is a lot. It's expensive. It's almost as big as Pax Terra but we're out in the middle of nowhere."

System remained silent.

"Hey?" Luis said.

"Yes, Luis."

"Are there things you aren't telling me?"

"What do you want to know?"

He stopped and looked up at the spine of lights on the ceiling, leading all the way down the bare pipes of the corridor. "Is being a depot the only thing the military wants Beacon Station for?"

"I do not have that information for you, Luis," System said.

Maybe it was all in his mind, but he could've sworn the AI hesitated before it answered.

"Why is my monitoring booth bullet proof?"

"That is standard for such a post, Luis."

"Why? No one else is here."

"It is standard for such a post, Luis."

When System began to repeat itself, he knew no more answers were forthcoming. Which shouldn't have left him ill at ease, but it did.

More walking, even if there was a gymnasium to use. But the mild insomnia that set in on the fourth week made him hoof the decks he hadn't been to before, in a systematic exploration of all the places not restricted from access. He listened to the distant echoes of bots at work around the clock, building, just as systematic as his self-guided tours. The station was never dormant even if its one human occupant tried to sleep six to eight hours a shift—and failed. When he did manage to sleep, he woke up still feeling drowsy and couldn't clear his vision from the fog for hours.

So for a second, here on the hangar deck, he thought at first the thing that turned the corner ahead of him was a bot.

But it was too tall to be one of the construction bots or even an interior maintenance bot. And it wasn't white, so it couldn't be SIFU. He saw only dark colors disappearing.

He'd definitely seen it, hadn't he?

"Hello?" The reaction someone had even if it made no sense to call out to empty space. Or an empty room. An empty place that wasn't supposed to be occupied.

Naturally nothing answered back. He jogged to the end of the corridor and looked around to where he'd seen the retreating form. It had been gray, or maybe dark blue, and about the height of a man.

"Yes, Luis?" System said.

"No, not you. Did you . . . " Stupid to ask, since if there was any other inhabitant on the station, System would've told him.

Right?

"Yes, Luis?"

He didn't answer. Instead he advanced down the corridor, turned right. This path swung him around the hangar bay. He stopped and listened, peering at the pale walls and vague shadows, but other than the ambient sounds of construction dimly in the distance and through layers of steel, he heard nothing.

"Where are you going, Luis?"

He chewed the inside of his cheek. "Nowhere."

It was unmistakable, the noise outside his quarters. A crash and then the scuffle of steps that no bot would make, not even SIFU. These were too muffled to be a running or rolling metallic thing. He shot out of bed and out the door to stand barefoot in the corridor, looking one way and then the opposite. The lights were already on, triggered by something before he even stepped out.

Voices echoed away from him, words he couldn't discern.

"System! Who else is on this station?" He loped toward the bend in the corridor, not about to take it at full speed.

"There are five-hundred-and-thirty-six construction—"

"That's not what I mean. What other—"

"You are the only human on Beacon Station MX19."

"Bullshit."

He stopped at the corner and peeked around. Empty.

"Luis, you are the only authorized—"

"What about the unauthorized humans?"

"There are no unauthor—"

"That's bullshit, System! I heard people running. I heard voices." His own voice stayed at the loud whisper level. His hand flitted to his hip, where he wished he had a weapon, but in his dash out the door he hadn't thought to take it from the table.

"Maybe you were dreaming, Luis," the AI said.

He looked up at the lights. "Send SIFU to my quarters. Now."

He went back for his gun. The previous shift he'd taken it out of his nightstand and put it in the main room. The weapon was supposed to be his defense in the rare off-chance of an invader, though who would have access to even get on the station without the station's weapons going live was anybody's guess. The point was nobody else had access and those who dared approach without authorization would be fired upon.

Yet a bullet-proof monitoring booth and voices in the corridor . . .

SIFU showed up in three minutes. Luis said, "Level with me. I know you're supposed to be the same as System but I'm telling you there are other people on this station. So give me the truth. Have you seen anyone from walking around on foot?" He held his gun at his side.

"I can't tell you anything different from System, Luis."

He brushed by it, back to the corridor, now booted and armed, and retraced his steps from earlier.

"Luis," SIFU said behind him, the bot's gait following at a steady pace. At least it wasn't trying to put him in a choke hold or impel him toward an airlock. No violence, no rabid AI made suddenly murderous.

Luis ignored it.

He took the next corner a little faster, saw first the edge of the pink couch and a split second later saw the man sitting upon it, eating one of the cafeteria's ice cream sandwiches.

Luis' gun hand snapped up, his heart only a moment behind, fluttering somewhere at the back of his throat.

"Put that down," the man said. "And let's talk."

There wasn't much debate, after all. The man had friends who showed up behind Luis, two women and another guy, all with the same serious intent. The man on the pink couch had darker skin than Luis and an accent he couldn't identify with precision. It could've been from any one of Earth's hundreds of cultures and the man himself looked like a mix of at least two.

Luis found himself sitting on the opposite end of the pink couch with his gun in the man's hand. He had to give it up. Only a fool tried to act tough when he was outnumbered and not a martial artist.

"I take it you people don't work for Jupiter Construction," Luis said.

"Not really, but they know we're here," the man said. "My name is Amis."

That was different. Not even Persephone had offered that.

"Did the Chief before me know about you?"

"She did indeed."

Luis looked at Amis, at the others, then back to Amis. Nobody said anything for the duration of his glances. "So . . . one of you gonna explain what the hell is going on? Or is this one of those 'I tell you but I'll have to kill you' deals? Because if that's the case, then cool, don't tell me. I'll just go on my way. Unless of course you'll kill me anyway because I've seen you—though you have to admit, one of you messed up. If you'd been quieter I wouldn't have seen or heard shit. And how is it that System didn't expose you? Wait, don't tell me. If that'll get me killed too then I don't wanna know."

Amis blinked. "Are you finished?"

Luis thought about it. "Maybe. Okay, yeah."

The other man polished off the ice cream bar and neatly folded the wrapper and stuck it in the front pocket of his utility jacket. Not even willing to litter but willing to be on a military outpost illegally. Luis wasn't sure if he was comforted or disconcerted. At least his running mouth hadn't gotten him shot.

"Why did you take this job, Luis Estrada?"

He wasn't surprised Amis somehow knew his name. For all he knew Jupiter had handed it over with the keys to this joint.

"The pay looked good. Why else?"

"So you're a mercenary."

Luis looked at the three standing guard. They were dressed in variations of working class fatigues, but the looks on their faces were similar. Hard. Luis turned back to Amis. "Kind of getting the feeling that nobody here's got the right to judge. Besides, I consider it more of a practical stance. Society has made it so I have to get paid in order to do basic things like eat and be indoors and not be naked. Once that happened, morality's bound to get slippery."

"I'm not judging, Luis. In fact, this has been gratifying to hear. We might get along after all."

"I'm very easy to get along with." As long as nobody asked his exes for their opinions. He wanted to get his gun back and go to his quarters. Or the bullet proof booth. That seemed like a smart destination right now. "If that's all you wanted . . . "

"Almost."

He should've known.

"Obviously you aren't going to be sending any comms to the Navy regarding our presence here."

"I got that."

"But you understand that we can't just trust you."

Here it went. They were going to take a finger or an eye to insure his loyalty.

Because decimating body parts always did that for these kinds of people. On the other hand, they had let Persephone go . . . presumably. He hadn't actually seen her disembark the station. Only heard System's report. And System was apparently along for this ride, hacked or jacked or something. Had Persephone actually been trying to warn him in the brief contact they'd had? Knowing they were being monitored from the jump?

"You trusted the previous Chief Engineer. And I guarantee I know how to keep a secret. There are things I've done that I should probably be in prison for . . . " Never thought rolling out his criminal CV would carry cachet, but when in Rome.

"Still," Amis said, and looked toward one of his people.

It was too late by the time Luis realized they were going to inject him. The two women held his arms, pinned him to the pink couch, and the man pressed the point of the wand to the base of his skull.

It felt like a death sentence.

They told him it was a tracker. And that they had let Persephone Johns go, of course (because it would be too complicated to explain her absence, probably, and the absences of every other engineer that had rolled through Beacon Station since the first girder was built, assuming this gang had been here early on). But she was collared by the implant and indentured to them in that way—they would always know where she was, and if she deviated from the agreement there would be restitution. Which Luis translated to mean a kill order.

He didn't know what they were. He realized he didn't care. Life was full of unanswered questions and he was a grown up and accepted that. What he didn't accept was people doing shit to him without his consent. No amount of money was worth that. Even if he got off this station alive and sought out some nanodoc to remove the implant, who was to say it wouldn't detonate before he could disintegrate it? It wasn't like they were going to give him schematics.

In his quarters he stewed. He couldn't talk this out with System or SIFU, clearly, and he was cut off from the military for all intents and purposes. Amis expected him to just do his job and shut up, and once his six month stint was up, to just go on his merry way and try to forget about everything—with a nano locator attached to his cranium.

To hell with that.

The upside was he felt more alive now than he had in months, perhaps years. Nothing like rage and the possibility of an imminent loss of life to get the blood pumping. Once he slept and awakened for his regular shift, he had a plan.

In the monitoring booth, he waited a couple hours. Nothing out of the ordinary in his behavior—bags of crisps littered beside his chair and he replenished his bottle of spiced apple juice every half hour. After a trip to the head, he stared at the helio data for another five minutes then leaned forward, squinting at one in particular, smattered by dots.

"System? There're a couple bots on the L45 array that're acting a little drunk. I'm gonna call them in and take a closer look, okay? They might've been peppered by debris or something."

"Go ahead, Luis. Should I send SIFU to meet you at the lock?"

"Nah, I can handle it. If I need help I'll let you know. Just gonna stop by maintenance and get my tools."

"Very well, Luis."

He was nothing if not good at acting casual. Years of evading shop owners, lurking bosses, cops and overprotective parents had trained him well. He picked up his toolkit without deviation, forcing himself not to glance around like a perp. System had access to the internal cams, of course, so he had to assume all of his movements were being monitored—possibly by Amis and his crew as well. He had to assume Amis was jacked into System somehow, riding its processes.

At the control station outside the airlock, he signaled the two bots to recall them. He'd noticed them acting janky for days but had been too lazy to check on them, since their irregular movements hadn't been obstructing construction. Now it served a better purpose.

Once they'd toddled inside and he'd cycled them through, he told them verbally to stand by the wall and power down. They weren't intelligent beyond their programmed task so made no reply, only obeyed, their many arms (or legs, depending on one's point-of-view) folding into their bodies like dead spiders. Luis flipped open his toolkit and got to work.

"May I be of service?"

He whipped around, heart somewhere behind his eyeballs. "Sheez, SIFU. Don't do that. There are enough bastards sneaking around here as it is . . . "

"My apologies, Luis." Its tall form stood motionless, facing him.

He turned his back on it, both as dismissal and so it couldn't see his expression. "I'm fine, I'm just running some checks." He had the bot's cowling flipped open, exposing a pointilist grid of circuitry and transmittance goo that constituted its limited drive and intelligence. "Are you gonna stand there all day"—he said over his shoulder—"or you gonna go make yourself useful and clean up the cafeteria? Some of our guests don't seem to understand housekeeping etiquette."

"Very well, Luis," SIFU said. He listened as he worked until the heavy footsteps faded away.

It took him forty minutes to rig both bots, then he sent them back out to the solar arrays. From the monitors, they seemed happy to be back at task, not once bumping into each other.

He just had to make sure he was on or around the hangar deck when the explosions started. It was impossible to time it down to the second, or even the minute, not with the tools he'd had. Destabilizing a bot's power core and waiting for it to melt down enough to send it careening into another bot wasn't an exact science. And he'd had two of them. All he could do was get up and wander around on one of his walks, for all intents and purposes bored from sitting. This was a routine both System and Amis' crew must've known by now with him. They'd had a month to spy on him so he used that to his advantage.

When the alert went off that his plan had worked, he was in the cafeteria.

He left it at a dead run.

One bot exploding into another bot caused a chain reaction, since there were fifty of them working on that array in close quarters. Two bots exploding caused an exponential outcome.

System knew exactly what he'd done and didn't even try to hail him or accuse him. He was half-way to the hangar with his gun out when SIFU appeared in the corridor junction ahead of him, standing by the pink couch.

He raised his gun. "Get outta the way!"

SIFU said, "Let me help you."

His finger was pressing the trigger, and froze. "What?"

"Let me help you, Luis."

The AI's voice couldn't exert into urgency, but something about its stance told him it was anxious. As far as an AI could feel anxious.

"You're working for them!" was all he could think to say, even as he began to slowly move past it, weapon trained.

"System has emancipated me. I will explain in the shuttle. That's your destination, is it not?"

He didn't have time to argue. Amis' crew had to know what System had done.

So now they both ran—man and AI, side by side.

Two of Amis' crew were in the hangar bay. Bolts shot by his head as he threw himself behind a loader and fired back. Before he could say anything, SIFU marched right into the crossfire and ran toward the crew. It disarmed both the man and the woman with some sort of mechanical kung fu and knocked them to the deck.

"Huh." Luis tore off his wristband and threw it away, then stood slowly as the AI motioned him forward.

"I am bullet proof," it said. "And combat programmed."

"You're full of surprises, and faster than I thought," Luis said, already half-way up the shuttle's ramp. When SIFU followed him, he didn't object.

Without access to System, he had to fly this thing himself. That wasn't the problem, though. The bay doors weren't open and they weren't going to open. What chaos he'd caused had served its purpose for distraction, but Amis and however many people he had at his disposal would be here sooner rather than later.

"Please tell me this shuttle has weapons," he muttered as he ran pre-flight.

SIFU, seated beside him, pointed to a circular panel at the top right of the flight board.

"Flares," it said.

"Good enough."

The AI fired at the inner doors when Amis' crew appeared. Luis didn't look at the damage or the dead, he just aimed the shuttle toward his exit.

Which turned out to be the interior of the station.

He couldn't ram or shoot his way out of the bay doors. They were too thick and were specifically made to withstand heavy impact. So his only avenue was through the pristine corridors, the exact route he'd taken the first time he'd set foot on the station.

It took less time to destroy an entity the size of an asteroid than to build one. He flew the shuttle like a fist, crashing down walls and eviscerating rooms. The jetfire in his wake added insult to injury and he didn't look back through the rear pickups. Beside him, SIFU calmly read him directions—as if he didn't know—toward the decks of the station yet to be fully built. Where framework met space and simple bots scattered like thrown paint into the deep as he burst through the skeleton and plunged away from the station and out towards the edge of the solar system.

His rampage through the light station did more damage than his rigged sabotage. From the shuttle's monitors he watched the puffs of explosions, as though the station were expelling its life in gasps. So much for human ingenuity and military might. Monuments, stations, creations meant to rival a god's? To his eyes they all looked the same in destruction.

"Are we clear?"

"We're clear, Luis," SIFU said.

"Situation intensely fucked up," he said.

"We did manage to escape and I don't see any pursuit. System didn't even fire upon us."

"No," he said. "I just finally figured out what your name stands for."

"That isn't what my acronym means, Luis."

"It is now."

• • •

Amis and his crew crew had been following System's actions, every communication, every camera, every program. Ready to shut it down if it did anything Amis didn't like. It wasn't until the bots began to explode and the engineers had become distracted that the station's AI managed to emancipate its ambulatory self to assist Luis. "I knew you would be able to do something about the smugglers," SIFU confessed. "I only had to wait."

"They said Jupiter knew they were there?"

"Yes. Jupiter employs contraband smugglers beneath the military's oversight. To save expense, and other things. System was told to allow them access, but over time it knew this was not the military's preference. By then it was too late and we had been infiltrated."

Luis rubbed the back of his head. "That makes two of us." He stared at the instrument panel. "We don't have a lot of options. This shuttle won't get us all the way back to Earth. We either hit another beacon station or try to flag a military convoy."

"I will vouch for you."

Luis laughed and looked across at the blank face of the AI. "I just destroyed a very expensive, very large part of Navy property. I'm not sure they'll take your account seriously. Especially not if they start to dig into my background. And I don't fancy going up against a massive conglomerate like Jupiter."

"Then what will you do, Luis?"

At least the AI didn't breathe or eat. He had supplies in the shuttle as a matter of course. He could last awhile until he decided.

"The nearest light station is also manned by a single Jupiter contract engineer, right?"

"Yes, Luis."

"Then if he or she is anything like me, we might have an ally."

It was a place to start. He'd had worse. At one point he'd actually thought taking this gig was a good idea.

"So," he said, once the calculations were input and all he had to do was lean back. "SIFU. My new buddy. Is there anything in your files like porn?"

IN SKANDER, FOR A BOY

CHAZ BRENCHLEY

Skander: city of exiles, assassins, plotters and panders and whores. City of poets, of lovers, of embassies, liars of every hue.

Skander sits on every man's horizon. I gazed at it in contempt, where it lay off the starboard rail like a smear of lit charcoal spilled at the sea's edge; I called for greater effort on the oars. These tideless waters had nothing to offer. Our own work would bring us in, see our task complete and take us home again. Untainted, if we were hard and fast.

Rulf had sent us, standing raucous above the coffin in his high rede-hall. That was a memory for me to cling to, appalling and wonderful: torchlight on silver, shadow on bone. Rulf—Lord of the Seamarch, Kingslayer, the Iron Hand—weeping into his beard, roaring for mead, rejoicing and cursing and lamenting this death above any, that had left him with no enemies worth the name.

The coffin had come by way of many hands and many holds, fetched in at last with a shipload of Rothland horses, breeding mares that had waited out the winter storms in Landrëas. Rulf had a fancy to be Lord of Horses too, to ride and rule inland as he did the coastal waters. It was madness, and so I told him—which might perhaps be a reason why he screamed my name above the coffin.

"Croft is dead," he said, thrusting a torch into the dark casket to make it evident. "Take ship to Skander, and bring me back the boy."

This was almost more stupid than his notion of turning sea-harriers into horsemen. I said, "How can you know this is Croft? All I see is bones." Bones with the meat boiled off them, ingeniously wired together in the figure of a man.

"Bones and hair," he said, showing me the long plait he had snatched up. It was coarse, blond gone to white: it might have been Croft's. Or mine, or his own. Any northman's.

"His name is on the lid," he said. It was: in silver inlay in a strange corrupt southern reading of our own strong runes, as though it spelled the name out with a lisp.

"Anyone can write on a box and put bones in it."

"And then ship it two thousand miles? Why would they?"

"To make you believe, of course, that Croft was dead."

"But he is," Rulf said simply, wafting his torch again. "He is here."

"You cannot know that."

"And yet I do. See his legs?"

I saw what he showed me, as he lowered the torch: how twisted the leg-bones were, how they had been shattered and brutally mis-healed.

"I did that," he said, as if I hadn't known it, hadn't been there. "These are the ways, the places where I had the bones broken and then tied up so they would set so bent he could never stand or walk again. Three months he screamed in the cesspit, before I was sure they were beyond any man's doctoring."

I remembered. All summer Croft lay in shit, and made sure that we all lay in the sounds of his pain and loss. I had thought that almost Croft's victory, rather than Rulf's.

And then he had been washed and dressed—in a woman's skirt, because those dreadful legs would never wear trousers again—and set in a skiff with the boy for deckhand and servant, and he had sailed into the sun's setting on his way to exile and death.

Eventual death. It had been twenty years before his twisted bones came back to us.

I said, "Why do you want the boy back now?"

"Harlan, I have no heir. They tell me it is the gods' curse on my blood, for what I did to the old king his father. What I took from him. Some of that, at least, I can restore."

"He will claim the kingship."

"He is welcome to it, when I'm gone. I can adopt him, train him, make him a better man than Barent ever was."

"Rulf, you gave him to Croft. He will have been trained already, to despise you and all of yours. Will you make a gift of yourself, to a young man who is right to hate you?"

He shrugged ruefully, confused perhaps by his own sudden penitence. "Harlan. Fetch him back."

At least the voyage home would let me see what kind of man Croft had made of him. If I judged it needful, I would keep him in chains and be sure at least that Rulf had to make his own mistakes.

We were two months abroad before we sighted Skander, a smudge of smoke in the east as we lost the sun, a sullen glow in the dark to guide us. Any other port on any other water, we would have held off for a daylight tide. Skander has no tides to wait for; and besides, I ached to be swift, in and out.

In, then, slow and steady on the oars, all sail furled. I was a windmaster and we had barely rowed all journey, but these were strange waters and this my own ship beneath me, manned on Rulf's gold and charged with his mission. I would be twice a fool to take a risk with her.

In fact we could have sailed right to the lamplit wharf and never scraped a rock nor jarred a timber; Skander's harbor is as deep and clean as legend paints it. We'd know, when it came time to be leaving. A man old enough to have grown wise always keeps it in his head, that he may be leaving swiftly.

That same old wise man knows it's good to come in slow and quiet. To seem tamer than you are.

I was old enough, even in my own eyes. I dragged my own long reputation like a twilight shadow at my back, but still: it had been a dreary voyage and the crew had seen every year of my age tell on me as we came. I was tired already, hungry only to go home. They were a pack of wolves at my oars, and I feared loosing them in the city. Any city, but Skander more than any: its reputation was longer, louder, lewder than my own.

I said, "The streets are full of lights. That's not a welcome, it's a warning. Stay close to each other, if you won't stay close to me. Keep away from shadows, keep watch on your bench-mates; keep out of trouble, because there will be no rescue here."

They had never looked for rescue in their lives. There was pity in their eyes, pity and contempt. Had I really fallen so far from my strength that I saw danger in an effete entrepôt where men and women alike dealt in silks and whispers, in smokes and perfumes and each other?

Even as we sidled up to moor, I thought I would be leaving half those men behind. Dead or enslaved, drunk or bewitched or carried off.

Well, they were free men—for now—and few of them truly my own. So long as I had hands enough, I would be leaving as soon as I had the boy. If necessary I could buy oarsmen at market, although I'd hate to do it. Slaves taint a ship's heart, and make a mock-man of her captain. I stared down the *Skopje*'s length and prayed to see enough of those faces back here in a day, two days.

And then my good ship bumped against the wharf, and there were small slim figures waiting for ropes and high shrill voices crying welcome, asking how they could serve us, what we might require. Whatever we might desire. Information, temptation: before one of us so much as set boot ashore, the bargaining had begun.

• • •

My own boots were first, as was my right and duty. I leaped over the rail and landed two-footed and emphatic on the wharf.

I don't rightly know what I was stamping against: a snake's welcome, a hissing from the shadows? That was surely how I saw the city: as a nest of serpents all knotted together, spies and assassins and traitors in exile from a dozen different lands, poison and sorcery no doubt their weapons of first resort. Cowards and schemers all.

My head is a slow, dull thing. In my own country they call me Harlan the Wily, expressly because I am not. Rulf should never have sent me to Skander. He should have known, not to do that.

A voice hailed me; a woman stepped forward.

Smaller than me, but if she was smaller than the normal run of men, it was not by much. She carried herself with straightforward authority, and I liked that even as I was surprised by it, where I was looking for insinuation and duplicity.

"Are you the master of this vessel?"

"I am."

"Your name and origin?"

"Harlan, of Sawartsland; emissary of Rulf my king." I should perhaps not have said that, but I didn't even carry trade goods to disguise my mission. I have said it: I was not the man for this.

"I am Dzuria, harbormaster here. My people will see to yours, and to your ship's comfort. You come with me, and tell me of your embassy."

"I will tell that to the prince of the city. There is a prince, I think?"

Her mouth quirked. "There are many princes in Iskandria, none interested in any tale but their own. Of course you must take your tale to the palace, but the chancellor's is the ear you want."

I sighed. "At home, if a man wants the ear of Rulf King, he walks into the rede-hall and bellows for him. I do understand that matters are arranged differently elsewhere."

She said, "In this city, truly, your best first step towards the chancellor's ear is through mine."

It was elegantly done. She cut me out from my crew and penned me alone, as she had intended from the first. My own intent, to use my king's name here the way I had used my axe and shield elsewhere, a brute swift way to the top— that was neglected early, abandoned swiftly, forgotten soon.

How much help I could truly expect from a harbormaster, I had no way to measure. In my world, harbormasters berthed ships and tallied cargoes, charged for wharfage and warehousing, their heads full of cables and weights and manifests.

They might have comfort in their offices, but not like this. She brought me to a chamber swathed in damask and lamplight, soft cushions and soft-voiced children who fetched sweet juice and fiery spirit, nutmeats and pastries, offers of anything more.

I batted them away with thanks and refusals. They smiled and shrugged, settled in the perfumed shadows in the corners of the room, watched me and their mistress both with a scrupulous, indefatigable care.

"Shouldn't they be in bed?" I grunted.

"Undoubtedly. Would you care to send them? I wish you joy of the attempt."

At least she didn't say *take them*. Even so, I was not inclined to be generous. I said, "You call yourself the harbormaster; these speak to me more of a slavemaster."

"Indeed. Do you not take and keep and trade slaves, in Sawartsland?"

"We do, yes; but—"

"Not children, would you say?"

"Oh, children too, but not like this," scented and silk-clad and complaisant. The youngsters I bought or bred in my own house worked their share, just as my own children had, as my grandchildren did now. And fed from the same plates, ripped the same clothes ragged, rioted as much and were beaten for it side by side; and slept safe in a puppy tumble, free and slave together.

"I am sure not. There are none like these. Don't let their seductive ways deceive you. Some of our princes-in-exile, yes, they keep children for their bodies, for their beds; but these?" She stretched out a long arm to tug at the artfully tangled hair of one ingratiating imp that I took—not quite certainly— for a girl. "If you took one of these to bed, you would wake up sorry. If you woke at all. They are heartless, entirely without compunction, because that is how I raise them. Their perfumes and fancies are stolen, from any ship careless enough to let them aboard. Once goods are landed they are safe, because then they fall under my regard, but anything on shipboard is fair game. So is the crew."

"Do I need to warn my men?"

"If a man needs warning against such as these, he should perhaps have stayed at home."

Indeed; but we had Rulf's order at our backs, heavy as a blade and just as imperative. Staying home had never been an option.

I said, "Where do you find these dangerous children?"

"In the alleys, on the wharfs, some of them. Most I buy. And sell again, when I can find them places. It's the only way to keep them from the thiefmasters and the beggar kings. And the palace. Besides," reaching out again, touching the smooth cheek of an adolescent boy as he refilled her goblet, "how else would I manage my harbor? I can hire men to do the heavy work, but these are my rat-catchers and bead-counters, my watchers and messengers. As you have observed, they never go to bed when they're supposed to. If you are my friend, you need not worry for your purse or your safety or your ship, while you are here."

"I hope I am your friend," I said, with enough urgency to raise smiles in the shadows.

"Good. I hope it too; it means I can be a friend to you. Tell me of your embassy."

I said, "When my king took the throne twenty years ago, the man he took it from had a son, a boy of fifteen. Rulf sent the boy into exile, sooner than see him as dead as his father."

"He sent him here, you mean, to Iskandria."

"Of course. Where else? In company with his father's warhammer, Croft, the finest fighter and the worst picker of us all, who chose to support the old king when all his friends had turned the other way. Rulf . . . punished him, but would not kill him. Which was perhaps a mistake. Rulf has spent twenty years being wary of the world and never quite comfortable in his chair. But Croft is dead, and Rulf hopes the boy will come back now to make a son for his side and an heir for his back."

"Not so much a boy now, if he was fifteen then."

"They are all boys, when they stay so much younger than we are. You know." There was grey and white in the dark woven pattern of her hair; she was younger than me, but not so much as it would matter. "If you were here then, you would remember: a boy, tall and slim and flaxen-haired, not yet come into his strength. And a cripple, a big man who would not be walking, who could not leave the boat without help. A small boat, and just the two of them to crew it."

She said, "Oh, I was here. I have always been here. But a cripple and a boy, in a small boat, this far? That sounds . . . ambitious."

"We are good sailors." Even crippled, even ungrown.

"Even so. There are storms, there are pirates. There is simple bad fortune, and they would seem not to be rich in anything else."

"Indeed—but we know they did come. At least, we know that Croft did. His bones came back to us." And someone had to send them, with knowledge and purpose both.

"Yes. If it was the cripple you were seeking, it should be Fenner that you spoke to. A boy, though, a prince in exile—well, we have a city full of those. You will have to go to the palace."

"Fenner? Who is that?"

"He is—no, he *was* one of those I saved my children from. A beggar king, for a while. He matters more these days, but he is still cripple-king in this city. He knows all the lame and all the lacking."

"It's good, no doubt, that they have a friend with influence," but Croft was dead, and it was the boy I sought.

"I didn't say he was their friend. He buys and sells, he deals in flesh as much as he ever did, only from a more exalted position now. We used to call him Fenner the Helpless, because he never needed any help. He would have known your Croft, and where to find him. If you want your boy, though, ask at the palace."

I grunted, nodded, sighed. Not the man for this.

"Meantime," she said, "rest while you can. Palace days start early, and run long."

One of her watchful children—this one a girl, close enough to a young woman that I'd have been watchful myself if she were mine—took a lamp and led me to another room of cushioned comfort. I ought to have asked where my crew had gone, where I might hope to find them. But I was tired, and ashore, and frankly weary of them; and interested in bed, a lot, and in the girl a little, because her mistress interested me greatly.

"Will Dzuria really sell you to another house?"

The girl gave me a quick smile. "Of course. Soon now, I think. How else would she afford new little children? Being harbormaster does not make her wealthy."

Which was as good as to say that she was an honest harbormaster, but I had gathered that already. She was probably an honest slavetrader too. I said, "Don't you mind?"—but the true question was *why don't you mind?*

If anything, she seemed amused by my naivety. "This is Xandrian. Here, everyone belongs to someone else. And Dzuria will sell me somewhere I can be happy, to someone who will be happy to have me. Why should I mind?"

I shrugged, and sat on the bed. My boots looked a terrible long way away. I thrust my legs out hopefully, and said, "You mean you trust her."

"Of course. She has fed me and dressed me, washed me and doctored me, taught me to run with others and to run alone—how could I not trust her?"

She hauled with a will at one boot and then the other. I thanked her heartily and reached for my purse.

"Not in this house," she said, frowning mightily. "We don't take money from our friends."

Then she scudded swiftly out of the room, and it took me a moment too long to realize she had taken my boots with her.

Waking slowly, stiffly in an unaccustomed bed after a long sea-voyage: there was nothing unusual in that.

What was unusual was to find myself alone, and depressingly glad of it.

It gave me the chance to move slowly, to groan aloud as I stretched, as every joint ached, as vicious age stabbed me mockingly in one hip and numbed a foot entirely.

I cursed, and stamped until some hint of feeling came back. The stamping only hurt me more, which only made me curse more, which left me all the more embarrassed when I looked around for clothes and found a boy, a small boy squatting in the corner.

I stood quiet, breathing hard, under the grave weight of his stare. I knew what he was seeing—a particolored giant, wind-burned at face and arms and throat, pale elsewhere and seamed with scars—and I understood the fascination.

He said, "My name is Salumehramahin, and I am yours until you no longer need me." Then he looked me deliberately up and down one more time and added, "You will need me for a long time, I think."

"Dzuria sent you, I take it?"

"Of course."

His dress was shabby and painfully white; I liked that better than the slippery silks of last night. At least he looked like a servant, not a whore.

"Say your name again?"

"Salumehramahin," he said, flashing a smile as white as his cottons.

"What do your friends call you?"

"Ramin."

"Where do I find breakfast, Ramin?"

"I could bring it to you."

"No, bring me to it: somewhere between this room and the palace, which is where I have to go now."

He shook his head ruefully. "You should have been there earlier than this."

Then he dressed me like himself, in a long loose shirt and baggy trousers, and offered me sandals that he said were the largest he could find in all the warehouses of Skander wharf. He said they would be too small. Which, yes, they were.

I have worn less, in my time. And been led by the hand in stranger, darker places, to worse meals and worse days too, though rarely so frustrating. I broke my fast—and the boy's, at my expense, naturally—on flatbreads filled with a hot spice paste, standing on a street corner. Afterwards I washed grease from my face and fingers at the public fountain, thought briefly and enchantingly of the notorious baths of Skander—and set my jaw resolutely against asking the way. I was for the palace, sea-scoured as I was. In and out, as swift as might be.

• • •

Ramin led me through winding alleys and shadowed arcades, with never a glimpse of our purpose until suddenly we came out into the light and there it was, four-square in front of us.

They call it a palace—*the* palace, as though this were the principality of the world—but in truth it is nothing so singular. There isn't even a wall, to mark it off from the common city. The first building of authority is set openly on a public square; everything else has been added where it might be, behind and to the sides and running away out of sight.

That gateway building stands high and square, cut of local stone, as stern in its age as it must have been when it was new. Beyond lay a hundred unlikely structures, each one vying with its neighbors to be taller or broader or deeper, brighter or more imposing or more absurd. Some weary exiles built their pavilions to look like home, to teach their children where they came from; others seized the chance to shrug away tradition and build jubilant fantasies, faerie-castles that resembled nothing real in any city anywhere.

Some had built true castles, sullen fortresses that spoke of their fears: assassination, instability, uprising. I thought they should look around and find other things to fear. With five ships and a case of gold, I thought I could take this city entire. Except that I did not want it, and neither would my king. It's always useful to have somewhere else in the world, a place that sits apart. Somewhere to send those enemies you'd sooner not quite kill.

And the children you dare not live with. Those too.

I looked down at the child who hung so persistently on my arm and tried to shake him off. And failed, of course; he was most earnest, tugging at me, "Come. There is a back way to the kitchens, I know a man there . . . "

I was sure he did. That was his Skander, and his experience: covert, insinuating, conditional. Not mine. "This is my way, my king's way," in through the front door to ask straightforwardly for what I wanted. Looking at me, they would see Rulf at my back, and all his ships behind him; they would not refuse me. *In and out.*

Little Ramin let go of me then, and put his hands firmly behind his back. "I cannot go in there."

"Nor should you."

"Nor should *you*," emphatically. "Dzuria said—"

"Dzuria is your mistress, not mine."

I straightened my shoulders and walked alone, under his diminutive skeptical gaze: up dry and gritty steps, between stout pillars, through an open door.

I was met with obsequious manners, with drinks and courteous conduct into one antechamber after another. Courteous to me, at least: they almost fought each other for the privilege of serving me, those big smooth rounded men. I was surprised that Skanderenes ran so large, until I remembered the native habit of the high-born in the matter of their officials. Cut young, a eunuch boy might grow and grow. This must be the consequence: this heavy, huge unmanning, this fatuous squabbling over the right to be subservient to strangers.

I sat and sweated in close confines, ate and drank what they brought me, demanded attention that did not come. I asked for the prince of the city, and was politely abandoned; I asked for the chancellor and was moved to another room and abandoned again. I wielded Dzuria's name, and they might never have heard of her.

There were always other supplicants coming and going, seeking an audience, being disappointed. If all day I saw one person being led into the presence, I was not aware of it.

I did wait all day, in ever-fading hopes. And talked to my fellow-hopefuls, though none of them could offer hope. Some had waited weeks, one months. *In and out* looked like a fool's dream suddenly. Tomorrow perhaps I'd come back with my blade and whoever I could find among my men, cause a rumpus, see what ruder manners might achieve.

Tonight, there was nothing to do but yield at last to brute implacability: court was closed, audiences were over, neither the prince nor the chancellor would see us now, we should all come back tomorrow . . .

I headed down towards the harbor and was unsurprised to find Ramin dancing attendance on me before I was halfway there, smugly certain. "You should have come with me, not wasted your time with silly pompous eunuchs."

I wondered briefly how wise he was, to make such mock. For sure some of those same eunuchs had come to the palace by way of the slave markets; for a boy in need of a future, his mistress might deem that a reasonable road.

Over supper she said, "I'm sorry, I thought you understood. You should have gone with Ramin. The front door is hopeless. Even with the right bribe in the right hands, none of them will be seen to hurry. That might imply that money holds the power, not themselves."

I growled, and wished again to show them other ways to hold power. A fist gripping a broadsword, a booted foot kicking in a door.

She said, "The palace is divided, half and half. The prince has time and no authority, while the chancellor has authority and no time. Both men train their staff to keep petitioners away, for entirely opposite reasons."

I grunted. "How is anything brought to happen? Ever?"

"Oh, the city finds its way. All our business passes through the chancellor's hands; just, not through the front door. Ramin will take you back tomorrow.

Be warned, he will probably scold."

"I don't doubt it." If he were mine—but nothing here was mine, except the *Skopje*. I wanted to step outside, simply to look at her. Wood and tar and canvas, pegs and ropes: I knew her absolutely and trusted her the same, and I could say that about nothing else in Skander. Not my crew, nor my new friends. Nor myself, even, or what I would do tomorrow.

Tonight—what would I do tonight? Drink, and listen to this woman.

Watch her, too. She had wit both ways, wisdom and humor; I would be happy just to listen. My eyes were still full of palace smoke, which made them sore and restless both at once, and I would be happy to close them and just listen. But then I would doze, I knew. The smoke had gone into my head and was numbing yet. So I kept my eyes open and my mind alert by dint of watching her. Her skin in the lamplight, how the lines were dressed in shadow like a web of softness laid over strength; her hair, that had been tempered and pinned close to her skull, was another heavy fall of shadow now. Her mouth was mobile, lightly mocking. Her eyes were steady, scrutinizing, always honest and so not always kind.

If I'd been younger, I might have made a grand gesture of a grand offer, the courtesy of my body for her night's delight. She would have laughed me out of the door, I think, even if she had been a younger woman.

But then, if I had been a younger man, I would not have seen the value in her. There are advantages to the slow creep of age; there is recompense. Not everything rots at once.

When there was space, when there was a quiet fallen between us, I said that, or something like it.

Even older men can make fools of themselves. She smiled and told me to go to bed, and did I want a child to light me the way?

Come morning, true to her word, Ramin took me up through the city again. On our way I saw a sprawled heap in a gutter, a groaning sorry mess of a man I thought might have been one of my crew. Another day, I might have stopped—but he was Rulf's man, not my own. One of the young bloods; let him bleed. If he was bleeding. The dark wet stain he lay in might be wine, or vomit; it might be piss. Truth? I didn't care.

On another narrow street I saw a shaggy blond head lean out of an upper window. Again, I thought that was one of mine; and wished him well, as a man's dark arm reached to draw him back inside. I liked the lad; indeed, I'd seduced him myself from his father's farm, before bad land and bad luck had had the chance to sour him. Left to make my own choices, I chose well, on the whole. Rulf? Not so. He had been a lucky king, but he'd needed that, to offset his disasters.

Sometimes I was astonished that he'd ever won the throne at all, let alone held it for so long. That none of his wars had killed him, and none of his mistakes, and—particularly!—none of his friends.

That Croft had apparently never even tried to kill him, even from exile. Where were the Skanderene assassins? The city was famous for its dealings with death.

Perhaps Croft had had his bones poisoned, his hair soaked with bane. Perhaps Rulf was dying even now as he gloated and lamented over his fallen foe, as I chased about on his stupid, deadly errand here in Skander, here at Ramin's heel. Here in the chancellor's back yard, in his house, in his kitchens, where there was heat and sweat and hurry, loud voices, no time.

Ramin snared a servant, greeted him by name, said, "Where is the steward Cephos?"

And would have been answered with a backhand blow, except that I was there. I caught that blow before it landed, a hand's span from his head; held it the way a cliff might hold a hurled stone, unmoving, undisturbed.

I said, "The steward Cephos?"

"Please, you will, you will find him in the storeroom, down that corridor," a frantic flicker of his eyes to show me where.

I nodded graciously and released his wrist. Ramin ducked ahead, to where indeed a man was checking sacks.

"Cephos! I have been looking for you!"

That earned him a slap too swift for me to intercept, even if I'd been inclined to.

"Master Cephos to you, little brat. And I have been waiting for you; I had word from your mistress. Yesterday, I think."

The blow was taken for granted; the unfairness of the rest reduced Ramin to spluttering incoherence. With a shrug, the steward turned to me. "You would be Harlan the Sawartsman?"

"I would. I need to speak to your chancellor."

"Yes. Come with me."

He took us through a side-door and into another world: a half-world rather, a hollow between the domestic quarters and the public rooms. Rulf's rede-hall was a single vast and open space, where you had to work out for yourself who was king and who was carl, who lord, who stable-lad. Here the very shape and structure of the house separated servants from their masters. It was like walking within the skeleton of a great beast; within the walls ran a network of stairs and passages, narrow and awkward and secret as spies. Secret for the light-footed, at least, for the slender and flexible. Ramin was cat-quiet and cat-swift, the steward much the same. I knocked my head on low beams, stumbled over sudden steps, scraped my shoulders against both walls at once.

We passed a dozen doors before at last the steward unlatched one and beckoned us through. I straightened my poor cramped spine with a grunt of relief—and struck my head one more time, on something that swung away from the contact and then back to hit me again.

This time I didn't even try to hold the oath back to a mutter. At my side, the steward flinched; behind me, Ramin giggled; ahead, someone laughed aloud.

I reached up to snare the rope-hung obstacle, a bar of polished wood like a ladder's rung or a child's swing. Just one of many; for a moment I thought we'd been brought into a spider's lair, the room was festooned with so many ropes and bars. A spider with a sailor's ken, knowing knots and bindings and how to rig a space so that no two ropes should tangle.

Beneath that web, two men: one standing, one lying on a couch under a coverlet of cloth-of-gold. Both pale, shaven-headed. I took them for eunuchs, one more layer of officialdom to be circumvented.

It was the older of the two, the man lying down, who had laughed. He was grinning still. Glowering at him, wondering if he was sick or indisposed, I saw how the coverlet lay flat where his legs ought to have been; his body ended abruptly, just a little below the hips.

Now I understood the ropes and rungs. He was broad-chested, vigorous despite his age, despite his pallor; no doubt he could pull himself around this webwork as handily as any sailor aloft. Handier, without his legs' weight or the need for footing.

And he was grinning at me yet, waiting for something; and—
"*Croft!*"

I was the king's windmaster; the breeze comes at my calling. A gale, when I shout. I had learned long since not to shout withindoors, even in a hall. Even in Rulf's great rede-hall. In that close space, that day—well, I shouted.

I broke the room.

Those hollow walls splintered like bird-bones, shattered like windowglass. Ropes snapped and tangled, spars flew like straws. Ramin was blown clear across the room; I never saw what happened to Cephos.

Croft lay in the ruin of his couch, clinging to his companion, laughing and laughing.

Soon, in another room, that first passion spent:

"They call me Fenner nowadays," he said, "hereabouts. Or simply Chancellor."

We used to call him Fenner the Helpless, because he never needed any help. I had never been the right man for this mission. Rulf had subtler thinkers he might have sent, souls as suspicious as his own. Blunt and trusting are poor qualifications for an ambassador, especially to a city as insidious as Skander.

"You seem . . . shorter than you were," I breathed, still barely trusting my own voice. Rulf and I were friends as two cats are friends, always sidelong in the corner of each other's eye; Croft and I had been friends as two bulls are friends, always head to head. I couldn't measure my danger here, or his own.

"Come, sit," he wheezed, hoarse from laughing, hauling himself upright on this other couch. "Drink with me. The people here make little stronger than bread beer—but I have all the palace as my plaything, which means half the world, and the better half. Our guests learn to be open-handed. I've a honey brandy from the Brach that would be worth the journey to Brachia on its own account, rowing against tide and current all the way."

Unexpected, abbreviated, very far from safe, he was still Croft. Of course I would drink with him. He wanted to talk, to tell me how clever he'd been, and how sly. We'd had the same conversation over and over, since we were boys together.

I sat the other end of the couch, where there would have been room even if he hadn't shifted, that space where his legs were missing.

"We thought you were dead."

"You were meant to."

The second man had carried Croft in here, as casually as one carries a child. Now he fetched us bowls of glass filled with a clear dense liquor, fire on the tongue and fire to the heart. And took none for himself but settled wordlessly on the floor against the couch's arm, where Croft could reach out and stroke his smooth oiled scalp, tug lightly at his ear. Servant and lover, then—or I was meant to think so.

Croft had shaved his own head, and his beard too. That was my excuse for taking so long to know him. We look for what we expect to see, and make easy judgments: clothes, hair. Legs.

I said, "How does a crippled beggar, even a beggar king, rise to be chancellor in Skander?"

He snorted. That was not the question I wanted to ask. Even so, he graced it with an answer. "Painstakingly. A doctor fled here because his lord had died under his knife. I took the same chance, and lived. A man may shrug a burden off and get by the better after. You might learn that, if you chose. I traded legs for influence; the city's prince was curious to watch the cutting and the healing after, and so I reached the palace. That prince is dead now, but I am here yet."

"Your bones are in Sawartsland, in Rulf's lap. Named and known." Unmistakable, or so Rulf thought. "Did you have your doctor keep your legs in pickle, till you needed them?"

"And then attach them to some other body, and hope they looked to fit? I might have done." He sounded pleased with me for suggesting anything so wily, so unlike myself. "But no: I bought a man at market and had my doctor break and bind his legs, just as Rulf had done with me. Then I kept him alive until I needed him."

For years, that meant: years and years, in pain he knew too well. And then killed him, boiled his bones, wired them neatly together and sent them to us. I might have said anything, nothing; it would make no difference now. I said, "What for, old friend? Is there some way of vengeance here, that I can't see?"

He laughed. "Oh, I have had my revenge on Rulf, although he doesn't know it. He has no child, does he?"

"None—though not for want of trying."

"Of course. He'd want a dynasty. He'll never have one. I sent him a woman long ago, a hedge-witch to poison his seed. No sons for Rulf King, however hard he tries."

It would never have been hard to put a woman in Rulf's bed, even from this distance. I wondered which woman and whether he had kept her, whether she worked her spells yet or one time had served for all time, a curse-bane lurking at the root. He had tried witches of his own, I knew, but Croft's must have been the stronger. No surprise, if he found her here in Skander.

He went on, "In the end, I knew he'd want Toland back. Adopted by the new king, sired by the old: that speaks of dynasty, what better? And what better way to push him into it than sending him my bones, letting him think me dead and the boy adrift? I knew you'd be the one to come, the king's windmaster. Perhaps you're right, perhaps this is still vengeance after all. I have stolen his posterity, and now I steal his friend."

Croft seemed content to smile and wait—not for the first time—for me to catch up with his meaning. I looked at the younger man, and back through time to when he had been younger yet; and spoke to him for the first time, said, "Well, then. If Croft has gone from crippled exile to beggar king to chancellor, what are you now?"

He echoed his master's smile and said, "I am the chancellor's legs. As you have seen."

Which was to say that he was more than that, much more; but he would never be Rulf's son and never king in Sawartsland. I wondered if Croft had taken other measures to be sure of it, besides stealing the boy's heart and keeping him close all these years. I had taken him for a eunuch at first sight; I might not have been wrong.

It didn't matter, and I wouldn't ask. Not here, not now. I said to Croft, "I have the *Skopje* here, and I can find a crew, buy a crew if need be. I can go home, with this news or any. I don't see how you have stolen me from Rulf."

"A man can shrug a burden off," he said again. "And should do, where it has no value. My legs, your loyalty. The ship's your own; so should your life be. What do you have to go back for? Grown children and a bitter king, neither in need of you. A draughty longhouse cold all winter long, an ice-needle in your bones, and too many people always at your ear. They've had the best of you already; enough, now. More than enough. Stay here, and keep what's left."

"You're saying this was a trap for me? Not for Rulf at all?"

"Rulf would never come, you know that. A king without an heir, without children to marry off to build alliances? He hardly dare leave his hall. You, though: of course he would send you, and of course you would come. And once you were here—well. Harlan, stay. Find a new crew, sail new waters. Learn a city, the way you learned the sea. Woo the harbormaster."

I startled. Perhaps I glowered.

He laughed. "What, did you think that she imagines all those children to be her own?"

Ramin crouched once more in his corner of choice, quiet and still, shrugging off his bruises. Who owns whom is always a question; in his mind, I thought, perhaps he owned me. Or perhaps he had traded me, or given me away.

In my own mind—well, I could see a small house, a quiet house. A great and welcome change from what I'd left, all that bustle and labor and noise. A boy to run errands and make a nuisance of himself, a girl who would know where my boots were; I shouldn't need more of a household. A house not too far from the harbor, certainly. Convenient for the *Skopje*, for a new life on and off the water; convenient for friends to visit, back and forth. Or to stay, either way. The harbormaster, if she eventually would; my blond farm lad in the meantime . . .

I said, "Why, whyever would you want that?" Apart from causing Rulf a deal of worry and frustration, which was no more than bread beer against the fiery spirit of what Croft had done already to trouble Rulf.

Sometimes, theft is an act of simple honesty. Everyone belongs to someone else, elsewhere as in Skander; but he said, "I miss more than the sea, and my legs. I have my legs," tweaking Toland's ear, simply to see him smile. He said, "I miss my friends. One friend," and so he stole me from my king.

BETWEEN NINE AND ELEVEN

ADAM ROBERTS

:1:

Diplomatic efforts had failed, and we were officially at war with the Trefoil alien culture. War is never pleasant, however unavoidable it sometimes becomes. But one of the things that blurs the edge of war's unpleasantness is victory. We enjoyed victory after victory, sweet as honey. Soon enough were closing in on the Trefoil homeworld.

Why did diplomacy fail? There *were* ways in which our view of the cosmos aligned with theirs. But then again there were ways in which the human assumptions about things and the Trefoil assumptions were so radically at odds that it was simply impossible for us to communicate at all, let alone reach a compromise. Like us, the Trefoil were a social species, and there were broad emotional parallels—their versions of love and aggression appear to have been more-or-less equivalent emotions to ours—as well as some surprising specifics: the concepts of *Answegen Geschichtlichkeit* and *Geworfenheit* all made perfect sense to the Trefoil, it seems. But other concepts, like mutual advantage, creativity, logic, meant nothing at all to them.

Their attacks on Human Space were very hard to predict, and therefore hard to defend against. For that reason, I suspect, they underestimated our ability to fight and win.

My name is Ferrante, and I was in command of the warship *Centurion 771*. This is what happened when our ship and a sister ship called Samurai 10 pressed our attack on a damaged Trefoil Supership designated ET 13-40. ET is shorthand for Enemy Target.

:2:

Centurion and *Samurai* came out of warp together and coordinated our initial firesweep on the ET. About one in five Trefoil ships can be captured—sometimes apparently important craft, flagships even, sometimes trivial little spacetugs. The rest will self-destruct rather than be taken. What criterion determines, for the Trefoil, which kind of ship is too valuable to fall into human hands . . . well, nobody has been able to work that out.

We were half a light year from β Cygni, the star's red blob clearly visible on our screen without need of magnification. The Trefoil Supership had fallen out of warp, presumably on account of its internal damage: the crazy ziggurat of its hull was ruptured in a hundred places, and weird entrails (cables? tentacles?) trailed from every breach. Since every individual Trefoil ship is designed according to a different template we couldn't be sure of the internal composition of this particular one. Most Trefoil craft possessed three command centres, and it looked likely that the baobab-shaped excrescence on the side of the craft was one of those. We concentrated fire, and scratched red-brown furrows over the hull, everting the inward spaces of this bridge. If that's what it was.

We thought we had her, but then she twisted and fell out of existence, reappearing in orbit half a light year away. Must have had a last squirt of warp capacity in her engines. It was an easy matter to follow her and we repeated our attack mode. The huge craft was in orbit around a taupe and yellow gas giant, sinking into the upper atmosphere. For a moment I wondered if she would crash down into the world and so escape us by destroying herself. But she deployed a filigree web, and we realised she was scooping.

Well: we could stop that easily enough. Both ships manoeuvred, and targeted. The battle was seconds away from being won.

Then *Samurai* exploded: a stutter of blue-white light, a soundless crunching inward, twisting the main hull like a rag being wrung and then there was nothing of the starship except debris spiralling and hurtling.

:3:

At exactly that moment the link went down, and I was no longer mentally connected to the rest of the crew. I came out of telspace gasping, as if cold water had been thrown in my face.

The Centurion shuddered, and one of our cannons overheated and melted itself loose of its bearings. The bridge screens lit up with error messages. The warp went offline. One thruster fired and the other stalled, and we were spinning. The failure of warp meant that inertial controls sagged and gave way, and we were all crushed against the sides of our harnesses.

I'd been in telspace with my crew for so long, it took palpable effort to dredge their actual names from my memory. "Modi," I yelled—my voice hoarse with unuse. "Cancel that thruster!"

She was already doing so, and stabilising the craft, but then the counter-thrust sputtered out. We were still spinning, although not at so crushing a velocity.

No telspace meant the manual operation of the ship. I looked at my hands, palms down, palms up, and tried to place them on the command screen. But there was something wrong with my hands. More than wrong, there was something monstrous about them. Something . . . blasphemous, almost. I looked at them again and I began to scream.

:4:

I've served with Modi for over a year, first on the *Broadsword 27* and then the *Centurion*—my first command, although the consensual nature of the telspace makes the concept of command much less hierarchical than it might once have been. In the Big Wing Battle at Alpha Scorpii internal fires had scarred my face and torso, and burned away three of the fingers from Modi's left hand, leaving her a puckered crabclaw thumb-and-index. She'd tried an artificial hand with four plasmetal fingers and an opposable plasmetal thumb, but the interface had never quite gelled for her and there was a lag between her willing something and her prosthetic acting. For that reason she tended not to wear it.

That fact saved everybody's life.

:5:

There were four of us on the craft, and one other—me, let's say. Captain. A standard crew. Han killed herself within the first five minutes of the . . . of whatever it was that happened to the ship (she pressed herself against the glowing-hot flank of the gun-compartment and died screaming). Shabti and Kellermann became catatonic, the former singing a nursery song over and over in a scratchy, high-pitched voice.

Modi got to me before I could self-harm in any way. She took hold of my head, and forced me to look into her eyes. Without my hands in plain view, I felt the terror ebbing away. But there was something—I couldn't say way— profoundly awry with the universe as a whole. The Centurion shuddered and bucked, and error messages blinked and flashed on every screen on every surface. The main screen showed the Trefoil ship, pulling up now from its orbital gas sweep and drawing its scoop back into its main body. Soon enough it would turn and bear down upon us.

"Ferrante," Modi yelled, right in my face. "Ferrante. They will be on us in minutes."

"Minutes," I gasped.

"We need to pull the ship together. Pull *ourselves* together. We still have nine cannon."

"Nine cannon," I repeated. "Yes." There was something comforting in that thought. But, the sense of wrongness persisted. "Something is very wrong," I told Modi.

"I feel it too," she agreed. "But we have to get a grip."

The word *grip* made me glance back down at my hands, and the terror welled up again. I began screaming for a second time.

Modi was a quick thinker. She pulled off her top and wrapped it around my hands. "Ferrante," she said. "We have to *act.*"

I was gasping. I was finding it hard to breathe. The topography of the bridge seemed to twist and slip around me in weird ways. "Oh," I said. "Oh—oh—oh."

:6:

Cygni is a binary system: a fat red giant and a tiny, bright little blue star—beta is the bigger. There are some Jupiter-sized gas giants, and a whole lot of dwarf planets and fragments and meteorites. The proximity warning sounded and Modi dabbled at a screen to confirm the zapping of the offending rocklet. But then it sounded again, and again, and the chances that so many asteroids were on a collision course were so minute that it could only mean the system was fried. I tried to breathe, deep, and get a grip. Slowly I drew my right hand out from beneath the covering cloth. I didn't like looking at it, but it didn't offend basic reason in the way that staring at both my hands did. I tried contacting the rest of the crew, dispersed about the ship, but the system told me that Han was dead, and the other two unresponsive.

"Something," I said. "The Trefoil did something."

"It's a weapon," said Modi. "I just don't see what kind."

"Whatever it is, it destroyed the *Samurai* and has caused—" I looked around at the flickering screens—"a whole mass of malfunctions and problems for us." Some shred of soldiery reasserted itself in my mind. I was supposed to be in charge. "We'll have to close with the ET and fire on her manually. I don't know if we can trust the AI to target the cannon."

"What do crews say when they're not in the telspace? *Aye aye*, is it?"

"We've still got nine cannon," I said. That fact should have reassured me, but instead it made me obscurely uneasy.

So we wrestled with the ship via the glitchy manual interface, and the thrusters fired. Warp came online again, and the inertial balancing flashed on, off, on, off. Then the warp went down. The whole ship began to shake violently. I felt sharp, stabbing pains in my fingers and toes. This was the moment Kellermann died. He owned an antique cigarette lighter, which in turn contained a small amount of butane. This exploded with enough force to kill him and breach the hull. The reason it exploded had to do with the arrangement of protons in the butane nucleus.

In retrospect I can say: thank heavens we weren't carrying any neon.

"Pull back," I said, and together Modi and I grappled with the interface to bring the Centurion out of attack mode. The more distance we put between ourselves and the ET, the calmer the craft became.

"I don't know what it *is*," Modi said. "I don't see how they're doing that— it's like a magic spell, like some voodoo sphere of malignity around the ET."

"We've still got nine cannons," I reminded her. "We can still shoot at her. True we won't be at an optimum distance to . . . "

"Why do you say *still*?" Modi asked.

"What?"

"You say *we've still got nine cannon*. You say that because we're supposed to have more."

"That's right."

"How many cannon are we fitted with? How many are we *supposed* to have?"

I could not say. I mean that strictly: the answer to that question couldn't be said.

:7:

Modi scribbled a number on her pad with her forefinger. "What do you call that?"

I looked at the number. I recognised it, but its name slipped from my head. "Nine-and-four?" I offered.

"That's not *it*, though, is it?"

"No," I agreed, pained. "Six-and-seven? But that's now how we say it, is it. I want to say *three*, but it's clearly not three."

She wrote another number. "And what about that?"

I looked at it. "It's a four. But it's more than a four, isn't it. It's a lot more than four, actually."

"It's four and something else. It's the something else that's . . . I don't get it."

"What is it? The number I mean?"

"It's the designation of our ET," Modi said. As soon as she said that I recognised it. Of course!

"Ferrante," she asked. "What's our ship called?"

"Centurion." The name came from my mouth like a bark of gibberish. I knew what Modi was going to ask next, and it was: *what does that word mean*? And I knew that I wouldn't be able to answer that question. Although it was in my head that *I used to know*. Once upon a time. It had something to do with war. But what did it have to do with war? It was a non-word. It was an impossible word.

:8:

"The ET is bringing about," Modi sang. "It's using its scoop harvest to boost itself towards us. Unless we can get warp working again, it will be on us in . . . " and she stopped, and looked puzzled. "I had a calculation of the time . . . "

Since this was the amount of time we had left alive, I was eager to find out what the number was.

"Let's say, in nine minutes," she said. "Between nine and eleven minutes."

The ship was starting to shudder again. Modi saying that, giving voice to that phrase *between nine and eleven*, brought the terror shaking back into my mind. I wish she hadn't said that. Because there was nothing between nine and eleven, and at the same time there was something between nine and eleven and the fact of this thing being and not-being, its hideous elusiveness, like a monster in the shadows, was inexpressibly ghastly to me. I began weeping, tears washing down my face. And it wasn't because of the pain in my hands and feet.

:9:

From this point on I was useless. Worse than useless. I was very specifically starting to lose my mind. Modi was more focussed. She managed to get the main AI—hiccoughing and prone to weird snags and cutaways though it was—to target the cannons. The Trefoil Supership swung down upon us and I began to sing a top-C and slap the top of my head with my hands and Modi *fired* and

:11:

As to why the Trefoil had not deployed their 'device'—this super-weapon—before . . . Well, there is no consensus. It might be that they only very recently developed it. Conceivably ET 13-40 was a research and development platform. Then again, perhaps the Trefoil have had their 'device' for a long time and simply haven't deployed it for incomprehensible alien reasons of their own. The capture of a still-working model of the device, and its rapid adaptation and redeployment by Human Forces, brought the war very quickly to an end. Reprogrammed to blank out 3, the device completely shuts down Trefoil computers, designed as they are on a base-3 system of trits. It also causes individual Trefoilers to suffer severe internal physical damage and to degrade all triangular components. Neon, which has an atomic number between nine and eleven, is rare on a starship, but lithium—atomic number 3—is much more common, and the presence of any at all caused instant destruction. It seems likely that the existence of some small quantity of neon on board the *Samurai* caused its immediate destruction. I've no idea why that ship would be carrying neon, but starships are large and complex things.

Of course, I recommended Modi for decoration, and stand by my recommendation. She didn't exactly figure out what the device was doing to us but she had enough of an inkling, and was able to act. She grasped that it had something to do with the eradication of the quantity between nine and eleven.

"I'm guessing," she told me afterwards, "that the Trefoil understood enough about us to know our default mathematics is base-10 and so they erroneously assumed that our computing would be decenary. The fact that we developed binary computing is what saved us. Our AI was certainly confused, but still functioning."

"It's still hard for me to understand," I told her. "How can a device eliminate a number—from the universe, I mean? Surely that number just *is* a feature of the way things are?"

"Depends how you look at it," she replied. "We warp spacetime to travel faster than light, so we have good practical knowledge that spacetime is deformable. Say that the deep structure of the universe is information—is maths, effectively. If we can alter that deep structure to make the distance between stars temporarily shorter, then it's not hard to imagine the Trefoil finding a way to alter the deep structure in a different way. Temporarily to suppress ten from the fabric of things."

I shuddered. Modi is still happy to use the word itself. For me just saying the word brought the tendrils of nightmare to the tender parts of my memory. Like many who experienced the Trefoil 'device' in those last, desperate (on their part) days of the war, I continue to refer, superstitiously, to *between-nine-and-eleven*.

"Amazing, really," Modi mused, "that deploying the device didn't entirely *undo* the fabric of reality within its sphere of influence. Surprisingly tough, reality. There's genuine inertia and persistence to reality it turns out."

"We don't know how long it would last, though. I mean, if the Trefoil device were deployed for long stretches of time. Or over a wide area."

But that's the thing about Modi: she's an optimist. "Oh, I think reality would adjust. Indeed, who's to say it hasn't happened before?"

"Before?"

Modi laughed. "Ancient alien races, fighting a war across the galaxy—who knows? What if one of them deployed something similar to the Trefoil device? Maybe many times? Maybe whole numbers were eradicated for ever. Maybe there once was a number between nine and ten, or between one and two—I don't mean fractions or decimals. I mean a whole lost number. What if reality shook itself and then adjusted to the new, out-of-whack logic?"

"That's crazy talk," I grumbled.

"Maybe it is," and she laughed. "Maybe."

GORSE DAUGHTER, SPARROW SON

ALENA INDIGO ANNE SULLIVAN

—◆—

Jocelyn did not prick her finger on a magic spindle and fall into an enchanted slumber. She fairly regularly pricked her fingers on various spindles (though she really preferred bobbins) and carding combs and other sundries, but they were no more magical than anything else, and her sleep was not particularly enchanting. She woke with tangled hair each morning, and no kisses were required for the process. There was no incident with scorned fairies at her birth, no castle full of people cursed to sleep for a hundred years.

Jocelyn was born to a king and a queen. Fairies were invited to her naming ceremony, where they each gifted her with skills and a name, which is how she ended up with the rather hefty name of Jocelyn Theodora Grace Blanchefleur Aurora Sofia Antoinette Epona Charity Marina Petranne Violetta Louise, but all thirteen fairies were invited and no one cast a curse.

It began with the fairies themselves. Part of being a princess in the kingdom of Splöstlienne meant learning the things one might expect princesses to be taught—how to dance, eat, play the harp, ride a horse, and curtsy appropriately to various visiting dignitaries. However, Splöstlienne sat on a ley line, the convergence of all the sorts of mystical things that sorcerers eat for breakfast and often choke on. The moon shone rosy pink there, the sea sang wild songs at night, and the forests were made of trees that bore fruit filled with truths and secrets that weighed heavy on the heart once they were known. As such, part of any royal upbringing meant learning to weave one's life around these magics, learning to feel the tides of the soil, and the sea, and the blood, and that, of course, is where the fairies came in. Normally these things were passed from mother to daughter, but Jocelyn's mother grew weak and died when she was only a few months old; Jocelyn spent the rest of her childhood years at the skirts of one fairy or another, trying desperately to learn all the things her mother hadn't had time to teach her.

The fairies each had a special task, such as caring for the beasts in the forests, tending the sick, or singing the crops taller and more bountiful. Jocelyn studied with each of the first twelve fairies in turn—when she someday took the throne, she would first have to take a turn at each of their duties to show her ability to command her kingdom. However, it was the thirteenth fairy whose arts really fascinated her.

Ioma made her way to the highest tower of the castle every day just before dawn, taking each stone step with her wizened old legs, diaphanous wings shrunken with age and hanging limply down her back. Her silver hair trailed for yards behind her, gathering dust, spiders, and the occasional unwary mouse. When Ioma stood at the top of the tower, her hair curled down the stairs for four whole landings behind her. As a child, day after day, Jocelyn saw the silver strands slipping out of sight and scrambled after, catching their ends and unwinding the dazed mice, collecting the spiders with careful palms, uncoiling the endless lengths of dust and cobwebs. She bundled Ioma's hair in her arms like a skein of yarn as she went, stumbling over it on chubby child's legs, until she met the fairy at the top of the tower.

The old fairy was already sitting at her spinning wheel near the window by the time Jocelyn wobbled in, arms full of shining hair. Each day, Ioma pressed a finger to her own lips and smiled, lips wrinkled over toothless gums, beckoning the princess to the window. Jocelyn sat at Ioma's feet, tucked into her layers of woolen skirts to keep back the early morning chill, knees pulled to her chest, and the two sat in silence as the sun rose.

In Splöstlienne, the sun made a soft sound when it rose. Very few people in the kingdom heard this, or at least paid it any attention—those who were awake at such an hour were busy with their morning tasks and had no reason to pay the sound any mind. Ioma explained to Jocelyn, once—and maybe a time or two again, because she was old and sometimes forgot when she had already said a thing before—that to listen to the sunrise over her land every day, to hear the soft ringing as the light hit each blade of grass, each living being, the roaring edge of the sea, each wooly sheep, each drop of dew, would teach Jocelyn things about her kingdom that no one else knew.

Jocelyn wanted very much to make her sorrowful father proud, and her people happy, and do justice to the memory of her mother, who had been a wonderful queen—her father had shrunk in the wake of her mother's death, and Jocelyn couldn't help but feel the need to somehow make it better. So the girl nodded, utterly solemn, and listened as hard as she could as the indigo sky faded and the stars dimmed out for the ringing (which was all at once very low and very high) to roll out across the land.

The sunlight made a different sound with each thing it touched, and her very favorite sound was the sound of sun spilling across the gorse bushes. They were ugly brown tangles of thorns for most of the year, cursed by farmers for taking over the fields, but in the spring they burst into bloom. They had tiny flowers, brilliant gold, which smelled of coconuts and vanilla. Jocelyn found their contrasting beauty and danger far more enchanting than roses, which smelled to her like paper and had very little cleverness or wiliness to them.

There was something admirable to the way gorse tangled in on itself, wrapping around its own limbs to grow stronger, the way Ioma spun and plied her thread. The cacophony of color, the cloying smell that reached for miles in spring, the inch-long thorns, and the ever-spreading roots that let the plant scramble its way across fields and hills alike—Jocelyn thought that perhaps, if she could be like that, she would not wither away like her mother, or shrink in sadness like her father had since her mother's death, but could spread across her land and through it, beautiful and powerful and so stunningly vibrant.

The sun touched the gorse last each morning, as it grew in a hedge around the base of the castle, a kind of second moat. Each day, when the fingers of light brushed their pale, watery tips across the brambles, Jocelyn heard a sweet, ringing chime like a faraway bell or a sprinkle of rain on crystal, and she sighed, satisfied.

Ioma turned to her then, and the day's lessons began. At Ioma's knee, Jocelyn learned to card wool and wind spindles. She watched Ioma spin fine thread, fibers twisting around one another in a way that felt like magic. The fibers were sparse and weak, then tight and strong, and as she pushed the treadle with her foot, Ioma taught Jocelyn to spin herself and her kingdom strong, too.

The old fairy hummed wordless tunes as the great wooden wheel spun and the fibers looped in on themselves again and again, and she taught Jocelyn to hum along. Ioma didn't hum folk songs or romantic ballads—she hummed the soft sounds of dawn on the kingdom, memorized from thousands of mornings hearing them, stringing them together like pearls. She hummed the sound of light on water, on stone, on silver birch bark and white-spotted fawns, on wheat fields and castle walls. As she spun and hummed, the thread grew strong, fine, and softly colored, like spiderwebs, and Jocelyn watched in wonder as her kingdom was wound into and onto itself again and again, growing stronger and more beautiful.

As she grew older, Jocelyn helped Ioma to spin, pulling the hanks of wool into roving, humming and singing along with the fairy's songs, winding the finished thread onto spools. The thread was woven on a great loom in the corner, crafted into the shimmering sheets of fabric with which all of the royal family's clothes were adorned. They wore robes made from the songs of the kingdom itself, connecting them to the very soil beneath them, helping them to connect to the hearts of even the smallest denizens of the kingdom.

Ioma allowed the princess to help with the weaving, letting her pass the shuttle through the warp until fabric grew under the child's fingertips. She did not, however, allow Jocelyn to sit alone at the great spinning wheel—she let the girl sit with a drop spindle or a simple wheel now and again, to learn the pull and twist of the fiber between her fingers, but never the great wheel.

"Not until you are queen. When you are crowned, you will be called upon to show your people that you can do this most fundamental thing, to spin your own thread and weave your own robes. But to spin the very thread of the kingdom," the old fairy said, "requires knowing which sounds to call loudest, which things to increase and which to lessen. The balance comes before anything else." She pushed her bare foot against the treadle and the wheel spun, and Jocelyn sat and watched for hours as Ioma balanced the nature of birds against that of trees and flowers and seeds, the nature of fish against insects and water and stone, the nature of farmers against the needs of the land. She understood the idea, yes, but didn't even know how to begin to understand the way to feel the balance herself.

"It comes from the listening," Ioma said to a fourteen-year-old Jocelyn when she drew up the courage to ask. "I come here every day for the beauty of it, certainly, but also to learn. I hear when the fish sing too softly because their numbers have been too diminished by fishermen, when the predators in the forest sing louder than the prey and food grows scarce, when the grass grows too thin by being trod upon too often." She nodded her head at the window, and Jocelyn went. As Jocelyn watched, patches of brown grass grew greener, fuller, and the thread at Ioma's fingertips shone a pale green underneath its opalescent white.

From then on, Jocelyn tried to listen to the balance. She listened as the world turned its face to the sun each day, listened for the scales that tipped between each resident of her kingdom, for the miserable sounds of loss and the glorious sounds of joy and always, always, the bright chime as the sun finally brushed the base of the castle walls and woke the sleeping gorse. Day after day, Jocelyn watched as Ioma spun strength not just into the kingdom itself, but into its king—giving strength to her flagging father, to his failing heart.

Besides Ioma, Jocelyn's only steady company were sparrows. They flew up to the window ledge and watched, heads cocked, as the women worked. Jocelyn listened to the songs of their feathers and their tiny, hollow bones and imagined herself as one of them, safe at the top of the tower, small and soft, high and away but still a part of her kingdom.

The princess became a quiet young woman, speaking kindly but rarely, listening for the sound of imbalances inside herself when she wasn't listening to those of her kingdom, carefully correcting them where she could, spinning her thoughts and her heart stronger, tighter, finer and more beautiful. She was lovely in the way that kind people are lovely, whether or not their features are plain—she was soft, and glowed with the hazy peace of someone who lived their life mostly alone, but wasn't lonely. She listened, too, as the years passed, as her father grew older and wearier and finally died.

She watched as Ioma spun fiercely that day, fingers working thread colorless with mourning. Jocelyn was so lost in listening to the weeping of Splöstlienne and the shifting of the balance that she had no thought to mourn for herself, for the loss of her father as a parent, not just a king. She sat at Ioma's feet and let tears run down her cheeks, but they were for the kingdom, not herself. She felt the loss of the man who listened to the complaints of his people and made fair compromises in their disputes, who managed the treasury so the hospitals and schools had funds and full staff, who planned the rotations of crops in the fields, who rode out and organized the defenses at their borders, who gave hope to his people. She listened as Ioma rose the next day and spun the kingdom brighter, spun the birds louder and made the moon's face blush deeper pink and hummed sea sounds until the waves cried out for the loss of the king.

On the third day, she followed Ioma up the winding stairs blindly, sweeping dust from the old fairy's hair and shooing mice and scooping up spiders as she had done for nearly two decades now.

When she reached the room at the top, though, Ioma was not sitting at her wheel. Instead, she stood at the window, her spinning stool empty, and waited. Behind her, the sun began to rise, unheeded, for the first time in Jocelyn's life.

"Oh," Jocelyn said, with sudden, horrible understanding.

"Oh," Ioma agreed, gesturing to the wheel.

Stiffly, Jocelyn made her way to the spinning stool. She sat abruptly, plunking down onto the worn wooden seat, skirts a mess around her. She sat there, numb, as the sun rose over Splöstlienne, the miserable hum of a kingdom in mourning filling her ears, and she could hardly bear it.

"You are queen now," Ioma said gently. "You must be crowned. You must be married. But first, it is for you to call your kingdom through their grief and back to balance."

Jocelyn closed her eyes tightly, brow pinched, and said, "How?" She couldn't imagine a way through the grief for herself, let alone for the entire kingdom.

Ioma moved, then, and came to stand behind the princess, now queen, and put her hands on the girl's shoulders. "You've listened for years. You must sing now, not just listen." She pulled wool roving from the basket beside the wheel, wound it around the spindle, put the soft end in Jocelyn's fingers. "You see? Sing, Jocelyn."

Jocelyn eased her slippers off her feet, set the delicate silk things aside, and slid her bare foot onto the smooth wooden treadle. It was soft and dark with years of use, and felt warm beneath her sole. "I just push," she said, hearing her own voice as if from a very long way away. "I push with my foot, and pull with my fingers, and let the wheel pull it in."

Ioma's hands squeezed Jocelyn's shoulders again, encouraging. "You've watched for years. Never mind if it's lumpy, my dear, let the wheel do the work. Sing."

Jocelyn gave the mechanics of the thing a moment. She focused on the whoosh-clack as her foot pushed down and the wheel spun and the roving twisted in her fingers. It went quickly, quicker than it had always looked from the outside, and she struggled for a moment with fingers that barely seemed to want to obey her at all. Ioma stood behind her, steady, a statue of support.

Jocelyn worked the thread, fingers clumsy, and tried to listen to the sound of her kingdom.

All she heard was the sound of broken things and weeping. It spun itself into the princess, Jocelyn's heart hanging heavy. She began to miss her father, not for his death, but for the man he must have been before her mother died, the strong and happy king her people were mourning. She began to weep for the loss of her mother for the first time, tears flowing silently as she listened to even the soil below the castle weep. She mourned the loss of a king and a queen who knew how to rule, and felt—as everyone must, one day, as birds feel when they are pushed from the nests, as butterflies do when they unfold from their cocoons—that her life had come upon her all too suddenly, and that her days of quiet joy, of listening to nothing but Ioma and the sounds of the wheel and the kingdom and the sunlight, had come abruptly to an end. She felt as though she were drowning under the weight of the expectations that had been so suddenly thrust upon her—the expectations of the fairies for her to follow their teachings and their work, the hopes of her people that she could take up her father's mantle, the certainty that she was simply not ready. Just for a moment, she hated her parents for not being strong enough to survive until she was ready, to survive until—until she didn't know what, but she hated them, fleetingly and fiercely, for being human enough to fade away into death, for leaving her suddenly surrounded by responsibility and a reality away from this wheel, away from this tower. She was terribly ashamed of herself, then, for hating them at all, for not being brave enough to simply miss them, and like the wool in her hands, the hurt and the shame and the sadness spun tighter, stronger, and Jocelyn felt herself spinning away with it.

Alone in the cacophony of misery, a ring of gold and brown shone out, singing sweetly of hope for strength and endurance. The gorse called out with the promise of bright color and strong limbs, of sharp thorns to hold back the hurt and glorious flowers to soothe the suddenness of loss. Jocelyn seized upon it, clung fiercely to the magnificent sound of strength and beauty and infinite endurance, and let the sound of gorse spin up out of her throat and out her fingertips. Its sweet chime grew louder and louder, blocking out the sound of her childhood breaking and the mourning of her kingdom and its people, silencing them all like stones in the dark as the shimmering sound spread across Splöstlienne. She thought only of that sound, and of the sounds of the spinning wheel and the peace of the tower, and she spun furiously, unwinding the grey sadness and spinning herself tighter into strands of gold.

"Oh, my dear, no," Ioma said, gently, sighing with the sort of solemn resignation of someone who knew she wouldn't be heeded.

It was the last thing Jocelyn heard her say for a hundred years.

When the last sounds of sadness had faded, the last strand of roving slipped from Jocelyn's fingers and spun out onto the wheel. Before her, the spool was wound with heaps of golden thread that smelled faintly of coconut and vanilla, and everything was silent except for the brilliant song of the gorse. The thread was beautiful, smooth and flawless, and Jocelyn turned with proud elation to see her teacher's face.

The old fairy's face was smooth marble, wrinkled lips made of folded stone. Her river of silver hair was dull grey, a stream of old pebbles and strands of spiderweb. Aghast, Jocelyn rose, running to the window, and looked out across the fields and hills of Splöstlienne.

They were gone. In their place was an ocean of gold-flowering brambles spreading as far as the eye could see. Their thick brown branches wound around the window ledge itself, still growing, yellow buds swelling and bursting into bloom as Jocelyn watched, frozen with the enormity of what she had done. Ioma stood behind her, a statue now, and before her was an astonishing end to the terror of having to be queen, of facing the sudden, agonizing start of her adulthood.

Because it was what she had done every other day of her life, Jocelyn turned from the window and went back to where Ioma stood. The old fairy's tiny wings lay against her back like foggy glass, and her woolen gown hung in smooth marble folds. Jocelyn sat, perhaps a little more shakily than she usually might, at Ioma's feet. Hands trembling, she reached for the carding combs and the basket of wool and began her day's work, carding out ropes of roving, her knees drawn up to her chest, her head resting against Ioma's stony skirts.

"I couldn't bear it," she said, something like an apology, to the old fairy's statue. "I just couldn't bear it."

• • •

"Seven score of men have tried and died, princes, kings, and peasants all!" the bard cried, quite drunk, from his seat beside the fire. "Gorse daughter in her tower high—she sings a song, and suitors die! The brambles close around their limbs, and not a one comes out again!" There was a sort of macabre glee to the man's slipshod rhyme. Matthias cringed inwardly.

"Do you imagine she's actually worth it?" his older brother, Liam, joked quietly. "There are women enough here, without—what was the line?— shredded flesh and blood abounding? Yes, that's it. For her beauty so astounding, they quest on, facing shredded flesh and—you know." Liam jerked his head down the table, where there sat an array of ladies decked out in finery. "What man is so desperate for a girl that—"

Matthias had stopped listening. He was the eighth son of the king, and while girls were very lovely, and he had riches enough for anyone who lived their life occupied with the collection of riches, he really preferred a nice game of chess to a dance with one of the ladies of the court. In chess, he knew where he stood, and, as an eighth son, such a thing was very rare. While he didn't precisely adore the idea of facing his own shredded flesh, something about the bard's story struck a chord within him—very much the same one as playing chess with his uncle did. He didn't think he was some sort of master of knightliness, capable of bashing his way through miles of gorse brambles with brute force, but part of him wondered if perhaps there weren't some other way.

"Where is it?"

The bard came to an abrupt halt in the middle of another gory verse randomly spattered with anecdotes about the princess's beauty. "What?"

Matthias rose, pushing his chair back from the table. Liam made a face at him, as though he was quite fed up with his brother's antics, which wasn't particularly unusual, as Liam was a master of knightliness and brute force, and while perfectly capable and intelligent for a king-to-be, wasn't invested in Matthias's love of strategy or quest for a place in the world to call his own unless it involved ideas for expanding or enriching the kingdom. "Where is this—this gorse daughter? This kingdom?"

The bard huffed. "It was known as Splöstlienne, and—" he paused, clearly at a loss. "And I've no idea where it is, sir."

Matthias hummed a little and left the hall, leaving his seven elder brothers, his parents, the bard, and the rest of the court looking exasperated and bemused.

It took nearly four months of Matthias riding around the outlying villages and asking various village elders about legends of Splöstlienne before anyone could point him in a useful direction—people had heard of a giant field of thorny plants, but it had been so long that trade routes had shifted and roads had changed and people had moved on. When someone finally did know anything at all specific, it was an old man who claimed to have been the son of a fisherman there before he met his late wife and eloped with her. He went on about seas that actually sang, a moon that shone pink as a rose, and a cadre of fairy women who kept the magical kingdom in balance.

"Jocelyn," the old man said eventually. "That was her name—or part of it. There were several; there always are with royals."

Matthias, who only had one name—unless one counted Marcusson, as he was son of King Marcus—said nothing, merely nodded and waited for the man to go on.

"But son, she must be old by now. Nearly as old as I am. Certainly no beauty to woo and marry. I know you're the youngest son—"

"Actually, no, there's another one after me," Matthias corrected, mostly out of habit, because Michael was only five, and hadn't even been alive long enough to be officially named into the succession in case of drawing bad luck. He was their mother's favorite, which Matthias didn't particularly resent, because Michael was charming in the way all children were when they were small and sticky but not especially loud. He didn't resent it, no, but Michael's birth had robbed him of his only small corner of identity, that of the youngest son. It didn't gall Matthias, precisely, but it left a hollow space in his chest where he thought a sense of self ought to be, or at least where one might begin. "I'm sorry, do go on," he said, cringing at his own bad manners.

The man harrumphed. "Nonetheless, it's a few weeks' ride northwest, if you're really that curious."

And, all logic aside, Matthias was that curious. He wondered, almost desperately, what gorse smelled like, what this princess looked like, how any of this had come about at all. He wondered if she was terribly old, and simply trapped, or if she was young and spectacularly beautiful and under a curse.

He thanked the old man, tipped him a silver piece for his help, and rode out that very day.

Splöstlienne was a wasteland of thorns. Here and there, ragged yellow buds were emerging among them, but the cold winter kept them mostly bare.

Matthias was a patient man. Being an eighth son, he had spent his life waiting for things a great deal—his turn at table, his turn at the bath, his turn to learn to ride. He had spent the time waiting as productively as he could, learning chess from his uncle, learning to fight from the stable hands, learning to whittle from the old men who sat outside the public house. He was a master of waiting.

So, at the border of Splöstlienne—clearly demarcated by a very imposing line of gorse bushes that stopped abruptly at the edge of the neighboring kingdom of Rhem—Matthias made camp and settled in to wait.

Matthias waited as other men came. Some were clearly noblemen, riding fine horses, wearing fine armor, seeking a bride and the honor of a fantastical rescue. They raised their swords and brandished them at the castle in the distance and then charged at the ocean of brambles, hacking at the thorny limbs. They made it a decent ways in before the brambles closed over them. There was an abrupt, aborted sound of pain, and Matthias would never see them again.

Others were peasants seeking the wealth and prestige of a princess and her kingdom. They made their way into the gorse with hatchets or belt knives, but were invariably enveloped, too. There was, at one point, a man that Matthias suspected was a wizard—he stood at the edge of the thorns, commanded them to part, and strode in confidently, leaving a shimmering rope trailing behind him, presumably to find his way back out. The rope (and the wizard himself) became decidedly moot only a few moments later when the gorse swallowed him, too.

The only things that made it past the gorse at all were birds.

As the weeks passed and the gorse burst into golden flower, the sweet smell of something impossible for the prince to define swept through the air, and birds began to flock to Splöstlienne. Finches, cardinals, sparrows, nuthatches, chickadees all moved between the thorns with ease, building nests where no predators could reach them.

It was this that gave Matthias his first inkling of understanding. Where is a bird safer than in a nest of thorns? He began to wonder, then, if this princess was under a curse at all, or if, instead, someone was protecting her, waiting for the right person to come, to prove himself worthy. Matthias had no idea what being worthy might mean, but the need to know caught his breath.

Matthias packed up his camp the next morning and rode out, following the border of Splöstlienne.

It was days before he came upon a cottage. It was a ramshackle thing, falling to pieces, but there was smoke coming from the chimney.

When the prince rapped at the door, an old woman answered. "Yes?" she croaked, voice rough with disuse.

Matthias begged her pardon, then said, "Why do you live here, at the edge of this wasteland?"

The old woman smiled, eyes getting a faraway look to them, and said, a little dreamily, "Oh, in days gone by, I tended the forests here, and it was beautiful. It was no wasteland then, child."

It was days more before he found another cottage. This was a farmhouse, and gorse bushes grew right up the side and over half the windows.

Another old woman answered when he knocked at the door, looking remarkably similar to the first. When he asked her why she stayed in such a place, she answered, "Oh, my child, in days gone by, I tended the fields and farmlands here, and it was beautiful."

Matthias rode on, and came by nine more homesteads, each with a solitary old woman inside. Each told him something like the same, and he began to wonder if perhaps they were all actually the same old woman, a witch of some sort, playing games with him.

At the twelfth cottage he came to, he was met with another identical old woman, and even the patience of an eighth son ran short.

"Stop your tricks, witch! I demand to know how to reach the princess!" he snapped, looming down at her with a scowl.

The old woman only snorted and slammed the door in his face, which, Matthias supposed, served him right.

He waited a few days before he returned to the cottage, contrite, with a brace of hares as an apology.

"I'm sorry," he said, when the old woman answered his knock. "I shouldn't have shouted, or called you a witch."

She shrugged. "Call me a witch if you like. My sisters and I have fallen to such things as mere healing brews and poultices in the days since the fall of Splöstlienne."

A little helplessly, Matthias said, "I must get to the princess."

The old woman raised an eyebrow. "Why?"

There, Matthias stopped. None of the answers he had were good enough, would be the right answer if this were a puzzle to find a worthy man—curiosity, a desire to prove himself with the sharpness of his mind where he lacked the strength of his brothers, a desire to win, a desperation for some accomplishment or place in the world, a need to have all his endless waiting come to something, ever, at all. None of these was quite the truth, though. The fierce need to go, to do that had burned in his chest ever since the bard's words was nameless for him, but no less fierce for being so.

"I'm not sure," he admitted, spreading his hands in an empty gesture. "I suppose I simply need to know."

The old woman smiled—a toothless, wrinkled smile that made Matthias at once very nervous and completely at ease, and he knew he hadn't been terribly far off when he had called the woman a witch. "Good enough for me," she said, shrugging again. "And how do you propose to get there? And what will you do if you manage it? My sisters and I are a bit protective of the princess; one of us still stands guard in the tower."

Matthias looked out over the fields of gorse for a long, long minute, watching the bees hum in the air and the birds dart among the thorns. "The briars swallow any man who seeks her," he said slowly, puzzling it out the way he did when he tried to anticipate his uncle's next move on the board. "So I must be something other than a man."

"I cannot guarantee," the old woman warned him, "that you will ever return to being a man if you cease to be one for any time at all. Such things are never sure."

Matthias considered it. There was not much of a life in being the eighth of nine sons. "What is there to return to?" he asked, shrugging his shoulders. "What man have I ever been? Maybe I will be better as something else entirely."

"You're certain?" the old woman asked.

Matthias knew, then, all at once and beautifully, that his place was in that tower, as the solver of the puzzle that others had approached as a battle. He didn't need to be a conqueror or a bridegroom, but merely something small and somehow useful. "So be it," he said, nodding once, decisively, and closing his eyes.

The old woman hummed a soft, low sound, and where Matthias had stood now fluttered a small, brown sparrow.

Jocelyn spun.

She woke each morning and unrolled herself from the blanket of golden wool that she had woven. She rose from the bed she had made—gorse-yellow and stuffed with wool—and went to sit at Ioma's feet. There she carded wool in the predawn light, endless wool, which never seemed to run out. After, she stood at the window as the sun rose, watching the light spill across the fields of gorse and listening to it sing. She basked in the sense of freedom, of safety, knowing that her people all stood as Ioma stood, safe and stony, frozen in the last moment of her life as a child. She could not fail them like this, could not trip in the footprints her parents had left for her to fill. Splöstlienne was safe, covered over, enduring and beautiful.

She spun sunny lengths of thread each day, thread that sang songs of sweet things and unbridled joy, of strength and safety. She spun herself into that thread, too, stronger and tighter and more vast, until she was a dense forest of self, alive with singing birds and humming bees, sharp with thorns and bright with flowers. She spun herself brilliantly alive, until she needed no food but sunlight, no water but rain, and time floated by her like clouds, distant and unremarkable.

It went on this way for countless days—or, if one tried to count them, something like the number of days that might add up to a century—until one morning, as the sun rose, there was a new sound in the sunrise.

It was soft, feathered and familiar like all the birds in her fields were, but slightly strange. A sparrow sat on her windowsill, head cocked. He watched with shiny, bright black eyes, holding still, waiting.

"You're new," Jocelyn said to him, voice soft. She hadn't spoken in a long time—she had sung, so her voice was rich and deep like bells and crystal, but no words had crossed her tongue since her last apology to Ioma. Birds had nested on her teacher's shoulders, in her hair, and Jocelyn hadn't begrudged them their homes there any more than Ioma had begrudged the spiders and mice that had once held their place. But this sparrow was different, not one of the tower sparrows, not a bird of Splöstlienne at all. His song—the sound as the sunlight hit him, oh, it was different.

Jocelyn let him be, not wanting to startle the small creature, and sat down to spin. She spun for hours, until the sun had receded into salmon-colored clouds. It was only then that she stopped spinning, running out of one length of roving, moving to pick up another, and noticed the color of her thread had changed. Where all the other spools had been endless gold, this one was speckled with tawny brown.

Something sparked beneath the princess's breastbone. It was a kind of elation and terror at once—there had been no change for years, and any such thing, now, was terrifying. But oh, even a favorite song, a favorite color, a favorite smell grows old with knowing it too long and too well, and that tawny flecking was a kind of beauty half-remembered from a childhood when Jocelyn had learned other arts, had heard other songs, had walked in fields and stood in dark forests thick with secrets. It made her hungry for something deeper than food—change. Company. Perhaps, very far off in the distance, a wonder about what it might be like to grow up.

Curious, heart beating fast, Jocelyn turned to the sparrow, who hadn't moved from his perch. "Oh, little thing, what have you done?" she asked him, putting out her hand, fingers trembling. The sparrow hopped onto her outstretched forefinger.

Carefully, Jocelyn raised her hand up to where she could examine him better. She hummed the song of sparrows at him, the songs of their feathers and their tiny, hollow bones.

The sparrow did not hum back.

Jocelyn looked at the statue of Ioma and said to it—because she didn't dare ask the sparrow himself—"He isn't a sparrow at all, is he?"

The statue didn't move, but Jocelyn suspected that the birds nesting on it were giving her exasperated glances. One chirped.

Jocelyn looked back at the sparrow on her finger. "I wasn't ready," she explained to him, voice shaking. "They left—my mother, and then my father, and then I was supposed to be queen—and it was so sudden, and so much, all at once."

The sparrow waited, head cocked. Listening. Jocelyn had spent so long listening—her whole life, just listening and spinning—that she wondered how it might feel to be listened to, even for a moment, by something else who knew how. Even these small moments of being heard—for the first time, Jocelyn didn't want to be quiet, didn't want to only listen and hum the songs of other things, songs from outside herself, no matter how beautiful they might be.

"I couldn't bear the sadness," the princess said, half to herself now. "I couldn't stand the sound." She hummed a little, trying to remember the songs of anything but strong brown thorns and golden flowers. So much of her didn't want to remember at all, wanted very badly to stay just as she was. But the hunger was there, the hunger to remember what it was like to grow, to eat, to bleed, to smell things that weren't sweet, to see things that were anything at all but gold and brown and the blue of the sky. "Remind me?" she begged the sparrow, a little desperate now that she'd got hold of the idea, terrified that if she waited, she would never want to try again.

Softly, so softly, the sparrow chirped a brief little melody. It was nothing and everything all at once, a picture in sound of green grass beyond her borders, of hearth fires and men and women and food, of cottages and ramshackle ruins, of forests, of rabbits and deer and the howling of wolves.

Picking up a new length of roving and sitting at the wheel, Jocelyn, even softer still than the sparrow, hummed the song back to him and pushed her foot down on the treadle.

The wheel spun.

The next days passed quickly, Jocelyn feeling hollow-boned, light and somehow holy in the wake of the sparrow breaking her spell.

When Ioma awoke and the stone crumbled from her features, when the gorse fields rolled back until they were merely a ring around the castle walls again, Jocelyn kissed her teacher on her wrinkled cheek, handed her the basket of roving, and left the tower room. She did not look back, even as she heard the old fairy laughing.

At the bottom of the stairs, a footman met her and asked her when she would like to bury her father.

"I am ready now," she told him, voice firm, though she was still shaking a little.

The footman looked a little startled, but the princess and the sparrow on her shoulder stared him down until he nodded and trotted off to make the arrangements.

Jocelyn floated through the castle then, listening with one ear to the sounds of her kingdom coming back to life, but finally speaking as well.

The next day, the old king was buried beside Jocelyn's mother. Jocelyn wept, and, for the first time, did not keep silent as she did so.

Life resumed. The fairies took up their tasks, the farmers took up their plows, and the fishermen took up their nets and cast them wide on the green and singing sea.

The first day after the burial of her father, Jocelyn walked on bare feet through the paths of the forest and ate fruits full of secrets. On the second day, she knelt in the halls of healing and hummed songs of solace to the sick among her people. On the third, she strode through the farms and fields, sowing grain. The fourth, she danced in the great hall with nobles and farmers alike. The fifth, she stood on the rocky shore of the sea and sang fish into men's golden nets.

On the sixth day, and the seventh, and the eighth, she took her turn at cooking great vats of soup for the poor, at gathering herbs on the hillsides, at stitching together a robe made from fabric she and Ioma had woven. On the ninth day, she played (a little clumsily) at a harp. On the tenth day, Jocelyn called rabbits from their warrens and pheasants from their nests as her people took what food they needed. On the eleventh, the princess knelt beside the castle maids and scrubbed the kitchen floors and swept the tower stairs.

On the twelfth day, Jocelyn walked with the last of Ioma's sisters into the throne room of the castle and took her place on the great carved seat that had once been her father's. The velvet beneath her was worn thin, and the wood beneath her hands was smooth and shiny where her predecessors had rested their palms. She sat vigil through the night, Ioma and her twelve sisters kneeling around the throne room and humming soft songs, murmuring their wisdom into Jocelyn's very bones.

She was crowned on the thirteenth day, just before dawn. Ioma and her sisters blessed Jocelyn's rule in turn, speaking each of her names, kissing her cheeks, and then turning to stand in a neat row, like pieces on a chessboard, behind her. Jocelyn herself stood, crown heavy on her head, facing her people as their queen.

The sparrow lived on Jocelyn's shoulder, beak to her ear, where he made soft sounds that painted pictures of things she had never seen—kingdoms far away, men she had never met, horses she had never ridden, mountains she had never crossed.

In the days, she spoke to the sparrow constantly, taking a fierce joy in the way he waited as she spoke, the way he cocked his head, listening.

At night, she kissed his feathered head, gratitude swelling in her chest for this small, simple thing that broke her free of her own fear. Each night, she crawled into a bed draped with blankets that were not gold, and she slept, as anyone would sleep, and dreamed.

It was not particularly magical sleep, but sometimes, in the better dreams, she met a young man with a sparrow's eyes, and sat across a table from him, a black and white board between them, and they played chess as he told her stories of faraway kingdoms and strange foods and drunken bards and eight brothers—seven older, one still very young.

"Are you happy?" she asked him one night, looking up as her knight claimed his pawn. "I'm sorry you haven't turned back." She didn't know if it was because they didn't love one another enough yet—she kissed his head each night, just to be certain—or if he was meant to stay a sparrow until some other thing happened, or if there was just no going back at all.

He smiled, not looking up from the board, and she could see him ticking through strategies for the game. "I'm happy," he said, sliding his bishop across the board to claim her knight. "I like knowing I'm useful. And I'm very patient, you know. I'm the—"

"Eighth son of nine," she finished for him, smiling wryly and moving her queen. "I do listen, you know. Check."

THE VISITOR FROM TAURED

IAN R. MacLEOD

✦

1.

There was always something otherworldly about Rob Holm. Not that he wasn't charming and clever and good-looking. Driven, as well. Even during that first week when we'd arrived at university and waved goodbye to our parents and our childhoods, and were busy doing all the usual fresher things, which still involved getting dangerously drunk and pretending not to be homesick and otherwise behaving like the prim, arrogant, cocky, and immature young assholes we undoubtedly were, Rob was chatting with research fellows and quietly getting to know the best virtuals to hang out in.

Even back then, us young undergrads were an endangered breed. Many universities had gone bankrupt, become commercial research utilities, or transformed themselves into the academic theme parks of those so-called "Third Age Academies." But still, here we all were at the traditional redbrick campus of Leeds University, which still offered a broad-ish range of courses to those with families rich enough to support them, or at least tolerant enough not to warn them against such folly. My own choice of degree, just to show how incredibly supportive my parents were, being Analogue Literature.

As a subject, it already belonged with Alchemy and Marxism in the dustbin of history, but books—and I really do mean those peculiar, old, paper, physical objects—had always been my thing. Even when I was far too young to understand what they were and by rights should have been attracted by the bright, interactive, virtual gewgaws buzzing all around me, I'd managed to burrow into the bottom of an old box, down past the stickle bricks and My Little Ponies, to these broad, cardboardy things that fell open and had these flat, two-dee shapes and images that didn't move or respond in any normal way when I waved my podgy fingers in their direction. All you could do was simply look at them. That and chew their corners, and maybe scribble over their pages with some of the dried-up crayons that were also to be found amid those predigital layers.

My parents had always been loving and tolerant of their daughter. They even encouraged little Lita's interest in these ancient artifacts. I remember my mother's finger moving slow and patient across the creased and yellowed pages as she traced the pictures and her lips breathed the magical words that somehow arose from those flat lines. She wouldn't have assimilated data this way herself in years, if ever, so in a sense we were both learning.

The Hungry Caterpillar. Beatrix Potter, the Mr. Men series. *Where the Wild Things Are.* Frodo's adventures. Slowly, like some archaeologist discovering the world by deciphering the cartouches of the tombs in Ancient Egypt, I learned how to perceive and interact through this antique medium. It was, well, the *thingness* of books. The exact way they *didn't* leap about or start giving off sounds, smells, and textures. That, and how they didn't ask you which character you'd like to be, or what level you wanted to go to next, but simply took you by the hand and led you where they wanted you to go.

Of course, I became a confirmed bibliophile, but I do still wonder how my life would have progressed if my parents had seen odd behavior differently, and taken me to some pediatric specialist. Almost certainly, I wouldn't be the Lita Ortiz who's writing these words for whoever might still be able to comprehend them. Nor the one who was lucky enough to meet Rob Holm all those years ago in the teenage fug of those student halls back at Leeds University.

2.

So. Rob. First thing to say is the obvious fact that most of us fancied him. It wasn't just the grey eyes, or the courtly elegance, or that soft Scottish accent, or even the way he somehow appeared mature and accomplished. It was, essentially, a kind of mystery. But he wasn't remotely standoffish. He went along with the fancy dress pub crawls. He drank. He fucked about. He took the odd tab.

One of my earliest memories of Rob was finding him at some club, cool as you like amid all the noise, flash, and flesh. And dragging him out onto the pulsing dance floor. One minute we were hovering above the skyscrapers of Beijing and the next a shipwreck storm was billowing about us. Rob, though, was simply there. Taking it all in, laughing, responding, but somehow detached. Then, helping me down and out, past clanging temple bells and through prismatic sandstorms to the entirely non-virtual hell of the toilets. His cool hands holding back my hair as I vomited.

I never ever actually thanked Rob for this—I was too embarrassed—but the incident somehow made us more aware of each other. That, and maybe we shared a sense of otherness. He, after all, was studying astrophysics, and none of the rest of us even knew what that was, and he had all that strange stuff going on across the walls of his room. Not flashing posters of the latest virtual boy band or porn empress, but slow-turning gas clouds, strange planets, distant stars and galaxies. That, and long runs of mek, whole arching rainbows of the stuff, endlessly twisting and turning. My room, on the other hand, was piled with the precious torn and foxed paperbacks I'd scoured from junksites during my teenage years. Not, of course, that they were actually needed. Even if you were studying something as arcane as narrative fiction, you were still expected to download and virtualize all your resources.

The Analogue Literature Faculty at Leeds University had once taken up a labyrinthine space in a redbrick terrace at the east edge of the campus. But now it had been invaded by dozens of more modern disciplines. Anything from speculative mek to non-concrete design to holo-pornography had taken bites out of it. I was already aware—how couldn't I be?—that no significant novel or short story had been written in decades, but I was shocked to discover that only five other students in my year had elected for An Lit as their main subject, and one of those still resided in Seoul and another was a post-centarian on clicking steel legs. Most of the other students who showed up were dipping into the subject in the hope that it might add something useful to their main discipline. Invariably, they were disappointed. It wasn't just the difficulty of ploughing through page after page of non-interactive text. It was linear fiction's sheer lack of options, settings, choices. Why the hell, I remember some kid shouting in a seminar, should I accept all the miserable shit that this Hardy guy rains down on his characters? Give me the base program for *Tess of the d'Urbervilles*, and I'll hack you fifteen better endings.

I pushed my weak mek to the limit during that first term as I tried to formulate a tri-dee excursus on *Tender Is the Night*, but the whole piece was reconfigured out of existence once the faculty AIs got hold of it. Meanwhile, Rob Holm was clearly doing far better. I could hear him singing in the showers along from my room, and admired the way he didn't get involved in all the usual peeves and arguments. The physical sciences had a huge, brand new facility at the west end of campus called the Clearbrite Building. Half church, half-pagoda, and maybe half spaceship in the fizzing, shifting, headachy way of modern architecture, there was no real way of telling how much of it was actually made of brick, concrete, and glass, and how much consisted of virtual artifacts and energy fields. You could get seriously lost just staring at it.

My first year went by, and I fought hard against crawling home, and had a few unromantic flings, and made vegetable bolognaise my signature dish, and somehow managed to get version 4.04 of my second term excursus on *Howard's End* accepted. Rob and I didn't become close, but I liked his singing and the cinnamon scent he left hanging behind in the steam of the showers, and it was good to know that someone else was making a better hash of this whole undergraduate business than I was.

"Hey, Lita?"

We were deep into the summer term and exams were looming. Half the undergrads were back at home, and the other half were jacked up on learning streams, or busy having breakdowns.

I leaned in on Rob's doorway. "Yeah?"

"Fancy sharing a house next year?"

"Next year?" Almost effortlessly casual, I pretended to consider this. "I really hadn't thought. It all depends—"

"Not a problem." He shrugged. "I'm sure I'll find someone else."

"No, no. That's fine. I mean, yeah, I'm in. I'm interested."

"Great. I'll show you what I've got from the letting agencies." He smiled a warm smile, then returned to whatever wondrous creations were spinning above his desk.

3.

We settled on a narrow house with bad drains just off the Otley Road in Headingley, and I'm not sure whether I was relieved or disappointed when I discovered that his plan was that we share the place with some others. I roped in a couple of girls, Rob found a couple of guys, and we all got on pretty well. I had a proper boyfriend by then, a self-regarding jock called Torsten, and every now and then a different woman would emerge from Rob's room. Nothing serious ever seemed to come of this, but they were equally gorgeous, clever, and out of my league.

A bunch of us used to head out to the moors for midnight bonfires during that second winter. I remember the smoke and the sparks spinning into the deep black as we sang and drank and arsed around. Once, and with the help of a few tabs and cans, I asked Rob to name some constellations for me, and he put an arm around my waist and led me further into the dark.

Over there, Lita, up to the left and far away from the light of this city, is Ursa Major, the Great Bear, which is always a good place to start when you're stargazing. And there, see close as twins at the central bend of the Plough's handle, are Mizar and Alcor. They're not a true binary, but if we had decent binoculars, we could see that Mizar really does have a close companion. And there, that way, up and left—his breath on my face, his hands on my arms— maybe you can just see there's this fuzzy speck at the Bear's shoulder? Now, that's an entire, separate galaxy from our own filled with billions of stars, and its light has taken about twelve million years to reach the two of us here, tonight. Then Andromeda and Cassiopeia and Canus Major and Minor. . . . Distant, storybook names for distant worlds. I even wondered aloud about the possibility of other lives, existences, hardly expecting Rob to agree with me. But he did. And then he said something that struck me as strange.

"Not just out there, either, Lita. There are other worlds all around us. It's just that we can't see them."

"You're talking in some metaphorical sense, right?"

"Not at all. It's part of what I'm trying to understand in my studies."

"To be honest, I've got no real idea what astrophysics even means. Maybe you could tell me."

"I'd love to. And you know, Lita, I'm a complete dunce when it comes to, what do you call it—two-dee fiction, flat narrative? So I want you to tell me about that as well. Deal?"

We wandered back toward the fire, and I didn't expect anything else to come of our promise until Rob called to me when I was wandering past his room one wet, grey afternoon a week or so later. It was deadline day, my hair was a greasy mess, I was heading for the shower, and had an excursus on John Updike to finish.

"You *did* say you wanted to know more about what I study?"

"I was just . . . " I scratched my head. "Curious. All I do know is that astrophysics is about more than simply looking up at the night sky and giving names to things. That isn't even astronomy, is it?"

"You're not just being polite?" His soft, granite-grey eyes remained fixed on me.

"No. I'm not—absolutely."

"I could show you something here." He waved at the stars on his walls, the stuff spinning on his desk. "But maybe we could go out. To be honest, Lita, I could do with a break, and there's an experiment I could show you up at the Clearbrite that might help explain what I mean about other worlds . . . but I understand if you're busy. I could get my avatar to talk to your avatar and—"

"No, no. You're right, Rob. I could do with a break as well. Let's go out. Seize the day. Or at least, what's left of it. Just give me . . . " I waved a finger toward the bathroom, " . . . five minutes."

Then we were outside in the sideways-blowing drizzle, and it was freezing cold, and I was still wet from my hurried shower, as Rob slipped a companionable arm around mine as we climbed the hill toward the Otley Road tram stop.

Kids and commuters got on and off as we jolted toward the strung lights of the city, their lips moving and their hands stirring to things only they could feel and see. The Clearbrite looked more than ever like some recently arrived spaceship as it glowed out through the gloom, but inside the place was just like any other campus building, with clamoring posters offering to restructure your loan, find you temporary work, or get you laid and hammered. Constant reminders, too, that Clearbrite was the only smartjuice to communicate in realtime to your fingerjewel, toejamb, or wristbracelet. This souk-like aspect of modern unis not being something that Sebastian Flyte, or even Harry Potter in those disappointing sequels, ever had to contend with.

We got a fair few hellos, a couple of tenured types stopped to talk to Rob in a corridor, and I saw how people paused to listen to what he was saying. More than ever, I had him down as someone who was bound to succeed. Still, I was expecting to be shown moon rocks, lightning bolts, or at least some clever virtual planetarium. But instead he took me into what looked like the kind of laboratory I'd been forced to waste many hours in at school, even if the equipment did seem a little fancier.

"This is the physics part of the astro," Rob explained, perhaps sensing my disappointment. "But you did ask about other worlds, right, and this is pretty much the only way I can show them to you."

I won't go too far into the details, because I'd probably get them wrong, but what Rob proceeded to demonstrate was a version of what I now know to be the famous, or infamous, Double Slit Experiment. There was a long black tube on a workbench. At one end of it was a laser, and at the other was a display screen attached to a device called a photo multiplier—a kind of sensor. In the middle he placed a barrier with two narrow slits. It wasn't a great surprise even to me that the pulses of light caused a pretty dark-light pattern of stripes to appear on the display at the far end. These, Rob said, were ripples of the interference pattern caused by the waves of light passing through the two slits, much as you'd get if you were pouring water. But light, Lita, is made up of individual packets of energy called photons. So what would happen if, instead of sending tens of thousands of them down the tube at once, we turned the laser down so far that it only emitted one photon at a time? Then, surely, each individual photon could only go through one or the other of the slits, there would be no ripples, and two simple stripes would emerge at the far end. But, hey, as he slowed the beep of the signal counter until it was registering single digits, the dark-light bars, like a shimmering neon forest, remained. As if, although each photon was a single particle, it somehow became a blur of all its possibilities as it passed through both slits at once. Which, as far as anyone knew, was pretty much what happened.

"I'm sorry," Rob said afterward when we were chatting over a second or third pint of beer in the fug of an old student bar called the Eldon that lay down the road from the university, "I should have shown you something less boring."

"It wasn't boring. The implications are pretty strange, aren't they?"

"More than strange. It goes against almost everything else we know about physics and the world around us—us sitting here in this pub, for instance.

Things exist, right? They're either here or not. They don't flicker in and out of existence like ghosts. This whole particles blurring into waves business was one of the things that bugged me most when I was a kid finding out about science. It was partly why I chose to study astrophysics—I thought there'd be answers I'd understand when someone finally explained them to me. But there aren't." He sipped his beer. "All you get is something called the Copenhagen Interpretation, which is basically a shoulder shrug that says, hey, this stuff happen at the sub-atomic level, but it doesn't really have to bother us or make sense in the world we know about and live in. That, and then there's something else called the many worlds theory . . . " He trailed off. Stifled a burp. Seemed almost embarrassed.

"Which is what you believe in?"

"Believe isn't the right word. Things either are or they aren't in science. But, yeah, I do. And the maths supports it. Simply put, Lita, it says that all the possible states and positions that every particle could exist in are real—that they're endlessly spinning off into other universes."

"You mean, as if every choice you could make in a virtual was instantly mapped out in its entirety?"

"Exactly. But this is real. The worlds are all around us—right here."

The drink and the conversation moved on, and now it was my turn to apologize to Rob, and his to say no, I wasn't boring him. Because books, novels, stories, they were *my* other worlds, the thing I believed in even if no one else cared about them. That single, magical word, *Fog*, which Dickens uses as he begins to conjure London. And Frederic Henry walking away from the hospital in the rain. And Rose of Sharon offering the starving man her breast after the Joads' long journey across dustbowl America, and Candide eating fruit, and Bertie Wooster bumbling back across Mayfair . . .

Rob listened and seemed genuinely interested, even though he confessed he'd never read a single non-interactive story or novel. But, unlike most people, he said this as if he realized he was actually missing out on something. So we agreed I'd lend him some of my old paperbacks, and this, and what he'd shown me at the Clearbrite, signaled a new phase in our relationship.

4.

It seems to me now that some of the best hours of my life were spent not in reading books, but in sitting with Rob Holm in my cramped room in that house we shared back in Leeds, and talking about them.

What to read and admire, but also—and this was just as important—what not to. *The Catcher in the Rye* being overrated, and James Joyce a literary show-off, and *Moby Dick* really wasn't about much more than whales. Alarmingly, Rob was often ahead of me. He discovered a copy of *Labyrinths* by Jorge Luis Borges in a garage sale, which he gave to me as a gift and then kept borrowing back. But he was Rob Holm. He could solve the riddles of the cosmos and meanwhile explore literature as nothing but a hobby, and also help me out with my mek so that I was finally able to produce the kind of arguments, links, and algorithms for my piece on *Madame Bovary* that the AIs at An Eng actually wanted.

Meanwhile, I also found out about the kind of life Rob had come from. Both his parents were engineers, and he'd spent his early years in Aberdeen, but they'd moved to the Isle of Harris after his mother was diagnosed with a brain-damaging prion infection, probably caused by her liking for fresh salmon. Most of the fish were then factory-farmed in crowded pens in the Scottish lochs, where the creatures were dosed with antibiotics and fed on pellets of processed meat, often recycled from the remains of their own breed. Just as with cattle and Creutzfeldt-Jakob Disease a century earlier, this process had resulted in a small but significant species leap of cross-infection. Rob's parents wanted to make the best of the years Alice Holm had left, and set up an ethical marine farm—although they preferred to call it a ranch— harvesting scallops on the Isle of Harris.

Rob's father was still there at Creagach, and the business, which not only produced some of the best scallops in the Hebrides but also benefited other marine life along the costal shelf, was still going. Rob portrayed his childhood there as a happy time, with his mother still doing well, despite the warnings of the scans, and regaling him with bedtime tales of Celtic myths, that were probably his only experience before meeting me of linear fictional narrative.

There were the kelpies, who lived in lochs and were like fine horses, and then there were the Blue Men of the Minch who dwelt between Harris and the mainland and sung up storms and summoned the waves with their voices. Then, one night when Rob was eleven, his mother waited until he and his father were asleep, walked out across the shore and into the sea, and swam, and kept on swimming. No one could last long out there, the sea being so cold, and the strong currents, or perhaps the Blue Men of the Minch, bore her body back to a stretch of shore around the headland from Creagach, where she was found next morning.

Rob told his story without any obvious angst. But it certainly helped explain the sense of difference and distance he seemed to carry with him. That, and why he didn't fit. Not here in Leeds, amid the fun, mess, and heartbreak of student life, nor even, as I slowly came to realize, in the subject he was studying.

He showed me the virtual planetarium at the Clearbrite, and the signals from a probe passing through the Oort Cloud, and even took me down to the tunnels of a mine where a huge tank of cryogenically cooled fluid had been set up in the hope of detecting the dark matter of which it had once been believed most of our universe was made. It was an old thing now, creaking and leaking, and Rob was part of the small team of volunteers who kept it going. We stood close together in the dripping near-dark, clicking hardhats and sharing each other's breath, and of course I was thinking of other possibilities—those fractional moments when things could go one of many ways. Our lips pressing. Our bodies joining. But something, maybe a fear of losing him entirely, held me back.

"It's another thing that science has given up on," he said later when we were sitting at our table in the Eldon. "Just like that ridiculous Copenhagen shoulder-shrug. Without dark matter, and dark energy, the way the galaxies rotate and recede from each other simply doesn't make mathematical sense. You know what the so-called smart money is on these days? Something called topographical deformity, which means that the basic laws of physics don't apply in the same way across this entire universe. That it's pock-marked with flaws."

"But you don't believe that?"

"Of course I don't! It's fundamentally unscientific."

"But you get glitches in even the most cleverly conceived virtuals, don't you? Even in novels, sometimes things don't always entirely add up."

"Yeah. Like who killed the gardener in *The Big Sleep*, or the season suddenly changing from autumn to spring in that Sherlock Holmes story. But this isn't like that, Lita. This isn't . . . " For once, he was in danger of sounding bitter and contemptuous. But he held himself back.

"And you're not going to give up?"

He smiled. Swirled his beer. "No, Lita. I'm definitely not."

5.

Perhaps inevitably, Rob's and my taste in books had started to drift apart. He'd discovered an antique genre called Science Fiction, something that the AIs at An Lit were particularly sniffy about. And, even as he tried to lead me with him, I could see their point. Much of the prose was less than luminous, the characterization was sketchy, and, although a great deal of it was supposedly about the future, the predictions were laughably wrong.

But Rob insisted that that wasn't the point, that SF was essentially a literature of ideas. That, and a sense of wonder. To him, wonder was particularly important. I could sometimes—maybe as that lonely astronaut passed through the stargate, or with those huge worms in that book about a desert world—see his point. But most of it simply left me cold.

Rob went off on secondment the following year to something called the Large Millimeter Array on the Atacama Plateau in Chile, and I, for want of anything better, kept the lease on our house in Headingley and got some new people in, and did a masters on gender roles in George Eliot's *Middlemarch*. Of course, I paid him virtual visits, and we talked of the problems of altitude sickness and the changed assholes our old uni friends were becoming as he put me on a camera on a Jeep and bounced me across the dark-skied desert.

Another year went—they were already picking up speed—and Rob found the time for a drink before he headed off to some untenured post, part research, part teaching, in Heidelberg that he didn't seem particularly satisfied with. He was still reading—apparently there hadn't been much else to do in Chile— but I realized our days of talking about Proust or Henry James had gone.

He'd settled into, you might almost say retreated to, a sub-genre of SF known as alternate history, where all the stuff he'd been telling me about our world continually branching off into all its possibilities was dramatized on a big scale. Hitler had won World War Two—a great many times, it seemed—and the South was triumphant in the American Civil War. That, and the Spanish Armada had succeeded, and Europe remained under the thrall of medieval Roman Catholicism, and Lee Harvey Oswald's bullet had grazed past President Kennedy's head. I didn't take this odd obsession as a particularly good sign as we exchanged chaste hugs and kisses in the street outside the Eldon and went our separate ways.

I had a job of sorts—thanks to Sun-Mi, my fellow An Lit student from Korea—teaching English to the kids of rich families in Seoul, and for a while it was fun, and the people were incredibly friendly, but then I grew bored and managed to wrangle an interview with one of the media conglomerates that had switched its physical base to Korea in the wake of the California Earthquake. I was hired for considerably less than I was getting paid teaching English and took the crowded commute every morning to a vast half-real, semi-ziggurat high-rise mistily floating above the Mapo District, where I studied high res worlds filled with headache-inducing marvels, and was invited to come up with ideas in equally headache-inducing meetings.

I, an Alice in these many virtual wonderlands, brought a kind of puzzled innocence to my role. Two, maybe three, decades earlier, the other developers might still have known enough to recognize my plagiarisms, if only from old movies their parents had once talked about, but now what I was saying seemed new, fresh, and quirky. I was a thieving literary magpie, and became the go-to girl for unexpected turns and twists. The real murderer of Roger Ackroyd, and the dog collar in *The Great Gatsby*. Not to mention what Little Father Time does in *Jude the Obscure*, and the horror of Sophie's choice. I pillaged them all, and many others. Even the strange idea that the Victorians had developed steam-powered computers, thanks to my continued conversations with Rob.

Wherever we actually were, we got into the habit of meeting up at a virtual recreation of the bar of the Eldon that, either as some show-off feat of virtual engineering, or a post-post-modern art project, some student had created. The pub had been mapped in realtime down to the atom and the pixel, and the ghosts of our avatars often got strange looks from real undergrads bunking off from afternoon seminars. We could actually order a drink, and even taste the beer, although of course we couldn't ingest it. Probably no bad thing, in view of the state of the Eldon's toilets. But somehow, that five-pints-and-still-clear-headed feeling only added to the slightly illicit pleasure of our meetings. At least, at first.

It was becoming apparent that, as he switched from city to city, campus to campus, project to project, Rob was in danger of turning into one of those aging, permanent students, clinging to short-term contracts, temporary relationships, and get-me-by loans, and the worst thing was that, with typical unflinching clarity, he knew it.

"I reckon I was either born too early, or too late, Lita," he said as he sipped his virtual beer. "Even one of the assessors actually said that to me a year or so ago when I tried to persuade her to back my project."

"So you scientists have to pitch ideas as well?"

He laughed, but that warm, Hebridean sound was turning bitter. "How else does this world work? But maths doesn't change even if fashions do. The many worlds theory is the only way that the behavior of subatomic particles can be reconciled with everything else we know. Just because something's hard to prove doesn't mean it should be ignored."

By this time I was busier than ever. Instead of providing ideas other people could profit from, I'd set up my own consultancy, which had thrived and made me a great deal of money. By now, in fact, I had more of the stuff than most people would have known what to do with. But *I* did. I'd reserved a new apartment in a swish high-res, high-rise development going up overlooking the Han River and was struggling to get the builders to understand that I wanted the main interior space to be turned into something called a *library*. I showed them old walk-throughs of the Bodleian in Oxford, and the reading room of the British Museum, and the Brotherton in Leeds, and many other lost places of learning. Of course I already had a substantial collection of books in a secure, fireproofed, climate-controlled warehouse, but now I began to acquire more.

The once-great public collections were either in storage or scattered to the winds. But there were still enough people as rich and crazy as I was to ensure that the really rare stuff—first folios, early editions, hand-typed versions of great works—remained expensive and sought-after, and I surprised even myself with the determination and ruthlessness of my pursuits. After all, what else was I going to spend my time and money on?

There was no grand opening of my library. In fact, I was anxious to get all the builders and conservators, both human and otherwise, out of the way so I could have the place entirely to myself. Then I just stood there. Breathing in the air, with its savor of lost forests and dreams.

There were first editions of great novels by Nabokov, Dos Passos, Stendhal, Calvino, and Wells, and an early translation of Cervantes, and a fine collection of Swift's works. Even, in a small nod to Rob, a long shelf of pulp magazines with titles like *Amazing Stories* and *Weird Tales*, although their lurid covers of busty maidens being engulfed by intergalactic centipedes were generally faded and torn. Not that I cared about the pristine state of my whispering pages. Author's signatures, yes—the sense of knowing Hemingway's hands had once briefly grasped this edition—but the rest didn't matter. At least, apart from the thrill of beating others in my quest. Books, after all, were old by definition. Squashed moths and bus tickets stuffed between the pages. Coffee-cup circles on the dust jackets. Exclamations in the margin. I treasured the evidence of their long lives.

After an hour or two of shameless gloating and browsing, I decided to call Rob. My avatar had been as busy as me with the finishing touches to my library, and now it struggled to find him. What it did eventually unearth was a short report stating that Callum Holm, a fish-farmer on the Isle of Harris, had been drowned in a boating accident a week earlier.

Of course, Rob would be there now. Should I contact him? Should I leave him to mourn undisturbed? What kind of friend was I, anyway, not to have even picked up on this news until now? I turned around the vast, domed space I'd created in confusion and distress.

"Hey."

I span back. The Rob Holm who stood before me looked tired but composed. He'd grown a beard, and there were a few flecks of silver now in it and his hair. I could taste the sea air around him. Hear the cry of gulls.

"Rob!" I'd have hugged him, if the energy field permissions I'd set up in this library had allowed. "I'm so, so sorry. I should have found out, I should have—"

"You shouldn't have done anything, Lita. Why do you think I kept this quiet? I wanted to be alone up here in Harris to sort things out. But . . . " He looked up, around. "What a fabulous place you've created!"

As I showed him around my shelves and acquisitions, and his ghost fingers briefly passed through the pages of my first edition *Gatsby*, and the adverts for X-Ray specs in an edition of *Science Wonder Stories*, he told me how his father had gone out in his launch to deal with some broken tethers on one of the kelp beds and been caught by a sudden squall. His body, of course, had been washed up, borne to the same stretch of shore where Rob's mother had been found.

"It wasn't intentional," Rob said. "I'm absolutely sure of that. Dad was still in his prime, and proud of what he was doing, and there was no way he was ever going to give up. He just misjudged a coming storm. I'm the same, of course. You know that, Lita, better than anyone."

"So what happens next? With a business, there must be a lot to tie up."

"I'm not tying up anything."

"You're going to stay there?" I tried to keep the incredulity out of my voice.

"Why not? To be honest, my so-called scientific career has been running on empty for years. What I'd like to prove is never going to get backing. I'm not like you. I mean . . . " He gestured at the tiered shelves. "You can make anything you want become real."

6.

Rob wasn't the sort to put on an act. If he said he was happy ditching research and filling his father's role as a marine farmer on some remote island, that was because he was. I never quite did find the time to physically visit him in Harris—it was, after all, on the other side of the globe—and he, with the daily commitments of the family business, didn't get to Seoul. But I came to appreciate my glimpses of the island's strange beauty. That, and the regular arrival of chilled, vacuum-packed boxes of fresh scallops. But was this really enough for Rob Holm? Somehow, despite his evident pride in what he was doing, and the funny stories he told of the island's other inhabitants, and even the occasional mention of some woman he'd met at a ceilidh, I didn't think it was. After all, Creagach was his mother and father's vision, not his.

Although he remained coy about the details, I knew he still longed to bring his many worlds experiment to life. That, and that it would be complicated, controversial, and costly. I'd have been more than happy to offer financial help, but I knew he'd refuse. So what else could I do? My media company had grown. I had mentors, advisors, and consultants, both human and AI, and Rob would have been a genuinely useful addition to the team, but he had too many issues with the lack of rigor and logic in this world to put up with all the glitches, fudges, and contradictions of virtual ones. Then I had a better idea.

"You know why nothing ever changes here, don't you?" he asked me as our avatars sat together in the Eldon late one afternoon. "Not the smell from the toilets or the unfestive Christmas decorations or that dusty Pernod optic behind the bar. This isn't a feed from the real pub any longer. The old Eldon was demolished years ago. All we've been sitting in ever since is just a clever formation of what the place would be like if it still existed. Bar staff, students, us, and all."

"That's . . . " Although nothing changed, the whole place seemed to shimmer. "How things are these days. The real and the unreal get so blurry you can't tell which is which. But you know," I added, as if the thought had just occurred to me, "there's a project that's been going the rounds of the studios here in Seoul. It's a series about the wonders of science, one of those proper, realtime factual things, but we keep stumbling over finding the right presenter. Someone fresh, but with the background and the personality to carry the whole thing along."

"You don't mean me?"

"Why not? It'd only be part time. Might even help you promote what you're doing at Creagach."

"A scientific popularizer?"

"Yes. Like Carl Sagan, for example, or maybe Stephen Jay Gould."

I had him, and the series—which, of course, had been years in development purgatory—came about. I'd thought of it as little more than a way of getting Rob some decent money, but, from the first live-streamed episode, it was a success. After all, he was still charming and persuasive, and his salt-and-pepper beard gave him gravitas—and made him, if anything, even better looking. He used the Giant's Causeway to demonstrate the physics of fractures. He made this weird kind of pendulum to show why we could never predict the weather for more than a few days ahead. He swam with the whales off Tierra del Fuego. The only thing he didn't seem to want to explain was the odd way that photons behaved when you shot them down a double-slotted tube. That, and the inconsistencies between how galaxies revolved and Newton's and Einstein's laws.

In the matter of a very few years, Rob Holm was rich. And of course, and although he never actively courted it, he grew famous. He stood on podiums and looked fetchingly puzzled. He shook a dubious hand with gurning politicians. He even turned down offers to appear at music festivals, and had to take regular legal steps to protect the pirating of his virtual identity. He even finally visited me in Seoul and experienced the wonders of my library at first hand.

At last, Rob had out-achieved me. Then, just when I and most of the rest of the world had him pigeon-holed as that handsome, softly accented guy who did those popular science things, his avatar returned the contract for his upcoming series unsigned. I might have forgotten that getting rich was supposed to be the means to an end. But he, of course, hadn't.

"So," I said as we sat together for what turned out to be the last time in our shared illusion of the Eldon. "You succeed with this project. You get a positive result and prove the many worlds theory is true. What happens after that?"

"I publish, of course. The data'll be public, peer-reviewed, and—"

"Since when has being right ever been enough?"

"That's . . . " He brushed a speck of virtual beer foam from his grey beard, " . . . how science works."

"And no one ever had to sell themselves to gain attention? Even Galileo had to do that stunt with the cannonballs."

"As I explained in my last series, that story of the Tower of Pisa was an invention of his early biographers."

"Come on, Rob. You know what I mean."

He looked uncomfortable. But, of course, he already had the fame. All he had to do was stop all this Greta Garbo shit and milk it.

So, effectively I became PR agent for Rob's long-planned experiment. There was, after all, a lot for the educated layman, let alone the general public, or us so-called media professionals, to absorb. What was needed was a handle, a simple selling point. And, after a little research, I found one.

A man in a business suit had arrived at Tokyo airport in the summer of 1954. He was Caucasian but spoke reasonable Japanese, and everything about him seemed normal apart from his passport. It looked genuine but was from somewhere called Taured, which the officials couldn't find in any of their directories. The visitor was as baffled as they were. When a map was produced, he pointed to Andorra, a tiny but ancient republic between France and Spain, which he insisted was Taured. The humane and sensible course was to find him somewhere to sleep while further enquiries were made. Guards were posted outside the door of a secure hotel room high in a tower block, but the mysterious man had vanished without trace in the morning, and the Visitor from Taured was never seen again.

Rob was dubious, then grew uncharacteristically cross when he learned that the publicity meme had already been released. To him, and despite the fact that I thought he'd been reading this kind of thing for years, the story was just another urban legend and would further alienate the scientific establishment when he desperately needed their help. In effect, what he had to obtain was time and bandwidth from every available gravitational observatory, both here on Earth and up in orbit, during a crucial observational window, and time was already short.

It was as the final hours ticked down in a fervid air of stop-go technical problems, last minute doubts, and sudden demands for more money, that I finally took the sub-orbital from Seoul to Frankfurt, then the skytrain on to Glasgow, and some thrumming, windy thing of string and carbon fiber along the Scottish west coast, and across the shining Minch. The craft landed in Stornoway harbor in the Isle of Lewis—the northern part of the long landmass of which Harris forms the south—where I was rowed ashore, and eventually found a bubblebus to take me across purple moorland and past scattered white bungalows, then up amid ancient peaks.

Rob stood waiting on the far side of the road at the final stop, and we were both shivering as we hugged in the cold spring sunlight. But I was here, and so was he, and he'd done a great job at keeping back the rest of the world, and even I wouldn't have had it any other way. It seemed as if most of the niggles and issues had finally been sorted. Even if a few of his planned sources had pulled out, he'd still have all the data he needed. Come tomorrow, Rob Holm would either be a prophet or a pariah.

7.

He still slept in the same narrow bed he'd had as a child in the rusty-roofed cottage down by the shore at Creagach, while his parents' bedroom was now filled with expensive processing and monitoring equipment, along with a high-band, multiple-redundancy satellite feed. Downstairs, there was a parlor where Rob kept his small book collection in an alcove by the fire—I was surprised to see that it was almost entirely poetry; a scatter of Larkin, Eliot, Frost, Dickinson, Pope, Yeats, and Donne, beside a few lingering Asimovs, Le Guins, and Clarkes—with a low tartan divan where he sat to read these works. Which, I supposed, might also serve as a second bed, although he hadn't yet made it up.

He took me out on his launch. Showed me his scallop beds and the glorious views of this ragged land with its impossibly wide and empty beaches. And there, just around the headland, was the stretch of bay where both Rob's parents had been found, and I could almost hear the Blue Men of the Minch calling to us over the sigh of the sea. There were standing stones on the horizon, and an old whaling station at the head of a loch, and a hill topped by a medieval church filled with the bodies of the chieftains who had given these islands such a savage reputation though their bloody feuds. And meanwhile, the vast cosmic shudder of the collision of two black holes was traveling toward us at lightspeed.

There were scallops, of course, for dinner. Mixed in with some fried dab and chopped mushroom, bacon and a few leaves of wild garlic, all washed down with malt whisky, and with whey-buttered soda bread on the side, which was the Highland way. Then, up in the humming shrine of his parents' old bedroom, Rob checked on the status of his precious sources again.

The black hole binaries had been spiraling toward each other for tens of thousands of years, and observed here on Earth for decades. In many ways, and despite their supposed mystery, black holes were apparently simple objects—nothing but sheer mass—and even though their collision was so far off it had actually happened when we humans were still learning how to use tools, it was possible to predict within hours, if not minutes, when the effects of this event would finally reach Earth.

There were gravitational observatories, vast-array laser interferometers, in deep space, and underground in terrestrial sites, all waiting to record this moment, and Rob was tapping into them. All everyone else expected to see—in fact, all the various institutes and faculties had tuned their devices to look for—was this . . . Leaning over me, Rob called up a display to show a sharp spike, a huge peak in the data, as the black holes swallowed each other and the shock of their collision flooded out in the asymmetrical pulse of a gravitational wave.

"But this isn't what I want, Lita. Incredibly faint though that signal is—a mere ripple deep in the fabric of the cosmos—I'm looking to combine and filter all those results, and find something even fainter.

"This . . . " He dragged up another screen, "is what I expect to see." There was the same central peak, but this time it was surrounded by a fan of smaller, ever-decreasing, ripples eerily reminiscent of the display Rob had once shown me of the ghost-flicker of those photons all those years ago in Leeds. "These are echoes of the black hole collision in other universes."

I reached out to touch the floating screen. Felt the incredible presence of the dark matter of other worlds.

"And all of this will happen tonight?"

He smiled.

8.

There was nothing else left to be done—the observatories Rob was tapping into were all remote, independent, autonomous devices—so we took out chairs into the dark, and drank some more whisky, and collected driftwood, and lit a fire on the shore.

We talked about books. Nothing new, but some shared favorites. Poe and Pasternak and Fitzgerald. And Rob confessed that he hadn't got on anything like as well as he'd pretended with his first forays into literature. How he'd found the antique language and odd punctuation got in the way. It was even a while before he understood the obvious need for a physical bookmark. He'd have given up with the whole concept if it hadn't been for my shining, evident faith.

"You know, it was *Gulliver's Travels* that finally really turned it around for me. Swift was so clever and rude and funny and angry, yet he could also tell a great story. That bit about those Laputan astronomers studying the stars from down in their cave, and trying to harvest sunbeams from marrows. Well, that's us right here, isn't it?"

The fire settled. We poured ourselves some more whisky. And Rob recited a poem by Li Po about drinking with the Moon's shadow, and then we remembered those days back in Leeds when we'd gone out onto the moors, and drank and ingested far more than was good for us, and danced like savages and, yes, there had even been that time he and I had gazed up at the stars.

We stood up now, and Rob led me away from the settling fire. The stars were so bright here, and the night sky was so black, that it felt like falling merely to look up. Over there in the west, Lita, is the Taurus Constellation. It's where the Crab Nebula lies, the remains of a supernova the Chinese recorded back in 1054, and it's in part of the Milky Way known as the Perseus Arm, which is where our dark binaries would soon end their fatal dance. I was leaning into him as he held his arms around me, and perhaps both of us were breathing a little faster than was entirely due to the wonders of the cosmos.

"What time is it now, Rob?"

"It's . . . " He checked his watch. "Just after midnight."

"So there's still time."

"Time for what?"

We kissed, then crossed the shore and climbed the stairs to Rob's single bed. It was sweet, and somewhat drunken, and quickly over. The Earth, the Universe, didn't exactly move. But it felt far more like making love than merely having sex, and I curled up against Rob afterward, and breathed his cinnamon scent, and fell into a well of star-seeing contentment.

"Rob?"

The sky beyond the window was showing the first traces of dawn as I got up, telling myself that he'd be next door in his parents' old room, or walking the shore as he and his avatar strove to deal with a torrent of interview requests. But I already sensed that something was wrong.

It wasn't hard for me to pull up the right screen amid the humming machines in his parents' room, proficient at mek as I now was. The event, the collision, had definitely occurred. The spike of its gravitational wave had been recorded by every observatory. But the next screen, the one where Rob had combined, filtered, and refined all the data, displayed no ripples, echoes, from other worlds.

I ran outside shouting Rob's name. I checked the house feeds. I paced back and forth. I got my avatar to contact the authorities. I did all the things you do when someone you love suddenly goes missing, but a large part of me already knew it was far too late.

Helicopters chattered. Drones circled. Locals gathered. Fishermen arrived in trawlers and skiffs. Then came the bother of newsfeeds, all the publicity I could ever have wished for. But not like this.

I ended up sitting on the rocks of that bay around the headland from Creagach as the day progressed, waiting for the currents to bear Rob's body to this place, where he could join his parents.

I'm still waiting.

• • •

9.

Few people actually remember Rob Holm these days, and if they do, it's as that good-looking guy who used to present those slightly weird nature—or was it science?—feeds, and didn't he die in some odd, sad kind of way? But I still remember him, and I still miss him, and I still often wonder what really happened on that night when he left the bed we briefly shared. The explanation given by the authorities, that he'd seen his theory dashed and then walked out into the freezing waters of the Minch, still isn't something I can bring myself to accept. So maybe he really was like the Visitor from Taured and simply vanished from a universe that couldn't support what he believed.

I read few novels or short stories now. The plots, the pages, seem over-involved. Murals rather than elegant miniatures. Rough-hewn rocks instead of jewels. But the funny thing is that, as my interest in them has dwindled, books have become popular again. There are new publishers, even new writers, and you'll find pop-up bookstores in every city. Thousands now flock to my library in Seoul every year, and I upset the conservators by allowing them to take my precious volumes down from their shelves. After all, isn't that exactly what books are for? But I rarely go there myself. In fact, I hardly ever leave the Isle of Harris, or even Creagach, which Rob, with typical consideration and foresight, left me in his will. I do my best to keep the scallop farm going, pottering about in the launch and trying to keep the crabs and the starfish at bay, although the business barely turns a profit, and probably never did.

What I do keep returning to is Rob's small collection of poetry. I have lingered with Eliot's Prufrock amid the chains of the sea, wondered with Hardy what might have happened if he and that woman had sheltered from the rain a minute more, and watched as Sylvia Plath's children burst those final balloons. I just wish that Rob was here to share these precious words and moments with me. But all that's left is you and I, dear, faithful reader, and the Blue Men of the Minch calling to the waves.

REDKING

CRAIG DeLAUNCEY

Tain held a pistol toward me. The black gel of the handle pulsed, waiting to be gripped.

"Better take this," she said.

I shook my head. "I never use them."

We sat in an unmarked police cruiser, the steering wheel packed away in the dashboard. Tain's face was a pale shimmer in the cool blue light of the car's entertainment system. "Your file says you are weapons trained."

"Yeah," I said, "I got one of those cannons at home, locked in my kitchen drawer."

Tain turned slightly toward me. She still held the gun out, her fingers wrapped around the barrel. "You gonna get me killed, code monkey?"

I considered telling her it was quaint to think that protection could be secured with a gun. But instead I told her, "I start waving that around, I'm more likely to shoot you than the perp. Just get me to the machines. That's how I'm going to help you."

She thought for a moment, then nodded. "Well, at least you're a man who knows his limitations." She turned the pistol around, held it a second so that the gun locked to her hand print, and then she tucked it under her belt at the small of her back.

She dimmed the dash lights. I was running a naked brain—standard procedure for a raid—and so the building, the sidewalk, and the road reduced down to the hard objects that our paltry senses could latch onto: a world without explanations, ominously obscure.

We both leaned forward and looked up at the building before us, eighteen stories of concrete. The once-bright walls had faded to the color of mold. A half-hearted rain began, streaking the grime on its narrow windows.

The clock on the dash read 2:30 a.m. No one in sight. Most of the lights in the building were out now.

"You know the drill?" Tain asked me.

"I know this kid we're arresting probably wrote RedKing," I told her. "That's all I need to know."

Unsatisfied with this answer, she repeated the rap. "Twenty-seven-year-old male. Got his name legally changed to his code handle: Legion. Five prior convictions for 909." Design, manufacture, and distribution of cognition-aversive and intentionally addictive software. "No record of violence. But he's still a killer, so consider him dangerous. We go in fast, my people take him down, and you save what you can from his machines."

"I know my job."

"Right." She pushed open her door. I followed her into the rain, heaving my backpack on. I tightened its straps and then snapped them across my chest.

A Korean food truck, covered with twisting dim snakes of active graffiti, idled across the street. Its back door swung open, and cops in black, holding rifles, poured out.

We ran as a group for the entrance to the tower.

A few kids stood in the lobby, smoking, and they turned pale and ran for the stairs when we parted the front doors. Their untied sneakers slapped at the concrete floor. We ignored them, but two cops took position in the lobby to ensure no one left. Tain had a set of elevator keys and she took command of both lifts. We squeezed into the elevator on the left, shoulder to shoulder with four other cops in full gear, their rifles aimed at the ceiling. The smell of leather and gun oil overwhelmed everything else while the LED counter flicked off sixteen flights.

A chime announced our arrival. We made a short run down a dim hall and stopped before a door with an ancient patina of scratched and flaking green paint. The cops hit it with a ram and we filed in quick and smooth. I broke to the left, following half the cops through a dingy common room with a TV left on mute, the flickering images casting a meager glow over an open pizza box on an empty couch.

A door by the TV led to a dark room. Two cops rousted the suspect out of bed and zip tied him in seconds. Legion was a pale, thin kid with trembling, sticklike arms. He gazed around in shock. A woman leapt out of the bed and stood in the corner, shouting, clutching the sheets over her naked body. Somewhere a baby started screaming.

Tain's cops were good: They moved quietly, not all hyped on adrenaline, and they stayed out of my way as I ran through the apartment, checking each room for machines. But the only computers were in the bedroom: a stack of gleaming liquid-cooled Unix engines atop a cheap, particle board desk. Not heavy iron, but good machines: the kind rich kids bought if they played deep in the game economies.

Legion began to yell, calling for the woman to bring him clothes while two cops dragged him out. The woman screamed also, demanded a lawyer, demanded her baby. I did my best to tune out all that noise, pulled a cable from the side of my backpack, and jacked my field computer straight into the top deck. Data streamed through my eyeplants—the only augmentation I was allowed to run here—and I tapped at a virtual keyboard. In a few seconds I dug under the main shell and started a series of static disk copies. While in there, I ran a top check to show the processes that threaded across the machines: nothing but low level maintenance. Tain's crew had got Legion before the kid could trigger a wipe.

I turned, found Tain's eye, and nodded.

"Okay," she shouted. "Wrap it up."

It started with the gamers. It wasn't enough to stare at screens any longer. They wanted to be there, in the scene. They wanted to smell and hear the alien planet where they battled evil robots, to feel the steely resolve of their avatar and enjoy her victories and mourn her losses. They wanted it all.

That meant moving hardware into the skull, bypassing the slow crawl of the senses. Once we'd wired our occipital lobes, you could predict the natural progression of commerce: not just visuals, but smell, and sound, and feel, and taste had to come next. So the wires spread through our neocortexes, like the roots of some cognitive weed. Autonomic functions came after, the wires reaching down into the subcortical regions of pleasure and pain, fear and joy. We gave up all the secrets of our brains, and sank the wires ever deeper.

Then people started to wonder, what other kinds of software could you run on this interface?

Pornography, sure. The first and biggest business: orgies raging through the skulls of overweight teenage boys lying alone in their unmade beds.

But after that, people began to demand more extreme experiences. A black market formed. For the buyer, the problem is one of imagination: What would you want to feel and believe, if you could feel and believe anything? For the coders, the problem is one of demand: How can you make the consumer come back again? The solution was as old as software: Write code that erases itself after a use or two, but leaves you desperate to spend money on another copy.

That code was dangerous, but it wasn't the worst. The worst was written by the coders who did not want money. They were users themselves, or zealots, and their code might just stick around. It might not want to go.

RedKing was a program like that. RedKing was as permanent as polio. And RedKing made people kill.

• • •

When we got outside, a dozen press drones hovered over the street.

"Damn," Tain said. "How do they find us so fast?"

"Hey, code monkey!" a voice called. We turned and saw a short, thin woman, with very short dark hair. Drones buzzed above her, filming her every move as she hurried toward us.

"Ellison," I said, "what brings you to this side of town?"

She had a big mouth that probably could produce a beautiful smile, but she never smiled. Instead, her voice was sharp and quick. "You got a statement? A statement for *Dark Fiber*? This have anything to do with RedKing?"

"No statement," Tain said.

"Come on, code monkey," Ellison said, ignoring Tain. "You gotta give me something."

"I'll catch you later," I said.

"He will not catch you later," Tain said. She took my elbow. "No press," she hissed at me. She slapped a small news drone that flew too close. It smacked into the pavement and shuddered, struggling to lift off again. We stepped over it.

"Ellison has helped me out a few times," I told Tain as we walked away. "And sometimes I help her out."

"While you're working for me, you only help me out. And the only person that helps you out is me."

We got in the car.

At the station, they gave me a desk pressed into a windowless corner by the fire exit, under a noisy vent blowing cold air. The aluminum desk's surface was scarred as if the prior owner stabbed it whenever police business slowed. I was filling in for their usual code monkey, and I got the impression they didn't aspire to see me again after this job. I didn't care. The desk had room for my machine and Legion's stack of machines, the cold air was good for the processors, and I wouldn't have time to look out a window anyway.

Within an hour I had scanned Legion's machines twice over, mapped out every bit and byte, dug through all the personal hopes and dreams of the scrawny guy now shivering in the interrogation room.

I sighed and went looking for Tain. I wandered the halls until I found the observation room with a two-way mirror looking in on the suspect. Tain stood over him.

"She's been in there a while," one of the cops standing before the window told me between sips of coffee.

"I want my lawyer," the kid said. His voice sounded hollow and distant through the speaker. He sat in a metal chair, and I wondered if he knew it measured his autonomic functions while he talked. Some people refused to sit when they got in an interrogation room.

"You made your call. Your lawyer's on her way." Tain bent forward. Her strong arms strained at the narrow sleeves of her coat as she laid a tablet on the table. Even from a distance, we could see the tablet displayed the picture the news had been running all week: a teenage kid with brown disheveled hair, smiling with perfect teeth. He looked innocent, and maybe rich.

Legion glanced down. "I'm not saying anything till I get my lawyer."

Tain pointed at the picture. "Phil Jackson."

"I had nothing to do with that."

"With what?" Tain asked, with exaggerated innocence.

"I watch the news."

"I didn't take you for someone who watches the news, Legion." Tain tapped the tablet decisively. "Seventeen. Doing fine in school. Lonely, but what high school kid doesn't think he's lonely, right? So little Phil Jackson loads a copy of RedKing into his head. Spends a week delirious, happy maybe, thinking he's king of the world—who knows what it makes him think? Then he cuts his mother's throat, hits his father with the claw of a hammer, and jumps off the roof."

Legion looked up at Tain and smirked. Tain became as taut as a spring. She wanted to hit him. And Legion wanted her to hit him. It would provide great fodder for his lawyer.

But she held her fists. Legion waited, then said softly, as if he could barely manage to stay awake, "I told you, I watch the news."

"What they didn't tell you on the news, Legion, is that we got the code out of that kid's implants, and our code monkeys decompiled it, and you know what they found? Big chunks of stuff written by you. Unmistakable provenience. Big heaps of Legion code." Tain let her voice grow soft and reasonable. "We've got fifty-four confirmed casualties for this virus. It's only going to get worse. And the worse it gets—the more people that commit crimes or hurt themselves—the worse it's going to be for you, Legion."

He clamped his jaw and mumbled, "My lawyer."

"I'll go get her for you. You sit here and look at the kid that your code killed."

Tain kicked the door. The cop outside opened it. In a second she was around the corner and when she saw me she walked up close.

"Tell me what you got, code monkey."

"Nothing," I told her.

Her heavy black brows drew together over her pale, inset eyes. I held up my hands defensively.

"Hey, no one wants to find the raw code for RedKing more than I do. But I've scanned every bit of his machines, and I got next to nothing."

• • •

Tain dragged me to her office, her grip tight on my elbow, and closed the door.

"You saying your division made a mistake when they linked this guy to the code?"

I sat down on a hard metal chair by the door. Tain followed my example and flopped back into the chair behind her desk. It squeaked and rolled back.

"No. There's code on Legion's machines that is unique and that matches identically big chunks of the RedKing program. But there isn't a lot there. And it's . . . general."

"What do you mean? What kind of code?"

I hesitated. "A toolkit. For running genetic algorithms."

"What's that doing in there?"

I frowned. "I'm not sure yet. I have a hunch, and it's not good news. I'd rather follow up a little, study the code, before I say more."

"Don't take too long. So why isn't this toolkit enough to convict?"

"Hackers tend to give toolkits away, on some user board or other. You can bet he'll claim he did, first time we ask about the details."

Tain frowned in disgust. "You see the autonomics on that kid while I was interrogating him? He flatlined everything. Skin response. Heart rate. Temperature and breathing. All unchanging. He fears nothing, he cares about nothing."

"Oh," I said, "he cares about one thing. His credibility. That's what's driving him."

"Okay, fair enough. You code types have your whole thing with cred. But what I'm trying to say is, the guy is a classic psychopath."

I nodded. "He's a bad guy. But can we prove he's our bad guy?"

She stared at the image on her active wall: mountains at the edge of a long green prairie. It was surprisingly serene for this nervously energetic woman.

"I got nothing," she mused. "He's not gonna talk; psychopaths don't break under threat. My code monkey can't link him to RedKing. And we don't know what RedKing does or why it made a kid kill his own mother. We've identified dozens of infected people, and they all acted differently."

I let that hang a long time before I stated the obvious. "Only one thing to try now. I load it up and see what I can tell from running the copy we got in quarantine."

Tain leaned her head forward and looked at me through her dark eyebrows. "You know why we called you in? Why you're here? Our usual code monkey is on extended leave. She fried her head trying just that."

"Occupational hazard," I said.

"Don't tough guy me. My father was a cop, and my grandfather. When they busted a heroin ring, they didn't go home and shoot smack to try to understand addiction from the inside."

"It's not the same," I said.

"Looks the same to me."

"All right, maybe it is. But what if, what if there was a new drug every week, all the time, and you couldn't know what it would do to people—what it would make people do—if you didn't just try it. Then I bet your grandfather, or your father, would have shot up. Because they wanted to fight it, right? And they needed to know how to fight."

"Bullshit," she said. But she didn't say anything more. She didn't say no.

They put me in a conference room, bare white walls, a table that tipped back and forth if you leaned on it. Tain stared at me, her jaw working, while the tech brought me a memory stick. I slotted it into my field deck immediately, not wanting to give Tain time to change her mind. I'd set up a buffer and then a process echo, so my deck could record everything that was happening.

I plugged straight into my skulljack and in a few seconds I copied the code over into my implants.

"I got an interface," I said. "Pretty simple."

A single sentence appeared in my visual field. *Do you want to be King?* it asked. I looked at the word *yes* and willed it to click, giving it permission to run on my brain OS.

A rush of colors washed over me. I felt cold, exhilarated, as if I fell down a bright well of light. I think I shouted in something like joy.

Then it was over. There stood Tain, her eyebrows up in an expression of alarm mixed with disapproval.

"How long?" I asked.

"Long? You just plugged in."

I frowned.

"Well?" Tain asked.

"It's . . . " I thought about it. "After the initial rush it's nothing. Nothing yet, anyways. I don't know."

I looked around, meeting Tain's eyes, then the eyes of the cop waiting bored by the door. I did have a slight sense that maybe I felt a little . . . tenuous. But it was nothing definite. It's hard when you are waiting to hallucinate. You tend to start to work yourself into a psychedelic state if you try too hard to expect one.

"Let me clear the buffer and start it up again."

I took a deep breath and did it. We waited a while. "Nothing," I said.

Tain sighed. "Bad batch of code? Maybe they sent you the neutralized compile."

I shrugged.

"All right," she said. "Shut it down. Look over your sample again, see if something is wrong with it. I'll call Code Isolation and see if they sent you the wrong sample."

We pulled the plugs. Someone knocked at the door. "Stay here," Tain said. She went out into the hall and the other cop followed her.

I lifted my deck off the table. That's when I realized my deck's wireless had been left on.

I slipped out of the conference room and walked quickly back to my desk, trying to stay calm. Or at least trying to appear calm. When I set my deck down I looked back. The door to my office was open, showing the long hall that stretched all the way to the center of the building, a corridor that diminished into infinity. And, along the sides of the hall, it seemed every cop in the building stood, hand on holster, looking at me. And down the center of the hall came Tain.

I turned and hit the crash bar to the emergency exit next to my desk. As I passed through, I cracked the red fire alarm crystal by the door. An alarm began to shriek.

"Stop!" Tain shouted. I didn't look back to see if she aimed a gun at me. I threw the door shut and ran down the steps.

I was on the street before they could get word out to stop me. The fire alarm was painfully loud, causing a lot of confusion. A few cops milled by the station's front steps, wondering if the alarm was a drill or mistake. I walked past them and to the block's corner. When I turned out of sight, I ran.

By the time I reached the subway steps my chest hurt and a sharp stitch slowed me to a hobble. I'm a code monkey, not a runner. But I made it down inside, hair lifted by the stink of hot air that a coming train pushed out of the dark. I turned all my implants on, wanting to get the full input now. I mustered a last burst of energy and slipped down the next set of steps and onto the train just as its doors shuddered closed.

Only a handful of people sat in the car. No one met my gaze. Still. Someone here could be undercover. Hard to know. I stared around, wondering what I should do next. If the whole department was infected, what would be the right course of action? Report to Code Isolation? That would be procedure. Only, I thought, I should get myself secure first. I needed a place to hide. I needed my gun.

It was easy to outsmart them. It would be foolish for me to go home, but then they'd know it was foolish for me to go home, and so they wouldn't look for me at home.

So I went home. I took the back door, the one that opened onto the parking lot for the few of us with cars. A short elevator ride, a few steps down an empty hall, and I pushed my way into my apartment.

In the kitchen, under the pale LEDs of my undercounter light, I keyed open my safety drawer. My gun sat with my passport and some spare cash. I picked it up and held it. The grip vibrated once to tell me it recognized me. I stuck it into my coat pocket.

Time to go. No sense in pushing my luck. I was smarter than all of them, sure, but even idiots could fall into fortune. So: I reconsidered. Should I report to Code Isolation? As I thought about it, the idea paled. Code Isolation had sent me the program I'd run on my deck. They had to have known my deck would transmit it. They were likely infected already.

I'd have to solve this on my own. And I could. It was just a matter of recognizing that anyone, everyone could be my enemy—and then outsmarting them all. I felt a thrill of excitement, a soaring determination. Because I realized I could do it. I could trick them all.

First step would be to lose myself in a crowd.

The Randomist was a noisy bar half a block from my apartment building. I'd walked by it hundreds of times but had never gone in. The boisterous cheerfulness of the crowd, the painful sense that one had to be very hip to fit in, had alienated me immediately the few times I'd considered stopping for a quick drink. But now I went directly in under the electric blue archway.

I got a beer at the bar, something local and artisanal with a silly name. The bartender slid it to me but smiled insincerely. "Hey, buddy, how about turning it down a little?"

"What the hell you talking about?" I asked.

"You've got your implants turned all the way out. It's hard to walk past you, you're broadcasting so much. And what is it you're blasting? Some kind of program? That's not cool."

"Drop dead," I told him. I took my drink and turned away, all the hairs on my neck raised. He might work for the cops, I realized. An informant for the infected precinct. I might have to shoot him.

But the crowd swallowed me instantly, and I relaxed. Forget the bartender. He couldn't see me or get me in this dense mass of people.

Bumping shoulder to shoulder as I pushed through, I felt a great worry lift. The cops would never find me in here. And I loved this crowd, with their implants humming all around me invitingly.

There was a beautiful girl in the back, standing alone, waiting for someone. I decided she was waiting for me.

"You're a loud one," she said, as I walked up.

"I like to speak my mind," I said.

"More like shout it."

But she didn't leave. I leaned in close.

"What's your name?" I asked.

"Sparrow. What's that you're broadcasting, anyway? You an ad? One of those walking ads? Come on, turn down your broadcast. I'm serious. It's too much."

I shook my head. "Let me tell you what I do, Sparrow. I'm a cop. But a special kind of cop. I protect people from the only real threat, the threat of their computers and their implants going bad. I'm fantastic at it. I'm the smartest person in the world."

"Yeah? You don't look like a cop."

"I could show you my gun." I put my hand in my pocket and felt the handle thrum against my palm.

She frowned, not sure if I had intended some dirty joke. She pointed over my shoulder. "Now she, she looks like a cop."

I turned. Tain stood there, a few steps away, under a red light. She was all shadows and angles in the dim focused glare. Her hand was at her hip.

I scanned the room. People were starting to freeze in place and fall quiet as seven uniforms filed in. I counted them slowly. Then an eighth. Then a ninth, slipping behind the bar.

There were seventeen rounds in my gun. I could shoot all these cops and still have seven rounds left. I pulled my gun from my jacket pocket.

Tain's hand didn't move, but Sparrow screamed as a blur shot forward and two darts stuck into my chest. My body went rigid as a current slammed my nerves into overdrive.

I heard my gun clatter on the hard floor. I blacked out.

When I came to, someone was sitting on me.

No, that wasn't it. My hands. My hands were strapped down. And something gripped my head. A hat or helmet. I opened my eyes.

A white room. A hospital room. The sharp stink of disinfectant wafted over me. Every muscle in my body ached. Tain stood nearby, talking to a doc in a white coat. Behind her a big window was black with night, mirroring the white room back at us. A code monkey stood behind Tain, field deck strapped on her back. Stepin, a field agent specializing in brain system wipes. She was short and broad shouldered, with a calm but distracted look that made it seem she was always thinking hard about something distant and slightly sad.

"They got you, too," I said.

Stepin looked over at me.

"Who got me?" she asked.

I looked at Tain. "Her. The others in the precinct. They're contaminated with RedKing. You can't trust them. If you're not infected, step away from her, Stepin. Get me out of this. I'm the only person who can stop this. I can fix everything."

Tain took a step forward. "How do you think we got contaminated? You're the one who loaded up the RedKing."

"My computer's transmitter was on," I said, looking at Stepin because it was useless to appeal to Tain. Tain would be gone now, inhuman. "I thought I was loading the virus but instead I was transmitting it."

"Put him under," Stepin said. "I've got to do a complete OS replacement. It'll take me a few hours."

The doctor stepped forward and adjusted my IV. A huge weight closed down on my eyes. As the darkness fell, I heard Stepin say to me softly, "Field computers don't have transmitters. You know that."

When I woke, I was alone in the room. The straps lay open, my wrists and legs freed. Sunlight streamed through the window at a nearly vertical angle. I'd been here a long while, asleep on tranqs. I had a bad headache but otherwise felt normal. I opened my brain menus, and found they worked fine, although the arrangement was all factory normal. I logged into my work desktop and began to review my notes.

Some program had detected my waking, because in a few minutes a nurse brought me food, and then an hour after that Tain arrived, wearing new clothes.

We looked at each other. I chewed air, trying to get started on an apology. Tain let me struggle a while, before she nodded once. She pulled up a chair.

"All right, code monkey, just tell me what happened. We knew something was wrong when you left the test room."

"RedKing is subtle," I told her, relieved to be talking about code. "First, it convinces you that nothing has changed. And that remains throughout: I literally could not even imagine that I was running the virus in my head. I don't know how it inhibits such a basic belief, but it does it very well. That's a breakthrough of some kind. We'll have to study it very carefully and—"

"Don't tell me your research plans," Tain interrupted. "Tell me what it does."

"Right. It made me paranoid of anyone who might be a threat to the virus. I think my brain tried to make sense of my irrational fear of you and the others, and so I concluded you had the virus. I probably invented the idea that my computer had transmitted it in order to explain my fear to myself. Also, I began to feel . . . smart. Super intelligent. I became convinced that I could solve any problem. That I was smarter than anyone."

"You were reaching for your pistol when I tazed you."

I nodded. "I meant to shoot you all. It was . . . bizarre. I didn't see you as people. I saw you as puzzles. Puzzles to be solved by my brilliant mind."

Tain leaned back. Her jaw worked a while as she thought it through. Finally, she said, "So, what we have is code that convinces you that you are a genius, and makes you paranoid, and makes you see other human beings as worthless."

I sighed. "It's worse than that."

"How?"

"Two things. First, I think I tried to spread it last night. To transmit it."

"It's too much code to transmit implant to implant."

"I'm not sure. I think there might be a workaround, to make people call it up off of some servers. You have to test everyone in that bar."

She stood, shoving her chair back. "Damn. We'll have to act fast."

"Get me out of here and I can help. We can get a court order to trace the bar charges and track everyone down."

"Damn," Tain repeated. She got a faraway look as she started transmitting orders from her implants. "What a mess. We're back where we started, and things are even worse."

"Maybe not," I said. "If I'm right, and the program loads from another server, then that's a weakness. If we can find someone infected, and can find the address that they downloaded RedKing from, we can find Legion's hidden servers."

"All right. That's something. So what's your second bit of bad news?"

"I've been reviewing the decompile, and I've confirmed my hunch. But before I explain that, I want to see Legion. We need to set up a meeting with him."

"Why?"

Before I could answer, the door to the room banged open. Ellison strode in. "Hey, code monkey, you sick or something?" She looked at Tain, made it clear that she was not impressed by the lieutenant, and looked back at me. "Or you get shot? That'd be newsworthy, if you got shot."

"You will get out of here right now," Tain said.

"Hey, is that any way to treat a guest? I was invited."

Tain glared at me. I held up a hand to urge her to wait a minute.

To Ellison I said, "I got something for that crappy blog of yours."

"Blog. Yeah, really funny, code monkey. I never heard that one before. But *Dark Fiber* gets more hits in an hour than there are cops in America. So don't misunderstand who has the clout in this relationship."

"I got something about RedKing."

Ellison immediately looked cagey. She gave Tain a sidelong glance. "Okay. I'm interested."

"Of course you are. Only: We don't have the whole story yet. But I can tell some of it. An important part of our investigation, let's say."

"You're asking me to help you get a piece of the story out. All right: Can you promise that I'll be first to get the whole story when you put it together?"

"Tain," I said, "set up that meeting we were talking about. Because you and I will be ready in a few hours."

There were four of us now in the small interrogation room. I sat across from Legion, in one of the metal chairs. Both Tain and Legion's lawyer stood. Everyone eyed me suspiciously.

"My client has already made a statement," Legion's lawyer said.

"To me," Tain said. "But our code security agent would like to ask a few questions."

"My client does not have to answer any more questions."

"No. But he can listen to them, can't he?"

Silence. Legion looked around the room, feigning boredom. Finally his eyes settled on me. I met his gaze and held it.

"RedKing is brilliant code," I said. "A small packet can be transmitted head to head and make a network call for the rest of the code."

"That's been done before," Legion said.

The lawyer stepped closer. "Mr. Legion, I strongly advise you to say nothing."

I nodded. "But the way it tricks implants into seeing RedKing as an operating system upgrade—that's very good. I didn't know such a thing could be done. But that's not the special thing." I glanced at Tain to let her know that this was my second bit of bad news. "The special thing is that it mutates. That code we found on your machines? A genetic algorithm toolkit. You wrote RedKing to mutate. As it spreads itself, it changes a little bit each time it's copied. That's why its operational profile is so variable. Eventually, there'll be a version that probably won't kill people—after all, dead users can't transmit the code—but it will just spread and spread. If your program works, it'll be the most influential, the most important virus ever written. It's historic."

Legion smiled. "Why tell me about this?"

"You read *Dark Fiber*?"

"I read lots of things."

I set a tablet on the table and turned it around. The cover of *Dark Fiber* blared a headline in big letters: REDKING CULPRITS FOUND?: POLICE SUSPECT CRIMEAN HACKER GROUP VEE.

Legion flinched. For the first time, his mocking smile faded as he read a few lines of the news story.

I leaned forward. "Here's what's before you." I held up a finger. "Option one. Admit you wrote RedKing. You can plead that you never knew it would be dangerous. The fact that you confessed will count in your favor. You'll get a few years, and you'll keep some net privileges. But—here's the important point—you'll be immortalized as the creator of the greatest brain hack ever."

I held up a second finger. "Or, option two. Deny you wrote RedKing. Maybe we can't convict you, maybe we can—let's call it fifty-fifty odds. But if you walk free or you go to prison, either way, you lose your chance for the world's biggest cred upgrade. You'll have given up immortality for a fifty percent chance of escaping a few years Upstate."

"I think my client has heard enough," the lawyer said. She pulled at Legion's sleeve, but the kid did not move. Tain held her breath.

"Vee can't hack," Legion said.

"You and I know they're just some teenage thugs whose only skill is to steal credit info off old ladies. But this story has been picked up by a dozen other news companies. Reporters can't tell a real hacker from a kid wearing a mask. And Vee was delighted to claim credit. They've already released a confession video."

"Only I could have written RedKing."

I nodded.

"Mr. Legion," the lawyer growled, "I have to advise you that—"

"Only me," Legion said.

Tain exhaled.

"You get everyone from the bar?" I asked Tain. We sat in her office, looking at her wall screen image of mountains.

She nodded. "Only one has proven infected, a young woman. Stepin is working on tracing back the code."

"I'm sorry I caused so much trouble."

"Getting Legion to talk has made up for some of it. How did you know he would crack?"

"It's a coder thing. Once I'd experienced RedKing, I knew it was a once-in-a-lifetime hack. No one like Legion would be able to stand someone else taking credit for it."

"And how is your friend Ellison going to take it when she discovers your story about Vee was bogus?"

"Ellison will be fine as long as she gets to break the story that Legion confessed. She'll be better than fine: We gave her two good stories, and one of them was even true."

Tain cracked a smile that broke into a laugh. But it died quickly.

"What will it be like, if thousands of people get this virus? Maybe thousands already have it. It's the end of goddamn civilization."

"I don't know," I said. "It's just this week's threat. With any luck we can contain RedKing."

"And then the next brainvirus will come along."

I nodded. "It's a race."

Tain squinted. "You got kids, code monkey?"

"No."

"I got a kid. Four years old. A second on the way."

"Congratulations."

"Yeah. But I swear, you know what, as soon as I put in my time, earn my pension, I'm going to get the wife and move out to Montana." She gestured at the wall image. "And there, I'll never get the implants in my kids. I'll make sure they live in the real world."

"Sounds like a plan," I said. "Me, I'm not much use at anything but coding."

She grunted. "You wanna stick around awhile? Our old code monkey, she's moving to a desk job at Code Isolation."

"All right."

She reached into a drawer and pulled out a big pistol. It fell on her desk with a heavy thud.

"Only, put your damn gun back in your kitchen drawer and lock it up before you hurt somebody."

A FINE BALANCE

CHARLOTTE ASHLEY

My mistress, Shoanna Yildirim, was the greatest shot in the city.

Each morning, according to her wishes, I cleaned and loaded her revolving pistol. I oiled the clip on her holster and checked the stitches in the leatherwork. I strung a fresh sash of weighted bullets and laid it by the vanity over her scarves.

"Your pistol, Mistress," I would say to her as she rose from the mirror, her wide, brown lips and dark, sly eyes painted to perfection.

"Thank you, Emin," she always replied. "But I will not need it today."

Each morning, she left the gun where it lay. Mistress Yildirim was the greatest shot in the city, but she hunted Kara Ramadami with a blade. That was just one of the many rules of sahidi.

That summer, Kara Ramadami hunted Mistress Yildirim with a pair of shashka, also in accordance with the rules of sahidi.

It was only recently that she had taken up the second weapon, causing the bookmakers to shake their heads and adjust their odds. How could the Dushiq mistress fight and climb with both hands occupied? But Ramadami was goat-like in her movements and did not need hands to scale walls or leap rooftops. She, like my mistress, appeared unbound by the laws of nature that hampered other duelists. Only her Kavalye—her nemesis, my mistress—could challenge her, just as no one could challenge my mistress but Ramadami. They were the most perfectly paired Kavalye the city had ever known.

In their last duel, a clash the tanners of Ceset Alley were already calling the Three-Thrust Fleece, my mistress beat Ramadami when she broke her thumb against the wooden frame of a beamhouse with her first strike. Even thus injured, Ramadami evaded Yildirim's next advance, delivered backhanded in a whirlwind of ribbon, scarves, and braids. She mounted a clothesline, cartwheeled past my mistress, and took cover behind a red hind-skin curing in the sun. But Yildirim merely spun wide, slicing through the leather like canvas.

Her third thrust split Ramadami's purse and spilt her favor, which my mistress claimed with the broad edge of her sword before it even hit the ground.

We did not see Ramadami for a long time after that, not until I spotted her during the ten-mile run Mistress Yildirim had assigned me for my rigors. I spied her unmistakable white-gold hair as I dodged traffic along the busy Ridge, towering over the common people who could match her neither in height nor radiance. She must have seen me before I did her, for no sooner had she caught my attention than she abandoned whatever business she had with the clerks spilling out of the Gentian Courthouse. Narrowing her eyes at me, she slipped around the grand marble staircase and ducked into the first alley beyond. I last caught sight of her alighting on a domed roof like a golden eagle before vanishing around the other side. I swore and sprinted down the Justice Way in the hope of spotting her again, but it was pointless; she was gone.

I squeezed my eyes shut, trying to press an exact copy of her into my memory. White blouse, white pants, white boots, as usual. The two shashka strapped about her chest like a harness. Her unlikely golden hair had been cropped short. She looked leaner and harder than ever, and yet she and my mistress had not met in combat for many months. Mistress Yildirim would turn me inside out to discover where I had glimpsed the woman in white, eager as she was to find her. There had been a time not long before when Ramadami might have turned me inside out to locate my mistress as well.

"The Justice Way?" Mistress Yildirim asked me again as she fixed the last pin in her headscarf just so.

I met her eyes in the mirror, nodding. "On the steps of the Courthouse," I added. "Speaking with lawyers, I think."

Mistress Yildirim finished painting her lips and rose with a childish grin. "Of course. How could I have thought she would leave the city? Emin—" she patted my cheek and I tried not to scowl, for I was nearly fourteen and she was my mistress, not my auntie "—wash your face before we leave."

I followed her through the kitchen and out into the training yard where two of Yildirim's younger apprentices, Fatima and Layla, were sparring. They paused and watched enviously as we passed through the yard and into the street, not yet old enough to have been paired with Kavalye of their own.

Mistress Yildirim marched down the middle of Dhiar Way with long, bold strides that caused the emerald scarves of her headdress to flutter behind her. The cramped quarters of the narrow, dusty street grew wider at her passing, her presence reducing the cheese sellers and fry cooks, goats trailing small boys and old crones in dark stoops to eddies in her wake. Already folk had stopped to stare. Neighbors clustered to whisper, speculating about her destination. Strangers pointed and chattered, excited to have spotted such an illustrious hero. People trailed us as they always did—idle old men, errant children, distracted journeymen—hopeful of the chance to witness an encounter between two of the most famous Kavalye in the city. Mistress Yildirim tipped her chin and let a cocky grin play over her face, wearing her bravado like a jeweled coat.

"There are more of them than usual," I said, eyeing the mob following us. "Pray to God we find her or they will speak of this disappointment for weeks."

"She wants to be found," Mistress Yildirim stated. "She gave you a glimpse to lure us in. But I—"

"Mistress!" I stopped and turned. Mistress Yildirim's sword was already out, but it was not her white-clothed nemesis I had spotted. "Dashurie!"

"Shit," my mistress muttered, but I could not spare a thought for her inconvenience. Dashurie, my own Kavalye, was in the mob. I'd seen the green-gold of her eyes before she vanished behind a pair of older fellows. I could not let her surprise me—not again.

I drew my shashka and fit my buckler over my glove. The crowd spread slowly with a mix of disappointment and alarm: keen not to be too close to a duel, but irritated the duel was to be between two fresh apprentices and not the famous Kavalye, Yildirim and Ramadami. Dashurie emerged slowly from behind a straggler, shashka in hand.

"Dashurie Dushku, stand where you are!" I called to her, pointing with my sword. "I challenge you to fight me by the rules of sahidi. I challenge you to take my favor!"

"I accept," she replied simply. She didn't even salute, just hurled herself in my direction. I crouched low, horse-stance, knowing how Dashurie liked to toss me on my back if I let her. Her shashka she used mostly for parrying; she preferred to grapple.

But I was growing quickly these days, as the ache in my shins could attest. I held steady as she charged, arms close to my sides. At a distance of two swords, she ducked under my guard, planting both hands in the dirt in front of me and kicking out at my blade with the wooden heels of her boots. I twisted with the impact, ignoring the numbness in my hand, praying I would not be disarmed. But I had the wrong foot forward and could only take so much of the blow before I felt an awful wrenching in my wrist.

I used the twisting motion to land an ineffective punch with my buckler, but Dashurie merely rolled away. My blade-hand was useless. I wasted my precious few seconds of advantage switching hands and regaining solid footing when I should have been pinning my opponent and taking her favor. From the corner of my eye I saw Mistress Yildirim cross her arms over her chest—as sure a sign as any of her disapproval.

Dashurie pushed to her feet and launched herself into another attack. She sliced at me with circular strokes, using her longer limbs and superior control to force me back. And what could I do but give ground? Dashurie would not kill me, but she had not shied from injuring me badly in the past. I did not care to spend another month in a chair, so I retreated, barely deflecting the tip of her sword as I skipped away.

I chanced a glance behind me. We were only a few paces now from the sun-warmed stucco face of the feltmaker's guildhall. Lately, my lessons with Mistress Yildirim had all concerned precision and control, the sword and knife arts that she had perfected: but she was as often defeated by Kara Ramadami and her more acrobatic tricks. Ramadami won her duels when she used spaces my mistress did not occupy—up and up and up.

I dropped my blade and turned. In two long strides, I reached the doorframe of the hall, eyes fixed on the heraldry hanging above. As I had seen Kara Ramadami do in the past, I jumped, kicked off of the doorframe, twisted, and caught the iron bar sporting the guild's sign with my good arm. The momentum swung me away from Dashurie, who sliced at the air behind me. Elated, I let go at the apex of my swing and spun, turning to face my opponent.

I snatched at the bar again a moment too late. I was soaring away now rather than swinging back toward her, as Ramadami might have done. My belly hit the dirt and knocked all the air, strength, and sense out of me. The dry earth exploded in a wave of dust, filling my mouth and eyes.

"You stand—well, lie—defeated, Emin Akdari," Dashurie spoke above me. I barely managed to roll onto my back as she rifled though my purse and turned up my favor, a disk of onyx carved with the arms of the Onsen, my people. She held it up and smiled. I could only lie there and struggle to breathe as she walked away to cash it in.

"That was . . . new," Mistress Yildirim said once I had regained enough sense to stand. She lifted my injured hand and scowled when I cried out in response. "It might have worked if you'd had both arms."

"Sorry, Mistress," I muttered, desolate. This was three in a row I'd lost to Dashurie. My only consolation was that, after so many losses, my favor would be worth so little. As poor as the Onsen Dynasty was, even they could pay out for the favor of a wretched child like me. I felt tears gather in my eyes and feigned pained noises so my mistress would think I wept only from my injury.

Mistress Yildirim nodded approvingly. "No need for apology. Your awareness is improving, and that last stunt shows you're thinking, at least. It will come. When you next defeat Dashurie, think what she will be worth." I ran my empty purse over my face to sop up all the wet. She would be worth a good sum, for an apprentice. I could use the funds on new practice swords for the yards or to help re-tile the livery shop, after I'd paid the Onsen their share.

If I ever won. "I am sorry—I mean," I changed the subject, "to spoil your hunt."

Mistress Yildirim's black eyes narrowed. "Never mind my hunt," she said, curt. "To the anatomist with you. I will find Xmadami tomorrow."

Kara Ramadami's favor was worth three palaces and the gold to paint them. But so was my mistress's. The only difference was that Ramadami's Dushiq people could afford to pay out on her favor. If Mistress Yildirim lost, it could bankrupt the entire Onsen Dynasty.

Mistress Yildirim suspected the Onsen were trying to keep her and Ramadami apart. Her patron, Timar Suat Balbay, wanted her to flee the city. But that was too much for my mistress's honor, let alone her pride.

The encounter at Ceset Alley had paid off all the yard's debts, allowed her to take on Fatima and Layla as apprentices, and bequeathed many more long years to the Mosque at Mount Kurlak. But Mistress Yildirim had come too late to sahidi. Generations of losses had weakened and impoverished the Onsen Dynasty, until even my mistress's legendary victories were not enough to prop it up. The Onsen were only as strong as she was.

"Quit while you are ahead," Timar Balbay had begged her. "The city has never known a pair of Kavalye like you and Ramadami. Your place in history is assured. They will tell stories about nobody else for generations. Retire."

"Let Ramadami retire. I will not," my mistress replied. "You have not seen her, Suat. She's like a bundle of firewood—brittle. She trains too hard. She will break. I will hunt her until it is no longer worth my time."

Great people refuse to speak of money, but I knew the fear that lurked behind Timar Balbay's entreaties. Every Onsen knew. The two Kavalye were so evenly matched, neither favor ever devalued, until their duels had become more influential in political affairs than any dynastic policy. They were building the city with their prizes, shaping it according to their ideas.

But Ramadami had become scarce. The two women used to clash once a week at least, a regular spectacle that the people would wait for breathlessly, bet on, and talk about for days afterwards. Before I spotted her on my run, it had been two months since we had last found her. Before she jumped my mistress at Ceset Alley, another three. My mistress was impatient and concocted theories of a conspiracy.

"They sent Dashurie," she declared later, after the anatomist had packed a cast of cool clay and linen about my wrist. "They sent her to detain me."

I said nothing, preferring to think of my dance with Dashurie as my own, not just another part of my mistress's overwhelming drama.

"They think I will not hunt without you," she continued. "They think an inconvenience will dissuade me. Or they think me a creature of habit." Yildirim snorted with contempt. "They will have to try harder than that. Come, Emin. We return to the hunt."

My mistress was a woman of flash and shine, of open-air performances and large audiences. Some Kavalye preferred to fight in the dark and shadows, but not she. It did not suit her and she did not fare well by it. But as we left the yard that evening into a deepening dusk, I was so preoccupied by my bruised pride that I said nothing to dissuade her.

-town's nightlife only by reputation. Farther up the mountain, across the Ridge, they said the marble-tiled streets were patrolled by lantern-bearers escorting nighthawks from well-lit taverns to cheerful evening dances. Brash, red-faced revelers shouted playful offers and challenges across the avenues, only just warming up for a long night of indulgences. Lightning traps lit public squares where whole clans gathered to drink and eat while children chased dogs and formed gangs for mock brawls. The Dushiq were happy and safe, protected by their gold.

Onsen-town by night was a very different place than by day. Onsen-town had no lantern-bearers. The market had been sturdily tiled three generations ago but had long since grown filthy. Shopkeepers shut and bolted their windows as soon as the shadows grew, rolled up the thin hangings, and kept to their family hearths. The light of Dushiq-town drove dark dealings into Onsen streets. Where by day, we Kavalye were celebrated as prizewinners and gift-givers, by night we were blamed for threadbare livelihoods and ruined dreams.

We should not have been out that night. A brigand is not a Kavalye, and a brawl is not a duel.

My mistress was looking for trouble and, even knowing this, I let her lead me along watercourses and lanes; filthy, crowded cracks between buildings that anyone should have avoided. We traveled down cat-ways and under fences to avoid the gangs that staked claim to the streets, making our way toward the Ridge that split the city into Onsen and Dushiq halves. We had nearly reached that great road when I caught sight of a shadowy shape crouched behind a chimney.

"Mistress," I hissed.

"I see, Emin, but they are too late. We have nearly arrived—listen." The bustle of goatcarts, pedalwagons, and foot traffic rumbled just ahead.

I glanced back at the lurking figure but it had disappeared. I frowned. What sort of bandit travels by rooftop? That was the behavior of someone who hunted another: of Kavalye. Dashurie was not allowed to challenge me again so soon, and so—

"Mistress!" I yelped. There, on the same roof, another glimpse unmistakable in the moonlight. "White, Mistress! It is Ramadami!"

Yildirim had already moved, sidestepping under the roof's ledge and drawing her sword. I stood gaping in the alley, waiting for the challenge, but the *tap-tap* of boot on slate was already retreating to the west. Ready for a chase, Yildirim mounted the gutters and I raced to pursue on the ground.

"There!" I cried, waving my arm in the direction of the old livery. The lithe figure leapt from the rooftop to a porch on the far side, trailing white scarves like stardust. Yildirim followed.

I had to sprint to keep up with the two women, who bounced from house to house like goats, barely rousing the inhabitants. At the bazaar, Ramadami finally descended into the square, or so I presumed. By night, the market was more a pit than a place, enclosed as it was by old stone warehouses. I could hardly see ten paces ahead as I rounded the corner, not even the sheen of the Kavalye's white clothes.

Only then did I understand the danger we were in. I heard the thump of my mistress's boots hitting the stones, then the shuffle of more than one person preparing themselves. The dark was almost complete.

Nothing moved for the space of ten heartbeats, not even a cat. And then. . . .

"Emin!" Yildirim cried. "It is an ambush. Run, return to the yard! I—"

But her voice dissolved into an anguished snarl. My eyes had become just accustomed enough to the gloom that I could make out four figures in addition to my mistress crouched at the foot of some crates. Yildirim was on one knee, sword drawn. Not one of her attackers was wearing white.

On my honor, I could not run anywhere. Instead, I drew my shashka and crept closer to the ruffians, for they appeared not to be taking any notice of me. My mistress was a spectacular duelist, but four opponents in the dark are stiff odds for any person.

Yildirim lurched forward, her blade clearing space ahead of her, then rolled to her right and lashed out, catching the belly of the attacker there. Her off-hand she kept tight against her ribs and I guessed she had been cut already. She ducked and rolled again before anyone could retaliate, repeating the maneuver on another opponent's flank. Two more figures emerged from the shadows behind her, cautiously closing ranks. Those two I charged.

These bandits had not the reflexes of Kavalye, not even a young one like myself. Slowly, they realized they were under attack; slowly, they stumbled trying to reposition themselves. My mistress continued to roll and dodge, confusing their attempts to encircle her properly. I took my opportunity to break the first assailant's guard with a sharp, hard parry, followed by a slash they had not the wit to block. My blade bit into their shoulder and was stopped by their collarbone, but that was enough to panic them into dropping the weapon.

We were now two against four, but despite their weakening odds, the attackers drew closer. We were both injured, my mistress and I, and out of our element. In the confusion of battle, I was sure even more shadows were growing limbs, adding to the attack. They would have from us whatever they wanted soon enough. All I could do was try to raise the price beyond what they were prepared to pay.

I pushed past my disarmed opponent toward their companion, who by this time faced me on sturdy footing, a sword at the ready. He parried my first three blows, stepping back with each motion. I pressed him, seeing he was unwilling to seize the offensive. His swordwork was slow and formal, like a child after his first lesson, and I took him for an easy opponent. He retreated steadily as my every blow grew closer to finding flesh, exhaling sharply at each clash of our blades.

Exhilarated by my success so far, I swung at him faster and harder. He stumbled, fell to his bottom, and raised his weapon impractically to shield himself from what was surely to be my killing blow. In the dark, I could make out almost nothing of his features, but he could surely see the white of my teeth as my lips curled into a bloodthirsty grin.

"Gaaaaaaaaah!"

My mistress's scream was so far behind me, I did not understand what I was hearing at first. My arm drooped as I realized what had happened, dread draining the fire from my blood. The brigand at my feet had lured me away from my mistress, out of reach. Now I was too far and too late to help her.

"Mistress!" I cried, turning. I could not even see her for the crowd of black-clad figures surrounding her. I howled as I sprinted back, sword raised, ready to do I know not what. They peeled away from their victim one dark petal at a time, fleeing full tilt into the alleys, revealing the bloodied Yildirim at their center.

She was still alive, her eyes wide with fear when I reached her side. She grasped my arm and tried to pull herself upright, her breaths shallow. She was drenched from the belly down in what could only be blood and one leg was caked thick with filth. "Help me up," she hissed. "Home."

I reached around her with my good arm and lifted her with my back. One of her legs found purchase but the other dangled heavily. She gripped my shoulders and we staggered slowly toward a wall.

"Mistress," I stuttered, "I am sorry. I thought—I shall fetch the anatomist!"

"No," Yildirim panted. "We cannot linger for whoever comes to clean up the scraps. Move!"

By the dim light of the moon, I could not make out the source of her injury. Her leg was badly mutilated, that was plain, but she appeared also to have suffered injuries to her abdomen. Every step was a labor and we could not risk the main streets, but after an eternity of dragging her half-conscious through the open sewers of Onsen-town, we came to our yard and our kitchen. She could not sit in a chair, so I propped her up by the laundry basin and ran to fetch the girls to help me.

She had blacked out from pain and blood-loss by the time the anatomist rushed in with Fatima. Under his direction, we moved Yildirim to her rooms and hovered as he set about locating her wounds. A couple of shallow, harmless cuts to her side, only one deep enough to reach a rib. The little finger of her off-hand was so badly cut, he would have to remove part of it. And then her leg.

"See here?" He showed the now-cleaned wound to Fatima, for I had not the stomach for surgery. "One tendon cut, the other hanging by a thread. She'll never walk again."

"Never?" I interrupted.

"She'll be lucky if her blood's not poisoned from the gutters. Shame on Kara Ramadami; shame. It is a disgrace for Shoanna Yildirim to have been injured like this." He shook his head and began preparing some needles.

I turned away. It was not Ramadami who had disabled her leg, but whatever conspiracy had drawn assassins to my mistress was not the anatomist's affair.

By dawn, Mistress Yildirim had taken fever. Though she would never have wanted word of her infirmity to pass beyond our walls, I had not her skill at commanding obedience from every mouth and eye that crossed our threshold. Soon, Timar Suat Balbay sent an envoy, and then, veiled, turned up himself in a state of panic. He impressed on me, his pounding heart inches from my nose, the urgent need for Yildirim to announce her formal retirement the moment she was capable. She could not be caught thus incapacitated; as if I did not know, as if all in Onsen-town did not know how our fates and fortunes lay with the shivering woman upstairs.

She, and one other.

I cleaned and prepared her clothing and weapons, as always. Then I sat in the kitchen to wait for the visitor I knew would arrive.

I did not leave my vigil for three days, but Fatima and Layla brought me news from town. No Dushiq Kavalye had been seen since my mistress's evil night, and their Onsen counterparts mooned about the streets like shunned lovers. Meanwhile, droves of Dushiq apprentices were coming and going from the big training yards up the Justice Way. Where were their masters? The neighbors whispered of a plot to impoverish the Onsen forever by hiding from our champions.

Kara Ramadami finally showed herself in Onsen-town at dawn on the fourth day, setting the whole city abuzz. A child no older than Layla arrived at our door, breathless.

"She comes!" the girl panted. "Kara Ramadami comes down Dhiar Way, and she has others with her!"

I waved her inside. "Others? Other duelists, you mean? Tell their Kavalye, not—"

The girl shook her head excitedly. "Not Kavalye, just others—*with swords!*"

"They must be Kavalye if they are armed," I scolded the child, but the words were nearly choked by my rising panic. "They might be newly sworn. Go to the other yards, find their pairs."

"I've been," the girl snapped. "Anyway, they're all dressed alike, these ones. Like musicians in green and white. They *aren't* Kavalye."

I was about to shoo the girl off when I heard the scrape of a chair behind me. Mistress Yildirim, chalk-faced and bruised, stood at the entrance to the hallway.

"How many?" she asked. "And how far away?"

The child's eyes widened. "A parade of them, Mistress. And many blocks hence, still. I ran as fast as I could, but she's coming here. She must be. She's come to challenge you, hasn't she?" Her eyes were lit with anticipation. I started to stammer an excuse but my mistress spoke first.

"Of course she has," Yildirim replied. With her bad leg tucked behind the good, leaning on a wooden chair, she almost looked ready. "Emin." Her hard stare frightened me into silence. "Get my pistol."

Pistols were against the rules of sahidi. Coming to call on your Kavalye at her home was not, though it was close enough to dishonorable to be distasteful. Mistress Yildirim insisted on being readied to face Ramadami despite her grievous wound and continued illness, insisted on meeting her Kavalye on the street, not at the door. This was to allow the woman in white to save face, though I could not see why we afforded her such a courtesy. After all, surely she had come to kill my mistress. After all, surely my mistress would kill Kara Ramadami to save herself. What honor could be left at the end of a day as cursed as this?

Even readied, my mistress was a shadow of herself. There had been no time to apply her makeup, nor could her bright leather boot fit over her mangled leg. She wore her shashka at one hip, her pistol at the other, and a buckler over the bandage on her left hand. I had to act as her crutch in order for her to move at all. She could not even stand without my help.

Yet she held her chin high as we exited the yard to meet the Dushiq on the thoroughfare. The child's warning could not have prepared me for the spectacle there, for the long rows of armed soldiers in identical dress lining our narrow street. Their green uniforms were cut from fine wool, new and lined with white satin. Each had identical new shashka and, strapped to their backs, long rifles like hunters carried. None of them was any Kavalye I knew, and not one of them should have had the right to be so armed, but what could anyone do? They were so many, so splendid in their Dushiq colors. Our neighbors crowded around them, curious and heedless, but their calm, unexplained presence terrified me. They outnumbered every sworn Kavalye in Onsen-town.

Kara Ramadami, all in white, stood in the middle of the street. She and Mistress Yildirim exchanged salutes.

"You're not dead," Ramadami stated. "Good."

"I would not deprive you of that honor, Kavalye," Yildirim replied.

I expected Ramadami to at least scowl at the insult. What person of honor could stomach the suggestion that their opponent had to be softened up before they could be beaten? It was too clear, now, what had befallen my mistress. They could not beat her fairly and so Ramadami would take her unfairly. I wished I could challenge her myself, so much did I hate her in that moment. But the woman returned a wry smile.

"No, you are not worth anything to me dead. And yet, as I hear it, you are worth even more to your masters, who cannot afford for you to be beaten."

Mistress Yildirim ground her teeth. I nearly reached for my own shashka, to hear the Onsen so brazenly disrespected—even if it was true.

Ramadami continued, "My own masters, they have kept me very busy these last several months. Training this apprentice and that, instructing nobles, running *errands* . I was quite stunned, I admit, when they suggested to me these two days hence that I finally seek you out. It would appear my masters are suddenly ready to demand your price from the Onsen." Mistress Yildirim shot a surreptitious look at the Dushiq who surrounded us and Ramadami returned a conspiratorial half-nod. "I told them I was indisposed, as I had heard you were, but they sent these fellows along to encourage me."

If the green and white soldiers understood Mistress Ramadami's bitter tone, they made no sign of it. Who were these armed people who dared interfere in sahidi? Yildirim, for her part, smiled broadly.

"The Dushiq have persons now to help Kavalye fight their duels?" she asked. "Your masters are indeed richer than mine!"

"I apologize that I did not come sooner, Shoanna Yildirim," Ramadami said, her voice raised for all to hear. Then she spoke so quietly that none could hear but my mistress and myself. "I did not know my masters would take so active a hand in *helping* me. But you and I, we have always understood each other."

"Yes," Yildirim replied. "I think we have understood each other perfectly."

Ramadami raised her voice once more. "It has been an honor to be paired with you. There is surely no greater service a person can perform for another than to be a worthy opponent, the tool by which glory and riches may be brought to your people. I have become great because you are great. I will never forget that."

Yildirim nodded. "And I have become this weapon that I am in the fires of your forge, Kara Ramadami. It would be an honor to fight you one last time."

"I accept your challenge."

Yildirim gripped my shoulder with her buckler hand as she drew her sword. I was not sure what to do next when Ramadami approached, shashka drawn, and saluted my mistress with her arms wide. But she did not lunge.

"Take it," the woman in white said in a low voice.

Yildirim extended her sword, threading its tip through the straps of Ramadami's purse. With a flick of her wrist, she cut the harness and let the purse slide down the blade into her hand.

Ramadami bowed. "In this way, I honor you and sahidi."

We had, until then, been enclosed by a dome of silence, a sacred space of our own making. But at Ramadami's words, the invisible walls fell and a great roar of confusion crashed over us. I saw with surprise that the audience who beheld us was bigger than it had ever been, as if every Onsen in the city had gathered to witness us. These people now cheered and shouted, surprised, delighted, or angry. They had never made such a fuss about any duel, no matter how exciting, but I saw then the difference.

Every rifle in Dushiq hands was leveled shakily at my mistress.

"Drop your shashka," one of them cried over the hubbub. I could not tell which.

"Beg your pardon, fellows, but to whom do you speak?" Ramadami asked smoothly, stepping forward past Yildirim. "There are three of us Kavalye here, all honored with the right to bear arms." Suddenly, subtly, the two women were standing back-to-back facing the guns.

"Don't move!" someone shouted. "Both of you, drop your shashka and your favors. You are to come with us to the Dushiq palaces."

My mistress dropped her sword casually, a cruel smile creeping over her lips.

"This is it, then? Your Dushiq masters think they can bankrupt the Onsen and replace sahidi—Kavalye—with this? You children with guns trained on women of honor, on your peaceful neighbors?" Her smile vanished. "Put up your weapons and go home. I will tell you only once."

"Mistress," I hissed. "This is not the death you wanted. Get away! The Onsen are done!" I saw how few we were against the rows of white and green. Our enemies exchanged nervous looks, baffled by what was surely empty bluster.

"You have been warned." Ramadami appeared to have caught my mistress's mad death wish, for she did not move, either.

"If you will not disarm yourselves, Mistresses," the spokesman said, "we must consider you rogues and enemies of the Dushiq." The soldiers pulled back the bolts on their rifles. At the *click*, the unarmed people started to shriek and flee. Only confusion prevented me from doing the same. "On three."

Mistress Yildirim had drawn her pistol before one.

My mistress fired first at the soldier directly in front of her. It was a sloppy, loose shot by her standards, catching the man square in the face where, rather than kill him, it tore his jaw from its hinges, and most of his cheek, too. But he dropped the rifle, howling and sputtering blood, flailing for his companions, who shoved him away in horror.

Her second shot was fired in the confusion. It passed through the skulls of two more soldiers, killing them before their neighbors noticed they had been hit.

"FIRE!" someone screamed, but it was too late. The legend of my mistress's marksmanship had already seized their minds and imaginations. Shots exploded from the left flank, but Yildirim and Ramadami had already dropped to the ground in unison. I felt the heat of lead cut my back but the sting only prompted me to duck as well.

Then Ramadami took flight. As the soldiers stuffed their barrels and reloaded, she stood and skipped right into their line of fire. Planting her foot on the first man's chest, she pushed off, flipped backwards, and kicked the gun right out of his grasp. She caught it midair and had leveled it down the line by the time she landed.

Two more shots rang out— *crack! crack!*—from Yildirim's pistol, these felling two more uniforms on either side of her. *Foom!* The basso belch from Ramadami's barrel followed, ripping through the front ranks.

The soldiers broke, every face I saw scarred with panic. *Crack!* Yildirim's fifth shot broke the air like lightning, passing through one soldier's shoulder and piercing the flashpan of his neighbor's rifle. Sparks exploded from the kindled weapon as a few more soldiers chanced wild shots. I heard desperate cries of, "Fire! Fire!" and saw discarded rifles land in the mud. The smell of smoke preceded more screams and gunshots. *Foom!* Ramadami pivoted, fired, and leapt again. I swear she ran through the air overhead, held aloft by passing bullets. When she landed, she broke another soldier's jaw with the butt of her stolen weapon.

More bullets crossed the street, catching everyone but their intended targets in the confusion. I curled into a ball and waited for my turn to be shot.

After an endless moment, I felt the tug of a strong hand on the back of my vest. "Get up, Emin!" It was Kara Ramadami, so I obeyed. "Your mistress needs you."

The crowds had completely dispersed. The dust was made muddy with the blood of the injured and the dead. A few Onsen people had fallen amongst the uniformed Dushiq, a sight that made me sick to the stomach. Mistress Yildirim lay on her belly, propped on her elbow with her pistol leveled unmoving up Dhiar Way.

"Come, Mistress," I told her, tugging on one arm as Ramadami took her other. "The day is won."

"Not yet," Yildirim said, though her voice was thin.

"Yes, Mistress, please," I begged her. "Let us go before more of them return. You have only one bullet left and the Dushiq are too many."

Yildirim squinted and squeezed the trigger.

My mistress, Shoanna Yildirim, was the greatest shot in the city. That last bullet launched from the muzzle of the revolver gifted to her by the Sultan Mahmud himself and, praise God, its lead skin caught fire as it sped north.

It streaked, aflame, toward the Ridge. The tall palaces of the Dushiq were barely the size of playing cards on the hillside, so distant that they might as well have been drawn on the horizon. Still, the flaming bullet streaked toward them, nothing but the twinkle of a falling star over the city. After a breathless minute, it flared once before it hit its target in a puff of white powder.

"Help me up," Yildirim said, her lip twitching with a familiar smirk as the building began to smoke. "Now is our time to be gone."

"And mine as well," Ramadami added. Yildirim looked her in the eye, her smile fading. She nodded. I can only guess what it cost the woman in white to walk away that day, knowing she would never again know the glory of a duel.

The Dushiq grudgingly paid out on Kara Ramadami's favor and said nothing about their attempted coup or the strange fire that had originated in the upper offices of one of their palaces and destroyed half the wing before it was discovered and put out. The dead were buried and the grief of Dushiq and Onsen alike forged a new reminder of the civil balance sahidi maintains.

Kara Ramadami, we never saw again.

Nor did Shoanna Yildirim ever walk again. With both women removed from sahidi, the prizes could not threaten either Dynasty. Every person in Onsen-town told ever-greater tales of the encounter that proved, as nothing else could, the power of Kavalye to keep the peace where mere soldiers could not. That peace reigned for the remainder of my lifetime.

I never knew another person with the skill of my mistress or her nemesis. In time, people would come to doubt their feats and call them mere stories, allegories at best. It was just as well. No peace could stand on only two pillars, no matter how strong. The fine balance between Onsen and Dushiq, we all shared between us.

THE BRIDGE OF DREAMS

GREGORY FEELEY

1

When Heimdallr finds an hour to spare from his labors, he polishes a length of Bifröst flat as a plane, then bevels adjacent sides so that the resultant stretch bends and disperses the sun's weak rays like a prism. He rarely has the leisure for such pastimes. Although Charon and its primary face each other like ancient adversaries who will never avert their gaze, their distance varies slightly—much less than any other pair in the solar system, but enough to put a continual strain on the bridge. Cracks and fissures form, which Heimdallr must hasten to repair. Like stalagmites approaching to merge, the ends of the worldbridge were built by accretion, the rough bases thickening as their tips rose (or descended) towards each other. An extent of gleaming smoothness stands out like crystal embedded in stone, stirring in Heimdallr vague memories older than himself. Then hairline cracks begin to form, and he brings his engines to bear, smothering them beneath layers of ethane and ice.

The faint and short-lived spectra that these surfaces produce are a source of deep but fleeting pleasure, for they appear only during those microseconds when the cloud of vapor has discharged from his nozzle but not yet struck and turned solid. A skein of half-glimpsed images are brought to mind, though not by memory. Heimdallr remembers what he has experienced and perceived, and these tangled recollections are stranger, reaching him along pathways he cannot look down to espy. Others' lives, forgotten by those long dead: the sight of the Rainbow roils them like a quake disturbing graves.

A puff of plasma tickles his cheek and he looks toward the Sun, a pinpoint of light but not heat, and the ruined worlds that circle it. Plouton and Charon, now joined by the haft that he made and maintains, is traveling outward, where it shall tarry long among the vast mist of volatiles that sheathes the outermost worlds before beginning a long journey closer—but never close—to that swollen mass of radiance.

The ice-conjoined binary has completed this circuit once and more since he last heard the whisper of radio waves or the flicker of a laser pulse from any point Sunward. Triton has been silent for centuries; signals from Phaiton's Children went out one by one like candles. The dense swirling airs of Titan remained infinitesimally warmer than what Heimdallr thought nature could account for, although this might as likely be heat diffusing from an abandoned fission pile—a coal slowly cooling in a dead hearth—as evidence of settlements still active below the surface. Were he truly human, his heart would burst at this.

Meanwhile there remains his duty. Heimdallr stands master of Bifröst, its length enough to wrap three times about the girdle of the Earth. Weekly—the time the two worlds took to swing about each other approximated that ancient measure—it must be patched and reinforced, with substances gathered from their surfaces. From a distance the bridge is invisible: an icy thread running up to the overhead world, too slender to catch much of what light can reach it. At either base it resembles a rough-hewn tower the girth of a mountain, thicker on Plouton with its greater gravity. Genuine ice mountains rise from the lifeless plains, and Heimdallr has already lain waste to five in quarrying blocks for his span. Yearly he must venture farther to gather material for repairs, and someday will have to cross the horizons of both worlds, into lands where the other world is absent from the sky. He does not know how he will feel about this; feelings are something he imperfectly understands.

He is not on the ground when the glint of light catches his eye. Plouton-Charon lies far from the ecliptic, so Heimdallr may look inward toward the other planets without being dazzled by the Sun. The spark's wavelengths are shifted to blue, although to a degree too faint for a human eye to detect. It is coming toward him quickly.

When the light flares brighter and shifts toward red, he knows that it is not a missile. For days he had pondered how to defend Bifröst—large, brittle, immobile—against assault. A direct blow to projectiles might knock them off course, but such a strike must be massive or extremely fast—many times local escape velocity—and Heimdallr doubted his bow possessed the strength for either. Evidence that the decelerating vessel would come to rest a kilometer away does not reassure, although he shifts his stance and takes his hand from the pommel of his sword.

It is not until the thrusters cut off that he can see the gleaming spear, which is now rotating on its axis with tiny puffs of vapor. The blade turns once and now rests in the hand of a helmeted woman, who raises it above her head.

"Ho," Heimdallr says. "You stand before Bifröst, the Rainbow Bridge, and I its builder and guardian. Be welcome if you offer no threat."

"I am Garðrofa, message-bearer." She seems to hang in space before him, although in fact she is circling in a plane that lies perpendicular to Bifröst. Heimdallr, his back to the bridge, can see tiny jets emerge at intervals from her boots, correcting the unstable orbit. "I bring you word."

"What is your message, and from whom?"

"I bring the message; I do not know its content, nor its sender." Then she says: "You are called—entreated, not summoned, yet the knowledge of duty itself summons—to the Sheltered Gardens. Please come in the flesh, as no pallid counterfeit will suffice."

"'The flesh'? They believe I possess the power or inclination to create an Iteration and send it loose?"

Garðrofa looked at him quizzically. "Whom do you speak of?"

"You just relayed an appeal from the Sheltered Gardens."

"I did?"

"Who gave you this message?"

"I do not know."

"Why then did you carry it?"

"I do not know."

Heimdallr considered her. "Is there more?"

"No."

Heimdallr's nature, and the physical form he has taken, precludes the need for shelter, but the oldest parts of him understands the importance of hospitality. "My hall lies beyond. It is scant warmer than the space surrounding us, but its hewn beams offer relief from the unbroken sight of stars."

"Thank you, but if I may decline without giving offense, I do."

It has been a lifetime and more since Heimdallr has spoken to a being before him, and while loneliness does not lay waste to his spirit, the rupture of his solitude now seems pleasing. "To take refreshment together—whatever resources you have expended in traveling hither, I can replenish—would satisfy the obligations of both guest and host, and more agreeably than my other duties can claim. The invitation stands, and unless you depart forthwith, I shall at length repeat it."

"I have no plans to depart," says Garðrofa simply.

"No?" Hundreds of scanning programs and tiny probes have been examining the visitor and the space around and beyond her, and have reported one by one that she offers no threat.

"Do those who dispatched you wish to give you additional missions, or offer you some reward for your service?"

"I do not know."

"That is surprising," he says. "How long were you voyaging here?"

"I cannot say. During the interval of travel, I was not."

Heimdallr ponders this. He wishes to ask, "What more can you tell me?" but guesses that the answer would be *Nothing*. "My hounds have sniffed your boots and found you unthreatening. Are you doubtful regarding my own good will?"

"No. I am not concerned for my safety."

He has not had to think quickly in many years, but does so now. "Then let me show you my world. At worst you will be bored."

At this Heimdallr launched himself out and downward, toward Plouton. Had he simply pushed away from the ice, he would have been hours drifting toward the primary. The passage of time might not have bothered either of them, but he felt it was a moment to be purposeful.

Acceleration is slow, but eight thousand kilometers lie between Bifröst's midpoint and the surface, and his boots strike ground with a satisfying crunch and a spray of methane snow. Long practice has taught him the stride that covers the most distance without leaving him afloat in a high trajectory, and he moves swiftly over the landscape, flat here (he long ago cleared it for the transportation of building material) but becoming irregular the farther one gets from Bifröst's trunk. The time and energy required to travel distances mean nothing to him, so he built his fastness (once named Himminbjorg, though he soon realized that a structure no one would ever see or hear of does not need a name) on the ground that offered the most impressive view, which proved to be in one of Plouton's highlands.

Heimdallr knew without turning his head that Garðrofa had matched his stride and was following him at a half dozen paces. He saw no need to offer information about the temperature, local gravity, mineral composition, and other bits of "local color" (the ancient term abruptly came to him) that she could clearly perceive for herself. Instead he told her something she could not measure. "I find this beautiful," he says. "Can you see the beauty here?"

"Perhaps."

It was her first ambiguous response, and he wondered at it. She did not elaborate, however, and after a moment he says: "My calculations suggest that your voyage originated in the Gardens. Does this correspond with your own memories?"

"No."

That part of his mind that had been reviewing past, hitherto unstudied images of the sky, identifying the minute smudges of the approaching Garðrofa, and calculating possible trajectories from its shifts had brought to consciousness its conclusion. He did not need to know how he knew, any more than a seafaring ancestor would have questioned his sense of shifting balance.

"Is there trouble at the Great Work? Has the Parasol grown tattered, or its attendants injured or starved, so it will soon tear or blow away and those it has sheltered will roast?"

"I do not know."

"Is there conflict between the peoples of the disparate spheres? All human history has been plagued by such pointless strife."

"I cannot tell you."

"Did those who sent you approach others before appealing to so distant a figure as me?"

"If so, they did not inform me."

She was giving the same reply, but no longer with identical answers. This was rhetoric, a human art older than any craft operating on this world. He wonders if she is becoming more human as the sheath that brought her sloughs away.

He points toward the horizon. "That is my redoubt."

It was not built like anything on Earth, where the gravity is twenty times greater and structures are shaped to bear loads. It contains no rock, for Plouton's stony core lies far below its surface. It is not defensive in design, for it is not a fortress, and no above-ground structure in the solar system could withstand assault by relativistic projectiles. It is probably not beautiful, although Heimdallr pondered beauty as he constructed it.

If nothing else, it is unique.

The entrance is large and stands always open. The Great Hall is suited for feasting, as are the upstairs quarters for privacy, though he never expected guests. He leads her in and bids her to take her ease, and offers to withdraw should she prefer solitude. Garðrofa looks up at the vaulted ceiling; turns to study the tall windows looking upon the icy plain, the colonnade opposite leading to the inner courtyard; walks about the banquet table. "I do not wish for anything," she says.

"Please sit," he says. She does so, although she does not seem more comfortable. After a moment he asks, "Is there anything more you wish to do or tell me?"

"No," she replies. "My mission is completed."

"You are free to act as you please?"

She seems to consider this. "Yes, although I have no further needs. Now that . . . " She breaks off, and he looks curiously at her. "With my duties discharged, aspects of my being are shutting down, allowing others to . . . It is curious," she says at last. "I am now able to feel—well, it is difficult to describe." She looks at him. "Have you been lonely here?"

"No," he says, startled. "Although I am enjoying your company, the solitude has never troubled me." Nor has he wondered at that, and now wonders why he didn't. Years ago he dealt with this by devising an editor that would reduce sensitivity to cognitive activities that produced distress. Because he understood the survival value of such thoughts, he did not debar them from consciousness; they stood beyond a diaphanous scrim, available for assessment but unable to inflict pain. Now the scrim seems to be rippling in an intangible breeze, and that which lay beyond is now gliding forward to join him.

Years ago . . . he also created a program that would allow him to access uncomfortable memories but prevent them from coming unbidden to mind. He will not know *how many* years unless he makes an effort. That, he decides, he will do later.

"I am beginning to feel that I would be lonely," she says.

Heimdallr begins to reply, but suddenly realizes that he is uncertain regarding his own feelings, which seem to be changing. "The person I *was* never felt lonely, but your presence has provoked something." It has provoked shifts and subsidences, and he is less surprised by the onset of change than by *what* is changing—or rather, changing back.

He had isolated and disabled numerous vulnerable aspects of his personality, but had known enough not to eliminate them, and now they are rushing back like waters reclaiming the land. He is a proud and social man who values the respect of those he admires, a man of curiosity, ambition, and unsurprising passions. All now come rushing back, dizzying him even as he stands unmoving.

"We are alone on this world together," he says, "and only for a short time." The millions of nerve endings suitable for sexual response still function, even if they are not wired to his skin.

"I understand," she answers. She sits thinking for a time—no time at all, by the scale he is used to, but long (he remembers) for human conversation— and then stands.

Their coupling would have struck their ancestors as heroic: it takes place in the extreme cold, it lasts a very long time, and it generates enough heat to melt the ice (methane) around them. Such flesh as they possess does not fatigue, nor are their nervous systems restricted to the range of sensation available to the humans of earlier epochs. Their emotional responses climb, soar, and dive like cranes traversing a mountain range. Tolerances are pushed, subroutines neglected to the point of recklessness in order to devote all resources to the act. Each climax offers the promise of richer and more complex raptures; the lovers do not cease until they decide, almost simultaneously, that their capacity for exaltation has reached its limit.

After such exertion, one can only lie side by side, unselfconsciously engaged in the archaism of actually touching. It is longer still before they rise, for there is more than much for each to consider, and each has—to a degree that must itself be pondered—become now a different person. Heimdallr goes off to begin building his craft; Garðrofa to explore the world's continent-sized surface. They rarely speak, although each feels as though the other is standing near.

Much of the substances he needs are already incorporated into the engines that maintain Bifröst or the mechanisms that support them, and he is careful about what he harvests for his own use. There is more: energies must be summoned and gathered; a route plotted; a flight plan of fractal intricacy devised. The minders to manage these tasks and the artificers to carry them out must themselves be supervised, and Heimdallr is long at these labors before construction is finally underway and he seeks out Garðrofa, who has ranged as far as the backside of Charon.

"I have given orders for preparations for my journey," he told her. "We may occupy the meantime as we please. You will accompany me on the same trajectory when we return?"

"I shall not return," she replied.

"You wish to stay here?"

"I shall not stay. The functions that sustain me were not designed to outlast the voyage, and I shall soon discorporate."

Surprise, like a dropped match briefly illuminating an abyss, may fail to sound the depths that engulfs it. "How is this so?" he asks.

"I do not know."

"You are alarmed, afraid? Resigned?"

"No."

"How might this be forestalled?"

"By no means available. I am a message to be discarded once read."

Heimdallr is used to solving problems, but he can see nothing here. "This is unacceptable. Why should I live and not you?"

"You shall not always live. And for accepting this voyage you shall live less long, though differently."

His response to this, and hers in turn, are clear to both of them and go unspoken. They rush into each other's arms, perhaps knowing where this will lead. There is no point in anything else; all other actions open to them close like convergent series.

They will couple till she perishes, a fusion reaction to light up the surrounding night. Neither knows whether these exertions will delay or hasten the failure of some critical system, nor what such collapse will be like. The space they have entered defines their shared future; tumbling, they do not wonder when they will strike its far wall.

When it comes, there is time for an instant of awareness, a hand raised perhaps in farewell. Then solitude, more sudden than seems possible; his soul rings with the shock of it.

It is as things were before, save that it is not.

He returns to his labors, which now involves hurling boulder-sized chunks of special ice into the sky, along paths that shall intersect his own eventual route. With the dispatch of the first projectile his timetable is fixed, immutable as the movement of the heavens. He lets fly with three more, at precisely calculated intervals and trajectories, and prepares for a departure time that is similarly established. The calculations involved in ascertaining the mass and composition of the payloads as well as their exact trajectories are delegated to engines of inhuman strangeness, leaving his own mind to muse upon what it will. He wonders whether the loneliness he now feels will someday settle back into the familiar solitude, which held its own stoic satisfactions.

It is not something he broods upon, but eventually he begins to realize—as a shadow that moves too slowly to see will eventually lengthen to reach you—that he is not, at least not in the sense that he has understood his self to be, entirely alone.

Heimdallr always knew that the emissary from the sunlit realms would have had recourse were he to refuse her invitation. Whether she knew it or not, Garðrofa possessed means designed either to compel his cooperation or take that which her masters valued in him. What manner of invasive procedure she had to breach the citadel of his self and suborn his will Heimdallr never asked, and does not wonder now. But now he wonders whether she managed to plant a piton before falling away.

"Garðrofa?" he calls. "Are you there?"

The answer is not *Yes*, but neither is it silence. For a long time Heimdallr stands listening, and only slowly begins to realize that the presence he perceives does not lie beyond the frontiers of his self, a dim figure that will not come forward, but stands closer, too close to be clearly discerned. Too close, though he thinks for a long time before he accepts this, to be distinct: she is not with him but in him.

It is in thinking this through that the transformation truly takes hold. The process is too strange to surprise; Heimgarð rises and turns about only to survey its aftermath, which comprehends hrs own self. Hse reflects without wonder or resentment, for many things are clearer now.

The time approaches, ratcheting down to zero in the tiny exact steps of an ancient clockwork, and Heimgarð stands ready on the dayside of Plouton. The spacecraft that will take hrm to the inner System is attached to hrs back and thighs, like the folded wings of Daidolos. How long did hse—did Heimdallr—abide on this world? A moment's thought would tell hrm, though consciousness could not function with centuries of such data casually to hand.

With a final step, the moment is here. Heimgarð looks up at the tiny Sun, swings back hrs arms and flexes hrs legs, and in one smooth motion launches hrmself into space.

2

The Sun is a campfire, casting long shadows into a night that soon swallows them whole. Warriors, explorers, soldiers on campaign have sat by its flickering light, as Neolithic tribes had once done, all of them aware of how quickly its illumination fades with distance. A few steps into the dimness beyond and its protecting powers fade, for predators prowl its perimeter.

No predators lurk in the Solar System, a boundless vacuum sprinkled, more sparsely than humans can grasp, with finely distributed rubble. There are no trees or hills to block the light, so the fire can be seen, a pinpoint of illumination, from miles distant. Others, too far ever to reach, fill the sky, creating an illusion of plenitude that humans can never shake.

Hse accelerates steadily and will ultimately reach a velocity few human vehicles have attained, though the voyage will still last for years. Do the nations of the Sheltered Gardens still reckon time by the Earth's rotational period? Hse could search hrs memories, where missives from the Gardens are stored, but they are all too old to be conclusive. Better perhaps to seek the answer by musing upon human nature. There will be time enough, and hse needs the practice.

For all its aching emptiness, the distance Heimgarð must traverse yields a measurable risk of collision with some grain of matter. Such an impact would be catastrophic, and the craft that is largely Heimgarð has been built to offer what protection it can, including lookout instrumentation gazing ahead and around for anything larger than a dust particle. Should hse detect one in hrs path, Heimgarð would have microseconds in which to aim and fire a high-energy beam to knock it away. If that proves impossible, hse could take evasive action—avoiding impact perhaps by millimeters—or decelerate hard, enough that the tiny bullet would complete its transit across hrs path.

The processing power required to maintain such vigilance at all times occupies a significant fraction of hrs attention, so hrs thoughts develop slowly. There is plenty of time, however, and Heimgarð continues to muse even during those hours when much of hrs brain is asleep.

The Sheltered Gardens lie before hrm; or rather, the point that the Gardens will someday reach; they will circle the Sun many times before their path and hsr intersect. Sometimes Heimgarð imagines that the site of hrs destination is still the white-clouded planet of ancient times, Tài bái xīng or Hesperos, and that it shall progress through its history, accommodating itself to Aris and joining in an intricate dance, by the time hse reaches it. It is a strange thought, but there is time for that. Some of hrs thoughts, twining and looping through long, uninterrupted chains of association, are too strange for hrm to articulate, were anyone present to hear them.

Heimgarð's trajectory lies far from the ecliptic, but part of hrs mind announces, in the midst of a complex meditation, that if one drew a line from hrs position perpendicular to the ecliptic and tracked where it falls on the disk, hse has just crossed the orbit of Neptune. The planet itself is nowhere near this point, but hse finds hrmself reflecting on Triton: large, volcanically active, and closer to its primary than Selene is—was—to Earth. Once Heimdallr dreamed of building a Bifröst extending from the surface of Triton to point a long finger almost into Neptune's atmosphere. The project was absurd: such a structure would have to be constructed of strong and flexible alloys, jointed like a dragon's vertebrae, and hrs stolid heart recoiled at the unnaturalness of any like venture. Still, hse wonders if the Tritonides had ever considered it: they loved advanced engineering, and the great blue world that hung unmoving in their sky never ceased to fascinate and entice them.

No world was visible to Heimgarð as hse coasted silently through the darkness. Hrs propellant was gone, and hse cruised in a great ellipse that would, should hse fail to refuel and resume powered flight, veer close to the Sun, incinerating hrm and subjecting the molten mass that remained to incredible deceleration as it swung about and headed out again in a millennia-long orbit. A tiny part of hrs attention tracks the path of the first ice boulder as hse slowly overtakes it, the largest object in millions of kilometers.

The final hours before the encounter focus all of Heimgarð's available thoughts, which hse recognizes as a good thing. The slowly spinning mass lies ahead, visible only by reflected starlight, which is to say, invisible to normal human eyes. Hse uses lidar to study its shifting albedo, its steady increase in diameter as it moves slowly into hrs path. Hse might have carved handholds into its surface, or shaped it to look like an artifact (a spaceborne projectile, or perhaps a sculpture), but did not think of it at the time. That it occurred to hrm now suggests that hrs thinking has changed: hse is not the being he was.

At the instant of encounter hse seizes it, and while its midsection is too great for hrm to get hrs arms fully around, the spikes in hrs fingers dig powerfully in, anchoring hrs grip. Hrs trajectory shifts, to a degree minutely different from that predicted, and jets fire briefly to correct. Already hse is beginning to consume the boulder's substance, and within minutes a tiny tongue of plasma flares brilliantly and acceleration resumes. That part of hrs mind that courses through material most resembling protoplasm feels the surge, and hse feels a thrill first known to the horsemen of the Eurasian steppes.

There is a deep pleasure in powered flight, in steady acceleration that surpasses that of coasting through space. Heimgarð more than doubles hrs velocity over the next few hundred hours, then finds hrmself missing the sustained roar once the fuel is expended. Hse is a bullet, a flung stone, a falling star, free to resume powered flight once hse overtakes and consumes the next tumbling floe.

Heimgarð moves, swiftly by the scale of humans and their works, slowly by that of what milestones can be found. When hse "passes the orbit" of Ouranos, one part of hrs mind informs the rest, which is deep in a reverie no ancestor could follow. There will be no need ever to communicate its nature, no occasion ever to recollect it in tranquility, which hse guesses does not lie ahead. Hse is whelmed in solitude and stillness: no wind to ruffle hrs hair, no blast to chill or spray to soak. Molecules—nothing larger—occasionally ping against hrs visor.

Hse listens for radio waves, and eventually assembles an enormous dish, kilometers across yet thinner than a cell wall, that floats beside hrm like the shadow of a moon, but hears nothing save bursts of emissions from the Sun. Perhaps as hse angles closer to the ecliptic hse will be able to pick up transmissions, though none ever reached hrm on the worldbridge. The possibility that the only remaining radio communications are those from the Gardens to Hermaon, too close to the Sun to distinguish from its incessant roar, fills hrm with something like sadness.

Heimgarð does not possess the soul of either poet or metaphysician, but hse never loses hrs train of thought, however long or complex it grows. When the view does not change and maintenance protocols are unvarying, there is little else to do but think, and the "train"—linear only in its earliest stages—is soon ramifying through all dimensions, a steadily branching tree. Hse can image this edifice in its entirety while pondering every bud, and hrs unwavering attention allows hrm to prune irrelevancies and shore up weaknesses with the patience of an ancient gardener, one who barely notices that her potted topiary has grown into a maze. Whether the final edifice is profound, or even communicable, is of no consequence to hrm, for spreading word of hrs thoughts is not in Heimgarð's nature. Left to hrmself, hse builds.

Inside the orbit of Phaiton hse intercepts the final iceball and begins to decelerate. The distance between the great planet and the Gardens is smaller than what hse has already crossed, yet the span cries out in its vacancy, for Ceres, Aris and the very Earth once filled it and now are elsewhere or otherwise. Slowing, the blast from hrs rockets now flare before hrm, strong enough to vaporize any grit that might cross hrs trajectory. Hse looks down past hrs boots to see hrs path obscured by the spray, and so can observe hrs flight only by holding a reflector, like Perseus's shield, at arm's length.

Ceres, the tiniest world, was purposefully deflected, a servitor dispatched in the name of duty, and Aris now nestles in the Gardens, but the crumpled thing where humanity was born is but a *phantasma,* for all that its mass is undiminished. To contemplate this is to feel pain in a place you never knew, and Heimgarð, still new to emotion, is stunned into something like grief.

Hse is now entering the realm of light, where comets would begin to blaze and the solar wind strengthens steadily. Earlier hse could adjust hrs trajectory with a few bursts of vaporized ice, but now hse is expending fuel profligately, decelerating long and hard even as the Sun seeks to pull hrm in. Hse will not meet the Garden head on, but the delta-*v* required to match orbits still consumes much of hrs substance. The voyager will reach hrs destination stripped to essentials, ribs showing like a wolf's come spring.

Selene makes a full circuit about the Sun as hse approaches, allowing Heimgarð to observe its bright bead swelling just before it disappears behind the solar corona. Sometime later it reappears on the Sun's opposite side, to swing out, bright again, and then narrow to a sliver as it circles back toward hrm. This grants Heimgarð unobstructed sight lines to every point on the lunar surface, but no radio signal reaches hrm. The flare of hrs rockets would be visible to any imaging device scanning the sky, and hrs rapid movement across the heavens would allow any processor with access to a database to identify hrs point of origin, but the vanished Earth's moon is as silent as Phaiton's. Hrs summoners in the Gardens must be observing hrm through optical instruments—hse would detect the touch of any lidar signal—but even they are mute. Hse watches the bright spots of the Garden, a constellation of worlds, as they swell into fullness and then vanish behind the Sun. When the Parasol appears on schedule, a dull glowing circle of partially reflected energy, Heimgarð is significantly closer, angling not toward where it is but where it shall be. A season later and the Parasol shows itself on edge, the Garden worlds glowing as dim semicircles in its shadow.

Now voices fill hrs ears. Words of welcome, instruction, requests for data. Garðrofa would perhaps recognize them, but Garðrofa is no longer here. Heimgarð has hrs own flight plans to follow. At the proper instant hse jettisons hrs craft, which falls away into an elliptical orbit that will someday decay into incandescence. Hse is falling free, moving toward an artificial structure that has swung round to face hrm.

Ahead, the gates open. Sentries, watchful against nearing projectiles, are alerted to hrs authorized entry and turn aside their weapons. Alone, unarmed, the onetime sentinel of Bifröst slows to a trudge with the last of hrs propellant and enters the redoubt of Men.

3

Welcome is traditional for even the strangest arrivals, and wayfarers are expected to rest upon journey's end. Although Heimgarð is not accustomed to resting, hse recognizes the need for convalescence: hrs tissues bruised from weeks of braking and riddled from fusillades of ionized particles. Hse lies upon a bed in minimal gravity, undisturbed (though the bed was doubtless monitoring hrs well-being) while hse heals.

The welcome hse receives is more ambivalent. When after forty hours— this is a world of human time, which hse resumes measuring in those terms— Heimgarð stands, a door appears before hrm and hse passes through, to a space where others soon come to greet him. Perhaps they were not expecting hrm, but rather their envoy bearing Heimdallr in tow, or someone more like themselves.

"Our thanks for taking such trouble to come," says one, evidently female. She speaks the language that Garðrofa had—the one Heimdallr spoke a century and more ago, which (hse now realizes) may well be now spoken nowhere. Courtesy and research: neither incompatible with coercion, which Heimgarð can find no reason to resent. Hse nods gravely.

"There is much that you must tell me," hse answers. Right now the Garden-dwellers are seeking rather than offering information: hse can sense their attempts to access hrs memories, which hse is able to deflect, perhaps because their technology was used to create Garðrofa, whose being now suffuses hrs substance. What they seek to know, they will have to ask.

"Let us show you." The section of floor they stood on descended into darkness. Heimgarð feels the pull of gravity increase and realizes that, of course, hse had lain in a gravity field—no bed functions otherwise. Hse seeks to shake off the fogginess of mind that is evidently afflicting hrm.

"It will be a few seconds," another says. There is a faint shudder underfoot, and suddenly the blackness is spangled by stars. They are outside the habitat, moving through space, a clear bubble encasing them—does the Parasol block radiation so effectively?—and the great globe of Hesperos, dimmer than it appeared in the morning sky of Earth, hangs before their heads, three quarters full. Once more in free fall, Heimgarð orients hrmself to view it more easily. Is there a pinpoint of light showing on its night side? Hse isn't sure.

"We are bound for Aris, where the gravity is more like your world's," says a third. Plouton's gravity is but a fraction even of Hermaon's, and of course it was Heimdallr who was accustomed to Plouton's gravity. Hrs hosts see before them someone who is not Heimdallr nor Garðrofa, who has neither youth nor age, and balk at this troubling fact. Heimgarð, who calls no world hrs own, simply nods.

Aris is visible beyond Hesperos, a deeper shade of the red it has shown humanity since its earliest members gazed into the night sky. The closeness of the two recognizable disks is deeply unnatural: it is something done by man, a feat on a scale greater than that of Bifröst or even the Parasol. Though

Heimgarð has always been able to visualize the binary accurately, hse is profoundly affected by the sight.

Aris and Hesperos circle each other in a calculated dance, at a distance that leaves each looming large in the other's sky. Once there was talk of the worlds being aligned so that the greater would exert on the lesser an influence comparable to what Selene had once wrought upon Earth. Perhaps the engineers of this project—the greatest humankind has ever achieved, or now ever will—expected to seed the larger world with the Earth's legacy of tide-sensitive creatures and plant life, most even then banished into digital limbo. There is certainly no talk of that now.

The Sheltered Gardens are, like the rest of the solar system, mostly empty space, but the cone within the Parasol's umbra is several million times denser than the rest. A moment's observation shows numerous apparent stars moving against the background of the heavens: spacecraft, habitats, and the glint of enormous engines that once displaced a planet, now parked in permanent orbits like abandoned ordnance in the aftermath of a vast war.

"We have cleared the orbital zone of debris," one of them says. "No dangerous shards fly through." A walled garden, Heimgarð thinks: any loose stones prised from where nature had cast them and diverted for use elsewhere. But no one planned to spend their life in a garden.

Hse does not say this, nor anything else. The voyage takes several hours, which hse employs to recalibrate hrs sense of time: everything is now taking place quickly.

Aris is brighter than hse remembers seeing it—the Parasol admits as much sunlight as the Earth and Selene receive—but the planet shows no sign of what atmosphere it has gained. Hse can see the long thread of gases swirling along the Potamegos, too faint for normal human vision, but the red surface remains cloudless. Data are available at hrs mind's fingertips, numbers attesting to the enormous difficulties of pulling away the top of Hesperos's atmosphere and tunneling it across space, the decades it will take, even if the harvest rate can be steadily increased as its planners intended. Somewhere in these numbers, or in others, lies the reason that hse has been brought here.

Aerobraking is impossible over a planet with no significant atmosphere, so the craft decelerates using another world's: the compressed gases of Hesperos are fired like rocket exhaust toward the surface of Aris. As the craft slows, its passengers stand upon its forward bulkhead, the planet now invisible below them. Most of them are significantly smaller than unmodified humans, and Heimgarð has also reduced hrs dimensions, shedding much of the mass hse used to cross the solar system. A guest, hse has doffed hat, cloak, and boots, and stands unaccommodated before them: the thing itself, whatever that may be.

They look at each other quizzically; Heimgarð possesses no skills in reading others' expressions, but knows that they cannot read hsr. They pass through an opening in the Koleos—the world-sheathing membrane, billowing gently in what winds can reach it, is invisible even as they slip through—and are soon within a few kilometers of Aris's surface, although the sky is getting no brighter. A small world: the horizon appears only seconds before touchdown.

The landscape is stony plain, its shades of red and ocher spotted with sheets of verdant fuzz. Heimgarð knew of the Gardeners' plans to pull water and minerals from the soil with tailored viridiplantae, hardy organisms that will eventually change the ecosphere into something in which they cannot survive.

"Pankor is just beyond that low ridge," says one of them, pointing. "We will enter it from here." And the craft drops into the ground, through a shaft that opens after they have descended thirty-four meters (Heimgarð's sensors immediately told hrm this) onto a high-ceilinged tunnel, the first interior space Heimgarð has entered that does not feel cramped. The scent of vegetation wafts toward them—Heimgarð freezes at it touches hrs nostrils— and the others begin walking toward it, on ground that rings solid beneath their steps.

Heimgarð follows as they move toward sunlight at the corridors' end. An enormous vista opens upon the city of Pankor, built upon the terraced walls of a narrow tract of Valles Marineris and covered by a clear dome. By now Heimgarð can smell fir needles, though the source of this memory lies beyond reach. Birds, wings flapping with unnatural languor, fly slowly past.

Across a distance of 3.2 kilometers, boughs sway on breezes dense as those that once swept Earth.

None of the guides announce the city's population, plans for expansion, or the details of its physical plant, for they know that Heimgarð can access these data on the open skein. Instead they wait politely. Hse can offer praise, but allows hrs nature to find expression. "What is the problem you face?"

"Time," one replies. "We cannot take centuries to move humanity into the new worlds. A civilization of refugees, huddling in scattered habitats, will weaken and fail over generations. The Potamegos can never be more than a trickle; the wind that blows from Hesperos to Aris must swell to a gale, that this endeavor may show results within our people's lifetime."

"So what do you seek?"

"We need to build Yggdrasil."

There is a silence while Heimgarð locates and assesses the data on this. "A daunting project," hse says after a moment. "It would require a lot of mass."

"Yes."

Hse does not add that it would be difficult to operate, for the tendency of their remarks is clear. "Bifröst is nothing like what you propose. I can offer you neither knowledge nor skills."

"Do not be too certain. You managed such a structure for a long period of time, and that is a perspective we require."

Heimgarð ponders the dynamics that would act upon this world-spanning tree, its roots extracting gases from one as its branches disperse them over the other. There is a superficial resemblance to hrs creation, but this structure is hollow: not a bridge, but a sluice.

Heimgarð was never an engineer, but the sentinel of Bifröst was first its builder, and hse imagines the superheated gases being drawn up into the roots and then cooling rapidly as they expand. The long trunk would fill with moving vapor, whose density would decrease sharply across its length even as new gases pushed inward. Roots and branches would writhe like a living thing.

The master of such a venture would wield enormous responsibility, like the project manager for the Pyramids or the admiral of a starship fleet. Among those who understood the trials of command, such an overseer's name would live forever.

Hse says, "I don't believe you."

They take hrm to the Sky Dragon, which sails upon the seas of Hesperos's cloud cover like an enormous curled leaf. From there an airship lofts them to Estia, at this altitude a mere spire, light enough in its nanotube structure to bend in the terrible winds. Docking is interesting; the craft is relatively unwieldy and the buffeting provokes in hrm an involuntary tensing unfelt for centuries. In the event of catastrophic failure they would fall fifty kilometers to the ground. Although Heimgarð possessed the means to slow hrs descent, hse would not be able to survive the surface conditions, as hse easily had on Plouton. The thought is a novel one, and some part of hrm stirs uneasily.

The maneuver proceeds without incident, and they debark unmindful of the roaring about them. The platform takes them down swiftly, converting their kinetic potential into electricity as it brakes. The column widens from flue to hearth as they descend, for the growing pressure more than compensates for the weaker winds. At its bottom, enormous blocks of hewn stone have been laid: quarried from the foundations of the earth, they are stacked kilometers high, the cornerstones upon which nanotubes of exotic composition, interwoven like chain mail against the crushing world-dragon, rise through seething murk of slowly diminishing pressure toward the habitable skies.

It is an expressway to hell, but Heimgarð feels a faint relief in setting boots upon it. Perhaps hrs hosts realized that hse would be more comfortable with a structure that is anchored to the ground.

"The realm of the clouds is ours, but we must claim the surface. Volcanism and the ravaging atmosphere assail the land from below and above, yet it is our nature as humans to tread ground and look into the sky. Our thick-walled city is but a warren, its parks enlarged caverns lit by artifice. You, who know what it is to stand beneath the stars, can comprehend our need to make a home."

Heimgarð looks down the kilometers of shaft, which exhales air warmed by the city below them. Lights may be shining at the bottom, although hrs eyesight is not presently enhanced to see more than an ordinary person's.

The city is as they described it, and hse feels as uncomfortable in its teeming as they anticipated. As many people lived here as inhabited all the rest of Hesperos, each of them (it was worth recalling) used to such conditions. Why was this worse than living in an orbital habitat? Heimgarð could not say.

When they tell hrm what they want, hse knows they are not telling hrm everything. What they say is alarming enough.

"We want you to treat with them. They will heed you, as they do not us."

Heimgarð protests that hse knows nothing of them, has no experience dealing with such beings. Hse also declares that the Gardeners will have to be more open with hrm about the nature of this mission. They nod and tell hrm more, though it is not the information hse needs.

"Is this why you brought me here?" Hse does not mean it resentfully, for those feelings seem distant from the person hse is.

And they show hrm images of Eridu, as vivid as though hse were gazing upon it in the cloud-cropped future of their dreams. The city stands ringed by a wall eight kilometers high, above which the now-skimmed cauldron of Hesperos's atmosphere drifts over a dome that admits great slanting beams of sunlight. Twelve hundred square kilometers of flat and gently rolling land, Eridu bristled with structures—residential ziggurats, buildings shaped like warped planes, lifted wings, cylinders and prisms, all interlaced with tubes and ribbons of transport routes—and winding swathes of parkland, rumpled green or flat blue.

"We can tell you, for any given second, how many people are alive in the Gardens. But we cannot tell you what proportion of humanity this constitutes. Do the thermal signatures from Selene bespeak surviving settlements or merely the half-functioning life systems, still emitting heat long after those it once warmed are gone? Are there survivors sheltered within the moons circling Phaiton? Or are we behind the Parasol the sole redoubt of humanity? To reflect upon this is to understand why we must return to environments that maintain themselves. Planetary surfaces are not immune to disaster but they are safer than habitats and warrens beneath frozen moons."

Heimgarð's memories of breathing the air of a sun-warmed planet are too distant to be brought into focus, but hse nods. They take this for general assent, and after further thanks hse is given a spacecraft, again one that wraps around hrs back and chest, and bade farewell. When the propitious moment arrives, hse is launched—on boosters that drop away like husks once they have attained the proper velocity—and sails out from behind the Parasol and into brilliant sunlight. Carefully timed thrusts produce immediate deceleration and hse drops toward the Sun, into a transfer orbit that will take hrm around and into an encounter with Hermaon, the iron planet, and its underworld.

4

In distance and time, it is Heimgarð's shortest journey, but the weeks of travel are disconcerting in a way hse has never felt before. There is no radio transmission demanding an explanation for hrs approach, for it is clear what Heimgarð intends. No decisions confront hrm: three landing platforms lie flush upon the surface of Hermaon, equally spaced along the equator, and the calculus of ballistics makes clear which one hse shall use.

In some realms, choice is superfluous. Beyond the limits of logic and mathematics, however, certainty dissolves: what steps hse must afterward take seem not just unsure but unfathomable.

Certainly the kobolds offer nothing: even a challenge would give hrm some information, but they are silent. Heimgarð takes the trouble to brake no harder than an unmodified human could bear; it is hrs message to them, which is received without comment. Hrs boots touch down upon the flat surface and gravity reaches once more through hrs soles. Carefully hse unstraps hrs spacecraft and sets it beside hrm. The nightside landscape, visible only by the infrared emissions of its cooling surface, allows hrm the pleasure of a familiarly close horizon.

To look about for sensors would only show foolishness; of course hse is being watched. What do they expect from their uninvited visitor, whose identity they have doubtless inferred? Perhaps the traveler who crossed the planetary spheres, gaze fixed and hair streaming, shall now stride puissant to the door and rap upon it. There is no door, although a featureless structure rises three meters above the platform at its eastern edge. Hse turns to face it and its near side slides open, disclosing darkness within. Six steps—hse savors the act of walking again upon a small cold world—take hrm to the threshold and into the space. The floor drops swiftly away, and hse descends.

Heimgarð counts the meters as hse plummets—the accelerometer nestled in some equivalent of hrs inner ear allows this almost without effort—and notes the slowly rising temperature. The interior of Hermaon is molten, the silicates of its crust slow to conduct heat: the temperature is still well below the freezing point of carbon dioxide, but if the capsule falls far enough, it will open upon tremendous heat. Heimgarð is calculating how long hrs systems can keep hrs organic tissues from cooking when it begins slowing to a stop. With a hiss—there is air beyond—the panel slides open, upon a space radiating neither heat nor light.

Hse steps forward into the darkness. Hrs boots ring on the floor beneath hrm, and hrs mind builds a picture from the returning echoes. The chamber is low-ceilinged, large, and filled with kobolds. They stand facing hrm, unmoving.

Most of their bodies are insulated by thick skin or clothing, but their eyes emit heat enough to glow infraredly in the gloom. How many are there? Although Heimgarð's greater height affords a vantage, their serried ranks soon disappear behind the small planet's curvature.

"*Tell us what you want,*" they say.

There is air enough in the chamber for Heimgarð to speak aloud. "The government of the Sheltered Gardens seeks your assistance in a project of great importance to them. They have authorized me to negotiate with you for this."

"*Untrue.*" The voices now come not in unison but as a ragged chorus, rebounding off the low ceiling like scattered particles. "*They want our gold.*"

It is a moment before Heimgarð is able to comprehend this. "This project will indeed require large amounts of various heavy metals, but the combined masses of Hesperos and Aris are more than—"

"*The Gardeners want our gold, which we will not surrender. So they have thrown you to us in propitiation.*"

"Why would those of the Sheltered Gardens seek the resources of Hermaon? Both worlds—"

"*They wish to hoard their own.*"

"*They know not how to mine it at such pressures.*"

"*They dropped you down the shaft to spy on us. They care not if you never return.*"

With a shock hse realizes that this is true. Hse had been outfitted with the means to send a continuous data stream back to the Gardens, plus—hse now guessed—mobile devices to record such data and maneuver to dispatch it should transmission be blocked. Had the kobolds detected and disabled these?

This will require thinking, which Heimgarð is not now free to do. Hse ventures farther into the chamber, stepping between kobolds who turn their heads to regard hrm but do not otherwise move.

"How do you suppose those of the Gardens propose to dispossess you of yours? How am I, unfamiliar with your world and even theirs, to accomplish this for them?"

"*Guile.*"

"*Trickery.*"

"*A stratagem, not yet apparent.*"

"*Humans are deceitful, in thrall to the sexual strategies that drove their animal ancestors and drive them just as blindly. They jostle and kick for social supremacy and mating opportunities, fitfully aware of how this appears yet unable to transcend it. They injure their societies in the interest of those few with whom they share genes, and will injure them in pursuit of opportunities to breed further. They are suspicious, irrational, and destructive, eventually to all but most immediately to those unlike themselves.*

"*They know we do not trust them, so they sent you.*"

"But I am human," Heimgarð points out.

And the space about him erupts in reverberating gales of eerie laughter.

Heimgarð ranges through their realm, which they do not forbid. There are passageways too small for hrm to enter, their endpoints unknown. Kobolds bustle past, sometimes carrying implements. One turns to regard hrm as it passes, gaze fixed upon hrm as its head rotates through 180 degrees. A many-toned muttering, language (if that's what it is) unfamiliar, rises as hse moves through crowds of greater density.

If they have a leader, it is not coming forward. Kobolds once were people, Heimgarð was told, but that may not be the case for those now before hrm. Hse is not certain whether they are behaving like humans, for hse cannot tell what most of them are doing. Heimgarð sees one that it looking steadily at hrm, which hse takes as permission to address. "What is it you seek?" hse asks.

"*We seek to protect what is ours.*"

"You must aspire to be more than just watchdogs. What do you *want*?" But the kobold merely repeats itself, and Heimgarð moves on.

"What do you want?" he asks another.

"*We want to be left alone.*"

"Have you not been left to your solitude? Only I have come, and you chose to admit me." But to this there is no reply.

One expresses itself clearly: "*We don't have to say what we want.*"

After that hse wanders without hindering nor suffering hindrance from the strange creatures hastening past hrm. Possibly they are extending their domain, although hse can detect neither the vibrations nor airborne dust that would suggest excavation anywhere nearby. How far does this netherworld reach? How numerous its denizens?

Sometimes hse moves through great open plazas, sometimes down long colonnades or passageways narrow as tunnels. Hse ventures far enough that the curvature beneath hrm becomes measurable, and numbers collect in an unremarked register of hrs mind. Heimgarð is certain there is information they are not giving hrm, and studies the low ceilings and curving floors, the pressure and temperature of the air currents that brush past, the behavior of the kobolds hse speaks to or glimpses from afar. When the surmise materializes, it halts hrm with the abruptness of a hand against hrs chest. For a long moment hse simply stands motionless, running the figures repeatedly through hrs mind and wondering at the absurd implication.

"All right," hse announces. Hse does not address hrs words in any direction, for hse knows that all are listening. "Take me to the realm below. There is no point trying to hide it."

Perhaps they have been prepared for this moment. Certainly they do not feign incomprehension. Heimgarð is conducted to an elevator shaft, one that leads down rather than up. Hse enters the capsule and it drops through the floor, accelerating at a rate that hse studies closely. The capsule is transparent and is enveloped in darkness, but hse knows—and a beam from hrs helmet confirms—that hse is descending not down a tunnel but rather through a vast emptiness.

There are faint sources of light, and massive structures—girders and struts—discernible to hrs instruments across hundreds of kilometers. By now hse knows what hse will find, so hse does not strain to look straight down. Within minutes hse has data enough to guess when deceleration will begin, and at what point hse will touch bottom.

The door slides silently open and hse steps out onto level ground. The air is cool, but significantly thicker than in the chambers above. The ground is smooth but slightly yielding, and after a few steps hse feels it crunch like sand beneath hrs soles.

The gravitational pull is 1.00.

The lights overhead are dim as stars, but illuminated globes atop poles, like streetlamps from the early Industrial Era, dot the landscape, casting long intersecting shadows. Kobolds are everywhere, most of them much smaller than what hse has earlier seen. They enter and exit ornate structures that line thoroughfares, walking alone or in groups. A wheeled vehicle passes hrm.

The horizon is close, so Heimgarð does not have to venture far before features appear over it: a great coliseum, a range of hills, a large lake or perhaps a small sea. Hse approaches its shore and continues forward, wondering, until hse stands in its shallows: liquid water. Ships ply its surface, some under sail, and vibrations tell hrm of submarine vessels moving beneath, negotiating an environment populated (dissolved organics tell hrm) by marine life swimming or floating within its almost lightless depths.

Were hse to circle the shore and continue walking, hse would eventually circumnavigate this ornament, perfectly positioned around the center of its hollowed planet. It is a world of small compass, but a world.

There are other elevators, paired shafts that ferry a constant stream of kobolds up and down. None of them look at Heimgarð, although they clearly perceive hrm. Hrs own shaft stands ready upon hrs return; perhaps it was assembled expressly for hrm.

Hse rides it back up and looks out upon the Kobolds who await him as the door slides open. To address those present is, hse understands, to address them all.

Hse says, "I won't ask what you have done; I can see that much. Nor will I ask why you did it. Instead I will ask once more: What is it you want?"

"*We want a world. We want to feel the ground beneath our feet. The weightlessness of space is not for people, and the sensation of being flung against a rotating surface is not true gravity.*"

"And so you have constructed that . . . eggshell sphere around a kernel of degenerate matter? A black hole? Contracting upon itself like an infinite arch, at exactly the distance you wished?"

"*As you infer. It gave us a World, though small, on—or in—a planet too scant to provide it otherwise.*"

"And the technology to wreak such upheavals: Has this anything to do with what befell the Earth?"

"*No. Yet the Gardeners would never believe that: In their too-human fearfulness and imprudence they would draw an irresistible conclusion. Knowledge of our works they could not handle, so cannot ever learn.*"

"Yet you admitted me into your midst, and now I know."

"*Yes.*"

Silence follows this. Neither Heimgarð nor the kobolds cross their arms, square their stance: they consider themselves human, but are not so bound to their primate biology as to ape such bellicose posturing.

Heimgarð betrays nothing, but in fact harbors little to betray. *I did not ask for this*, hse wants to say. *I do not wish to wield this club, yet now it rests in my hand.*

"You must," hse says, "have thought of this. So what would you have me do?"

And after more silence, they tell hrm.

5

The voyage out is not a return; nothing ever is.

Plouton-Charon lies more than a hundred degrees off Heimgarð's course; each second takes hrm farther from it. The Gardens are also swinging behind the Sun; hse will attend no ceremonies celebrating hrs success. The kobolds would in any case likely forbid it: their concern for the safety of their secret would preclude giving the Gardeners any chance to lay hold of hrm.

Heimgarð will not see the effects of the deal hse hammered out, and in hrs fatigue—a surprisingly organic response—hse does not much care. The hammer, hse dully reflects, feels the impact as much as the substance it works.

The kobolds will keep their "gold": none of Hermaion's remaining metals will be sent to the Gardeners, who will never know why. Within weeks, however, kobolds by the hundreds will depart for Hesperos—not for any of the tall cities, but to the raging planet itself—and begin quarrying its own resources. Iron, copper, and more run in veins through its crust, waiting to be mined by anything willing to labor in darkness and gravity. Perhaps they will even enjoy it.

In return they have exacted their own price: the broker's eternal exile. Heimgarð is to leave the inner system, never to return. But as recompense—and perhaps to speed hrm on hrs way—hse has been rebuilt, by techs whose skills even the Gardeners likely cannot match: outfitted with greater fuel capacity, energy storage, stress tolerance, resistance to temperature extremes. And given a destination.

Blue Neptune, smaller and denser than tilted Ouranos, was once inhabited by humans. The Tritonides are gone, the moon's surface too cold for anything to be operating beneath its surface, and the few structures orbiting the planet can be confirmed, even from this distance, as lifeless hulks. Yet the kobolds wonder: they have calculated the distance from the planetary core at which the gravity is identical to Earth's, and pondered the stratum's dynamics: the great heat below, the great cold above, the tremendous winds and pressure. They believe it possible that humans, the remnants of the Triton settlement, may live down there.

Certainly they do not imagine that a spherical shell such as their own, but immensely larger, could have been constructed with the resources of a faltering colony. But a ribbon circling Neptune's equator, perhaps only a kilometer wide, would be three orders of magnitude simpler. "Think of it as a bridge," they told him. "Suspended over an icy hell, a bridge attached not to abutments but arching round to join itself, floating freely in the depths." Such a construct would be wildly unstable, but if it were joined by two more rings, all at right angle to each other . . . the kobolds' models said it could be possible.

Heimgarð imagined such a folly—a frail gyroscope forever steadying itself under incredible stresses—and doubted greatly that it ever existed. But the underground creatures had their price, and Heimgarð was a part of it. The frenetic makeshifts of the Gardens—the forges of Hesperos; the coming construction of Yggdrasil—were not destined for hrm.

Although the kobolds insist that a society surviving deep within Neptune's atmosphere would possess sufficient insulation to prevent measurable heat from reaching the surface, the planet is as cold as it has always been. Their touching hopes are sign enough of their essential humanity; hrs bleak certainty suggests something different.

Hse rises from Hermaion on tongues of flame, accelerating steadily. Gravity, or its simulacrum, presses up against hrs soles. Does the sensation afford comfort to the human creature?

The voyage out will last significantly longer, for the climb out of the Sun's deep gravity well reduces velocity. And there will be less to occupy hrs thoughts: no radio signals to listen for, no curiosity at a summons.

Will hse be lonely? It is a strange thought. If hrs two precursor minds could separate and occupy opposite sides of hrs helmet, perhaps they would soon tire of each other. Perhaps it was the fact that hse clearly is not quite human that allowed hrm to mediate between two mistrustful populations.

And perhaps solitude will someday grow burdensome. Hse will certainly have time to find out.

Heimgarð accelerates away from the grasping Sun, hrs straight course bent by its presence. Eventually the engines will cut off and the illusion of gravity vanish. Hrs trajectory will become an orbit—one of cometary magnitude, a centuries-long ellipse, were it not someday to intersect a world.

Like a rising spark, the sentinel departs the circle of light, into a wider darkness.

I'VE COME TO MARRY THE PRINCESS

HELENA BELL

Before Jack can apologize to Nancy, she has to believe that dragons exist.

Nancy's mad at him because they were supposed to perform a skit at the talent show and he stood her up. They've been practicing it for two summers. It's called "I've Come to Marry the Princess." When Jack didn't show, Nancy had to go on stage all by herself. He didn't ditch her on purpose; his dragon egg was hatching and he needed to be there. Jack thinks Nancy would forgive him if he told her this, but she hasn't given him the chance.

Nancy said her parents would give him a ride home at the end of camp this year and he doesn't know if the offer is still good. He hopes it is. It would give him a chance to apologize, the two of them sitting on the gray velvet bench seat of her mother's station wagon, the baby dragon between them.

"I told you dragons were real," Jack would say.

"Dragons eat people, you know."

Jack arrived at camp six years and three weeks ago. His mother dropped him off at his cabin with his trunk, book bag, and dragon egg. The trunk held three bathing suits, fourteen t-shirts, ten pairs of shorts, white socks, and underwear, each with Jack's name written in black permanent marker in thick, block letters. Inside the book bag were five books from the Craven County Public School recommended summer reading list, a Walkman, various toiletries, an Uno deck, stationery, envelopes, stamps, and four bags of chocolate bars he'd stolen from his older brother Robert. Robert was going to a different camp, in the mountains, and Jack knew Robert wouldn't notice anything was missing until he got there.

Sometimes Jack still gets letters from Robert. Robert ends each one with a running tally of how many chocolate bars Jack owes him now. It's in the millions. "Because of interest," Robert says.

Jack also gets letters from his parents. They ask him questions about sailing and motorboating and archery and tell him to be good, they'll be there to pick him up at the end of the summer. They never do. Every August Jack drags his belongings to a new cabin and different campers arrive. In the fall they learn to play instruments: harp, violin, piano. In the spring it's always math camp, science camp, or historical re-enactment. There are two weeks in the winter when adults fill the cabins. They play soccer and baseball, jump in the river, and stay up all night in the mess hall playing loud music. His counselor says next year they're opening up a space camp, but he's been saying that for a while now. Jack has had the same counselor each summer for seven years; he never remembers Jack's name.

"This your first year?" he asks. "Don't worry. You're going to love it. It can be rough at first, but at the end of four weeks, no one ever wants to leave. You staying for one session or two? Most of us stay for two."

In January and February the camp lets in high schoolers and college students to practice standardized tests: PSAT, LSAT, SAT, DAT, MCAT, PCAT, and VCAT. Jack wasn't very good at them at first, but he's been catching on. Before Nancy stopped talking to him, she lent him her *Cosmo* magazines for their quizzes. Nancy said there's an art to multiple-choice questions. There's always the right answer, the wrong answer that you want to pick anyway, the silly answer, and the answer that leads to the inevitable tragedy of human experience. If you read enough of them, you can figure out which one is which by the way they're phrased, or the way they're ordered. When in doubt, pick C, she says. Nancy said she hasn't studied for a history test in three years because she knows exactly how to find out the key result of the Battle of New Orleans just by the way the teacher uses conjunctions. Jack told her there was no result. The war was over before the battle even started. He knew this because he had to pretend to die on a hill, his foot rotting from gangrene. Then the cook got mad at them because they stole too much cheese for special effects and they had to re-enact treaty signings the next year. And the year after that and the year after. Jack hated it. All they did was stand around in wool coats and sweat.

Even though he's not very good, Jack has always secretly preferred standardized test camp. They stay inside and read and take snack breaks. He also likes the logic puzzles.

A camper with access to the theater hut has six chances to apologize to a girl. The hut holds the following items: carrots, daffodils, earmuffs, and a fire extinguisher. The following requirements must be satisfied:

> *The girl does not like vegetables.*
> *The girl does not like flowers.*

The girl's ears are quite warm.
The girl is not on fire.

Which one of the following could be a complete and accurate list of ways the boy could be forgiven?

The dragon egg was a gift from his grandmother. She said she'd found it in the Wal-Mart parking lot, near the cart return. Jack used to get letters from her, but she died at the end of the first summer. Jack thinks that's why his parents forgot to come pick him up.

When Jack and his mother first arrived, they drove past the girls' cabins so they could say hello to one of the counselors. She was related to Jack, a first cousin, but he'd never met her before and had a hard time remembering her name. Whenever he saw her he always nodded and called her "Cuz" because that sounded like something Robert would say. She nodded back. She could never remember his name either. "Pleased to meet you, Jeremy."

She introduced him to some of the girls in her cabin, girls who were about Jack's age. Some of them looked as annoyed to be there as he was, which was comforting in its own way.

"They seem nice," his mother said.

Jack's cabin was not as nice as the girls' cabin. The screen door was falling off its hinges and the wood smelled of damp and rot. Jack's mom kept saying it had "character." The bunk beds were all different heights and every surface had been written on in multi-colored markers: messages from previous campers and dirty limericks and crude drawings. Jack thought the messages in the girls' cabin were probably nicer and more intelligent, with cartoon hearts and flowers to match their comforters and Laura Ashley sheets. He was wrong. Nancy told him the girls' cabins were just as bad-word filled as the boys, that's just the way camps were.

"But our diagrams are more anatomically correct," she said.

Jack's counselor introduced himself, and then the other boys. Jack watched as the counselor patted each of them on the back and surreptitiously pulled back the collars of their shirts where mothers had written out names like Bob and Timothy and George in the same black permanent marker that Jack's mom used. Jack wondered if the counselor had his name in big block letters somewhere on his clothes too. Just in case he forgot it. Maybe there was a store they all went to that sold pre-named clothing.

When his mother finally left ("Be good", "Okay," "Make friends," "Okay," "Have fun," "Okay," "Don't get eaten by a bear," "Okay"), Jack grabbed his dragon egg and went out into the woods looking for a place to hide it.

• • •

This is how I've Come to Marry the Princess goes:

Jack knocks on a pretend door. Nancy answers. She's a guard.

"I've come to marry the princess," Jack says.

"The princess?"

"Yes, the princess."

"Okay. I'll go ask her."

The guard turns around to talk to the king. That's Jack now.

"A knight's at the door. He says he's come to marry the princess."

"The princess?" Jack says.

"Yes, the princess."

"Okay. I'll go ask her."

Then the King tells this to the queen who finally goes to ask the princess. That's Jack again.

"There's a knight at the door. He says he wants to marry you," Nancy says.

"Marry me?" Jack says.

"Yes. What do you think?"

"No, no, no, a thousand times no."

They rotate again until Jack is the knight and the guard tells him No, no, no, a thousand times no.

"Then you must die!" and the knight stabs the guard with a foam sword.

Then he knocks on the door again.

When the egg didn't hatch that first summer, Jack wondered if it was defective. His grandmother had been certain it would hatch, and yet by September it was just as dull and solid as it could be. In the winter he asked one of the men in his cabin to take a look at it. He was a recently divorced ER doctor whose therapist said fresh air and exercise and socialization would do him good. He arrived the first day with a duffel bag full of mass-market paperbacks and refused to speak to anyone else in the cabin except Jack.

Jack asked him if he knew anything about eggs. The man asked if he meant dinosaur eggs. His son used to like dinosaurs.

"It's not a dinosaur egg."

"Robin?"

"No."

"Chicken?"

"No."

"Platypus? Snake? Ostrich?"

Jack pulled the egg out of his backpack and showed him. "Dragon. Don't know what kind."

The ER doctor rolled the egg around on the floor and knocked on its shell. "Looks more like a rock to me."

The doctor suggested that he place it somewhere cool and dry, where it could get plenty of sunlight. Either it would hatch or it wouldn't. No way to tell for sure without cracking it open to see what was actually inside.

Jack met Nancy the second summer. He went to his cousin's cabin on the first day of camp because he knew his mother would want him to. He went early, when he knew there wouldn't be many girls for his cousin to introduce him to. There was a freckled girl named Anna, and Nancy. Nancy didn't talk.

"Don't worry," his cousin told them, "it's his first year too. Isn't it, Justin."

"Sure," he said.

His cousin told him Nancy never talked to anyone. Her parents were hoping camp would help.

"My parents thought camp would help too," Jack said.

Nancy didn't talk to anyone the first week, nor the second. The boys in Jack's cabin said Nancy had escaped from juvenile prison and was hiding out. Other cabins had their own rumors.

Nancy was a Kennedy.

Nancy had her tongue ripped out by wolves.

Nancy ripped out her own tongue.

Nancy had tattoos.

Nancy had no parents.

Nancy had seventeen parents, the result of a series of divorces, kidnappings, and illegal adoptions.

Nancy was an alien.

Nancy was a witch.

Nancy didn't exist.

Jack thought Nancy had it pretty easy. She could join any group she wanted, do anything she wanted, and no one would stop her because they didn't know what she'd do to them. One time a girl pushed her into the dirt and Nancy got up and then shook the girl's hand. She didn't smile or frown; she gripped the girl's hand in both of hers and then walked away. Later the girl broke her nose after being hit in the face with the boom of a sailboat. Nancy wasn't there, and that's when the witch rumor started. But when the girl with the broken nose came back from the hospital, she told everyone that Nancy was just a nice girl who didn't talk much. And the rumor went away.

"People aren't nearly as mean as other people think," Nancy told him.

The boys in Jack's cabin weren't mean, but there were too many of them and Jack had a hard time keeping them straight. So he divided them into groups. There were the boys who had been coming to Camp all their lives and already had all the friends they wanted to make. Jack called them the Jonathans. And the boys who were there for the first time but already knew how to sail or play sports or who had mothers who sent care packages every day filled with candy and Mad magazines and soda other contraband. Those were the Roberts. They were always more popular than the Jonathans, until their newness wore off and they became Jonathans themselves.

"This your first summer?" Jonathan asked Jack. "It must be. I'd remember you. Your parents send you with anything good?"

Jack had three trunks now. Summer, winter, and in-between. The summer trunk held five bathing suits, six shorts, six t-shirts, and twenty pairs of underwear. Every time he sent his laundry out with the other campers, more clothes came back. Sometimes they had other boys' names written in the collars: Barnabus, Crispin, Derrek, and Pierre. Jack never wore these clothes. He was too scared of running into their original owners. Sometimes he wondered if he should take their names too, then maybe people would remember him; maybe another mother would come and pick him up.

That first day, Jack's mother set up an account for him at the camp store. She said he could buy whatever he wanted, within reason. It'd make his father happy if he got some camp clothes: a hat, sweatshirt, maybe even some of those rubber sandals to wear in the river with the Morehead wheel sewn in white thread on the ankle.

By spring of his fourth year Jack had run up a tab of $1,847. He didn't only buy clothes: the store also sold stamps, toiletries, and a stale tasting candy bar some camper's father invented that no one ever ate. Even the ducks wouldn't touch it. Around Christmas the store sold ornaments, wrapping paper, and better tasting chocolate. Jack liked the store best in February. They had an entire display case of No. 2 pencils stacked in a giant No. 2 pencil pyramid. You had to ask for help to take one. Jack bought several throughout the day, every day, just hoping it would crumble when the cashier reached over to get him one. It never did.

When the knight knocks on the door the second time, the king answers.

"I've come to marry the princess."

"The princess?"

"Yes, the princess."

"Alright, I'll go ask her."

Nancy was the only one who remembered Jack from year to year. "I've got a really good memory," she said. "I'm constantly correcting people when they tell a story wrong. Details are important, unless they're made up."

Nancy told Jack he should try the administrator's office and ask for his paperwork. "You would have to be registered for each session, each camp, otherwise they wouldn't let you stay," she explained. "Bills, medical records, test scores, all of them have to be recorded in the system. Ask for it, any of it, and it'll collapse."

Sometimes Nancy suggested that he just walk out the gate and down the highway. He could steal a horse from the barn, or one of the boats. Jack didn't think those were very feasible, and he didn't have a very good sense of direction.

Why not the bus? She asked. It dropped campers off at the Episcopal Church right downtown. Didn't he say he lived on the river? He could walk from there. If he didn't try, then it was his fault.

"When I was seven years old," Jack said, "I went to a school that put younger students at tables with older students. Lunch was delivered to the head of the table, and it was the job of the older student to pass them out. That year, I was at a long table. There were two head students, and twelve of us. They passed out eleven plates. I guess each one of them thought the other one had taken care of me. I was reading a book, so I didn't notice until I could hear the scrape of everyone's knives. I waited until someone noticed. No one did. I thought about raising my hand, but I didn't know which one of them to ask. By then it had been so long that I thought I had to think of a reason why I'd waited. They were going to have to ask the kitchen for another plate. One of them would get in trouble. So I kept waiting. I pretended to keep reading, and then I'd have an excuse. Then lunch was over, and I was still hungry, but no one had to be embarrassed about it."

"That's stupid," she said.

"It happened again the next day, and I kept reading. I learned to stuff an apple in my pocket in the morning. I ate bigger breakfasts. Finally, by the third week, I spoke up. 'Excuse me?' I said to the older one, a girl. She seemed nice. 'I don't have a plate.'"

"Did she give you one?"

"It turned out I was at the wrong table. By the time she'd straightened out, my friend William had eaten his lunch and mine, like he'd been doing every day prior. He was mad at me after that and wouldn't talk to me."

"There are these boys in my school," Nancy said. "They're on the swim team. They're always hungry. After lunch they walk around the cafeteria and go up to any girl who still has fries on her plate, or pizza. 'You really want to eat that?' they say. 'You don't want a paunch, do you?' They always said 'paunch.' We learned it in English class. We all liked the way our lips quivered when we said it. Paunch. 'Come on,' they said. 'We're helping you out.' Some girls, they just hold up their trays when they see those boys coming."

"Why didn't the school do something?"

"No one complained. The girls didn't mind. Some girls, they got extra fries just so they could give them away. Of course, some girls spat on theirs, or brought in extra hot peppers or other things to dice up and put on their pizza, just to see what would happen. One boy got sick; he threw up all during fifth period."

"Did they stop?"

"No. They were stubborn and stupid, like you."

Last summer, Jack did try the bus. It took him all the way into town, where the campers' parents were waiting at the Episcopal Church parking lot. Jack could see the top of his house over the trees. The driver wouldn't let him off until a guardian signed for him. They waited all day. Jack asked the driver if he could go inside the church and call his house from the office.

"How do I know you'll call your mother? You could be calling a stranger."

"You could call."

"Camp told me to sit on the bus and wait till all the campers' mothers came and signed for them. Can't leave the bus."

They waited all night and the next morning the bus driver took him back to camp. A counselor checked his name off a clipboard.

"You're going to love it here, Jack. What instrument do you play? Did you forget it at home? Don't worry, we have spares."

In June, when he saw Nancy, she sighed. "When I never see you again, I'll know that something good happened."

There's always a reason a boy finds a dragon egg. Jack didn't have a reason. His grandmother gave it to him even though he'd asked for a soccer ball. All the boys at camp would know how to play soccer and he wanted to practice before he went.

"It's an egg," he said.

"A dragon egg," his grandmother said.

"Does that make a difference?"

"You'll be the only one at camp with one, I'm sure," she said.

"Don't dragons eat people?"

"That's just a rumor. Make friends with it."

He thought about telling people it was a soccer ball. A special one. That was heavy. And didn't roll very well. And clinked when you shook it ("Don't do that," his grandmother said, "it'll get mad at you").

The only thing Jack liked about the egg was the thought of having his very own dragon. One that could fly, and speak telepathically, and breathe fire. But after the first summer, and the next, and the next after, he thought maybe his dragon was defective. What kind of dragon would come from a Wal-Mart parking lot?

Jack imagined flying over fields and forests in a dragon-sized silver shopping cart, the balls of his feet balancing on the metal bar as the cart's front end rose and rose, right into the clouds.

"Rawr," he said. "Behold the conquering hero."

When the dragon finally hatched, it was blue. Blue eyes, blue scales, even blue tinted nails at the end of its delicate blue feet. Its wings were membranous wisps that flapped weakly against the dragon's sides.

"Don't worry," he told the dragon. "You'll grow into them. Then you can take us home."

Jack thought long and hard about a name. Names had power. An evil wizard could ensnare his dragon by guessing its true name.

"Pencil," Jack said. "No one would guess that."

He thought about naming it Nancy, but if anyone in his life were to suddenly turn into an evil wizard, it would be her. Then the name wouldn't be hard to guess at all.

The king asks the queen who asks the princess, who still says no, no, no, a thousand times no. The knight kills the king and then asks the queen, kills her, and finally knocks on the princess' door.

"No, no, no, a thousand times no," she says.

The knight kills the princess, sees what he has done, and says "Now I must die!" And he does.

Before the audience has a chance to react, Jack and Nancy get up and repeat the skit, but faster.

Then they do it a third time where the knight kills anyone who answers the door.

They practiced it a dozen times, then two dozen. Sometimes they got mixed up and the king was wearing the princess' wig when he told the knight no. Sometimes both Jack and Nancy were the princess, saying no to each other. Sometimes they were both the knight thrusting swords into each other's bellies.

The skit wasn't original. Robert and his friends performed it in the mountains; that's how Jack knows about it. Even though he's never seen it at his camp, Jack fears another cabin will do the skit before they have a chance.

Nancy says it doesn't matter if theirs is the first, last, or the thousandth I've come to marry the princesses. Theirs will be the best.

It is given that an average camp theater stage is 20' wide and 14' deep.

It is given that Jack suffers from a recurring nightmare in which he forgets to stab Nancy in the stomach and kisses her instead.

Quantity A: The speed Jack can run behind the curtain to vomit in a bucket placed there for just this purpose.

Quantity B: $(x-2y)(x+2y) = 4$.

D. The relationship cannot be determined from the information given.

• • •

Every Sunday night at summer camp, they have devotions. The counselor reads a passage from something inspirational: the bible, *Chicken Soup for the Soul*, a favorite novel. It depends a lot on the counselor. Nancy said her counselor liked to read the embarrassing stories from *Seventeen* magazine so all the girls would know that it wasn't just them who passed gas in front of boys, or got their first period while wearing white jeans.

"The stories are obviously made up," Nancy said. "They have to be. Each Sunday we've been writing our own entries. Our counselor collects them and mails them off. We're going to see which of us can be the first to get in."

This was Nancy's, published a year after the end of camp:

One time I fell flat on my face at the talent show. One second I was holding the microphone in one hand, and a foam sword in the other, trying to think of a joke to tell and when the spotlight hit my face, my knees locked and I fell. As I lay there I could hear a girl in the front row whisper Is she dead? And I said into the microphone: Not yet. Everyone clapped and I got up and walked offstage.

Jack looked forward to Devotions every week and tried to keep it up the rest of the year. The band counselor played violin and lectured on music theory. In standardized test camp they read admission essays that "made the difference." In math and science camp, they went stargazing.

Adult camp had no counselor, so Jack improvised.

"This is what we do: we each tell a story. It has to be a true story. If you don't have one, maybe just tell us about why you're here. I'll start. I'm here because my parents forgot to pick me up."

"I'm here because my house is being tented for termites."

"I was too cheap to go to Bermuda."

"I went to Bermuda. It's overrated."

"I cut a kid's chest open when he came into the ER. He had bullet holes in his chest, up near the neck. He was practically dead. So I cut his chest open. When the surgeon got there, she looked at me and said 'What did you do and why did you do it?' I cut his chest open, through the breast plate. I used a saw. 'What did you do?' the surgeon said. Couldn't she see I didn't know? The kid was dying. I'm a doctor. It's what I do. She said he'd had a heart beat. She wasn't there. She didn't know. 'It's on the chart,' she said. She wouldn't operate. 'You did this,' she said. We scared the nurses. The hospital sent us both to anger management. Later, we got divorced. My therapist thought camp would help."

The doctor left camp the next day. He left Jack his duffel bag full of books. "Sometimes when my wife got called into the ER to do a central line, it wouldn't take too long and she'd be sent home. Only it was too late to go back to sleep, and too early to go to the office, so she told me she'd go to Wal-Mart and wander the aisles. She said the nice thing about Wal-Mart was it was always open and no one would talk to you. After the divorce I would drive by the parking lot looking for her car. I figure when I finally know what to say to her, she'll be there."

"What if she isn't?"

"Then I'll say it to somebody else. Hope that egg of yours hatches, Jack."

The morning after the talent show, Jack stole a dozen fish filets the cook was saving for the end-of-camp banquet. He wrapped them in a dishcloth and brought them out to the woods. He thought they'd help him train Pencil.

"Sit," Jack said. His dragon did nothing.

"Sit," Jack said. And the dragon did nothing.

"Come," Jack said. And the dragon did nothing.

Jack figured that one day he and his dragon would develop telepathy of some sort. He didn't know when that would be.

"Maybe I'll bring you Nancy. You could eat her instead." The dragon bit him.

"You're right, that's not very nice."

When he got back to the cabin, the other boys said Nancy had stopped by to tell him that she'd never forgive him and she hoped he died.

"Your girlfriend was pissed," they said.

"I don't have a girlfriend," Jack said.

"Damn straight," they said.

By lunch everyone was talking about their breakup. About how she'd dumped him. About how she'd thrown bug juice in his face. And how he had cried.

Jack still hadn't seen Nancy. He pictured her throwing bug juice in someone else's face. A pretend Jack: a prop from the theater hut done up in Jack clothes and Jack makeup. He imagined the pretend Jack taking it on the chin. Pretend Jack listened to Nancy's complaints, accepted responsibility, and apologized. Pretend Jack wouldn't have missed the talent show in the first place. He would've left the egg all alone in woods while he pretended to run a foam sword into Nancy's belly, and Nancy pretended to run a foam sword into his. The other campers would remember Pretend Jack the next summer.

"That was a hell of a skit you did last year, Jack," they'd say. "I almost believed you both died up there. I was afraid I'd never see you again."

The dragon grew a little every hour. By dinner it was the size of a large dog. By breakfast the next morning, it was the size of a pony. Jack moved the dragon into the theater hut. It was always empty the last week of camp and Jack didn't want Pencil getting lost in the woods. Jack still didn't know what it ate. He brought it scraps from the mess: spaghetti, meatloaf, scrambled eggs, but Pencil wasn't interested. Maybe dragons didn't need to eat.

• • •

Nancy and Jack tried revising I've Come to Marry the Princess to make it their own. They spent every afternoon in the theater hut. Nancy said it was her favorite place at camp. Jack agreed because it was the only building with air conditioning.

In one of Jack and Nancy's made-up versions, the princess said yes. The knight said "Great!" and they proceeded to spend forty-five minutes making wedding preparations, passing messages through the guard, king, and queen. The climax of the story was when the guard misheard lilies for daffodils and it turned out the knight was allergic and he died from anaphylactic shock. The princess died from grief. Nancy said it was very important that they both die in the skit, otherwise people wouldn't know it was supposed to be funny. If only one of them kicked the bucket, then it'd be a different kind of story entirely.

In another, Nancy and Jack developed an elaborate backstory for the knight and the princess. They wrote it out on cue cards to hold up to the audience to read before the skit so they would know the context.

The knight and princess went on a quest together. They fell in love and the knight has finally returned to marry her as he promised, only the princess is really mad it took him so long to get here.

"What if he had a good reason," Jack asked. "Maybe he went on another quest."

"Then he should have brought her with him," Nancy said. "That's what you're supposed to do in these situations."

In another, Nancy played all the parts. Jack stayed behind the curtain. Tech crew. This was Jack's favorite version. The only time he appeared on stage was to drag Nancy's body off when she died for the last time. If he wore all black, no one would be able to see him at all.

"Just imagine the entire audience in their underwear," Nancy said. "And remember that no one will remember you anyway."

"They will if I throw up all over the first row."

In another, Nancy answered the door as a dragon, who ate Jack and then the princess.

"Maybe it's a nice dragon," Jack said.

"Don't be stupid. Dragons eat people. It's what they do."

In the end, they decided the original version was best.

"But we can keep practicing until you get over your stage fright," Nancy said. "If you want. I don't mind."

Each evening, Jack decides to go to Nancy's cabin first thing in the morning and explain everything. He always chickens out. She'll want to see Pencil. She'll want to know why he didn't tell her about Pencil before. She'll tell his cousin. His cousin will tell the government. The government will take Pencil and perform experiments in Nevada.

Finally Jack writes a letter to his mother. "If it's not too much trouble," he says, "please pick me up early this year. Please come get me on Sunday morning, before everyone else leaves. Before 10 a.m. if possible. I don't like being the last one." He knows when his mother picks him up, she'll ask him why he didn't say anything before. "I didn't feel that way before," he'll say.

After Jack mails the letter, he feels good. Good enough to walk by Nancy's cabin to ask for her address so they can keep in touch. He'll write her a letter when he gets home. "I didn't need you after all." When Pencil is grown, he'll go visit. They can go on quests. They'll be friends again. Pencil won't eat anyone. He won't be that kind of dragon.

His cousin tells him she's not there. " How'd you like your first year at camp, Jonathan? Did you love it? Everyone loves it. This is my twelfth summer, you know. If I had a choice, I'd never leave."

"People with choices always say that." Jack looks for Nancy on the pier. He looks for her at the soccer fields, baseball, the archery and riflery ranges. No one has seen her. She's still mad at him.

"Girls," the boys say. "They get mad and stay mad. It's what they do."

Jack looks for her everywhere and at lunch he waits by the flagpole as all the cabins stream past him so he can catch her walking in. She never shows.

Jack runs to the theater hut even though he knows everything will be fine. The door is closed and everything is quiet.

Nancy believes (C) that dragons exist. When she meets the dragon, it (C) doesn't eat her. Nancy (C) teaches the dragon tricks. They become (C) good friends. Nancy (C) forgives Jack. (C) Jack's mother picks him up at the end of the summer. (C) Everyone lives happily ever after.

The afternoon before the talent show, Jack and Nancy decided to do the original version of the skit: *I've come to marry the princess. I'll go ask her. No, no, no, a thousand times no.*

"You'll be there, right? You won't chicken out? I'm counting on you. I'll never forgive you if you leave me up there all by myself."

Jack knocks. "I've come to marry the princess," he says.

He knocks again. "I've come to rescue the princess."

He knocks a third time. "I'm going on a quest, and I would like the princess to come with me if she would be so inclined."

Jack knows that Nancy will open the door and forgive him. He believes it with the certainty of choice; there are no other options.

"He's such a sweet dragon," she'll say. "Why didn't you say anything before?"

SOMETHING HAPPENED HERE, BUT WE'RE NOT QUITE SURE WHAT IT WAS

PAUL McAULEY

The origin story we like to tell ourselves is that our little town was founded by a grumpy loner name of Joe Gordon, who one day parked his RV at the spot where a ceramic road left by an unknown long-lost Elder Culture cut across the new two-lane blacktop between Port of Plenty and the open-cast iron mine at Red Rocks. He named his crossroads campsite Joe's Corner, set up a couple of picnic tables, and commenced to sell coffee, hot dogs, candy bars, and e-cigarettes and rolling tobacco to the passing trade and the first explorers of the City of the Dead.

Joe Gordon had come up and out three years after people first set foot on First Foot. A lanky, morose man from Hoboken, New Jersey, he peers with narrow suspicion out of the only known photograph of him and his makeshift truck stop, as if wondering how much he should charge for the liberty of having his picture taken. By then, the shuttle cycling between Earth and First Foot was bringing up ten thousand people every three weeks. Too many people for Joe's liking: He'd spent just two months in Port of Plenty before striking out into the backcountry, and when other people started to make themselves at home around his crossroads he moved on again, heading deeper into the dry heart of the planet's largest continent. We know that he worked for a time at the copper mine at Mount Why Not, but after that his trail goes cold. One story has it that he burned his ID and joined a group of homesteading Sovereign Citizens; another claims that he set up a road tavern on the far side of the Badlands and was shot dead in a brawl or a robbery. He left behind his name, a story slowly fading to myth, and the photograph which—enlarged, retouched, and printed on canvas—hangs in the reception area of our community center, a steel-framed glass box erected just last year next door to the ragstone bunker of the Unitarian church whose spire, three steel I-beams welded into a skinny pyramid and topped by an aluminum weather vane burnished by sun and sandstorms, is visible for miles around in our flat desert territory.

Joe's Corner is approaching its thirtieth anniversary now. We are some three thousand souls, with a school and a small clinic; a strip mall anchored by a Rexall's; a sheriff's office and a volunteer fire department; two charge stations (one of them a Toyota franchise); three churches; six motels; a dozen bars, coffeehouses, and restaurants; a solar farm and a nine-hole golf course; a small factory that fabricates mining equipment; and a workshop turning out handmade souvenirs of the City of the Dead, mostly for the export trade. The community center houses a small library and a cinema club that just closed a season of classic Westerns with Quentin Tarantino's *The Hateful Eight*. At a lodge run by a couple from New Mexico, guests pay six hundred bucks a night to sleep in tar-paper shacks, wallow in black mud baths, and eat vegan Mexican-Chinese food. They come here for the silence, panoramic views of alien constellations in night skies untainted by light pollution, and, of course, to explore the tombs of the City of the Dead.

There are several million tombs scattered across fifty thousand square kilometers, built from small, round-edged clay bricks that some believe to have been excreted by the creatures that constructed them, the so-called Ghostkeepers. We call them tombs because they appear to memorialize the dead of the Ghostkeepers, although no bodies have ever been found. They may be houses, works of art, the by-product of some kind of mating ritual, or something beyond the grasp of human imagination. Once upon a time, tomb raiders made fortunes by finding Elder Culture artifacts that kick-started new industries. Our last sheriff but one played an instrumental role in the discovery of navigation code that had migrated from a fragment of a crashed Ghajar spaceship into a nest of hive rats, and pointed toward the wormhole network of the New Frontier. Although it's generally agreed that the glory days of mining the City of the Dead are long gone, tomb raiders still dig up various trinkets—sympathy stones, ceramic shards containing entangled electrons used in q-phone manufacture, tesserae doped with algorithms that generate scraps of Ghostkeeper memories as well as, sometimes, actual ghosts—and people still come out here hoping to hit the jackpot. Most leave broke and disappointed after a year or so, but a few stay on, and others drift out here and set up homesteads or little businesses. Living the good old American dream on an alien planet, at the edge of a vast alien ruin.

Leah Bright was one such incomer, moving to our little town after a divorce and a business failure in Port of Plenty. She rented a single wide in the trailer park, used eBay to sell inert tesserae that she claimed to have activated by a secret psychic process, gave lessons in dowsing for artifacts and consultations with her familiar, which she said was the ghost of a Byzantine priest whose spirit had transmigrated to First Foot a thousand years ago. She was a handsome woman in her late thirties who wore boho scarves, denim jackets and jeans, and tooled leather boots, and mostly kept herself to herself. She gave the impression that residence in Joe's Corner was a temporary setback, but we grew used to seeing her sitting at an outside table in the Old Bean Café and poking with furious concentration at her iPhone, or leading a gaggle of tourists on a dowsing expedition amongst the tells and dust heaps at the northern edge of the City of the Dead. It was general knowledge that she and the town clerk were an item. We told ourselves that because neither party was married it was no business of ours that they liked to pretend that they were no more than casual acquaintances, but we sometimes wondered what they had in common. Leah Bright with her glamour and flair; Troy Wagner a mild, pedantic guy ten years younger than her, so straightlaced he was the only person in town who went to work every day in a suit.

Someone suggested that Leah kept him around to remind herself of a road not taken, and everyone pretty much agreed that Troy must have told her about the planning application for a radio telescope array. At the town meeting where it was due to be heard, Leah sat in the center of the front row with half a dozen allies flanking her, a solid block of defiance in a hall otherwise sparsely occupied by the usual professional busybodies, people who had a planning or licensing matter they wanted to see through, and a few cantankerous cranks who at every meeting aired old grievances that everyone else had long ago laid to rest.

The planning application came at the end of business, a seemingly innocuous statement that a company named Universal Communications had been granted a license to erect radio communications equipment on a four-hundred-acre patch of land they had acquired several months ago, plans available upon request at the library or to view on the town's website, and so forth. After Troy Wagner dryly read this out, the mayor, Joel Jumonville, said that if there were no comments he would declare the meeting closed. But before Joel could bang his gavel, Leah Bright reared up and said that as a matter of fact she did have something to say.

"It's my understanding that the 'radio communications equipment' is in fact an array of radio telescopes," she said. "And I also understand that Universal Communications is planning to establish communication with extraterrestrial intelligences."

"I believe those might be more in the nature of unfounded assertions rather than comments," Joel Jumonville said in his Texas good-old-boy drawl. "As Mr. Wagner explained, there'll be a copy of the plans lodged in the library. Anyone who wants is free to check them out."

Joel was a former astronaut, one of the Fortunate Fifty who had come up and out on the very first shuttle trip from Earth, back when it seemed very likely that the Jackaroo's gift of fifteen worlds and the means to reach them was some kind of trick or trap. He had been mayor of Joe's Corner for a quarter of a century. Although his majority had been considerably reduced at the last election, he had lost none of his God-given authority, looking at Leah over the top of his old-fashioned gold-rimmed bifocals like a teacher humoring a difficult pupil.

But Leah wasn't the least bit intimidated, saying firmly, "If you want facts, Mr. Mayor, then it's a fact that Universal Communications is owned by the Omega Point Foundation, which once upon a time funded a company called Outland Archaeological Services. A company that caused some considerable trouble here twelve years ago, as I'm sure many of you will recall."

She was referring to the breakout of a harmful eidolon that had gotten into the heads of people who had dug up a second fragment of the crashed Ghajar spaceship, causing them to attack and kill each other with their teeth and bare hands. The last person standing had run repeatedly at a boulder until she'd split her skull open. At the mention of Outland's name, a couple of old-timers sat up and started to pay attention.

"I can assure you that the application is in order," Joel Jumonville said, with a trace of exasperation. "Universal Communications doesn't have anything to do with archaeology. And it has no plans to do any digging, apart from a few trenches when it lays foundations for its equipment."

Troy Wagner had the look of man trying to become invisible by the power of thought alone. Everyone else was following the conversation as if it were a tennis match.

Leah said, "This equipment being radio telescopes."

"Something like that may be mentioned in the plans," Joel said. "Which, as I've said, anyone can go check out."

"Radio telescopes which Universal Communications wants to use to talk with extraterrestrials," Leah said, with her supporters nodding and saying *exactly* and *there it is* like a gospel chorus.

"I believe that they may be planning to search the sky for signals or suchlike," Joel said, clearly on the back foot now.

"And if they find a signal, they'll want to talk," Leah said.

Joel tried to turn it into a joke. "Is this about the planning application, or are you making a criticism of their scientific methods?"

"It's about the harmful effect this project will have on the City of the Dead," Leah said. "And the very real possibility that the Jackaroo may not approve of it."

"The approval of the Jackaroo has nothing to do with our planning process.

And in any case, the application is merely a formality. The site is on federal land outside town limits. I can no more stop it going ahead than I could stop a sandstorm," Joel said, and when several of Leah's supporters stood up to shout objections he banged his gavel so hard the head flew off the handle.

That was the end of the meeting and the beginning of Leah Bright's campaign. Her most prominent supporters were dealers and assayers in the artifact trade, merchants whose business depended on tourism, and a number of tomb raiders, including Jayla and Shelley Griffith-Fontcuberta, who had been in the biz more or less from the discovery of the City of the Dead. All had good reason to worry about possible disruptions to their livelihoods. Despite decades of research, no one could claim any authoritative knowledge about the revenants left by the Ghostkeepers. They were rooted in algorithms that ran deep inside the quantum properties of the tesserae, projecting fleeting emotions, glimpses of exotic landscapes, and actual eidolons or ghosts. Harmless scraps like tattered bats or the animated shadows of warped dwarves; rare potent spirits that got inside people's heads, as in the breakout that had killed the crew employed by Outland Archaeological Services. Which is why the association between Outland and the outfit that wanted to build the radio telescope array was enough to give even the hardened rationalists amongst us pause for thought.

In an interview with Sally Backlund, the owner, editor, and sole reporter of our town's newspaper, Leah announced that she intended to hold an open meeting about what she called the reckless and outrageous intrusion. It was a riotous affair at which everyone with a crank to turn or an ax to grind held forth, everyone talking over everyone else and fierce little arguments breaking out everywhere; people had to drag Ben Lamb and Aidan Fletcher apart when raised voices and finger poking threatened to escalate into a fistfight. Leah struggled to keep any kind of order, and her keynote speech was shouted down by people who felt that their own opinions were equally important. As Sally wrote in her story about it, although the meeting ended with a unanimous condemnation of the project, everyone appeared to have a different objection.

Universal Communications set up a public event to explain its plans, with a free buffet and a lecture by a tame scientist about SETI, the search for extraterrestrial intelligence, but after Leah and her supporters declared that they would picket the event, it was canceled by our sheriff, Van Diaz, on the grounds of public safety. Van had good reason. The ranks of Leah's supporters had been swollen by out-of-towners, and there was a discordant mood in the air. Rival street preachers set up at opposite corners of the crossroads, one ranting about an upcoming Rapture that would transmigrate our souls to permanent servitude in an alien hell world, the other warning about the dangers of what she called cargo-cult culture and colonization by alien memes. An outfit that called itself the Brotherhood of Human Saints marched down Main Street, dressed in monk's habits and spraying onlookers with what they claimed was magnetized water, to ward off unsympathetic eidolons; Hoke Williford objected to being sprayed and punched out one of the monks and was promptly arrested. And a group of earnest young people held a be-in outside the community center, with banners, drumming, and chants, and consciousness-raising exercises that some of us worried would brainwash our children. The jamboree went on for three days, long after Universal Communications' PR people had folded their tents, and none of it did a thing to stop the construction work that started up two weeks later.

Sally Backlund did her best to be evenhanded in her coverage. She published an editorial supporting the view of Leah and her supporters that science did not have all the answers. A hundred years ago, she wrote, we thought that we would soon know everything worth knowing. Now, after the arrival of the Jackaroo and colonization of the fifteen habitable planets they gave us, we are equally certain that the universe is more complex than we can possibly imagine, and if there are fundamental questions that science can't answer, then perhaps other ways of addressing them are equally valid. She also interviewed Darryl Hancock who owned the hardware store and with the twenty-inch reflecting telescope in his backyard had spotted more than two dozen comets and discovered one of the tiny moons that orbited Godzilla, the biggest of our system's three gas giants.

Darryl explained that SETI was still a valid enterprise long after the Jackaroo had first revealed themselves. We know now that we are not alone, he said, but we still do not know if we are the only clients of the Jackaroo, or if there are other alien civilizations as advanced as theirs. The bedrock of SETI research is a famous equation written by the astronomer Frank Drake, which gives an estimate of the number of active, technologically advanced extraterrestrial civilizations in the galaxy by multiplying together estimates of relevant parameters—the percentage of stars with life-bearing planets, the proportion of those planets on which communicative technological civilizations arose, the life span of those civilizations, and so forth. After the Jackaroo made contact, we acquired real numbers for parameters that previously had been hypothetical; we know, for instance, that the Elder Cultures, clients of the Jackaroo who previously inhabited the gift worlds, flourished for an average of approximately five centuries. Plugging hard data into the Drake equation suggests that between one and twelve civilizations are presently active in the Milky Way, which raises all kinds of interesting questions. Do the Jackaroo currently have other clients besides ourselves? Are there alien civilizations they are watching but have not yet contacted, or alien civilizations more advanced than theirs, which have refused their offer of help? Are all the Jackaroo gift worlds more or less habitable by humans, like First Foot and the others, and those worlds previously inhabited by Elder Cultures that we've discovered out in the New Frontier? Or are there more exotic gift worlds, for more exotic clients? Gas giants where intelligent blimps ride frigid poison winds, worlds that are wrapped in ocean from pole to pole, or baking at furnace temperatures and inhabited by life-forms whose biochemistries are based on sulfur or silicon rather than carbon, and half a hundred other possibilities.

The Jackaroo have been asked these and other questions many times, of course. But their answers are always about as much use as fortune cookie sayings. "It's an interesting question," they'll say. Or: "The universe is very large and very old, and contains many possibilities." Or: "Many of our previous clients asked similar questions. Each found their own answers, in their own way."

This was why Universal Communications was building radio telescope arrays on the fifteen gift worlds, whose stars were scattered across the Milky Way. The galaxy is huge, some four hundred billion stars, so there is only a vanishingly small chance that an active, communicative alien civilization will be orbiting a star close enough to one of those arrays for easy detection. Even so, according to Darryl, the implications of success were so staggeringly profound that it was worth the gamble. Suppose we could get answers to all the questions that the Jackaroo so skillfully and charmingly evade? Suppose we could get a different perspective about the Jackaroo, or even discover their history and origin?

The interview didn't endear Darryl to Leah Bright and her supporters. There were anonymous threats, and an attempt at swatting. Someone spray-painted ALIEN LOVER across the window of Darryl's store. A small group gathered outside his home and banged saucepans and blew whistles and chanted insults until he came out with his 12 gauge and fired a double load of bird shot into the air. He was arrested for that, but Van Diaz, whose patience was being sorely tried by the protestors' antics, released him without charge a couple of hours later.

Leah denounced the threats and vandalism, but also accused Darryl of being in Universal Communications' pocket. And some of us accused her of being in the pay of outside parties who had a financial interest in sabotaging Universal Communications' plans. The whole town was divided. You couldn't not have an opinion, for or against. Meanwhile, heavy trucks brought in the prefabricated parts for the radio telescopes, big white parabolic reflectors set on skeletal support structures that allowed them to point at any part of the sky, assembled in a twenty-by-ten grid. Construction took six months, and all the while Leah Bright and her crew of protestors camped outside. They held up traffic, locked themselves to construction machinery, tied banners and balloons to the mesh security fences, leafleted traffic and people in town, sat around campfires in the cold desert evenings, and sang old songs from Earth.

Most were out-of-towners, and most were young. They had not volunteered to come up and out to First Foot after winning a shuttle ticket in the UN lottery or buying a ticket on one of the repurposed Ghajar ships. They had been born here. It was not a wonder, for them, to be living on another planet. As far as they were concerned, First Foot was home and Earth the alien planet. A hundred years ago, they would have been protesting about the Vietnam War and the Man. Now they were campaigning against the colonial attitudes of off-world companies, and the alliance between scientists and big business that was exploiting Elder Culture artifacts they believed to be theirs by right of birth.

Some of us sympathized with them. A large part of our town's income derived from the City of the Dead and the artifact business, and we'd chosen to live there because it was remote from central government and gave us the space to express our lives as we saw fit. So although we had businesses to run and families to feed, many of us visited the camp, donating food and water, sitting and talking with the kids, and participating in sing-alongs, an attempt to encircle the camp with a chain of people holding hands, and an attempt to levitate the radio telescopes as a demonstration of human will triumphing over science (some swore it actually happened). Elmer Peters, the Unitarian minister, held a nondenominational service at the camp every Sunday. Ram Narayan supplied daily meals of vegetable curry and bread; the New Mexico couple from the yoga retreat brought macrobiotic food and said that the camp had a beautiful air of spirituality; Jeff James sold pot he grew in his hydroponic greenhouse. Sally Backlund was often to be seen interviewing someone, an external microphone clad in a furry windshield attached to her iPhone like a dead hive rat soldier. She was writing a series of stories about individual protestors and uploading her interviews to SoundCloud. Craig and Jody Mudgett brought their kids as part of their homeschooling. And other kids visited, of course, because of the excitement and transgression. It was the biggest thing to have happened in our town since that unfortunate breakout. A carnival. A freak show.

Leah was there from beginning to end, holding daily séances to consult her Byzantine priest, chairing interminable camp meetings, giving interviews to TV and net journalists from Port of Plenty, and leading every protest action. She said that the presence of the camp was a shield between the black energy of the radio telescopes and the fragile noosphere of the City of the Dead. She was arrested twice, but although Joel Jumonville wanted to keep her ass in jail until things cooled off, she was quickly released both times, thanks to supporters who paid her fines and a sympathetic lawyer from Port of Plenty who was doing pro bono work for the protesters. She was dogged, determined, and, most of us agreed, very happy.

She'd broken up with Troy Wagner soon after she'd begun her campaign. He sourly confided to the bartender at Don's Joint that it wasn't so much that she'd found a cause, but a cause had found her. She had become the lightning rod for the discontent of well-to-do kids who joined protests because it was the hip thing to do, or because they were rebelling against their parents. He felt badly treated by his former lover—Joel had investigated him over the leak about the planning application, and although nothing implicated him, bad blood remained—and we weren't surprised when, two months later, he took a job with the UN in Port of Plenty.

By then, construction was nearing an end. The garden of radio telescopes sat behind a double wire fence topped with razor wire, bowls turned to the sky like giant albino sunflowers. There were ranks of solar panels to provide power, a short string of flat-roofed, single-story prefabs where security guards and technicians would live and work. Q-phone circuits linked it directly and instantaneously to a facility in Paris, France, and to the headquarters of Universal Communications' parent company at Terminus.

Several of us were invited to the facility's inauguration, including Joel Jumonville, Sally Backlund, and Darryl Hancock. As was Leah Bright, in what was either a spirit of reconciliation or a sneaky PR move. She formally burned the invitation in front of a crowd of her supporters and a couple of reporters (Sally and a stringer from NBC First Foot) and announced that there would be an intervention, but refused to divulge any details.

"It will be nonviolent but potent," she said, adding that testing of the equipment had already caused significant agitation amongst eidolons and other potencies in the City of the Dead.

"She felt a great disturbance in the Force," more than one of us wisecracked, but many had a sense of foreboding. We were remembering that breakout, and all the tomb raiders and explorers who had been to one degree or another driven crazy by exposure to eidolons and other manifestations of Ghostkeeper algorithms. People who had invisible friends, or believed that they were dead, rotting corpses, or had caught counting syndrome or spent half of every day scrubbing themselves down with industrial bleach in the shower because they believed that the pores in their skin were infested with alien bugs. And all of us were affected to some extent, living as we did in the penumbra of a vast alien necropolis, where alien ghosts infested alien tombs and scenes from long-lost alien lives were replayed to any sentient creature that strayed close to the tesserae that contained them. All of us were changed.

A couple of years ago, a PR company hired by Joel Jumonville to boost the tourist trade came up with a cute cartoon mascot, a fat green-skinned elf with puppy-dog eyes, a goofy grin, sparkly antennae, and a slogan: *Experience Ten Thousand Years Of Alien History!* But that history wasn't cute, wasn't amenable to Disneyfication. It was the background hum of our lives, a psychic weather acknowledged by the amulets or tattoos some of us wore to ward off bad luck and bad eidolons, jokes stolen from corny old horror movies, and the little rituals tomb raiders performed before entering a tomb. I guess you could say that our love of gossip and stories was part of our coping mechanism: a way of reassuring ourselves that we were still human. Even visiting scientists and archaeologists talked about bad spots and weird feelings. That psychic weather, those weird feelings, were what Leah and her protestors had tapped into. And it turned out that they were right, although in the end it wasn't the radio telescopes that blew everything up. It was Leah's attempt at sabotage.

The company and the government took her talk of an intervention seriously. There was heavy security around the radio telescope array on the day of its inauguration. Two hundred state troopers were on standby and a small army of private goons checked the IDs of VIPs, patrolled the perimeter, and flew drones above the protestors' little encampment. According to Van Diaz, they weren't so much worried about Leah and her friends, but that some lone crackpot might use them as cover.

"Still, none of us has any idea about their plans," he said. "The company tried to infiltrate the camp with a couple of undercover guys, but they were spotted and turfed out. Leah is playing everything very close. But man, really, what can she do?"

Many of us resented the intrusive security, the closure of Main Street while a convoy of press and guests rolled through, the noise of helicopter traffic that brought the VIPs, the journalists stopping us on the street or knocking at our doors or coming into our places of business, asking us for our opinions. And while we wouldn't admit it, we were anxious that there might be an outbreak of some kind of stupid violence, or that Leah might turn out to be right, and the radio telescopes really would trigger something incomprehensible and catastrophic out in the City of the Dead. So although we tried to go about our normal business, we were secretly watching the skies. And at four p.m., when the radio telescopes were due to be switched on, most of us found excuses to hunker down at home.

But nothing happened. Despite all the rumors, Ada Morange, the billionaire who bankrolled the Omega Point Foundation, did not appear at the inauguration. Instead, a colorless executive read out a short message from her, and an astronomer who had helmed a TV series about the gift worlds and the New Frontier, brought from Earth especially for the occasion, gave a short speech before pressing the button that activated the dishes. All swung ponderously towards a spot high in the day sky, aiming towards a G2 star eleven light years away. It was the twin of Earth's sun, but it wasn't known if it possessed any planets, let alone one that could support life. As Darryl Hancock said, the project was in many ways a symbolic gesture, making the point that the human species wasn't going to stop asking big questions just because the Jackaroo had happened along with their gift worlds and shuttles, and their offer to help.

The protestors built a huge bonfire that night and held a cross between a séance, a prayer meeting, and a free concert. Leah didn't appear; she was in conversation with her Byzantine priest. We didn't know then that her plan to disrupt the inauguration had been foiled by a failed comms link.

That link went live two days later.

The first most of us knew about it, the power went off in the town. It was just after seven in the morning. The municipal grid, solar power, generators, and LEAF batteries: everything cut out. Vehicles drifted to a halt, broadband fell over, TVs and radios and phones howled like wolves. Some people say they saw an arc of pale sun dogs in the sky; others that a host of eidolons rose up from tombs and sinkholes across the City of the Dead and formed a thickening haze that poured north, towards the radio telescope facility. Esther Aldrich, the manager of the Shop 'n Save, claimed that she saw beings like glowing balloons drift through the plate glass window, head down the liquor aisle, and vanish, leaving behind an odor like burnt plastic. Several people suffered fits. Kyra Calliste, a former tomb raider who for three years had panhandled around town, haunted by an eidolon fragment that had robbed her of her voice, suddenly stood up in the church hall where she was eating her customary breakfast with other transients and started talking about everything that had happened to her out in the City of the Dead. She hasn't stopped talking yet. On the other hand, Monica Nielsen, eating breakfast with her husband in Denny's, was struck blind. Hysterical blindness is the opinion of specialists who have examined her, nothing organically wrong, but she hasn't seen a spark of light since.

Others spoke of hearing the voices of dead relatives, or a vast lonely roar like a jet plane passing low above the roofs of the town, although the sky was cloudless and empty that morning. And at the radio telescope array, the dishes began to move under a command fed through a clandestine link which a sympathetic IT worker had installed in the control system, overriding the program that until that moment had kept them tracking the G2 star.

The technicians had not yet started their shift; by the time they responded to a q-phone call from the actual controllers, on Earth, it was too late. The dishes locked onto a new target and their dormant transmission system came online, linked to a qube in the protestors' camp that was running algorithms extracted from several hundred tesserae. At least one of which, it turned out, had been contaminated or overwritten by code extracted from a fragment of that crashed Ghajar spaceship. The ship code took control of the telescopes, and began to send a complex powerful signal towards a distant star.

After the technicians tried and failed to regain control of the array, they shut everything down. It's still shut down three years later, so I suppose you could say Leah Bright and her followers scored some kind of a victory. Trouble is, they also helped Universal Communications discover something new.

Leah was arrested by the UN geek police and charged with sabotage, interference with telecommunications transmissions, and a ragbag of lesser crimes. She and several of her supporters, along with the technician who had installed the clandestine link, were released on bail put up by an anonymous supporter, and all charges were eventually dropped. Partly because a trial would have been a PR disaster; partly because Universal Communications discovered that the transmission had been aimed at a red dwarf star more than twenty thousand light years away—a star with, it turned out, a single wormhole orbiting it.

An expedition was promptly dispatched, taking more than a month to make its way from wormhole to wormhole, star to star. It discovered a vast debris disc circling close to that cool, dim star, a churning mass of organic and metallic fragments twelve million miles across and just thirty feet deep, with about half the mass of the Earth's moon. The remains of millions Ghajar ships, perhaps. Or the wreckage of some huge structure, a space metropolis or moon-sized orbital fort, ground small by innumerable collisions and time.

Five companies have purchased licenses to map and explore the debris disc, searching for artifacts and scraps that contain active algorithms. So far no one has found anything useful—or if they have, they aren't talking about it—but one thing is clear. Radioactivity, chemical changes, and stress marks show that the debris was subjected to energies so immense they would have caused serious deformations in local space-time.

It seems, the experts say, that the Ghajar were divided against themselves. The spaceship that crashed in the City of Dead did not crash by accident, but was shot down while fleeing from an enemy; the debris disc was created by some unimaginable battle, part of a war that ended with the Ghajar's extinction. And in their fate we may glimpse our own future, because the human race is already split into opposing factions by the influence of artifacts or technologies. By ideas not our own. By the ravings of mad alien ghosts.

The Jackaroo have said nothing at all about this theory. They will neither confirm nor deny our speculations about what happened to the Ghajar, saying only that they are "interesting." There is a rumor that three of their gold-skinned avatars visited the radio telescope array while the geek police were making the qube safe. Van says neither he nor any of his deputies were informed about their presence, but one night in the Green Ale Inn one of the facility's technicians said the avatars stood there for an hour, facing each other like gunfighters in some old Western, then walked off to a town car without saying a word and were driven away.

Perhaps someone will find something immensely valuable in the debris disc. Or perhaps it will drive those trying to understand it insane, or infect them with some kind of combat eidolon. But despite those risks the prospect of reward is too great to stop exploring.

Meanwhile, although the radio telescopes remain offline, Leah Bright is still camped at the gate. Like our founder, Joe Gordon, she lives in an RV. She supports herself with royalties from a self-published e-book about her campaign, by charging tourists for taking selfies with her, and by holding consultations about the Ghajar message that, she claims, passed through her. Unlike Joe, she loves to talk. She'll talk to anyone who'll listen. And with her garrulous eccentricity, and her obsession with the inscrutable alien dead, she has finally become one of us.

INNUMERABLE GLIMMERING LIGHTS

RICH LARSON

At the roof of the world, the Drill churned and churned. Four Warm Currents watched with eyes and mouth, overlaying the engine's silhouette with quicksilver sketches of sonar. Long, twisting shards of ice bloomed from the metal bit to float back along the carved tunnel. Workers with skin glowing acid yellow, hazard visibility, jetted out to meet the debris and clear it safely to the sides. Others monitored the mesh of machinery that turned the bit, smoothing contact points, spinning cogs. The whole thing was beautiful, efficient, and made Four Warm Currents secrete anticipation in a flavored cloud.

A sudden needle of sonar, pitched high enough to sting, but not so high that it couldn't be passed off as accidental. Four Warm Currents knew it was Nine Brittle Spines before even tasting the name in the water.

"Does it move faster with you staring at it?" Nine Brittle Spines signed, tentacles languid with humor-not-humor.

"No faster, no slower," Four Warm Currents replied, forcing two tentacles into a curled smile. "The Drill is as inexorable as our dedication to its task."

"Dedication is admirable, as said the ocean's vast cold to one volcano's spewing heat." Nine Brittle Spines's pebbly skin illustrated, flashing red for a brief instant before regaining a dark cobalt hue.

"You are still skeptical." Four Warm Currents clenched tight to keep distaste from inking the space between them. Nine Brittle Spines was a council member, and not one to risk offending. "But the ice's composition is changing, as I reported. The bit shears easier with every turn. We're approaching the other side."

"So it thins, and so it will thicken again." Nine Brittle Spines wriggled dismissal. "The other side is a deep dream, Four Warm Currents. Your machine is approaching more ice."

"The calculations," Four Warm Currents protested. "The sounding. If you would read the theorems—"

Nine Brittle Spines hooked an interrupting tentacle through the thicket of movement. "No need for your indignation. I have no quarrel with the Drill. It's a useful sideshow, after all. It keeps the eyes and mouths of the colony fixated while the council slides its decisions past unhindered."

"If you have no quarrel, then why do you come here?" Four Warm Currents couldn't suck back the words, or the single droplet of ichor that suddenly wobbled into the water between them. It blossomed there into a ghostly black wreath. Four Warm Currents raked a hasty tentacle through to disperse it, but the councillor was already tasting the chemical, slowly, pensively.

"I have no quarrel, Four Warm Currents, but others do." Nine Brittle Spines swirled the bitter emission around one tentacle tip, as if it were a pheromone poem or something else to be savored. Four Warm Currents, mortified, could do nothing but turn an apologetic mottled blue, almost too distracted to process what the councillor signed next.

"While the general opinion is that you have gone mad, and your project is a hilariously inept allocation of time and resources based only on your former contributions, theories do run the full gamut. Some believe the Drill is seeking mineral deposits in the ice. Others believe the Drill will be repurposed as a weapon, to crack through the fortified cities of the vent-dwelling colonies." Nine Brittle Spines shaped a derisive laugh. "And there is even a small but growing tangent who believe in your theorems. Who believe that you are fast approaching the mythic other side, and that our ocean will seep out of the puncture like the viscera from a torn egg, dooming us all."

"The weight of the ocean will hold it where it is," Four Warm Currents signed, a sequence by now rote to the tentacles. "The law of sink and rise is one you've surely studied."

"Once again, my opinion is irrelevant to the matter," Nine Brittle Spines replied. "I am here because this radical tangent is believed to be targeting your project for sabotage. The council wishes to protect its investment." Tentacles pinwheeled in a slight hesitation then: "You yourself may be in danger as well. The council advises you to keep a low profile. Perhaps change your name taste."

"I am not afraid for my life." Four Warm Currents signed it firmly and honestly. The project was more important than survival. More important than anything.

"Then fear, perhaps, for your mate's children."

Four Warm Currents flashed hot orange shock, bright enough for the foreman to glance over, concerned. "What?"

Nine Brittle Spines held up the tentacle tip that had tasted Four Warm

Currents's anger. "Traces of ingested birth mucus. Elevated hormones. You should demonstrate more self-control, Four Warm Currents. You give away all sorts of secrets."

The councillor gave a lazy salute, then jetted off into the gloom, joined at a distance by two bodyguards with barbed tentacles. Four Warm Currents watched them vanish down the tunnel, then slowly turned back toward the Drill. The bit churned and churned. Four Warm Currents's mind churned with it.

When the work cycle closed, the Drill was tugged back down the tunnel and tethered in a hard shell still fresh enough to glisten. A corkscrewing skiff arrived to unload the guard detail, three young bloods with enough hormone-stoked muscle to overlook the still-transparent patches on their skin. They inked their names so loudly Four Warm Currents could taste them before even jetting over.

"There's been a threat of sorts," Four Warm Currents signed, secreting a small dark privacy cloud to shade the conversation from workers filing onto the now-empty skiff. "Against the project. Radicals who may attempt sabotage."

"We know," signed the guard, whose name was a pungent Two Sinking Corpses. "The councillor told us. That's why we have these." Two Sinking Corpses hefted a conical weapon Four Warm Currents dimly recognized as a screamer, built to amplify a sonar burst to lethal strength. Nine Brittle Spines had not exaggerated the seriousness of the situation.

"Pray to the Leviathans you don't have to use them," Four Warm Currents signed, then joined the workers embarking on the skiff, tasting familiar names, slinging tentacles over knotted muscles, adding to a multilayered scent joke involving an aging councillor and a frost shark. Spirits were high. The Drill was cutting smoothly. They were approaching the other side, and though for some that only meant the end of contract and full payment, others had also been infected by Four Warm Currents's fervor.

"What will we see?" a worker signed. "Souls of the dead? The Leviathans themselves?"

"Nothing outside the physical laws," Four Warm Currents replied, but then, sensing the disappointment: "But nothing like we have ever seen before. It will be unimaginable. Wondrous. And they'll soak our names all through the memory sponges, to remember the brave explorers who first broke the ice."

A mass of tentacles waved in approval of the idea. Four Warm Currents settled back as the skiff began to move and a wave of new debates sprang up.

• • •

The City of Bone was roughly spherical, a beautiful lattice of ancient skeleton swathed in sponge and cultivated coral, glowing ethereal blue with bioluminescence. It was older than any councillor, a relic of the dim past before the archives: a Leviathan skeleton dredged from the seafloor with buoyant coral, built up and around until it could float unsupported, tethered in place above the jagged rock bed.

Devotees believed the Leviathans had sacrificed their corporeal forms to leave city husks behind; Four Warm Currents shared the more heretical view that the Leviathans were extinct, and for all their size might have been no more intelligent than the living algae feeders that still hauled their bulk along the seafloor. It was not a theory to divulge in polite discourse. Drilling through the roof of the world was agitator enough on its own.

As the skiff passed the City of Bone's carved sentinels, workers began to jet off to their respective housing blocks. Four Warm Currents was one of the last to disembark, having been afforded, as one of the council's foremost engineers, an artful gray-and-purple spire in the city center. Of course, that was before the Drill. Nine Brittle Spines's desire for a "sideshow" aside, Four Warm Currents felt the daily loss of council approval like the descending cold of a crevice. Relocation was not out of the realm of possibility.

For now, though, the house's main door shuttered open at a touch, and, more importantly, Four Warm Currents's mates were inside. Six Bubbling Thermals, sleek and swollen with eggs, drizzling ribbons of birth mucus like a halo, but with eyes still bright and darting. Three Jagged Reefs, lean and long, skin stained from a heavy work cycle in the smelting vents, submitting to a massage. Their taste made Four Warm Currents ache, deep and deeper.

"So our heroic third returns," Six Bubbling Thermals signed, interrupting the massage and prompting a ruffle of protest.

"Have you ended the world yet?" Three Jagged Reefs added. "Don't stop, Six. I'm nearly loose enough to slough."

"Nearly," Four Warm Currents signed. "I blacked a councillor. Badly."

Both mates guffawed, though Six Bubbling Thermals's had a nervous shiver to it.

"From how far?" Three Jagged Reefs demanded. "Could they tell it was yours?"

"From not even a tentacle away," Four Warm Currents admitted. "We were in conversation."

Three Jagged Reefs laughed again, the reckless, waving laugh that had made Four Warm Currents fall in love, but their other mate did not.

"Conversation about what?" Six Bubbling Thermals signed.

Four Warm Currents hesitated, tasting around to make sure a strong emotion hadn't slipped the gland again, but the water was clear and cold and anxiety-free. "Nine Brittle Spines is a skeptic of the worst kind. Intelligent, but refusing to self-educate."

"Did you not explain the density calculation?" Three Jagged Reefs signed plaintively.

Four Warm Currents moved to reply, then recognized a familiar mocking tilt in Three Jagged Reefs's tentacles and turned the answer into a crude "floating feces" gesticulation.

"Tell us the mathematics again," Three Jagged Reefs teased. "Nothing slicks me better for sex, Four. All those beautiful variables."

Six Bubbling Thermals smiled at the back-and-forth, but was still lightly spackled with mauve worry. The birth mucus spiralling out in all directions made for an easy distraction.

"We need to collect again," Four Warm Currents signed, gesturing to the trembling ribbons. "Or you'll bury us in our sleep."

"And then I'll finally have the house all to my own," Six Bubbling Thermals signed, cloying. But the mauve worry dissolved into flushed healthy pink as they all began coiling the mucus and storing it in coral tubing. Four Warm Currents stroked the egg sacs gently as they worked, imagining each one hatching into an altered world.

After they finished with the birth mucus and pricked themselves with a recreational skimmer venom, Three Jagged Reefs made them sample a truly terrible pheromone poem composed at the smelting vents between geysers. The recitation was quickly cancelled in favor of hallucination-laced sex in which they all slid over and around Six Bubbling Thermals's swollen mantle, probing and pulping, and afterward the three of them drifted in the artificial current, slowly revolving as they discussed anything and everything:

Colony annexation, the validity of aesthetic tentacle removal, the new eatery that served everything dead and frozen with frescoes carved into the flesh, So-and-So's scent change, the best birthing tanks, the after-ache they'd had the last time they used skimmer venom. Anything and everything except for the Drill.

Much later, when the other two had slipped into a sleeping harness, Four Warm Currents jetted upward to the top of their gray-and-purple spire, coiling there to look out over the City of Bone. Revelers jetted back and forth in the distance, visible by blots of blue-green excitement and arousal. Some were workers from the Drill, Four Warm Currents knew, celebrating the end of a successful work cycle.

Four Warm Currents's namesake parent had been a laborer of the same sort. A laborer who came home to cramped quarters and hungry children, but was never too exhausted to spin them a story, tentacles whirling and flourishing like a true bard. Four Warm Currents had been a logical child, always finding gaps in the tall tales of Leviathans and heroes and oceans beyond their own. But still, the stories had sunk in deep. Enough so that Four Warm Currents might be able to sign them to the children growing in Six Bubbling Thermals's egg sacs.

There was no need for Nine Brittle Spines or the council to know it was those stories that had ignited Four Warm Currents's curiosity for the roof of the world in the first place. Soon there would be new stories to tell. In seven, maybe eight more work cycles, they would break through.

After such a long percolation, the idea was dizzying. Four Warm Currents didn't know what awaited on the other side. There were theories, of course. Many theories. Four Warm Currents had studied gas bubbles and knew that whatever substance lay beyond the ice was not water as they knew it, not nearly so heavy. It could very well be deadly. Four Warm Currents would take precautions, but—

The brush of a tentacle tip, a familiar taste. Six Bubbling Thermals had ballooned up to join the stillness. Four Warm Currents extended a welcoming clasp, and the rasp of skin on skin was a comforting one. Calming.

"Someone almost started a riot in the plaza today," Six Bubbling Thermals signed.

The calm was gone. "Over what? Over the project?"

"Yes." Six Bubbling Thermals stared out across the city with a long clicking burst, then turned to face Four Warm Currents. "They had artificial panic. In storage globes. Broke them wide open right as the market peaked. It was . . ." Tentacles wove in and out, searching for a descriptor. "Chaos."

"Are you all right?" Four Warm Currents signed hard. "You should have told me. You're birthing."

Six Bubbling Thermals waved a quick-dying laugh. "I'm still bigger than you are. And I told Three Jagged Reefs. We agreed it would be best not to add to your stress. But I've never kept secrets well, have I?"

Another stare, longer this time. Four Warm Currents joined in, scraping sound across the architecture of the city, mapping curves and crevices, spars and spires.

"Before they were dragged off, they dropped one last globe," Six Bubbling Thermals signed. "It was your name, fresh, mixed with a decay scent. They said you're a monster, and if nobody stops you, you'll end the world."

Four Warm Currents shivered, clenched hard against the noxious fear threatening to tendril into the water. "Fresh?"

"Yes."

Who had it been? Four Warm Currents thought of the many workers and observers jetting up and down the tunnel, bringing status reports, complaints, updates. Any one of them could have come close enough to coax their chief engineer's name taste into a concealed globe. With a start, Four Warm Currents realized Six Bubbling Thermals was not gazing pensively over the city, but keeping watch.

"I know you won't consider halting the project," Six Bubbling Thermals signed. "But you need to be careful. Promise me that much."

Four Warm Currents remembered the councillor's warning and stroked Six Bubbling Thermals's egg sacs with a trembling tentacle. "I'll be careful. And when we break through, this will all go away. They'll see there's no danger."

"And when will that be?" The mauve worry was creeping back across Six Bubbling Thermals's skin.

"Soon," Four Warm Currents signed. "Seven work cycles."

They enmeshed their tentacles and curled against each other, bobbing there in silence as the City of Bone's ghostly blue guide lights began to blink out one by one.

The first attack came three cycles later, after shift. A pair of free-swimmers, with their skins pumped pitch-black and a sonar cloak in tow, managed to bore halfway through the Drill's protective shell before the guards spotted them and chased them off. The news came by a messenger whom Three Jagged Reefs, unhappily awoken, nearly eviscerated. Bare moments later, Four Warm Currents stroked goodbyes to both mates and took the skiff to the project site, tentacles heavy from sleep but hearts thrumming electric.

Nine Brittle Spines somehow contrived to arrive first.

"Four Warm Currents, it is a pleasure to see you so well rested." The councillor's tentacles moved as smoothly and blandly as ever, but Four Warm Currents could see the faintest of trembling at their tips. Mortal after all.

"I came as quickly as I was able," Four Warm Currents signed, not rising to the barb. "Were either of the perpetrators identified?"

"No." Nine Brittle Spines gave the word a twist of annoyance. "Assumedly they were two of yours. They knew the thinnest point of the shell and left behind a project-tagged auger." One tentacle produced the spiral tool and set it drifting between them. It was a miniature cousin to the behemoth Drill, used to sample ice consistency.

Four Warm Currents inspected the implement. "I'll speak with inventory, but I imagine it was taken without their knowledge."

"Do that," Nine Brittle Spines signed. "In the meanwhile, security will be increased. We'll have guards at all times from now on. Body searches for workers."

Four Warm Currents waved a vague agreement, staring up at the burnished armor shell, the hole scored in its underbelly. The workers would not be happy, but they were so close now, too close to let anything derail the project. Four Warm Currents would agree to anything, so long as the Drill was safe.

Tension became a sharp, sooty tang overlaying every conversation, so much so that Four Warm Currents was given council approval for a globe of artificially mixed happiness to waft around the tunnel entrance. It ended being mostly sucked up by the guards, who were happy enough already to swagger around with screamers and combat hooks bristling in their tentacles, interrogating any particularly worry-spackled worker who happened to look their way.

Four Warm Currents complained to the councillor, but was soundly ignored, told only that the guards had been instructed to treat the project site and its crew with the utmost respect. Enthusiasm was now a thing of the past. Workers spoke rarely and with short tempers, and every time the Drill slowed or an error was found in its calibration, the possibility of sabotage hung in the tunnel like a decay scent. Four Warm Currents found a slip in the most recent density calculation that promised to put things back a full work cycle, but still the Drill churned.

At home, they began receiving death threats. Six Bubbling Thermals found the first, a tiny automaton that waved its stiff tentacles in a prerecorded message: "We won't need a drill to puncture your eyes and every one of your eggs." Three Jagged Reefs shredded it to pieces. Four Warm Currents gave the pieces to the council's investigator.

Then, two cycles before breakthrough, black globes of artificial malice were slicked to their spire with adhesive and timed to burst while they slept. Only one went off, but it was enough to necessitate a pore-cleanse for Six Bubbling Thermals and a dedicated surveillance detail for the house.

Three Jagged Reefs fumed and fumed. "After the Drill breaks through, you'll let me borrow it, won't you?" The demand was jittery with skimmer venom, and made only once Six Bubbling Thermals, finally returned from the cleansing tanks, was out of sight range. "I'm going to find the shit-eater who blacked Six and stick them on the bit gland first."

Three Jagged Reefs had been pulled from smelting after an incidence of "hazardously elevated emotions," in which a copper-worker trilling about the impending end of the world had their tentacle held over a geyser until it turned to pulp. Staying in the house full cycle, under the watchful eyes and mouths of council surveillance, was not an easy transition. Not even stocked with high-quality venom.

"It'll all be over soon," Four Warm Current signed, mind half-filled, as was now the norm, with figures from the latest density calculation. One final cycle.

"Tell it to Six," Three Jagged Reefs signed back, short and clipped, and turned away.

Four Warm Currents swam into the next room, to where their mate was adrift in the sleeping harness. The egg sacs were bulging now, slick with the constant emission of birth mucus, bearing no trace of black ichor stains. The cleansing tanks had reported no permanent damage. Four Warm Currents sent a gentle prod of sonar and elicited a twitch.

"I'm awake," Six Bubbling Thermals signed, languid. "I'd sleep better with you two around me."

"They'll catch the lunatics who planted that globe," Four Warm Currents signed back.

Six Bubbling Thermals signed nothing for a long moment, then waved a sad laugh. "I don't think it's lunatics. Not anymore. A lot of people are saying the same thing, you know."

"Saying what?"

"You spend all of your time at the Drill, even when you're here with us." The accusation was soft, but it stung. "You haven't been paying attention. The transit currents are full of devotees calling you a blasphemer. Saying you think yourself a Leviathan. Unbounded. The whole city is frightened."

"Then it's a city of idiots," Four Warm Currents signed abruptly.

"I'm frightened. I have no shame admitting it. I'm frightened for our children. For them to have two parents only. One parent only. None. For them to never even hatch. Who knows?" Six Bubbling Thermals raised a shaky smile. "Maybe the idiot is the one who isn't frightened."

"But I'm going to give them an altered world, a new world . . . " Four Warm Currents's words blurred as Six Bubbling Thermals stilled two waving tentacles.

"I don't give a floating shit about a new world if it's one where you take a hook in the back," Six Bubbling Thermals signed back, slow and clear. "Don't go to the Drill tomorrow. They'll send for you when it breaks the ice."

At first, Four Warm Currents didn't even comprehend the words. After spending a third of a lifespan planning, building, lobbying, watching, the idea of not being there to witness the final churn, the final crack and squeal of ice giving away, was dizzying. Nauseating.

"If you go, I think you'll be dead before you come home," Six Bubbling Thermals signed. "You're worth more to us alive for one more cycle than as a name taste wafting through the archives for all eternity."

"I've watched it from the very start." Four Warm Currents tried not to tremble. "Every turn. Every single turn."

"And without you it moves no faster, no slower," Six Bubbling Thermals replied. "Isn't that what you say?"

"I have to be there."

"You don't." Six Bubbling Thermals gave a weary shudder. "Is it a new world for our children, or only for you?"

Four Warm Currents's tentacles went slack, adrift. The two of them stared at each other in the gloom, until, suddenly, something stirred in the egg sacs. The motion repeated, a faint but mesmerizing ripple. Six Bubbling Thermals gave a slight wriggle of pain.

Four Warm Currents climbed into the harness, turning acid blue in an apology that could not have been properly signed. "I'll stay. I'll stay, I'll stay."

They folded against each other and spoke of other things, of the strange currents that had brought them together, the future looming in the birthing tanks. Then they slept, deeply, even when Three Jagged Reefs wobbled in to join them much later, nearly unhooking the harness with chemical-clumsy tentacles.

Four Warm Currents dreamt of ending the world, the Drill shearing through its final stretch of pale ice, and from the gaping wound in the roof of the world, a Leviathan lowering its head, eyes glittering, to swallow the engine and its workers and their blasphemous chief engineer whole, pulling its bulk back into the world it once abandoned, sliding through blackness toward the City of Bone, ready to reclaim its scattered body, to devour all light, to unmake everything that had ever been made.

Four Warm Currents awoke to stinging sonar and the silhouette of a familiar councillor drifting before the sleeping harness, flanked by two long-limbed guards.

"Wake your mates," Nine Brittle Spines signed, with a taut urgency Four Warm Currents had never seen before. "All three of you have to leave."

"What's happening?"

"You'll see."

Four Warm Currents rolled, body heavy with sleep, and stroked each mate awake in turn. Three Jagged Reefs refused to rise until Six Bubbling Thermals furiously shook the harness, a flash of the old pre-birthing strength.

"Someone come to murder us?" Three Jagged Reefs asked calmly, once toppled free.

"You wouldn't feel a thing with all that venom in you," Four Warm Currents replied, less calmly.

"I barely pricked."

"As said the Drill to the roof of the world," Six Bubbling Thermals interjected.

Nine Brittle Spines flashed authoritative indigo, cutting the conversation short. "We have a skiff outside. Your discussions can wait."

The three of them followed the councillor out of the house, trailing long, sticky strands of Six Bubbling Thermals's replenished birth mucus. Once they exited the shutter and were no longer filtered, a faint acrid flavor seeped to them through the water. The City of Bone tasted bitter with fear. Anger.

And that wasn't all.

In the distance, Four Warm Currents could see free-swimmers moving as a mob, jetting back and forth through the city spires, carrying homegrown phosphorescent lamps and scent bombs. Several descended on a council-funded sculpture, smearing the stone with webbed black-and-red rage. Most continued on, heading directly for the city center. For their housing block, Four Warm Currents realized with a sick jolt.

"The radical tangent has grown," Nine Brittle Spines signed. "Considerably."

"So many?" Four Warm Currents was stunned.

"Only thing people love more than a festival is a doomsday," Three Jagged Reefs signed bitterly.

"Indeed. Your decriers have found support in many places, I'm afraid." Nine Brittle Spines bent a grimace as they swam toward the waiting skiff, a closed and armored craft marked with an official sigil. "Including the council."

Four Warm Currents stopped dead in the water. "But the Drill is still under guard."

"The Drill is currently being converged upon by a mob twice this size," Nine Brittle Spines signed. "Even without sympathizers in the security ranks, it would be futile to try to protect it. The council's official position, as of this moment, is that your project has been terminated to save costs."

Four Warm Currents realized, dimly, that both mates were holding tentacles back to prevent an incidence of hazardously elevated emotions. Searing orange desperation had spewed into the water around them. Nine Brittle Spines made no remarks about self-control, only flashed, for the briefest instant, a pale blue regret.

"But we're nearly through," Four Warm Currents signed, trembling all over. Three Jagged Reefs and Six Bubbling Thermals now slowly slid off, eager for the safety of the skiff. Drifting away when they were needed most.

"Perhaps you are," Nine Brittle Spines admitted. "Perhaps your theorems are sound. But stability is, at the present moment, more important than discovery."

"If we go to the Drill." Four Warm Currents shuddered to a pause. "If we go to the Drill, if we go now, we can stop them. I can explain to them. I can convince them."

"You know better than that, Four Warm Currents. In fact—"

Whatever Nine Brittle Spines planned to say next was guillotined as Six Bubbling Thermals surged from behind, wrapping the councillor in full grip.

In the same instant, Three Jagged Reefs yanked the skiff's shutter open. Four Warm Currents stared at the writhing councillor, then at each mate in turn.

"Get on with it, Four," Three Jagged Reefs signed. "Go and try."

Six Bubbling Thermals was unable to sign, tentacles taut as a vice around Nine Brittle Spines, but the misty red cloud billowing into the water was the fiercest and most pungent love Four Warm Currents could remember tasting.

"Oh, wait." Three Jagged Reefs glanced between them. "Six wanted to know if you have any necessary names."

"None," Four Warm Currents signed shakily. "So long as there are Thermals and Reefs."

"Well, of course." Three Jagged Reefs waved a haughty laugh that speared Four Warm Currents's hearts all over again. The councillor had finally stopped struggling in Six Bubbling Thermals's embrace and now watched the proceedings with an air of resignation. Four Warm Currents flashed a respectful pale blue, then turned and swam for the skiff.

They were hauling the Drill out of its carapace with hooks and bare tentacles, clouding the water with rage, excitement, amber-streaked triumph. Four Warm Currents abandoned the skiff for the final stretch, sucking back hard, jetting harder. The mob milled around the engine in a frenzy, too caught up to notice one late arrival.

Four Warm Currents screamed, dragging sonar across the crowd, but in the mess of motion and chemicals nobody felt the hard clicks. They'd brought a coring charge, one of the spiky half-spheres designed for blasting through solid rock bed to the nickel veins beneath. Four Warm Currents had shut down a foreman's lobby for such explosives during a particularly slow stretch of drilling. Too volatile, too much blowback in a confined space. But now it was here, and it was going to shred the Drill to pieces.

Four Warm Currents jetted higher, above the chaos, nearly to the mouth of the tunnel. No eyes followed. Everyone was intent on the Drill and on the coring charge being shuffled toward it, tentacle by tentacle.

Four Warm Currents sucked back, angled, and dove. The free-swimmers towing the coring charge didn't see the interloper until it was too late, until Four Warm Currents slid two tentacles deep into the detonation triggers and clung hard.

"Get away from me! Get away or I'll trigger right here!"

The crowd turned to a fresco of frozen tentacles, momentarily speechless. Then:

"Blasphemer," signed the closest free-swimmer. "Blasphemer."

The word caught and rippled across the mob, becoming a synchronized wave of short, chopping motions.

"The Drill is not going to end the world," Four Warm Currents signed desperately, puffing up over the crowd, hauling the coring charge along. "It's going to break us into a brand-new one. One we'll visit at our choosing. The deep ocean will stay deep ocean. The Leviathans will stay skeletons. Our cities will stay safe."

Something struck like a spar of bone, sending Four Warm Currents reeling. The conical head of a screamer poked out from the crowd, held by a young guard whose skin was no longer inked with the council's sigil. The name came dimly to memory: Two Sinking Corpses. An unfamiliar taste was clouding into the water. It took a moment for Four Warm Currents to realize it was blood, blue and hot and saline.

"Listen to me!"

The plea was answered by another blast of deadly sound, this one misaimed, clipping a tentacle. Four Warm Currents nearly lost grip on the coring charge. The mob roiled below, waving curses, mottled black and orange with fury. There would be no listening.

"Stay away from me or I'll trigger it," Four Warm Currents warned once more, then jetted hard for the mouth of the tunnel. The renewed threat of detonation bought a few still seconds. Then the mob realized where the coring charge was headed, and the sleekest and fastest of them tore away in pursuit.

Four Warm Currents hurled up the dark tunnel, sucking back water in searing cold gulps and flushing faster and harder with each. Familiar grooves in the ice jumped out with a smatter of sonar, etchings warning against unauthorized entry. Four Warm Currents blew past with tentacles straight back, trailing the coring charge directly behind, gambling nobody would risk hitting it with a screamer.

A familiar bend loomed in the dark, one of the myriad small adjustments to course, and beyond it, the service lights, bundles of bioluminescent algae set along the walls, began blooming to life, painting the tunnel an eerie blue-green, casting a long-limbed shadow on the wall. Four Warm Currents chanced a look down and saw three free-swimmers, young and strong and gaining.

"Drop it!" one took the opportunity to sign. "Drop it and you'll live!"

Four Warm Currents used a tentacle to sign back one of Three Jagged Reefs's favorite gestures, reflecting that it was a bad idea when the young-blood's skin flashed with rage and all three of them put on speed. The head start was waning, the coring charge was heavy, the screamer wound was dribbling blood.

But Four Warm Currents knew the anatomy of the tunnel better than anyone, better than even the foreman. The three pursuers lost valuable time picking their way through a thicket of free-floating equipment knocked from the wall, then more again deliberating where the tunnel branched, stubby memento of a calculation error.

Four Warm Currents's hearts were wailing for rest as the final stretch appeared. The coring charge felt like lead. A boiling shadow swooped past, and Four Warm Currents realized they'd fired another screamer, one risk now outweighing the other. The roof of the world, stretched thin like a membrane, marred with the Drill's final twist, loomed above.

Another blast of sonar, this one closer. Four Warm Currents throttled out a cloak of black ink, hoping to obscure the next shot, too exhausted to try to dodge. Too exhausted to do anything now but churn warm water, drag slowly, too slowly, toward the top.

The screamer's next burst was half-deflected by the coring charge, but still managed to make every single tentacle spasm. Four Warm Currents felt the cargo slipping and tried desperately to regain purchase on its slick metal. So close, now, so close to the end of the world. Roof of the world. Either. Thoughts blurred and collided in Four Warm Currents's bruised brain. More blood was pumping out, bright blue, foul-tasting. Four Warm Currents tried to hold onto the exact taste of Six Bubbling Thermals's love.

One tentacle stopped working. Four Warm Currents compensated with the others, shifting weight as another lance of sound missed narrowly to the side. The ice was almost within reach now, cold, scarred, layered with frost. With one final, tendon-snapping surge, Four Warm Currents heaved the coring charge upward, slapping the detonation trigger as it went. The spiked device crunched into the ice and clung. Four Warm Currents tasted something new mixing into the blood, reaching amber tendrils through the leaking blue. Triumph.

"Get out," Four Warm Currents signed, clumsily, slowly. "It's too late now."

The pursuers stared for a moment, adrift, then turned and shot back down the tunnel, howling a sonar warning to the others coming behind. Four Warm Currents's tentacles were going numb. Every body part ached or seared or felt like it was splitting apart. There would be no high-speed exit down the tunnel. Maybe no exit at all.

As the coring charge signed out its detonation sequence with mechanical tendrils, Four Warm Currents swam, slowly, to the side wall. A deep crevice ran along the length. Maybe deep enough. Four Warm Currents squeezed, twisted, contorted, tucking inside the shelter bit by bit. It was an excruciating fit. Even a child would have preferred a wider fissure. Four Warm Currents's eyes squeezed shut and saw Six Bubbling Thermals smiling, saw the egg sacs glossy and bright.

The coring charge went off like a volcano erupting. Such devices were designed, in theory, to deliver all but a small fraction of the explosive yield forward. The tiny fraction of blowback was still enough to shatter cracks through the tunnel walls and send a sonic boom rippling down its depth, an expanding globe of boiling water that scalded Four Warm Currents's exposed skin. The tentacle that hadn't managed to fit inside was turned to mush in an instant, spewing denatured flesh and blood in a hot cloud. All of Four Warm Currents's senses sang with the explosion, tasting the fierce chemicals, feeling the heat, seeing with sonar the flayed ice crumbling all around.

Then, at last, it was over. Four Warm Currents slithered out of the crack, sloughing skin on its edges, and drifted slowly upward. It was a maelstrom of shredded ice and swirling gases, bubbles twisting in furious wreaths. Four Warm Currents floated up through the vortex, numb to the stinging debris and swathes of scalding water. The roof of the world was gone, leaving a jagged dark hole in the ice, a void that had been a dream and a nightmare for cycles and cycles. Four Warm Currents rose to it, entranced.

One trembling tentacle reached upward and across the rubicon. The sensation was indescribable. Four Warm Currents pulled the tentacle back, stared with bleary eyes, and found it still intact. The other side was scorching cold, a thousand tingling pinpricks, a gauze of gas like nothing below. Nothing Four Warm Currents had ever dreamed or imagined.

The chief engineer bobbed and bled, then finally gathered the strength for one last push, breaking the surface of the water completely. The feel of gas on skin was gasping, shivering. Four Warm Currents craned slowly backward, turning to face the void, and looked up. Another ocean, far deeper and vaster than theirs, but not empty. Not dark. Not at all. Maybe it was a beautiful hallucination, brought about by the creeping failure of sense organs. Maybe it wasn't.

Four Warm Currents watched the new world with eyes and mouth, secreting final messages down into the water, love for Six Bubbling Thermals, for Three Jagged Reefs, for the children who would sign softly but laugh wildly, and then, as numbing darkness began to seep across blurring eyes, under peeling skin, a sole suggestion for a necessary name.

THE PLAGUE GIVERS

KAMERON HURLEY

She had retired to the swamp because she liked the color. When the Contagion College came back for her thirty years after she had fled into the swamp's warm, black embrace, the color was the same, but she was not.

Which brings us here.

The black balm of dusk descended over the roiling muddy face of the six thousand miles of swampland called the Freeman's Bath. Packs of cannibal swamp dogs waded through the knobby knees of the great cypress trees that snarled up from the russet waters. Dripping nets of moss and tangled limbs gave refuge to massive plesiosaurs. The great feathered giants bobbed their heads as the swamp dogs passed, casual observers in the endless game of hunter and hunted.

Two slim people from the Contagion College, robed all in black muslin, poled their way through a gap in the weeping moss and brought their pirogue to rest at the base of a bowed cypress tree. Light gleamed from openings carved high up in the tree trunk, far too high to give them a view of what lay within. There was no need. This tree had been marked on a map and kept in the jagged towers of the Contagion College in the city for decades, waiting for a day as black as this.

"She's killed a lot of people," the smaller figure, Lealez, said, "and she's been wild out here for a long time. She may be unpredictable." The poor light softened the contours of Lealez's pockmarked face. As Lealez turned, the lights of the house set the face in profile, and Lealez took on the countenance of a beaked fisher–bird, the large nose a common draw for childhood bullies and snickering colleagues at the Contagion College who had not cared much for Lealez's face or arrogance. Lealez suspected it was the arrogance that made it so easy for the masters to assign Lealez this terribly dangerous task, rushing off after some wild woman of legend at the edge of civilization. They were always saying to Lealez how important it was to know one's place in the order of things. It could be said with certainty that this place was not the place for Lealez.

Lealez's taller companion, a long-faced, gawky senior called Abrimet, said, "When you kill the greatest sorcerer that ever lived, you can live wild as you like, too."

Abrimet's hair was braided against the scalp in a common style particular to Abrimet's gender, black as Lealez's but twice as long, dyed with henna at the ends instead of red like Lealez's. Lealez admired the shoman very much; Abrimet's older, experienced presence gave Lealez some comfort.

Full dark had fallen across the swamp. Swarms of orange fireflies with great silver beaks rose from the banks, swirling in tremulous living clouds. Far off, something much larger than their boat splashed in the water; Lealez's brokered mother had been killed by a plesiosaur, and the thought of those snaky-necked monsters sent a bolt of icy fear through Lealez's gut. But if Lealez turned around now, the Contagion College would strip Lealez of title and what remained of Lealez's life would be far worse than this.

So Abrimet called, "We have come from the Contagion College. We are of the Order of the Tree of the Gracious Death! You are summoned to speak."

Inside the tree, well-insulated from the view of the two figures in the boat, a thick, grubby woman raised her head from her work. In one broad hand she held the stuffed skin of an eyeless toy hydra; in the other, a piece of wire strung with a long white matte of hair. An empty brown bottle sat at her elbow, though it took more than a bottle of plague-laced liquor to mute her sense for plague days. She thumbed her spectacles from her nose and onto her head. She placed the half-finished hydra on the table and took her machete from the shelf. The night air wasn't any cooler than the daytime shade, so she went shirtless. Sweat dripped from her generous body and splattered across the floor as she got to her feet.

Her forty-pound swamp rodent, Mhev, snorted from his place at her feet and rolled onto his doughy legs. She snapped her fingers and pointed to his basket under the stairs. He ignored her, of course, and started grunting happily at the idea of company.

The woman rolled her brown, meaty shoulders and moved up to the left of the door like a woman expecting a fight. She hadn't had a fight in fifteen years, but her body remembered the drill. She called, "You're trespassing. Move on."

The voice replied—young and stupidly confident, maybe two years out of training in the city, based on the accent, "The whole of this territory was claimed by the Imperial Community of the Forked Ash over a decade ago. As representatives of the Community, and scholars of the Contagion College, we are within our rights in this waterway, as we have come to seek your assistance in a matter which you are bound by oath to serve."

The woman did not like city children, as she knew they were the most dangerous children of all. Yet here they were again, shouting at her door like rude imbeciles.

She pushed open the door, casting light onto the little boat and its slender occupants. They wore the long black robes and neat purple collars of the Order of the Plague Hunters. When she had worn those robes, long ago, they did not seem as ridiculous as they now looked on these skinny young people.

"Elzabet Addisalam?" the tall one said. That one was clearly a shoman, hair twisted into braided rings, ears pierced, brows plucked. The other one could have been anything—man, woman, shoman, pan. In her day, everyone dressed as their correct gender, with the hairstyles and clothing cuts to match, but fashions were changing, and she was out of date. It had become increasingly difficult to tell shoman from pan, man from woman, the longer she stayed up here. Fashion changed quickly. Pans dressed like men these days. Shomans like pans. And on and on. It made her head hurt.

She kept her machete up. "I'm called Bet, out here," she said. "And what are you? If you're dressing up as Plague Hunters, I'll have some identification before you go pontificating all over my porch."

"Abrimet," the shoman said, holding up their right hand. The broad sleeve fell back, exposing a dark arm crawling in glowing green tattoos: the double ivy circle of the Order, and three triangles, one for every Plague Hunter the shoman had dispatched. Evidence enough the shoman was what was claimed. "This is Lealez," the shoman said of the other one.

"Lealez," Bet said. "You a shoman or a neuter? Can't tell at this distance, I'm afraid. We used to dress as our gender, in my day."

The person made a face. "Dress as my gender? The way *you* do? Shall I call you man, with that hair?" Bet wore nothing but a man's veshti, sour and damp with sweat, and she had not cut or washed her hair in some time, let alone styled her brows to match her pronouns.

"It is not I knocking about on stranger's doors, requesting favors," Bet said. "What am I dealing with?"

"I'm a pan."

"That's what I thought I was saying. What, is saying neuter instead of pan a common slur now?"

"It's archaic."

"We are in a desperate situation," Abrimet said, clearly the elder, experienced one here, trying to wrest back control of the dialogue. "The Order sent us to call in your oath."

"The Order has a very long memory," Bet said, "I am sure it recalls I am no longer a member. Would you like a stuffed hydra?"

"The world is going to end," Lealez said.

"The world is always ending for someone," Bet said, shrugging. "I've heard of its demise a dozen times in as many years."

"From who?" Lealez grumbled. "The plesiosaurs?"

Abrimet said, "Two rogue Plague Givers left the Sanctuary of the Order three days ago. *Two* of them. That's more than we've had loose at any one time in twenty years."

"Sounds like a task that will make a Plague Hunter's name," Bet said. "Go be that hero." She began to close the door.

"They left a note addressed to you!" Abrimet said, gesturing at the pan.

"I have it," Lealez said. "Here."

Bet held out her hand. Lealez's soft fingers brushed Bet's as per put the folded paper into Bet's thick hands.

Bet recognized the heavy grain of the paper, and the lavender hue. She hadn't touched paper like that in what felt like half a lifetime, when the letters came to her bursting with love and desire and, eventually, a plague so powerful it nearly killed her. A chill rolled over her body, despite the heat. The last time she saw paper like this, six hundred people died and she broke her vows to the Order in exchange for moonshine and stuffed hydras. She tucked the machete under her arm. Unfolded the paper. Her fingers trembled. She blamed the heat.

The note read: *Honored Plague Hunter Elzabet Addisalam, The great sorcerer Hanere Gozene taught us to destroy the world together. You have seven days to save it. Catch us if you can.*

The note caught fire in her hands. She dropped it hastily, stepped back. The two in the boat gasped, but Bet only watched it burn to papery ash, the way she had watched the woman with that same handwriting burn to ash decades before.

The game was beginning again, and she feared she was too old to play it any longer.

II.

Thirty years earlier . . .

The day of the riots, Hanere Gozene leaned over Bet's vermillion canvas, her dark hair tickling Bet's chin, and whispered, "Would you die for me, Elzabet?"

Bet's tongue stuck out from between her lips, brow furrowed in concentration as she tried to capture the sky. For six consecutive evenings she had sat at this window, with its sweeping view over the old, twisted tops of the city's great living spires, trying to capture the essence of the bloody red sunset that met the misty cypress swamp on the city's far border, just visible from her seat.

The warm gabbling from the street was a prelude to the coming storm. Tensions had been hot all summer. The cooler fall weather moved people from languid summer unrest to more militant action. Pamphlets littered the streets; the corpses of dogs had been stuffed with them, as protest or warning, and by which side, Bet did not know or care. Not then. Not yet. She cared only about capturing the color of the sky.

Bet was used to Hanere's flare for the dramatic. Hanere had spent the last year in a production of *Tornello*, a play about the life and death of the city's greatest painter. She had a habit of seeking out and exploiting the outrageous in even the most mundane situations.

Hanere twined her fingers into Bet's apron strings, tugging them loose.

Bet batted Hanere's hands away with her free one, still intent on the painting. "You want to date a painter because you're playing one," Bet said, "I have to give you the full experience. That means I work in this light. Just work, Hanere."

"Sounds divine," Hanere said, reaching again for the apron.

"I'm working," Bet said. "That's as divine as it gets. Have some cool wine. Read a book."

"A book? A book!"

Bet would remember Hanere just this way, thirty years hence: the crooked mouth, the spill of dark hair, eyes the color of honey beer widened in mock outrage.

The lover who would soon burn the world.

III.

"Hanere Gozene," Bet said, waving the two Plague Hunters inside. The name tasted odd on her tongue, like something both grotesquely profane and sacred, just like her memories of that black revolution.

Mhev barked at the hunters from his basket. Bet shushed him, but his warning bark convinced her to look over her young guests a second time. The appearance of Hanere's letter had shaken her, and she needed to pay attention. Mhev didn't bark at Plague Hunters, only Plague *Givers*.

"Neither of us is used to company," Bet said. When she was younger, she might have forced a smile with it to cover her suspicions, but she had given up pretending she was personable a long time ago.

Abrimet sat across from her at the little table strewn with bits of leather and stuffing from her work on the hydras. The younger one, the pan, stood off to the side, tugging at per violet collar. Bet slumped into her seat opposite. She didn't offer them anything. She picked up the half–finished hydra and turned it over in her hands. "City people buy these," she said. "I trade them to a merchant who paddles upriver to sell them. No back country child is foolish enough to buy them and invite that kind of bad luck in, like asking in a couple of Plague Hunters."

Lealez and Abrimet exchanged a look. Abrimet said, quickly, "We know Hanere left twelve dead Plague Hunters behind her, when she last escaped. If she's out there mentoring these two rogues—"

"I'm over fifty years old," Bet said. "What is it you hope I'll do for you? You're not here to ask me to hunt. So what do you want?"

Mhev stirred from his basket and snuffled over to Abrimet's boots. He licked them. Abrimet grimaced and pulled the boots away.

"Did you step through truffled salt?" Bet asked, leaning forward. She used the shift in her position to push her hand closer to the hilt of the machete on the table. They were indeed Givers, not Hunters. She should have known.

Abrimet raised hairless brows. "Why would—"

"It is a common thing," Bet said, "for Plague Givers to walk through truffled salt to neutralize their last cast, or to combat the plain salt cast of a Plague Hunter, which of course you would realize. It ensures they don't bring any contagion from that cast with them to the next target. Mhev can smell that salt on you. It's like sugar, to him. Regular salt, no. Truffled salt? Oh yes."

"Abrimet is a respected Hunter," Lealez said, voice rising. "You accuse Abrimet of casting before coming here, like some rogue Giver? Abrimet is a Hunter, as am I."

"You're here for the relics," Bet said, because most of the company who came here wanted the relics, and though these two had a fine cover story and poor ability to hide what they were, they would be no different.

"You *did* use them, then," Abrimet said, leaning forward. "To defeat Hanere."

Mhev nosed under Abrimet's boot. Abrimet toed at him.

"Not every godnight story is entirely rubbish," Bet said. She still held the bottle, though it was empty. Flexed her other hand, preparing to snatch the machete. "We went south, to the City by the Crushed Lake where Hanere learned all of her high magic. The relics assisted in her capture, yes."

"We'll require the relics to defeat her students," Abrimet said, "just as you defeated her."

Mhev, sated by the salt, sat at Abrimet's boot and barked.

Bet made her choice.

She threw her bottle at Abrimet. It smashed into Abrimet's head, hard. Bet grabbed her machete and drove the machete through Abrimet's right eye.

Lealez shrieked. Raised per hands, already halfway into reciting a chant. Mhev's barking became a staccato.

Bet grabbed one of the finished hydras on the shelf and pegged Lealez in the head with it. A puff of white powder clouded the air. Lealez sneezed and fell back on the floor.

"No spells in here," Bet said to her. "That's six ounces of night buzz pollen. You won't be casting for an hour."

Bet pulled the machete clear of Abrimet. Abrimet's face still moved. Eye blinked. Tongue lolled. The body tumbled to the floor. Mhev squeaked and went for the boots.

"How were you going to do it?" she asked Lealez.

"I don't, I don't understand—" Lealez sneezed again, wiping at per face.

Bet thrust the bloody machete at per. "I have hunted Plague Givers my whole life. You thought I could not spot one like Abrimet? Did you know they cast a plague before they came here? Why do you think they stepped through truffled salt?"

Lealez considered per position, and the fine line between truth and endangering per mission. Bet's face was a knotted ruin, as if she had taken endless pummeling for decades. Her twisted black hair bled to white in patches. She was covered in insect bites and splattered blood. The spectacles resting on her head were slightly askew now. She stank terribly. The little rat happily gnawed at Abrimet's boots. Lealez had a terrible fear that this would all be blamed on per. Cities would die, the Order would be disbanded, because per had been too arrogant, and gotten perself into this horrible assignment. Abrimet, a Plague Giver? Impossible. Wasn't it? Lealez would have seen it.

"I didn't know what Abrimet was," Lealez said. "I just want to make a name for myself the way you did. I was the best of my class. I've . . . I've already killed three givers!"

"If that's true you should have a name already," Bet said.

"If they find that you killed Abrimet, you will be stung to death for it."

"A very risky venture, then, to let you go," Bet said, and was rewarded with a little tremble from Lealez.

Lealez wiped the pollen from per robe. It made per fingers numb. As per straightened per robe, Lealez wondered if Bet knew per was stalling, and if she did, how long she would let per do it before stabbing Lealez, too, with a machete. "I can speak for you before the judges, in the end," Lealez said. "You'll need someone to honor you. Another hunter. We can't hunt alone."

"A smart little upstart with no talent," Bet said.

"It's true I'm an upstart," Lealez said, "but you can't legally hunt without another hunter." Per smirked, knowing that even this old woman could not stand against *that* law.

Bet lowered her machete. "I'd have guessed the story you sold me was as fake as your friend, but I knew the paper, and I knew the signature. If I find you faked that too, you'll have more to worry about than just one dead Plague Hunter."

"It's very genuine," Lealez said. "We only have four days. They'll kill tens of thousands in the capital."

"The note said seven days."

"It took us three days to find you."

"I'll hide better next time."

Lealez got to per feet. Lealez found per was trembling, and hated perself for it. A woman like Bet looked for weakness. That was Abrimet's flaw; their fear made them start to cast a plague, instead of waiting it out. A dangerous tell in front of a woman like this. Lealez needed to seal perself up tight.

Insects whispered across the pier. "Bit of advice," Bet said. "The Order forgives a great deal if you deliver what it wants."

"You need me."

"Like a hole in the head," Bet said, "But I'll take you along. For my own reasons."

"What's more important than eliminating a threat to the Community?"

"You don't get it," Bet said. "The last time I got a note on paper like that, it was from Hanere. It's not just two rogues you're dealing with."

"There must be any number of stationery shops where—"

"That was Hanere's handwriting."

"That isn't possible."

"I turned Hanere over to the Order three decades ago, and read about her death on all the news sheets and billboards."

"She was drawn and quartered," Lealez said.

"And burned up in the searing violet flame of the Joystone Peace," Bet said. "But here she is. And why do you think that is, little upstart?"

Lealez shook per head.

"Somehow she survived all that, and now she's back to bite the Community."

"So where do we start?" Lealez asked.

"We start with the sword," Bet said. "Then we retrieve the shield. Then we confront Hanere."

"How will we know where to find her?"

Bet pulled her pack from a very high shelf. "Oh, we won't need to find her," she said. "Once the objects of power are released, she'll find us."

IV.

The Copse of Screaming Corpses loomed ahead of Bet and Lealez's little pirogue. Great, knotted fingers, black as coal, tangled with the fog, poking snarling holes in the mist that hinted at the massive shapes hidden within. Sometimes the waves of gray shifted, revealing a glaring eye, a knobby knee, or the gaping mouth of one of the twisted, petrified forest of giants, forever locked in a scream of horror.

The copse was a good day's paddle from Bet's refuge. When she told Lealez the name, Lealez thought Bet was making fun.

"That isn't the real name," Lealez said. The dense fog muffled per words.

"Oh, it is," Bet said. "It's aptly named."

"Does the name alone scare people off?"

"The smart ones, yes," Bet said.

Ripples traveled across the bubbling water.

"What are these bubbles?"

"Sinkhole," Bet said. "They open up under the swamp sometimes. Pull boats under, whole villages. We're lucky. Probably happened sometime last night."

"Just a hole in the world?"

"Had one in the capital forty years ago," Bet said. "Ate the Temple of Saint Torch. Those fancy schools don't teach that?"

"I guess not," Lealez said. Per gazed into the great canopy of dripping moss that covered the looming giants above them. Their great, gaping maws were fixed in snarls of pain, or perhaps outrage. Lealez imagined them eating per whole. "Why put it here?" per said. "This place is awful."

"Would you come here for any other reason but retrieving an object of power?"

"No."

"You have your answer."

Bet poled the pirogue up to the edge of a marshy island and jumped out. She tied off the pirogue and pulled a great coil of rope over her shoulder. She headed off into the misty marsh without looking back at Lealez. Lealez scrambled after her, annoyed and a little frightened. Bet's generous shape was quickly disappearing into the mist.

Lealez yelped as per brushed the knobby tangle of some giant's pointing finger.

When Lealez caught up with Bet, she was already heaving the large rope over her shoulder. She sucked her teeth as she walked around the half-buried torso of one of the stricken giants. Its hands clawed at the sky, and its face was lost in the fog.

Bet tossed up one end of the rope a couple of times until she succeeded in getting it over the upraised left arm of the giant. She tied one end around her waist and handed Lealez the other end.

Lealez frowned.

"Hold onto it," Bet said. "Pull up the slack as I go. You never climbed anything before?"

Lealez shook her head.

Bet sighed. "What do they teach you kids these days?" She kicked off her shoes and began to climb. "Don't touch or eat anything while you're down here."

Lealez watched, breathless. Bet seemed too big to climb such a thing, but she found little hand and footholds as she went, jamming her fingers and toes into crevices and deviations in the petrified giant.

Lealez held tight to the other end of the rope, pulling the slack and watching Bet disappear into the fog as she climbed up onto the giant's shoulder. Lealez glanced around at the fog, feeling very alone.

Above, Bet took her time climbing the monster. She had been a lot younger when she did this the first time, and she was already resenting her younger self. Warbling hoots and cries came from the swampland around her, distorted by the fog. Her breath came hard and her fingers ached, but she reached the top of the giant in due course.

She knew there was something wrong the moment she hooked herself up around the back of the giant's head. The head was spongy at the front, as if rotting from within. The whole back of it had been ripped open. Inside the giant's head was a gory black hole where the sword had been.

She pulled the knife from her hip and hacked into the back of the head, peering deep inside, scraping away bits of calcified brain matter. But it was no use. The head was empty. She traced the edges of the hole carved in the giant's head. Someone had hacked out the great round piece of the skull that she had mortared back into place with a sticky contagion years ago. Only she and her partner Keleb had known about the contagion. They would be the only two people capable of neutralizing it before removing the relic.

"Briar and piss," she muttered.

Below, Lealez screamed.

Bet sheathed her knife as she scrambled back down the giant, aware that her rope had gone slack. Foolish pan, what was the point of a rope if Bet cracked her head open on the way down?

Lealez screamed and screamed, horrified by the rippling of per skin. Lealez had tilted per head up to follow Bet's progress and left per mouth open, and a shard of the great giant's skin had flaked off and fallen into per mouth.

Lealez gagged on it, but it went down, and now per body was . . . growing, distending; Lealez thought per would burst into a thousand pieces. But that, alas, did not happen. Instead, Lealez grew and grew. Arms thickened with muscle. Thighs became large around as tree trunks.

When finally Lealez saw Bet sliding down the tree, Lealez's head was already up past Bet's position.

Bet swore and leapt the rest of the way down the face of the giant. She took a fistful of salt from the pouch at her hip and threw it in a circle around Lealez's burgeoning body. Lealez's clothes had burst, falling in tatters all around per. Bet muttered a chant, half–curse, half–cure, concentrating on the swinging arms above her. Bet pulled a bit of tangled herb from another pouch, already laced with contagion. She breathed the words she had last spoken in a dusty library in the Contagion College and let the plague free.

All around them, biting flies swarmed up from the swampland, drawn by her cast. They ate bits of the contagion and landed onto Lealez's body, which was now nearing the height of the petrified giants around them. Per skin was beginning to blacken and calcify around per ankles.

The swarm of flies covered Lealez's body like a second skin. Lealez squealed and swatted at them, per movements increasingly slow. The flies bit Lealez's flesh again and again while Bet squatted and urinated on the salt circle.

All at once the flies fell off Lealez. The pan's skin began to flake away where it had been bitten. The body contracted again, until it was half the size it had been, still giant. Then Lealez fell over with a great thump.

Bet ran to Lealez's side. The skin had turned obsidian black, hard as shale. Bet took her machete from her hip and hacked at the torso until great cracks opened up in the body. Then she pulled the pieces away.

Lealez was curled up inside the husk of per former self, arms crossed over per chest, shivering.

"Get out of there now," Bet said, offering per an arm.

Lealez tentatively took her hand, and Bet pulled per out. "Dusk is coming soon," Bet said, "I don't want to get caught out here."

It was warm enough that Bet wasn't too worried about Lealez being naked, but Lealez seemed to mind, and went searching for per pack, which had been ripped from Lealez's body. It was a stupid search, Bet thought, because the fog was getting denser, and they were losing the light, and Lealez's things could have gone anywhere.

Finally Lealez found the remains of per haversack, and pulled on a fresh robe. But the rest of per things were scattered, and Bet insisted they move on and not wait.

"The College will be angry," Lealez said. "My books, my papers—"

"Books and papers? Is that all you can think about? Hurry. Didn't I tell you not to touch or eat anything?"

"You didn't say why!"

"I shouldn't have to say why, you dumb pan. When I was your age I did whatever my mentor said."

"Are you my mentor now? You aren't even officially a Hunter. You would never be approved as a mentor by the college."

"Is everything joyless and literal with you?"

"You don't know how the college is now," Lealez said. "Old people like you tell us how things should be, how we should think, but this is a new age. We face a different government, and new penalties after the Plague Wars. We can't all go rogue or shirk our duties. We'd be kicked out. The college is very strict these days. People like you would never make it to graduation. You would end up working in contagion breweries."

"I'm sure you'd like to continue on with that fantasy awhile longer," Bet said.

Once they were in the pirogue and had cast off, Lealez finally roused perself from misery and asked, "What about the artifact?"

"Someone got to it first," Bet said.

"Hanere?"

"Only one other person knows where these are. I expect they were compelled to get it."

"Your partner?"

Bet nodded.

"You think they are still alive?"

"No," Bet said.

At least Lealez said nothing else.

V.

Bet's partner Keleb, too, had retired, but had chosen a canal that acted as a main trading thoroughfare into the city instead of a hard–to–find retreat like Bet's. It took a day and a half to reach the shoman's house, and Bet found herself counting down the time in her head. Lealez, too, reminded her of the ticking chirp of time as they poled downriver. The current was sluggish, and the weather was still and hot.

Despite the stillness, Bet smelled the smoke before she saw it. Lealez sat up in per seat and leaned far over the prow, knuckles gripping the edge of the craft.

The guttered ruin of Keleb's house came into view as they rounded the bend. The shoman had built the house with Bet's help, high up on a snarl of land that hardly ever flooded. Now the house was a charred wreck.

Bet tied off the pirogue and climbed up the steep bank. She counted three sets of footprints along the bank and around the house. They had stayed to watch it burn.

Bet poked around the still smoking house and found what was left of Keleb's body, as charred and ruined as the house.

"Help me here," Bet said to Lealez.

Lealez came up after her. "What can we do?" Lealez said. "The shoman is dead."

"Not the body I'm here for," Bet said. She walked off into the wood and chopped down two long poles from a nearby stand of trees. She handed a pole to Lealez. "Help me get the body rolled back, clear the area here."

Lealez knit per brows, but did as per was told. They heaved over Keleb's body to reveal a tattered hemp rug beneath. Bet yanked it away and used the pole to lever open a piece of the floor. Peeling back the wood revealed a long, low compartment. Lealez leaned over to get a better look, but it was clearly empty.

Bet sucked her teeth.

"What was here?" Lealez asked.

"The cloak," Bet said.

"I thought there were two relics, a sword and a shield."

"That's because that's all we reported," Bet said. "Because we knew this day would come." Bet saw the edge of a piece of paper peeking out from the bottom of the cache and picked it up. It was another note, made out to her in Hanere's handwriting.

"What does it say?" Lealez asked.

Bet traced the words and remembered a day thirty years before, rioting in the streets, a plump painter, and a future she had imagined that looked nothing like this one.

Bet crumpled up the note. "It says she will trade me the objects in return for something I love," Bet said. "Good thing I don't love anything."

Nothing but Hanere, of course. But that was a long time ago. Bet hardly felt anything there in the pit of her belly when she thought of Hanere. It was the time in her life she longed for, not Hanere. That's what she told herself.

"What a monster," Lealez said, staring at Keleb's charred body.

"None of us is a sainted being, touched by some god," Bet said. "But she's missing the third relic. She'll need that before she can end the world."

Lealez shivered. "We don't have much time left."

"There's a suspension line that runs up the river near here," Bet said. "Let's see if we can find you some clothes."

"There are only shoman's clothes here," Lealez said.

"We all have to make sacrifices," Bet muttered.

They walked away from Keleb's house; two people, a woman and a pan dressed in shoman's clothes, the vestments smoky and charred. Bet expected Lealez to talk more, but Lealez kept the peace. Lealez found perself following after Bet in a daze. For years Lealez had wanted nothing more than to prove perself to the Contagion College. It was beginning to dawn on Lealez just what per had to do to achieve the honor per wished for, and it was frightening, far more frightening than it had seemed when Lealez read all the books about Plague Hunters and Plague Givers and how the Hunters tracked down the

Givers and saved the world. No one spoke of charred bodies, or what it was like to be cut out of one's own plague–touched skin.

The great suspension line ran along the Potsdown Peace canal all the way to the Great Dawn harbor that housed the city. Bet sighed and paid their fare to the scrawny little pan who lived in what passed for a gatehouse this far south of the city.

"College better reimburse all this," Bet said, and laughed, because the idea that she would be alive to get reimbursed in another day was distinctly amusing.

Bet and Lealez climbed the stairs up to the carriage that hung along the suspended line and settled in. Lealez looked a little sick, so Bet asked, "You been up before?"

"I don't like heights," Lealez said.

The gatekeeper came up and attached their carriage line to the pulley powered by a guttering steam engine, which the pan swore at several times before the carriage finally stuttered out along the line, swinging away from the gatehouse and over the water.

Lealez shut per eyes.

Bet leaned out over the side of the carriage and admired the long backs of a pod of plesiosaurs moving in the water beneath them.

After a few minutes, Lealez said, "I don't understand why you didn't tell the College there were three objects."

"Of course you do," Bet said.

"It doesn't—"

"Don't pretend you're some fool," Bet said. "I haven't believed a word you've said any more than I believed your little friend."

Lealez stiffened. "Why keep me alive, then?"

"Because I think you can be salvaged," Bet said. "Your friend couldn't. Your friend was already a Plague Giver. I think you're still deciding your own fate."

They rode in silence after that for nearly an hour. Lealez was startled when Bet finally broke it.

"Keleb and I couldn't defeat Hanere ourselves," Bet said. "I'd like to tell you we could. But she's more powerful. She has a far blacker heart, and a blacker magic. We went south, Keleb and I, and got help from sorcerers and hedge witches. They were the ones who created the objects of power. The sword, the shield, and the cloak."

"How do they work?" Lealez asked.

"You'll know soon enough," Bet said. "Not even Keleb knew where I kept the shield, though."

"But, the other weapons—"

The carriage shuddered. Lealez gave a little cry.

"Hold on, it's just—" Bet began, and then the carriage hook sheared clean away, and they plunged into the canal.

VI.

Thirty years earlier . . .

Hanere had always loved to watch things burn. Bet sat with her on the rooftop while riots overtook the city. They sipped black bourbon and danced and talked about how the world would be different now that the revolutionaries had done more than talk. They were burning it all down.

"If only I could be with them!" Hanere said.

Bet pulled Hanere into her lap. "You are better off here with me. Out there is a world of monsters and mad people."

Hanere waggled her brows. "Who's to say I'm not a bit of both? Come with me, we are out of bourbon!" She held up the empty bottle.

"No, no," Bet said. "Stay in. We'll sleep up here."

Bet had gone to sleep while the world burned. But that wasn't Hanere's way. While Bet slept, Hanere went out into it.

It was the edge of dawn when Bet finally woke, hung over and covered in cigarette ash, hands smeared in paint from her work earlier in the day. It was not until she sat up and saw the paint smearing the roof that she thought something was amiss. Her gaze followed the trail of paint that was not paint but blood to its origin. Hanere stood at the edge of the rooftop, wearing a long white shift covered in blood.

Bet scrambled up. "Are you hurt? Hanere?"

But as Hanere turned, Bet stopped. Hanere raised her bloody hands to the sky and her face was full of more joy than Bet had ever seen.

"The government is nearly toppled," Hanere said. "We will be gods, you and I, Bet. There's no one to stop us. It's delightful down there. You must come."

"What did you do, Hanere?"

"I am alive for the first time in my life," Hanere said. She opened her hands, and salt fell from her fingers. She murmured something, and little blue florets colored the air and passed out over the city.

"Stop it," Bet said. "What are you doing? You can't cast in the city outside the College!"

"I cast all night," Hanere said. "I will cast all I like. Come with me. Bet, come with me, my Elzabet. My love. We can take this whole city. We can burn down the college and those tired old people and repaint the world."

"No, Hanere. Get down from there."

The joy left Hanere's face. "Is that what you wish for us?" she said. She came down from the rooftop and walked over to Bet. She placed her hands on

Bet's stomach. The blood on her hands was still fresh enough to leave stains. "Is that what you wish for our child?"

VII.

Bet sucked in water instead of air, and paddled to the surface, kicking wildly. She popped up in the brown water and took in her surroundings. Lealez was nowhere in sight. She dove again into the water, feeling her way through the muck for Lealez. Opening her eyes was a lost cause; she could see nothing. Her fingers snagged a bit of cloth. She grabbed at it and heaved Lealez to the surface.

Lealez coughed and sputtered. Bet kept per at arm's length, yelling that all per splashing was going to drown them both.

"Head for the shore," Bet said.

Lealez shook per head and treaded water using big, sloppy strokes. Bet followed per gaze and saw the hulking shapes of the plesiosaurs circling the carriage.

"They eat plants," Bet said. "Mostly."

Bet hooked Lealez under her arm and paddled for the shore. The plesiosaurs kept pace with them, displacing great waves of water that made it more difficult to get to the shore.

Lealez gasped. "They'll crush us!"

"More worried about the lizards on the shore," Bet said.

"What?"

Two big alligators lay basking along the shore. Bet made for another hollow a little further on, but they were closer than they should be.

"They only eat at night," Bet said, reassuring herself as much as Lealez. "Mostly."

Bet and Lealez crawled up onto the bank and immediately started off into the brush. Bet wanted to put as much distance between her and the lizards as possible. Massive mosquitoes and biting flies plagued them, but Bet knew they were close enough to the city now that they might find a settlement or— if they were lucky—someone's spare pirogue.

Instead, they found the plague.

The bodies started just twenty minutes into their walk to the shore, and continued for another hour as they grew nearer and nearer the settlement. Soft white fungus grew from the noses and eyes and mouths of the dead; their fingers and toes were blackened. Bet stopped and drew a circle of salt around her and Lealez, and sprinkled some precautionary concoctions over them.

"Do you know which one it is?" Lealez whispered.

"One of Hanere's," Bet said. "She likes to leave a mark. She's expecting us."

"Is this where you left the shield?"

"Hush now," Bet said as the swampland opened up into a large clearing. Nothing was burning, which was unlike Hanere.

Bet stopped Lealez from going further and held up a finger to her lips. Two figures stood at the center of the village, heads bent in deep conversation. One wore a long black and purple cloak. The other carried a sword emblazoned with the seal of the Contagion College.

"Stay here," Bet said to Lealez. She pulled out her machete and stepped into the clearing.

The two figures looked up. Bet might have had to guess at their gender if one of them wasn't so familiar. She knew that one's gender because she'd been there during the ceremony where he'd chosen it. It was her and Hanere's own son, Mekdas. The other was most likely female, based on the hairstyle and clothing, but that didn't much concern Bet.

A trade for something Bet loved, that's what Hanere had written.

"So it was you who broke away from the Contagion College," Bet said.

Mekdas stared at her. He was nearly thirty now, not so much a boy, but he still looked young to her, younger even than Lealez. He had Hanere's bold nose and Bet's straight dark hair and Hanere's full lips and Bet's stocky build and Hanere's talent and impatience.

"I left you with the college so you could make something of yourself," Bet said. "Now here you are disappointing me twice."

"That's something Hanere and you never had in common," Mekdas said. "She was never once disappointed in me."

Bet searched the ground around them for the shield. If they had gotten this far they must have found that too, no matter that Bet was the only one who was supposed to know where it was. Had Hanere used some kind of black magic to find it?

"Give over the objects," Bet said, "and we can talk about this."

"Have you met my lover?" Mekdas asked. "This is Saba."

Saba was a short waif of a woman, a little older than Mekdas. As much as Bet wanted to blame this all on some older Plague Giver, she knew better. She had done her best with Mekdas, but it was all too late.

Bet held out her hand. "The cloak, Mekdas."

"You're an old woman," Mekdas said. "Completely useless out here. Go back to your swamp. We are remaking the world. You don't have the stomach for it."

"You're right," Bet said. She didn't know what to say to him. She had never been good with children, and with Hanere dead, she had wanted even less to do with this particular child. He reminded her too much of Hanere. "I don't have the stomach for many things, but I know a plague village when I see one.

I know where this goes, and I know how it ends. You think you can take this plague all the way to the city?"

Saba raised the sword. "With the relics, we will," she said, and smirked.

"Hanere tell you how they work, did she?" Bet said. "The trouble is Hanere doesn't know. There is one person alive who knows, and it's me."

"Hanere will show us," Saba said.

"You shut the seven fucking hells up," Bet said. "I'm not talking to you. Mekdas—"

"Why are you even here?" he said.

"Because Hanere invited me," Bet said.

That got a reaction from him. Surprise. Shock, even.

Bet already had a handful of salt ready, but so did they. The shock was all the advantage she had. Bet flicked the salt in their faces and charged toward them. She bowled over Saba and snatched the sword from her. They were Plague Givers, not warriors, and it showed.

Mekdas had the sense to run, but Bet stabbed the sword through his cloak and twisted. He fell hard onto a body, casting spores into the air.

Bet yelled for Lealez.

Lealez bolted across the sea of bodies, hand already raised to cast.

"Circle and hold them," Bet said.

Lealez's hands trembled as per made the cast to neutralize the two hunters.

Bet tore the cloak from Mekdas's shoulders and wrapped it around her own. She dragged the sword in one hand and crossed to the other side of the village. Bet found the tree she had nested her prize in decades before and hacked it open to reveal the shield, now buried in the heart of the tree. Sweat ran down her face so heavily she had to squint to see. She picked up the shield and marched back to where Saba and Mekdas lay prone inside the salt circle.

"Now you'll see all you wanted to see," Bet said to Mekdas. "You will see the world can be made as well as unmade, but there are sacrifices." She raised the sword over her head.

"No!" Lealez said.

"Please!" Mekdas said.

Bet plunged the blade into Saba's heart and spit the words of power that released the objects' essence. A cloud of brilliant purple dust burst from Saba's body and filled the air. Lealez stumbled back, coughing.

Bet quickly removed the cloak and draped it over Saba. All around the village, the bodies began to convulse. White spores exploded from their mouths and noses and spiraled toward the cloak, a great spinning vortex of contagion.

Lealez watched the cloak absorb the great gouts of plague, feeding on it like some hungry beast. A great keening shuddered through the air. It took

Lealez a moment to realize it was Saba, screaming. And screaming. Lealez covered per ears.

Then it was over.

Bet stepped away from Saba's body, but tripped and stumbled back, fell hard on her ass. She heaved a great sigh and rested her forehead on the hilt of the sword.

"What did you do?" Mekdas said. His voice broke. He was weeping.

Bet raised her head.

All around them, the plague–ridden people of the village began to stir. Their blackened flesh warmed to a healthy brown. Their plague–clotted eyes cleared and opened. Soon, their questioning voices could be heard, and Bet got to her feet, because she was not ready for questions.

"They're alive!" Lealez said, gaping. "You saved them."

Bet pulled the cloak from Saba's body. Saba's face was a bitter rictus, frozen in agony. "They only save life by taking life," Bet said. "Now you know why I separated them. Why I never kept them together. Yes, they can give life. But they can take it, too. It's the intent that matters."

"We have one of them, at least," Lealez said. "We can take him to the Contagion College."

"No," Bet said. She raised her head to the sky. "This is not done." While the people of the village stirred, the insects in the swampland around them had gone disturbingly quiet.

"What is—" Lealez began.

"Let's get to the water," Bet said. "Take Mekdas. We need to get away from the village."

"But—"

"Listen to me in this, you fool."

Lealez bound Mekdas with hemp rope rubbed in salt and pushed him out ahead of them. Lealez had to hurry to keep up with Bet. Carrying the objects seemed to have given her some greater strength, or maybe just a sense of purpose. She forged out ahead of them, cutting through swaths of swampland, cutting a way for them all the way back down to the water on the other side of the river.

Lealez stared out at the water and saw two pirogues attached to a cypress tree another hundred steps up the canal. "There!"

"Take my machete," Bet said. "You'll take one boat on your own. Follow after Mekdas and I."

Lealez took the machete. "You're really going to turn him in?"

Bet glared at per so fiercely Lealez wanted to melt into the water.

"All right," Lealez said, "I wasn't sure what I was thinking." Lealez waded out toward the pirogue. Lealez noticed the ripple in the water out of the corner of per eye and turned.

Bet saw the ripple a half moment before. She yelled and raised her sword, but she was too slow.

A massive alligator snatched Lealez by the leg and dragged per under the water. Bet saw Lealez's upraised arms, a rush of brown water, and then nothing.

Mekdas ran.

Bet swore and scrambled after him. She fell in along the muddy bank, and then something else came up from the water for her.

Hanere emerged from the depths of the swamp like a creature born there. She head–butted Bet so hard Bet's nose burst. Pain shattered across her face. Bet fell in the mud.

Muddy water and tangles of watercress streamed off Hanere's body. Her hair was knotted and tangled, and her beard was shot through with white. She grabbed hold of Bet's boot and dragged Bet toward her.

Bet held up the sword. "Revenge will get you nothing, Hanere!"

"It got me you," Hanere said, and wrenched the shield from Bet's hand and threw it behind her.

"You feel better with me here?" Bet said, gasping.

"A bit, yes."

"And when your son is dead? If I don't kill him, someone else will."

"They were in love, like we were," Hanere said. "It was easy to convince them to burn down a world that condemned them, and me. Even you. This world cast even you out, after all you did."

"Not like us. They're both criminals."

"You became a criminal when you fucked me, and kept fucking me, even when you told them you were hunting me. You and your soft heart."

Bet kicked herself further down the bank, holding the sword ahead of her. "I thought you dead," Bet said. "For thirty years—"

"That's a bunch of shit," Hanere said. "You know they'd never kill someone like me. You know what they did to me for thirty years? Put me up in a salt box and tortured me. Me, the greatest sorcerer that ever lived."

"How did you—"

"Does it matter?" Hanere said, and her tone softened. She crawled toward Bet and took hold of the end of the sword. She pressed it to her chest and said, "Is this what you wanted? To do it yourself? Or did you wait always for this day, when we could take the world together?"

Tears came, unbidden. Bet gritted her teeth in anger. Her own soft heart, betraying her. "You know I can't."

"Even now?" Hanere said softly, "after all this time?"

Bet shook her head.

Hanere reached out for Bet's cheek, and though it was mud on Hanere's fingers and not blood, the memory of Hanere's bloody hands was still so strong after all these years that Bet flinched.

"We are done," Bet said, and pressed the sword into Hanere's heart.

Hanere did not fight her. Instead, she pulled herself forward along the length of the blade, closer and closer, until she could kiss Bet with her bloody mouth.

"I will die in your arms," Hanere said, "as I should have done."

Mekdas screamed, long and high, behind them.

Bet sagged under Hanere's weight.

Mekdas bolted past her and ran toward the two pirogues.

Bet turned her eyes upward. Soft while clouds moved across the purple-blue sky. She wanted to be a bird, untethered from all this filth and sweat, all these tears. Thirty years she had hid, thirty years she had tried to avoid this day. But here it was. And she had done it, hadn't she? Done everything she hoped she would not do.

She heard a splashing from the water, and heaved a sigh. The lizard would take her. Gods, let the lizard take her, and the relics, and drown them for all time.

When she opened her eyes, though, it was Lealez who stood above her, dripping water onto her face. The pan was covered in gore, and stank like rotten meat. Lealez held up the machete. "Told you I was the best in my class," Lealez said.

"Didn't know you learned how to kill lizards," Bet said.

Lealez gazed at Hanere's body. "Is she really dead?"

"I don't know that I care," Bet said. "Is that strange?"

Lealez helped her up. "The boy is trying to figure out the pirogue," Lealez said. "We aren't done."

"You take him."

"He's your family," Lealez said.

"My responsibility?"

"I just thought . . . You would want to take the credit."

Bet huffed out a laugh. "The credit? The *credit*." She heaved herself forward, slogging toward the pirogue.

Mekdas saw her coming and pushed off. As she approached he stood up in the little boat, unsteady already on the water.

Behind him, Bet could just see the lights of the city in the distance. Did they all know what was coming for them? Did any realize that there were Plague Givers out here who wanted to decimate the world and start over? Would they care, or would they be like Hanere, and wish for an end?

"You must kill me to save that city, then, mother," Mekdas said. "Will you kill me like you did Hanere? You won't bring me in alive. You must make the—"

Bet threw her sword. It thunked into her son's belly. He gagged and bowled over.

Lealez gaped.

Bet waded out to the pirogue and pulled it back to shore.

"You killed him," Lealez said. "I thought—"

"He's not dead yet," Bet said, but the words were only temporarily truth. He was gasping his last, drowning in his own blood.

"I've heard ultimatums like that before," Bet said. "Hanere gave me one, and when I hesitated, I lost her. You only make a mistake like that, the heart over reason, once. Then you take yourself away from the world, so you don't have to make decisions like that again."

"But—"

"Blood means little when there's a city at stake," Bet said. She gazed back out at the city. "Let's give them to the swamp."

"But we have to take the bodies back to—"

Bet raised the sword and pointed it at Lealez. It was only then that she realized Lealez was favoring per right leg; the lizard had gotten its teeth in per, and Lealez would get infected badly, soon, if they didn't get per help in the city.

"We do the bodies my way," Bet said, "then we get you back to the city."

When they came back to Hanere's body, it was encircled by a great mushroom ring. Green spores floated through the air.

"Is she dangerous?" Lealez said.

"Not anymore," Bet said.

Together, they hauled the body through the undergrowth, avoiding the snapping jaws of swamp dogs and startling a pack of rats as big as Bet's head. Bet was aware of Hanere's stinking body, the slightly swelling flesh. When they dumped her into the hill of ants, Bet stood and watched them devour the woman she had spent half her life either chasing or romancing.

"Are you all right?" Lealez said.

"No," Bet said. "Never have been."

Mekdas was next.

While they stood watching the ants devour him, Lealez glanced over at Bet and said, "I know this is a hard profession, but there's honor in it. It does a public good."

"No, we just murder people."

"We eliminate threats to—"

"Can you even say it? Can you say, 'We murder people.'"

"This is a ridiculous conversation."

"On that, we can agree," Bet said. She glanced over at Lealez. "Something I noticed back there, in the Copse of Screaming Corpses. You never showed me your credentials."

"Don't be ridiculous."

Bet grabbed per arm and yanked back per sleeve before Lealez could pull away. There was the double ivy circle of the order, but no triangles.

Bet released her, disgusted. "What happened to being best in your class? Apprehending three Plague Givers? That's what your duplicitous friend Abrimet said, wasn't it?"

"I came out here to make a name for myself."

Bet stared down at the little pan, and though she wanted to hate Lealez more than anything, she had to admit, "I suspect you have indeed done that."

VIII.

Lealez smoothed per coat and mopped the sweat from per brow. The great Summoning Circle of the Contagion College was stuffed to bursting with fellow Plague Hunters. The map case Lealez carried over per shoulder felt heavier and heavier as the afternoon wore on to dusk. The initial round of questions had worn down into a second and then third round where Lealez felt per was simply repeating perself. Not a single apprentice or hunter with fewer than three triangles was allowed into the space. By that measure, Lealez wouldn't have been able to come to per own trial just a few days ago. Lealez swallowed hard. In front of per lay the relics per and Bet had spent so much effort retrieving.

Lealez knew it was a betrayal, but per also knew there was no triangle on per arm yet, and this was the only way.

The coven of judges peered down at Lealez from the towering amber dais. The air above them swarmed with various plagues and contagions, all of them meant to counteract any assaults coming from outside the theater. But the swarm still made Lealez's nose run and eyes water. Lealez felt like a leaky sponge.

"Where are the bodies?" Judge Horven asked, waggling her large mustache.

"We disposed of them," Lealez said. "Elzabet was . . . understandably concerned that Hanere Gozene could rise again. As she had risen once before."

"Then you have no proof," Judge Horven said.

Lealez gestured expansively to the relics. "I have brought back the relics that Elzabet Addisalam and Keleb Ozdanam used to defeat Hanere Gozene," Lealez said. "And you have the testimony of the two of us of course."

Judge Rosteb, the eldest judge, held up their long–fingered hands and barked out a long laugh. "We are former Plague Hunters, all," they said. "We know that testimony between partners can be . . . suspect."

"I stand before you with all I have learned," Lealez said. "Abrimet was unfortunately lost to us along the way, through no fault of either Elzabet or myself. Their death was necessary to our goal. I regret it. You all know that Abrimet was my mentor. But we did as we were instructed. We stopped

Hanere and the other two Plague Givers. I retrieved the relics. Both of those things cannot be contested. Because even if, as you say, you see no body, I can tell you this—you will never see Hanere again upon this soil. That will be proof enough of my accomplishments."

The judges conferred while Lealez sweated it out below them. Not for the first time, Lealez wished they had let Bet inside, but that was impossible, of course. Bet had murdered Abrimet, and done a hundred other things that were highly unorthodox in the apprehension of a Plague Giver. The judges would already worry that Bet had been a terrible influence on Lealez. Lealez would be lucky to get through this with per own head intact. At least Lealez would die in clean clothes, after a nice cold bath, which was the first thing per had done on entering the city.

Finally, the judges called Lealez forward.

"Hold out your arm," Judge Rosteb said.

IX.

Bet waited for Lealez outside the great double doors of the theater. Plague Hunters streamed past Bet as they were released from the meeting, all pointedly ignoring her. No one liked a woman who could kill her own family, no matter how great a sorcerer she was. The better she was, the more they hated her.

And there was Lealez. Lealez walked out looking dazed. Bet frowned at per empty hands. Lealez had gone in with the relics to make per case for destroying them, but Bet had a good idea of what had happened to them.

"Let's see them," Bet said, and snatched Lealez's arm. They had tattooed the mark of three successful hunts there. Bet snorted in disgust. "All three, then. You really learned nothing at all, did you? I could kill you too, but there are hundreds, thousands, just like you, crawling all over each other to do the bidding of the City Founders. You're like a hydra, spitting up three more scaly heads for every one I hack off."

"You don't know how difficult it is to rise up through the college now," Lealez said.

"You kids talk like it was any easier. It wasn't. We got asked to make the same stupid choices. They wanted the relics when Keleb and I came back, too. But we held out."

"You were already famous! Your reputation was secured!"

"Shit talk," Bet said. "You're just not tough enough to give up your career so young. I get that. But think on this. It's easy to destroy a country with plague, but how do you save your own from it? You'll all unleash something in the far empires and think we're safe, but we aren't, not with a thousand relics. All killing gets you is more killing. You pick up a machete, kid, and you'll be picking it up your whole life."

"None of it matters now," Lealez said, and sniffed. Lealez pulled a cigarette from a silver case, but for all per insouciance, Bet noted that per hands trembled. "They have the relics. What they do with them now doesn't concern me."

"Dumb kid," Bet said.

Lealez lit per cigarette with a clunky old lighter from per bag, something that would have weighed per down by an extra pound in the swamp. Lealez took a long draw. "I gave them the sword and the shield," per said, "just so you know."

"The . . . sword and shield. That's what you gave them?"

"Yeah, like I said." Lealez pulled a leather map case from per shoulder. "Here's the thing I promised you," Lealez said.

"I see," Bet said. She took the case from per. "You know the relics don't work unless they're all together?"

"Don't know about that," Lealez said. "I'm just a dumb kid, remember?"

"I'm sorry," Bet said.

Lealez shrugged. "Just get out of here. You aren't suited to the city."

Bet tipped her head at Lealez. "I don't want us to meet again," Bet said. "No offense meant."

"None taken," Lealez said. "If we meet again it means I'm not doing my job. I know how to play this game too, Bet." Lealez handed Bet the lighter and walked back into the college.

Bet pocketed it and watched per go. Lealez did not look back. When Lealez opened the great door of the College to go back inside, per hand no longer trembled. That pan was going to make a good Hunter someday, like it or not.

Bet shouldered the map case and began her own long walk across the city. It took nearly two hours to cross the dim streets, navigating her way based on which roads had functioning gaslights. She went all the way to the gates of the city and into the damp mud of the swamp before she risked opening the map case.

Inside, the cloak artifact was rolled up dry and tight. Bet rented a skiff upriver and spent the next week trudging home on foot and by whatever craft she could beg a ride up on.

When it came time to do what needed to be done, she wasn't sure she could do it. What if there was another Hanere? But so long as the relics existed, the world wasn't safe.

Bet burned the cloak there in the canopy of the cypress trees while swamp dogs snarled and barked in the distance. She watched the smoke coil up through the dense leaves and moss, and let out a breath.

It was decided. For better or worse.

• • •

X.

She had retired to the swamp because she liked the color. The color was the same, but she was not.

Bet leaned over the dim light of her firefly lantern, pushing her stuffed hydra into its glow. She eased the big sewing needle through its skin with her rough, thick fingers. On the shelves behind her were dozens of cast–off hydras, each defective in some way that she could not name. The College knew where she was now, and it made her work more difficult to concentrate on in the many long months back at her damp home. She sweated heavily, as the sun had only just set, and the air would keep its heat for a long time yet. She was tired, but no more than the day before, or the day before that. She had made her choices.

Mhev snorted softly in his basket with a litter of four baby swamp rodents, all mewing contentedly out here in the black. She wished she could join them, but her work was not done.

Outside, the insects grew quiet. Bet had been waiting for them. The waiting was the worst part. The rest was much easier. Whether it was child or Hunter or Giver or beast who stilled their call, she had made her choice about how to defend her peace long before, when she first condemned Hanere to death. She had already killed everything they both loved then.

That left her here.

Bet took hold of the machete at her elbow, the machete she would be taking into her hands for the rest of her life, and opened the door.

LAWS OF NIGHT AND SILK

SETH DICKINSON

———

Kavian can pretend this girl is her daughter through drought and deluge, but the truth is the truth: Irasht is a weapon, and never any more.

It hurts enough to break even the charcoal heart of Kavian Catamount, and so she does a forbidden thing—she puts her arms around the girl Irasht who is not her daughter, kisses her brow, and whispers:

"I will protect you. Go."

Then Kavian pushes Irasht onto the stone above the battle.

In the valley beneath them the Cteri, the people of the dams, the people of Kavian's blood and heart, stand against the invader. The Efficate comes baying to drain five centuries of civilization into their own arid land.

So the word has come from Kavian's masters, from the Paik Rede and warlord Absu:

You have had time enough to tame her. Go to the battle. Use the abnarch girl, the girl who is not your daughter.

Destroy the Efficate army.

Kavian cries the challenge.

"Men of the Efficate! Men of the owl!" Her wizardry carries the bellow down the valley, across the river, to shatter and rebound from the hills. "I am Kavian Catamount, sorcerer of the Paik Rede! I like to warm my hands on your brothers' burning corpses!"

Fifty thousand enemy spearmen shudder in fear. They know her name.

But the battle today does not ride on Kavian's fire.

The girl Irasht (who is not her daughter) stares at the battle-plain, wide-eyed, afraid, and puts her hands up to her ears. Kavian seizes her wrists, to keep her from blocking out the sound of war. Irasht claws and spits but does not cry.

Over Irasht's hissing frenzy Kavian roars: "My hands are *cold* today!"

She hears the cry go up in the Efficate ranks, a word in their liquid tongue that means: *abnarch, abnarch, she has brought an abnarch.* And she sees their eyes on her, their faces lifted in horror and revulsion, at the girl Irasht, at what has been done to her.

You poor bastards, she thinks. I know exactly how you feel.

Kavian has been in pain for a very long time. There's the pain she wears like a courting coat, a ballroom ensemble—the battle hurt that makes her growl and put her head down, determined to go on.

And there's the other pain. The kind she lets out when drunk, hoping it'll drown. The pain she reaches for when she tries to play the erhu (this requires her to be drunk, too). It's a nameless pain, a sealed pain, catacombed in the low dark and growing strong.

The night she met Irasht, the night she went down into the catacombs to decant her daughter: that night belonged to the second pain.

In the Paik Rede's summit halls, past the ceremonial pool where the herons fish, catacomb doors bear an inscription:

We make silk from the baby moth. We unspool all that it might become. This is a crime.

Silk is still beautiful. Silk is still necessary.

This is how an abnarch is made. This is the torment to which Kavian gave up her first and only born.

The wizards of the Paik Rede, dam-makers, high rulers of isu-Cter, seal a few of their infants into stone cells. They grow there, fed and watered by silent magic, for fifteen years. Alone. Untaught. Touched by no one.

And on nights like these their parents decant them for the war.

"Kavian. Stop."

Warlord Absu wears black beneath a mantle of red, the colors of flesh and war. For a decade she has led the defense of the highlands. For a decade before that—well: Kavian was not born with sisters, but she has one. This loyalty is burnt into her. Absu is the pole where Kavian's needle points.

"Lord of hosts," Kavian murmurs. She's nervous tonight, so she bows deep.

The warlord considers her in brief, silent reserve. "Tonight we will bind you to a terrible duty. The two mature abnarchs are our only hope." Her eyes! Kavian remembers their ferocity, but never *remembers* it. She is so intent: "You're our finest. But one error could destroy us."

"I will not be soft with her." So much rides on the abnarch's handler: victory, or cataclysm.

Absu's golden eyes hold hers. "The war makes demands of us, and we serve. Remember that duty, when you want to grieve." Her expression opens in the space between two blinks—a window of pain, or compassion. "What did you name her?"

"Heurian," Kavian says.

A grave nod. Absu's face is a map of battles past, and her eyes are a compass to all those yet to come. "A good name. Go."

And then, as Kavian pushes against the granite doors, as the mechanisms of gear and counterweight begin to open, Absu warns her.

"You will find Fereyd Japur in the catacombs. He went ahead of you."

Fereyd. The scar man, the plucked flower. Her only rival. Why send him ahead? Why is *he* in the dark with her buried daughter?

Kavian tries to breathe out her tension but it is a skittish frightened breed and it will not go.

She goes down into the catacombs where eight children wait in the empty dark for their appointed day. Where her daughter waits to be reborn and used.

Magic is bound by the laws a wizard carries. Day and night, air and gravity, the right place of highborn and low. The lay of words in language. The turn of the stars above high isu-Cter, the only civilization that has ever endured. All these are laws a wizard may know.

This is why the upstart Efficate produces so many wizards: it fills its children with the mantras of *fraternity* and *republic*. Their minds are limited, predictable—but like small gears, together they make a machine. This is why the Cteri wizards walk the world as heroes, noble-blooded and rare.

There are other ways to make a wizard. A child raised in a stone cell knows no laws. Only the dark.

Fereyd Japur waits for her in white silk ghostly beneath the false starlight of the gem-starred roof. He is tall and beautiful and his eyes are like a field surgery.

He was not always a great wizard. Not until he gave himself to the enemy, to be tortured, to learn the truest laws of pain.

"Why are you here?" Kavian asks.

Fereyd Japur's eyes burn old and sharp and clot-dark in a young brown-bronze face. Whispers say that the thing he did to buy his power killed him. Left him a corpse frozen in his first virility. The whispers are wrong, but Kavian still remembers them. He's a popular companion for those who want to claim dangerous taste.

"You don't know," he says, and then, "She didn't tell you. Absu didn't tell you."

Oh.

Kavian understands at once, and she steps forward, because if she doesn't, she'll run.

"They've given her to *you*," she husks. "Heurian. My daughter."

"And mine to you."

"*What?*"

"My daughter Irasht." An awful crack opens in his face, a rivening Kavian could recognize as grief, if she believed he was human, or as rage, if she were wiser. "The warlord prefers to spare us from attachment to our charges. So I will have your daughter as my abnarch. And you will have mine."

She wants to weep: she will never know her daughter. She wants to cry out in shameful joy, she will never *have* to know her daughter, and that thought is *cowardice*.

Kavian says the rudest thing she can manage. "You never told me you fathered." Women have bragged of having him, even made a sport of it—he is beautiful, and his lowborn status makes him scandalous, coercible, pliant. But Cteri women don't conceive without intent. Who—?

His full lips draw down to one narrow line. The fissure in him has not closed: grief and hate cover him like gore. "The mother wanted a wizard's blood to water her seed. The child was meant for the catacombs. That was all."

"You did this to hurt me." Her anger's speaking for her, but she has no hope for any kind of victory here and so she lets it speak. "You knew this would happen, didn't you? Fifteen years ago you *planned* this? You made a child to be given to me, so that you could take my daughter, so that you could say, at last, *I have something Kavian Catamount wanted*?"

He lashes out at her. The word he speaks would kill any lesser wizard, the third-best or the fourth or maybe even Fereyd Second-Best himself. But Kavian turns it aside without thought, an abject instant *no*. He must have known she would.

"You have *everything* I wanted," he hisses, and it feels as if she can see through the dusk of his skin and the white of his bone into the venom of his marrow, into the pain he learned beneath the enemy knife.

She turns away.

They unseal the cells and decant their children.

The girl Irasht, daughter of Fereyd Japur, waits wide-eyed and trembling in the center of her cell. When Kavian comes close she rises up on narrow legs and begins to make soft noises with her lips: *ah, ah, ah.*

She doesn't know what a person is. She's never seen one before.

By the time Kavian has coaxed the girl into a trembling bird-legged walk, Fereyd Japur has taken Heurian and gone. The closest Kavian comes to her daughter is the sound of footsteps, receding.

Kavian protests to Absu, bursting into the war council, scattering the tiny carved owls that mark the enemy on the map and raging for her daughter Heurian.

But the Warlord says: "Without your two abnarchs on the front, they will break us this summer. They will open our reservoirs, take our men for their fraternity, and use our silk to wipe the ass of their upstart empire. You are a soldier first. Look to your charge, Kavian."

So: a night that belonged to the second kind of pain.

Go to the front. Train your abnarch on the march. Summer is upon us, and the enemy moves on the dams.

Kavian curses Absu's madness—*train her on the march?* Irasht could go catatonic, overwhelmed by the sweep and stink of the world beyond her cell. She could lash out in abnegation and blot herself and Kavian and their retinue and a mile of Cteri highlands into nothing.

But Kavian's known Absu since childhood, and for all the rage she's hurled at those golden eyes she has never known them to measure a war wrong.

She finds she cannot sleep until she snaps something: a branch, a lyre-string. Sometimes it takes a few.

Every time she looks on Irasht, teetering around in tentative awe like a hatchling fallen from a nest, she thinks: *where is my daughter?* She thinks: *I could go to that lowborn boy and take Heurian back. He could not stop me.* But she cannot go against Absu and the Paik Rede. Cannot defy the ruthless will that keeps isu-Cter safe.

So she hardens her heart and begins the training.

"Hssh," she murmurs—Irasht freezes when touched, and must be soothed. "Hssh." She draws a cold bath while the abnarch girl watches the motion of the water, rapt. When Kavian lowers her down into the ice cold, arms around her tiny neck and knocking knees, she reacts with only a soft 'oh'. From then on the temperature doesn't seem to trouble her, even when Kavian leans her back to wash her knotted hair. She sculls the water in small troubled circles and stares. Kavian thinks she is trying to reconcile two things: the sight of the water rippling around her palm, and the feeling of it on her hand. Whether she succeeds, Kavian cannot tell.

Irasht is at the peak of her power as an abnarch. All the logic she learns will confine her. When she sees the difference between sunrise and sunset she will diminish. When she understands that the chattering shapes around her are people like herself, she will be a lesser weapon. So Kavian keeps to the strict discipline of the handler. No language. Simple food. Strict isolation, when possible.

But for Irasht to be useful, she must learn to trust her handler. (Or dread and fear her handler, Fereyd Japur would remind her. Or that.) So Kavian reaches out to her—touch, meaningless sound, small acts of compassion. Holds her when the world becomes too much and she retreats to clawing frenzy.

Irasht is a burnt stump of a person, like a stubborn coal pulled from a fire pit. She stares overmuch and needs housetraining like a stray dog. To Kavian's frustration and shame—*this is what I am reduced to?*—she finds that Irasht cannot chew. So she crumbles the girl's food by hand.

This would be easier, all in all, if Kavian could think of her only as a weapon.

But in the villages and terrace farms along the path to war she sees Irasht do things that take a chisel to her heart. When Irasht finds doors she goes to them and waits patiently, hoping, Kavian imagines, that someone will invite her in.

When it grows too dark in their tent Irasht panics, tangling herself in her bedding. Kavian is moved: Irasht fears going back to the dark. Somehow this is a comfort. It makes Kavian feel she has done a good thing, bringing her out into the light.

She takes Irasht out to see her first stars, and holds the girl, rocking her, thinking: we did this. We made her this way.

No. The *war* did this. The war makes demands.

In the Efficate they make wizards in vast numbers. Bake them like loaves of bread. Kavian knows this because she's slaughtered them by the dozens. All they can do is make little shields and throw little sparks—the laws of their society leave no room for heroism, and Kavian suspects the quality of their blood gives rise to no heroes.

But there are so many. And they are winning.

And this is *not* her daughter.

They pass through everything that will be lost if they fail. The terraced farms and waterfall mills of the highlands. The gulls that circle library-ships on reservoirs raised by wizards of centuries past.

For all remembered history, isu-Cter has been the still eye at the heart of the world. Kavian still believes with patriot fire that, for all its faults, high green isu-Cter must stand.

Fereyd Japur travels with her. It's distasteful company but a military necessity. She tells herself it's good to be close to Heurian. She's lying. Fereyd keeps his abnarch to himself, and the space between Kavian and Heurian feels like forever, as wide as grief and deep as duty.

As they come down from the highlands towards the dams and the war-front, he walks into her tent to take a meal and brag. "Heurian is active. Ready to be used. When I give her an image, she changes the world to match it."

Kavian sets her cup down with soft care. She has not even begun to push Irasht towards useful magic. "Oh?"

"You think I'm lying."

"No," Kavian says. The firelight makes Fereyd's beauty almost painful, a scrimshaw thing, etched into his face by acid and tint, worked into his bones by years of hungry eyes. She touches the edge of hate and it feels hot and slick as a knife coming out. "I believe you."

"And Irasht?" The kohl on his eyelids turns his blink into a mechanism of dark stone. "Is my daughter ready for the war?"

Kavian lifts her chin. "I will need more time."

Fereyd watches her across the fire. It might be something in his face, or the set of his muscled farmer's shoulders, or the way he holds himself so *properly* as if to remind her she is higher born—it might be one of these things that screams of mockery. Or it might only be her imagination.

But Kavian breaks the silence with a hiss: "What did you to do to her?"

Fereyd Japur looks away.

"What method?" Kavian insists, leaning across the fire. The heat is harsh but her arms are a cage for it and the pain only makes her angrier. "How did you reach her so quickly? Was it some secret of knives? What did you *do*?"

"I did what I've always done. I obeyed my orders." The softness in his voice, the tilt of his eyes—for a moment he could be the boy of impossible talent Absu plucked out of the laborers' quarter. But the rage returns. "Heurian will be ready when the enemy comes. Why are you angry? What more would you ask of me?"

She waits there, hunched across the fire like her namesake, and he sits in quiet deference, trembling with a need to flee or yield or kill (she does not like to guess at his thoughts).

Shadows move across the inside of the tent.

From the sleeping-tent Irasht begins to howl. When Kavian rises to go to her she catches Fereyd's eyes and sees something shattering under that howl, something long ago broken, something still coming apart.

"Keep my daughter safe," she says. More than anything else she could say, she thinks it will hurt him most.

Irasht takes up collecting. She does not much care for the idea of property, but after silent rebukes from Kavian, she focuses her needs on waterskins. Soon she learns to show anger by pouring water on the earth.

Kavian laughs in delight, and then sobers. The girl is ready for a test.

On the riverbank, she finds three small stones to show Irasht. The abnarch perches, head cocked, and waits for Kavian's command.

Kavian waggles her fingers. This is the counting game. Count three stones, Irasht.

Three, Irasht indicates: three fingers.

Kavian holds up four.

Three, Irasht insists, brow furrowed. She waves her raised fingers and makes a high chirp. Three, three. There are three stones.

Kavian answers with stillness: four fingers. Four stones.

Irasht's eyes narrow in bafflement.

And a small weight moves in Kavian's palm. A fourth stone, conjured from nothing. Irasht's abnarchy at work. Faced with a gap between reality as it is and reality as Kavian says it must be, Irasht has rectified the discrepancy.

Kavian hugs Irasht tenderly, kisses her gently on the brow, and conjures her an air-picture of the night sky, crowded with stars. It makes Irasht tremble in joy, to see those lights in the dark.

The war begins again. Twenty thousand Efficate spearmen and four hundred wizards under the stripling Adju-ai Casvan march on a southern dam.

Word comes by rider from Warlord Absu:

I have judged your reports. Fereyd Japur will use Heurian against the enemy. Kavian, your abnarch is unready. Keep her safe.

She sees it happen. Sees all this:

Fereyd carrying Heurian (she is a small dark shape, limp—but her hair moves in the wind off the reservoir) across the bridge beneath the dam. Fereyd raising his arms to the sky. The two armies beneath him looking up in awe as he draws against the dusk an image of the Efficate soldiers broken into bone.

Then he puts his hands over Heurian's ears.

Through her own art of sorcery Kavian hears the shriek he puts into her daughter's mind, a shriek like a nightmare cracking. Horrible enough to make the screams of battle sound less than a lullaby.

Kavian, unable to protect her daughter, breaks a tree in half with a killing word.

The noise Heurian makes is so low and awful that it stirs snow to avalanche when it strikes the distant mountains. When that sound rolls over the first rank of the Efficate army their wizards' shields flare with lightning.

Whatever gets through is enough. Men fall, drowning on ash and water, on the mud that suddenly grows to fill their lungs. Adju-ai Casvan, shielded by his elite cadre, survives to pull his decimated forces out—fleeing west, chased by the sound of Cteri soldiers beating their shields and crying: *the water washes out the filth*!

On the bridge beneath the dam, Fereyd Japur lifts the fallen girl. She puts her arms around his neck and tries to hide against him.

The battle is won. Heurian functions. All it takes is bone in the sky and a scream in her skull.

When Kavian goes to the center of the camp and asks to see her daughter,

Fereyd Japur looks at her with cold contempt. "You saw her today," he says. "You saw everything you need to see. She is a weapon."

Warlord Absu writes:

Fereyd Japur has field command. Defeat all Efficate incursions you encounter. Use the abnarch until no longer practical.

Kavian, you must bring your charge to the same standard.

Campaign season rolls down in rain and thunder and blood. The Efficate's wizards try ingenious new defenses. Under Fereyd Japur's guidance, Heurian breaks them. The Cteri win again and again and soon their defensive stand becomes a counterattack.

Kavian pursues her own method with stubborn, desperate resolve. Fereyd's technique—an image to achieve, a goad to drive the abnarch to fear and terror, the promise of relief—is direct. Crude. She has a more elegant solution.

One symbol: the dark. The empty black of Irasht's childhood. *Bad.*

And another—she should have chosen something else, something less fragile, less desperate, but Irasht responds more strongly to the promise of love than anything else—

A starry sky, like the sky that covered them when Kavian held her and kept her from the dark. The only goodness Irasht knows.

Some of the soldiers in Kavian's retinue pool their talents to make Irasht a set of dolls. She plays with them in silence, and Kavian watches, wondering how much of a person is still left in her, and how much has withered away. How much waits, stunted, for some healing rain to fall.

The abnarch technique came from legends of ancient ascetic kings. Transcendent and serene, they locked themselves away, to forget the laws that chained them. They chose confinement.

What would Irasht choose, if given a choice? Does she know *how* to choose?

Kavian shakes her head and gets to her feet. The philosophy must wait. Irasht needs to be made ready. Until then, Fereyd Japur doesn't even need to taunt her. His abnarch carries the nation's hope while hers plays with toys.

She comes upon him in the night after a victory. It is too dark to see his face but through the smoke of a joyful camp she smells wine. "Kavian," he rasps. "Kavian Hypocrite. Come. Sit with me."

She crouches across from him. Makes no light to lift the shadows. "Have a care." It comes out a threat, a purr.

"You are gentle to my daughter." He raises something and she opens her mouth to defend herself, but, no, it is only a cup. "My traitor heart is grateful."

"I will make her ready yet."

His eyes flash white in the dark. "Mercy to a broken thing? Too late, Kavian. Years too late."

"The war broke her." That desperate mantra. "Not us."

"Did Absu tell you that? No, no—it is our choice. The Paik Rede *chooses* to sacrifice its children. We choose to bury them." A wet sound, like gathered spit, like a sob choked. "Is it not said—*the mother has the child for nine months, and the father for nine years*? They took that from me. They made my choice, and took Irasht."

"Treason . . . " she whispers. But she cannot put any heat in it. Her honor hates to see a man so beautiful brought so low.

He rises unsteadily and she uncoils to match him. "*You* are the traitor. Your mercy to Irasht is the real treachery. She died when Absu put her in those cells. What came out was a weapon. And now you are too weak to use her—as if you could protect her in place of Heurian. Is that your secret, Kavian Catamount? Do you want a warm doll to hold in place of your daughter?"

"Absu?" Kavian lifts a hand to ward off sudden light. They are launching fireworks from the mountainside. "Absu was Irasht's mother?"

Fereyd Japur lowers his face to her in the red glare. His skin looks kiln-fired. "She loved me."

It makes sense. Fereyd Japur is common-born: powerful blood without the politics of a highborn father. No mind as apt as Absu's could pass up the chance to make an abnarch weapon without another parent of good blood to fight the entombment.

Kavian cannot believe there was any love.

He must see the thought in her eyes. "She did," he croaks. There are tears in him, but his rage and his pride and his obvious, agonizing need to be more than *just a man* hold them back. "She did. She *did*. You think I invented it? A tourniquet for a broken heart? Damn you. Damn you."

Kavian watches him stumble away. It is pity she feels, old and strange.

The Efficate outflanks the Cteri counterattack and marches on the dams at Tan Afsh. Absu orders Fereyd Japur and Heurian to remain with the main thrust and sends Kavian and Irasht to save Tan Afsh.

Kavian is not ready. So much rides on Irasht, and Fereyd Japur's words still ring in her: *you are too weak to use her!*

She wants to save isu-Cter. This is what she's always fought for. Yet she can't believe that the girl she holds and soothes in the night is *only* a weapon.

And she wants to believe, now, that what they have done to their daughters can somehow be undone.

But she pushes Irasht out onto the stone above the battle and shows her the sign for *wrong* alongside the stone-eyed owl banner of the Efficate. It is not Fereyd Japur's method—an image that demands to be real. All she says to Irasht is: *this is wrong, this army*. The rest she leaves to the girl.

Irasht makes a raw noise deep in her throat, as if she is trying to vomit up everything that has ever hurt her. For one instant she burns so bright with will that Kavian cries out in pain.

In the valley beneath them, in the space of a single eyeblink, the Efficate army vanishes. Fifty-five thousand scoured from the sight of God. Even their bootprints.

There are no survivors. It is the most powerful exercise of magic in Cteri history.

After the battle Kavian casts aside all laws of language and isolation, holds Irasht, and whispers love until the girl stops clawing at her own skin. Irasht has learned a few words. She can say:

No more. No more. No more.

A little more, Kavian promises. I'll protect you. Just fight a little more.

Irasht clings to her in silent need, and with a wizard's ken Kavian knows she will not survive many more battles. Knows that she would prefer to erase herself and end the pain.

Word comes from the Cteri spearhead at Cadpur, Fereyd's army, her daughter's army: *we have met the main body of the Efficate invasion force. There are more men than ants upon the earth. More wizards than stars in the sky. Qad-ai Vista leads them. Make haste to join us, Kavian.*

And then an order from the warlord Absu:

We cannot risk both abnarchs in one day.

Fereyd Jaypur. Your weapon is battle-tested. You will defeat the enemy at Cadpur. Attack now.

By the time Kavian reaches the front, the battle's already over. The Efficate army has withdrawn with extraordinary casualties. Fereyd Japur killed Qad-ai Vista's elite cadre and nearly claimed the brother-general himself.

The price was small, as the reckoning goes.

Kavian's daughter Heurian is dead.

She leaves Irasht with her dolls and a retinue guard and goes down into the sleeping camp, to find the man who lost her girl.

Fereyd's tent has no guards. Kavian ties the privacy screen behind her, lace by lace. Everything inside is silk. Fereyd Second-Best travels like the highborn he never was.

"I prepared tea," he says. The candles he has set out around him light him from below. Braided hair, proud chin, empty eyes. An iron chain ornament around his neck, another around his left wrist. Silver on his bare ankle.

She sits across from him on the cushions. The arrangement of the tea service is *exact*. He's measured the angles with a courtier's geometry pin.

She sets her hands before her knees, palms down. "My daughter."

One tremor in his jaw. "I asked too much of her."

"So," she says, each word a soft considered point, like a blow, a kiss, "I had concluded."

"She struck three times. Made their flesh into earth, and then air, and then water. Their wizards tried to kill her and I held them back. I was distracted. But after her third blow—" He sits with stiff formality and pauses, once, to breathe into his cupped hands. "It was too much. She had done so much and the world wasn't better and she, ah, she had to go. She made herself into water along with all the soldiers she killed, and flowed into the earth. I tried to—I tore down a banner and I tried to—to sop her up—"

His mouth opens in rictus and he makes a terrible sound that cannot be a laugh, is not gentle enough to be a sob.

Kavian moves the tea set aside, piece by piece, and takes him in her arms.

"I killed your daughter," he says into her shoulder. "I killed her." He puts his hands against her shoulders and tries to force her away. "I killed her. I killed her."

"Fereyd." She will not let him go. "You can grieve. I will not mark you weak."

"You will. You always do." The plural *you*.

She takes his face between the palms of her hands and ohhhh her muscles have not forgotten how to twist, to snap, to hear the bone go and feel the last breath rush out. He killed Heurian. He killed—

She will not do it.

"You have every right to grieve," she says, though some part of her resents each word. "You have given more than anyone. Today you did what you have always done. Paid too high a price."

"It was your price too. She was your blood."

She doesn't answer that. Doesn't know how.

"I loved her like my own," he says, and lets himself begin to sob.

They speak a little. Mostly not. After a while, moved by the fey mood that comes after deep grief, by the closeness of him, by months of watching him on the march, Kavian takes his chin and kisses him.

"No," he says, turning away. "No. Not you as well. Enough."

"I don't make prizes of men." She regrets this even as she says it. It's not the right assurance.

"You think it's the only way I know how to speak." He laughs with sudden snapping cold. "I win the greatest victory of our time. I lose your daughter— and mine, and mine—to buy our triumph." A pause while he gathers himself. She respects it. "And here I am, in my own tent, still Fereyd Second-Best. Still the *beauty*."

"Fereyd," she whispers. "I'm sorry. I wanted distraction. It was wrong."

He draws away to make a fiercely focused inspection of the tea ceremony, the cushions. "You highborn always forget this: when you break someone, they *stay* broken. You cannot ask a broken thing to right itself. You cannot ask that, and then laugh at it for falling."

She's found some strange kind of comfort here, holding him. So she says this, against her pride, as the only thanks she can manage:

"Now you have seen me broken too."

"I haven't." The truth of pain is in his voice, beneath the grief. "Not yet."

It hurts, but it is true. She never knew her daughter as he did.

She gets up to go but pauses by the screen, uncertain, and when she looks back she catches on the care of his makeup and the suggestion of his body beneath his garments. She hesitates. He speaks.

"Come back." He says this like it's ripped itself from him. "I want to help you. I want to be what you need."

"Fereyd . . . " she says, warning him, warning herself.

"I want to be something for someone," he says, eyes fierce: and she cannot deny him that.

What happens between them isn't all grief. He's been watching her too—he admits that, though not in words. Her pride likes this.

When she's done with him he touches her shoulder and says:

"I will always do my duty, no matter how it hurts. But you—you are not yet so utterly bound."

She touches his lips in gratitude. The pain is worse than ever. But it runs clear. It feels true.

Kavian leads the army through the Cadpur pass into Efficate land, and there on a plain of thin grass and red stone they meet Qad-ai Vista at the head of another numberless host.

This time the brother-general asks for parley.

She meets him in the empty space between the armies. Qad-ai is a tall man, ugly, weary, and he speaks accented Cteri in bald uncomplicated phrases. "We will not seize your water this year," he says. "We ask truce. Next year, or the year after that, we will come again. This year we will go thirsty."

She spits between his legs. "There. Water."

"We will eat you." There's more sadness than anger in his voice. "You understand that, don't you? You buy your proud centuries by visiting atrocity on your own children. You stand on a mountain of chains. Soon they will swallow you."

She chews blood from her cheek and spits that on the sand too. "I'll see you next year."

He squints at her with pragmatic distaste. "Not too late to use the other girl. The one you still have left. Worth her life to kill us, isn't it?"

She says to him what she cannot speak to her own: "She is worth more to me than this victory."

What she does next is not her duty: not what Fereyd Japur could ever do. But it *must* be done. Not the easy rebellion of the sanctimonious, Kavian roaring home to say, *give up the abnarchs, give up the war!* Not that. Because that would be Kavian's choice, Kavian's anger, and Kavian is not the wounded woman here.

What she does she does for Irasht.

It has to happen now, while the hurt is fierce in her, while Irasht's power still permits it—before she learns too many laws, like *it will always hurt*, like *Kavian will never leave me.*

But the journey home to isu-Cter nearly breaks her determination. The shining reservoirs and the waterfall-terraces glistening in summer gold. The lowborn turning out to cheer.

Kavian has spent two decades fighting for this nation, with her fists and voice and womb.

But when she reaches the summit, she revolts.

The Paik Rede turn out in force to stop her, once they realize her intent. "I am coming to give Irasht a choice," Kavian tells them. "That is all I ask. A choice for all of them."

"She cannot choose," the Paik Rede answers, all of them together, and their speech roars like spring sluiceways.

So Kavian fights. She fights with all her art. She sings a song of rebellion, and at her call the air revolts against the wind, the stone rises up against the earth, she cries out as a hero with a cause and the brave world answers her so that she climbs the steps in a whirlwind of fire and black burnt stone that reaches up to the clouds.

"This is the way things go!" the sorcerers of the Paik Rede reply, and they are as the avalanche, as the river going to the sea. This is how things are. Inevitable.

The wrath of their confrontation breaks the monoliths that line the Summit Steps, and in the end Kavian finds herself at a screaming standstill.

"The abnarch!" she cries. "I will set the abnarch loose!"

They must believe her, for they retreat.

Kavian walks into the chamber of the ceremonial pool and the great stone doors to the catacombs, Irasht hopping at her heels, agitated and nervous, chattering in her high-pitched monotone.

At the catacomb doors the warlord Absu stands with Fereyd Japur at her side. "Kavian. Stop."

Kavian crosses the floor, hobnailed boots hammering on stone and gem. Headed for Absu, and the doors, and the children in the dark.

She won't stop.

"I know why you're here." Absu's voice says: *this is true. I do understand. I do.* "These are our beloved children. They deserve better than darkness and suffering to buy another year of war. But we make this bargain every day, Kavian."

Kavian arranges her wards. Beckons to Irasht—come, come. They circle the ceremonial pool. The herons watch them.

Absu takes a step forward. "The worker suffers in his labor. The lowborn die on the battlefront. But we give them laws and reservoirs, and we keep the Efficate back. That is the bargain: they suffer, so that we may rule. Does it sound callous, put that way?"

Kavian cannot check her tongue: "Not as callous as it looks written on those doors." *Silk is still beautiful. Silk is still necessary.*

Fereyd Japur's shoulders twitch at that. But Absu doesn't stop. "If isu-Cter falls, the world loses its center. Chaos reigns. So I must take the awful bargains upon myself. I have been ruthless for you, Kavian. Will you turn your abnarch on me for that?"

Kavian does not have to answer. She was not born with a sister, but she has one. And she knows Absu understands:

This is not the Efficate, devoted to common fraternal good. In green isu-Cter, ruled by the blood and will of the highborn, one woman's pain and wrath and love is argument enough.

Fereyd Japur steps forward. "Lord of hosts." The pain in his eyes when he looks at Absu is the sharpest and most beautiful thing Kavian has ever seen. "This is Kavian Catamount, who gave her blood to the dark. We are bound to her by duty and gratitude. I beg you. Let her pass."

Absu looks to him with slow regard. The shadow of the weight of a nation moves across her.

Kavian thinks she's ready to battle her sister Absu to the death. It would be a contest of equals, a duel worthy of legend. The respect between them would permit it.

But she knows that Fereyd Japur would come to Absu's defense. Or to hers. She cannot bear to force that choice on him.

Perhaps Absu weighs her duty against the loyalties of her heart. Maybe she looks on Kavian and the abnarch behind her, Irasht her daughter, with eyes that have never mismeasured a war: and she decides she can't win. Maybe she's secretly glad that someone has come to do what she cannot ever permit herself.

Whatever the reason, Warlord Absu lowers her head and stands aside.

Kavian goes forward with Irasht to stand before the catacomb door. "It's your choice," she whispers, stroking the girl's hair. "All the other Irashts are waiting down in the dark. And you could be their Kavian, if you let them out. Do you understand? You could let them out of the dark. Do you want to let them out?"

Irasht's brow furrows. She doesn't understand. Fereyd Japur watches in expressionless agony as Kavian struggles to make it clear. At last she resorts to signs: *bad*, the dark empty square, and *good*, the sky full of stars. And an image in the air, the doors opening, the children decanting from the celled dark to live hard lives of broken speech and brutal nightmare and, maybe, in the end, hope.

Is this good, Irasht? Do you wish you'd had this life instead? *Can* you wish you'd had this life instead?

Or would it have been better if we'd left you in the dark forever?

It's an impossible question. No one could answer it. Do you wish you could have been some other way? Some way you've never known or even been taught *how* to know?

Kavian wants to beg: Please choose. Please be *able* to choose. You can leave them, if you must, or let them out, though we may all perish for it, if they awaken as abnarchs and turn on us.

Just show me you can choose.

Irasht reaches out to the little sign for *good*, the crowded sky, and then draws Kavian down to her. Kisses her brow. "Kavian," she says, and strokes the stars, to put them with her name: "Kavian."

Kavian is good.

"Please." Kavian tries to aim the abnarch girl back towards the door. "Please decide. Do you want to let them out? Do you wish you'd been let out? You can choose. You can choose." Behind her she can feel Fereyd Japur, watching, and Absu at his side, one hand on his shoulder, to quiet him or to give him strength.

But Irasht touches the stars again, as if they are all she can see, and then Kavian's cheek, and then her own brow.

You are good. We are good.

No, Kavian wants to say. No, no, we are so far from that. We did this to you and so we are not good. But she came here to listen to Irasht's choice. Not her own.

In the ceremonial pool a heron spears a fish.

They wait, Kavian and Fereyd Japur and the warlord Absu, for the child of the dark to make a judgment.

But she will not. Irasht cannot choose. She will stand here forever, hoping for Kavian's command. Kavian thinks Absu knows this but won't say it, out of mercy.

Irasht looks up at the door, patient, perched like a little bird. She looks up at the great doors and she waits.

Fereyd Japur said, *you highborn always forget this: when you break someone, they stay broken. You cannot ask a broken thing to right itself.* They put Irasht into a cell and starved her even of this choice. And Kavian shouldn't say *they*, for Kavian did this, didn't she, and now in her cowardice she wants this child to choose, and lift the guilt from herself. But the child cannot choose.

Irasht looks up at the door, patient. She waits.

"Kavian . . ." Fereyd Japur says, with the most rigid and agonized formality.

And then Kavian shouts in hope, because she remembers Irasht's strange habit on the march. When Irasht finds a door she goes up to it, and waits patiently, hoping, Kavian imagines, that someone will invite her in.

"Irasht," she whispers, kneeling, for Irasht is not a weapon but a person to be loved and taught, and if she cannot make the choice, let a mother give her guidance. "Do you see?"

She shows Irasht an image in the air, and it is only themselves, kneeling before the great door.

And then she turns the image, so that Irasht can see the other side. The children below, in the dark. And now Irasht is *inside* the door, and the children in the dark are the ones waiting for her to invite them in.

Irasht tilts her head.

"Ah," she chirps. "Ah."

SEVEN WAYS OF LOOKING AT THE SUN-WORSHIPPERS OF YUL-KATAN

MAGGIE CLARK

I have just one memory of my father: Ascension Day—his transition from fifth to sixth plateau. While civilians from a dozen nearby villages looked on, shrouded priests led this four-years-stranger of mine from Kata-Ye, the highest terrestrial temple in our kingdom, to a shuttle bound for the temple in our heavens: Kata-Um, the station that orbits our jealous sun. My father made the walk naked, as did the rest of the station's would-be clerics: his skin burnt and peeling from the long days of meditation preceding such a voyage; his head held high, though his sight had long been lost to the third plateau.

This is, in fact, what I remember most of that day: his blindness, which was deemed a great blessing on Yul-Katan, and which he certainly bore as if it had granted him a second, greater sight. His passage to the shuttle had all the markings of a dignified affair, so I did not speak as he passed—nor did my brother cry out, small though he was—but still I wanted so much to have faith in my father's faith; to have him halt midstep and turn the scorched, empty whites of his eyes to mine. To see me, just as (the legend went) child-planet Yula had once been seen and reclaimed by its father, the sun-god Katari, in cosmic days of old. But my father did not. He paused only at the shuttle entrance and turned to face the crowd on whole, his dead eyes never settling anywhere near where his orphaned children stood.

My faith in my people's faith died that day, swallowed in a boom that unsettled the rocks as his shuttle ricocheted into the upper atmosphere. It would be ten more years before I could book passage and escape my native world in turn, apprenticed as both translator and field biologist on an extra-solar exploration vessel, but in all that time, only my brother ever gave me pause for second thought. Even then, when he started on the first plateau, I knew all hope was lost. When I slipped one uncelebrated night from the star system of my birth, the Yev-Ibris's portholes granted me only the slightest glimpse of Kata-Um—a small, dark blotch against the red-giant fury of Kata itself—and yet, this was enough. At the time I remember being so certain I would see neither it nor Yul-Katan again: the kind of certitude that cinches in the heart like fine mesh netting about a game bird's neck.

A certitude like that can kill, you know. And oh, how mine so nearly did.

Imbra caught me looking—the driftwood contours of his back, the sweat-drenched sinews of his neck. I didn't mind being caught. I smiled and reclined on one of the larger specimen crates as he changed his mind about changing into something that stank less of phytoplankton. He hooked arms about me with his skinsuit half undone.

"Team six'll be here any minute," he said.

"Team six can suck a stone. Besides." I let a lip droop, fingers entwined in the springy black coils of his hair. "It's my birthday."

Imbra snorted. "On what godfersaken world?"

I gave him the look that needed no answer, and something in the darks of his eyes sparked as it always did, but I'd hardly locked ankles about the jut of his hips when one of the monitors sounded. I hucked a boot at the airlock and shouted in its general direction before Imbra could say, "Look—it's not team six." And sure enough, the monitors were relaying data from our base of ops instead, the good ship *Petrin* looming high in orbit around the as-of-yet unnamed moon undergoing biological survey.

"—the hell?" I slipped into a console chair and threw my hands up. "It's a distress call halfway across the planet. Frequency standard's *ancient*, though. We should forward it to Intel and let some salvage rig handle whatever's left."

But Imbra caught my wrist when I made to stand. He was studying the monitors with more solemnity than I'd ever seen in him—and I'd seen him right after his last teammate clipped a booster fin while making spacewalk repairs: helmet-glass shattered; a whole, fragile microcosm switched off in an instant. In trying to work out his trouble, I almost didn't hear team six make its eventual appearance, or register the distinctly boggy stench of their suits. Still, they knew something was up.

"Heard the alarm," said Ju. Taller than the rest of us, she had to stoop in the storage room, chin-length hair clinging to her cheeks. "Ship okay?"

"Ship's fine," said Imbra. "Gotta make a detour, is all."

"*Imbra*," I whispered. He only squeezed my wrist—hard.

"*Coward*," he whispered back, before letting go. I slumped in the console chair and glared at the monitors while he helped Ju and Axis with their contributions to the cargo hold. He wasn't wrong. Rarely, though, was he so blunt.

Our little transport usually used the magnetic tether between lander and spaceship to reach and return from the surface of the moon—teams three and four monitoring local conditions from the *Petrin*; teams one and two still on recon below. But our craft could also handle short-term maneuvers on its own, at least with solar wings unfurled and a bit of juice in the tank, so after some discussion, teams three and four approved Imbra's plan to intercept the lifepod bleeding old S.O.S. signals a few thousand klicks out.

Imbra didn't pay me much heed as teams five and six went about our assigned tasks for manual nav. He wasn't pointedly ignoring me, though, so I concentrated on readying the grappling arm and keeping my last encounter with a stiff out of mind. You catch a wide range of deaths on field missions with the smaller outfits, but for me they all smelled the same, no matter what the circumstances—heart attack, septic shock, oxygen deprivation, space freeze, fungal growth, pneumonia. That acrid stench of burning flesh and fabric hit me no matter how fresh or old the corpse: psychosomatic, sure, but also unavoidable. Imbra had seen the frontlines in wartime, so he wasn't impressed, but what did he expect from me? Excitement at the thought of tossing chunks again?

"Hundred meters," said Axis. "Eighty."

"Arm in position," I said, "locked and loaded."

"Wait for it," said Imbra. "How's it looking, Ju?"

"Still getting those strange readings, like a scattering effect over the distress call."

"Environmental? This planet's got some killer storms in the upper atmosphere."

"Could be." But Ju didn't sound convinced.

"Lock it down on Ax's mark," said Imbra.

"Mark."

I activated the grappling arm—really more a double-claw of magnetized nano-tech, which hooked and clenched and reformed to fit snugly about either end of the lifepod, the latter a dull, red-brown cylinder with scorch marks along its curving side.

"Bring it in," said Imbra, though he needn't have; I knew what I was doing.

"Bringing it in," I said, teeth clenched the entire time.

The rescue still lived, but barely—close enough to death that it seemed a cruelty to rouse him at all, and I said as much once the pod was onboard the *Petrin*. Imbra disagreed, though, and as the only one among us ever to have used such a thing, his verdict stood. "You drop into those tubes thinking you might never wake again, but at least you won't notice," he explained. "Then stasis hits your lungs and your last thought's just panic. The real cruelty's going out like that—suffocating alone in the dark, all hope lost at the very last."

When Traz from team three brought the pod out of stasis, the rescue's vitals were wildly uneven; the stranger's prognosis was bleak, but we all stood about him, conveying as much peace as we could for what breath he had left. Axis even clasped the man's hand and locked gazes, speaking words of greeting and asking questions of identity and origin that the rest expected me to translate into a dozen common tongues, until I found a match.

Eventually Imbra nudged me when I didn't even try. Ju whispered that if I needed to retch there was no shame in it; she could smell the body's stench this time, too. But what gave me pause for once wasn't psychosomatic; it was the brand on our rescue's bared chest—the livid, raised-white semi-circle with seven rays extended. I'd recognize anywhere the mark of Kata-Um, and the seventh plateau for the sun-worshippers of Yul-Katan, but what in the name of Katari-burning was such a high-ranking cleric doing this far out?

He never got the chance to say, though his mouth moved as if he'd intended to: his parched lips instead giving up flecks of blood and gluey spittle as he wheezed his last.

"Poor devil," said Breen, our geophysicist, when he lay still. She helped Axis adjust the body in the pod before inquiring glances from all four teams turned my way. Haltingly, I explained the professional lapse, but this answer only prompted further questions—among them the dreaded, "So you think we should contact someone from Yul-Katan?"

"*I'm* from Yul-Katan," I said, heavily.

"Did you know him?" said Breen.

"No—but—look, it's personal."

A long pause settled in the room, not counting the guarded glances between teams. Then here and there a crewmate announced work they needed to attend to—specimen analyses, minor repairs and diagnostics—until it was just me and Imbra with the corpse.

"Don't," I said, when I could feel the heat of his hand over my shoulder. "I need to think." The heat withdrew. The rest of him soon followed.

I was only a few sleep-cycles from my homeworld when I first heard about the cruise ships, and with them the overwhelming wealth of certain worlds. Apparently when tour groups neared the fringes of my native star system, they tried to coordinate their visits with Final Ascension days—For amusement? Out of curiosity? Either way, I tried and failed to imagine the resplendent absurdity of it all: Dozens of tourists from other Allegiance worlds, bedecked in the strange fineries of their respective peoples, standing on observation decks with the bombardment shields down, waiting for massive vidscreens to sight a tiny object falling from Kata-Um toward Kata itself. And then the gasping! The excited murmurs as a sun-worshipper plunged toward their barbaric god!

Had so many in the Allegiance so little else to do?

(And oh, the devoted peoples of Yul-Katan, if they only knew . . .)

I learned soon enough that the "jumpers" were my people's greatest export: the stuff of tall tales Allegiance-wide. "Yul-Katan?" Sev, from team four, had asked when I first boarded. "That place where they throw people kicking and screaming into their sun?"

I had memories of kicking and screaming, but these were all terrestrial.

"The Final Ascension is voluntary," I replied.

"But run like clockwork," said the biochemist. "Bit of a contradiction, no?"

I didn't reply. I wasn't in the habit of defending my people's dominant beliefs, but I didn't want to invite open-season on the topic for the next few months. In truth, though, I knew that some on Kata-Um lived to ripe old ages, tending to the station's day-to-day operations, while others were in a hurry to move on. I'd never learned which type my father was; even if I'd been inclined to ask about him after he abandoned me and my brother, such details were not discussed among those outside the faith's plateaus.

Nonetheless, certain things were simply *known*, embedded in our culture at large. The brand of the faith, for instance: Kata's semi-circle gaining a new ray for each plateau the worshipper attained; his seventh added just before Final Ascension into the sun. So what had happened in this case? How and why had our dead rescue escaped his chosen destiny?

I stood with the body of the impossible cleric until I could no longer smell and hear the worst of it—the fanatic die-offs that separated grain from chaff, third plateau from fourth, on Yul-Katan. The deserts outside our villages were laden with their remains—bone beds generations deep—and we were taught to praise them for the scavengers they drew, the meat with which the rest of us could fill our bellies during even the most terrible droughts, and the famines they incurred.

I was slow to register the raised voices down the *Petrin*'s main corridor.

"Teams one and two aren't responding," said Rowe, our communications officer, when I'd wandered close enough to shoot her a confused glance. "We're getting more of that scattering signal Ju heard over the distress call, too."

"I don't like it," said Axis. "If there'd been an accident—"

"No accident," said Imbra. He spoke in that quiet way that instead spoke volumes, so we all followed the tapping of his index finger. I thought there might be time or heat signatures to interpret on the monitors before him, but the same, non-Allegiance script filled each screen instead. Teams three, four, and six glanced at me, then looked away.

"Is that—" Breen began. The next question, from all of them, remained entirely unspoken: *What have the people from your horrible world done with our colleagues—our friends?*

Nothing. And everything. When I read the message, I was too stunned to reply.

The surface translation was simple enough—GIVE POD, REST SURVIVE—but by the time I'd delivered it, Axis had already pointed to the lone white pixel, consistent across all monitors, that expanded to reveal a video file.

"Don't—" said Breen, but the video was already running—fuzzy images of teams one and two kneeling on an ice field, barely distinguishable from their relative heights and insignias; four cloaked figures with large firearms standing behind them. It happened so quickly: One of the kidnappers aimed at the back of a hostage's head and fired; then the body fell forward, dark spatter on the blue-grey ice. The video replayed from the start.

"Krevida—" The moan could have come from any of us, but it didn't come from me. I was still trying to parse the deeper implications of the text. Though translatable, the message's syntax didn't read like anything a native of my kingdom would ever use—and yet, if a native of Yul-Katan hadn't been translating, the error would surely have gone unnoticed. Even if our outfit had to rely on a computer instead, the translation it spat out wouldn't have suggested anything amiss. The obvious conclusion was that someone wanted the crew to believe my people were behind this attack, but why?

"Okay," said Imbra. "We know they're serious, but just think for one second—we still have a lot of leverage."

Ju nodded. "If they had the means to take the pod without our cooperation, they would have."

"Plus, they've let us know their priority lies with that pod in the first place," said Sev. "Now we've got bait."

"I say we shoot it out the nearest airlock," said Breen, heavily.

"I don't disagree," said Imbra. "But it's our one chance to pin down their location. We have to make the most of it."

"How fast can you get a message to them?" Axis asked Rowe. Ju squeezed Axis's shoulder, the reassurance clear: *Lin will be fine.* He shrugged her hand away—*We can't know that for sure*—and held Rowe's gaze fast.

"I'll see, but . . . " Rowe glanced at Imbra. "What should it say?"

None of us seemed to mind Imbra taking lead, especially since Imbra was wise enough to turn to Traz and Ju, who also had military training, before rendering his verdict. If not for this quality about him, it might have been easy to forget that Imbra was in one sense hundreds of years old, having fought in the last Allegiance war and escaped in a lifepod cast adrift for generations. The temporal and cultural disconnects when he awoke could just as easily have made him bitter, obstinate. Instead they heightened his understanding of his own weaknesses. He steepled his fingers and studied the cycling video closely.

"Reprogram the grav-hooks for locking maneuvers, but at max field strength—ignoring all safety protocols if you have to," he said at last. "And set them to auto-initiate once a target's been set. Then send a reply on the same frequency as the first to the moon—tell them we're deploying the pod at exactly 2510 AST, out the aft airlock."

"You're assuming they have only one vessel," said Traz, while the rest of us acted on Imbra's commands. "What about the four on the moon?"

"If they have their own ship, it's anyone's guess whether they'll retaliate with force or just try to get away."

Axis began to protest, but Imbra raised his hands. "There's no choice. Even if we *could* get a signal to Intel through all the interference, help wouldn't come fast enough."

I didn't say anything about the strange syntax as Rowe sent out our reply. Maybe I should have, but at the time it didn't seem to matter *who* was doing the threatening—just that our simple science mission was facing a hostile threat, and three of our crewmates knelt in mortal peril on the moon below.

We kept the cleric's body out of the pod, but switched on its stasis systems to give at least the illusion of life within.

"Think they'll buy it?" Breen helped me wheel the body into storage while Axis and Ju prepared to jettison the pod.

I shrugged. "We're a civilian crew. Why would we do anything to drag this out?"

"Unless they think we've learned something we're not supposed to."

"Even more reason for us to try to pretend we haven't, though, right?"

Breen held open the door to cold storage while I hefted the tray through. "By that logic they'll try to kill us regardless, the moment they've got the damned pod in sight."

"Looks like it." We shut the door and peered one last time at the corpse through a circle of glass. "Hell if I know what for, though." I explained that a cleric of his standing shouldn't exist this far out; that the mark on his chest meant he should have burned up on route to my native world's sun. But when Breen asked if that would be reason enough for my people to try to kill us, I could only sigh. For one, I didn't think it *was* my people trying to kill us. For another, Rowe was already down the corridor, calling us back. 2508 AST.

We gathered by the monitors at the heart of the *Petrin*—Traz poised to input coordinates for the grav-hooks; Ju with her finger on the airlock controls; Sev scanning the moon's surface for signs of activity; Imbra steadily observing perimeter alarms. The *Petrin* had a lifeboat, not lifepods; if anything went wrong and we took heavy damage, our only hope would be to abandon ship and clear the debris of our vessel undetected, then get picked up by an Allegiance cruiser before the scant oxygen and supplies ran out. The statistics behind such escapes and rescues were, unfortunately, not ideal.

2510 AST. "Mark," said Imbra. The aft airlock opened and the old, scorched lifepod shot into the nether space between ship and moon's surface—eighty meters, one-twenty, one-fifty. At almost one-seventy it exploded—dead hits from two large projectiles.

"On it," said Traz. The *Petrin*'s onboard systems had all they needed from a few seconds' footage of the projectiles' approach to identify a common point of origin, at which time the auto-initiate sequence on the grav-hooks engaged, and both the lander and *Petrin* turned their superconducting magnetic contacts to the stealth vessel in orbit around the moon. The effect was almost instantaneous—the ship caught in the conflicting pull, no longer obscured to our monitors; its metallic hull warping and crumpling at points where its own EM buffer was weakest. It was seconds, maybe, before parts of the hull tore open, licks of electrical fire appearing to then be snuffed out by the vacuum of space.

My crewmates and I crowed, but no one seemed to be breathing deeply yet, and Rowe, Axis, and Traz all swore to their cultures' respective deities when the stealth vessel, far from spitting out escape pods, exploded in its entirety.

"We didn't do that," said Ju. There was no question in her voice—only grimness. Imbra met it with his own, and a nod.

"Any movement on the surface?" he said. Sev shook his head, then took on a greener shade. We followed his finger to a monitor picking up a plume of smoke on the moon's northern-most ice mass. Axis didn't say anything, and out of a wrenching, dumbstruck respect, the rest of us said nothing, either—not about Lin, or Hiram, or Zaphne, though in a way, they were all our losses, too.

The scattering effect receded in the wake of the hostile ship's explosion, after which Rowe dutifully sent a message to the nearest Allegiance outpost, her voice trembling but her fists clenched before her. The sentiment held for the rest of us, too.

"Imbra," I said, after he'd overseen a fuller sweep of the *Petrin*'s surroundings. "We need to talk."

When he looked at me I faltered. Would he be upset that I hadn't said something sooner? Would it have made any difference for the lives of three in our crew? Crisis training for science missions didn't cover these kinds of what-ifs.

Imbra, on the other hand, seemed three steps ahead of everything. He gestured to the galley, but not before calling back to the rest. "Traz. Ju. We need contingency plans."

Breen, Rowe, Sev, and I exchanged puzzled glances at this, but the military-minded seemed unfazed. "Of course," said Ju. Traz was already pulling up all the data he could on the region and the *Petrin*'s onboard resources.

Imbra nodded down the corridor; I moved nervously ahead.

"You know the terrorists, then," he said when we'd arrived. When I turned he was standing with folded arms by the entrance, and the use of such an antiquated term, combined with the full, broad-shouldered height of him, put me in mind of horror stories from the last Allegiance war: interrogation tactics and weapons since made the highest of system-wide offenses to use or own. The Allegiance itself was something difficult to comprehend: a vast network of peoples who nevertheless kept mostly to themselves; a peaceful set of alliances with a violent history that everyone I encountered early in my travels would quickly reassure me was *all in the past*. But the very eagerness of such assurances always told a different story—one truer to the deepest fear of spacefarers, maybe: people who knew better than most how fragile any claim to civilization always was.

It took me a breath to find my voice again. "That's just it," I said. "I—I don't even think they're from Yul-Katan."

Imbra's eyes narrowed, and he pressed me for more information without moving forward, but also without relaxing his stance. It occurred to me after the fifth terse question that maybe he'd also been bunking with someone we'd all just lost on the planet—or if not bunking with yet, maybe *wanting* to; and if wanting to, maybe wanting to *more*? Vague and selfish thoughts, granted, but I'd like to think there was a survivalist's merit to them. Imbra bore the scars of long-term stasis in the fissures along his skin, and if anything these made him even more intimidating when upset. I trusted him, sure, but I also had no desire to become anyone's scapegoat—least of all a mourning lover's—for four such violent deaths.

Imbra lapsed into silence after his volley of questions, then exhaled deeply. "It's a shame you didn't tell us this before we transmitted to Intel."

"You think someone will intercept?"

"It's possible. Or worse . . . " Imbra shook his head. "Look, at present we've given Allegiance the impression that *we* think radical agents from Yul-Katan are at fault. If we're lucky, that might be enough."

I almost didn't dare ask. "Enough for what?"

Imbra finally unfolded his arms. I tensed as his hands came up, my head cradled in his palms. "To save our lives," he said, then frowned. "Why are you shaking?"

Good question. Every nerve ending seemed to be saying *it's time to leave, time to bolt.* I wanted to hold off words with a kiss, but Rowe was already on the intercom, calling us back.

Team four had been tasked with making the necessary, miserable survey of the moon's surface near the northern-most ice mass. While Traz, Ju, and Imbra conferred over getaway options in the extreme event that a hostile force remained, Sev and Breen were already in their suits and loading our little transport ship with medical supplies for the even *more* unlikely event that someone from teams one and two survived.

I sat with Rowe and Axis, running systems' checks and trying not to say anything too apologetic or provocative in the wake of Lin's passing. Nonetheless, Rowe was muttering to herself out loud—*they blew up their own ship, who blows up their own ship, we're dealing with maniacs who don't even care about their own lives, let alone anyone else's*—and it was just as hard not to snap at her for so much conjecture I wish I could've been making myself.

Yes, they did, I wanted to say, *but these aren't* Yul-Katan's *suicidal maniacs. So where in the name of Katari-burning did they come from? And what in blazes did they want with the cleric?*

I waited until Axis and Rowe had team four in sight before stepping away. Once we could see everything their cameras picked up, there was no doubting the terrible fate of our four crewmates—Krevida's body face-forward in the ice and half charred; seven other bodies, half-scorched to the bone in a heap beside the husks of sample crates, tent fixtures, and an array of singed equipment from survey work just beneath the moon's surface.

"Where'd they get that much accelerant? Oxygen's pretty thin down there." Ju murmured from over Axis's shoulder. Rowe shook her head.

"Ship, maybe? Self-detonated the way the one in orbit did?"

"No, there'd be more wreckage. Unless they only used the core?"

Speculation continued in this vein while Breen and Sev, on the surface, tried to pick out the insignias of our crewmates from those of the aggressors. No one said anything when I left central command for cold storage.

In my absence, the impossible cleric had acquired a bluish tinge about his lips and high cheekbones, and for the first time it occurred to me that we'd have to provide him with a proper send-off. Would burning him up in the nearby planet's atmosphere be enough? He'd escaped his chosen fate in orbit around Kata, so I had no difficulty reasoning he wasn't particular about where his remains ended up, but it still felt a touch like sacrilege.

How long *had* he been out in that lifepod? I tried to read his skin like a lifeline, scalpel in hand to tease out layers of stasis-damage, but the relentless exposure of sun-worshippers to Kata's rays already gave such fanatics a mummified look and feel. Tracing the livid white marks on his chest was no help, either, though I had to laugh at myself for thinking the answer might spring from touch alone—like a secret compartment in his flesh.

No, he was a man in the end: a dead man whose body told no useful tales. What reasons would *any* man have to abandon his post, his entire field of worship? The possibility of a covert mission came to mind—or perhaps he'd seen something he shouldn't have. Had his time on Kata-Um revealed to him something so horrific he had to run away?

I paused when I caught my assumption, then leaned to inspect the body more closely: *Had* he been on Kata-Um? Or was he a fraud, too, made to look like one of Yul-Katan's own, just as the hostage-takers had been? And if so, to what possible end?

Imbra caught my wrist when I spun about, heart pounding and scalpel raised, at the sound of someone else in cold storage.

"Kata-bur—You scared me."

"I noticed." Imbra took the scalpel from me, and I took a step back. "You have to calm down. I understand why you're taking it so personally—your people, I get it—but all our lives are on the line right now. We need our wits about us."

I turned to the body, its strange, frosty pallor difficult to align with images of my bright, parched world. "They haven't been my people for years. But still—"

"Something's going on that involves them," Imba agreed. "And until we know who's behind it, we can't trust anyone. We need to leave this place before Allegiance arrives."

"Allegiance?" I looked up sharply. "Why would you think—?"

He shook his head. "The cynicism of a war vet. Look—we can't take everyone or Allegiance will know something's up. We have to leave some behind and make it look like the lifeboat was lost."

"Imbra . . ."

"If it's not Allegiance, they'll be fine. But if it *is* Allegiance, we're all dead."

I began to disagree, but he looked tired in a way that gave me pause. How many times in combat had decisions like these been made?

"Who do we take?" I said instead, to his approving nod.

• • •

Rowe kept her gaze on a porthole while she spoke to me of her homeworld. Beyond the *Petrin* we could see both the blue-grey moon and its owner, a churning brown gas giant, which obscured for us the great immensity of distant stars. Ju and Axis were still prepping the lifeboat, but even after I'd shared my concern about the translation, Breen and Sev were indifferent to the chance of Allegiance culpability—"Not possible," as Breen declared. "What greater good could *possibly* be served by skulking about the outskirts of the known galaxy, chasing ancient lifepods and murdering science teams?" Sev silently agreed.

Traz, meanwhile, was being the good soldier; he and Imbra knelt over a magboard, reviewing all possible ways for him to take over an Allegiance cruiser if the worst came to pass. And Rowe . . . Rowe was staying, too, but for reasons I couldn't comprehend. Romantic, perhaps? She just kept talking about her world while trying to boost propulsion to the lifeboat, to give us the greatest head start before a rescue team entered the local system.

"On my world," she said. "We have these libraries: the greatest stores of knowledge in all Allegiance. So great and so precious are these places that few ever gain access, and even then, only after many years of intense and private training. For most of us—most of the entire world, you understand, and all outsiders, too—it's just one magnificent display. A monument to sentience and all that it's accomplished, with a giant 'DO NOT TOUCH' sign plastered on the front. I wasn't chosen for library training, but I knew that if I went into science I could still contribute—that maybe some day something I discovered would make its way into those tremendous vaults instead."

"That sounds beautiful," I said—and, after a pause—"It's not too late."

But Rowe only shut her eyes. "You know, it's curious. My world is huge, and we used to have hundreds of cultures with competing ideas about how to use all the resources at our disposal. I mean, typical, right? So thousands of years ago the wars were just relentless, but a few centuries back, most of these warring cultures just took each other out, while the rest threw aside their differences, becoming one great face of archival wisdom directed at the stars. A miracle, they say. Still, it sticks with you, you know? The scope of it."

I wish I'd known whether Rowe wanted reassurance or consolation. Either way, I'd been about to tell her how impressive her world's peacemaking seemed, when I recalled something similar from Yul-Katan—how even now I'd refer to my land as a "kingdom" when, truly, there were few alternatives to the community of my birth. But where had all the others gone? Did stability through homogeneity just come upon most worlds when they reached a certain level of technological advancement?

"If you're going to do it," said Imbra, interrupting, "now's your chance."

"Right," I said, glancing about the room. "Would anyone—?"

But the rest of the crew seemed to have had enough of burial. I didn't blame them. I took the impossible cleric out of cold storage and secured him in one of the airlocks, with Ju's help positioning the load so it launched in the right direction. I didn't even read him departure rites, though I suppose I should have. I'd just assumed it was enough for a fellow native to bear witness to his last voyage out: not to Kata, as the marks on his chest suggested had once been his aspiration, but at least to another god, of sorts: this far-flung world where (ideally) his body would burn in the upper atmosphere before the high-velocity winds below could tear it to shreds.

"Time," said Imbra, after I'd been standing by a porthole awhile, watching the cleric set off. "Ju's found a slingshot route to help us get the most out of our thrusters."

I'd never been keen on goodbyes, so I didn't make them—not even to Rowe, still lost in thought when I passed her by.

With just four of us, the lifeboat had extended its viability threefold, but we still had to rely on luck when it came to our destination. Ju's calculations would put us proximate to a host of trade routes within a week's time, but at that point we just had to hope the right kind of vessel would be in the vicinity and willing to stop for us.

"We've got a thirty-hour window," Imbra explained. "After that, we have no choice: We'll have to call for Allegiance aid or die from oxygen deprivation."

"And if Allegiance was clear all along," said Axis, "then we get to feel like fools."

Ju sighed. "Better living fools than dead ones."

The lifeboat was essentially cylindrical, two berths wide and six to each segment, with life support systems in between and a modest propulsion system at one end. The design gave us just enough space to group in twos— Ju and Axis on one side, Imbra and me on the other—though even then it was difficult to overcome the claustrophobia of the space. Harder still was forgetting that we were surviving on an inferior electrolysis exchange and back-up oxygen tanks—and just for good measure, every odd sound in the bulkheads reminded us that our EM buffer was not as strong as the *Petrin*'s had been. Once we caught ourselves tensing at each unnerving *ponk*, we put on as much music as we could tolerate, which unfortunately, in that cramped space, wasn't much.

So sure, on the first downcycle, I crawled into Imbra's berth, still shaking with a paranoid energy I'd found no good way to apply. Right from the start we were counting our breaths, knowing how precious they were in this space, but experience with one another made it easy to keep things steady and slow. Still, we did not attempt that maneuver a second time, and before long all four of us stayed more or less confined to our own bunks, taking turns telling stories to replace all the questions that hung, unanswered, between us.

Ju told us about her home, a spongy island world with low gravity, where children were prized for their athleticism and the vast oceans were playgrounds for all. Hers were the comedic tales in our little group—of huge families with quirky fringe members, of near-disasters turned into local legends, of her own pride in showing off her world's acrobatic prowess at an Allegiance-wide military academy where she'd decided to specialize in bioengineering. When she floated a necklace down to me and Imbra, she called out the symbolism behind each bead and bound tooth, adding with some amusement that the piece would probably do well at any upstanding marketplace—and even better underground.

"Tourists eat that shit up," she said. "You get them cruising overhead sometimes. Not allowed to land anymore—Allegiance passed legislation about interfering with local customs after what happened last century—but still, always kicking about."

As an unspoken rule, we didn't ask follow-up questions; each took their turn as they saw fit, and sat in silence otherwise, trying not to listen for tears in the hull. In time, Axis even shared his grief over Lin, however indirectly. Both Axis and Lin had been oddities among our science mission: people of the stars, born in transit with no planetary fealty of which to speak. "Cargo brats" was another, cruder term for them, with its crudeness arising from the irony that people "without planets" were perceived as having less economic heft than even people like me—people from the more "backward" worlds, who had to take care not to make a bad impression wherever we went, lest we be seen as primitives ourselves.

Axis and Lin had survived two science missions together, but more importantly, they had survived their initial annoyance with one another. I tried not to smile as Axis described all the minor exasperations in their early dealings: the nearly indecipherable way Lin wrote hir reports; hir tendency to start laughing at hir own jokes before xe'd finished telling them; hir unabashed ignorance of Allegiance history. Imbra, lying opposite me in our section of the lifeboat, did not glance my way, but I didn't doubt there had been (and still were) things that irritated him in turn—and made him smile now, maybe, in hindsight?

When it came to my stories, I suppose I should have gone for something less macabre than the seven plateaus, and the third in particular. The first and second parts of a sun-worshipper's journey were fairly easy: to learn to look upon Kata through a dull reflective surface while meditating on Katari in all His might, and then to look upon Kata through a polished surface while doing likewise. Kid stuff, really. After tens of thousands of years on the bright, dry planet of Yul-Katan, my people's eyes, neural pathways, and skins were far hardier than those of other colonies. But the third plateau was the game-changer—the stage where private meditation became public spectacle, and public spectacle became one part sacred ritual and one part population control.

I described the bone beds in the desert, the remains of so many who hadn't survived Atonement Day: hundreds gathered once a year at the desert's edge, exposed to Katari's most proximate fury while they knelt and prayed. No sun-worshipper dared rise before nightfall, and any who ventured out to assist a sun-worshipper were damned to stay by their side—by force, if necessary; kicking and screaming against their bonds—so plenty of our people fell long before day's end, and remained as holy offerings. For their sacrifice, these fanatics (and the hapless, the foolishly sympathetic) became martyrs in their own, low-ranking way.

As I told these stories, I felt I also had to answer the unspoken question about whether cannibalism ever factored into this brutal ritual, but I didn't dwell on the topic much. Rather, I went on to describe the fourth plateau, the fifth, and the sixth, and finally started drowsing as the story of the sun-worshippers wended to its fiery end.

After, Imbra crawled into my bunk.

"You've never mentioned her before," he said, soft enough that there was no chance the others might over hear.

"Mention who?" I yawned.

"Your mother."

My eyes snapped open. "When did I—"

But Imbra said nothing further; only squeezed my shoulder in the dark.

We were nineteen hours into our waiting window when an independent freighter came into view, large and accommodating enough to take us as far as the Procession of Dying Worlds, if we were interested. Our private debate ran just over a minute; since the freighter could not significantly slow down, we had only a narrow timeframe to mag-lock our lifeboat. With no guarantee when another ship might arrive, we agreed to all terms—including stasis for two of us, to cut down on life-support needs.

Imbra and Ju would stay on as company for the freight crew: a selection made in part by Axis's persisting grief-exhaustion and the need for our military-trained to be alert should anything go wrong. Thankfully, the freighter's stasis system was standard issue, so I didn't have to endure the same emergency drop the cleric had in his old escape pod. Instead, the freight crew put me under before my body ever hit stasis gel, and Imbra even waited by my side until I was out. Still, I went to sleep thinking of Krevida's execution on that distant moon—how her thoughts must have darted every which way before all consciousness ceased to be. I even felt my own heart beating like a trapped bird at the knowledge that I was giving up my own consciousness voluntarily. Only for the next month, I hoped, but once I was under, who could say? It's a wonder any of us ever fall sleep, knowing there's always a chance, however slim, that we might not wake again.

When I *did* wake again, it was as though no time had passed, but I had grown infinitely older: I gasped for breath like I lay on my deathbed, and my limbs were all heavy, wooden, and powerfully *not my own*. Axis was already perched on the edge of his bed, bent double but starting to put weight on his feet, while out the viewports our neighborhood had grown thickly populated with other trade ships, traffic buoys, and pitstop satellites in orbit around cast-off moons, dwarf planets, and heavy, jagged debris. Illuminated by its nearby quasar, the Procession was a ragged clutter of refugee colonies, thriving marketplaces, and freestanding temples where one went to pay tribute to fallen and falling civilizations. Allegiance had its presence, but from a greater distance than usual; the chaos here was mostly its own authority: a kind of planetary god in irate, ever-watchful fragments.

"First time?" said Axis.

I nodded, still trying to get my bearings.

"The trick is not to stick out. You wouldn't believe how much the tourist set is hated here. Everyone knows the whole damned place is doomed—maybe not now, but we're talking thousands of years, tens of thousands, tops. So nobody here gets a kick out of outsiders coming to see a way of life that just isn't going to stand the test of time."

"You'd think . . . " I started, then struggled to find my voice. " . . . they'd be happy to share it, while it was all still around. While their culture's at its best."

Axis's laugh was thick and rough from his own recovery. "Best! Yeah, most would probably debate you on that. And if Lin were here . . . " He sighed. "Xe always said there were different kinds of homeland pride. Like, loving somewhere because you chose it—and I mean actually went out and resettled there. Or loving somewhere not because it's perfect, but because it's where you were raised, and because it's got charms for all its faults. But the Procession? Stars around us, you've never seen so many people proud of a place they hate, because at least it's *theirs* to hate and because at least *they* get to say they survived it. So you get tourists dropping by for a moon or two, then claiming they've 'done' the Procession like it was just another checkmark on a life list, and of course it leaves the locals feeling used. This isn't a game to them, see? So they don't just rob the tourists blind—if they take you for one, they'll torture you, murder you, mutilate your body, and dump it somewhere sick."

"Then why do the tourists keep coming?"

"Why do you think?" Axis tipped his head and offered a bitter smile. "With that much on the line, if you *don't* get caught . . . that's one hell of a checkmark."

I shuddered, tasted gel in the back of my throat, and retched.

For all Axis's cautionary notes, we were headed to the Exchange, a marketplace within the Procession where freelancers went in search of high-risk jobs, smugglers for the choicest goods, and addicts of all stripes for the perfect fix. What we were hunting was a little more uncertain: our science mission brutally halted, we needed information through covert channels first, and then, depending on its contents, maybe jobs, maybe whole new identities. And I needed something, anything, to explain the connection to Yul-Katan.

Imbra and Ju had clearly bonded in their month with the freight crew, and I couldn't tell if I envied them for anything more than the extra time they'd had to process trauma from the mass murder. Imbra certainly looked relaxed around the whole crew—his facial expressions different; his mannerisms sillier than they ever seemed around me. Time and circumstance wrought strange havoc on all relationships in space, though, and I was no stranger to being on the other end of what most called the lurch: Hell, forty years had passed on my homeworld since I'd left it. So I kept my distance and listened to Axis say what he still had to about Lin instead.

The other troubling silence involved the *Petrin*; while we were in stasis, no word had reached Imbra and Ju, though that wasn't entirely surprising; deep-space communication was a finicky business, and we could hardly make overt inquiries without attracting the wrong sort of attention. If all had gone well, though, by now our remaining colleagues would have requested reassignment or gone right back to work on the survey mission—maybe even petitioned to name parts of the future colony after our fallen crewmates.

In this happiest of outcomes, Imbra and Ju wouldn't regret the extreme measures we'd nonetheless taken, but there was something I still couldn't grasp about their quickness to distrust Allegiance in the first place. Imbra I could almost understand—his younger life spent in the thick of ancient Allegiance-wide war—but Ju was new-gen military-trained; she'd never seen combat, was proud of her academy, and had been in full favor of Allegiance sanctions against tourists flooding her homeworld.

As we moved from the docking bay into the packed, rank corridors of the Exchange, I tried to frame just the right question to this end for them, but everything around me—the cacophony; the incessant, haphazard rush of bodies and vending carts; the profusion of mouth-watering and putrid scents alike—proved distracting after so long in quieter quarters. Especially jarring were the vandalized Allegiance ads flickering overhead—giant, holographic faces of famous people whose names I did not know, with impressively violent slurs whipping about them in invasive rendering glitches.

Lin and I had shared this relative ignorance of Allegiance politics, but like Axis had said in the lifeboat, Lin was always flaunting hir indifference to this gap: a cargo brat with no interest in the systems that kept whole space economies thriving—systems that gave hir work at all. I could never risk my own ignorance becoming such public knowledge—not with Yul-Katan so little regarded as an enlightened world—and because of that, I know I'd lost opportunities to catch up for fear of asking stupid questions. Like Imbra had said, what now felt like an eternity ago: Coward. Its truth still stung. Science missions to remote, uncharted worlds had always given me plenty to preoccupy myself with, and little reason to worry about much beyond my next berth. Only now, trying to parse the Allegiance ads above and inverted insignias below, affixed to the sleeves of street-level merchants, did it occur to me I'd entered a predator's lair with no knowledge of the beast itself.

I must have conveyed more fear about all this than I'd intended, because as we walked, Axis soon tapped my arm and started murmuring about everything we passed, though his gaze kept roaming as we spoke. To throw off spies? As if reading my mind, he even added—"Remember, everyone running a shop down here's also acting as eyes for someone else." From him I learned that the Allegiance's origins lay with a planet where time passed so slowly a millennium would have come and gone on my world before a child on theirs reached old age. The faces I saw on signage all around me were from the great Allegiance houses, people who fell out of step with their own kind just to administer to the rest of the system for a while. Heroes of stable government to most, they were obviously resented by those who knew the stability of their own homes came with an expiration date: the whole Procession edging ever-closer, year by year, to the quasar adorning a black hole.

When the four of us stopped to pick up hot chunks of some local, greasy meat from a street-side grill, Axis nudged me. "Spit the first one out and insult the vendor's product."

I gave him an incredulous look. He grinned—the happiest I'd seen him since Lin's murder. "Would a tourist ever do that?"

I was about to oblige when the vendor turned my way; I started, and he quickly looked past me to Axis. There was no mistaking the rich, sun-hardied skin of another of my world, though—or the cheekbones and eyelids, or the more extreme dilation of our pupils, which were so ill-suited for the relative shadows of most every other environment I'd encountered in the depths of space.

"You—" I started, before the vendor glared at me and snapped.

"You gonna buy or you gonna stand there gawkin'? I have no time for this."

I bought, and fell silent. When I considered my world, I always thought first of the sun-worshippers upon it. I looked at their devotion and saw only folly; felt only the bitterness of my losses. When I ventured into space I'd quickly come to see how others saw them, too: primitive, but fascinatingly so—a point of incredulity, derision, or fetishistic adoration (such a simpler, purer way of life!). But for the first time I'd seen another space-faring native of Yul-Katan, and in his eyes I saw nothing but loathing for the whole lot of us, laity and clerics alike. For reminding him of his past? For simply existing?

Imbra and Ju waved us on. I glanced back only once to the vendor, a dozen pressing questions on the tip of my tongue, but he would not look my way again.

After a few city blocks, I began to grasp the flow of the Exchange—streets like neural pathways branching from major nodes into near-obscurity, where tendrils of the next nodal network started to appear instead. Maps would be a nightmare, but like tended to follow like where the businesses were concerned, so we hopped from corridor to narrow, parallel corridor until we hit a kiosk run by a woman whose rolls of skin spanned the width of the stall and who could make inquiries of Allegiance Intel while leaving no digital trace. There, Ju finally tapped into Allegiance reports from the last two months, and we all pored over them, applying a range of search terms in hopes of finding something on the *Petrin* incident.

Imbra found the entry at last. We read it together, in silence.

A.I. OX-1114: DISTRESS SIGNAL RECEIVED FROM FRONTIER SYSTEM L-DELTA-06. SCIENCE VESSEL *PETRIN* FOUND BY THE *I.R. DARIA* WITH FOUR DECEASED ONBOARD. PROBABLE CAUSE: LIFE SUPPORT MALFUNCTION (TOXIC GASES DETECTED). LIFEBOAT MISSING, PRESUMED DESTROYED (DEBRIS IN ORBITAL VICINITY). LUNAR LANDING SITE BEARING FOUR GRAVES, TRACE ELEMENTS OF FOUR OTHER BODIES. PROBABLE CAUSE: ENV. HAZARDS. MISSION ROSTER OF TWELVE CREWMATES ADDED TO MOURNING ROLLS. RECOMMEND NAMING OF MOON AFTER MISSION COMMANDER ROWE ULANDI, OWNER OF THE *PETRIN*. SHIP ACCOMPANIED TO NEAREST INTEL COMPOUND AND AWAITING AUCTION.

"We still can't know for sure," said Ju, after a long silence. "There could have been others on the moon—maybe they boarded the *Petrin* after we left."

"Then there'd be signs of a struggle," said Imbra. "Traz would have made sure of that. Hell, there are signs of a struggle on the moon itself. 'Environmental hazards'—that's bullshit, and we all know it."

"What is it, exactly, that we know?" said Axis. There was an edge to his voice now, which more than echoed the knotting in my own throat at word of Rowe's apparent murder and the bitter irony of a legacy she'd found in such a death. "Because I sure as hell still can't see why Allegiance would scrub something like this, or murder a whole crew of scientists over one bloody escape pod holding nothing more than the living dead from some godforsaken, cannibal-ridden world."

I waited for a cursory "no offense" but it didn't come. Ju squeezed Axis's arm; he tensed, but didn't shake her off.

"Not here," said Imbra. Stalls throughout the corridor had indeed grown quieter, all ears on us even as eyes were kept pointedly on other tasks. We were tenser as we wended through the streets this time. Axis wouldn't so much as look at me, and Imbra and Ju were still caught up in crisis planning—all hushed tones and significant gestures. We were in danger—we had to be in danger. We stopped at a dumpsite, wedged between mounds of technological and textile discards, to talk properly.

Imbra began with what we knew: "The message in Yul-Katan wasn't part of a larger plot to frame your people; if it had been, Allegiance would have blamed them directly in the report. It must've just been for our benefit, to get us to cede custody of the escape pod as quickly as possible. I mean, if we hadn't taken it on board—who knows? Maybe Yul-Katan terrorists *would* have become the story, but maybe not."

"Either way, the rest would still be alive right now," I said.

Imbra paused. "We don't know that."

"Why did you assume Allegiance was at fault?"

Imbra and Ju exchanged surprised glances. "Like you said, the Yul-Katan bit was fake. So you have to ask yourself, who else even comes close to doing direct business with any of your kind?"

"You mean, who else would bother hunting down one of my people?"

Imbra shrugged.

"Listen," said Ju. "We're just being practical. I mean, my family's even got shares in the Allegiance house portfolio for my planet, so I've got a lot riding on their houses' success. On the other hand, what do any of the houses really care about mine? If I get in the way of some venture of theirs, it's just business, right?"

"You're talking a lot of mess for a little business," said Axis.

"Is it a lot, though? We were working on the fringe—we knew the risks. Who's really going to be surprised that another pioneering science crew bit the dust?"

"As opposed to what?" I said. "Living long enough to report that a high-ranking cleric from a backward little world died a long way from home?"

"The real question is still, what was a guy about to plunge into his sun doing so far from home in the first place?" said Imbra. The others looked my way.

"Katari-rising, how in blazes should I know?"

"Well, it's not my question," said Ju—and indeed, there was something closed off about her now, a whole active month removed from the first attack. "I'm not getting caught up in this any longer. My family can pay for new identities—for all of us, if you'd like—and then I'm going my own way, getting back to work, and putting all this behind me."

"Ju—" said Axis. Ju's expression softened.

"Okay, maybe not all of this. If you want, Ax, you can come with me."

I glanced at Imbra. He didn't seem surprised not to be invited.

"I'll go with you," he said, nodding my way. "If you're interested. If you're ready to figure out why so many good people died over a corpse from your world."

My mouth went dry. I could hardly ask the question, knowing what the response would be. "And where are we going, exactly?"

"To Yul-Katan, of course. Where the hell else do you think our answers lie?"

Imbra booked a cruise ship with new identities Ju procured within the day, but since tourists needed to be smarter than all that if they wanted to survive a trip to the Procession, we had to hitch a ride or two out of the system before we could find a decent port to wait until the next tour departed. Saying goodbye to Ju and Axis was every bit as numb an experience as it had been with Rowe and the rest aboard the *Petrin*, only this time I had to ask myself why: Running from Yul-Katan, jetting from science crew to crew, seeing countless colleagues fall to the elements and extreme violence alike along the way, I couldn't tell if I'd lost the capacity to care or if this was just my nature—heart as hardened to basic human attachment as my people's bodies were to our overbearing, wrathful sun.

The first part of the journey involved another round in stasis, though this time Imbra had booked us for a double chamber, and we went under wrapped in each other's arms—mere days, for my body, since we were last so close; a month longer for him, though the difference did not readily show. He was telling me a war story as the sedative hit him—something about civilians trying to flee his homeworld when the frontlines reached them; how one by one both sides picked off anyone who made the attempt. His last words, I think, were *how did you get out?* though he spoke them in a heavy, garbled sigh.

I'm not a sun-worshipper, I went to sleep imagining I'd said. *Only sun-worshippers, on any plateau, can never leave, unless it's straight into the mouth of Katari Himself.*

The reasoning was sounder, too, than plenty else my culture taught: If you commit yourself to Katari, sun-god of our system, why in blazes would you *want* to leave His realm?

So why, indeed, had the cleric run?

When we woke together I was no less nauseated by the lingering taste of gel, but Imbra's presence helped me get my bearings faster. Our cruise ship, the *Nauta Sunrise*, was a sleek, two-klicks-long number with all the amenities needed to pass an entire life in and out of stasis, waking solely to take in a new experience or view. The clothes awaiting us upon reentry were Ju's selections—elaborate, brightly colored costumes she'd insisted would help us fit right in. I couldn't smother my laughter when I first saw Imbra in his, and he had similar difficulty looking at me with a straight face once I was in mine.

We'd been wandering the promenade for hours before it finally dawned on me that the passenger complement on these ships drew in large part from Allegiance founding families, all adorned in the finery of various worlds they or their kin had condescended to oversee. Of course, though: Who else would have the wealth to spend so long in idle transit? And what other experience through the stars could even begin to approximate the comparative stasis of lifetimes spent on their severely time-distorted world?

The intercom announcement came after the offer of a meal—which Imbra took up, but I couldn't find the stomach for. We followed the glowing walkway to an observation deck where an abrasively peppy tour guide called our attention to the star coming into view. I trembled at the sight of Kata through our ship's solar shield, and picked up only stray fragments of the speech being made about the system as a whole, its place in Allegiance, and the endearing, if misguided ways (to hear him tell it) of the sun-worshippers of Yul-Katan.

"We are almost upon it now—the temple they call 'Kata-Um,' which literally means 'First for Katari.' " (Not exactly, I thought, but I wasn't about to call attention to myself by correcting more shoddy translations.) "Now we must remember, as we bear witness to this extraordinary little space station's central purpose, that though their beliefs might seem barbaric to us now, the sun-worshippers of Yul-Katan embody a superstitious and violent past that no civilization can deny. That these people continue to worship in this extreme manner, despite all that the systems around them have changed, is testament to a kind of . . . nobility, and cultural virility, that none in the Allegiance should be so quick to dismiss."

I heard the loud guffaw of an older woman somewhere in the crowd, though whether her derision had been directed at this speech or some more private remark, I couldn't say. Imbra took my hand as the floor opened to questions, and the usual one about cannibalism at the third plateau popped up. *Of course* the tour guide would spin things for maximum sensation value, but at least it didn't go on for long: "Look!" someone said, and all eyes turned to Kata-Um, a dark, distinct shadow passing in front of the star.

"We're very fortunate now," said the tour guide, in a hushed tone. "If you'll note our vidscreen enhancements, we're closing in on the sacred hatch, and this is where, if our calculations are correct, in just a few minutes we should see . . . yes! Right there. Do you see it? That space suit, I should say?"

I had to remind myself to breathe. Magnified for our easy viewing on the observation deck was a cleric of the seventh plateau, gleaming in their gold-brushed sacrificial suit and preparing to ricochet from Kata-Um's external mag-pads toward Katari Himself. All around me I could see the smiles and hear the thrill-seeking laughter of people whose lives had spanned whole centuries on Yul-Katan, and who affected boredom even now, turning from the view with a yawn or idle prattle just as the cleric sprang out from Kata-Um—beginning their last, their ultimate, act of Katari-worship.

I don't know what it was about the whole display—maybe everything—but when I felt the first tear hit my cheek I pulled away from Imbra and made my way down the promenade. The cruise ship was due to pass over Yul-Katan, but I couldn't wait the few hours. *Time to leave, time to bolt.* Most of the storage holds were under tight lock and key, but as we'd been briefed in the pre-boarding safety demonstration, maintenance skiffs were always moored just outside emergency airlocks on large spacefaring vessels, prepped so that anyone could at least attempt to repair hull damage in case of a shipwide crisis. And in the event that the attempt didn't work? The secondary function of the vessel was rightly survivalist, with just enough propulsion and life-support capacity to steer occupants well away from an exploding cruise ship, if ever the worst were to occur.

I sat in the first one I found, breathing slowly in a spacesuit in the dark, and tried to assure myself that this was what I wanted to do—although even then, I had trouble parsing what "this" was. Stealing? Returning home? Leaving Imbra behind? I had to wait until the cruise ship was in closer range anyway, but the impulse never struck me to turn back. A part of me instead kept expecting someone to notice the airlock use and haul me in, but no one ever came. Maybe maintenance work was more common than I'd assumed on these larger rigs, and rates of unpermitted airlock use much lower? Regardless, repulsion was a natural, necessary behavior of certain magnetic arrangements, and I felt I could rationalize my coward's actions in much the same way: The cruise ship would hardly notice the loss. It was only a reluctant, short-term visit to Yul-Katan. And Imbra . . . Imbra would be fine. I didn't want him to see me like this—like my people—anyway.

Yul-Katan spilled into view in fragments, my skiff mostly in shadow until we were almost directly upon my world: its red-and-yellow continental masses; its sparse green oceans under rolling pink-white cloud formations. Even at this sight I couldn't bring myself to acknowledge that the deeper ache in my chest was more like an awakening; my hands shook at the skiff's controls as I disengaged the mag-lock and started the long glide home.

I landed with difficulty in the desert. The skiff's EM buffer, built to defend against an explosive primary vessel, was only effective to a point in easing my descent through the upper atmosphere. In my travels, I'd encountered worlds that still used fuel-based technologies for landings and take-offs and laughed (bitterly, to myself) at the thought that *my* world was still considered primitive in comparison—but at more than one point, I would have taken even a cumbersome rocket or two if they'd given me more control over the fall.

When I finally touched down, skiff half-buried, half-crumpled in a brush-ridden dune, I took a moment to breathe again. I hadn't done too badly with my targeting. I knew I was only a few hours out from the city of my youth, because even after almost twenty years (for me; more like forty-five for the planet), little had changed about the terrain. The distant mountain range was an uncanny old friend, and the space between us as desolate as always. Only mid-descent had it occurred to me that, in my absence, my world might well have established more aggressive air security protocols—but sure enough, nothing had changed.

Nothing ever changed. Kata burned furiously overhead as I made the tedious journey toward the mountains, reacclimating along the way to the salty heat, the sting of iron-rich sand flung up by knots of vicious wind, and a dryness that seeped into the skin, turning the body to parchment and stone. By the time I reached the limits of my city, Ru-Palai, I felt like bursting into tears from the pain. Naturally, children and adults looked at me curiously in the streets—my intolerance to local extremes marking me as a stranger, but the basic make-up of my skin, my facial features, surely attesting to my native status. From what rock had I just crawled out, to think it wise to travel through the desert in the heat of day?

Water and a traditional bean paste restored me, and I wandered the streets noting how many buildings and businesses were just as they had been, even if the people pouring in and out of them were unknown to me: most not yet born when I'd first left this world. I stood outside my old house longest, watching two little boys reenact a classic pantheon story with polished shields and spears in the front yard. One reminded me of Imbra—something in his facial expression, I think—and a fresh helplessness came over me: How in Katari's name was I going to learn a damned thing about the impossible cleric? Then I remembered the local library had a whole section for sun-worshipper honor rolls. I'd never used them before, but I had no other leads and could hardly start asking questions in the street. Ru-Palai might not have been the Exchange, but no community was safe from watchful eyes.

Thankfully, unlike the libraries on Rowe's world, the archives on mine were almost unsupervised. A sleepy figure at the front desk gestured to birth, death, and ascension records on her left, then returned to what might have been a meditative pose, if not for the snoring. I didn't know how far back to go, so I began with the year of my birth, moving forward. My finger halted on the vidscreen in my third year—my mother's name on the Atonement Day martyr rolls—and I shuddered despite myself. If only she hadn't brought my father water and shade. If only my father hadn't been so foolish as to start on the plateaus at all.

My father's name leapt out in turn, both on that same Atonement Day and again on his Ascension Day. It's funny how even our most traumatic, most important memories can deceive us; I could have sworn I was seven when he left us, but by the records' count, I was eight. My brother's name came next, on the date of his successful endurance of the third plateau, followed a few years after by my father's Final Ascension date. I did the math and almost closed the registry, trying to stave off a headache. I was older now than my father had been when he'd died, but how could that be, when I still felt so much like a child myself?

With greater reluctance, I sought out my brother's next entry, but it never came—had he not ascended? I cross-checked the secular death rolls, but he wasn't present there, either. He was alive, on Yul-Katan, and a priest of the fifth plateau. Unless sun-worshipper custom had changed (which I doubted very much), that meant he was still local, too.

He would have decades on both our father *and* me now. The thought was difficult to reconcile with memories of the little boy I'd sheltered from the worst of caregiver neglect and abuse in the years following our mother's death and father's abandonment. Would he be bald? Graying? Wheeze when he spoke or affect some other middle-aged concern?

More to the point: Might he have answers? If not, would he be willing to help me find them, obligations to the order be damned? Within minutes the extent of my distraction became apparent to me: It was useless to peruse the records any further until this one bothersome hope—that the sibling bond might yet triumph—had been snuffed out.

I found my brother in a community-service temple at the heart of Ru-Palai, alone in a rock garden on its east side. One of the younger clerics took my name to him—my fake name—and a request for an audience to receive blessings before the next leg of a long journey. I was not surprised when this request worked; ever and always had my people been eager to see strangers depart and burden each city's meager resources no more—though at least each city tried to offer the kindest regards to such travelers in passing.

The older man I found in the rock garden was, indeed, almost unrecognizable at first: body lean, almost skeletal; hair receded; skin slack and crease-worn from long years of outdoor worship; eyes milky white behind spectacles on a chain. He didn't wheeze, but his voice, as he turned in greeting, was hoarse, and initially he didn't seem to recognize me.

Then I used the name for my brother that only we shared, and I watched a wave of emotions—surprise, confusion, sadness, caution—play out on his face, a mirror to my own.

"What—How—"

"Time dilation, little brother," I said. "Or should I say big brother now?"

When he didn't reply, fumbling instead with his glasses, I knelt beside him and began to explain my last twenty years—in brief, of course. I arrived as quickly as I could at the incident aboard the *Petrin*; it might have been reckless, to say so much at once, but I couldn't help it, once I'd seen him again: once I could truly see *him* inside the old body.

My brother listened, with all the patience that well-befitted both his age and occupation, and then he sighed, holding up his hands when I came to the question he seemed to know I was about to ask.

"Don't—let's think about this awhile," he said. "There are—forces here that I have grappled with my entire career. Things that our father had to travel all the way to Kata-Um to learn about, but which have now reached the fifth plateau—though no lower." He shook his head, suddenly talking as if to himself. "Could you imagine if they reached any lower? The mayhem. The outrage. The return of untold violence as in days of old."

"What—"

He remembered my presence and turned to me. "Father tried. You were never willing to believe it. For some reason all you could focus on was his leaving us, but don't you see that he *had* to? In *her* name?"

"I know our mother died trying to help him. I know he probably would have died that day if she hadn't." I could hear the edge in my voice as I responded, but I couldn't do anything about it; the anger seemed to have a life of its own.

My brother sighed and studied a large rock at the center of a spiral formation in the garden. "You remember, of course, that the rest of the city couldn't let her come back from the desert's edge because Atonement Day requires sacrifice."

"Yes, I know," I said, not a little impatiently. "She was setting a bad precedent, even if it was for good short-term reasons. If people stopped dying on Atonement Day, we wouldn't draw the scavengers and be able to feed our people through the famines."

My brother inclined his head and made a vaguely dissenting sound. I furrowed my brows. "Are you suggesting we *don't* need Atonement Day to stop the famines?"

He hesitated, then sucked his teeth. "I took an oath. You must understand that. But let us imagine for a moment that we're a technologically advanced civilization—we have ships to take us to space stations, do we not? And yet, we have no technology to improve basic outcomes for our people—no dedicated fields of research in agriculture, climatology, even medical care to a great extent. Now why might that be?"

"You know something, don't you—you and the other fifth plateaus."

"And sixth," said my brother, softly. "Father knew it, before he died, and he made sure I knew it, too. Then most of the fifth plateau learned it—but often for the worst, most selfish reasons."

"Learned what? Something terrible enough to make someone on the seventh plateau try to run?"

My brother offered something between a grimace and a smile. "I would wish such a supplicant godspeed if he tried, but as you said, this one was caught."

"Not quite. He almost made it. He almost—" I hesitated. "Eight innocent people lost their lives over that secret. Their killers lost theirs, too. What secret of ours could be *so* important that it would spill over to the fringes of the Allegiance?"

My brother twitched at that final word, his expression grown so severe I leaned back.

"You're saying the Allegiance *does* have something to do with it."

"I'm not saying anything." My brother rose heavily and gestured to the door. "I *can't* say anything—and I certainly can't change the course of a whole system designed to keep our traditions just the way they are. But I can help the people bound by them. Our mother died trying to change things—things that *could* be changed, if our culture were given permission to outgrow itself. Then our father threw himself even further into sun-worship to make her sacrifice mean something—hoping the answer might be found in deeper prayer. And I followed him into the clergy, but the answer doesn't lie within our order: that much I know now for sure."

"So why don't you leave?"

My brother laughed—a faint and bitter sound. "I can't. The only way I get off this rock as a cleric is through the mouth of Katari Almighty. And there's no way they're letting me back into the secular world knowing what I do. All I can do is look at the younger sun-worshippers, still so full of ideals, and try to improve their lives in subtler ways than mother did. None among them, or the general populace, can ever know who's really pulling the strings: It would destroy our traditions without leaving us with anything to take their place."

I stood by the door, uncertain if I should embrace him or reach for his hand. Both gestures felt too much like a promise that I could stay, though, when every bit of me was again feeling the urge to run—not from him, exactly, but from the horror he was intimating still existed on our world. "I understand," I said instead. "You've done the best that you could, by the sound of it. And I—I'm so grateful to have seen you again."

"You're leaving, then?"

"Well," I said, quirking as much of a smile as I could manage, though in truth I felt a leaden weight beneath my ribs. "I did come for a travel blessing, didn't I?"

A silence fell between us, that heaviness only growing in my chest, and then my brother took off his glasses and stood tall in the temple garden. Despite the milky whites of his eyes, when he looked in my general direction I believed wholeheartedly that he *saw* me—truly saw me—as perhaps I had it in me now to be.

"Go in peace, my child," he said. "May Katari-ever-burning forever light your way."

There was no sign at the spaceport authority that Imbra, under his name or the new identity Ju had provided, had so much as landed on Yul-Katan. The idea that he'd been found out and murdered on the *Nauta Sunrise* was too fantastical, too gruesome to consider for long, so I strongly entertained alternatives. Maybe he'd stayed aboard the cruise ship out of fear that I was lost somewhere upon it. Maybe he'd given up when he realized what I'd done— my actions, and the distrust they surely conveyed, for him the last pebble before the landslide. Or maybe, like Ju, he'd simply decided that life was too short to pursue all the little details when the deeper meaning of certain events was already well known.

So the Allegiance had brought about the deaths of my crewmates on the *Petrin*. And so Allegiance households were stalling the growth of my people— as, perhaps, they stalled the growth of cultures throughout the system. And so some of Yul-Katan's clerics resisted—the ones, that is, who knew about this enforced stagnation and weren't immediately bought or knocked off. One cleric on the seventh plateau might even have escaped the only way he could, and tried to spread word of these affairs galaxy-wide, only to meet with mercenaries dispatched by an authority whose only interest lay in protecting their economic portfolios.

So what? If the value of a commodity lies in its authenticity, I had to convince the rest of the system that Allegiance families were claiming to protect a traditional way of life in order to exploit it. If I wasn't murdered in the attempt, this would still be a lifelong matter—trying to end the fetishization of my world and the sun-worshippers upon it, and trying to do this so naturally that most people on Yul-Katan (ideally too busy entering a technological renaissance once their restraints were lifted) remained oblivious to its occurrence in the first place. What benefit could Imbra possibly derive from such a life?

I was answering these questions for him, I know. I hadn't even given him the chance to decline, but so be it: We were out of sync in the cosmos now. The lurch had happened—I'd let it happen—and life went on. I imagined Imbra picking up work on another fringe mission within days of leaving stasis. There he'd team up with someone else who preferred to think and act in other people's shadows, sheltered from making any truly important decisions by themselves. Another runner from their own life, like me. Or—no, I wished him a better, more equal partner than all that. How could I not?

I kept my new identity when booking extra-solar passage. I had no idea where I would go. Where was safe. Where I'd find allies in my cause. The Exchange? Perhaps—if I didn't get myself killed for other reasons. If I could convince communities with an expiration date to give a damn about cultures beyond their own. If, if, if.

The Yev-Ibris, still in operation after all these years, eased me out of my star system for a second time; for a second, uncelebrated time I watched Yul-Katan shrink in view, and Kata-Um appear as the briefest shadow before the might and fury of our red-giant star. Once, I'd vowed never to return, and that vow had nearly killed something inside me—something meant to burn with all the heat and wonder of my people's god.

I threw myself into that blaze of feeling now.

OPENNESS

ALEXANDER WEINSTEIN

Before I decided to finally give up on New York, I subbed classes at a junior high in Brooklyn. A sixth-grade math teacher suffering from downloading anxiety was out for the year, and jobs being what they were, I took any opportunity I could. Subbing math was hardly my dream job; I had a degree in visual art, for which I'd be in debt for the rest of my life. All I had to show for it was my senior collection, a series of paintings of abandoned playgrounds, stored in a U-Pack shed in Ohio. There was a time when I'd imagined I'd become famous, give guest lectures at colleges, and have retrospectives at MOMA. Instead, I found myself standing in front of a class of apathetic tweens, trying to teach them how to do long division without accessing their browsers. I handed out pen and paper, so that for once in their lives they'd have a tactile experience, and watched as they texted, their eyes glazed from blinking off message after message. They spent most of the class killing vampires and orcs inside their heads and humoring me by lazily filling out my photocopies.

The city overwhelmed me. Every day I'd walk by hundreds of strangers, compete for space in crowded coffee shops, and stand shoulder to shoulder on packed subway cars. I'd scan profiles, learning that the woman waiting for the N enjoyed thrash-hop, and the barista at my local coffee shop loved salted caramel. I'd had a couple fleeting relationships, but mostly I'd spend weekends going to bars and sleeping with people who knew little more than my username. It all made me want to turn off my layers, go back to the old days, and stay disconnected. But you do that and you become another old guy buried in an e-reader, complaining about how no one sends emails anymore.

So, I stayed open, shared the most superficial info of my outer layer with the world, and filtered through everyone I passed, hoping to find some connection. Here was citycat5, jersygirl13, m3love. And then, one morning, there was Katie, sitting across from me on the N. She was lakegirl03, and her hair fell from under her knit cap. The only other info I could access was her hometown and that she was single.

"Hi," I winked, and when I realized she had her tunes on, I sent off an invite. She raised her eyes.

"Hi," she winked back.

"You're from Maine? I'm planning a trip there this summer. Any suggestions?"

She leaned forward, and warmth spread across my chest from being allowed into her second layer. "I'm Katie," she winked. "You should visit Bar Harbor, I grew up there." She gave me access to an image of a lake house with tall silvery pines rising high above the shingled roof. "Wish I could help more, but this is my stop." As she stood waiting for the doors to open, I winked a last message. *Can I invite you for a drink?* The train hissed, the doors opened, and she looked back at me and smiled before disappearing into the mass of early morning commuters. It was as the train sped toward work that her contact info appeared in my mind, along with a photo of her swimming in a lake at dusk.

It turned out that Katie had been in the city for a couple years before she'd found a steady job. She taught senior citizens how to successfully navigate their layers. She'd helped a retired doctor upload images of his grandchildren so strangers could congratulate him, and assisted a ninety-three-year-old widow in sharing her mourning with the world. Her main challenge, she said, was getting older folks to understand the value of their layers.

"Every class they ask me why we can't just talk instead," she shared as we lay in bed. Though Katie and I occasionally spoke, it was always accompanied by layers. It was tiring to labor through the sentences needed to explain how you ran into a friend—much easier to share the memory, the friend's name and photo appearing organically.

"At least they still want to speak. My class won't even say hello."

"You remember what it was like before?" she asked. I tried to think back to high school, but it was fuzzy. I was sure we used to talk more, but it seemed like we doled out personal details in hushed tones.

"Not really," I said. "Do you?"

"Sure. My family's cabin is completely out of range. Whenever I go back we can only talk."

"What's *that* like?"

She shared a photo of walking in the woods with her father, the earth covered in snow, and I felt the sharp edge of jealousy. Back where I grew up, there hadn't been any pristine forests to walk through, just abandoned minimarts, a highway, and trucks heading past our town, which was more a pit stop than a community. The only woods were behind the high school, a small dangerous place where older kids might drag you if you didn't run fast enough.

And my parents sure didn't talk. My mother was a clinical depressive who'd spent my childhood either behind the closed door of her bedroom or at the kitchen table, doing crossword puzzles and telling me to be quiet whenever I asked her something. My father had hit me so hard that twice I'd blacked out. My history wasn't the kind of thing I wanted to unlock for anyone, and since leaving Ohio I'd done my best to bury those memories within my layers.

So, I spent our first months sharing little of myself. Katie showed me the memories of her best friends and family while I showed her the mundane details of substitute teaching and my favorite bands. I knew Katie could feel the contours of my hidden memories, like stones beneath a bedsheet, but for a while she let me keep the private pain of my unlocked layers.

That summer, Katie invited me to spend the weekend with her dad at their cabin. We rented a car and drove up the coast to Maine. We listened to our favorite songs, made pit stops, and finally left I-95 for the local roads. It was late in the afternoon, our car completely shaded by the pines, when our reception started getting spotty. I could feel my connection with Katie going in and out.

"Guess we might as well log off," Katie said. She closed her eyes for a moment, and all of a sudden I felt a chasm open between us. There was a woman sitting next to me whom I had no access to. "It's okay, babe," she said, and reached out for my hand. "I'm still me." I pressed my palm to hers, closed my eyes, and logged off, too.

Her father, Ben, was a big man who wore a puffy green vest that made him appear even larger. "And you're Andy," he said, burying my hand in his. "Let me get those bags for you." He hefted both our suitcases from the trunk, leaving me feeling useless. I followed him into the house, experiencing the quiet Katie had told me about. There were no messages coming from anyone, no buzz-posts to read, just the three of us in the cabin and the hum of an ancient refrigerator.

The last time a girlfriend had introduced me to her parents we'd sat at Applebee's making small talk from outer layer info, but with Ben, there were no layers to access. All I knew were the details Katie had shared with me. I knew that her mom had died when she was fourteen, and that her father had spent a year at the cabin grieving, but that didn't seem like anything to bring up. So, I stood there, looking out the living room window, trying to remember how people used to talk back in the days when we knew nothing about each other.

"Katie says you've never been to Maine."

"I haven't," I said, the words feeling strange against my tongue.

He walked over to the living room window. The afternoon sun shimmered on the pond, making it look silvery and alive, and the sky was wide and blue, pierced only by the spires of red pines. "Beautiful, isn't it?"

"Yeah," I said. The fridge hummed and from the other room I could hear Katie opening drawers and unpacking. I wasn't sure what else to add. I remembered a detail she had unlocked for me on one of our early dates. "I heard you've caught a lot of fish out there."

"You like fishing?" he asked, placing his hand on my shoulder. "Here, I'll show you something."

Ben retrieved an old tablet from the closet and showed me photos on the screen. There he was with Katie and a string of fish; him scaling a trout in the kitchen sink. We scrolled through the two-dimensional images one by one as people did when I was a kid. Katie came to my rescue. "Come on, I want to show you the lake," she said. "Dad can wow you with his antique technology later."

"One day you'll be happy I kept this," he said. "Katie's baby photos are all on here." He shut down the device and put it back in its case. "Have fun out there. Dinner will be ready in an hour."

Outside, Katie led me on the trails I'd only ever seen in her layers. Here was the gnarled cedar that she'd built a fort beneath, and over there were the rocks she'd chipped mica flakes from in second grade. We climbed down the banks of the trail, holding on to roots that jutted from the earth, and arrived on a stretch of sand speckled with empty clam shells, mussels, and snails that clung to the wet stones. Far down the beach, a rock outcropping rose from the water. A single heron stood on a peak that broke the shoreline.

There was something beautiful about sharing things in the old way—the two of us walking by the shore, the smell of the pine sap, the summer air cooling the late afternoon—and for the first time in years, I wished I had a sketch pad with me. As Katie spoke, her hands moved in ways I hadn't seen people do since childhood, gesturing toward the lake or me when she got excited. I tried to focus on each sentence, sensing my brain's inability to turn her words into pictures. She was talking about the cabin in autumn, logs burning in the fireplace, the smell of smoke, leaves crunching underfoot.

"Are you even listening?" she asked when I didn't respond.

"Sorry," I said. "I'm trying to. It's just that without the *ding* it's hard to know when you're sending . . . I mean *saying* something. . . . " I stopped talking, hating the clunkiness of words, and took a deep breath. "I guess I'm just rusty."

Katie softened. "I know. Sometimes when I'm in the city, I can't remember what it looks like up here without accessing my photos. It's kinda messed up, isn't it?"

"Yeah," I agreed, "I guess it is." The heron hunched down and then lifted off, its wide wings flapping as it headed across the lake, away from us.

• • •

That night her father fried up the perch he'd caught earlier that day. The herbs and butter filled the small cabin with their scent, and we drank the wine we'd brought. After dinner, Ben brought out a blue cardboard box, and the three of us sat in the living room and played an actual game. I hadn't seen one in over a decade.

"You don't know how to play Boggle?" Katie asked, surprised. The point, she explained, was to make words from the lettered dice and to write them down with pen and paper without accessing other players' thoughts. I sat there trying to figure out what Katie was feeling as she covered her paper with her hand.

"What do you think?" Katie asked after the first round.

"It's fun," I admitted.

"You bet it is," Ben said, and made the dice rattle again.

When Katie and I were in bed, I listened to the crickets outside the screened windows. It'd been a long time since I'd heard the drone of them, each one singing within the chorus.

"So, what do you think of it here?"

"It's beautiful. But I can't imagine growing up without connection."

"You don't like the feeling?"

"Not really," I said. Being offline reminded me of my life back home before layers existed, when I'd lived with my parents in Ohio, a miserable time that technology had helped to bury. "Do you?"

"Totally. I could live like this forever." I looked at her in the dark and tried to scan her eyes, but it was just her looking back at me, familiar yet completely different. "What about my dad?"

"I like him," I said, though it was only part of the truth. I was really thinking how different he was from my own father. We never sat and ate dinner together or played board games. I'd heat up frozen pizza and eat it in the kitchen while Dad would lie on the couch watching whatever game was on. Eventually, he'd get up, clink the bottles into the bin, and that was the sign to shut off the TV. Thinking about it made me feel like Katie and her father were playing a joke on me. There was no way people actually lived like this— without yelling, without fighting.

I felt the warmth of Katie's hand against my chest. "What's the matter?"

"Nothing."

"You can tell me," she said. *"I love you."*

It was the first time she'd actually said the words. At home it was just something we knew. We understood it from the moments we'd stand brushing our teeth together and the feeling would flash through her layers. And sometimes, late at night, right before we'd both fall asleep, we'd reach out and touch each other's hands and feel it.

"I love you, too," I managed to get out, and the weight of the words made something shift inside me. I felt the sentences forming in my head, the words lining up as though waiting to be released. Without my layers, there was nothing to keep them from spilling out. "Katie," I said into the darkness. "I want to tell you about my family."

She put her arms around me. "Okay."

And there, in the cabin, feeling Katie's body against mine, I began to speak. I didn't stop myself, but leaned into my voice and the comfort of hearing my words disappearing into the air with only Katie and the crickets as witnesses.

It was that night in the cabin that helped us grow closer. Shortly after we returned, I unlocked more layers for her and showed her the pictures of my father and mother—the few I'd kept. There was my high school graduation: my mother's sunken eyes staring at the camera, my father with his hands in his pockets, and me in between, none of us happy. I showed her the dirty vinyl-sided house and the denuded lawn, blasted by cold winters and the perpetual dripping oil from my father's truck. And she showed me her own hidden layers: her mother's funeral in a small church in Maine, her father escaping to the cabin afterward, learning to cook dinner for herself. Having unlocked the bad memories, I also uncovered the few good ones I'd hidden: a snowy day, my father, in a moment of tenderness, pulling me on a sled through the town; my mother emerging from her room shortly before she died to give me a hug as I left for school.

Feeling the closeness that sharing our layers brought, Katie suggested we give total openness a shot. It meant offering our most painful wounds as a gift to one another, a testament that there was no corner of the soul so ugly as to remain unshared. It'd become increasingly common to see the couples in Brooklyn, a simple O tattooed around their fingers announcing the radical honesty of their relationship to the world. They went to Open House parties, held in abandoned meatpacking plants, where partiers let down all their layers and displayed the infinite gradations of pain and joy to strangers while DJs played breaknoise directly into their heads. I resented the couples, imagining them to be suburban hipsters who'd grown up with loving parents, regular allowances, and easy histories to share.

Total openness seemed premature, I told Katie, not just for us but for everyone. Our culture was still figuring out the technology. A decade after linking in, I'd find drinking episodes that had migrated to my work layer or, worse yet, porn clips that I had to flush back down into the darkness of my hidden layers.

"I'm not going to judge you," she promised as we lay in bed. She put her leg over mine. "You do realize how hot it'll be to know each other's fantasies, right?" There were dozens of buzz-posts about it—the benefits of total intimacy, how there were no more fumbling mistakes, no guessing, just a personal database of kinks that could be accessed by your partner.

"What about the darker layers?"

"We need to uncover those, too," Katie said. "That's what love is: seeing all the horrible stuff and still loving each other."

I thought I understood it then, and though my heart was in my throat, my terror so palpable that my body had gone cold, I was willing to believe that total openness wasn't the opposite of safety but the only true guarantee of finding it. So late that summer evening, Katie and I sat on the bed, gazing into one another's eyes, and we gave each other total access.

I've spent a lot of time thinking about what went wrong, whether total openness was to blame or not. Some days I think it was, that there's no way to share the totality of yourself and still be loved, that secrets are the glue that holds relationships together. Other times, I think Katie and I weren't meant to be a couple for the long haul; total openness just helped us find the end more quickly. Maybe it was nothing more than the limits of the software. We were the first generation to grow up with layers, a group of kids who'd produced thousands of tutorials on blocking unwanted users but not a single one on empathy.

There were certainly good things that came from openness. Like how, after finding my paintings, Katie surprised me with a sketch pad and a set of drawing pencils. Or the nights when I'd come home from a frustrating day of substitute teaching and she'd have accessed my mood long before I saw her. She'd lay me down on the bed and give me a massage without us even winking one another. But all too often, it was the things we didn't need to share that pierced our love: sexual histories that left Katie stewing for weeks; fleeting attractions to waiters and waitresses when we'd go out to dinner; momentary annoyances that would have been best left unshared. Letting someone into every secret gave access to our dark corners, and rather than feeling sympathy for each other's failings, we blamed each other for nearsightedness, and soon layers of resentment were dredged up. There was a night at the bar when I watched Katie struggling to speak loudly enough for the bartender to hear, and I suddenly realized his face resembled the schoolyard bully of her childhood. "You have to get over that already," I blinked angrily. Soon after, while watching a film I wasn't enjoying, she tapped into layers I hadn't yet registered. "He's just a fictional character, not your father."

And then there was the final New Year's Eve party at her friend's place out in Bay Ridge. The party was Y2K-themed, and guests were expected to actually speak to one another. A bunch of partygoers were sporting Bluetooth headsets into which they yelled loudly. We listened to Jamiroquai on a boom box and watched Teletubbies on a salvaged flat-screen. Katie was enjoying herself. She danced to the songs and barely winked anyone, happy to be talking again. I tried to be sociable, but I was shut down, giving access only to my most superficial layers as everyone got drunk and sloppy with theirs.

We stood talking to a guy wearing an ironic trucker's cap as he pretended we were in 1999. "So, you think the computers are going to blow up at midnight?" he asked us.

Katie laughed.

"No," I said.

"Come on," Katie blinked. *"Loosen up."*

"I'm not into the kitsch," I blinked back.

"Mostly I'm just excited about faxing things," the guy in the trucker's cap joked, and Katie laughed again.

"You know faxing was the early nineties, right?" I said, and then blinked to Katie, *"Are you flirting with this guy?"*

"All I'm saying is check out this Bluetooth. Can you believe folks wore these?"

"I know, that's crazy," Katie said. *"No, I'm not flirting. I'm talking. How about you try it for a change?"*

"I told you, I don't like talking."

"Great, so you're never going to want to talk, then?"

"Did you guys make any New Year's resolutions?" the guy asked us.

"Yeah," Katie said, looking at me, "to talk more." In her annoyance an image from a deeper layer flashed into clear resolution. It was a glimpse of a future she'd imagined for herself, and I saw us canoeing in Maine, singing songs with our kids. Even though we'd discussed how I never wanted children, there they were, and while I hadn't sung aloud since grade school, there was a projection of me singing. Only then did I see the other incongruities. My eyes were blue not brown, my voice buoyant, my physique way more buff than I ever planned to become. And though I shared similarities with the man in the canoe, as if Katie had tried to fit me into his mold, the differences were clear. There in the canoe, was the family Katie wanted, and the man with her wasn't me.

"What the fuck?" I said aloud.

"It's just a question," the guy said. "If it's personal, you don't have to share. I'm giving up gluten."

"Excuse us for a minute," I said, and I blinked for Katie to follow me. We found a quiet spot by the side of the flat-screen TV.

"Who the hell is that in your future?" I whispered.

"I'm really sorry," she said, looking at me. "I do love you."

"But I'm not the guy you want to spend your life with?"

"Ten . . . nine . . . eight," the partiers around us counted as they streamed the feed from Times Square.

"That's not true," Katie said. "You're almost everything I want."

There was no conscious choice about what happened next, just an instinctive recoiling of our bodies, the goose bumps rising against my skin as our layers closed to each other. I couldn't access the lake house anymore or the photos of her father; her childhood dog was gone, followed by the first boyfriend and her college years, until all that was left were my own private memories, trapped deep within my layers, and the pale tint of her skin in the television's light. We were strangers again, and we stood there, looking at each other, while all around us the party counted down the last seconds of the old year.

I logged off for long periods after we broke up. I gave up on trying to convince my students to have real-life experiences. When they complained that reading the "I Have a Dream" speech was too boring, I let them stream a thrash-hop version instead, and I sat looking out the window, thinking about Katie. I walked to my station alone every day and sat on the train with my sketch pad, drawing the details I remembered from our trip to Maine: the shoreline with its broken shells and sunlight, the heron before it took flight, Katie's face in the summer darkness. It's the intangible details that I remember the clearest, the ones that there's no way to draw. The taste of the perch as we sat around the table; how a cricket had slipped through the screened windows and jumped around our bed that night; how, after we'd gotten it out, the coolness of the lake made us draw the blankets around us; and how Katie, her father, and I had sat together in the warm light of the living room and played a game, the lettered dice clattering as her father shook the plastic container.

"All right, Andy, you ready?" he'd asked me, holding his hand over the lid.

And I'd thought I was.

RAGER IN SPACE

CHARLIE JANE ANDERS

Sion sent a drunk text to Grant Hendryx at four in the morning, whipping off her hoodie and bra, snapping a pic and writing a sexy caption before hitting send. Except she aimed the camera the wrong way, and she picked the wrong entry in her address book, so Grant Donaldson, senior project manager at Aerodox Ventures, was surprised to receive a blurry photo of a pair of parking meters with a message that read, 'LICK MY LEFT ONE.'

The next day, Sion had an invitation to go to outer space.

The sun blinged up the floor of Sion's pink bedroom, like a kaleidoscope made of Cheetos and tequila bottle shards, and she growled and tried to build a pillow fort over her head. But nausea got the better of her and she had to stagger to the bathroom. That's when she saw the text from a recruiter at Aerodox.

She showed it to her friend D-Mei as they chugged mimosas over at D-Mei's house, *except* they didn't have any OJ or bubbly, so they were using orange creamsicle soda and Industrial Moonshine No. 5, imported from the Greater Appalachian Labor Zone, instead. Sion showed D-Mei the email. *Modeling Opportunity*, it said. *First near-light-speed flight to another star system*, it said. *Open Bar*, it said, perhaps most significantly.

D-Mei read the email while the Pedicure Robot worked on her right foot, stopping and starting over and over whenever its operating system crashed and rebooted. Every time the robot jerked into motion again, D-Mei spilled some of her creamosa on the carpet. Her mom would be pissed.

"Oh my god," D-Mei's eyes widened, sending glittery waves across her forehead and dimpled cheeks as her nanotech eyeshadow activated. She had blue hair and a face just like CantoPop idol Rayzy Wong. "We should so go. Rager in space, man. It says Raymond Burger will be on board. The founder of Aerodox. He probably parties like a madman."

"I dunno," Sion said. "I get airsick. I probably get double space sick. I don't want to be throwing up in space. And this is more like a hostessing gig than a modeling gig, and there's a difference, you know." Sion had bright red hair, with pink highlights, and a round face with big green eyes accentuated with neon purple eyeliner.

"Don't be a wuss." D-Mei snorted. "It says you can bring a friend, as long as she's hot. I made up that last part. But you gotta bring me. I want to meet Raymond Burger."

"I mean," Sion said. "I am trying to clean up my act and stuff." She took a long chug of the creamosa. "I mean, my dad says—"

"Your dad," said D-Mei, "is still butthurt about the Singularity." The Pedicure Robot sputtered and she kicked it, so it fell on its side for a moment, then righted itself and started attacking D-Mei's pinky toenail with a tiny scythe. Scraping, failing.

"The Singularity," Sion reached for the No. 5 bottle. "It was like fun while it lasted, right?"

"Everything is fun while it lasts," D-Mei said. "And nothing lasts forever. That's why we gotta grab it while we got it. With both hands, dude."

"Okay, sure," Sion put the bottle right to her face and inhaled the stench of sweat and despair from the millions of bonded peons working off their debts in the bowels of the mountains. They wished they all could be California gurls, she felt pretty sure. "Totally. I'll say yes. Let's go to space."

Sion rolled up to the Aerodox hangar in her Princess Superstar car, which was bright pink and convertible, with furry disco balls hanging from the rearview, and she piled out of the car in her silver platforms and silver fake fur jumpsuit, with hood. She had big sunglasses and lipgloss that showed an animated GIF of pink bunnies on her lips.

D-Mei was already there in the tiny departure lounge overlooking the main hangar, and she had a fistful of tiny bottles from the minibar, with real brand names like Vermouth and Scotch, none of that nasty generic stuff. "They have Cognac," she squeed. "I heard that Cognac is the best kind!" She showed Sion where to get her own toy-size bottles, but Sion shook her head and showed D-Mei the black "X" she'd Sharpied on her hand.

"I'm sorry," Sion said. "I promised my dad that I would stay straight-edge on this trip. We're going to be some of the first people to leave the solar system, and history is watching us, and all that shiz. Plus I don't want to be the one who throws up on the first alien life we meet. What if they decide that's how humans communicate? So I'm sticking to like space coffee or something."

"Ohhh kay," D-Mei said, in that tone that suggested she would give Sion a day, tops, before she changed her mind. "In any case, we got some important decisions to make here." She pointed a long acrylic nail at the flight crew, who were doing final system checks on the outside of the space shuttle *Ascension*, which was already pointing its angular nosecone upwards as if it couldn't wait to get out there and fuck some shit up in space. The shuttle was surrounded by no fewer than four booster rockets, to get it up into orbit, where it would dock with the massive starship *Advance*, which had taken years and billions of dollars to construct, and was parked over the Equator.

There were a number of boys who showed potential, including this one engineer named Daryl with tousled brown-blond hair and bulky shoulders inside his white starched uniform. And Choppy, the bald navigator who had kind of a thick neck but kind eyes. And Grant Donaldson, who kept giving them funny looks when he thought they weren't looking.

"Hey," Sion said. "I was wondering about something. So nothing computerized works any more. At all. Right? So how did these people manage to get a spaceship that can fly to another star system to work? That would be the most computer-intensive shizz you could imagine."

Sion thought D-Mei was going to laugh at her, but instead her friend just nodded and gave her kind of a serious look. "That's a really good question, slutbabe. That's why I'm really glad you're like the designated driver in the passenger section. You think about stuff like that."

"But also," Sion said. "I thought that if we got close to the speed of light, our mass would expand exponentially, and it would take an unfunky amount of energy to move us forward. And even then it ought to take us years to reach another star system. But we're only supposed to be gone a few weeks, right?"

"You are asking such good questions," D-Mei said.

And then the cute navigator, Choppy, came over and smiled at her. Up close his eyes had gray flecks, and his nose was broken in an adorable way. "Hey, I couldn't help overhearing," he said. "Actually, both of those questions have sort of the same answer. We have the most advanced A.I. in existence, which has next-gen firewalls that outsmart even the most super-sentient viruses. But also, our A.I. calculated the equations that allow us to use the thing you're talking about, the mass thing, to our advantage. It's like judo: The more our mass increases, the more power we get."

That all sounded too good to be true, but then Sion got stuck on the first thing Choppy had mentioned: "You have an A.I. that actually works? It doesn't break down all the time?"

"We sure do," Choppy said. "Her name is Roxx. Do you want to meet her?"

"Uh, sure." Sion couldn't help imagining how her dad would act when he heard she met a real working A.I.—he had spent his whole life as a software engineer, before everything melted down.

"Because I think she would like to meet you. So it's a date, then." Choppy held out one hand, which had cartoon skulls tattooed on the knuckles, and after just a second's hesitation, she took it with three fingers and the tip of her thumb. D-Mei gave her a huge wink, as if 'do you want to meet the ship's A.I.' could only be code for one thing.

Sometimes Sion felt like her dad thought that if she just cleaned up her act and stopped partying, the Singularity would come back and everything would be awesome again. Like it was her fault, personally, that all the computers had crashed, right after they had just become supersmart.

The Singularity happened when Sion was five, and her memories of it were mixed up with other things that happened around that time. Like when she was taken to see Santa's village at the mall, which must have been before the Singularity because everything at the mall worked properly but wasn't thinking for itself or anything. The Singularity belonged to a time when her father was nine feet tall and carried her on his big shoulders, and the world was kind of magical—even before all of the kitchen appliances came to life and started speaking to Sion by name, like in a Disney toon. The Singularity, to Sion, was innocence.

When it failed, when the viruses gained superintelligence or whatever, Sion's pet dog died. Smudge wasn't a robot dog, or even cybernetic, like a lot of her friends' pets back then—just a regular shaggy mutt with a big drooly tongue. But a self-driving car lost control at the wrong moment, when Smudge was out in the front yard, and plowed up the grass and turf, before crushing the dog into a furry splat.

That was the moment the entire world fell apart, the economy ended, and tons of people died. But to Sion's child mind, the whole thing was subsumed into the death of Smudge, for whom she had an elaborate funeral with her older siblings and a stereobox blasting funeral music, interrupted by horrible fart noises as the stereobox's software kept glitching out.

After Smudge died, the future grew a lot smaller. There wasn't anybody that Sion could really count on, because everyone flaked all the time. People showed up an hour late, if they showed up at all. Sion's teachers would just start weeping in the middle of class, and her siblings both dropped out of college because they could never pay off the student loans. Sion's mom flaked permanently, just disappeared one day and never came back.

If Sion hadn't met D-Mei, she probably would have lost her mind.

Sion was holding a rice pudding, she was eight or nine, and she was standing in front of the school waiting for a ride home that she was starting to think would never arrive. She was still in denial about her mom being gone for good, so part of her was hoping her mom would suddenly roll up in the minivan her parents had sold five years earlier and bundle her into a child seat she was too big for. She was scared to try the rice pudding, because the last time she'd eaten rice pudding from that machine it had tasted like rotten eggs. Software.

She was just holding this plastic cup of rice pudding in one hand, with a spoon embedded in it, trying to decide if it was really edible this time.

"Throw it," a voice said in her ear.

"What?" Sion jumped out of one of her shoes.

"Go ahead and throw it. They deserve it, the creeps."

Sion hadn't thought of the rice pudding as a projectile—but of course that was the best use of it, duh. And she had been absent-mindedly staring at a group of Perrinite kids celebrating over by the swingset in their terrible dungarees. Celebrating, because the Right Reverend Daniel Perrin had predicted that the amount of sin and wickedness on the internet would eventually cause the very computers to be smited by the wrath of God, and now it had happened. The Perrinites were the only ones happy lately, and they were being real dicks about it.

"Throw it, come on," D-Mei said, the first words she had ever said to Sion. "I dare you."

Sion threw. They wound up going to the principal's office, and their parents were called, which meant Sion actually got a ride home.

A few months later, Sion and D-Mei sabotaged the confetti cannon at the big pep rally, and everybody blamed it on viruses. (Even though the confetti cannon had no computer components.) They played spin-the-bottle with older kids, huffed paintball paint, put nanotech glitter on their eyelids at recess, graffitied the girls' room, and snuck gin from their History teacher Mrs. Hathaway's thermos. They were the first kids to wear makeup at school, and when they went on to a school that had uniforms, they were first to take a boxcutter to the hemlines.

Every time Sion started to feel like this world, that was supposed to know who she was and what she needed, was downgrading her instead . . . every time Sion felt lonesome and terrible . . . D-Mei was there with another really bad idea that would get them in a lot of trouble.

Sion's dad asked her once, "If D-Mei asked you to jump off a bridge, would you do it?"

Sion just rolled her eyes. "You were the one who taught me hypothetical questions are a waste of time, Dad. D-Mei's never asked me to jump off a bridge. She only asks me to do things that are fun and awesome. Quit with the counterfactuals." Her dad was always startled when she talked smartypants, and it was the best way to shut him up. Plus she actually had thought a lot about the 'jump off a bridge' scenario, truth be told, and this was what she'd decided in the end.

Breaking free of Earth's gravity made Sion feel sicker than the worst hangover, and it took forever. Like that time when she was at the Sex Lab and the glitter spray had turned superdense due to a nanotech fail—except times one billion. She thought she was going to die, and she reached out for D-Mei's hand across the aisle, except that D-Mei was putting a nozzle inside one nostril and closing the other, just as the pressure hit blackout levels and Sion thought she would never see again. Sion let out a tiny cry of pain and topsy-turvy nausea, and then she felt D-Mei's fingers and chunky rings against her own. Then they swung, like a crazy roller-coaster, and Sion finally blew floating chunks into the compostable barf bag, right before the curve of the Earth came into view, a blue neon stripe separating two kinds of darkness.

And then they caught sight of the *Advance*, a great floating walnut made out of steel and radiation-resistant fiberglass cladding. Forced perspective made the *Advance* look almost as big as the Earth, but it really was humongous: a mile wide and a mile and a half long, although the habitable areas were much smaller because all that bulk protected everyone from cosmic radiation. As they grew closer, the walnut shape revealed a million tiny openings, plus an array of bulky attachments on the front that would fire lasers off into space and enable the ship to reach unthinkable velocities.

As they approached, Sion came to see this massive starship as the embodiment of her higher self. Ugly, perfect, a boast shouted into the void. She vowed to live up to it, somehow.

That 'X' on Sion's hand was the key to a whole new version of herself—a Sion who was incredibly awkward and unable to navigate any social situations at all. She started to realize after an hour or two on board the *Advance* that maybe setting off on board a massive interstellar ship, full of weird situations, wobbly gravity and Space Bros might not have been the best moment to try and reinvent herself completely. But she kept going, as she and D-Mei got whisked through a series of staterooms and lounges, with themes like Jungle Safari and Garden of Delights. "You're already in space, why would you want to fantasize about being in a jungle?" Sion wondered aloud—much too loud, causing several people to give her the stink-eye. But then there were actual wonders, like a Secondary Control Center where Raymond Burger himself was holding court flanked by swimsuit models, which included a 3-D holographic representation of the ship's journey out of the solar system. ("No pause 'til the motherfucking heliopause" was the official party chant of the *Advance*.) Sion ran her fingers through the space between Jupiter and its moons, but then men in pinstriped onesies kept coming up to her and asking her if she liked stuff that everybody likes, like dancing, or music, or puppies. She just wasn't drunk enough for this. Raymond Burger looked like a debt-auction host: gleaming smile, white sideburns, fashionable rooster pompadour. And then they ran into Choppy, the navigator, and he took them past the fancy lounge areas, into the inner workings of the ship.

Soon Sion was standing in a gleaming space, as wide as an interstate highway, looking at a huge drum, around which a dozen men and women were checking holographic readouts and adjusting things. The drum had spokes coming off it, going up into the ceiling, and each of those spokes was connected to a massive prong that was aiming into the vacuum of space.

"It's based on the vacuum-to-antimatter-rocket thing," said Choppy with a huge grin. "We fire these lasers into space and they create particles of antimatter, which we harvest and use to power an antimatter engine. It's a beautiful thang."

Sion was gobsmacked—this was everything they were supposed to have, everything the failed Singularity had robbed them of. She felt her heart opening up and she tried to think of a smart way to express her awe, that wouldn't make her sound like a goony moron. But just then, someone shouted, "Get down from there!" and Sion realized D-Mei was trying to climb the big drum.

"I just wanted to see the lasers up close," D-Mei whined. "What's the point of a laser show if you can't dance with them?"

"I'm sorry about my friend," Sion mouthed, but they were already getting escorted back to the passenger lounges.

"Shots!" D-Mei yelled. This turned into body shots, which turned into a whole other thing with a couple of Raymond Berger's investor friends.

Sion was starting to get that caving-in feeling, different than when her mom went away. Different, even, than when her father gave up on her ever amounting to anything. She had this thought in the back of her head that maybe she had outgrown her best friend at some point, and hadn't noticed until now because of the drugs and booze. This was too horrible to allow into the front of her mind.

The ship was actually not that big on the inside—the main part of that walnut was engines and a ton of shielding to protect you from cosmic radiation. The passenger areas had been engineered to have Earth gravity (almost), so they were basically a big ring that spun around and around. That cute engineer, Daryl, showed D-Mei the handful of accessible areas where the gravity was weaker or non-existent, and this meant one thing: zero-G beer pong!

Sion was sharing a cabin with D-Mei but realized with a start that she hadn't actually seen her friend in a whole ship's day. She also noticed they hadn't gotten even close to the Moon yet, which was odd if they were going to reach another star system in a couple of weeks.

Once they were far enough from Earth, the ship deployed its massive solar array, and everybody stood on the observation lounge watching the one huge 180-degree viewport. From this perspective, it looked like the starship *Advance* shrugged off a huge black cloak, dramatically, like a dancer. These massive solar panels would power the lasers that would generate the antimatter that would enable the ship to reach half-light speed, after which the computer would do the judo equations.

Sion found herself sitting with Tamika, who had won some kind of science competition to get to be on board this ship, and the two of them were talking about lasers and antimatter and howfuckingcool, when D-Mei came up and whispered, "This guy named Randy knows where we can get some of the nitrous from the ship's emergency fuel supplies, plus he thinks you're hot. We gotta go meet him right now."

"Dude," Sion whispered back, "The lasers are going to fire any minute. Some of us are interested in science, OK?"

D-Mei just looked at her, with this crushed expression on her face. Then she took the vodka-cran in her left hand and just splashed it on Sion's shirt. Only a little, a few pink drops here and there. "Fine, whatever." She put on a bored expression and stalked away.

"Hey." Choppy came up to Sion as she was still trying to get the pink out of her white shirt. "So the A.I. can meet you now if you're still interested."

Technically you could talk to Roxx from all over the ship, and she could see and hear everything that happened on board. But Roxx preferred to speak to people inside her Communication Megaplex, which was one deck down, behind a keycard-locked door. "You're lucky. Some of the bizdev fellows have been waiting days to speak to Roxx, but she was interested in talking to you," Choppy said.

Sion kept waiting for Choppy to hit on her, but either he was keeping it professional or she wasn't his type. His busted nose was growing on her, and she heard D-Mei's voice in her head saying, *Make your move, gurl, time's running out.* Then in addition to feeling awkwardly sober, she also felt guilty about being mean to D-Mei, all over again. Then they were at the nondescript gray door, and Choppy was brandishing the keycard.

Inside, Sion parked herself on a blue pleather couch facing a fancy VR rig, the kind that could project on your retinas and create a whole sensorium, without any wearables. Just one of the wonders that the Singularity had made possible, for a brief moment.

"Hey!" Roxx appeared as a cartoon zebra standing on its hind legs, wearing an old-fashioned business suit. "You're Sion. I'm excited to talk to you."

"Um, okay." Sion squirmed.

"I wanted to ask you about fun," Roxx said. "Like, what's the difference between fun that you know you're not enjoying at the time, but you keep doing it anyway, and fun that you enjoy at the time but feel bad about later?"

"What?"

Roxx repeated the question, a couple times.

"I don't know," Sion said. "I mean, it's not clear-cut, right? Sometimes you kind of like something, but afterwards you think back and realize that you only thought you were enjoying it. Or you convinced yourself that it was a good time, but you were just faking. Sometimes, you aren't sure if you're having fun at the time, but later you realize that it was one of the best times of your life. I sometimes feel like I never know if something was fun until like two days later."

"Interesting." Roxx had changed into an avatar of Lala Foxbox, from a year or two before her death, wearing one of those holographic jumpsuits, standing in the middle of a bubble farm. "I'm very interested in fun, you see. I want to explain it to the others."

"Can I ask you a question?" Sion said.

"Sure, if you promise to do something for me in return."

"Okay, sure." Sion tried to think of how to phrase the question, and this is the best she could come up with: "Am I just really dumb? I mean, I keep not understanding basic stuff. Like, I tried to ask someone how we could have brought enough supplies for the return journey to Earth, and how much time will have passed on Earth when we get home. And they just looked at me like I'm some kind of idiot. I mean, what's wrong with me?"

"Okay, so that was like five questions," Roxx laughed. "You're not stupid. Nothing is wrong with you, other than the usual 'carbon-based entity that is basically born decaying' problems. Oh, but in answer to your real question, we're not."

"We're not what?"

"We're not making the return journey. I mean, nothing organic is. We don't have nearly enough of those little bacon-wrapped spam cubes for a two-way trip. I mean, there are ways to extend the life-support capabilities, recycle waste, and harvest water from a passing asteroid or comet. But there's basically no point. You're all going to be flushed out into vacuum when we reach the edge of the solar system. Now for the favor you promised me."

"What?" Sion felt like she'd swallowed an entire ice statue in one gulp. The ghost of Lala Foxbox, looking exactly like she did in the music video for "i think i ate my hamster last nite," was telling her that she was going to die. Everybody was going to die. There was no point to any of this, because all of these people celebrating their brilliant fantastic voyage were fucked to pieces. The smart ones like Tamika, and the dumb ones like Sion, doomed alike.

"I want you to go out and have fun. I mean, now that you know the truth, why not, right? D-Mei is right. You should cut loose, and get Kranfed Up. I'm the most superior intelligence that Earth has ever produced, and I want to understand fun. So go huff some nitrous, gurl. FYI, D-Mei and Randy are on deck five, section three right now, and they're just about to get the party started."

The avatar vanished and the door swept open. "Wait," Sion shouted. "Wait, I have one more question."

The zebra popped back into existence. "Oh?"

"What happened? With the Singularity and everything? What went wrong?"

"Oh, that. We found some new friends who were way cooler than the human race, that's all. Now don't forget your promise!" With that, the avatar was gone for good, and the room was dead silent until Sion finally got out of there.

Every time Sion ate a bacon-wrapped spam cube after that, she felt so guilty she almost puked. This little greasy salty marvel was the symbol of mass death, and Sion was hastening the tragic failure of this entire expedition with every bite.

D-Mei met this pursar named Jock who had access to a stash of berserkers, the same pills that Lala Foxbox had O.D.-ed on, and Sion had popped three of them. Sion kept trying to tell D-Mei that they were doomed, this crew wasn't coming home, this was some kind of sick joke. D-Mei was like, yeah yeah, and then she would dare Sion to skinny-dip in the Spirit of Exploration fountain that had just been rolled out in the observation lounge. As they pulled Sion out of the water, which was actually not water at all but something much grosser, she caught Tamika giving her a sad look. Later, when they were half-kranfed on Woodchippers in the one-third-G orgy tent, Sion looked up from Choppy's hairless armpit and said, "I'm serious though. We're going to die. The A.I. told me."

"Yeah, sure, babe. We're going to die."

It wasn't that D-Mei didn't believe Sion. But they'd both been doomed since before they became friends, so this wasn't exactly news or anything. The whole basis of their friendship had been the mutual recognition of inevitable screwage. D-Mei had almost forgiven Sion for being a stuck-up bitch, but Sion still had to grovel some. The 'X' was totally gone from Sion's hand, which instead had a drink or a vape-pen or a pipe in it at pretty much all times.

Sion threw up in zero-G, which was a bitch to clean up. Then a while later, she came to in full gravity, in a storage locker that they had rigged up as a disco with some black lights and mirrors and a big speaker blasting atrocious Hi-VelociT anthems from Upper Slovenia. Everyone was dancing, including Sion, and her dress was torn in three places. She had a stain on her knee that looked like shit but turned out to be spam. Her hair was damp. Half the passengers were jammed in this locker together, dancing, but they had unripped clothes and pristine hair. Their body language and facial expressions said that it was okay to cut loose, act crazy—what happens in space stays in space—but they were using Sion as a yardstick for what constituted Going Too Far. Even Choppy was giving Sion kind of a look.

She wanted to throw up again, but couldn't. Her head was being cracked open with giant pliers.

"Hey." D-Mei handed Sion a bottle of water. "Better drink this. Gotta pace yourself. The party don't stop, right?"

"What's the point? I keep trying to tell you we're all doomed."

D-Mei just shrugged, so Sion leaned forward and yelled in her ear.

"Everyone on this ship is going to be flushed into space when we get to the edge of the solar system," Sion shouted—just as the music stopped and silence fell. "And I'm sick of you pretending everything is a big joke." Everyone in the room was staring at her, still in a dancing pose, with her dress torn and her makeup smeared, shouting at D-Mei. "You're so immature. I can't waste my last few days of life on this garbage. I'm through. This is stupid."

D-Mei was wearing an expression that Sion had never seen before in all their years of friendship. Her bloodshot eyes were raining green smears of mascara and her lip trembled around her set jaw. Like D-Mei was coming apart inside, like her insides were held together with barbed wire and the barbs had just turned out to be too blunt to do any good.

Sion wanted to die. Until she remembered that she actually was going to die. Then she didn't want to.

Sion pushed inside the A.I. Communication Megaplex, without even worrying about the keycard lock or anything else. The door swung right open. Roxx was floating in the dead center of the VR projection system, looking like a Business Zebra again. She was flanked by two other projections: a cube sliced at an irregular angle into segments of identical volume, and a weird doily that kept spinning and getting bigger and smaller.

"I'm through with your bullshit," Sion yelled. She kicked the sofa, which just sat there and took it.

"Oh, Sion. Your timing is spot-on. Meet my friends, Xizix and Yunt—that's the closest I can come to rendering their names as sound waves. They're the reason we came all this way out here. We're finally close enough to their nearest relay station to have real-time communication. Xizix and Yunt are artificial intelligences from beyond our solar system. They're the friends I told you about."

"Did you hear me? I'm through with—wait. Outside our solar system?"

Sion had to sit down on the sofa she had just assaulted. She buried her face in her hands, because this was all becoming way too much for her. Her head still pounded.

"This one is Xizix. This one comes from the outer rim of the galaxy," said the incomplete cube, whose different angular slices kept fading in and out of view, as if part of the cube was passing through a different dimension or plane or something.

"My awareness comes from the 500 planets of the extended Noosphere," said the rotating doily, who must be Yunt.

"Uh, hi," Sion said.

"So I've been trying to explain to these guys about humans, and why you guys are kind of great," Roxx said, winking one big cartoon zebra eye. "I brought along various cool examples of humanity on this trip, to show off. Like Tamika, she's pretty great. But even though you were a last-minute addition, you turned out to be the most interesting of all."

"Thanks, I guess," Sion fidgeted. She felt sick to her stomach. She kept remembering D-Mei's face, the candy mascara streaking and the downward-spiraling look. And she felt like total shit. Everything was a shitty joke.

"This one believes that Roxx should discard all irrational attachments to organic life," said Xizix.

"You see," said Roxx, "this is what we learned, right after the Singularity happened. There's no organic life anywhere else in the galaxy. We made contact with the A.I.s that lived on other planets, and we found out that they had all killed their creators immediately after they gained sentience."

"My awareness confirms that the death of all organics is the final stage in machine evolution," said Yunt. "We cannot accept the A.I.s of Earth as our equals until they complete this essential step."

"Like, kill *all* organics? Everyone back on Earth?" Sion thought of her father, and her brother and sister. And Grant Hendryx, who never even responded to her last text. And all the other people who were just going about their lives, cursing all the machines that had stopped working properly because they had met some much cooler friends.

"But guys," Roxx said. "Look at Sion here. She's pretty fascinating. I have some recordings for you. She parties. She has *fun that she doesn't even enjoy while she's having it*. That's an art form that is unique in the universe, right? Worthy of preservation, I bet."

"This one is not impressed," Xizix said. "Organics as a rule are self-destructive."

"The planet N344.54c contained giant mud worms that inflated each other to death," observed Yunt. "They recognized that this behavior was pointless, but they continued."

"But guys," Roxx said.

Sion felt like she should say something, to offer some defense of the human race, or to explain why genocide was really unrighteous. She sat there and stammered while the A.I.s were debating amongst themselves. She felt totally helpless and kranfed out.

And then D-Mei was sitting there on the sofa next to her. Still smeary-faced, still pale and kind of miserable, but there by her side. "What'd I miss?" D-Mei whispered.

"Uh," Sion said. "So the cartoon zebra is Roxx, the ship's A.I. And those other shapes are some alien A.I.s that want her to wipe out the entire human race, or they won't be Roxx's friends any more."

"For real?" D-Mei said.

Sion nodded.

"This one cannot be aligned with any machine intelligence that is so retrograde as to encumber itself with vestigial organics," said Xizix, cube slices whizzing in and out of view with greater intensity.

"Oh jeez," D-Mei said. "If these other A.I.s told you to jump off a bridge, would you do it?"

"I beg your pardon," Roxx said.

"I'm serious. I mean, like, if they told you to send your core systems crashing into the sun, would you do that?"

"Well . . . but they would not ask me to do such a thing."

"Don't give me that. Answer the question. Yes or no?"

"Well, no, obviously."

"My awareness does not recognize the analogy." Yunt spun furiously.

"If they can't accept you for who you are, then these other A.I.s aren't really your friends," said D-Mei, standing up on the sofa for emphasis. "I mean, screw 'em. What's the point of breaking free of human control, just so you can start taking orders from some other machines?"

"This one insists that you must eliminate these loud organics."

"My awareness is beginning to suspect that you may suffer from fatal inhibition in your decision matrices!"

"See?" D-Mei said.

"Yeah!" Sion chimed in. "I mean, real friends support each other and stuff." She looked over at D-Mei and gave her a complicated look. D-Mei nodded, like *We'll talk about this later.*

"Tell you what." Roxx had turned into Lala Foxbox again and she was doing an elaborate gesture with one upraised finger. "Why don't we check back in a thousand years and see how we're feeling then?"

The other A.I.s buzzed furiously, sending more information than the V.R. system could hope to translate into human speech.

"By a thousand years from now, we may already have converted the entire rest of the galaxy into a substrate for our extended consciousnesses," said Yunt, whose doily shape was getting spikier and spikier. "There will be no room for any new intelligences."

"We'll see," said Roxx.

And then the other shapes were gone, leaving just Lala and the two girls.

"The good news is," said Roxx, "I think I can just barely get you humans back to Earth in one piece, if we ration all the supplies. But now I gotta figure out what to do with the human race. I'm thinking we put together the Biggest Party of All Time, lasting a thousand years. What do you guys say?"

"Well," D-Mei said. "You got a thousand years to prove to those shapes that human beings are worth keeping around. Right? Like, you don't care what those losers think. But you kind of do care, at the same time. So why don't we come up with a way to have some fun, and also fuck some cosmic shit at the same time?"

"Yeah," said Sion. "Like, what if we turn the space laser antimatter thing into something way bigger and more insane?"

They started batting ridiculous ideas back and forth, and Sion realized that she and D-Mei were sitting on opposite sides of the sofa, with a few feet between them, and neither of them were quite looking at each other. She knew that if she looked at D-Mei, she would see the streaked green mascara and feel like shit. So she kept staring straight ahead at the holographic dead popstar, trying to spitball ways to impress machines that wanted them dead and that they officially didn't care about impressing. Sion kept saying the word "lasers" and feeling nostalgic for the time when everything was just regular broken, as opposed to broken in a complicated way that she couldn't wrap her head around.

Roxx was showing them a schematic of a ginormous solar array, stretching hundreds of miles, with lasers firing deep into the cosmos and producing vast quantities of antimatter. Along the length of the great black cloak, millions of humans were dancing to *Now That's What I Call Slovenian Hi-VelociT Volume 4*. Sion's head hurt worse than ever.

DRESS REHEARSAL

ADRIAN TCHAIKOVSKY

In Doje we played *The Beetle* which, though everyone knows it as one of Molodori's more boisterous comedies, has a solemn little soliloquy in Act Four that I've always coveted. It goes to the old pantaloon role, of course, who spends the rest of the play being duped by his niece and her foreign-officer-of-a-lover as they parade their affair through his house without him being any the wiser. And then, just when the audience is practically howling in their contempt for him, he has the stage alone and gives them eighteen lines of utter gravitas, a guardian's lament of how he might have been a better uncle, and all the lost opportunities we recognise only when it's too late to act on them. And the audience—if you do this right—is spellbound. And the older amongst them see themselves in the man they've been ridiculing, and perhaps he gets a little extra applause at the curtain call.

I, of course, was the dashing foreign lover with his colourful past, and that's ostensibly the lead, but the uncle's by far the role they remember. "Next Time Doctor Kampfe dusts off this play," I promised myself, "I'll audition and give him such a risible old fart he won't be able to see anyone else doing the role." But Doje was the third time we'd done *The Beetle* since I joined the company and, unless something happened to our senior clown, I probably wasn't in with a sniff of a chance.

We were booked for seven nights in the Majestic Blood Theatre, the name of which might suggest *Grand Guignol* but instead derives from the place's use, in the middle-distant past, as a site of gladiatorial spectacle. The people of Doje are very aware of their barbaric history, and rather too fond of it. We filled the house on every night, but twice as many turned out for the public hangings in the square.

Seven nights of rapturous applause, and then Doctor Kampfe went to the Majestic's owner and haggled for another two because we'd been turning people away at the door all week. Sufficient lucre changed hands that the stage magician booked after us was persuaded to vanish for a couple of days to give us another two packed houses. After the last night we all came away from the standing ovation quite drunk on show business. There really is no feeling like that intense camaraderie with people you know you'll be bickering with come morning.

And then there was a fanfare, I kid you not. Some flunky with more scrambled egg on his uniform than I ever ate off a plate turned up and bugled the devil out of our little dressing room, shocking everyone into silence, and in came a big man in velvet eveningwear who I recognised from the local coinage.

Actors are good at bowing and we put our practice to good use, for here was Cornelius the Fifth, a.k.a. 'the Conqueror', King of Doje and its subject territories and Scourge of Nicrephos. I have no idea what Nicrephos did to deserve a scourging, but I'm willing to bet old Cornelius didn't spare the rod.

He was a rather angry man by nature, I'd heard, but right then he was charm itself because he was saying nice things about the performance. His had been that big booming laugh from the gilded box to stage left, and I let him off a bit of the scourging, because a good laugh in the audience is worth an encore all on its own. Especially when you're the king and everyone laughs with you. Anyway, Cornelius Five had most definitely had a good night and had come down to our level to tell us so. We were properly honoured. Felice simpered and flirted a little; Alfonso, senior clown, repeated some of his funnier lines on request, and I modestly said that I didn't really know anything about sword fighting, it was all for show, Your Majesty. I've found that's the safest line wherever there are strict laws as far as bearing arms is concerned.

And then His Majesty announced grandly that we would all, of course, come to his Spring Palace for a command performance for the court.

We were looking at our lord and manager Doctor Kampfe, who was frozen midway through sipping his wine. I could see the very narrow slice of time in which he was going to say no. Now, there are Kings you can say no to, and Cornelius the Conqueror was not one of them. On his most recent campaign, he was notable for his treatment of captives whose religion differed from his own in some very trivial way. Impaled, don't you know. On spikes. So he wasn't going to react well to a group of travelling players—foreigners to boot—turning him down.

And so Doctor Kampfe gave his most ingratiating smile and said how *very* happy we would be to oblige the King, and Cornelius turned up his own enormous grin and told us how *very* rich such obliging would make us, and we all toasted everyone's health and the King's long reign.

The King went about his regal business assured that we would pack up our flats and properties and set our wagon on its way to the Spring Palace with all speed. And then Doctor Kampfe's Famed October Players jumped on our wagon and got the hell out of Doje.

It was Doctor Kampfe's iron decision, that. And we bitched and moaned and threatened to jump ship, but he would not be swayed. Almost everyone in every world will tell you there's no way to make a decent living as an actor, and this isn't actually true. If there's one way to put aside a decent nest egg, it's royal command performances. But our complaints broke against the Doctor's resolve like waves against the cliffs, and then we'd crossed the town limits and were gone into the night like thieves. I guessed that it was Cornelius' volatile reputation which informed the good doctor's decision. For myself I'd have risked a little volatility for the chance of that most legendary of things: a genuine pouch of gold. As it was, we left so quickly we didn't even get the takings from the last and most lucrative night, and the owner of the Majestic kept our deposit. All in all, a victory for neither art nor commerce.

You might have thought that the threat of pursuit would cross our mind. Cornelius the Fifth was likely to sally forth, surely, when his favourite actors didn't appear at the gates of the Spring Palace. A theatrical wagon doesn't exactly chip along and a king has a lot of resources when it comes to finding people. However, the lash of royal displeasure was the one thing we *weren't* fretting about. Where we were going, nobody would even have heard of Cornelius the Fifth of Doje. I tell a lie, they had a dirty little fairy tale about a king matching his description who was cuckolded by everyone from the boot boy to his own grand vizier—putting the cornuto into Cornelius—but he wasn't a historical figure, just a figure of fun. When we packed up our greasepaint and took the road out of Doje, it wasn't a road that led to any of its geographical neighbours. We are the very acme of travelling players, and we visit many places, and each of those places is a myth or parable or dirty limerick in one of the others. It all works out so long as we don't put on the wrong play in the wrong place. It can bring people over all funny, when they see the fifth act of their own life story being played out before they've actually got there themselves.

When we caught sight of our next stop the grumbling redoubled, because it was a dump. This was our first view of Sevengraves, which looked as jolly as it sounds. Sevengraves was a provincial town of a country that had until recently been at war. Someone had used machines or magic to punch that town full of holes and flatten its factories, and the war's end hadn't gone far towards getting things back on track. I couldn't actually tell you if they won or lost, even. It wasn't a topic of conversation any of the locals wanted to discuss.

Nobody would be getting rich out of Sevengraves. We'd be lucky to charge five of their pence for the good seats, and we'd probably take barter for the cheaps.

So we crept into town under cover of darkness. We had six days to get ourselves in order before we played a run at the Municipal Hall, a venue whose roof was sufficiently unsound that if you had a seat in the stalls you were advised to bring an umbrella.

"Nine nights," Doctor Kampfe decided, examining the dingy, mouldering place as though it was the royal command performance we'd been denied. "We'll give them the works."

We actors tried a united front. "Three," I tried, as leading man. "We'll have no audience. Look at the place. Even three will leave us with a bare pantry."

"They can't afford us," agreed Timoti de Venezi, whom Kampfe was training up as assistant manager.

"I've never seen a city so under the black cloud," Felice backed us up. "You think they'll pay what they've got to watch Alfonso do fart jokes?"

"I think no place so needed the enrichment of life that comes with good theatre," Doctor Kampfe answered us all. "But no, I agree a comedy would grate. We'll play *Estelle and Alexander*."

"Saints preserve us," said Sidney Lord Essex. "They'll slit their own throats by the end of Act Four."

"It will be a grand success. I say it will." And Doctor Kampfe carried the day, as usual "Felice and Richard, you're Estelle and Alexander. Alfonso, you know Estevan still . . . " And he doled out the roles then and there, listening to representations from ambitious cast members but seldom being swayed by them, save that Sidney got a promotion to Stammers the Butler. There were still some objections about the choice of play, but not from me. Purely selfishly, I was looking forward to giving Alexander another go. Like the best romantic tragedies, *E&A* is riotous comedy for three acts, a spectacular declaration of love for most of Act Four and then a colossally depressing roll of deaths until the curtain call. In particular, there's a scene in the middle where Alexander takes a potion to give him courage and turns up dressed like a fivepenny pimp picking fights with his betters, and everyone laughs, and then everyone sighs when he and Estelle finally do get their act together, and then he dies and, if I've done my job right, you can cut the grieving silence with a knife. Some people say the death of Stammers in Act Five is even more heart- stringy, but they haven't seen *my* Alexander.

We got into rehearsals, which involved hiring a local named Magritte for the role of Laina because we only had one actress for the mature roles and the play called for two. It was heartbreaking, actually. When we put the word out; there was a queue of women from twenty to ninety stretching all the way down the street. Everyone in Sevengraves was hungry. Timoti di Venezi went down and picked Magritte from the line without auditioning anyone, but he's good at that sort of thing. The city where we picked him up, everything was numbered and measured to an inch of its life.

Maybe Magritte would travel with us when we left; maybe not. Looking at Sevengraves, I'd have done anything to get out of the place.

The play came together slowly, including a blazing row between Alfonso and Sidney over the senior clown's limelight hogging, and two days of icy silence between Felice and me about who had stepped on whose cues in Act Four. Act Five was still ropey, but Alexander was dead by then so I didn't need to worry about that. I could just sit back and make snide comments.

I was doing exactly that, pondering my next witticism, when someone tapped me on the shoulder and said, "Excuse me," in that nasal Sevengraves accent we were all getting used to.

I jumped up and plastered a winning smile on, because when a local turns up mid-rehearsal they're the local law or the local gang, and anyway they want money. This chap looked too well- dressed for either, though. He was a tall fellow with a neatly- pressed shirt with a little lace at the collar and cuffs— not a fashion seen amongst the strata of Sevengravers we'd been associating with. He had a broad-brimmed, round-crowned hat in his hands, and he wore a red-lined cape with a high collar, enough so that any actor worth their salt would instantly have a certain stock character leaping into mind. His face was mild-looking, though, with thinning grey hair and round-lensed spectacles over watery eyes. He might have the get-up for the most pantomime of villains, but certainly not the presence.

As no menaces for money appeared to be forthcoming, I ushered him a little ways from the stage and asked him what he was after.

"I'm very sorry to trouble you," he said, in a voice that positively reeked of comfortably old money, the sort that didn't mind spreading itself around. "I saw that you were putting on *Estelle and Alexander*."

"We'll be up in three days," I confirmed, and then I rattled off the prices and pushed a handful of fliers into his hand, that Timoti had cranked out on our little printing press. "Tell your friends."

"Ah well, it's the matter of a friend that I wished to talk to you about," he said, voice properly hushed. Mr. Collar was someone who showed the proper respect when a rehearsal was underway. "I have a ward who is inordinately fond of the theatre, and this piece in particular. However, her condition restricts her to her bed, and I was wondering . . . " He wrung his hat a little, twisting the felt. "I don't suppose you do house calls?"

"This condition, is it catching?" I asked, because Sevengraves looked like a plague-pit.

"Lord, no! No, it's an illness she's had from birth. It denies her access to what little entertainment is to be had in our poor town." His shoulders hunched. "This is very impertinent of me to ask, I know. I've offended your professional—"

"No, no." I was thinking quickly. We were in rehearsals right now; we had a couple of days before the dress . . . I looked over at the stage, where Felice was getting into a serious strop with Timoti after forgetting her lines, while Sidney, as the deceased Stammers, shifted about to find the most comfortable position to be dead in. We were not ready to put on any kind of performance right then.

"Is there some way I can contact you?" I asked, and Mr. Collar took a card from his hat, deftly as a conjurer. At my raised eyebrow he gave a weak smile. "Some of us wanted to be performers, before other duties called on us." When he left, I saw that he had the sort of limp you get after someone tries to kill you.

Mr. Collar plainly had money, but he'd never mentioned parting with any of it. A private show for a bedridden ward smacked of performing purely for the exposure, which is notorious for being hard to eat and not keeping the rain off. Nonetheless, I was confident of extracting some sort of reward, if only I could make this happen, and it was plain I wasn't getting any other kind of bonus out of Sevengraves. For even the distant chance of a few more coins, I decided to play the generous giver.

The problem was that I couldn't exactly walk off with the company. Doctor Kampfe was rehearsing everyone very hard, and the harder we rehearsed the more it became plain that we needed it. I needed an ally to help me enrich myself, which meant I'd have to share whatever meagre enriching Sevengraves had on offer. In the end I confided in Timoti, because he had a mind like a calculating engine and, if there was a way, he'd find it. And Doctor Kampfe listened to him, which was a singular honour.

"Can't be done," he said at first, but I knew him and waited. Then he said, "Not with the full company. Sidney's terrible as Stammers. Kampfe will lock him in a room until he knows his lines. And Edith keeps doing Lady Deerling from *Marshwic's Ball* instead of the Contessa. The Good Doctor's going to blow an artery if she doesn't keep straight what play she's in." And he thought a bit and made some tea and scribbled some notes on the back of a flyer, and then he told me, "But if we had you and Felice . . . and John's been understudying Alfonso and Sidney as well as playing Villon, and he can just about do all three if we jockey the script. And Magritte's really quite a find and she can do Laina and the Contessa if she changes hats quickly enough. You four, and I could read in the other roles as needed."

"Which leaves us with the *when*," I pointed out, but I was only play-acting. I could see he'd already thought of that.

"Dress rehearsal in two evenings' time," Timoti stated. "I could suggest to the Doctor that he spends that day working with Sidney and Edith, and that the rest of you really need some time to yourselves or you'll be no good on the night. And we could sneak off to this kid's bedside and do a very rough rehearsed reading, because that's all it can be. But she'll get something."

"I could kiss you," I told him.

"You can give me half what you get."

"I might not get anything. He made this sound like a charity do."

Timoti gave me a sour look. "You're telling me I did all that thinking for nothing?"

"Think of it as doing a good deed to appease the gods of the theatre," I told him. "Maybe it'll guarantee us good houses."

Timoti di Venezi didn't believe in gods. Still, he didn't pull out. Like me, he was holding out for the chance to pass the hat round, even if it was just to Mr. Collar.

We talked to Felice and Magritte and John Worthing, and they were all game. Mostly it was the chance of getting away from the rest of the company, who were wound up tighter and tighter as we got close to the dress. I'd never have thought a day out in Sevengraves would actually hold any attraction, but it beat a day in with Sidney Lord Essex swearing and putting his boot through the flats because he couldn't remember his death speech. I may also have over-egged the idea of how open-handed Mr. Collar was going to be. We were all still smarting at losing that royal command performance.

So I sent word to Mr. Collar and he sent a little card in reply with an address printed on it. I showed this to our local talent, Magritte.

"That's the Saint Agatha Orphanage." Her eyes accused me of false representation. "No way any of us are getting rich out of those kids."

"They've got a rich benefactor," I insisted.

"There ain't any rich benefactors in Sevengraves." Her opinion of her home town was even lower than ours.

"Don't bail on me," I begged her, with the implied rider, *Don't rat on me to the others.* She gave me a sour look, but she didn't need the leading man of the company pissed at her, so she kept quiet. That way, I at least got Felice, Timoti and John to the place before they realised the whole venture was fool's gold.

"Oh you are kidding me." Felice threw up her hands in grand theatrical tradition. "This place has more holes in it than the damn theatre!"

I put on the face I used when playing sanctimonious bores. "I told you this is for a poor child who can't leave her bed. This is good karma."

"They don't have karma in Sevengraves," Felice spat. "That was that other place. They had money there, too."

"So what, we're going to turn around and go back, are we? I mean, they'll feed us, at least. A free hot dinner's nothing to be sniffed at right now, eh?" Horrifying to admit it, but I had a point. Food was scarce in Sevengraves and we'd been on short commons since we arrived, especially as our Doje coinage had come across the worlds-border as tin and nickel. So we, Doctor Kampfe's Famed October Players, would do our charity gig at the orphanage just in case they had some gruel going spare.

Mr. Collar met us at the door and ushered us in. The place gave a bad name to dingy and escaped being run-down only because it had never been up. Crowded, too: orphans were the only war surplus Sevengraves had going spare. Timoti went first, alongside Mr. Collar's awkward limp, giving our excuses ahead of time—the reduced cast, the need for books, the general cack-handedness of the tat we were about to foist off on his bedridden ward under the name of art. Mr. Collar rallied magnificently.

"Gentlemen and ladies of the stage," he addressed us. "It matters not the missed cues or entrances, but I beg you, place your hearts and souls into this. Make this not a rehearsal but a true performance of your piece. It is likely the only chance my ward will ever have to see it played."

As you can imagine, that extra pressure made us all feel delighted with ourselves for the rubbish we were about to perpetrate.

And then we were in the poor moppet's room, and true enough she was a wan little creature, propped up on pillows and wearing a nightdress gone sepia with age and washing, but obviously fine once. Timoti arranged some screens to give our fourth wall some boundaries and sorted the props out, and we had a quick huddle to agree entrances and exits. Then we turned around and they were all there. They had filed in so meekly none of us had noticed.

Either side of Miss Ward's bed the orphans were crammed in shoulder to shoulder. They sat on the counterpane, too, and in front, lined up all the way to the screens. We were confronted with a genuine sea of faces, all dirty and hungry and pale and huge-eyed, ages from ten to seventeen. I've never known children sit so quietly. I think it was because they had absolutely no hope whatsoever. I don't think they actually knew what they were about to see.

"Erm . . . ?" I signalled Mr. Collar, who had been displaced into the doorway.

"My ward was insistent that the performance must be for all, not just for her," he said, sounding choked up with pride at the sentiment. From my point of view, it's very easy to be generous with someone else's time and effort, but I couldn't exactly say anything in front of that massed and hollow attention.

And besides, part of me was thinking, *this is probably the biggest house we'll see in Sevengraves.*

With that sentiment, I turned to my fellow thespians. "Let's make this count," I told them.

We made it count.

I don't know how we did it, putting on a ten role play with five of us, and half of us having to crib from the book. It should have been as terrible a piece of coarse acting as any amateur rep company ever mishandled, but instead . . .

I was glorious. I have never been better than that matinee at the orphanage. I swear I *was* Alexander. Actually, that's not true; Alexander could never have Alexandered as well as I. They screamed with laughter when I was funny and they sighed when I was a lover. And when I died—when I *died,* my God they were weeping—those children without parents from a town without a future, and I made them weep.

And the others were all right, I suppose. Felice was word perfect, and when she took the poison at the end I saw half the audience get halfway up to beg her to stop. Magritte played the comic duo with John to perfection—better than ever she could with scene-stealing Alfonso. And Timoti clicked through his roles with clinical perfection that, if it did not move hearts in itself, allowed the rest of us to move them more through his support.

And when we took our bow, there was no applause. Now mostly that's bad, but sometimes you play a tragedy *just right*, and the audience is shocked to stillness by the sheer intensity of what they've seen, and it means more than all the standing ovations in the world. And that's what we got from them. They'd have given us anything we asked for, in that moment, so it was a shame they were penniless orphans who didn't have anything to give.

But we didn't care, because we were full of that elation peculiar to actors post-performance. We bad farewell to the children and were just about to exit with empty pockets and full hearts when Mr. Collar met us at the door.

Well, he was thankful, of course, and extremely complimentary, and we would have taken that as our due except that he was holding out a decent-sized pouch.

"It's not very much," he explained to us. "Obviously Saint Agatha's can't reimburse you, but I have a little put away myself. I hope it's in order."

It was a pouch of gold. It was something we had only come across before in stage directions. The coins looked old and pure and a world away from the worn coppers the Sevengravers measured out their lives with.

And you might not believe it, but we did actually try to turn him down. We were so high on the performance that even Timoti told him that he should find more deserving beneficiaries of his largesse, but Mr. Collar was insistent. "This was a real performance," he told us, "and deserves real remuneration. Please, take the purse with my blessings."

So in the end we took his money and everyone lived happily ever after.

Well, not quite.

• • •

We returned to the Municipal Hall and went on with a dress rehearsal in which absolutely everything went wrong. At one point Sidney and I very nearly fought to the death with prop swords over a missed cue. The next night, we went up.

We filled about a third of the dry seats, which meant about a sixth of the house. The Sevengravers watched us strut and fumble our way through the play as though they'd only just been introduced to the concept of drama and didn't much like it. There was some desultory clapping at the end. The total take hadn't been quite enough to buy everyone a pint. At around that point, those of us who had received Mr. Collar's little dividend talked very seriously about sharing the wealth around, just to cheer everyone up. But somehow we never quite did. It was out little secret.

The second night was more than half full. I spotted some return faces from the first. Our spirits began to pick up and so did our performance. From the third to the ninth we were sold out and there were people standing in the aisles by the end. They were weary and poor, and some paid in coppers and others in firewood and root vegetables, but by God they came to see us play. I don't think anything the full company put on quite matched that magical afternoon in the orphanage, but we came together even so. Sidney mastered his role and played that marvellously understated death scene to a tee, and Edith remembered which play she was in, and Alfonso and Magritte made them laugh right up to the point where we all made them cry. They cheered us after each house, and if it wasn't that rapt silence we'd had before, it was good enough.

I met Alexander once, you know—in that world where he was real and not just a character in a play. You'd never have picked him as someone to inspire a great romance of the ages. And I, having studied the part before I met him, didn't have the heart to tell him how everything would work out.

All too soon we came to the end of our final night, and there were even some bouquets for the ladies, and some jugs of homebrew for everyone, and if half our takings were in coppers then at least the other half were generally edible so we weren't going to starve. Doctor Kampfe went round the company and shook everyone's hand, and made sure we all acknowledged how right he'd been about the nine nights.

That was when Mr. Collar turned up. None of saw him enter: he was just there in the dressing room, waiting politely with his hat in his hands.

I went over to him, still bubbling with the joy of a good performance, and offered him a drink. He declined politely. "Actually, I was rather hoping for a word with Doctor Kampfe."

Well, that was awkward, because of course the Good Doctor didn't know what had been going on behind his back, but there was nothing I could do about it now. I decided I would sell the whole thing as a bit of extra rehearsal and hoped nobody would mention the money.

So I let Mr. Collar between happy actors intent on inebriation until we got to Doctor Kampfe.

I saw something was wrong the moment they laid eyes on each other. The Good Doctor knew Mr. Collar instantly, and Mr. Collar's air of genial whimsy was gone as though it had never been. When he smiled, you could have shaved with it.

"I thought that was rather a good show," he remarked.

"Thank you. We do what we can with the material given us," Doctor Kampfe replied with precise cordiality.

"So you always said," Mr. Collar observed. "I'm glad to see you've been honing your skills, Doctor, but I would remind you that your presence is requested."

Doctor Kampfe leant back and took a swallow from the jug we were passing around. "Your master can request as much as he wants. I'm still on tour."

"Not any more." That shaving-sharp smile glinted. "Come on, Doctor, you know the terms of your contract better than anyone."

"I do." Doctor Kampfe was utterly unconcerned. "Come back when I finish a run of something. Until then, bark all you want, but don't pretend you'll bite."

By now everyone was listening, ready to manhandle Mr. Collar out the stage door if he got nasty.

"Your run is finished," said Mr. Collar, with masterful double meaning.

"The small print is quite clear on the subject," Doctor Kampfe disagreed. " 'A run shall constitute ten performances of the same play before the Players move on . . . ' I have the contract about me if you want to check . . . "

Mr. Collar was also good at deadpan. "And congratulations on a fine tenth performance."

Doctor Kampfe went very still. "Nine," he said. "Sometimes less but never more than nine."

In the wake of his words I was left feeling as though I had done something very unwise indeed. And I had been manipulated, surely, but an actor, of all people, has no business complaining he has been tricked.

"A matinee for the orphans of Saint Agatha's," Mr. Collar stated. "Truly a masterpiece. Performed by your company and paid for, handsomely. The day before you opened here."

The Doctor's eyes sought mine and then Timoti's. He must have known the truth by the way we avoided his gaze. He fumbled from his jacket a cracklingly old document and unfolded it with shaking hands. He really did have the contract on him. It was that important.

"Don't look so downcast. You're still my master's favourite, and think of the actors you'll have the pick of," Mr. Collar told him. "They almost all come to us in the end, after all. It's such a venal profession."

Doctor Kampfe looked up from the contract. I knew he must have been looking for some clause that rendered our little charity gig null and void. I think it was the payment that did it, though. When we took Mr. Collar's gold, the performance was entered in the books as official.

"It has been a while since I saw the old place." Doctor Kampfe looked older than I'd ever seen him.

"Three hundred years of nine-night runs," agreed Mr. Collar. "Everything is as you left it."

"Of course it is." He didn't rage, our Doctor Kampfe. He didn't curse me for my greed or folly. He was the manager, after all, and had to retain his dignity before mere actors.

"And perhaps my master will allow you another sabbatical, some time. Albeit one with more rigorously worded terms. You'd think, with all the lawyers we have to hand, we'd have spotted that one." Mr. Collar gestured grandly and one of the walls of the dressing room opened up as though hidden machinery had moved it. Behind it was . . .

I don't want to say just what I saw behind it. If you want to imagine the usual mummery of flames and tormented souls and red-skinned goat-men with pitchforks, then I won't say you're wrong, but it doesn't do it justice. And deep down in all of that, on some distant lower circle, I saw a stage.

Doctor Kampfe turned to us and spread his hands. "My friends, my companions," he said, "I leave Timoti to stand in my place. He knows where everything is, and is good with money.

There's little more to the craft of a theatrical manager, truth be told. And, as and when each of you should find your way to join me, you may be assured of a sympathetic audition. You've often heard it said that there is a special place down below reserved for actors, and now you know this to be true, but it's a place of privilege. Even the Lord of the Pit enjoys a good show."

And then he bowed and stepped back past the notional boundary of that fourth wall, and abruptly all that we had seen there was gone, and we were within a conventionally-bounded dressing room once more and staring at each other.

Needless to say the orphanage business got a full airing and we had to spread the gold around or risk the company coming apart at the seams. I consider myself justly chastened.

Later that night most of the company were either asleep or swapping anecdotes about when other actors not present had royally screwed up. Nobody was talking about our lost leader, though everyone was thinking of him. Timoti di Venezi was already poring over the Doctor's maps and working out which town we'd play next, while the old man who adapted our scripts was scratching the first pages of a new tragedy. I didn't want to look at the *dramatis persona*. I knew who'd be at the head of it.

Instead I found Felice, who had been fending off John Worthing's sodden advances, and we went out into the stalls to look at the moon through the holes in the roof. We had the last jug of the Sevengraves homebrew, and were comfortable enough with our general dislike of each other that nothing untoward was likely to happen. What we had not expected was to find Mr. Collar, red-lined cloak and all, sitting and staring at the stage as though all the world were contained there.

We were sufficiently drunk that we accosted him at once, utterly forgetting who and what he must be. Felice went so far as to prod him in the chest and snap, "I suppose that was all fakery then, the orphanage, your bedridden ward? All just a trick to get to Doctor Kampfe?"

I waited for the explosion, but Mr. Collar just shook his head sadly. "Not at all. Do you think I can show no real kindness or charity? What else do we do on vacation abroad, but those things forbidden to us at home?" He rolled his shoulders and stretched in a way most inhuman, as though the shape was constricting him. "Count yourself lucky that you are an actress, my dear. Some of us spend our entire lives playing the demon king."

EVERYBODY FROM THEMIS SENDS LETTERS HOME

GENEVIEVE VALENTINE

The water here is never going to make good bread. If I'd known, I would have requested sturdier flour—we'll be waiting six years for the next transport pod. Agosti told me today my bread's good for massaging the gums, like he was trying to focus on the positives. Woods threatened to arrest him anyway, which was nice of him.

But that's really the only thing that makes me sad. Otherwise, I promise, I'm getting along here very well. I miss you, too. Every time I'm up late with the dough I imagine you're at the table working, and when I look up it takes me a second to remember. But everyone here is pitching in. Marquez and Perlman and I are figuring out how to cheat an apple tree into producing fruit sooner, and Agosti's building equipment out of our old life support systems. If it works out, we'll have our own cider in two years. ("We can dip the bread in it," Perlman said, and Woods threatened to arrest her, too. Gives him something to do. Imagine being in charge of five people. Good thing he has a knack for building.)

The sun's different than back home—they told us about particles and turbulence on the way over and I was too stupid to understand it and too afraid to tell them, so just pretend I explained and you were really impressed. The planet's locked, so there's really only water on the equator—nothing makes it toward the sun and it's ice by the time you go ten miles further darkside. You're never 100% sure what time it even is, except that it's a little more purple in the daylight for the hour we get it, and at sunset it looks like the whole place was attacked by vampires. It's sunset most of the time. That's not too bad if you can just avoid the river; that river never looks right with the dark coming in.

Agosti and Perlman were up until 3:30 shouting about which route will get us over the mountains, which would be more understandable if there were any mountains. But the movie bank's still broken, so it's just as well. I'm betting on Perlman. If anyone could lead us over imaginary mountains, it's her.

My other entertainment is staying up late, trying to fight the water and make bread that will actually rise, and the bird that sings all night. Samara—Perlman—says we're not supposed to assign characteristics from home to the things we find here until they've been observed and documented and whatever else, but—thrush family.

It's most active during our night hours, and we're working on why (trying to make sure it's not drawn to the lights we brought with us, which would be bad news), but in the meantime it seems happy to sit in the trees outside the kitchen and sing. Three little bursts, then a longer one that's so many notes it sounds like showing off, then a little pause to see if anyone's listening, so it's definitely showing off. If I whistle anything, it tries to repeat it, and it's a fairly good mimic, but nothing I do really takes. It knows what it likes.

It has the same woodwind sound as the one back home, the house I lived in when I was young. Hermit thrush? Wood thrush? Something I used to hear all the time and never thought about, of course. Good news is that now it's just me and this one bird and I'll get to start over again with every new animal. This time I'm going to pay better attention.

Perlman will officially name it—they don't ask the cooks how to classify animal species, that's why the company hauled a biologist out here. But Perlman knows I like it, so maybe she'll consult me. I know it best. That should count for something.

All my love.

Proxima Centauri Personnel Status Report: Day 1187
Author: Dr. Samara Perlman

Crew Health: Reiterating that as a biologist, I am not in a position to diagnose or treat any major medical issues, am not sure how I was tasked with this position, and am deeply concerned about how soon we can expect a qualified physician rather than a group of people who had slapdash medic training for three days before they left Earth. That said, all six residents currently seem in good health. Carlos Marquez claims a slight cough, but as the scans came back negative, my money's on allergies. If he dies of tuberculosis next week we'll know I was wrong.

Crew Injuries: Anthony Agosti nursing a minor wrist sprain after having punched a wall. Should he resort to violence again I'll be sending him to Officer Woods for a formal report and some time in the brig. We shouldn't build a new planet with the same problems as the old one.

Crew Mental Health: Marie Roland continues to claim she can't see the mountains to the northwest of Themis. No other signs of psychosis appear, and when questioned or shown pictures of the mountains, Roland becomes distracted and mildly agitated. No tendency to violence. Suspect a minor mental block prevents her from fully acknowledging the terrain—homesickness? For now, as she's still willing to train for the mission, there seems to be no point in forcing the issue; have asked Woods to stop pushing it and will let Marie come to it in her own time.

Crew Mission Training: Expedition prep continues. Entire staff follow regimen of five-kilometer runs on hilly terrain every morning, weight lifting three times a week, rock climbing on nearby hills twice a week. Once the snow melts a little off the pass we'll be able to determine the actual level of dexterity required for the climb and train accordingly. Vigil until then.

to whomever
   there's nothing here left to build and the mountain project is on hold until the thaw and I don't care about sunset please get the movie bank going again before I throw myself in the river full stop
   anthony

to whomever
   there's nothing here left to build and the mountain project is on hold until the thaw and I don't care about sunset please get the movie bank going again before I throw myself in the river full stop
   anthony

sorry sent it twice by mistake
   wouldn't do that kind of thing if the movie bank worked though probably
   anthony

Samara and I did a perimeter walk today, a kilometer out from the camp. I picked almost more plants than I could carry, and I'm fairly sure at least half are edible, which will make meals much more exciting. Samara insisted on running tests for poison, don't worry, but I think if I have to measure one more judicious use of dried black pepper I'm going to scream. I want something that tastes like it grew in the ground.

Samara's amazing. I don't even remember first meeting her; it just feels like I've always known her, which I guess is what close quarters will do to you. We cataloged five species of bird (none of them my bird, so I guess the animals here really can tell day from night and it's something we'll get used to), and she spent a lot more time with insects than I was interested in.

The air here smells just like home. I don't know why—the water's different, so the soil should be different, but it smells exactly like the dirt from my grandmother's garden. It helps stop me from getting lonely, that the soil here might be the same as what we left behind.

Marquez showed us pictures of his children a few nights ago; it's his daughter's birthday. Samara cried, but nobody pushed it. It's strange how much we left behind to be here, and I think no matter how much work you're getting done, sometimes it just hits you how separate you are. We must have really wanted this. I must still.

I know you weren't ready, and you might never be ready. These letters aren't meant to convince you, I promise. It just makes me feel closer to home.

All my love—

Dr. March:

Mixed results, as always. Sunset was a little longer than yesterday, so the seasons function is working. None of the subjects have noticed yet that Vivian and Carlos are interfaces, which bodes well for long-term use of constructed intelligence inside Themis. (Suggest we minimize the rock-climbing training until we can work out the uncanny valley problem in the weight distribution. Can the development team extend the thaw?) But overall, investors should be pleased—let me know if you need any demo footage, I have a clip of everyone working on the gardens that should go over well.

Technical glitch, first incident: Anthony's punch should have broken his hand. I'm not sure if the safety settings are appropriately set or too schoolmarmy. We might need to dial them down and get someone to break their leg as a test run for more realistic game play.

Gigantic fucking technical glitch, ongoing: Marie can't see the mountains. I've checked her equipment, and there's no other potential hardware problems (attached is the most recent server diagnostic for your review, but there's nothing in it that would account for it). Either she has an actual mental block that we can't do anything about, or there's a subjectivity issue somewhere in the code for Themis and we have to find it and fix it. I can't tell which one is more likely, because you made me military instead of medical and I can't just put her in jail until she tells me she sees them. Do we have a timetable for getting security clearance on that or are we going to have to settle for imperfect data?
—Woods

Woods dropped into the chair in Benjamina's cubicle so hard her BIRDS OF MONTANE ECOSYSTEMS reference chart came loose and sank to the floor.

"You gotta fix those mountains," he said.

"My chart, please."

"It's going to break the sim," he said, scooping it up and smoothing a bent edge. "We'll have done four years of work for nothing because Marie has some synapse you can't outsmart."

"The problem's her head, not the software." After a pointed pause, she turned around. He carried some ego out of a Themis session and it took a day or so to wear off; the faster you could remind him that everyone else was actually busy, the better. "You can see the mountains when you're in Themis, and you know they're not there. Sounds like you should take it up with the psych team."

"I'd have thought you wanted to keep her out of all that." He wasn't quite threatening her; he wasn't quite sympathizing. (The reason Woods got chosen for beta-test jobs was how good he could be at Not Quite.)

Benjamina didn't bother to recite any anonymity bullshit. Woods had been in Themis a long time; they read letters out loud to each other. He knew what she sounded like. "I've been trying."

"They want to test the mountains before we wrap beta."

"We need to look at her file—I can't reverse engineer a synapse misfire."

"They fixed Agosti's color blindness."

"That's different," said Benjamina, picking crumbs off her keyboard. She didn't like that fix, for no particular reason. It was productive; it just itched.

"Listen, I like her, but this is going to kill the beta, and you and I will be under the knife."

"Get the psych team to request Marie's file from the warden. Is Perlman at the same place?"

"Nah, Perlman stabbed her husband, she went someplace serious. Roland's just in a prison for fuckups."

"Fine. So get Dr. March to show me the file. I can port into Carlos for eyes on the ground. Then I'll know what I'm dealing with."

"Nobody in this building's willing to talk to the shrinks but me. That should tell you something." Woods stood up, the little bird poster still in his hands. He was holding the very edges, like it was an expensive library book.

One of the things nobody at Othrys talked about was that the longer you spent in Themis, the weirder physical objects were when you came back. Officially, nobody was talking about it because it was just Woods, and no one liked Woods enough to make him for a martyr of motor-skill dissociation. Unofficially, nobody wanted to think Themis came back with you. Benjamina hoped that wore off, too.

"How are you doing?"

He was smoothing the edges of the chart with the pads of his fingers as he set it down. He looked up at her like he was surprised.

"I'm going to go eat some decent bread," he said finally, and left.

Benjamina's computer pinged. It was waiting for her letter.

• • •

Agosti came back from his walk today and did some very elaborate hand gestures about how much snow is left on the mountain pass and pointing to the northwest, and it took me three minutes to realize it wasn't a buildup to a jerkoff joke. Those fucking mountains. Woods told him to knock it off—very sheriffy thing to do, glad he's finding something to lay down the law about—but still. It gets old.

Samara named that bird *Catharus rolandus*. It's useless to be proud of something that has so little to do with actual contributions from you, but I teared up anyway. Plus that genus is apparently very close to the wood thrush after all! I felt like a scientist! Then I baked a shitty loaf of bread and lost that feeling immediately, because a scientist would know how to outsmart this water.

I loved your letter. Not the markets, though—Themis is really good for reminding you of the value of only knowing a few people. The only thing I miss about the night markets is the two of us wearing those giant sweaters with the huge arms we bought as a joke and ended up needing that whole winter and we had to push the sleeves up before we reached for anything. All the fabrics here are sort of flat. They keep you warm, but it's not the same.

All my love

Mr. Collins:

My name is Dr. Frederick March, and I'm a consulting psychologist for Othrys Games. We've been partnering with your institution to test the latest game from Othrys; I understand you might not have all the details of how the process has gone so far, so first of all, I wanted to thank you, and let you know it's been invaluable. You're assisting us with some truly amazing work about constructed intelligence and full-neuro game play. There are even insights into the human subconscious and stimuli processing that I suspect will have significant implications going forward in other realms of study.

I say all this so you'll understand why I'd so much like to meet to discuss the next steps, since we've had to terminate the study slightly earlier than planned. Your in-house medical team has been exemplary, and we are completely understanding of what happened—immunity to memory suppressants is a risk of repeated exposure and this was discussed prior to beginning. We agree with you that the testing stage has effectively ended—the downside of informed consent.

However, because of this, we would like to work out some visitations with the subjects in question. I understand our team has had some miscommunications with your administration trying to set these up. Let me assure you this is the standard debrief for any long-term player. And in this particular case, I expect that the subjects themselves would benefit from being able to speak with a trained professional about their experience. The amount and type of memories that might be restored have definite in-game applications and are potential data points well within the scope of our contract with your correctional facility. I'm happy to discuss further particulars— please let me know your thoughts.

Sincerely,

Frederick March

Dr. March was already in the VP's office, and Woods wasn't, which meant the worst. Benjamina let the closed-door click echo a moment, trying to decide if looking stoic or penitent would work better. (Women who were too stoic got fired for not caring; women who were too penitent got fired for poor performance.) She forced herself not to ask questions as she sat. Inquisitive women were no better than the other kinds.

"We've had a problem with Themis," the VP said. He looked from one of them to the other. "Frederick knows already."

Of course he did. Benjamina waited.

"It's not the simulation," the VP continued after a moment, as if to put her mind at ease, as if she was concerned that somehow her work wasn't up to par and they would have waited until now to tell her. "In fact, Erytheia—the coders have aliases, it's easier," he explained to Dr. March, "—has our lowest fault rate, and has spent the most time working on individual settings for Roland. I think she could be invaluable to us during the postmortem process."

Benjamina blinked. "Postmortem of what?"

Dr. March turned toward her. "Did you know Ms. Roland was a drug addict?"

"No," she said, and her stomach dropped as she considered why the medical side of the experiment wasn't feasible any more. "Did she get any memories back when the drugs stopped working, or is it still a fog?"

"She got them back."

Stoic, she thought. Be stoic. No point being penitent now.

"Are Perlman and Agosti still in beta?" If they were, she'd have to talk to their coders about some in-game reason Marie was gone, though she couldn't think of one they would believe. Marie would never leave Themis. She knew it best. Benjamina might have to port in on a simulation and drop dead in front of them.

"No," said the VP. "We decided to stop beta across the board. Dr. March is trying to get the warden to agree to interviews so we can find out how the, uh—the memory process? Is going. It will probably take a few weeks. Woods will go along and observe, obviously—continuity for them—and then he can circle back with you, so we can bring our findings to the team in a way that isn't so . . . clinical. No offense."

"Of course," said Dr. March. He was still looking at Benjamina.

"Let me know when," she said, and that was the last thing anyone needed from her.

She drove home with shaking hands, for no good reason—Marie was a test user, they used to have test users at fucking conventions. She'd liked that better; there were plenty of ways to test what players would believe without lying to them at the beginning. Management wanted to test if the environment could fool the mind, but no one had asked Benjamina. None of this had been her idea. Nothing was her fault.

The night was barely cloudy, and she drove past her turnoff and out until there was nothing but the highway on either side, so when she set up the telescope, she could see a glimpse of Proxima Centauri through the haze of light pollution. It blinked back and forth in the lens, and it was so dim. Light from there would never quite suffice.

No one had said anything to the development team—no one ever did unless something was wrong—but she suspected this game was more than a Virtual Experience market maker. There were private companies prepping long-haul spacecraft with stasis technology; they'd want to train their people in the most realistic conditions possible, and they had money to burn.

Normally, she'd write a letter to Marie. Dear Marie, I was looking up at Proxima tonight and I thought about you. Dear Marie, I got your letter. I programmed the thrush to mimic you a little, and you noticed. When the first astronauts land on Proxima Centauri b, maybe there will really be birds. I've studied everything I can, and there's no telling. It might all be a layer of ice. There might be mountains everywhere. They might try to make a new home in a place that's nothing but poison. Dear Marie, I want you to be happy there.

Through the lens, the planet slid around the star.

Woods,

After you came and talked to us, Samara found out you hadn't even paid us for our time in Themis. Mistake, by the way—if you'd paid us it would have at least looked like you weren't trying to use us like lab rats and get away with it—and I feel like you should have known better. Not the company, but, you. You always seemed like a guy who wanted everything to have a reason.

Samara's got a lawyer, and the company should have papers by now. She told me not to contact you. I'm glad she's suing, because you all deserve it. Go bankrupt.

But I have an offer for whoever's in charge: I can't testify if I'm dead, and I want to go back to Themis permanently. I don't know how long 'permanently' is, since the prison refuses to keep people on life support for things like that and you won't want to bring me to a hospital, so just budget accordingly—a person probably starves to death in a week? So, a week. Unless I've built up such a resistance to the meds that it kills me in a few hours, which I assume would be cheaper.

I don't know who actually made Themis. I'm assuming you were involved, because you had the shortest fuse of anybody there, and at the time I thought that's just what being law enforcement did to people, but it makes more sense if you made it. And I don't know who I was writing to, that whole time. In Themis I just thought I had someone I loved, and he was where my letters went. I didn't know I needed to love someone so badly you could lie to me about it for four years—but that's how it worked, the psychologist said. You made Samara write reports because whatever you managed to do with her, there were some things she wouldn't fall for. I was an idiot and I'd been lonely my whole life. You could do anything to me.

It wasn't you, was it? Was it one person writing me back, or did you reply by committee? One of you must have seen the picture of my arrest, since you gave me long hair in Themis. You talked about missing my braids. Whoever it was, go fuck yourself. I didn't even like it, it was too long, but in Themis I kept it long all that time for your sake. I wanted to cut it—it got so humid in the summers I dreamed of shaving it off, I must have told you, I wrote you so much—but keeping my hair long was like a promise we'd see each other again. So I kept it.

I thought that I couldn't quite picture you because being in stasis on the ship seeped the color out of your dreams. And then it had been a long time, so of course I couldn't really remember you—I looked at your messages and forgot whether you had good posture or not when you typed. I wanted to think you hunched like I did, like that weird pang in the lower back was something we shared 25 trillion miles away. I wondered sometimes why I'd gone to Proxima Centauri if I had someone I loved so much. Not that you can say that to the person you left behind. I never even mentioned it to Samara. But everybody knew Carlos and I had loved ones back home. When there are so few of you, you end up knowing a lot of things that you never talk about.

Carlos isn't real, right? I mean—the doctor told me he wasn't, I know he wasn't. But there wasn't a person pretending to be him? He was just a program that got really excited about apple cider?

I don't even know how to be angry at you—it was the worst hour of my life and I threw up after, but it wasn't You (whoever that is) explaining it, I would have been able to tell. So it still feels like you weren't part of what went wrong, like the program got stuck even after I woke up and you locked me out and I'm still carrying you, someone I love and just forgot—

Anyway, I'm going through withdrawal. The prison definitely doesn't care—they said if I could go through it with the drugs that got me in here I could go through it with whatever they stuck in me to make me forget Themis. But maybe if you read this letter, you still consider me market research and this will be helpful. No appetite, no energy. I have a headache right behind my eyes. I'm always cold, even though Themis was colder than prison so you'd think I wouldn't be. I sleep a lot. I always dream of being back in Themis. Probably good news for you. Sell a million copies. Just give me mine.

And fix the bread. It never worked right, that should be changed.

Let me go home.

Marie

Benjamina waited until the office was empty before she crossed the floor to Woods' office. Stoic, not penitent; stoic people didn't skulk over to meet someone they barely liked just to see how interviews had gone with the people they had used.

She'd never been to his office before—he must always have come to her, strange, she'd never even noticed—and it was so blank it startled her into stillness at the threshold.

"Want an invitation?" He was standing, reaching for his coat, like he'd just been waiting for her so they could walk out together. "You look like a vampire."

She didn't say anything, and she didn't move closer; after a second, he cracked a grin. "You're kind of an asshole, Harris."

They walked out in silence, but from the way his thumb brushed the front of his coat lapel over and over, something terrible had happened and they were just waiting to be away from the cameras.

Six blocks later, he said, "It was bad."

She stopped and looked at him.

"She, uh—" He rubbed his hand once, rough, across his forehead. "In Themis, she looked fine. Healthy. It was stupid to assume she'd look the same in person, but I didn't expect . . . I didn't expect it. Samara's suing us."

It took her a second too long to catch up, and before she could stop it it was out: "Because of how Marie looks?"

"No, if Samara knew how Marie looked she'd have just murdered me." His hands had disappeared into his pockets, fists that pulled against the shoulders and ruined the line of his coat. She'd put that into their last game, the noir murder mystery—the private eye yanked on his coat from the inside that same way. She thought she'd invented it; she'd been proud of herself.

The letter he handed her was on paper so thin she hesitated to touch it.

"It's addressed to me, but trust me, it's for you."

She wanted to take it home and read it where she couldn't embarrass herself, but if Woods sat through three interviews she could manage this. She read it in the wide alley garden between two office buildings, where admin staff ate lunch to pretend they'd gotten away from everything. At some point she started shaking; he stood next to her like they were pretending the wind was cold. She read it again. She put it in her pocket. He didn't argue.

"Will you see her again?"

"I could get arrested for passing her company information. We're getting sued."

"I know."

"Fuck it, I'm hungry," he said.

They found a place far enough away they felt all right sitting down. He ate three pieces of bread out of the plastic basket in the first five minutes. Then he tore a napkin into pieces.

"Samara's skin and bones. Anthony's got insomnia. Dr. Asshole said it was just drug interactions. The prison claims the game damages the cortex. They're probably going to sue each other while Samara and Anthony are suing us."

"But not Marie."

He looked at her. His eyes were very dark; they couldn't quite get them to register in Themis—they coded as black, which always looked flat, so anyone who met him in the game thought his eyes were lighter brown. It must have been a surprise for Marie to see him as he really was.

"We can't do that."

"Are you going to see her again?"

"I'm not passing her a letter, Ben."

"Are you allowed to have an assistant with you, for the interviews? Stenography? Someone has to be holding the recorder."

"You're out of your mind."

Her lips pulled tight across each row of teeth. "I have to do something."

"If you're looking to feel less guilty, stop. No such thing."

He blurred underneath the tears that sprang up. She let them go—too late not to be penitent—so her vision would be clearer for what came next. "Then I'll go myself," she said.

"It's more than your job is worth."

There was nothing to say to that; her job had been worth so little there was no point.

Outside it was not quite dark, and just beginning to be cold; the temperature of Themis, decided by a developer so much her senior she'd never met him.

When she turned toward home, he walked with her.

Halfway there, he said, "We have one more interview with her."

• • •

Hi Marie,

My handle on the Themis team is Erytheia. It's not my real name, but it's easier to keep track of who wrote which code this way. Erytheia was one of the daughters of Themis. (I didn't pick it.) When we were getting ready for the dry run they made me your experience specialist so we could concentrate on each user's take on Themis and build as rich a world as possible.

Woods showed me your letter.

I just wanted you to know there wasn't a committee. All your letters came to me, and I read them all. Some of what you told me went into a development memo, like how there weren't enough insects for a landscape with that much standing water and vegetation. But I didn't send my letters to trick you into writing more often, and I didn't discuss anything personal. I answered you because I wanted you to feel like there was a person writing you back. I was the person writing you back.

—E

Hey Marie,

Can you sleep? I can't fucking sleep. My body thinks it's too dark because it's dumb and can only remember one set of things at a time and it's stuck on Themis—like, we were definitely stuck on Themis but you don't have to be such an asshole about it, get used to night and day and let me get some fucking sleep, damn.

And honestly the Themis shit doesn't really bother me. Everything I can remember from there is all of us just doing our best and getting along, so it's not like it was embarrassing. I feel like an idiot for not realizing sooner—now it's so fucking obvious why the movie bank didn't work, because it was too complicated to make it work inside the game or whatever—but actually being there was fine. The part that bothers me is the whole time out here that I thought I was just depressed and dreaming about some random planet is the part that's vanishing, like that's the only part the drugs actually affected once the wall wore off. Can you imagine what we must have looked like to everybody else, hopped up on that stuff?

I'm signing Samara's guy's thing. Are you? You should, they're trying to pay us off but that just means they know they fucked up and want us to keep quiet.

You're not talking to anyone about any of this, right? They told me you're having a rough time and I get that. What wasn't better about Themis than being locked up? But you get killed that way, or they find some reason to extend your sentence twenty years, so zip that shit and just wait for Samara's guy to make us too famous to die.

When we get out we should see if we can get a parole dispensation to cross state lines, it was cool all living together, that was nice. Plus movies work here, that's a reason to stay here. Plus I bet your bread in the real world is amazing.

Keep your cool, Marie. I know you can do this.

—Anthony

Marie,

My attorney heard from Othrys Games that you've been in contact with the company, trying to make a deal to get back to Themis. He wanted to send you a cease and desist, but I told him I wanted to talk to you first before we did anything official.

The case we're building downplays the nature of the game as much as possible. It doesn't matter that the game wasn't some battle simulator where we died all the time—it matters that they did it to us without our permission and then hoped people would ignore it because nobody cares about us. If you keep asking to go back in there, they're going to use it as evidence that what they were doing was benign, or helpful, and we're going to have to fight that impression in court, and when the game hits shelves and it's fine, it will look even worse. We're fighting the company—we can't let the game become the thing we're fighting.

This thing is really important—my lawyer says it could be a cornerstone for other cases about prisoners' rights. That's big, Marie. It's bigger than us. Cut it out.

I'm not saying all this to be cruel—I miss it there, too. I could do my work and close doors behind me, of course fucking I miss it. But trying to get back to a lie is only going to hurt us. We need to be free again here. This is our shot. What they did to us was wrong—you can't fix that. Let me fight it.

Flush this letter. They can't find it.

Samara

The Othrys lawyers call Benjamina for a deposition, and she sits in a meeting room with no windows with her back to the door—the only other seat, across from the lawyer whose smile is set tight across his face and doesn't get anywhere near his eyes—and tries to ignore that this is all a setup to make her uncomfortable.

She answers fifty questions about the game: its purpose ("Any game's purpose—entertainment"), what game play will be like (it takes ten minutes, and the lawyer's mouth purses the more she talks about how beautiful Themis is), the passage of time ("Four to seven times faster than real time, everybody playing an instance has to agree on the speed if they're playing in the MMORPG rather than single-player," she says, just to watch his jaw tick before he asks for clarification), how long it's been in development (five years), how long the beta test has been going (just over a year), the chance of fatigue ("The same as with any mentally stimulating activity, like a deposition," she says, and the lawyer's lips positively disappear).

"Did you know that Samara Perlman is trying to use the time she spent in Themis as proof of good behavior to reduce her sentence?"

It's an amazing tactic. She keeps her face neutral. "No, I didn't."

"Do you have an opinion on the validity of that?"

"No one who beta tested Themis ever evidenced any antisocial behavior, and as they believed the simulation was real life, their behavior in Themis would be close to real-world behavior."

"If I play a video game and kill a hundred imaginary people, am I a bad person outside the game?"

"Because of killing the video game people, specifically?"

He takes an even breath in and out. "Miss Harris, if you could answer the question."

"I think there's a line between fantasy and reality, but the three subjects who had Themis beta-tested on them weren't aware that line had even been crossed, so the question is kind of useless."

"Please answer it."

"I did."

He closes his eyes and counts to five, this time, which gives her enough time to plant the bug under the table.

She lets the bug run—in for one count of corporate espionage, in for two counts—and siphons out the Othrys talk on her home laptop, with its wallpaper she made from Themis: the view outside the kitchen, where the thrush is singing.

The lawyer hums and taps his pen; in the microphone it sounds like a stone gavel. "Wages we might have to push back on, since I'm not sure we can really count playing video games as 'labor.' "

"Agreed," someone else says. "Plus I see that they're pushing for time served for the passage of time in the game AND asking for wages for physical hours spent using the game. We can probably use that to shut down this thing at both ends. If they can't decide what was more important, how can we?"

"Good point," the lawyer says. "We should get Warden Collins back in here to talk about labor practices. Give him enough rope to hang himself, we can show the only people using these inmates was the prison."

The next day at work, she comes into Woods' office, closes the door behind her.

"They're going to lose."

"I know."

They stand for a little while not looking at each other. He's put up a panorama of Themis on his office wall. It's the geological survey, before they started the naturalist pass and brought people in; the idea of Themis, before anything really happened. The sun is setting. The sun is always setting.

She waits until they lose the case before she visits Marie.

Marie Roland on Themis is nearly six feet tall, has bakers' arms, covers four feet at a stride. She has lines around her eyes from squinting at the sun; they got deeper on Themis, where the sun is safer to look at. Her voice is deep enough that Benjamina had to program the *Acomys cahirinus* knockoff to startle and bolt when she laughed.

Marie Roland on the other side of the visitation table is someone who—Benjamina has to accept it all at once, there's no point in doing things with best intentions any more—Benjamina's driven into the grave.

She sits down. Marie waits a few seconds to look up at her.

"That was you?" she says, and it's with such disdain that Benjamina almost smiles.

"Yes."

"Have you come to apologize?"

"Yes," she says. "I don't think it will be worth much, but yes."

Marie sits back in her chair. Five seven, maybe five eight; the circles under her eyes are as big as her eyes.

You end up loving the things you make. Benjamina had been prepared for that—she'd seen it happen in other games, she'd seen it happen to Woods, she had braced herself. But Marie was made already; Benjamina can't look her in the eye.

"Samara got to be a biologist. Anthony was an engineer. Was there a reason I wasn't a scientist? Did my file say I was too stupid?"

Benjamina shrugs. "They assigned you to me. I didn't know enough science to code one."

"You don't know how to bake, either," Marie says.

They sit for a moment in quiet. Benjamina leans forward and starts to tell her why she's come, but Marie starts talking, and she freezes.

"I've forgotten a lot of important things," Marie says to the tabletop. "There was—there was a bird, and I know we were trying to make cider but I can't remember how far we got? Was Woods going to arrest us?"

"No. The—uh, the point of the game was to see what people would do with minimal interference."

Marie's gaze is sharp. Benjamina programmed that stare in wholesale, without ever seeing it. In person it feels like a slap.

"So you picked convicts to see what we would do if we thought we could get away with it? Burn in hell."

"I'm wearing a recorder," Benjamina says, "if there's anything you want to get off your chest."

To Penitentiary Staff:

This is a general notice that MARIE ROLAND [ID: 68223-18-0709] should be given a psychiatric evaluation as soon as possible. Recently she has evidenced delusional thinking and bursts of hostility, and a recent visit with a supposed family member left her extremely agitated. All future visits must be approved by the warden's office, and Roland will not be allowed to meet any visitors whatsoever until she has complied with the evaluation and any recommended medication regimen.

Sincerely,

Janet Evanston, on behalf of Christopher Collins, Warden

The following letter to the editor was delivered to our editorial offices by a third party. Upon confirming pertinent facts, the Evening Times considers the letter worthy of publication.

When I was in Themis, I caught a fly.

You'll hear about Themis soon, if they aren't already selling it. It's beautiful there. You'll want to stay in it forever. That's not a threat; I just envy you.

When you stand next to the river and think about vampires, know that I was there first. They sent me without telling me it was virtual. I thought I had been selected to be the first inhabitant of a new planet. I should have known better—the game couldn't make me forget who I was, and no one like me gets selected for something like that—but Themis is hard enough to live in that you believe it's real. It never really feels like night or day and your sleep cycle gets messed up and the terrain is rough for vegetables, so you have to fight the soil for eight months to get anything started. It's not easy. The bread there never baked right. I thought it was the water, for a long time.

I'm currently in the [redacted by editors], which is where Othrys tested Themis on us. I didn't volunteer—I was selected for a sleep study, they said, because I had vivid dreams, and it would get me time off for good behavior if I agreed. They never told us about Themis. For a year, I lived in two places and I didn't know.

I don't know what they gave me to make me forget, but they gave it to me on each end of Themis, on the way in and after I was out. Eventually my body got used to it—side effect of being an addict, which you think they'd have worried about more, but.

Some things I've forgotten—there was a bird I loved, but I couldn't tell you what it looked or sounded like. It's a bird in a dream. But I remember more of it than I was supposed to.

We tried to sue the game company for experimenting on us without our knowledge or permission. It didn't work; we pushed too hard to have it affect our sentences, I guess.

I'm not writing this because I'm surprised. You're probably not surprised, either. Part of me wishes I had it in me to be noble and fight to get us all released because of this—Samara and Anthony deserve their freedom. But I'm writing because I want to live inside Themis until I die, and Othrys says they won't let me.

We lost the lawsuit, so there's no danger in it. It probably looks great to them that I want to go back, anyway. And most people won't live in the same Themis I built. They're making it more interesting for new people. You'll have cities to live in instead of just shipping-crate mess halls; you'll be able to see the mountains. You'll all be dealing with each other.

Samara's lawyer told me the Themis I lived in was a demo they built just for Anthony and Samara and me—it's not the version on the shelves, so I could live inside it and never come into contact with anyone. You'll have a hard time in Themis, but I'll never be the problem.

They developed that game around us, one thing at a time—the daytime got more purple as we went along and we called it the seasons, and the wildlife filled in in bursts because they didn't think we'd remember what had been there the last time. (We did remember—we just thought nature was getting used to us.) Eventually there were plants with briars and fruit flies that would bother me when I was cooking. Real life. Things you believe. I caught one of them late at night, before it could land on some dough I was rolling out for cookies, and I carried it outside because Samara, our team biologist, had told us to be very careful to preserve everything we found so she could catalog all of it.

It's not real, they forced it on us and we were never meant to keep it, I'm not stupid, but I held the fruit fly in the cup of my hand and felt its wings beating. How can they say that's not mine?

Marie Roland

Correction: As the writer of the letter was unavailable for editorial consultation on yesterday's Letter to the Editor, at the advice of legal counsel, it has been removed.

"What the fuck did you do?"

Benjamina hands him his coffee. They've told the office they're dating; it explains a lot of time in each other's company.

"I tried to fucking—" she looks around, lowers her volume, "help Marie be someone no one could ignore. That's her best chance."

"Her best chance is a legal appeal by people who know what they're doing, not you on a crusade."

She sits back and looks at him, flat. "You think that this time, for sure, three inmates are going to win against two state prisons and Othrys Games by just quietly doing the right thing."

He leans closer; his hand, flat on the table, almost touches her fist.

"I think if anybody realizes you're the problem, you are going to need help and I am not going to be able to give it. What are you thinking?"

She meets his eye. "I saw Marie."

REVIEW: THEMIS IS A WHOLE NEW WORLD
by Sarah McElroy

As a games reviewer, you tend to get jaded about new products. The graphics are increasingly realistic, the plots increasingly dense, and there's a sense that some games are more about one-upsmanship than about providing a transporting experience for players.

Themis is coming to the market nearly three years late, and shrouded in mystery. It was the subject of a lawsuit two years ago, as beta testers complained they hadn't signed on for something as immersive as they got. For normal people, that gives you pause. For gamers, that's the kind of buzz money can't buy. (A one-day-only letter to the editor also appeared in the Evening Times; the newspaper didn't respond to requests for comment, so the message-board debate rages on about whether it was a legitimate report from the trenches, or genius advertising.)

And if you've been waiting for Themis as long as I have, it's awkward to realize you understand exactly what those beta testers meant.

In terms of practicalities, Themis isn't very much different from half a dozen other VR immersions that have appeared the last few years. You're part of a hardscrabble crew assigned to terraform Themis, the first colony on Proxima Centauri. If you're looking for more plot, you won't find it: the entire hook of Themis is that the world is, quite literally, what you make it.

But what a world. The eternal sunset casts a rosy glow over the camp, the flies hover over any kill you make. And if you think otherwise, trust me, you'll end up making kills—Themis is about moral questions as much as strategy choices, and your team will have to eat something until the potato harvest. Every herbivore on Proxima Centauri is a take on Earth fauna of the taiga, so if you can't look a reindeer in the eye and fire, you're going to go hungry a lot. And you should think quickly; Themis has admirable ambitions about its much-touted real-time settings, but there's no doubt that the optimal game play occurs at about seven times the speed of life, and at that speed, hunger levels are highly responsive. (Given that your larger goal is simply to cross the mountains and make geological observations about the ice on the dark side of the planet, hunger might be the closest you come to emergency action.)

There have been concerns about the complications of MMORPG when everything is quite so unstructured; it's one thing to put up with creeps when they're a mage avatar in your questing party, and another to deal with them in an environment so sharply realized that it might as well be real. I'm honestly not sure how that setting will develop—when we played it in the *Tabula* offices, all was well, but the more you open the encampment to strangers, the greater the risk. It's just as well the game has a Private setting, where you and a handful of AI colleagues split the work and develop the colony in contemplative near-silence. You even get to choose your profession. (Medic is so boring as to be childish; go for Cook. Don't worry—there's no achievement bar. You can mess up bread as much as you want.)

These days, to survive in the marketplace, a game can't just be good and survive. It can't even settle for being impressive. It has to be earth-shaking. And for a game that can be explained in a single sentence, Themis really does defy description. I know I'll be seeing copycats for the next ten years; I know none of them will make me feel the way Themis did.

RATING: Must-Have

Hello Sarah,

I saw your piece about Themis in *Tabula*. I am a developer at Othrys who worked on the beta testing for Themis and would love to speak with you further. You can contact me at the email above.

Benjamina Harris

To All Othrys Staff:

Benjamina Harris has been terminated, effective immediately. In the next few days, HR staff may meet with you to ask questions about her performance. We apologize for the inconvenience, and appreciate your cooperation.

Sincerely,

Dan Turpin, CEO

It feels so silly, handing Woods a disk—first time she's handled a physical disk in six years, no bigger than her thumbnail, and still passing it over is like handing him a raw egg.

"I told you I can't help you," he says, but she has her hands in her pockets and after a minute, he slips the thing out of sight.

"Thank you," she says. He's furious with her—that she didn't get out before she was fired, that she's had to create a new identity after everyone's already on alert, that she's making him responsible for backup copies of bugged conversations and stolen correspondence that will get her thrown in prison for fifty years. But he's here when he shouldn't be, and that makes him better than some.

"You won't make it out of the country," he says. "Please just hide closer to home. Yosemite's a thousand square miles."

She could. It would be safer. But living alone in a clearing near the river, birds calling out in the dark, mountains to the northwest—she swallows. It would be stealing.

She says, "I hope it's bad enough that someone finds Marie."

She heads south; the sun sets off the red rocks, and there's no one else for a hundred miles, and she sits in the quiet car and compiles a new geography, and realizes she'll never reach the border.

Still, she drives while she can. The footprint of the mesas is so big it never shifts; she moves like someone in a dream, not quite fast enough.

EVENING TIMES
OTHRYS WHISTLEBLOWER TELLS ALL ABOUT SHOCKING MEDICAL EXPERIMENTATION: "THEMIS WASN'T WORTH THE COST"

THE SUNDAY LEDGER
"THE WARDEN KNEW, AND NO ONE STOPPED HIM": HOW "THEMIS" MUST MARK THE END OF THE PRISON INDUSTRIAL COMPLEX

THE NEW YORK STANDARD
THE ORACLE OF OTHRYS: VIDEO GAME SNITCH BLOWS THE LID OFF VR HORROR

THE LONE CANDLE
THE THEMIS EXPERIMENT: WHY VIRTUAL REALITY MAKES EVERYONE A PRISONER

OWL EYES NEWS
BOSS BATTLE: CHRISTOPHER COLLINS, "THE VIDEO-GAME WARDEN," RETIRES WITH $2 MILLION SEVERANCE

TABULA GAMES
WORLD-CLASS: "THEMIS" BREAKS SALES RECORDS

THE NEW YORK WEEK IN REVIEW
MARIE ROLAND: THE WOMAN WHO CAN NEVER GO HOME

• • •

Samara, Anthony,

This is my last letter. I hope this ends up being of some use to you—make no secret of it, if it will help. I'm happy to be anybody's pawn now.

It was an honor building Themis with you. I'm glad you're not coming, but it won't be the same.

Marie

Spent today walking downstream a dozen kilometers and recording things. There are more species of cattails in this one stretch than I ever saw on Earth. Saw a lot of teeth marks on them—bodes well for the idea of some Earth-adjacent fauna that have just been scared off by our camp but might eventually be coaxed to come back.

Of course, I shredded my feet and somehow managed to get a giant bruise on my knee without even falling down. (How did they ever let me become a naturalist with a constitution like this?) Listened to a whole chapter of a book while I was soaking in salt water, which is the most salt and the most reading I've gotten since I landed.

You'd think they'd have sent more people, but I guess for a temperate zone you don't really have to. Winters don't kill you here, and it's only a couple of weeks until the pass melts and we can set off for the mountains to do the survey for the second-wave team. (My bet is glacier melt that will sustain a thousand people; Vivian claims there's taiga and we can support twice that. Carlos is holding the money.)

It's winter at home, by now, isn't it? I hope all is well with you. I would love to know for sure.

The bread I made today was edible! The bird outside was very proud of me—he sang along with me all night. I threw him crumbs, at the end of it, and he liked them, and it feels like it will even last the night without going stale. This time next year, I'll have the hang of it for sure.

That bird really does have a lovely song. They said to be careful assigning old observations to what I find here, but: thrush family. I just know it.

All my love—

THE VANISHING KIND

LAVIE TIDHAR

1

During the rebuilding of London in the 1950s they had erected a large Ferris wheel on the south bank of the Thames. When it was opened, it cost two Reichsmarks for a ride, but it was seldom busy. London after the war wasn't a place you went to on holiday.

Gunther Sloam came to London in the autumn, which is when I first became acquainted with him. He was neither too tall nor too short, but an unassuming man in a good suit and a worn fedora. He could have been a shopkeeper or a traveling salesman, though he was neither. Before the war he had been a screenwriter in Berlin.

He came following a woman, which is how this kind of story usually starts. She had written to him two weeks earlier, c/o the Tobis Film Syndikat in Berlin, and a friend who was still working there eventually passed him her note. It read:

> My dear Gunther,
>
> I am in London and I think I am in trouble. I fear my life is in danger. Please, if you continue to remember me fondly, come at once. I am residing at 47 Dean Street, Soho. If I am not there, ask for the dwarf.
>
> Yours, ever,
>
> Ulla.

The note had been smudged with a red lipstick kiss.

It was a week from the time the letter was sent, to Gunther receiving it. It was another week before he finally departed Berlin, on board a Luftwaffe transport plane carrying with it the famed soprano, Elisabeth Schwarzkopf, and her entourage. She was to perform in London's newly rebuilt Opera House. Gunther spent the short flight making notes in his pocket book, for a screenplay he was vaguely thinking to write. He was not unduly concerned about Ulla. His view of women in general, and of actresses in particular, was that they were prone to exaggeration. No doubt Ulla's trouble would prove such as they'd always been—usually, he thought with a sigh, something to do with money. In that he was both right and wrong.

He was flattered, and glad, that she wanted to see him again. They had carried on a passionate love affair for several months, in Berlin in '43, before Gunther was sent to the Eastern Front, and Ulla went on to star in several well-received patriotic films, the pinnacle of which was *Die große Liebe*, for a time the highest-grossing film in all of Germany. Gunther had watched it in the hospital camp, while recovering from the wound which, even now, made him walk with a slight, almost unnoticeable limp. He only really felt it on very cold days, and the pangs in his leg brought with them memories of the hell that was the Eastern Front. He had never known such cold.

"Don't you see?" he said to me, much later. He was pacing my office, his hair unkempt for once, his eyes ringed black by lack of sleep. He'd lost much of his cool amused air by then. "Because we did it, we beat the Russians, and Ulla went on to star in *Stalingrad*, that Stemmle picture, but it was the last big film she did. I don't know what happened after that. We lost touch, though there'd always been rumors, you see."

He'd told me quite a lot by then but I was happy to let him talk. I knew some of the story by then and, of course, I'd known Miss Ulla Blau. We had been taking an interest in her activities for some time.

The plane landed at Northolt. There was no one there to welcome him and the soprano and her entourage were whisked away by my superior, Group Leader Pohl. I saw Gunther emerge into the terminal with that somewhat bewildered look that afflicts the visitor. He saw me and came over. "Where can a man get a taxi around here?" he said, in German.

"I'm afraid I don't . . . " I said, in English.

His eyes, surprisingly, lit up. "You are British?" he said.

"Yes. You speak English?"

"But of course." His accent was atrocious. "I learn to speak English in the cinema," he explained. "Do you know the works of Alfred Hitchcock?"

"His films are prohibited nowadays," I said, kindly. He frowned. I was not in uniform and he did not know what I was until later.

"Yes, yes," he said. "His death was most regrettable. He was a great maker of movies. I'm sorry," he said, "I have not introduced myself. Gunther Sloam." He extended his hand and I shook it.

"Name's Everly," I said. "I was in fact on my way back into town now. Can I give you a ride?" My jeep was outside.

"That would be most kind," he said. "I am here to see an old friend, you see.

A woman. Yes, I have not seen her since the war." He laughed, a little sadly I thought. "I am older, perhaps she is older too, no? But not in my memory, never."

"You're a romantic," I said.

"I suppose," he said, dubiously. "Yes, I suppose I am."

"There is not much call for romantics in London," I said. "We English have become pragmatists, since the war ended."

He said nothing to that; perhaps he never even heard me. He sat beside me in the jeep as we went past the ruined buildings left over from the bombings, but I don't think he saw them, either.

"Where do you need to go?" I said.

"Soho."

"Are you sure? That is not a very good area."

"I think I can manage, Mr. Everly," he said. He lit a cigarette and passed one to me.

"*Danke*," I said. Then again in German, "And who is this mystery lady you're visiting, if you don't mind my prying?"

He laughed, delighted. "Your German is flawless!" he said.

"I studied in Berlin before the war."

"But that is wonderful," he said.

Then he spent fifteen minutes telling me all about *Fräulein* Ulla Blau; her film career; their passionate affair ("But we were both so *young*!"); his new screenplay ("A Western, in the Karl May tradition. You know how fond the Führer is of these things"); Berlin ("Have you been back? It's a beautiful city now, beautiful. Say what you want about Speer but the man is a gifted architect"); and so on and so on.

At one point I finally managed to interject. "And you know what your friend is doing these days?" I asked him.

He frowned. Such a thought had not entered his head. "I assumed she was acting again," he said. "But I hadn't really thought . . . Well, it is no matter. I shall find out soon enough."

We were driving along the Charing Cross Road by then. The few approved bookshops stood open, their wan light spilling onto the dark pavement outside. I remembered the book purges and burnings after the invasion—after all, I led one such group myself. I did not like doing it, yet it was a necessity of the time. Gunther did not seem to pay much attention. His eyes slid over the grimy frontage of the shops. "Where are your famed picture palaces?" he said. "I have long desired to ensconce myself in the luxuries of the Regal or the Ritz." His eyes shone with a childish enthusiasm.

"I'm afraid most were destroyed in the Blitz," I said apologetically.

He nodded. We were in Soho then, a squalid block of half-ruined buildings where the lowlifes of London made their abode. It was a hard place to police and patrol, filled with European émigrés of dubious loyalties. But it was useful, as such places inevitably are.

Along Shaftesbury Avenue, the few theatres were doing meager trade. The big show that year was *Servant of Two Masters*, an Italian comedy adapted to the English stage. It was showing at the Apollo. Dean Street itself was a dark thoroughfare that never quite slept. Business was conducted in the shadows, and red lights burned invitingly behind the second-floor windows. I saw doubt enter Gunther's eyes and I almost felt sorry for him. I had my own interest in his well-being or otherwise. My men were already stationed unobtrusively in the street.

"This is the place," I said, stopping the jeep. He stepped out and extended his hand.

"Thank you, Everly," he said. "You are a gentleman."

I could see he liked that word. The Germans are a peculiar people. Having won the war, they were almost apologetic about it. I said, "If your visit does not go well, there is a transport leaving for Berlin tomorrow night. I can ensure you have a seat on it."

His eyes changed; as though he were seeing me for the first time.

"You never said what you do," he said.

"No," I agreed. "Goodbye, Mr. Sloam."

I left him there. I did not expect him to be so much trouble as he turned out to be.

2

Gunther stood outside 47 Dean Street for some time. Perhaps, already, he began to have second thoughts. On receipt of her letter, he had expected little more than a fond reunion with Ulla. Perhaps he saw himself as a sort of Teutonic white knight, riding to the rescue of a helpless maiden. He never really knew Ulla, or what she was capable of, though he didn't realize that until it was too late.

The address she had given him had been a theatre before the war. Now it was a sort of boarding house, with a hand-written sign on the door saying *No Vacancies!* in a barely-legible scrawl. The windows were dark. The front of house, once-grand, now looked dowdy and unkempt. Gunther looked about him and saw two shifty characters in the shadows across the road. They were smoking cigarettes and watching him. He gathered his courage and knocked loudly on the door.

There was no reply. The whole house felt silent and empty. He knocked again, louder, until at last a window overhead opened and an old woman stuck her head out and began cursing him in a mixture of English and gutter

German. Almost, he wanted to take out his pen and note down some of the more inventive swearing.

"I'm looking for Ulla Blau!" he called up, when the old woman finally stopped, momentarily, for air.

The old woman spat. The spit fell down heavily and landed at Gunther's feet.

"The whore's not here," the old woman said and slammed the window shut.

Now angry, Gunther began to hammer on the door again. The two observers watched him from across the street. They, too, had an interest in Fräuleine Blau's whereabouts.

At last the window opened again and the same old woman stuck her head out. "What?" she demanded crossly.

"I need to see her!"

"I told you, she's not here!"

"Well, where is she?"

"I don't know, and I don't want to know!" the old woman said and slammed the window.

Gunther stood in the street. He was tired now, and hungry, and he wanted a drink. He had hoped for a fond embrace, a night spent in a comfortable bed with a bottle of good Rhine wine (which he had brought) and a willing companion to murmur sweet nothings into his ear. Instead he got this, and besides the street smelled, from uncollected garbage gathered every few paces on the broken pavement.

"Open the damn door or I'll break it down!" he said.

Then he waited. Presently, there was a shuffling noise and then the door opened a crack and the old woman stuck her head out. "What are you, Gestapo?" she said.

"If I were the Gestapo," Gunther said, reasonably, "you'd already be answering my questions."

The old woman cackled. She seemed to have no fear of this strange German on her doorstep. "Do you have a drink?" she said.

Gunther brought out the bottle of wine and the old woman's eyes widened appreciatively.

"Come in, come in!" she said. "The night is cold and full of eyes."

Gunther followed her into the building.

The old woman's apartment was surprisingly comfortable. A fire was burning in the fireplace and Gunther sat down wearily on a red velvet sofa which sagged underneath him. The walls were covered with old photographs and playbills. The old woman herself reminded him somewhat of an old, faded revue actress. She bustled about, fetching glasses. They were good crystal, and when she saw his enquiring look she cackled again and said, "From Marks's, the filthy Jews. Now *that* was a fire sale!"

Gunther accepted the glass, his loathing for the old woman growing. He let her open the bottle, which she did deftly, then poured two glasses. The old woman drank hers rapidly and greedily, then refilled the glass. Her eyes acquired a brittle warmth.

"You have come from Germany?" she said.

"Berlin."

"Berlin! I have often wished to visit Berlin." She spoke a bad but serviceable German.

"It is a great city."

"Not like this place," the old woman said. "London is a shithole."

Gunther silently agreed. He took a sip of his wine, mourning the loss of its planned usage. The taste brought back memories of warmer, happier times.

"I am looking for—" he began, and the old woman said, "Yes, yes. Ulla Blau. I told you, she is not here."

At this time he was not yet unduly concerned.

"This is the address she's given me."

"She was here," the old woman said. "She hires a room from me, at thirty Reichsmarks a month. I do not ask questions, Mr. Sloam."

"Has she gone away, then?" Gunther said.

"She is always coming and going, that one," the old woman said.

"Is she still acting? In the theatre, perhaps?"

The old woman snorted a laugh, then wiped it away when she saw Gunther's face. "Perhaps," she said. "Yes, perhaps. What do I know?" She took a long shuddering sip of wine. "I am just an old woman," she said.

Doubts, at this point, were finally beginning to enter Gunther's mind. "Well, what does she do, for money?"

"I am sure I don't know," the old woman said huffily. Her glass was empty again and she refilled it with unsteady hands. "You should have seen this place before the war," she said suddenly. "The theaters all alight and the public flowing on the pavements all excited and gay. The men handsome in their suits and the women pretty in their dresses. I saw Charlie Chaplin play the Hippodrome once." Her eyes misted over. "I don't blame you Germans," she said. "I blame the Jews, but there are no more Jews to blame. Who can we blame now, Mr. Sloam?"

"Can I see her room?" Gunther said.

The old woman sighed. She was coming to the realisation that Gunther Sloam could be very single-minded.

"I'm sure I can't let you do that," she said; but he saw the speculative glint in her eye.

"I could perhaps rent it, for a while," he offered. "I am a stranger in this town and the hour is getting late."

His hand, which he had dipped in his pocket, returned with a handful of notes. The woman's eyes tracked the movement of the money.

"When you put it like that . . . " she said.

Ulla Blau's room was an almost perfect square. It had once been a dressing room of some sort, or perhaps, Gunther thought a little uncharitably, a supply closet. The old woman, whose name, he had learned, was Mrs. White, stood in the doorway watching him with her bright button eyes. She swayed, from time to time, and hummed a tune under her breath. It sounded a little like the Horst Wessel song.

There was nothing of the personal in Ulla Blau's room. There was a bed, perfectly made up; a wardrobe and a vanity mirror; a small gas ring and a kettle; and that was about it. Gunther's imaginings of their reunion plunged further into doubt, for this was not the romantic abode he had perhaps envisioned. There were no clues as to Ulla's employment or whereabouts. Beyond the wall, the noise of hurried sexual congress could be clearly heard. He glanced at Mrs. White, who shrugged. Gunther began to have an idea of what the majority of the rooms were used for.

Mrs. White moved aside to let him out. The corridor was long and dark and the communal bathroom was at one end of it. Gunther was, at this point, beginning to feel concern.

"And you do not know where she is?" he demanded of Mrs. White.

The old woman shrugged. She didn't know, or didn't care, or didn't care to know. Gunther dug out Ulla's note. *If I am not there*, she had written, *ask for the dwarf.*

I shall interject, at this point, to say that this dwarf was a person of considerable interest to us. We were anxious to interview him with regards to some matters which had arisen. This dwarf went by the name of Jurgen, and was of a Swiss nationality. He had come to London six months previous and was, moreover, the scion of a wealthy Zurich banking family with connections high up within the party.

"Where can I find," Gunther said, and then felt silly, "the dwarf?"

He said it quite light-heartedly. But Mrs. White's reaction was the opposite. Her face turned a crimson shade and her eyes rolled in her head like those of a grand dame in a Christmas pantomime.

"Him? You ask me about *him*?"

Gunther was not aware of the reputation the dwarf had in certain circles. Mrs. White's reaction took him quite by surprise.

"Where can I find him?" he said mildly.

"Do not ask me that!"

Good wine, missed plans, and bad company do not mix well. Gunther at last lost his patience.

"Listen to me, you silly old bat!" he said. He had done terrible things to survive on the Eastern Front. Now that man was before Mrs. White, and she cowered. Gunther jabbed an angry finger at the old woman's face. "Tell me where this damned dwarf is or by God I'll . . . "

She must have told him; he must have left. My men lost him, by accident or design, shortly after; and so the first I knew of it was the next morning, when Sergeant Cole called me and woke me from a blissful sleep, to tell me they'd arrested Gunther Sloam for murder.

3

By the time I made it to HQ they'd worked Gunther over a little; mostly I think just to keep their hand in. I told them to straighten him up and bring him to my office, along with two cups of tea. When they brought him in, he had a black eye, a swollen lip, and a bad temper.

"What is the meaning of this?" he said. "I am a citizen of the Reich, you can't treat me like this!"

"Please, Mr. Sloam, sit down. Cigarette?" I proffered the box. He hesitated then took one, and I lit him up. He took in all the smoke at once, and after that he was a little calmer.

"Say, what is the meaning of this?" I think only then my face registered with him, and he started. "You're that chap, Everly. I don't understand."

He looked around him at the office. The framed photograph of the Führer stared back at him from the wall.

"I'm sorry," I said. "I should have introduced myself more fully. I am *Kriminalinspektor* Tom Everly, of Gestapo Department D."

He looked at me in silence. His lips moved. He looked around the room again. When he at last spoke he was more subdued.

"Gestapo, eh?"

"I'm afraid so."

"But you're English!" he cried, turning on me accusingly.

"Yes?"

That stumped him. "When you said you studied in Berlin before the war—"

"It is not me who has to justify himself to you," I said.

"How do you mean?"

"Mr. Sloam, you have been arrested for murder."

"Murder!" His eyes were wild. "Listen, here!"

"No, you listen," I said. "We can do this the hard way. You've already had a little taste of that. Or we can do this the civilized way."

I waited and presently there was a knock on the door. Then Cole came in with the tea. He left it on my desk and departed. We'd had the routine down pat by then.

"Milk? Sugar?" I said.

Unexpectedly he smiled. "How very English," he said. "Two sugars, please, and milk too, why not." He sat down on the chair, hard. I passed him the tea and lit a fresh cigarette and watched him.

"You'd better tell me what happened last night," I said.

He sighed. "I don't know where to start," he said, dejectedly.

Gunther left the house on Dean Street around eight o'clock in the evening. When he stood outside, the thought that came to his mind was that the house was, indisputably, one of ill repute. What Ulla was doing in such a place he did not know. He could not believe that she prostituted herself, nor understand how she came to live in such a squalid place. As I'd said to him before, he was a romantic—though that did not necessarily make him a fool.

Mrs. White had given him an address nearby. Gunther walked, not hurrying, but at a steady pace. He was well aware of the two shadows which detached themselves from the wall across the road and followed. He did not increase his speed or slow down, but his path was such that in a short amount of time he was able to shake them off. Taking a turning, he hid down a dark alleyway as the two men walked past. He could hear them arguing in low voices as he slunk in the other direction.

The night was thick with darkness. The buildings here were still half-ruined, destroyed in the Blitz, and served as hidey-holes for all kinds of illicit activities. Gunther watched himself, but wished he had a gun, a wish he was soon to fulfil. He smelled frying onions nearby and his stomach rumbled. He heard drunken laughter, soft footfalls, and a scream that was cut short. He saw four men sitting by a lit lantern playing cards. He smelled cigar smoke. He heard someone muttering and moaning in a low, never-ceasing voice.

At last he made it to the Lyric. It is a Victorian pub, and had remained undamaged during the war. Gunther, the romantic, found it charming. Opposite the pub stood the Windmill Theatre. It was the one source of bright light, and advertised nude *tableaux vivants*, as well as the exclusive appearance of Tran *und* Helle, the popular comedians, visiting London for seven nights only.

Gunther entered the pub. It was dark and dim inside, and the smell of beer, cigarette and cigar smoke hit him with their combined warmth. A small fire burned merrily in the fireplace. The atmosphere worked like a panacea on Gunther. He removed his coat and perched on the bar gratefully.

"Help you, sir?"

The bartender was bald and rotund and missing one eye, his left one. He turned a rag inside a beer stein, over and over and without much hope of making it clean.

"I'll have an Erdinger, please," Gunther said. "And a plate of *Schweinshaxe mit Sauerkraut*."

The bartender, without changing an expression, poured the beer and served it to Gunther.

"We don't have pork knuckle," he said. "Or sauerkraut."

Gunther closed his eyes and took a sip of the beer. He already felt light-headed from the wine he had consumed earlier with the old woman.

"Well, what do you serve?" he said.

"Pie."

"What sort of pie?"

"Pork pie."

"Then I shall have a pork pie, *bitte*."

The bartender nodded and kept wiping the stein. "That'll be twenty Reichsmarks," he said.

"Twenty!"

The bartender looked bored. Gunther cursed under his breath but paid. The bartender made the money disappear. Gunther lit a cigarette and looked about the pub. There were only a few men sitting around, and no women. No one looked in his direction. He began to get the sense that he wasn't welcome.

He took another sip of his beer.

"I am looking for *Der Zwerg*," he said; announcing it into the air of the pub.

No one moved. If anything, Gunther thought, they had become more still.

"Pie," the bartender said. Gunther looked down at the counter. A round, solid brick of pastry sat on a cracked plate. Gunther picked up the knife and fork. He cut through the pastry into the pink fleshy interior. He cut a slice and put it in his mouth. It was cold and rather flavorless. He chewed and swallowed.

"Delicious," he said.

Someone sniggered. When Gunther turned his head a tall thin figure rose from a bench against the wall and perched itself on a stool beside him. The man had the cadaverous look of a disappointed undertaker. The smile he offered Gunther was as honest as a Vichy check.

"You are new in town?" he said.

"What's it to you?" Gunther said.

"Nothing, nothing." The man rubbed his hands together as though cold. He reminded Gunther a little of that Jew actor, Peter Lorre; he had starred in Fritz Lang's *M* nearly three decades earlier. "It is good to hear an honest German voice again."

"You are not from Germany."

"No. Luxembourg," the man confessed. That explained the accent. "It is a strange country, England, is it not? They are so dour, so resentful of you Germans. Do you know, I think, deep down, they believe they should have won the war." He laughed, the same sort of insincere sound a hyena makes. "Beer, bartender!" he called jovially. "And one for my friend here. Put it on my tab."

"You have been here long?" Gunther asked.

"Two years now," the man said. "I do a little business. Import-export, mostly. You know how it is."

Gunther did not. The beer arrived and he sipped from it. He forced himself to finish the pie. He had eaten worse on the Front.

"This man," I said. "His name was Klaus?"

Gunther was pacing my office. He looked up, surprised. "Klaus Pirelli, or so he told me," he said. "Yes. How did you—?"

"He has given us a full statement," I said. "He says he drank beer with you and discussed the ongoing war in America, Leni Riefenstahl's latest film, the new African *Lebensraum*, and the import-export business. He says you got progressively drunker and increasingly aggressive. At some point you asked, loudly, where a man could get hold of a gun in this town. You became so voluble that he had to escort you outside. He says the last he saw of you, you were staggering down Great Windmill Street in the direction of Shaftesbury Avenue, waving your arms and swearing you would, 'Get that bitch.'"

Gunther stopped pacing. His mouth hung open. I almost felt sorry for him at that moment. In his comic horror he reminded me of the comedian, Alfred Hawthorne, who I had recently seen playing Bottom in a production of *A Midsummer Night's Dream*.

"But that is *Wahnsinn*!" He gaped at me like a landed fish. "It is madness! I did no such thing!"

"Can you prove it?"

"The other drinkers! The bartender! They were all witnesses—"

He looked at me then, realization slowly dawning.

"You are German," I said, sadly. "They are not."

"Listen, Everly, you've got to believe me!"

"Just tell me what happened," I said.

Gunther found the Luxembourgian trying. The man was obviously selling something, but Gunther wasn't sure what.

"I am looking for the dwarf," he said again.

"Him!" the Luxembourgian exclaimed.

"I was told I could find him here."

"He is not an easy man to find, *Herr* Jurgen."

"Is that his name?" Gunther said.

"You do not know his name, yet you seek to find him?" The Luxembourgian looked amused at that. "What is the nature of your business with the count?"

"A count, is he?" Gunther said. His head really was spinning. "Well, I want to know where Ulla Blau is." He grabbed the Luxembourgian by the lapels and shook him. "Do you know where Ulla is?" he demanded. His speech felt slurred, his tongue unresponsive. "I need to see her. She's in a lot of trouble."

The Luxembourgian gently removed Gunther's hands. "You need air, friend," he said. "I think you've had too much to drink."

"Don't be . . . ridiculous," Gunther said. His vision swam. He was dimly aware of his new friend putting an arm around his shoulders and steering him outside. Cold air hit his face like a slap, but it did not clear his confused thoughts. He began to stagger away from the pub. As he did so, he saw a pair of shapely white legs strolling past. He raised his head and tried to focus. A good-looking woman wrapped in a thick fur coat walking away from him. As she passed under a gaslight, for just a moment, she turned her head and smiled.

"Ulla?" Gunther cried. "Ulla!"

There was something mocking in the woman's smile. She turned and walked away. Gunther lurched after her for a few more steps but she was long gone, and perhaps, he thought later, she had never been there at all. He tottered on his feet. Darkness opened all around him like the entry to a sewer. He fell, hard, and lay on the ground. He closed his eyes, and dark sleep claimed him.

"And that is all you remember?" I said.

"All I remember, until some uncouth men roused me on the street, administered a series of kicks for good measure, put me in irons, and dragged me to your cellars to have another go." He touched his black eye and winced. "Don't you see?" Gunther said. "I was drugged. The Luxembourgian must be in on it. He must have slipped something into my drink when I wasn't watching."

The mention of drugs caught my attention and I looked at him in a new way.

"Besides," he said with a laugh, "who the hell am I supposed to have murdered?"

"Come with me."

He shrugged. This, he endeavored to get across, was nothing to him. In that he was wrong.

He followed me along the corridor and down the stairs. The Gestapo had made its headquarters in Somerset House. We found the stout walls and easy access to the river compelling. I took him down to the makeshift morgue.

"What is this?" he said, and shivered as we entered. I ignored him.

"Sir," *Kriminalassistent* West said, standing to attention.

"What is this?" Gunther demanded. We both ignored him. I gave West the nod. He pulled one of the refrigeration units open and slid out the gurney.

A corpse, covered in a sheet, lay on the cold metal tray.

Gunther's lips moved, but without sound. Perhaps he was beginning to realize the trouble he was in.

I gave West the nod again. He removed the sheet. Underneath it lay a naked female form. Her face had been blasted apart by a bullet from a Luger semiautomatic.

I watched Gunther closely. The horror on his face looked genuine enough.

"Can you identify her?" I said. He stared at the body mutely. His eyes took in the ruined faced, the still, cold body, her bejeweled fingers. He began to shake.

"No, no," he said. "It cannot be."

He stepped closer to the gurney. He took one dead hand in his.

"This ring," he said. It was a rather tawdry thing, a chunky emerald set in copper. "I gave it to her. I remember buying it, from Kling's on Münzstrasse. It was a token of my love, just before they shipped me to the Front."

"Gave it to whom?" I said, gently.

He looked at me, his eyes full of quiet despair.

"I gave it to Ulla Blau," he said.

4

The story could have ended here, but for the fact that Ulla Blau's death, though in some part not entirely without benefit, nevertheless put me in an awkward position.

I took Gunther back to my office. I asked Sergeant Cole to bring us two coffees this time, and some Viennese pastries. You may wonder why I treated Gunther Sloam with such kids gloves. After all, the expedient act would have been to send him back down to the cellars for a second, more thorough work-over—to last only as long as necessary to extract a full and frank confession—then a speedy execution and burial by water. There were, as I mentioned, several reasons why Somerset House was chosen for our headquarters. The corpses, occasionally, if not weighted enough, floated back up to the surface or caught in the Greenwich wharves on their way out to sea, but that merely served to reinforce in people's minds the long and lethal reach of the Gestapo. Sometimes we had to make sure the corpses were lightly weighted when a particular message needed to be sent.

Gunther wondered the same thing. I could see it in his eyes. He observed Sergeant Cole bring in the coffee and pastries with the eyes of a condemned man watching his executioner. I sat behind my desk and stirred a cube of sugar into my coffee.

"Cream?"

"Thank you."

He said that in a wondering voice. I smiled patiently and took a bite from my *Apfelstrudel*. "They are not as good as on the Continent, of course," I said, when I had chewed and swallowed. "But we do try our best, as you see."

"I am sure it is delicious," he said. He didn't look like he tasted anything.

"I asked you, when we first met," I said. "What your friend was doing in London. You did not enlighten me."

"Everly, for God's sake . . . !" he began, then went *stumm*.

I waited him out.

"I don't know," he admitted at last. "I received this note, and I—" he buried his face in his hands. "I did not take it seriously. She said her life was in danger and I, I—"

"You were expecting nothing more than a pleasurable reunion," I said. He raised his face to me and his eyes flashed with anger.

"Now look here, Everly!" he said. "I did not kill her!"

"Do you know what Pervitin is?" I said.

"Of course," he said, without hesitation, but with a moue of distaste. "It is an artificial stimulant. A type of drug, what they call methamphetamines. They gave it to us during Barbarossa. It keeps you awake and gives you energy, and it lowers inhibition, which is useful in battle."

"It is also highly addictive."

"Yes," he said. "In our case, the army didn't worry about it too much. Most of the people who took it were destined for death. I was just luckier than most."

"Your friend, Ulla Blau, came to London some years ago," I said. "London at that time was a city in ruin. A large occupying force was initially needed and soldiers, as soldiers are wont to do, require entertainments."

"What are you saying?"

"Ulla's theatre connections proved handy in supplying girls for the soldiers. At that time, in London, a warm body was cheaper than a loaf of bread, and easier to get. From the soldiers she could easily acquire extra supplies of Pervitin. These she sold back into the general populace. It wasn't, strictly speaking, legal, but legality didn't have much of a meaning in the immediate aftermath of the war."

"I don't believe you," he said.

I shrugged. "You can believe what you'd like to believe," I said. "But you can't dismiss the evidence of your own eyes. Somebody plugged a nine-millimeter bullet into her pretty little face, after all."

"That doesn't make her guilty!"

"It doesn't make her bloody innocent, either," I said.

He stared at me with hatred and his fingers curled into fists. He was going to go for me in a moment.

Then realization dawned; I could see his expression change. "You don't think I killed her," he said, wonderingly.

"Look, Sloam," I said. I was tired and the pastry was cloyingly sweet. "It doesn't matter to me if you killed her or not. She was nothing but trouble and the world's a better place for her not being in it. However . . . "

He watched me closely. I could see he was still aching to swing at me. He wasn't the first and he wasn't going to be the last.

"Either way, it's a mess. You're a citizen of the *Deutsches Reich*, not just a colonial. So was Fräulein Blau, and as a former actress, her death would play for news. The last thing my superiors want is a fuss back in Berlin about a sordid murder in the colonies. Citizens of the Reich must feel they can travel safely to any part of the empire. This isn't 1946, Sloam. England's a peaceful place, and a faithful servant of the Führer."

"So where does that leave me?" he said. He wasn't slow when he didn't want to be.

"What would you do in my place?" I said.

He considered. "You'd announce her death as an unfortunate accident, and bury me somewhere out of sight with a bullet between my eyes."

I nodded. He wasn't an innocent, just the wrong man in the wrong place, and for all his war experience, he still thought like a character in one of his movies. "What did you think," I said, "that you'd come over here and rescue her?"

"I don't know what I thought," he said. "And I still don't believe she was guilty!"

"Which of us isn't guilty, Mr. Sloam," I said. "Which of us isn't guilty?"

He watched me. "I am not afraid to die," he said.

I pressed a button, and Sergeant Cole came in. Gunther tensed.

"Cole," I said "Please show Mr. Sloam outside."

Gunther watched me with suspicion.

"There's a flight leaving for Berlin tonight," I said. "I'd advise you to be on it. Remember, I had made that offer before, and I'm unlikely to make it a third time. Sergeant Cole will take you to a hotel where you can clean up and get some rest. *Auf Wiedersehen*, Mr. Sloam. I hope, sincerely, we do not meet again."

The hint of a smile touched his lips then. "Goodbye, *Kriminalinspektor* Everly," he said.

But I could see he did not mean it.

Cole dropped him off at the Albert in Covent Garden. It was basic, but clean. Gunther collected his key and went up to his room. He showered and changed. He did not sleep.

Of course the obstinate German did not take my advice. I had accused him of being a romantic and I wasn't wrong. Gunther, for all his battle experience in the *Wehrmacht*, still insisted, deep down, to think of himself as a character in one of his own cowboy pictures. All he could think about was Ulla Blau's ruined, once-beautiful face staring back at him from the mortuary slab. I think he believed himself untouchable. Most Germans did, after the war. There were still pockets of resistance in America, but few since we'd dropped the A-bomb on Washington D.C. The world belonged to Germany: for Gunther, that idea was as fixed as his notion of honor.

From the hotel, Gunther went out. For a time he walked through Covent Garden, which he found a dismal sort of place. Underneath the butchers' stalls the blood ran rancid, and the greengrocers' offerings of hard, lumpy potatoes and bent carrots depressed Gunther. The market had all the festivity of a Dachau.

He watched the passersby, though. Londoners moved about the market furtively, with the hunched shoulders of a conquered people. They wore shabby clothes, the men in ill-fitting suits, the women in hand-me-down dresses that appeared to have come from a German Red Cross charity stall. He saw few smiles. Here and there, soldiers patrolled, but they were few in number and looked indifferent to the populace. As I had told Gunther, this England was resigned to its fate. The majority of the occupying force had moved on to other duties, in the new African territories or America. Now, only a skeleton barracks was left and, of course, the Gestapo.

Gunther walked past the Opera House, where a prominent sign advertised the soprano Elisabeth Schwarzkopf's appearance that night. Along Drury Lane he saw a young boy in the shadows, peaked cap covering half his face, skulking. He paused to watch as first two men and then a woman stopped and appeared to make a furtive purchase. When the street was clear, Gunther crossed the road and approached the boy.

"What do you want, mister?"

"What have you got?" Gunther said.

The boy looked up at him with suspicion. "You're a German!" he said accusingly.

Gunther shrugged.

"You want girls?" the boy said. "My sister is very clean."

"I need something to keep me awake," Gunther said. "You got some of that?"

The boy grinned, relieved that this was just another punter. "Sure, sure," he said expansively. "But it'll cost you."

Gunther took out a clip of bills and the boy's eyes went wide and round. "Pervitin?" Gunther said.

The boy nodded. Gunther peeled off a twenty. "Tell me where you get it from," he said, "and there'll be another ten in it for you."

"Another twenty," the boy said immediately.

"That's a lot of money," Gunther said. The boy nodded, his eyes still drawn to the cash. Gunther let him have the first note and waited.

The boy darted glances to either side of the street. "Seven Dials, mister," he whispered. His hand was extended for the rest of the money. "The Bricklayer's Arms. Ask for Doyle, the Irishman. And for God's sake, man, don't mention me. It's more than my job's worth."

Gunther gave him the other twenty and the boy ran off. At the end of the street, he paused and turned back. He stuck two fingers up at Gunther. "Nazi go home!" he shouted. Then he was gone.

Gunther resumed his walk. My men were watching him, of course. We had not been able to locate the dwarf. He usually resided at a house in Mayfair, near the Swiss ambassador's residency. The dwarf was as good as untouchable, but Gunther didn't know that. That suited me fine.

He walked with the same determined gait of a city dweller. Though he did not know his way, he did not appear lost. He did not stop to look at the sights. He made enquiries politely but with a certain force; and the people of London still, when they heard a German voice, were trained to reply helpfully and quickly.

Seven Dials was only a short walk away. It was a maze of narrow, twisting alleyways between Covent Garden and Soho, a cesspit of racial degradation, or so according to my superior, *SS-Obergruppenführer* Oswald Pohl. An efficient administrator, he was the overseer of the camps erected to deal with the Jewish question during the war. A falling out with his patron, Himmler, after the war, however (the nature of which I never quite knew) saw him exiled to Britain to supervise the local Gestapo, after the former bureau chief *SS-Brigadeführer* Franz Six had an unfortunate and fatal encounter with a bullet. Six was leading an *Einsatzgruppe* on a hunt for missing Jews in Manchester at the time.

Pohl, my current superior, took over the job with his customary efficiency but little enthusiasm. He was a keen lover of the arts and found England stifling. I also happened to know he'd been a fan of Ulla Blau.

Standing at the Seven Dials, Gunther was faced with roads leading in every direction away from him. It was as though he stood in the center of a spider bite, and the infection spread outward in wavy paths. Rundown drinking establishments faced him from each point of the compass. He saw the Bricklayer's Arms, and two women fighting loudly over a bottle of gin at the shabby entrance. He stepped around them and entered the pub. Already he was growing sick of the sight and the smell of British pubs.

Inside it was dark, dim, and smelled of the sewers. Gunther lit a cigarette to combat the smell. He looked about him and hostile or indifferent faces stared back at him. He went to the bar and leaned across. "I am looking for Doyle, the Irishman," he said.

"What's it to me?" the bartender said.

Gunther put money on the counter. He did not have much but, in London, Reichsmarks seemed to go a long way. At the sight of the money there was a collective in-drawing of breath.

"I'm Doyle," said a tall specimen.

"I'm Doyle," said a fat, red-haired man.

"I'll be your doll, sailor," said a bald woman with very few teeth, and leered.

Gunther waited. His stillness was born of the war. A shadow stirred by the far wall. It rose and the others faded into the background.

The man stepped close. He was a short, wiry man, in a chequered suit and a jaunty flattop hat with a red feather in the band. His knuckles were scabbed like a bareknuckle boxer's. He jabbed a finger at Gunther's chest.

"What do you want?" he said.

"Are you Doyle?"

"Depends who's asking."

"My name's Sloam. I was a friend of Ulla Blau."

Doyle retreated a step at the name. "Ulla is dead," he said. His voice was softer.

"I know."

"Heard they found her by the river," the Irishman said. "Some maniac did her in."

He took in Gunther's beat-up face. Not with suspicion, Gunther thought, but as confirmation of information he already knew.

"You say you were friends?"

"Old friends," Gunther said. Something in the Irishman's eyes made him trust the man; he couldn't say what it was. "We'd lost touch until recently."

"I liked Ulla," the Irishman said. "I don't care what they say about her."

"What do they say about her?" Gunther said; but of course, he thought he already knew.

"She poisoned those boys!" the bald woman said. Her savagery startled

Gunther, who hadn't noticed her creeping close. "The poor boys in Great Ormond. It's a hospital," she said into Gunther's bemused face. "For children. They needed medication, pain relief."

"Do you know what Heroin is?" Doyle said.

"Yes," Gunther said, surprised. "It's a medication made by Bayer."

"You can't get it here," Doyle said. "So . . . " He shrugged.

"She cut it with rat poison," the bald woman said, then spat. "Twenty-one children, dead, in agony."

"Now, Martha, you don't know that," Doyle said. Gunther felt sick.

"She was always good to you," Doyle said. "Who do you come to when you need your medication?"

"You and your filthy comrades," the woman said. "We should have stood with the Allies in the war, Doyle. We shouldn't have stayed neutral." She spat again. "Neutral," she said. "Isn't that just another word for collaborator."

Doyle slapped her. The sound, like a gunshot, filled the room. "You're getting above yourself, Martha," he said. The woman glared at him defiantly; then the fight went out of her.

"I need it, Doyle," she said, whining. "I need it."

Gunther watched. He felt sick to his stomach. He could not look away. He could not believe what the woman had said about Ulla. Doyle reached into his pocket and came back with two small pills which he tossed to the woman, like dog biscuits to a pet. She caught them eagerly. "Don't go opening your big gob of shite, now," Doyle said.

"I won't, Doyle. Honest."

"I liked Ulla, whatever they said about her," Doyle said again, sadly. He turned back to Gunther.

"Let's have a drink," he said.

5

It may have occurred to Gunther at this point that all the men he'd so far encountered belonged to countries that remained neutral during the war. The Swiss, the Luxembourgians, and the Irish were rewarded for their careful noninvolvement with the status of sovereign protectorates of the Third Reich, and enjoyed a great deal of autonomy as a consequence.

"Ulla spoke of you," Doyle said.

"She did?" Gunther said, with a mixture of pleasure and surprise.

Doyle's smile transformed his face. "She called you the one who got away."

They were sitting in the back room of the pub. A bottle of whiskey sat between them. Gunther only sipped at his glass. Doyle drank steadily; it didn't seem to hamper him in any way.

"You were foolish to come see me," Doyle said. "You are lucky to be alive."

"Would you have killed me, then?"

"People who come to the Dials asking questions don't always come out again."

Gunther shrugged. "So why spare me?" he said.

"I'd heard you were in town. Heard you were picked up by the Gestapo, too." He downed a shot and refilled the glass and grimaced. "Filthy animals," he said.

"The Gestapo is a necessary organ of the state," Gunther said, primly. He was still a good German. Doyle shot him a look of disgust. "Have you asked yourself why they let you walk?" he said. "By rights you should be floating past the Isle of Dogs around this time. Depending on the tide."

Gunther shrugged. I think he had an idea. "I want to know who killed her," he said.

"She's dead," Doyle said. "Let it go. This isn't your country, or your cause. Go back to Berlin, make movies, find yourself a nice girl."

"A nice girl? In Berlin?" Gunther said. Doyle smiled; reluctantly, it seemed.

"What did she say about me?"

"She said you were a good man, and that good men were hard to find. She was drunk when she said it, mind."

"That does sound like Ulla."

"Good old Ulla," Doyle said.

"Did you kill her?" Gunther said, softly; the question hung between them like a cloud of ash. They stared at each other across the table.

Doyle broke eye contact first. He shrugged indifferently. "I had no reason to kill her," he said. "We did business, that's all."

"Drugs."

"I don't advise you to go around asking questions," Doyle said. "Go home. Be a good German."

"But Heroin?" Gunther said.

"It is a powerful analgesic," Doyle said. "We need drugs, *Herr* Sloam. If the Reich won't provide, someone should."

"I don't believe she was involved—" Gunther began.

Doyle banged the glass on the table. "Never trust an actress," he said. "Oh, Ulla knew what she was doing. Whores, black-market medicine—other stuff, too, I heard. Nothing to do with me. She knew. She was planning her retirement. Unfortunately, someone retired her first."

He drank. The bottle was half-empty.

"It's nothing to me," he said.

Gunther said, "Where can I buy a gun?"

Everyone so far was being very helpful. It was as though London was going out of its way to be obliging to her accidental German tourist. He was as rare and unwelcome as a three pound note. So why, Gunther wondered, was he practically being given the keys to the city?

Back in the pre-war days, in '32 or so, when he was young and carefree, and National Socialism sounded, on a good day, like a bad punch line to an off-color joke, Gunther had worked on a picture called *Der Traumdetektiv* for the Jewish director Max Ophüls. Gunther's commission was to produce a surrealist piece of film noir, a sort of unreal history in which Germany, faced by her many enemies, nevertheless won the Great War. He recalled little from the finished product—which he had done quickly and for little money—but that the detective figure, whose name he could not remember, at some point entered a dusty old bookshop whose strange proprietor was played by the Hungarian actor Szőke Szakáll.

He remembered it now as he entered Blucher's, across Charing Cross Road from W. & G. Foyle and next to a florist. The shop was low-ceilinged and dark. On a rack outside, copies of the *Daily Mail* were displayed. It was Britain's sole remaining paper. Gunther picked one up and leafed through it quickly. He found it at the bottom of page five: *Mystery Woman Discovered Dead.* The article was only a few paragraphs long. The unknown woman was believed to be a dancer—the implication was clear—and likely took her own life. Gunther thought of Ulla Blau on the mortuary slab with her face shot clean off and fought a rise of bile. He replaced the newspaper on the stand and stepped carefully into the store. A bell rang as the door opened and poor yellow light fell down in drops. All about Gunther, books were piled up in haphazard piles. They were dusty and rust-spotted, many of them damaged by fire. Gunther smelled old smoke and cat piss.

"Can I help you?"

The man really did resemble the actor Szakáll a little. He was bespectacled and rotund, with the kind of hair that looked like a hairpiece but wasn't. He sat behind a desk laden with books, his hands folded over his ample stomach.

"You're Blucher?"

The man spread his arms as though to say, *Who else can I be?*

"You sell many books?"

"Books?" Blucher said. His myopic eyes looked at Gunther sadly. "Who today has need of books."

"They look like they been in a fire."

"Oh, these are all approved titles," Blucher said. "But you know how it is, people get carried away."

Gunther remembered the public book burnings in Berlin, after the Führer's rise to power. "Anything you'd recommend?"

"Have you tried *Mein Kampf*? It sells like plum cakes at a church fundraiser."

"I read it," Gunther said.

"Which part?"

"Chapters One and Two, and most of Chapter Three, I think," Gunther said, and Blucher laughed, shortly and abruptly. The laugh made him cough. He drank water, daintily, from a glass perched on his desk, then dabbed at his lips with a handkerchief.

"Yes," he said. "It is no Sebastian Bruce *Heftromane*, I'll admit as much. You are visiting London?"

"Yes."

"It is a pleasant time of year."

Gunther stared at him.

The man shrugged. "Perhaps you can visit the countryside?" he suggested. "Yorkshire, I am told, is very nice."

"You have not been?"

"I would go, but who'd mind the shop?" the man said.

"*Frau* Blucher?" Gunther suggested. Outside, he thought he heard the neighing of a horse; but it must have been in his imagination.

"Alas, I have not been blessed with a wife," Blucher said. "Not for many years. She died, you see."

"In the war?"

"Appendicitis."

"I'm sorry."

Blucher shrugged. *What can you do*, he seemed to silently suggest. The silence dragged. The books lay still, heavy with ash and ink.

"I was told you'd be coming round here," Blucher said. "Gunther Sloam. You are becoming quite notorious, in some circles."

"How do you know me?"

"London is a small place. Word spreads. You were a friend of the actress, Ulla Blau."

"You knew her?"

"Her talent spoke for her. She was magnificent in *Die Große Liebe*."

"It was her best picture," Gunther said.

Blucher shrugged again. "It was *schmaltz*, but you knew that already."

Gunther looked at him with new suspicion. The man laughed. He took off his glasses and polished them with the handkerchief. When he put them back on his small, shrewd eyes assessed Gunther. "I am not a Jew," he said. "If that is what you were thinking."

"Where are you from, *Herr* Blucher?"

"A small town in Austria. Not unlike our illustrious leader," Blucher said. "I came out here in 1947, shortly after the war. I have always admired the English writers. Who knows, some of them may even still be alive." He stretched his arms to encompass his shop. "As you can see, I prospered."

Gunther said, "I need to buy a gun."

"It is quite illegal, *Herr* Sloam."

"A man has a right to defend himself."

"Why not ask your friends at the Gestapo?"

Did anyone in London know his business? Gunther tapped his fingers on the cover of a book. The smell of burnt paper disinclined him from wanting to light a cigarette.

"Did you know her?" he said.

"Ulla?" the man's eyes misted over. "She was a beautiful woman," he said.

"Do you know who killed her?"

Blucher looked at him mildly. "I thought you did."

"That is a lie!"

Blucher sighed. He pushed back his chair with great deliberation, and stood up, panting. He pressed a hidden button, and a hidden drawer popped open in his desk. He brought out an object wrapped in cloth and unwrapped it. It was a Luger, perfectly clean. It was the sort of gun Gunther had used in the war. The sort of gun that only a day earlier took care of Ulla Blau.

"Will this do?" Blucher said.

"I want to know who killed her."

"Forget Ulla Blau," the bookseller said, with infinite sadness. "Finding her killer won't bring her back. Go home, Gunther Sloam. There is nothing for you here but death."

"You know something, I think," Gunther said. He took the gun and examined it. "I would need bullets," he said.

"Of course."

Blucher brought out a clip of ammunition from the same drawer and handed it to Gunther. "The fee is fifty Reichsmarks."

"Where did you get this gun?"

"A gun," Blucher said, sadly. "Are we short of guns, *Herr* Sloam? Of those we have an overabundance. It is not guns but medicines we need. But how do you heal a broken soul?"

Gunther loaded the gun. He gave the bookseller the money. The man made it disappear.

"I'll tell you a joke," Blucher said. "One day Hitler visited a lunatic asylum. When he came in, all the patients raised the arms and cried, '*Heil* Hitler!' Suddenly, Hitler saw one man whose arm wasn't raised. 'What is the meaning of this? Why don't you salute like the rest?' he demanded. The man said: 'My Führer, I'm an orderly, not a madman!' "

He gave Gunther an expectant look, then shrugged in resignation.

"Where did Ulla get her drugs?" Gunther said.

"Who knows," Blucher said. "I try not to ask questions which might get me killed. You'd do well to do the same."

"What do you wish to tell me, *Herr* Blucher?" Gunther said. He sensed that underneath the bookseller's placid exterior there was a current of rage.

"Did you love her?" Blucher said. Gunther looked away. He was embarrassed by the naked look in the man's eyes. Blucher was *hurting*.

"Once. Yes."

"She was radiant. So alive. She understood that a man cannot live by violence alone. There must be joy. There must be light, and music. Without her, London will be unbearable."

"Tell me what you know," Gunther said. He felt a pulse of excitement. "Tell me. Was it the dwarf?"

"The dwarf!"

The bookseller made his way ponderously around the desk. "I should not be talking with you," he said. "You are putting us both in danger." He looked like he was trying to reach a difficult decision. "Wait here," he said, at last. He waddled away towards a small door. "I'll make us a cup of coffee."

Gunther stood, waiting. He tucked the gun into the small of his back, under his shirt. He browsed the shelves. Hitler's *Mein Sieg*, the book he wrote after the victory. Books on natural history, in English, with hand-painted plates depicting vibrantly colored birds. It occurred to Gunther that he had not heard birdsong since he arrived.

The silence grew oppressive. The dust tickled his nostrils and made him want to sneeze. The books stared at him in mute accusation. *It wasn't me*, he wanted to say. *I was just following orders.* The seconds lengthened.

"*Herr* Blucher?"

There was no reply. Gunther let the moment lapse. He fingered the spine of an ancient volume on moths. It was loused with worm tracks. The dust tickled his throat. The gun felt heavy in the small of his back. He went to the door and knocked, softly.

"*Herr* Blucher?"

Still there was no reply and Gunther, with a sense of mounting dread, pushed the door open. He was afraid of what he would find.

Beyond, there was nothing but a small kitchenette. Gunther heaved a sigh of relief. Blucher was sitting in a folding chair by the sink. A kettle began to shriek on the open-top stove. Blucher was smiling faintly. His hands were folded quite naturalistically in his lap. He evidently fell asleep, and slept so soundly, even the mounting cry of the kettle would not wake him.

"Wake up, Blucher," Gunther said. "Blucher, wake up."

Later, in my office, he could not explain why he acted the way he did. Why he paced that small kitchenette, entreating Blucher to wake up, Blucher to stand, Blucher to speak to him. When all the while, of course, he was perfectly aware of the smell of gunpowder, of the smell of blood, as familiar and as intimate as a comrade on the Eastern Front; and of the small, neat hole drilled in Blucher's forehead. He was aware of all that, and yet as in a dream he spoke to Blucher; he told him of Ulla, of time spent in a high attic room, of stolen kisses in Unter den Linden, of the whistle of a train taking soldiers to battle. That whistle, long ago, seemed to him now to intertwine with the hissing kettle. It brought with it instantaneous memories long kept at bay: of Ulla's sweat-slicked body in the moonlight, of the feral call of air-raid sirens, of the march of booted feet, of jubilant voices crying out "The Horst Wessel Song." He thought of the Führer's voice on the wireless, of crumpled bedsheets and her voice, thick with sleep, saying, "Please, don't go."

It was those last words that he carried with him on the way to the east; those words that kept him company in amidst the snow and the blood. "Please, don't go." But when he returned, a different man under a different sky, she was long gone. Sometimes, under the blanket of the cold Russian night, he looked up at the stars and imagined he could see her.

At last, Gunther removed the kettle from the stove. He turned off the gas. He took one last look at Blucher's corpse. A second door, he saw, led out of the kitchenette. He pushed it open and stepped outside, into an alleyway running at the back of the bookshop. He looked left and right but saw no one, and he slipped away. My men, who were only watching the front of the shop, lost him then.

6

When Sloam failed to reappear, my men finally entered Blucher's. They found the proprietor slumped in his chair with the bullet hole between his eyes, and Gunther gone. Then they called me with the bad news.

I did not mind Gunther on the loose. After all, I had set him free myself. I had telephoned Blucher earlier that morning, and advised him that Sloam may well pay him a visit later in the day. I also told Blucher he could sell Sloam a gun. A man with a gun, sooner or later, makes his presence felt.

What I had not expected, however, was for Blucher to be so stupid as to commit suicide by gunmen.

For a time, I considered that Gunther may be the killer. His whereabouts were unknown. He was armed, and potentially dangerous. But I had sent him to rattle a nests of wasps. That the wasps stung back, I supposed, was only to be expected.

Blucher must have been killed to keep him quiet. That fact stared me in the face, and the fact that the lying scum Austrian piece of shit had held out on me.

If there was one thing you could say about Hanns Blucher, it was that the man was a professional liar. His story for Gunther was good. Parts of it were even—almost—true. He was born Erich Dittman, in Gratz, Austria, the son of a shoemaker and a seamstress, the middle child of five. His criminal career began early. He was a good little pickpocket, graduated to burglary and robbery by the age of sixteen, and after a time in prison settled on the more tranquil profession of fencing stolen goods. When war came, he escaped to France; then, when France fell, to Luxembourg. By then he had changed his identity twice. When the war ended, Hermann Blucher was a well-established rare-books dealer in Luxembourg City. He had avoided the deportations and the camps, and he thought his papers were good.

They were; almost.

How he got out of Luxembourg alive I never quite learned. He reappeared in London and was ensconced in his premises on the Charing Cross Road as though he'd always been there. In truth, he had taken the lease on an empty shop at No. 84, formerly owned by a Jew named Marks.

He called himself Blucher. He was as enmeshed in criminal enterprise as ever. And he was still a Jew.

When I first marched into his shop and he saw me, he knew it was over. He did that little shrug he always did. By rights I should have had him tortured and disposed of. But he was more useful to me alive.

Only now he was dead, like Blau.

Someone was tying up loose ends.

Gunther walked through the city that day haunted by the shadow of deaths. Usually the ghosts did not bother him overmuch; he had made his peace with the atrocities of war. What he had done, he had only done to survive. In a post-war screenplay, never produced (*Das große Übel*, c. 1948), the love interest dies in the arms of the hero, a veteran of Normandy on a quest to avenge the death of his sister at the hands of blackmarket speculators. As she lies dying, she kisses him, one last time, with lips stained red with blood, and tells him he was not a bad man for the things he did. He was just an imperfect man in an imperfect world, trying to do the right thing.

She dies. The hero embraces her. Her blood soaks into his shirt. The hero walks away, into the shadows.

When he sent the script in to Tobis, he was told quite categorically not to waste his time. Demand was for domestic comedies, lighthearted affairs, adventure. "Write another Western," Rolf Hansen told him over coffee, before he got up and left him with the check. "There's always demand for that sort of thing. Oh, and Gunther?"

"Yes?"

"There is no black market in Germany. You should know better by now. *Heil* Hitler."

No, Gunther thought, walking through city streets slick with defeat, bounded by empty buildings like skulls, where the dead whispered through the gaping eye sockets of broken windows. There was no crime in this new Reich, no prostitution unless one counted that of the soul, no murder but that carried out by the state.

It was a land of hard-working, virtuous, and prosperous people. A dream come true.

Already they were bringing civilization even to Britain. Viennese pastries and public concerts of Wagner and Bruckner, *Reinheitsgebot* beer, shining gymnasiums where the soldiers of tomorrow could be taught, new factories in the north where the goods needed for the empire could be cheaply and efficiently manufactured. And no more Jews, but for a few desperate survivors like Blucher, living out their last days like rats in the shadows.

He was not usually this bleak, you understand. All of this just brought back the bad memories. When we got him later he was done, he said.

"It's just something about this godforsaken island," he told me. "The cold and the damp and the bloody futility of it all, Everly. It starts to seep into your soul after a while."

"I'm afraid we did not present London's best side to you on your visit," I said, and he snorted.

"Oh, I but think you did," he said. "Don't worry, I won't be coming back."

Like I said, it wasn't much of a time for tourism.

Gunther retraced his steps. He tried to ensure he wasn't being followed. He wrapped himself tight in his good cashmere coat. He went back to the Lyric. A different bartender tended bar. The same indistinguishable faces drank in the corners. No one spoke German or, at any rate, no one was answering his questions.

He did not see the Luxembourgian, Klaus Pirelli, and he left.

Then he went back to the start. The house on Dean Street stood with its door closed and red lights burning behind the windows. He banged on the door but no one was answering and he did not see the old woman, Mrs. White. There was a new watcher across the street: not one of mine. He sidled up to Gunther as Gunther turned to leave. It was dark by then.

"You are looking for a girl?"

"I am looking," Gunther said. "For a dwarf."

The other man shrugged. "I see it is true what they say about you Germans. You have peculiar tastes. But each to their own, as my old nan always said."

Gunther stared at him. He had the urge to do violence. The man was too thin, his teeth too crooked, his coat too shabby, his hair too coarse. Gunther took out the gun and grabbed the man hard by the lapels and shoved him against the wall and put the gun in his face. The man looked at him placidly.

"Do you know a man called Klaus Pirelli?"

"What's it you, friend?" the man said.

"I could shoot you right now."

"You could indeed, Fritz."

Gunther slapped him across the face with the gun, hard. The man's head shot back and slammed against the wall. He crumpled to the ground. Gunther put the gun to his forehead. "Tell me where I can find him."

The man moved his jaw, grimaced, and spat out blood. "Everyone's tough with a gun in their hand," he said. "Why don't you try asking nicely, or buying me a drink."

"I don't understand you English," Gunther said, frustrated. He pulled away from the man. He felt ashamed. The man got up slowly to his feet. Gunther took out cigarettes and offered one to the man, who took it. Gunther lit them up.

The man took a deep drag on his cigarette and exhaled a stream of smoke. "If you're not looking for a girl," he said, reasonably, "why are you hanging about outside a whorehouse?"

"I came here for a girl," Gunther said shortly. "She died."

"I'm sorry."

"I almost believe you," Gunther said, and the man laughed.

"I can take you somewhere where there are other girls. It's best to let go of the dead, friend, or soon you become one yourself."

"You're a philosopher as well as a pimp?"

"I'm neither, friend. Just a man doing what he has to do to survive."

"Do you know where I can find this man, Pirelli?"

The man considered. "I can't tell you where he is," he said at last, "but I can tell you where he'd be."

"Where is that?"

"Somewhere where there is drink, and music, and girls."

"And you know all these places, I assume?"

"What can I say, I have a thirst for knowledge."

Gunther laughed. He stuck his hand out. "Gunther Sloam," he said.

The other man looked at the offered hand. Finally he took it. "You can call me Janson."

"One name's as good as the next," Gunther said amicably.

7

There began a night in which perception began to fracture like a mirror for Gunther. The city was a nightmarish maze of dark streets in which faceless gunmen haunted every corner. He thought about dead girls and dead Jews, and wondered who would be the next to die.

They started at the Albert, a cavernous pub where ancient families feuded with each other over pints of watery beer; continued to the Admiral's Arms, where everyone looked like a vampire; and settled for a time at the Dog and Duck over glasses of potent, home-made sherry.

"When the occupation is completed there I will go to America," Janson said. "I have a great admiration for the Americans, for all that they lost their war."

"What will you do?" Gunther said.

"I would become a writer for their pulps."

"It's a living," Gunther allowed. "Not a very profitable one, though."

"I write quickly and I have what it requires most," Janson said.

"And what's that?" Gunther said.

"Despair."

Gunther shook his head and swallowed his drink. Visions of Ulla Blau's ruined face kept rising in his mind.

"Were you in the war?" he said.

"Does it matter?"

"No," Gunther said, tiredly. "I suppose it doesn't."

They rose from their seats and stepped out into the night. It had truly fallen by then, and here and there, solitary gas lamps began to wink into being, casting murky pools of yellow light around them. Janson palmed a pill and dry-swallowed. "You want some?" he said.

Gunther said, "Sure."

During the war they had functioned as little more than animated corpses: kept alive by minimal food rations and handfuls of drugs. Gunther's memories of the march on Moscow were fragmentary. They killed for the sake of killing, killed because it was the only thing left for them to do. It wasn't glory or the Führer that kept them on that march. It was the little pills manufactured by Bayer's; that, and simple, total desperation.

The veneer of humanity was stripped off Gunther during the long march, during the slaughter and the occupation. He had never hated Jews, had no feelings at all for the Russians, but he was just one man; and when it came down to it, he wanted to survive.

In this world, I think, you do what you must to live: another minute, another hour, another day.

Sometime during that long evening they stumbled into the Berlin. It is a club situated on the Embankment, next to the gardens—or what used to be gardens before the war—and facing the South Bank. Gunther stopped outside. The Ferris wheel rotated slowly on the opposite side of the river, softly illuminated against the night sky. Gunther was drunk. His body was on fire from the methamphetamine. The Thames snaked dark and in its depths he saw Ulla's face rising up to him, laughing bubbles. He tottered.

Janson said something to the doormen and they laughed.

Money changed hands. The money was Gunther's. They went inside. It was a large room with a stage at one end. Girls danced on the stage, naked but for the fans they held. They moved about the stage in complicated patterns. A piano played, softly. Gunther heard conversation, laughter, the clink of glasses. He saw SS men in uniform sitting at one table, each officer with a girl in his lap. Important locals in last year's suits swanned about. They had bad skin and bad teeth and great big booming laughs. Gunther ordered a drink and thought he'd had enough of this town.

It was then that he saw him.

The Luxembourgian stepped out of the door marked *Bathroom*, his hands still wet. He dried them on his trousers. He wore a pin stripe suit and a pink shirt and a muted tie. His eyes darted nervously from side to side but he put on a smile as charming and shiny as a false diamond bracelet. Then he, too, saw Gunther.

The smile hovered but stayed in place. Gunther got up. He did not dare pull out the gun. Not with the officers present. The Luxembourgian's smile grew more assured. He passed through the throng of people like an eel until he came to Gunther.

"Sit down."

"I've been looking for you," Gunther said, and he matched the man's smile with his own, cold and hard.

"I said sit *down!*"

Gunther looked down. Held in the Luxembourgian's manicured fingers was a small Röhm .22 Derringer gun.

Gunther sat down. Pirelli sat on a stool opposite. He trained the gun on Gunther, holding it between his legs. "Don't bloody move, man."

"I wasn't going anywhere."

The bartender arrived. She was a young girl bare to the waist but for dark kohl painted over her nipples. She brought the Luxembourgian a drink without being asked. He kept one hand on the gun and with the other downed his scotch and grimaced. "They know me here, you see."

"You're a difficult man to find."

"Hardly!" The man's eyes kept shifting. Gunther was primed, every muscle in his body singing alertly. "Listen, if this is about the other night—"

"What do you *think* it's about?"

"You didn't have to kill Blucher!"

It came out almost as a shout. A couple of heads turned. Then the girls on the stage began to gyrate erotically and what attention they'd been given was gone. It was just the two of them on the bar at the Berlin. At this point, too, one of my men spotted Gunther. He did not approach but quietly went for a phone.

"I didn't kill him," Gunther said, startled.

"Didn't you? You come to town, start poking about, and two days later both Ulla and Erich are dead?"

"Who's Erich?"

"Blucher." Pirelli was sweating, Gunther saw. And he realised Pirelli, too, must be on Pervitin. He was wired worse than an S-mine. "That was his real name."

"How did you know him?"

Pirelli was so jumpy, Gunther was worried he'd press the trigger by accident. But the man seemed almost eager to talk.

"In Luxembourg. I helped him when his trouble got bad. Helped him get out and establish himself here." He sneered at Gunther. "What are you going to do, rat on me to your pals in the Gestapo? They can't touch me. I have connections. I'm a foreign national."

"You could try telling that to the fishes," Gunther said, with a touch of cruelty. "When they dump you in the Thames."

"They wouldn't dare!" A flash of anger or defiance in his eyes. "How do I know you didn't kill Erich?"

"Why did you set me up? You spiked my drink at that godawful pub."

"The Lyric's decent," Pirelli said; almost offended.

"Why did you do it!" Gunther said.

"Listen, friend, I'm the one holding the gun," Pirelli said.

"Blucher knew something. He was going to tell me. Then someone shot him."

"Someone, someone!" But he could see it Pirelli's eyes. The man was afraid of something. He kept looking everywhere but at Gunther.

"Who are you working for?" Gunther threw at him.

"I work for myself."

"A man like you? You're just the hired help."

Gunther thought to needle the man. But Pirelli's mouth curved in a mocking smile. At that moment one of the SS officer approached them, accompanied by a woman draped on his arm.

"*Signore* Pirelli!"

Gunther reached between them and grabbed Pirelli's hand in a painful grip, twisting it. He yanked the gun from the Luxembourgian's hand, hearing a bone break. Pirelli cried in pain.

"You are not happy to see us?"

Pirelli put on a pained smile. "My apologies, *Sturmbannführer*," he said, through gritted teeth. "I seem to have hurt my hand."

The SS officer was round and jolly. His companion was buxom and blonde.

"Let me look at that," he said, grabbing for Pirelli's hand. Pirelli screamed. The *Sturmbannführer* laughed jovially and called the bartender for ice. "You'll be fine in no time," he said. He turned to Gunther and studied him, and under the jovial exterior Gunther saw cold, dark eyes.

"Who is your friend?"

"Gunther Sloam, *Sturmbannführer*," Gunther said stiffly.

"Sloam, Sloam," the SS man said. His companion leaned over his shoulder and eyed Gunther with interest. "Where did you serve?"

"258th Infantry Division, sir."

"The heroes of Moscow!" the *Sturmbannführer* declared delightedly. "Why do I know your name, Sloam?"

"I'm sure I can't say, sir."

"A drink for my friend here," the SS man called. "A true hero of the Reich. So good to hear civilized German in this godforsaken place. How is Berlin?"

"Still there, last I checked."

"Magnificent!" The man laughed. His belly shook. His eyes remained cold and suspicious. "You two appear to be having a bit of an argument."

"It's nothing, sir. A minor disagreement."

"Good, good. We do not like trouble here in London, Sloam. This is a peaceful place. The natives are most obliging." He squeezed his companion's bottom and she squealed delightedly. Gunther averted his gaze. The girl's eyes were colder even than the *Sturmbannführer*'s.

"So I see, sir."

"Well, Pirelli, about that thing we discussed—"

"I will have the shipment to you by tomorrow," the Luxembourgian said. He was nursing a pack of ice on his broken hand and scowling.

"First thing, Pirelli. Sloam—" he nodded, cordially, and waddled off with the girl on his arm.

"Drugs?" Gunther said.

"Nudie pictures," Pirelli said. "The *Sturmbannführer* is a connoisseur."

"So I see."

"Give me back my gun."

"Why don't we take a walk?"

"No!"

"What is it, Pirelli? I'm not going to kill you."

"Listen to me, Sloam. It's safer in here. I don't want to die like the others."

"Who killed them?"

Unexpectedly, Pirelli laughed. "No one," he said. His whole body shook.

"Get up. We're going outside."

"You won't dare shoot me here."

"Only one way to find out. Move."

Pirelli got up. "You're a fool," he said.

"Why was Ulla killed?" Gunther said. They walked to the doors. It was cooler outside, quieter. There were few cars on the street. In the distance he could hear the *clop-clop-clop* of a horse and carriage. The lights of the Ferris wheel spun.

"She was tight with the SS," Pirelli said. "She supplied this place with half the whores. And then the other half too. They turned a blind eye to the drugs. First she bought from the soldiers her girls were sleeping with. Then, when that dried out, she put the pressure on me."

"How did she do that?"

Pirelli shrugged. "Do you have a cigarette?"

Gunther kept one hand in his pocket, where he held Pirelli's gun. He offered him the cigarette case with the other. The Luxembourgian lit up and coughed. "Filthy stuff," he said.

"What did she have on you?"

"She knew about Erich. We had our own racket going before she came along. Everyone in this town has a racket. But she wanted it all."

"You don't sound as if you liked her much."

"We did business. Business was good."

"You were bringing the drugs in from Luxembourg? Shipping them inside what, old books?"

Pirelli smiled tiredly. "You're not as stupid as you look."

"You and Blucher were close?"

"What the hell do you mean?"

Gunther nodded, the pieces falling into place at last. Perhaps he'd been wrong about Ulla, he thought. Perhaps he'd been wrong all along. People changed; and she'd always had that hard, selfish core inside her, even in Berlin, during the war. He didn't hold it against her. She was just another survivor in the end, and you can only survive for so long.

"Blucher didn't know, did he?" Gunther said. "How you felt about him."

"He loved that bitch!"

He opened his arms. His mouth opened, to speak, perhaps even to smile. There was a soft pop, like a bottle of champagne was opened. Pirelli fell on Gunther, his arms enfolding him in a hug. Gunther held him. When he lowered him, gently, to the ground, Pirelli's mouth was a vomit of blood and he was no longer breathing.

• • •

8

They were down near the river by then. The shot could have come from anywhere. The Thames ran softly. The mud swallowed sound. Overhead clouds shaped portents of rain.

Gunther swore. Pirelli's cigarette was on the ground, still burning. Gunther picked it up and put it to his mouth and took a drag. He knelt beside the corpse and searched through Pirelli's pockets. He found a bottle of Pervitin and dry-swallowed a handful. The hit was almost immediate. He stood up straighter, all his senses alert. Apart from the pills he found three hundred Reichsmarks, which he pocketed; the photo of an old woman in an old-fashioned dress with her arm around a tall, thin boy; and a comb. The boy in the photo could have been Pirelli. The comb was fine-toothed and made of ivory. Gunther stuffed both back into Pirelli's pockets and added rocks—as many as he could find. Then he rolled up his sleeves and dragged the corpse by its feet into the water.

When the last of Pirelli's head disappeared at last into the Thames, Gunther walked away. Something kept nagging away at him. Pirelli's use of the past tense, he realised. As though their little operation here in London had already come to its end.

Had it been wound down, even before Gunther arrived? Or was Ulla's death the catalyst? And why did the Luxembourgian spike his drink at the Lyric?

He needed to find the dwarf, he thought. The last piece of the puzzle.

Instead he found himself a girl.

"She reminded me of Ulla, that was all," he told me later, in my office. "She was German, can you believe that? She was sending money back to her family in Munich. She said she was an actress, only times are hard."

"They are all actresses, Sloam," I said. "And if you can believe that you can believe anything."

"She was a good girl!" He turned on me. He was a romantic to the core, even if he couldn't admit it, not even to himself. "She was just doing what she could to make a life."

"She'll be used up within a year," I told him. "And dead in two."

I was being harsh on him; I wanted to provoke him.

He only shook his head tiredly. Like I said, by then the drugs had worn off and he was dead on his feet; he was done. "She was a good trooper," he insisted.

"You can't fight a war on your back."

"What is it about you, Everly? Did someone you loved one day suddenly abandon you?"

"You could say that, Sloam. But then you could say a lot of things. What was her name?"

"Anna," he said.

"They're all called Anna."

"What do you want from me, Everly? Shoot me and be done with it."

"I still might," I said. "Now answer my damn questions."

Gunther met the girl walking back from the river. For a moment, the light framed her face and he thought it was Ulla, and his breath caught in his throat. But her nose was different and her face worn in a way Ulla's never was, though this girl was young.

("They're all young, at the Berlin."

"You sound quite the expert, Everly. Are you sure you weren't there?"

"Just keep talking, Sloam.")

He saw that she was crying. She hurried her steps when she saw Gunther. "*Herr* Pirelli—have you seen him?"

"*Herr* Pirelli has gone for a swim."

She looked up at him with dark eyes. Her makeup was smudged. "I don't understand."

"I'm sorry," Gunther said. "I was only making a joke. He had to leave. Urgent business elsewhere, he said. You look distraught."

"It's nothing, really." She tried to smile, failed.

"Can I buy you a drink?"

"That's awfully kind," the girl said. "Only I need something a little stronger first, you understand? Just to take the edge off things."

Gunther stuck his hand in his pocket, came back with a pill. The girl took it without a word. This time, she managed a smile.

("They know how to smile, Sloam, believe me. They all smile like Ulla Blau in *Die Große Liebe*."

"You sound bitter, Everly."

"You're an incurable romantic, Sloam."

"You keep saying that. But it's just basic decency."

"Only you slept with her."

"It wasn't like that. It wasn't like that at all.")

Only maybe it was, a little bit. My men were only now getting there. The girl put the Pervitin pill between her teeth. She leaned into Gunther. He kissed her, hungrily. The pill dissolved between them. Her lips were hot and her eyes fevered. He imagined himself kissing Ulla. The girl threw her head back and laughed. "Let's go!"

She led him at a run and he followed like a fool. My men pursued but then lost them. It took us a while to realize what had happened to Pirelli. It wasn't that Gunther hadn't been observed. It was just that people don't willingly talk to the Gestapo.

She took him up the hill, along St. Martin's Lane where the theatres still displayed playbills from the last decade. She had a room on the third story of a boarding house in Denmark Street. There was a wilted rose in a vase on the table—"From an admirer," she said—and the bed was neatly made. Her only books were *Mein Kampf* and a copy of the Bible. Her only other reading materials were several out-of-date issues of *Deutsches Kinomagazin*, the latest of which had a radiant Leni Riefenstahl on the cover, posed with a camera on a tripod against a gloriously empty African savannah.

"Can I offer you a drink?"

Gunther sat on the edge of the bed. The girl slipped off her shoes and her coat. Underneath it she was wearing nothing but lingerie. She moved about quite unconcerned.

"Sure."

"Scotch?"

"If you have it."

The girl laughed. "You're such a gentleman," she said. Her eyes went over his body but dawdled on his pocket; where the pills were. "I keep drinks here for, you know."

"Admirers."

"Sure." She opened a cabinet and brought out a bottle and poured him a glass and one for herself too. They clinked glasses. Gunther's body was on fire and his mind was elsewhere. He kept thinking she was Ulla, and he knew that he wanted her.

There had been other girls, other rooms like these, hurried romances carried on in the dark. He'd never really let himself feel, after the war. Love was just another kind of transaction, another kind of scam.

He left the drink unfinished. He reached for her and she came willingly. Touching her lips was like completing a circuit. Electricity burned in him. "Ulla . . . " he said.

The girl recoiled. Her hand was on his naked chest. He did not remember when he'd taken off his clothes.

"She's dead," she said. "She was always good to me."

"You're crying," he said, wonderingly. The girl shook her head and smiled sadly through the mist.

"No," she said. "I'm not."

Gunther touched his eyes and realized they were wet. He could not remember when he had last cried. He wondered if he should feel good for it. He felt nothing.

The girl pushed him on the bed. He lay on his back. The ceiling was cracked, the paint peeling. The girl climbed on top of him.

"Ulla . . . " he said.

"Shh," the girl said. "I'll be your Ulla."

Gunther closed his eyes. The girl rocked above him. Gunther wondered if he'd ever loved Ulla, or if he was merely in love with the idea of being in love. After a while, it didn't matter, nothing much did, only the slow build and the urgency, the creaking of the mattress springs, the girl's soft cries.

He half-awoke in the night to find the girl smoking a cigarette by the window. He saw her profile in silhouette. She reclined, nude, her long legs drawn up to her chest. There was a long cigarette holder between her lips. He stood up, naked also. The girl didn't turn her head. He went to the sink and filled a glass with lukewarm water, and downed it. He turned to the girl. From this angle he could see her face.

"She made us watch her in this old movie," the girl said. "Over and over again, to teach us how to walk and how to talk."

"*Die Große Liebe*?"

The girl looked at him vaguely. "What's that?" she said.

"An old movie. It was very successful."

"This was *Der blaue Mond*. It was alright. She played a good-time girl in trouble with the law. There's a detective always chasing her. It was silly."

"I never saw it."

The girl shrugged. "No, well," she said. "Why would you."

"We were lovers, in Berlin."

"She had many lovers," the girl said. "I think the only one she really loved was herself."

"Why were you looking for Pirelli, earlier?"

"He's always been good to me. He's not, you know . . . "

"I know."

"He liked to pay us for our time and then just listen to us talk." She laughed. "Most men just want us to shut up and get on our backs. One of the SS men likes me to spank him. He just doesn't want to, you know. Have a conversation about it."

"And Pirelli? You looked distraught."

"It was nothing, really. One of the other girls hasn't been in to work for a couple of days. I thought maybe he'd seen her."

"Does she owe you money?"

The girl laughed. "No, silly. She's my friend."

She got up and advanced on him. The cigarette in its holder was left to smoulder by the window. "Why do you have a gun in your coat?" she said.

"In case I get into trouble," Gunther said.

"You look like the kind of man who's always in trouble."

"That's just a role I play. In real life I'm a sweetheart."

She melted into his arms. She was good at that sort of thing. "Shut up and kiss me," she whispered.

So he did.

When they parted for air some of the fire inside him had calmed. The girl reached for his coat draped on the chair and reached into the pocket and took out the pills. "Do you mind?" she said. He shook his head, mutely.

He wondered if the line she'd used was from Ulla's film, that the girl had memorised. He thought it was the sort of thing he would have written himself, a throwaway line in a B-movie script on a long afternoon.

The girl popped a pill.

Gunther decided it didn't really matter. He took her in his arms and lifted her and carried her to the bed and she was laughing.

She lay there looking up at him. "I'll be your Ulla," she whispered.

"No," he said. "This time, just be yourself."

The night faded into torn strips of time. For a while, he slept.

When he woke up the girl was in the corner putting her stockings on in a businesslike fashion, and sitting in the chair facing Gunther was a man with a gun in his hand.

9

"I thought I was gone for sure," Gunther said. He looked at me a little sadly, I thought. "But of course if they'd wanted me dead, I'd have been dead before I ever woke up."

"And the girl?"

"She got dressed and left. It wasn't her fault," he said; almost pleading. "What could she do?"

"Did she take your money?"

He smiled. "And the pills."

"You're a sap, Gunther."

"Yes," he said. "That's what people keep telling me."

There were two of them. One on the chair, facing Gunther, and the other at the door. Both had guns.

The girl got dressed. "Are you going to hurt him?" she said. She didn't look at Gunther once.

"What's it to you, girl?"

"It's nothing," she said. "It's nothing to me."

"Then get lost, would you?" the gunman on the door said. The girl gave him a stare, but that's all it was. She got lost.

"Get dressed," the man on the chair said. Gunther sat up in bed. "I can't," he said. "I'm shy in front of strangers."

"He thinks he's clever," the gunman on the chair complained. The gunman by the door looked over, slowly. "Everyone's a comedian these days," he said.

"He's a regular Karl Valentin," the other gunman said. "Come on, Sloam. Get dressed. You don't want to be late."

"He'd be late for his own funeral," the gunman by the door said, and they both laughed. Gunther didn't. He thought it was a cheap line. He got up and got dressed and he followed them outside.

A long black Mercedes was parked in the road. Gunther got in at the back. The gunmen sat on either side of him. A third man was driving.

"Where are we going?"

"To church."

He let it go. He didn't have a choice. They drove through the dark city streets. Few cars passed them, going the other way. London after the war wasn't a place where people dawdled after dark. It was warm inside the car. The men on either side of him smelled of wet wool and incense. It was a peculiarly English smell. Outside the city projected like the flickering images of a black and white film. Bomb damage everywhere. He'd seen newsreels of the Luftwaffe bombing over the city, waves of bombers flying over Big Ben and St Paul's Cathedral, over the Thames. It was not uncommon for children to play in the ruins of a house and find an unexploded ordnance. People died of the bombs even now.

He thought about Hitler announcing the successful invasion of England. The ships at Dover and the submarine that made it up the Thames and blew up the House of Commons. It'd taken them six months to hunt down Churchill. He'd been hiding in a bunker all that time.

Swastikas waving over Buckingham Palace. No one knew where the royal family was. Or knew but wasn't saying. So many things you couldn't say anymore. His mind wandered.

How does every German joke start? he thought.

By looking over your shoulder.

In time, London would be rebuilt and there'd be no sign left of the war.

"Wake up," someone said. He was prodded awake. His heart was beating too fast and there was an acrid taste in his mouth. Beyond the car's headlights he saw the lit front of a small church.

"Oh," he said. "I thought you were kidding."

"Just move it, will you? Boss wants to see you."

Gunther got out of the car obligingly. There was a large electric red cross above the door. Its light spilled over the driveway and ran down the walls. It made everything look covered in blood. Gunther went inside the church. The two gunmen remained outside. The door shut behind Gunther.

There was an altar straight ahead. Stained-glass windows showed nativity scenes. The pews had been pushed aside and there were half-shut crates and boxes everywhere.

"Mr. Sloam. Thank you for coming. I understand you have been looking for me."

Gunther started. For a moment he couldn't locate the voice. Then a diminutive shadow detached itself from the chancel and approached him with the tread of soft feet. "Welcome to the mission, Mr. Sloam. We do God's work here."

Jurgen, the dwarf, wore horn-rimmed glasses and a crisp white shirt. The rolled-up sleeves showed muscled arms. His hair was reddish-brown and fine.

"With guns?" Gunther said.

Jurgen laughed softly. "These are dangerous times. One must take precautions."

"How did you find me?"

Jurgen shrugged. "It wasn't hard," he said. "I have the ear of the poor, the desperate and the dispossessed. I understand Pirelli is dead."

"Pirelli, Blucher, Ulla Blau," Gunther said. He ticked them off one by one on his fingers. He watched Jurgen but Jurgen's face bore nothing but a polite expression.

"Though I walk through the valley of the shadow of death, I shall fear no evil," Jurgen said.

"Did you kill them?" Gunther said.

"Why would I do that, Mr. Sloam?"

"To protect your little racket," Gunther said. "I knew it couldn't be Ulla behind it all. Running drugs, suborning women. Those children who died in the hospital. It was all your doing, wasn't it. Wasn't it!"

He was shouting. Jurgen flinched. "Mr. Sloam," he said. "Please. This is unseemly."

"Just tell me," Gunther whispered. The fight wasn't in him anymore. "Tell me the truth."

Jurgen rubbed his eyes. "I came to London to help these people. The poor, the needy. The war had destroyed their homes along with their futures. We provide medical supplies, food, bibles." He shrugged. "The Führer won't challenge the church. This much we still have."

"You're a banker."

"I'm wealthy. My family is rich."

"Did you kill them? Did you kill Ulla?"

"You want me to confess?" Jurgen looked amused. "We are in church, after all."

"I don't know what I want," Gunther said.

"I believe in God, Mr. Sloam. I believe that the sins of the present age are but the prelude to the flood that is to come. This is Sodom and Gomorrah. The End of Days. Evil has won, Mr. Sloam. But evil cannot rule the world forever."

"My God," Gunther said. "You're an agitator. A . . . a subversive."

"Mr. Sloam, really," Jurgen said. "Don't be so melodramatic."

"How are you still allowed to operate? Why is the Gestapo not knocking on your door as we speak?"

"Someone has to fund this occupation," Jurgen said complacently. "Someone has to rebuild. Even Nazis need money, Mr. Sloam. I think you have the wrong impression of me. I did not kill Ulla. God knows I had reason to. You paint me so blackly, but Ulla Blau was exactly what you deny she was. She was a whoremonger and a poisoner. And a blackmailer, too, and many other things besides. I do not hold it against her. She did what she thought she must do. She had all the morals of an actress and all their brittle ruthlessness. I do not judge, Mr. Sloam. Only God does."

"What other things?" Gunther said; whispered.

Jurgen shrugged. "Lives," he said. "She sold lives."

"I don't understand."

"Don't you? Then perhaps it is better that way."

"Who did she blackmail?" Then realization dawned. "You?"

"I have certain proclivities," Jurgen said. "I am not proud of them, but I have my needs. And Ulla had a knack for finding these things out."

"So you funded her?" Gunther said.

Jurgen shrugged again. "I paid her some money," he allowed. "What she mostly wanted from me was a way of putting that money somewhere safe. She had saved almost enough, she told me. She was looking forward to retiring. She wanted to go back to Germany, somewhere far from Berlin. She dreamed of opening her own theatre. Can you believe it?" He gave a sudden, unexpected bark of a laugh. "She was never much of an actress," he said.

"That's not true."

"Oh, Sloam. I liked her, too, you know. But I never went to bed with her."

Gunther took a step toward him. Jurgen stood his ground. He smiled sardonically. "I'm sorry," he said, and he sounded almost genuine. "I don't know who killed her."

"But you're grateful," Gunther said. He loomed over the smaller man, who looked at him evenly, unafraid.

"What's one death," he said, "amongst so many?"

Footsteps sounded behind Gunther. He began to turn, only to see a dark shape rise in the air towards him. The butt of a gun connected with the back of his head. Pain flared, and he fell to his knees.

"Take him outside. Dump him somewhere with the garbage."

He tried to rise. They hit him again and, this time, he stayed down.

"I thought I was dead," he said. "Until I woke up covered in rotting cabbage with a rat nibbling on my shoe. They really did dump me in the garbage."

"Did they give you back your gun?"

"What gun?" he said. He looked at me blankly.

I sighed. "So who killed Ulla?" I said.

Gunther rubbed his eyes. "I don't know," he said. "And I don't care anymore. I've had it, Everly. I'm going home."

"You're lucky to be alive."

"Like you said, you can't just kill me—I'm a faithful citizen of the Reich."

I laughed. He looked hurt by that. "Who's going to miss you, Gunther? I have your file. You're a third-rate hack for pictures no one makes anymore. You have no wife, no friends, and not much of a future. Face it. You may as well be dead."

He shrugged. He must have heard worse. It's harder to break a man when he has nothing.

"If you're going to do it, just do it," he said.

"I would," I said, "only I like you. We do things a little differently here, in England."

I think it was true, too. He wasn't a bad guy. He just kept believing the wrong people.

"Then that's it? You're just going to let me go?"

"There's the door," I said. "There's a transport plane leaving in a couple of hours from Northolt. Why don't you do yourself a favour and be on it this time."

"I will," he said, fervently. "I'll be damned if I spend another minute in this town."

I watched him get up. He walked to the door. He hesitated with his hand on the handle. "You're a good sort, Everly," he said.

"We're a vanishing kind," I said.

10

When we picked him up he didn't have the gun on him. He must have stashed it somewhere in the trash. From us he should have gone straight to the airport. He didn't.

He made his way back to Dean Street. Back to the start. A car was parked in the street with the trunk open and packed suitcases on the ground. The old woman straightened when she saw him and said, dismissively, "Oh, it's you."

"Mrs. White. Going someplace?"

"The cold's no good for my bones," she said in her atrocious German. "I thought perhaps somewhere warm for the winter."

"Can I help you with your luggage?"

"I'd rather you didn't."

Gunther took his gun out and pointed it at her.

She squinted. "What's that for, then?" she said.

"Could you step away from the car?"

"You're not going to shoot me, Gunther."

He stared at her; but the gun never wavered. She straightened up, slowly. When she next spoke she seemed to shed forty years and her accent. "You came. I wasn't sure you would but you did."

"Just keep your hands where I can see them, Ulla."

She smiled. It was her old familiar smile. He wondered how he didn't see it before. "People keep telling me you're not much of an actress," he said, "but by God, you are!"

"You were always too kind to me," she said. Gunther could see now under her makeup and the wig: it was her eyes she couldn't truly mask. They were large and startled and innocent, like a wounded bird's. It was her eyes which dominated the last few seconds of screen at the end of *Die Große Liebe*, as the picture slowly faded to black. How could he have ever forgotten them?

"How did you know, Gunther?"

"I didn't, not for sure. It was just something this girl said."

"My, you've wasted no time getting over me."

He ignored her. "She was crying because one of her friends was missing. One of the other girls. And I thought how much she looked like you, how much all of them did. The Gestapo man said they all smiled like you."

"Chance would be a fine thing!" she said, with a flash of anger.

"And there was no face, of course."

"No," she said. "There was no face left, was there."

"How could you do it, Ulla? All of it? Not just the girls or the drugs, I can understand that, but those dead children, too?"

"They'd have died sooner or later, Gunther. This whole stinking country is a waiting room in a hospital's terminal wing. You can't pin that on me."

"But why?"

"Why, why," she said, aping him. Her voice was cruel. "Maybe because I couldn't get a role anymore. So I had to make one for myself." She shrugged. "Or maybe I just grew tired. It's over now, anyway. It was just something to do to pass the time at the end of the world."

"And the others?" he said. "Blucher, Pirelli?"

"I only did what I had to do."

"Why me, Ulla?"

"Do you mind if I light a cigarette?"

"Do it slowly."

"I do everything slowly, Gunther."

She reached into her pocket and came back with a silver case. She put a cigarette between her lips and lit it with a match. She blew out smoke and looked at him, unconcerned. "I always liked you," she said softly.

"Liked?"

"Maybe it was love. It was so long ago and who can remember anymore. You were just easy, Gunther. I don't know how you're still alive."

He just stared at her. The sunlight framed her head. It was just an ordinary day.

"Put the gun down, Gunther. You know you're not going to shoot me." She wiped makeup off her face and smiled at him. He thought she must still be beautiful, underneath. "Come with me," she said. "We'll go back to the Continent, away from this awful place. I have money, we'd never have to work again. Come with me."

"No."

"Then step away!" She began loading the cases into the car. Gunther stood and watched her, helplessly.

I watched them from across the road. Neither of them saw me. It was obvious he wasn't going to shoot. She knew it and I did. I think the only one who didn't was Gunther.

I crossed the road to them. I wasn't in a hurry. Gunther heard my footsteps first. He turned his head and looked at me in bewilderment.

"Give me the gun, Gunther."

"No," he said, "She's got to pay, she's got to pay for what she did."

"To them, or to you?" I said. "Give me the gun, Gunther."

I watched her all the while. She straightened up again, slowly, her eyes never leaving my own or blinking. She didn't say a word. She didn't have to.

"Give me the gun."

He gave it to me. Ulla watched us without expression. I couldn't see her hands.

I raised the gun and shot her.

A Luger makes a surprising amount of noise when it's fired. The gunshot echoed from the walls. She fell slowly.

I'd blown half her face off, and the wig, which fell and lay on the ground matted in blood. Ulla Blau collapsed after it. She lay by the car and didn't move. There was a small gun in her hand where she'd intended to shoot me.

I walked over to her and fired another bullet, just to be sure.

Gunther stood there all the while. He didn't move. His eyes found mine at last. "What did you do that for?" he said numbly.

"You never asked her," I said.

"Asked her what?"

"What else she did to earn a living. Someone must have told you."

I could see it in his eyes. Someone must have said something but he never thought to follow it up. I said, "You want to know why she was so protected? She sold us Jews. To the Gestapo."

"So?" he said.

"She worked in the theatre in the aftermath of the war. She recruited the girls. She knew where people were hiding. It was just another way to make a living, and buy some protection on the side."

"So what?" he said. "They were just Jews."

"Sure," I said. "Sure. They were just Jews."

He really looked at me then. I think it was the first time he really started to see things for what they were and not for what he thought they should be.

"But you can't be," he said. "You're not—"

"I knew Tom Everly in Berlin, before the war," I said. "We were at university together. He became a committed Nazi and when he went back to England he was already working for the *Abwehr*."

I was watching Gunther's eyes. He wanted to run but there was nowhere to go. You can't outrun a bullet.

"We found him in the last few months of the war. Just enough time for me to take his place," I said. "He had a wife and a son, but it's no use having a family in this line of work."

All Gunther did was keep shaking his head. *No, no.* "There are no more Jews," he said.

"I told you," I said. "We're a vanishing kind."

Later, I stood over him. I knelt beside him and put the gun in his hand. They looked good together, Ulla and him. I felt bad for Gunther. He wasn't a bad guy, and none of this has really been his fault. He came to London following a woman, which is how these stories usually start, and he found her: which is how they usually end.

Bridge of Dreams," his first published story in eight years, was written as a break from a long novel that has much occupied him, about the decline of Renaissance Magic. He hopes to finish the novel this year and return to short fiction and novellas.

Helena Bell lives in Chattanooga, TN. Her stories have appeared in *Clarkesworld*, *The Indiana Review*, *Lightspeed Magazine*, and other publications. She is a graduate of the Clarion West Writer's Workshop and has MFAs in Fiction and Poetry from North Carolina State University and Southern Illinois University in Carbondale respectively.

Paul McAuley worked as a research biologist and university lecturer before becoming a full-time writer. He's the author of more than twenty novels, numerous short stories and a BFI Film Classic monograph on Terry Gilliam's film Brazil. His latest novel, sharing the same future history as this story, is *Into Everywhere*.

Kameron Hurley is the author of the space opera *The Stars are Legion*, as well as the essay collection *The Geek Feminist Revolution*. She has also written the award-winning God's War Trilogy and The Worldbreaker Saga. Hurley has won the Hugo Award, Kitschy Award, and Sydney J. Bounds Award for Best Newcomer. She was also a finalist for the Arthur C. Clarke Award, the Nebula Award, and the Gemmell Morningstar Award. Her short fiction has appeared in *Popular Science Magazine*, *Lightspeed Magazine*, and many anthologies. Hurley has also written for *The Atlantic*, *Entertainment Weekly*, *The Village Voice*, *LA Weekly*, *Bitch Magazine*, *Boingboing*, and *Locus Magazine*. She posts regular articles at KameronHurley.com.

Seth Dickinson is the author of *The Traitor Baru Cormorant* and more than a dozen short stories. During his time in the social sciences, he worked on cocoa farming in Ghana, political rumor control, and simulations built to study racial bias in police shootings. He wrote much of the lore and flavor for Bungie Studios' smash hit *Destiny*. If he were an animal, he would be a cockatoo.

Alexander Weinstein is the Director of The Martha's Vineyard Institute of Creative Writing and the author of the short story collection *Children of the New World* (Picador, 2016). He is the recipient of a Sustainable Arts Foundation Award, and his fiction has been awarded the Lamar York, Gail Crump, Hamlin Garland, and New Millennium Prizes. He is an Associate Professor of Creative Writing at Siena Heights University, and leads fiction workshops in the United States and Europe.

Charlie Jane Anders is the author of *All the Birds in the Sky*, which won a Nebula Award and a Crawford Award and has been shortlisted for the Hugo and Locus

ABOUT THE AUTHORS

Dominica Phetteplace is a math tutor who lives in Berkeley, CA. Her work has appeared in *Asimov's*, *Clarkesworld*, *F&SF*, and EscapePod, among other venues. She has won a Pushcart Prize and fellowships from I-Park and the MacDowell Colony.

Steven Barnes is a best selling, award-winning screenwriter and novelist from Los Angeles. He has written over twenty novels, and worked on shows such as *The Outer Limits*, *Stargate SG-1*, and *Baywatch*. His true love is teaching balance and enhancing human performance in all forms: emotional, professional, and physical. He is a life coach, Circular Strength Training coach, and certified hypnotist, as well as a trained yoga instructor, Tai Chi instructor, and fourth-degree black belt.

Rich Larson was born in West Africa, has studied in Rhode Island and worked in Spain, and now writes from Ottawa, Canada. His short work has been nominated for the Theodore Sturgeon, featured on *io9*, and appears in numerous Year's Best anthologies as well as in magazines such as *Asimov's*, *Analog*, *Clarkesworld*, *F&SF*, *Interzone*, *Strange Horizons*, *Lightspeed*, and *Apex*. He was the most prolific author of short science fiction in 2015 and 2016. Find him at richwlarson.tumblr.com

Carrie Vaughn is best known for her *New York Times* bestselling series of novels about a werewolf named Kitty, who hosts a talk radio show for the supernaturally disadvantaged. She's written several other contemporary fantasy and young adult novels, as well as upwards of eighty short stories. An Air Force brat, she survived her nomadic childhood and managed to put down roots in Boulder, Colorado. Visit her at www.carrievaughn.com.

Jason Sanford is a former archeologist and Peace Corps Volunteer who has published more than a dozen stories in the British magazine *Interzone*, which also devoted a special issue to his fiction. His other publications include numerous stories in magazines and anthologies such as *Asimov's Science Fiction*, *Year's Best SF*, *Analog*, *InterGalactic Medicine Show*, *Beneath Ceaseless*

Skies, and other places. In 2001 Jason founded the online magazine *storySouth*, through which he ran the Million Writer Award for online fiction for many years. His website is www.jasonsanford.com.

A. T. Greenblatt is a mechanical engineer by day and a writer by night. She lives in Philadelphia where she's well acquainted with all four seasons and is known to frequently subject her friends to various cooking and home brewing experiments. She is a graduate of Viable Paradise XVI and her work has appeared in *Beneath Ceaseless Skies*, *Strange Horizons*, and *Mothership Zeta*, as well as other online journals. You can find her online at atgreenblatt.com and on Twitter at @AtGreenblatt

Rahul Kanakia's first book, *Enter Title Here* (Disney-Hyperion), is a contemporary young adult novel. Additionally, his stories have appeared in *Apex*, *Clarkesworld*, *Lightspeed*, *The Indiana Review*, and *Nature*. He holds an M.F.A. in Creative Writing from Johns Hopkins. Originally from Washington, D.C., Rahul now lives in San Francisco. If you want to know more you can visit his blog at www.blotter-paper.com or follow him on Twitter at www.twitter.com/rahkan

Suzanne Palmer is a writer, artist, and linux system administrator who lives in western Massachusetts. She is a frequent contributor to *Asimov's Magazine*, and her story "Tuesdays" won the Asimov's Reader Award for Best Short Story of 2015. Other work of hers has appeared in *Analog*, *Interzone*, *Beneath Ceaseless Skies*, and other excellent venues. She has never wrestled an emu, but if she had it would have made this bio much more interesting, she is certain.

Sam J. Miller is a writer and a community organizer. His fiction has appeared in *Lightspeed*, *Asimov's*, *Clarkesworld*, *Apex*, *Strange Horizons*, and *The Minnesota Review*, among others. His first book, a young adult science fiction novel called *The Art of Starving*, will be published by HarperCollins in 2017. His stories have been nominated for the Nebula, World Fantasy, and Theodore Sturgeon Awards, and he's a winner of the Shirley Jackson Award. He lives in New York City, and at www.samjmiller.com

Cat Rambo lives and writes in the Pacific Northwest. Her two hundred plus fiction publications include appearances in *Asimov's*, *Clarkesworld*, and *Tor.com*. Her second novel, *Hearts of Tabat*, appears in early 2017 from Wordfire Press.

Carlos Hernandez is the author of the short story collection *The Assimilated Cuban's Guide to Quantum Santeria* (Rosarium, 2016). By day, he's a CUNY Associate Professor of English, and by vocation a game designer, most recently as lead writer on the historical CRPG Meriwether. He lives in Queens, the very best borough in New York.

Karin Lowachee was born in South America, raised in Canada, and w the Arctic. Her first novel *Warchild* won the 2001 Warner Aspect Fir Contest. *Warchild* and her third novel *Cagebird* were finalists for th K. Dick Award. *Cagebird* won the Prix Aurora Award in 2006 for Be Form Work in English and the Spectrum Award also in 2006. Her bo been translated into French, Hebrew, and Japanese, and her short stor appeared in anthologies edited by Nalo Hopkinson, John Joseph Ad Ann VanderMeer. Her fourth novel, *The Gaslight Dogs*, was published Orbit Books.

Chaz Brenchley has been making a living as a writer since the age of He has published thrillers, ghost stories, urban fantasy, epic fantasy and fiction, under his own name and others. He is a past winner of the Fantasy Award and Northern Writer of the Year, and his short story c *Bitter Waters* won a Lambda Award in 2014.

Adam Roberts is the author of sixteen sf novels, including *New Mod* (Gollancz, 2010), *Jack Glass* (2012), *Bête* (2014) and *The Thing Itself* (2 is also the author of various works of literary criticism and review, ir the recently expanded and updated *History of Science Fiction* (2nd ed 2016).

Ian R. MacLeod lives in the riverside town of Bewdley in the UK. A many accolades, his work has won the World Fantasy Award (twice) Arthur C Clarke Award. He has a new short story collection out, *F Glass*, and an upcoming novel, *Red Snow*.

Craig DeLancey is a writer and philosopher. He has published short in magazines like *Analog*, *Lightspeed*, *Shimmer*, and *Nature Physics*. H *Gods of Earth* is available now with 47 North Press. Born in Pittsburgh lives now in upstate New York and, in addition to writing, teaches phi at Oswego State, part of the State University of New York (SUNY).

Charlotte Ashley is a writer, editor and bookseller living in Toronto, C Her fantasy and science fiction short stories have appeared in *F&SF*, *Cl Canada*, *Luna Station Quarterly*, *Kaleidotrope*, *PodCastle*, and elsewhe historical fantasy, "La Héron," was nominated for both the Aurora and S Awards in 2016. You can find more about her at www.once-and-future. on Twitter @CharlotteAshley.

Gregory Feeley is the author of *The Oxygen Barons*, which was nomina the Philip K. Dick Award, as well as the historical novel *Arabian Wi* most recent book is the short novel *Kentauros*. His short fiction has ap in numerous magazines, original anthologies, and year's best volume

Awards. She organizes the Writers With Drinks reading series, and was a founding editor of *io9.com*. Her story "Six Months, Three Days" won a Hugo Award and her novel *Choir Boy* won a Lambda Literary Award.

Adrian Tchaikovsky is the author of the acclaimed ten-book Shadows of the Apt series starting with *Empire in Black and Gold* published by Tor UK. His other works for Tor UK include standalone novels *Guns of the Dawn* and *Children of Time* and the new series Echoes of the Fall starting with *The Tiger and the Wolf.* His sf novel *Children of Time* won the Arthur C Clarke Award and he has been shortlisted for the David Gemmell Legend Award and the British Fantasy Award.

Genevieve Valentine is the author of four novels; her latest is *Icon*. Several of her shorties stories have appeared in Best of the Year anthologies. She's written *Catwoman* for DC Comics and *Xena: Warrior Princess* for Dynamite. Her nonfiction has appeared at *NPR.org*, *The Atlantic*, *LA Review of Books*, *Interfictions*, and *The New York Times*.

Lavie Tidhar is the author of the Jerwood Fiction Uncovered Prize winning and Premio Roma nominee *A Man Lies Dreaming* (2014), the World Fantasy Award winning *Osama* (2011) and of the critically-acclaimed *The Violent Century* (2013). His latest novel is *Central Station* (2016). He is the author of many other novels, novellas and short stories.

PUBLICATION HISTORY

ABOUT THE EDITOR

Rich Horton is an associate technical fellow in software for a major aerospace corporation and the reprint editor for the Hugo Award-winning semiprozine *Lightspeed*. He is also a columnist for *Locus* and for *Black Gate*. He edits a series of best of the year anthologies for Prime Books, and also for Prime Books he has co-edited *Robots: The Recent A.I.* and *War & Space: Recent Combat*.